THE
UNWILLING

KELLY
BRAFFET

mira

mira™

Recycling programs
for this product may
not exist in your area.

ISBN-13: 978-0-7783-8824-1

The Unwilling

This edition published by arrangement with Harlequin Books S.A.

For questions and comments about the quality of this book, please contact us at
CustomerService@Harlequin.com.

Mira
22 Adelaide St. West, 40th Floor
Toronto, Ontario M5H 4E3, Canada
BookClubbish.com

Printed in U.S.A.

Praise for *The Unwilling*

"Brilliantly executed. *The Unwilling* is about sharing joy, and sensing fear and cruelty, and caring beyond ourselves. Kelly Braffet managed to make an adventure story about empathy."

—*Vanity Fair*

"Kelly Braffet is extraordinary... Familiar yet entirely unique, *The Unwilling* is the sort of story that seeps under your skin and pulses there, intimate and vibrant and alive. Fantasy at its most sublime."

—Erin Morgenstern, *New York Times* bestselling author of *The Starless Sea* and *The Night Circus*

"Suspenseful, magical, wonderfully written, and never predictable, Braffet's first foray into speculative fiction is an essential addition to all epic-fantasy collections."

—*Booklist*, starred review

"Drips with atmosphere and intrigue... Braffet's tale is a study in suffering and cruelty but also in determination... Readers who enjoy complex characters will find much to savor here."

—*Publishers Weekly*

"Braffet has a real gift for dialogue, and Judah's quick cleverness is a constant joy... Readers will fall in love with the contemplative pace, brisk dialogue and rebellious heroine of *The Unwilling*."

—*BookPage*

"A juggernaut of an epic fantasy novel with ingenious, thrilling twists and turns. Put this on the shelf beside Naomi Novik and George R. R. Martin."

—Kelly Link, award-winning author of *Get in Trouble*

"A viscerally powerful book. Full of complex and compelling characters, this is the story of the corruptions of power and the strength it takes to resist... An incredible, brilliant story."

—Kat Howard, author of *Roses and Rot*

"Gorgeously told, at once a sweeping epic and an intimate portrait of being trapped in an oppressive regime. Meet your new favorite fantasy writer."

—Gwenda Bond, *New York Times* bestselling author of *Stranger Things: Suspicious Minds*

For Zelda

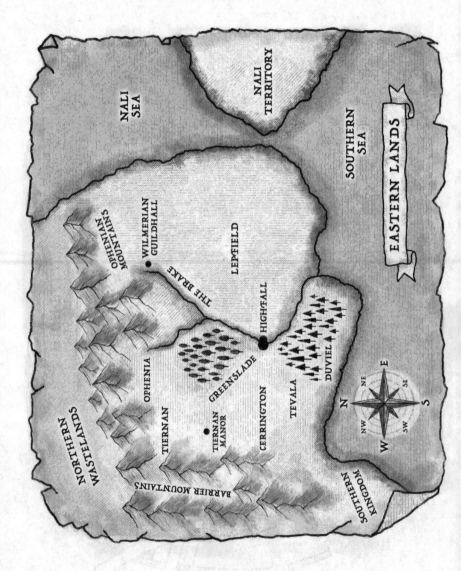

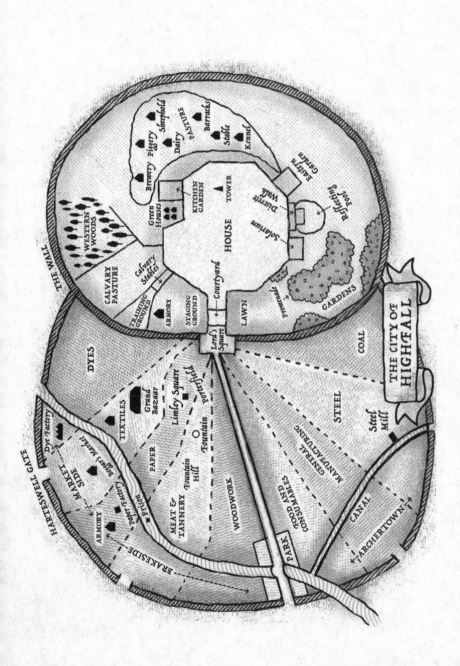

THE CITY OF HIGHFALL

PROLOGUE

On the third day of the convocation, two of the Slonimi scouts killed a calf, and the herbalist's boy wept because he'd watched the calf being born and grown to love it. His mother stroked his hair and promised he would forget by the time the feast came, the following night. He told her he would never forget. She said, "Just wait."

He spent all of the next day playing with the children from the other caravan; three days before, they'd all been strangers, but Slonimi children were used to making friends quickly. The group the boy and his mother traveled with had come across the desert to the south, and they found the cool air of the rocky plain a relief from the heat. The others had come from the grassy plains farther west, and were used to milder weather. While the adults traded news and maps and equipment, the children ran wild. Only one boy, from the other caravan, didn't run or play: a pale boy, with fine features, who followed by habit a few feet behind one of the older women from the other caravan. "Derie's apprentice," the other children told him, and shrugged, as if there was nothing more to say. The older woman was the other group's best Worker, with dark hair going to grizzle and gimlet eyes. Every time she appeared the herbalist suddenly remembered an herb her son needed to help her prepare, or something in their wagon that needed cleaning. The boy was observant, and clever, and it didn't take him long to figure out that his mother was trying to keep him away from the older woman: she, who had always demanded he face everything head-on, who had no patience for what she called *squeamishness and megrims*.

After a hard day of play over the rocks and dry, grayish grass, the boy was starving. A cold wind blew down over the rocky plain from the never-melting snow that topped the high peaks of the Barriers to the east; the bonfire was warm. The meat smelled good. The boy had not forgotten the calf but when his mother brought him meat and roasted potatoes and soft pan bread on a plate, he did not think of him. Gerta— the head driver of the boy's caravan—had spent the last three days with the other head driver, poring over bloodline records to figure out who between their two groups might be well matched for breeding, and as soon as everybody had a plate of food in front of them they announced the results. The adults and older teenagers seemed to find this all fascinating. The herbalist's boy was nine years old and he didn't understand the fuss. He knew how it went: the matched pairs would travel together until a child was on the way, and then most likely never see each other again. Sometimes they liked each other, sometimes they didn't. That, his mother had told him, was what brandy was for.

The Slonimi caravans kept to well-defined territories, and any time two caravans met there was feasting and trading and music and matching, but this was no ordinary meeting, and both sides knew it. After everyone had eaten their fill, a few bottles were passed. Someone had a set of pipes and someone else had a sitar, but after a song or two, nobody wanted any more music. Gerta—who was older than the other driver— stood up. She was tall and strong, with ropy, muscular limbs. "Well," she said, "let's see them."

In the back, the herbalist slid an arm around her son. He squirmed under the attention but bore it.

From opposite sides of the fire, a young man and a young woman were produced. The young man, Tobin, had been traveling with Gerta's people for years. He was smart but not unkind, but the herbalist's son thought him aloof. With good reason, maybe; Tobin's power was so strong that being near him made the hair on the back of the boy's neck stand up. Unlike all the other Workers—who were always champing at the bit to get a chance to show off—Tobin was secretive about his skills. He shared a wagon with Tash, Gerta's best Worker, even though the two men didn't seem particularly friendly with each other. More than once the boy had glimpsed their lantern burning late into the night, long after the main fire was embers.

The young woman had come across the plains with the others. The boy had seen her a few times; she was small, round, and pleasant-enough looking. She didn't strike the boy as particularly remarkable. But when she came forward, the other caravan's best Worker—the woman named Derie—came with her. Tash stood up when Tobin did, and when they all stood in front of Gerta, the caravan driver looked from one of them to the other. "Tash and Derie," she said, "you're sure?"

"Already decided, and by smarter heads than yours," the gimlet-eyed woman snapped.

Tash, who wasn't much of a talker, merely said, "Sure."

Gerta looked back at the couple. For couple they were; the boy could see the strings tied round each wrist, to show they'd already been matched. "Hard to believe," she said. "But I know it's true. I can feel it down my spine. Quite a legacy you two carry; five generations' worth, ever since mad old Martin bound up the power in the world. Five generations of working and planning and plotting and hoping; that's the legacy you two carry." The corner of her mouth twitched slightly. "No pressure."

A faint ripple of mirth ran through the listeners around the fire. "Nothing to joke about, Gerta," Derie said, lofty and hard, and Gerta nodded.

"I know it. They just seem so damn young, that's all." The driver sighed and shook her head. "Well, it's a momentous occasion. We've come here to see the two of you off, and we send with you the hopes of all the Slonimi, all the Workers of all of our lines, back to the great John Slonim himself, whose plan this was. His blood runs in both of you. It's strong and good and when we put it up against what's left of Martin's, we're bound to prevail, and the world will be free."

"What'll we do with ourselves then, Gert?" someone called out from the darkness, and this time the laughter was a full burst, loud and relieved.

Gerta smiled. "Teach the rest of humanity how to use the power, that's what we'll do. Except you, Fausto. You can clean up after the horses."

More laughter. Gerta let it run out, and then turned to the girl.

"Maia," she said, serious once more. "I know Derie's been drilling this into you since you were knee-high, but once you're carrying, the clock is ticking. Got to be inside, at the end."

"I know," Maia said.

Gerta scanned the crowd. "Caterina? Cat, where are you?"

Next to the boy, the herbalist cleared her throat. "Here, Gerta."

Gerta found her, nodded, and turned back to Maia. "Our Cat's the best healer the Slonimi have. Go see her before you set out. If you've caught already, she'll know. If you haven't, she'll know how to help."

"It's only been three days," Tobin said, sounding slighted.

"Nothing against you, Tobe," Gerta said. "Nature does what it will. Sometimes it takes a while."

"Not this time," Maia said calmly.

A murmur ran through the crowd. Derie sat up bolt-straight, her lips pressed together. "You think so?" Gerta said, matching Maia's tone—although nobody was calm, even the boy could feel the sudden excited tension around the bonfire.

"I know so," Maia said, laying a hand on her stomach. "I can feel her."

The tension exploded in a mighty cheer. Instantly, Tobin wiped the sulk off his face and replaced it with pride. The boy leaned into his mother and whispered, under the roar, "Isn't it too soon to tell?"

"For most women, far too soon, by a good ten days. For Maia?" Caterina sounded as if she were talking to herself, as much as to her son. The boy felt her arm tighten around him. "If she says there's a baby, there's a baby."

After that the adults got drunk. Maia and Tobin slipped away early. Caterina knew a scout from the other group, a man named Sadao, and watching the two of them dancing together, the boy decided to make himself scarce. Tash would have an empty bunk, now that Tobin was gone, and he never brought women home. He'd probably share. If not, there would be a bed somewhere. There always was.

In the morning, the boy found Caterina by the fire, only

slightly bleary, and brewing a kettle of strong-smelling tea. Her best hangover cure, she told her son. He took out his notebook and asked what was in it. Ginger, she told him, and willowbark, and a few other things; he wrote them all down carefully. Labeled the page. *Caterina's Hangover Cure.*

Then he looked up to find the old woman from the bonfire, Derie, listening with shrewd, narrow eyes. Behind her hovered her apprentice, the pale boy, who this morning had a bruised cheek. "Charles, go fetch my satchel," she said to him, and he scurried away. To Caterina, Derie said, "Your boy's conscientious."

"He learns quickly," Caterina said, and maybe she just hadn't had enough hangover tea yet, but the boy thought she sounded wary.

"And fair skinned," Derie said. "Who's his father?"

"Jasper Arasgain."

Derie nodded. "Travels with Afia's caravan, doesn't he? Solid man."

Caterina shrugged. The boy had only met his father a few times. He knew Caterina found Jasper boring.

"Healer's a good trade. Everywhere needs healers." Derie paused. "A healer could find his way in anywhere, I'd say. And with that skin—"

The boy noticed Gerta nearby, listening. Her own skin was black as obsidian. "Say what you're thinking, Derie," the driver said.

"Highfall," the old woman said, and immediately, Caterina said, "No."

"It'd be a great honor for him, Cat," Gerta said. The boy thought he detected a hint of reluctance in Gerta's voice.

"Has he done his first Work yet?" Derie said.

Caterina's lips pressed together. "Not yet."

Charles, the bruised boy, reappeared with Derie's satchel.

"We'll soon change that," the old woman said, taking the satchel without a word and rooting through until she found a small leather case. Inside was a small knife, silver-colored but without the sheen of real silver.

The boy noticed his own heartbeat, hard hollow thuds in his chest. He glanced at his mother. She looked unhappy, her brow furrowed. But she said nothing.

"Come here, boy," Derie said.

He sneaked another look at his mother, who still said nothing, and went to stand next to the woman. "Give me your arm," she said, and he did. She held his wrist with a hand that was both soft and hard at the same time. Her eyes were the most terrifying thing he'd ever seen.

"It's polite to ask permission before you do this," she told him. "Not always possible, but polite. I need to see what's in you, so if you say no, I'll probably still cut you, but—do I have your permission?"

Behind Derie, Gerta nodded. The bruised boy watched curiously.

"Yes," the boy said.

"Good," Derie said. She made a quick, confident cut in the ball of her thumb, made an identical cut in his small hand, quickly drew their two sigils on her skin in the blood, and pressed the cuts together.

The world unfolded. But *unfolded* was too neat a word, too tidy. This was like when he'd gone wading in the western sea and been knocked off his feet, snatched underwater, tossed in a maelstrom of sand and sun and green water and foam—but this time it wasn't merely sand and sun and water and foam that swirled around him, it was *everything*. All of existence, all that had ever been, all that would ever be. His mother was there, bright and hot as the bonfire the night before—not her

15

face or her voice but the *Caterina* of her, her very essence rendered into flame and warmth.

But most of what he felt was Derie. Derie, immense and powerful and fierce: Derie, reaching into him, unfolding him as surely as she'd unfolded the world. And this *was* neat and tidy, methodical, almost cold. She unpacked him like a trunk, explored him like a new village. She sought out his secret corners and dark places. When he felt her approval, he thrilled. When he felt her contempt, he trembled. And everywhere she went she left a trace of herself behind like a scent, like the chalk marks the Slonimi sometimes left for each other. Her sigil was hard-edged, multi-cornered. It was everywhere. There was no part of him where it wasn't.

Then it was over, and he was kneeling by the campfire, throwing up. Caterina was next to him, making soothing noises as she wrapped a cloth around his hand. He leaned against her, weak and grateful.

"It's all right, my love," she whispered in his ear, and the nervousness was gone. Now she sounded proud, and sad, and as if she might be crying. "You did well."

He closed his eyes and saw, on the inside of his eyelids, the woman's hard, angular sigil, burning like a horse brand.

"Don't coddle him," Derie said, and her voice reached through him, back into the places inside him where she'd left her mark. Caterina's arm dropped away. He forced himself to open his eyes and stand up. His entire body hurt. Derie was watching him, calculating but—yes—pleased. "Well, boy," she said. "You'll never be anyone's best Worker, but you're malleable, and you've got the right look. There's enough power in you to be of use, once you're taught to use it. You want to learn?"

"Yes," he said, without hesitating.

"Good," she said. "Then you're my apprentice now, as much

as your mother's. You'll still learn herbs from your mother, so we'll join our wagon to your group. But don't expect the kisses and cuddles from me you get from her. For me, you'll work hard and you'll learn hard and maybe someday you'll be worthy of the knowledge I'll pass on to you. Say, *Yes, Derie.*"

"Yes, Derie," he said.

"You've got a lot to learn," she said. "Go with Charles. He'll show you where you sleep."

He hesitated, looked at his mother, because it hadn't occurred to him that he would be leaving her. Suddenly, swiftly, Derie kicked hard at his leg. He yelped and jumped out of the way. Behind her he saw Charles—he of the bruised face—wince, unsurprised but not unsympathetic.

"Don't *ever* make me ask you anything twice," she said.

"Yes, Derie," he said, and ran.

PART I

CHAPTER ONE

Judah didn't like the Wilmerian guildsman.

She, better than anybody, knew that it wasn't a person's fault what they looked like, so she wasn't bothered by the sweat that coated his bald head and dripped from his nose in the hot, crowded hall. His rough-spun robes smelled like a freshly dug grave but she could overlook that, too. Guildsmen lived by strange rules. Maybe the Wilmerian Guild had prohibitions against bathing, even before state dinners; their guildhall and gas mines were in the high plains to the north, and for all Judah knew, water was scarce there.

The Wilmerians had made clayware, long before mining gas, and the guildsman had introduced himself as Single-Handled Ewer. He turned his sweating nose up at the dazzling array of food on the table, the cheeses and roasts and candied fruits and Judah's favorite sticky spiced duck; he produced a crumbly gray-brown shard of what appeared to be clay from the depths of the grave-dirt robe, put it between his teeth and actually began to *nibble*; and even all of this, Judah could overlook. Although he made it hard, the way he closed his eyes in apparent ecstasy and, too loud, proclaimed that the Wilmerians would not touch any food of the world until they had ingested their sacred portion of earth. Most people had reasons for what they did, even if those reasons were bizarre. And Judah herself had been thought bizarre often enough to judge strangeness gently, too.

But once the guildsman had downed a few glasses of wine—nothing in his guild vows about that, apparently—he'd started to stare at her hair, and that, Judah couldn't forgive. In this land of monotonous corn silk, the dark, almost-purple mass always drew stares, but Judah didn't have to put up with it from somebody with clay in his teeth.

Do I have something in my hair? she'd asked coolly, and he'd said, *I apologize. It's just so...odd.*

The courtier sitting on her other side wasn't much more appealing. Like all courtiers, he was greased and polished, his hair heavy with pomade and kohl thick around his eyes. At least the Wilmerian mostly kept his smell to himself; the courtier's perfume made her eyes water. The best she could say for him was that he didn't seem to be overindulging in the drops that were the courtiers' drug of choice these days; it amused her to watch the ornate jeweled vials pass from hand to hand with what she assumed was supposed to be subtlety, but she was less amused by the prospect of having one of the blurry-eyed droppers sitting right next to her.

For weeks, the Wilmerians had been crawling over the newest part of the House like cassocked beetles, installing the gas lamps. By the lavender light of the new sconces, the guildsmen and courtiers assembled in the hall appeared faintly cadaverous. In the front of the hall, on the dais, where Gavin looked bored and Theron looked scared and only Elly was able to fake the proper level of interest, the Guildmaster was talking. "Such a privilege it has been," he said, with enthusiasm as genuine as Elly's interest, "to visit the very heart of the Highfall, the hidden treasure that is the great House of Lord Elban. We are honored to add our tiny light to its legendary brilliance."

Speaking of brilliance, the diamonds in the courtier's ears were too large. She wondered if wearing diamonds that ostentatious meant the courtier could actually afford them, or if he just wanted the other courtiers to think he could.

"It is with humility that we work with the things of the earth, and with humility that we offer our small wares to those who will use them to bring light to the still-dark corners of our world." The Guildmaster, short, square and robustly corpulent despite the Wilmerians' ostensible asceticism, beamed at Gavin's father. "And who fits that description better than Lord Elban?"

Cheers and applause rose at this, as they were supposed to. The great Lord Elban, in his gilded chair at the center of the dais, merely nodded. He was tall and lean, with white hair that flowed down over his shoulders and skin that wasn't much darker. Even his blue eyes were so pale as to be nearly white. He wore nothing but black, which heightened the effect. Those he skirmished with on the southern border called him the Wraith Lord. Judah couldn't remember where she'd heard that. It didn't seem like the sort of thing she was supposed to know. On balance, she would rather be down here on the floor, squeezed in between the courtier and the guildsman, than up on the dais, anywhere near him. He made her think of a bird rather than a wraith: something cruel that waited. Like a carrion crow. Maybe the effect was different when he was charging toward you on a warhorse.

The Guildmaster's speech went on and on. He must not have been paid for the lamps yet. Judah's dress fit her badly. As always, it was one of Elly's, made over. She was hot and uncomfortable, and she wanted to leave. She'd been late getting dressed and there hadn't been time to braid back her hair and the Wilmerian wasn't the only one staring at it. At her.

"I don't know why the Seneschal is making me go," she'd complained to Gavin the night before. "Nobody cares if I'm there. Nobody will even talk to me. I'm just Judah, the witchbred foundling."

She didn't exactly mean it as a negative. She was mostly amused by the way the staff wouldn't quite look at her and the courtiers couldn't quite look away. Still, Gavin had scowled. "Tell me who calls you witchbred. I'll have them executed."

"Kill the whole House, then," she'd said, "and most of the courtiers."

"Could you do that?" Theron had asked, curiously.

Gavin ignored his brother. "You're no foundling. You're my foster sister. And the courtiers had better get used to seeing you, because someday, when I'm Lord of the City, I'm going to make you—I don't know, Lead Chancellor in Charge of Keeping Me Sane, or something."

"I thought that was the Lady of the City's job," she'd said, and Elly, playing solitaire by the window, said, "Leave me out of this."

It wasn't Gavin's fault that she was eating in such odious company. The Seneschal, dressed in his usual gray, stood behind Elban, but she could still feel his eye on her. Anything inappropriate that she did would earn her a lecture, and twenty-two years of the Seneschal's lectures had bored her into a reluctant obedience, or at least a moment's consideration as to whether her intended bad behavior was worth the tedium of another one. Escaping this room was certainly worth it. She intended to do so at the first possible opportunity.

More applause. The Guildmaster had finally shut up. Now Elban rose, and a thick and instantaneous blanket of silence fell over the hall. Elban's face—otherwise as handsome as Gavin's—bore a crosshatch of old battle scars, earned honorably or otherwise, that left it craggy and granitic. "The Guildmaster has spoken well," he said. "This House is the jewel of Highfall, and Highfall is the jewel of the empire I have spent my entire life building. Every province, guild and noble family stands united under my banner, from the Barriers in the east to the sea in the west, from the border of the Southern Kingdom to the dead lands of the north. We are powerful. We are prosperous."

Another cheer from the courtiers. And it did sound nice when he said it that way, using words like *united* and *prosperous*. Darid, the House stablemaster, had told her that Elban's cavalry horses came back covered in blood, when they came back at all.

"But we must be vigilant," Elban continued, and the cheers died. "There are evil forces at work in our city, seditionists who would eat away at us from the inside like woodworm. Who would work against Highfall's best interests by disrupting our factories and starving our workers; who would even sink so low as to sabotage the very Wilmerian envoy we celebrate tonight, claiming their gas lines carry poison. Even worse, they spread lies about our soldiers. Calling the expedition across the Nali Strait a rout, saying they stumbled home in defeat. Yes, stumbled!"

Elban called anyone who disagreed with him a seditionist. The word had long since lost any meaning, but derisive jeers filled the air. Not that the courtiers cared about the soldiers; they just liked to jeer.

"The Nali expedition was designed to draw out the Nali, to test their capabilities. It was a resounding success." Elban's icy eyes swept the room. "Were lives lost? Yes. Such is the nature of war. Those lives were freely given. We learned much at the Battle of the Nali Strait. We learned that the Nali are unnatural, inhuman. More like insects than men. Like insects, they would invade, and they would devour, even swarming over Highfall itself if they thought they could."

More jeers. Elban held up a finger; the jeers stopped. "In two months, I will cross the Nali Strait again. With the knowledge gained from the last campaign, and the marvelous ever-burning fire of the Wilmerian Guild, we will do more than defeat the Nali on their own shores. We will sweep them from the world like the infestation they are. We will annihilate them."

He spoke without emotion, but the crowd leapt to their feet with a deafening cheer. The Wilmerian to Judah's right did so a bit drunkenly, the courtier to her left with courtier-like reserve and panache. None wanted to be caught lagging. None wanted to be seen cheering less exuberantly than the rest. Judah stood, too, but she didn't bother to clap or cheer. A door opened; the musicians came in. With the musicians came drummers and with the drummers came fire-dancers, spinning pots of flame on cords around their bodies. Another wave of cheering broke over the hall and the horrible new gaslights were extinguished. The orange light of the flame-pots shifted and swung crazily in the darkness.

It was the distraction Judah was waiting for. When the lights came back up, she was gone.

Despite the gas lamps, deep shadows nestled between the pillars lining the gallery outside the hall. Judah shivered; the wide neckline of her poorly cut dress left most of her shoulders exposed. She could hear the quiet slip of her pinching, uncomfortable court shoes on the flagstones. Outside, the rosebushes stretched thorny fingers against the window and the spitting snow glinted in the purple light.

Another cheer erupted from the hall.

She wandered through the liminal quiet, considering. She could go to the stables, where Darid might let her muck out stalls or oil tack or do some other small, useful thing; but her court shoes would dissolve within minutes in the snow and mud, and her boots were a long walk away, back in her room. Besides, the stablemen might be having their own celebration. Guildspeople, with their odd clothes, assumed names and forced piety, were never much liked by outsiders, and the Wilmerians were cruel to their horses. Darid had lost more than one night of sleep trying to keep their starved, overworked beasts alive—because he loved horses and didn't want them to suffer, but also because a dead horse would mean a dead stableman, another head on the spikes in the kitchen yard. Once the Wilmerians left, their horses would suffer again, but Darid's stablemen wouldn't. That was worth celebrating. Darid was kind to her, but she knew she made the stablemen nervous, and didn't want to intrude.

Meanwhile, most of the rooms in the huge, sprawling House would be empty. As long as she avoided the kitchens, which would still be frenzied from the feast, she could do anything, go anywhere: the library, the catacombs, the portrait hall. She could go to the council chamber and dance on the massive wooden table; she could sit in Elban's throne and issue imaginary proclamations. *The wearing of perfume by courtiers is now forbidden. Chocolate caramels will be served with all meals. Everyone caught wearing heels of three inches or higher will be summarily beheaded.*

Then she heard a noise. She was never sure afterward exactly what kind of noise it was: the swish of heavy fabric, a rough drunken breath. Maybe it wasn't a noise at all, but the faint smell of dirt. Whatever it was, something inside her sent up a warning. She tensed, and turned.

It was the Wilmerian. He'd followed her out of the hall. The hood of his cassock was down. His eyes were watery and unfocused and his jaw hung slack. She probably wouldn't have heard anything if he'd been sober. An alarming thought.

"Bertram." His voice sounded breathless, with none of the aloof piety it had held earlier.

"I'm sorry?" she said, carefully.

"Bertram. Before I took my vows. My name was Bertram."

The back of her neck prickled. "All right."

"You have to give up everything when you join a Guild. Even your name. I—" He hesitated, and took a step closer. The words tumbled out of him all in a rush. "I want to touch your hair."

"No," she said.

Bertram's thin lips were dry and as she watched, he licked them. His hands reached out like talons, those bleary eyes glued to her hair. "They say you're witchborn. That you stole Lady Clorin's soul. Killed her."

Judah hadn't heard exactly that variation before. She didn't believe in witches and she didn't believe in souls, but this didn't seem like the time to mention it. He stood between her and the open end of the gallery; the only door behind her led to the chapel, and was no doubt locked. She'd been stupid. She should have circled around him as he spoke so he couldn't trap her. Even if she did manage to bolt past him, her shoes weren't made for running any more than they were made for snow. Drunk he may have been, but he could still probably catch her, and if he caught her she would be well and truly caught. The Wilmerians were all broad-shouldered. Judah was sturdy but small. The gaslight above her burned steady with its creepy purple glow. Six months ago, it would have been an oil lamp, or a torch, and she could have thrown it at him. Now she had nothing.

"Hair like blood," he said. "It looks soft. Is it soft?"

She imagined Bertram's fingers sliding into her hair—questing, invading, clenching, pulling—and decided that her head would be on a spike before she let him touch her. He came closer.

Suddenly, she heard boot heels. Not Gavin's or Theron's formal leather boots, but hard wooden soles, with the staccato clip of high heels. The pomaded courtier who'd sat on Judah's other side appeared over Bertram's shoulder: neither young nor old, earrings sparkling in the gas lamps and visage unsullied by anything so common as emotion. Only the wryest lift of an eyebrow suggested that there was anything odd about the scene before him.

Bertram hadn't seen him yet. His fingertips brushed against Judah's hair just as the courtier, sounding bored, said, "Guildsman. Lady Judah," and then the guildsman's whole body flinched, as if he'd been doused in cold water.

He snatched back his hand and his face filled with horror and shame. Staggering backward, he said, "Forgive me."

"Forgive you?" the courtier said with benign interest. "Whatever for?" But Bertram was already stumbling away down the gallery, a tangle of coarse robes and fumy sweat. The courtier watched him go, then turned back to Judah, one eyebrow lifted in what looked like curiosity. Contemplating the poisonous hay he could make of what he'd seen, probably. It was what courtiers did.

Quickly, Judah circled him, putting the length of the gallery at her back. Normally, no courtier would acknowledge her existence, let alone chase her. But for all she knew, this particular courtier was as drunk as Bertram. Surely there was an aphorism in that. From the grasp of the guildsman to the grip of the courtier.

"You should be more careful. It's a strange night." Mocking, but they all sounded like that, so it was impossible to tell if the mockery were directed at her. His kohl-lined eyes drifted up to the gas lamp overhead. "And oddly lit."

"The House is full of drunk courtiers," she said, bolder with an escape route at her back. "Nothing strange about that."

The corner of his mouth moved. "Nothing particularly safe about it, either. You might find yourself running into unsavory characters. You might find yourself owing them favors." Courtiers trafficked in favors, and reputation, and fear.

"A favor? In exchange for walking down the hall? Seems like a low threshold."

"Oh," the courtier said, "but think of the rumors."

"I try not to. Good night, lord courtier." Giving him a wide berth, Judah walked past him and away, acutely conscious of his gaze on her back.

"Good night, foundling," she heard him say, as she left the gallery by the first flight of stairs she came to. As she climbed them, she felt something scratch the inside of her wrist, like a fingernail drawn across the skin. She ignored it. For now.

Up a broad marble staircase, down a twisting narrow one: nothing in the House was straightforward. Generations of City Lords had lived there, and it had been built and rebuilt and demolished and built again. The floors were flagstone or cool ceramic or, in one room, copper, although nobody remembered why. She passed gas lamps and oil lamps, dark corridors where you were meant to light a torch or carry a lantern and even darker ones where nobody respectable had passed in years. She navigated by feel and memory and, when there were windows, starlight. Eventually she made it back to the rooms where she and Gavin and Theron had lived since birth and Elly had lived since she was eight. The suite was modest enough, just two bedrooms with a shabby parlor between them. It was tradition that the Lord's heir stayed in his childhood rooms until he married or took power, but normally those childhood rooms were lovingly tended by loving nurses who'd been lovingly chosen by loving mothers. Gavin and Theron's mother, Clorin, was dead, and in the absence of the loving mother the system had fallen apart. The sofa was losing stuffing and the curtains were riddled with moth holes; the silk on the walls was threadbare and the furniture still bore every scratch and dent from their childhood. Nobody, including them, had ever thought to replace any of it.

Tucked away in each bedroom was a tiny alcove, meant for a nurse or a handservant and big enough for a narrow bed and not much else. As the irrelevant second son, Theron slept in one alcove, and as the mostly unwanted witchbred foundling, Judah slept in the other. (Or was supposed to; half the time she slept with Elly, who didn't mind sharing.) Now all three rooms were empty, because everyone else was still stuck down in the hall being official. Unwanted foundling status had its advantages. The ashes in the fireplace were cold. Nobody had laid a new fire. Judah did, and lit it; then she kicked off her useless court shoes, slid into the pair of Theron's old boots she'd claimed as her own, put on her coat and went out onto the terrace while the room warmed.

The snow had stopped. They were on the quiet side of the House, high above the ground. The pasture stretched below her, weird and blue with light reflecting off the snow. To the far left, she could just see the inky black puddle of the orchard and the western woods beyond it; across the pasture, just barely, she could make out the haze of brush and ivy that marked the edge of the Wall. The Wall was flawless white stone, impossibly high, eternal and unyielding. The ground rose slightly on this side of the House, so from their terrace the Wall loomed almost as high as the House itself. On the other side, the Wall was just as high, but the ground there sloped downward. From a certain height the smokestacks and spires of the city could be seen bristling above the Wall like a poorly hidden beast. The city had a name—Highfall—but Judah rarely thought of it as anything other than the city or *outside*. People lived there, down among the steeples and high gabled roofs, under the dim glow of the underlit clouds. They tended the ceaseless fires that kept the factories running; they bought and sold, worked and rested, lived and died. A sluggish river called the Brake wound through the city, full of water from other places: places like Tiernan, where Eleanor was born, and the provinces where the courtiers were from, and all of the lands that Elban had invaded or annexed or simply strode into and claimed with his army at his back. All of the place-names she'd seen on maps, all of the lakes and mountains and peninsulas and oceans.

And somewhere out there, among the dark and the fires, was the place where she'd been born—or so she'd been told. Somewhere lived people with the blood-colored hair and black eyes she could not disguise; people who were solid and round instead of lithe and delicate, whose noses were strong and sharp instead of buttonish like Elly's or straight like Gavin's. She didn't even know which direction to look. She had no sense of the city; she had no memory of being there. Twice a year, on each solstice, the four of them were taken to the small antechamber built into the Wall, where a balcony city-side overlooked the Lord's Square. When she thought of the city, it was the Square she pictured: grand manors, graceful linden trees waving like the fans the lady courtiers carried these days, the same sea of pale golden-haired people dressed in their best and most vivid colors surging below. Never among them did she see hair or eyes like hers; always, Elban's red-and-gold banner hung from every window ledge and lamp-post. The air felt thicker in the Square, and smelled faintly of burning from the factories.

Elban's solstice speeches tended to follow the pattern of the one he'd just given the Wilmerians: so much conquest already, more to come, steadfast in the face of evil, glory and glory and riches and glory. When the speech was done, the four of them were herded out onto the balcony. If she listened closely to the cheers from the gathered masses, she could pick out voices calling Gavin's name, and Elly's. Sometimes, for reasons she didn't understand, she might even catch her own. Rarely poor Theron's, but she didn't think he'd ever noticed. The crowds and the noise made him feel sick and it was all he could do to stay on his feet. The height did the same to Elly and Judah had her hands full, keeping the two of them upright. Gavin claimed to hate solstices, too—although he always seemed to stand a bit straighter when the crowd chanted his name—but even so, they all had to appear. Protocol, the Seneschal said. Gavin said it was to prove they were still alive.

There were no crowds beneath her now, and the air that blew in from over the Wall, wherever it blew from, was crisp and alive. From here she couldn't hear the calls of the coach-men who waited in the courtyard to carry the city-dwelling courtiers back to their manors, or the rattle of their wheels on the cobbles. After the crowds and heat of the hall the cool silence was a relief. She felt the scratch on her wrist and ig-nored it again.

In time, the terrace door creaked open behind her, and she heard the faint hush of silk. "How did you manage to get away so quickly?" Elly said.

"Misdirection." Judah leaned against the railing. "Ducked out when the dancers came in. How'd you escape?"

The blonde girl, whose dress fit perfectly and whose hair was dressed with rubies, didn't step through the door. The railing was high and solid and the terrace itself much wider than the balcony over the Square, but Elly still preferred to stay inside. "Gavin told the Seneschal I was sick from the wine, and he let me go. He said I have to work on building up my tolerance, though."

"He didn't give you a bottle to get started on that, did he?"

"He did not."

"You should have taken one anyway. You were drinking Sevedran up there. Down in the pit, we were practically drinking vinegar."

"It all tastes like vinegar to me." Elly yawned. "Gavin said to stop ignoring him."

"Being ignored is good for him."

"I've always thought so. You're lucky you got out when you did. I had to dance with the Guildmaster. He smells like a sick sheep."

"How do you know what a sick sheep smells like?"

"I grew up in Tiernan. I've forgotten more about sheep than you'll ever know. Anyway, you're the one he should have danced with. He was full of questions about you."

"Did he ask you if I stole Lady Clorin's soul?" Judah said.

"Not in so many words." Elly arched her back in a stretch, or as much of one as her dress would allow, and groaned. "Gods, I'm so glad they're leaving. My mother would be horrified to learn that she sent me five hundred miles away from Tiernan and I still ended up doing blackwork until my hands ached. I've never been so glad to see the back of anything as I was that altar cloth."

"I suggest being talentless. The Seneschal never asks me to make state gifts."

"Only because people think they'll end up cursed. By the way, there's some cake inside for you. It's good, it has that cream in the middle."

"Thanks."

"Also by the way," Elly said, and her voice sounded so casual that Judah knew that whatever she was about to say had been on her mind for the entire conversation, "who was the courtier sitting next to you tonight?"

Oh, but think of the rumors. Judah remembered the nastiness in the corridor and suppressed a shudder. "No idea. Why?"

"He was watching you," Elly said merrily. "And he left at the same time you did. I think that's why Gavin was so desperate to know where you were. He thought you had a new friend."

Judah grimaced. "Blech."

"It's nice to have friends." Elly's voice was gently mocking, but Judah couldn't tell if she was making fun of Gavin, or the courtier, or Judah herself. Pulling her shawl more tightly around her, Elly said, "Well, my face hurts from smiling. I'm going to bed."

"I'll stay out a while longer."

"Don't bother waiting up for Gavin. When I left he was surrounded by courtiers." Elly lifted a hand in a wave, then went inside.

The scratch came again. More insistently this time. Down in the great hall, Gavin was drawing a fingernail against the blue-veined skin on the inside of his wrist, a complicated swirl that meant, simultaneously, *Where did you go?* and *Are you okay?* and *Can I stop worrying about you?*

Judah sighed, pulled up her own sleeve, and scratched. *Fine. Home. Bored.*

The response came almost immediately. *Good. Stuck here. See you later.*

Once, she would have waited for him. Once, he could have

been counted on to come back before dawn. The terrace was quiet and peaceful, and she couldn't quite shake the memory of the Wilmerian's voice.

They say you're witchborn. They say you stole Lady Clorin's soul.

She'd been carried into the House in a midwife's basket. Lady Clorin had been laboring with Gavin for three days, and the midwife was supposed to be the best. The maid who recommended her said she brought special skills, unsurpassed. And Clorin had survived, so maybe the midwife did bring special skills, but she'd also brought the newborn Judah, wrapped in an old piece of toweling and still wet with blood. Lady Clorin had lost five babies by the time she'd had Gavin—two dead in their cradles, one born dead, and two more not even making it that far—and she was softhearted. She'd asked the midwife what would become of the tiny baby girl.

The midwife shrugged. "Nobody wants girls. Might be able to find a brothel to take her in. Otherwise, the Brake."

Clorin told the old woman to leave the baby with her instead. The Seneschal saw no harm in it. Elban didn't care, so the Lady of the City was allowed to keep the new baby as if it were a kitten. Judah and Gavin slept in the same crib, fed from the same nurses, played with the same toys. Even when Judah's hair turned its disturbing garnet color and her infant-blue eyes deepened to black, Clorin delighted in her two babies. Judah couldn't remember who'd told her that, but she had the distinct impression that it was true.

When Judah and Gavin were barely two, Theron had been born, and Clorin had died of it. This, nobody had ever talked to her about, but Judah suspected that probably, by the time Theron came along, Elban and the Seneschal had realized they'd made a mistake. She suspected that was probably why Theron had come along, when by all reports Clorin was frail even before Gavin, and never fully recovered from his birth. Nobody would have considered it strange that two infants who slept in the same crib would share the same illnesses, but the books Judah had read on the subject suggested that well before two, babies could walk, and fall down, and bump into things. Well before two, then, someone would have noticed that when Judah fell down, Gavin's knee bruised, too. She wondered, sometimes, how they must have confirmed it: had they snatched her from Clorin's arms and put her in a snowbank to see if Gavin shivered? Had Clorin watched as they cut Judah's tiny heel to see if Gavin bled? She wondered also about the nurse who'd been keen enough to notice (because it would have had to be a nurse; nobody else would have spent enough time with them): who she was, how long she'd been allowed to live. If they'd killed her quickly, or if she was among those silent members of the House staff who'd had their tongues cut out for convenience's sake, creeping about doing tasks that didn't require speech.

She rarely indulged in such thoughts. There was no point. Years had passed before she realized that the bond was unique to the two of them. Years more passed before she understood that the bond was why she was allowed to live in the House as she did, why she was allowed to live at all; why the fiction was maintained, at solstices, that she was a treasured member of the family and Elban's dead Lady's pet, when in fact he could hardly look at her without sneering. When she was eight there had been long, awful days in Elban's study when the limits of the bond had been tested. Those were days she tried not to think of at all. The scars, she told herself, were like the bond. They had always been there. They always would be. There was no point thinking about them.

She preferred to think of days spent playing on the parlor carpet in the sun, back when its colors had been bright and alive. Toy soldier campaigns under the table. Dirt-smeared, feral afternoons in the orchards and pastures, Theron frowning along behind and sneezing from the dust. They explored the old wing, uninhabited for generations save for spiders and sparrows and mice, and prowled the catacombs, tiptoeing with delicious dread past the crypts that held Gavin and Theron's dead ancestors as marble busts of their occupants watched with stone eyes. Carrying flickering lanterns, they'd found the aquifer deep in the living rock that supplied the House with fresh water, and fled from the vast lightless stillness of it, giggling to hide their nervousness. Judah was never afraid in the dark because she could always feel Gavin somewhere in it. Over time the scratch code evolved and then each knew exactly where the other was, and what they were doing, and what they might do later. When they had a tutor, they used the scratches to snicker over his bad teeth or hairy ears (their tutors were never women) but most of the time, they had no tutor. Most of the time, they were ignored, and they were happy.

Now, none of them were ignored. Now, Gavin trained with the House Guards every day; at night, if there was no state event like the Wilmerian dinner, he either went to Elban's study to listen to the old man talk about his campaigns, or did who knew what with the courtiers. Theron was supposed to train, too, but his poor eyesight and complete lack of killer instinct led him instead to spend most of his time hiding in the secret workshop he'd set up in the old wing. Eleanor, who would eventually be Lady of the City and Gavin's wife, sat in the Lady's Library for hours, reading protocol manuals and etiquette guides and the social diaries of Ladies long dead. Judah spent her days avoiding the Seneschal, who apparently spent his hunting for her so he could tell her about new things she wasn't allowed to do: read freely in the main library, nose about freely in the map room, make a spectacle of herself in front of the courtiers.

But she was still allowed to sleep, and sleep she did, in her tiny alcove off Elly's room. When she woke the morning after the Wilmerian dinner, Elly and Theron were already gone. Gavin sat on the threadbare sofa in the parlor, gray patches shadowing his eyes; but he smiled when he saw her. "Very sneaky last night. What makes you think you get to be free when none of the rest of us do?"

"Not my fault if I'm clever enough to escape." She dropped into the sprung, leaking armchair that she liked best. "Pour me some coffee, Lordling?"

"I'm too important to pour coffee."

"Too hungover, you mean. Elly said the courtiers got hold of you last night."

"They did indeed. Stumbling all over themselves to ingratiate themselves with the future Lord of the City. Stumbling, period, if they'd had enough drops."

"Sounds awful," she said.

He grinned and leaned forward to pour her coffee. Let the courtiers high-comb their hair, decorate themselves with gems and kohl and scent: Gavin was twice as handsome with none of the effort. Judah knew him too well to be impressed by his future on the throne, but even she had to admit that he'd practically been made to order for the role, except for the awkward matter of her. "All joking aside," he said, handing her the chipped cup she always used, "what happened to you last night? You didn't answer when I scratched."

Pain transmitted best between them but strong emotion would, too, particularly if it generated a physical response. Thinking of the Wilmerian filled her with something slithering and uncomfortable, and without bothering to examine her reasons, she knew she didn't want Gavin to know what happened. "Nothing. I came back here and enjoyed the quiet."

"Really."

"Really." She picked up a bun from the tray on the low table between them.

He let a breath's worth of silence pass. "Did your new courtier friend enjoy the quiet with you?"

She threw the bun at him. It had been stale, anyway. "Go hang."

"It wouldn't be the worst thing in the world for you, you know," he said with a laugh. "The rest of us are busy all the time now. It'd give you something to do."

"I have plenty to do. How late did Theron stay last night?"

"Not much longer than you. He said the smoke from the fire dancers made his chest feel tight. Funny how that never seems to happen with the torches and acids in his workshop."

"Maybe it does. Maybe he just thinks that's worth it."

Gavin's annoyance would have been obvious even without the scowl. "He snuck out early this morning. If he put half the effort into actually training that he puts into avoiding it, he'd be commander of the army already."

It wasn't annoyance he was feeling, after all, Judah realized; it was anger. In a few years, Theron would be commander of the army anyway, no matter how ill-suited he was for the job. That was what the second son did. Gavin had always been frustrated by his brother's refusal to prepare for the role, but somehow this felt different. She narrowed her eyes. "Why are you so angry at him?"

Gavin chewed his lip for a moment. "He needs to start showing up to training. He needs to at least try."

"It doesn't matter how hard he tries. He still won't be able to see past the end of his arm."

"All the same." His usually-easy grin seemed forced. "I didn't know I was angry enough for you to feel it. Sorry.

When he's not there, I feel like I have to try twice as hard. And I already try pretty hard. So."

That didn't feel entirely true but Judah decided not to press it. "You could try a little harder not to get hit. If I'm going to end up with all the bruises anyway, they might as well put me down there with a sword."

Gavin's smile caught and spread to his eyes. "You'd be terrifying in battle. If you came at me with a weapon, I'd give you whatever you wanted. The whole country. Anything."

"Make it so, Lordling. You were just saying that I needed something to do."

"And you were telling me to go hang." He yawned. "Speaking of training, I should get down to the field. My hangover pass won't last past noon."

"So go."

"I am. I'm going." He stood up. Then he stopped. "Jude—last night, after you left...you felt sort of strange."

She put on a puzzled expression. "Strange, how?"

"Your heart was beating fast." He shook his head. "I don't know. Strange. You're sure everything was okay?"

"No. I had to go to a state dinner and sit between a courtier and a zealot. It was horrible."

"Duly noted. Anyway, that's why I sent Elly after you. Not that she minded leaving—but I wasn't just being nosy." Leaning down, he took an apple from the bowl on the table, and kissed the top of her head. "See you later."

"Don't get hit with anything," she said.

"Talk to Theron for me," he said in return.

The House didn't feel as empty as it had the night before. Their rooms were in one of the older, more run-down sections, but there were still guest rooms nearby, and the halls were full of kitchen staff and skittish pages rushing by with trays. Judah even passed a few courtiers, who either ignored her or sneered at her. Those who were truly talented at court-craft managed both. Many of them believed the story about the midwife was a lie, that she was a Southern Kingdom hostage or some illicit offshoot of Elban's, but even if there'd been no mystery about her origins, the courtiers would have sneered. They made it quite clear that the least she could do was dress decently, even if she couldn't actually be decent.

The courtiers could sneer all they wanted. Elban was healthy and strong, but when a man waged war the way he did it was wise to keep on the good side of his heir; Gavin wanted her left in peace and, with the exception of the occasional unpleasant incident like the one with the Wilmerian, he was mostly indulged. So was she. She wore what she wanted—the plainest dresses possible, Theron's old boots, Gavin's old coat—and didn't always bother to braid her hair, even though she knew how much the color disturbed people when she let it go wild. She left state dinners early, didn't bother with lessons, and wasn't asked to make the traditional crafts of her home province for visiting dignitaries. What province would that be, anyway, and what arcane and frightening crafts would it produce? Nobody knew, and nobody was quite sure, and even though nobody officially believed in witchcraft anymore, nobody was willing to risk it.

Judah made her way to the oldest section of the House, which stood at the building's proper center, like the hub of a wheel. More than one ruling family ago, the hub had been the entire House; later Lords had built around it, wanting more spacious rooms with better views and smoother glass, until it was completely surrounded. The last Lord to actually occupy the old section had been Gavin's several-times-great-grandfather, Mad Martin the Lockmaker: Mad, because he spent the last years of his life defending himself against imaginary assassins, and Lockmaker because in his madness, he'd covered every door and cupboard with beautiful, intricate locks that opened with spinning brass wheels or complicated patterns of glass gemstones or even musical notes. After Mad Martin died (of old age, reportedly) his heir had tried and mostly failed to open them. Then he'd tried to remove them, and when that failed, too, he'd had some of them hacked apart, leaving huge axe-shaped gashes in the doors. Eventually he'd given the job up as too much work, built the new council chamber that Elban still used, and abandoned the old section entirely. By then, most of its windows had been bricked over, anyway. The old part of the house was dark and old-fashioned, and nobody much minded losing it. With no particular ceremony—at least, none that was recorded—the wooden door that had once been the front entry was closed for the last time and sealed with a big, clumsy lock.

Which Theron had picked, effortlessly, when he was ten. Back then, on cold or rainy days, they'd stolen food from the kitchen and spent hours wandering the abandoned halls, where nobody ever thought to look for them. But as the years passed, the empty rooms and decaying towers that had inspired such excellent imaginary adventures held less and less appeal. Theron was the only one who came here now. Theron loved puzzles and devices as much as Mad Martin had, and he soon set himself to opening all of the elaborately locked cabinets and boxes. Most held nothing but dust and dead mice, but in others he found strange clockwork devices, which he took back to the room he'd claimed as his workshop, and tried to fix. If pieces were broken, he repaired them. If pieces were missing, he experimented with shapes and materials until he found a replacement. Elly had a music box in her room that he'd actually managed to bring back to life, a lovely golden nightingale perched on a branch. When the key was twisted, the leaves on the branch waved as if in the wind, and the nightingale sang. The song was halting and in an uncomfortable key that nobody used anymore, but the music box was Theron's greatest triumph.

The door to his workshop was hidden behind a tapestry. Judah had never had the heart to mention the pointlessness of the gesture; the marks left by Theron's repeated passage from the main door to the workshop were obvious, anyway, and even if they weren't, nobody ever came to find him but the three of them. Nonetheless, Theron wanted the door hidden, and so it was. Even if most of the time, as now, the door was propped open and the tapestry tied back to let in air. Inside, Judah found Theron bent over his workbench, his glasses slipping down his nose and some complicated metal thing in front of him. His coat lay across a high stool. Each individual lump of spine was visible through his thin shirt. She coughed and scuffed her boots loudly and still, when she said, "Hi," Theron jumped.

"Don't sneak," he said crossly. "You startled me."

"Sorry." Startling Theron was as easy as breathing. Judah leaned on the bench next to him and watched him poke at the metal thing. It was all spinning gears and colored glass bits. The glass bits seemed to wink like eyes and the whole thing made Judah think of a patiently crouched spider. But Theron gazed down it with all the fervor and devotion of a guildsman. His hands, so often fumbling and uncertain, were quick and sure as he adjusted a cog inside the body of the thing with a tool that appeared to be, and probably was, a sewing needle fixed onto the handle of a dinner knife. "What's that?" she said.

"I don't know," he said.

"What's it do?"

"I don't know."

"Then how will you know when you've fixed it?"

"I won't," he said, "unless you shut up for five seconds."
Theron was long and thin from head to toe. There was something of a bird about him, normally; not the carrion crow that
Elban made her think of, but something sparrowy and quick
to flit away. Folded onto his stool as he was now, he reminded
her more of a stick insect. His blue eyes were stormier than
his brother's but warmer than his father's. Behind their long
lashes they shone with intelligence and, at the moment, irritation. The workshop was the only place where Theron felt
confident enough to risk being annoyed. Judah loved him this
way, and so she waited.

The workshop occupied the base of one of the old-fashioned towers that nobody bothered to build anymore. The
door that led up into the tower was seldom open. Most of
the time it was blocked by a chest Theron had lugged there
from someplace, although now the chest stood in the middle
of the room and the doorway was clear. They'd tried once
to climb the narrow stone staircase that spiraled up into the
cobweb-draped dimness; at least, Gavin, Judah and Theron
had. Elly, terrified by the height of the thing, wanted nothing to do with it. They teased her for refusing to climb trees
but in the case of the tower they'd had to concede her point,
because before they'd climbed two full loops around, they
came to a place where the stairs had mostly fallen in. Usually,
the towers held nothing but old furniture, anyway, so they'd
given up. But Theron had been taken with the wide shelves
and workbenches built into the curving walls of the tower's
lowest level, and had claimed it as his own. The single greasy,
smeared window opened onto an empty space, open to the air
but walled off on all sides; Theron called it a light well, but
the light that passed through it was thin and almost useless. It
was probably just an architectural oversight. There were lots of

those in the House, places where old and new met and hadn't joined seamlessly: corridors that dead-ended, rooms with uneasy corners and awkward ceilings. The bottom of the light well was thick with brambles. They'd never found a way in, but they hadn't tried very hard.

The view, or lack thereof, didn't matter to Theron. He rarely looked out the window. Many of the locks opened with codes, so he'd dedicated one side of the room to code breaking, and piled the benches there high with books he'd stolen from the library and messy stacks of ink-spotted paper he'd scavenged from wherever he could. On the other side, where he was working now, he kept his tools, most of which he'd built or stolen or also scavenged. Older than old, some of them, and rough with corrosion for all that he'd purloined vials of acid to eat away at the crud.

Eventually, he put down the needle tool he was using. "All right. Did you want something?"

"A few things. To make sure you survived dinner last night, for one thing."

"I seem to have."

"Also, Gavin says you have to start showing up for training."

"Gavin doesn't get to tell me what to do." Theron returned to his table, surly. "Not yet, anyway."

Judah lifted her hands, palms out. "I'm only the messenger. He seemed pretty determined about it, though. Might be easier to go and get him off your back."

"Easier. To go down to the training fields and present myself as a target for the murderous lunatics Elban calls his guards? No thanks."

"Not all of them are Elban's." Elban's personal guard wore scarlet badges on their chests. The House Guard wore white. The army was made up of a mix of the two. In theory their loyalties were separated—they pledged different oaths—but the distinction was trivial. "Listen, I don't blame you. But at some point, you're going to have to deal with them." Judah couldn't think of anyone more poorly suited to command a fighting force than Theron. He didn't like crowds or loud noises and when he was frightened or nervous, he stuttered. "You know Gavin won't let anything happen to you."

"Oh, good. My brother is watching out for me. I'm so relieved." Theron picked up the needle tool again and bent back over his device, but his movements had gone aimless. "Who was that courtier you left with last night?"

Judah blew out a disgusted huff of air. "If this is what happens when I leave a room five minutes before a complete stranger, I'll be more careful next time."

"Well, Gavin certainly spends enough time with them. And you two being as thick as you are—and, really, I mean that in all possible senses—it's not unreasonable to think you'll start, too."

"I loathe the courtiers."

"Gavin used to say the same."

"He has to play nice."

"Does he." Theron's tone was dry.

She experienced a moment of dislocation: in her head, Theron would be forever fourteen and gangly. But the Theron before her, with his wary expression and patchy unshaven beard, seemed much older than the twenty he was, even. "Don't be oblique. You're bad at it. If you have something to say, say it."

"He has one courtier friend in particular. I don't know her name." With distaste he added, "She's very pretty."

"Better the courtiers than the staff." This distinction had been the subject of many an argument between Gavin and Judah, particularly since she'd become friendly with Darid and learned more about staff life. Lady courtiers had family, position and power to protect them; the staff girls had nobody. She was relieved, if a bit surprised, to hear that any of what she'd said had sunk in.

But Theron's disgust was clear. "He's marrying Elly. He shouldn't be spending time with other women."

"Maybe not, but—Theron, nobody expects that. Not even Elly. Gavin is who he is. The courtiers are who they are. They're horrible. He's not. It'll all work itself out eventually." She resisted the urge to ruffle his hair. "Gavin can be a little oblivious sometimes, but he's not a bad person. And he really will keep an eye out for you on the training field. You know that."

"Give up. I'm not going down there unless he drags me."

"He might."

Theron only shrugged. "In the meantime, maybe you'll let me get back to work."

So that was what she did.

The previous spring, she'd walked past the House stables during weaning. The cavalry stables, on the other side of the House, were all shouting and drills and massive stomping warhorses; those, she avoided. But there were foals at the House stables. She'd been unobtrusively watching them for months: their first wobbly explorations of the paddock, their games of tag and chase, the way their mothers bent soft noses down to theirs. But that day, weaning day, was different. The foals she'd grown to recognize paced nervously, squealing and bolting and tossing their heads in distress. Every time one approached the gate, the stablemen drove it away with cries and waving arms. The mothers were nowhere in sight.

All Judah had known was that the foals were upset, that they wanted to leave the paddock and couldn't. She'd glared at the stablemen perched on the split-rail fence, who shifted uncomfortably. A few of them did something with their hands, a sort of slashing motion. Much later, Darid told her that cityfolk used that sign to protect against the evil eye—not that they would admit to believing in it, but just to be on the safe side. He'd been the one who'd finally approached to ask what she wanted. She hadn't known he was Darid then; he was just the head stableman, as blond-haired and blue-eyed as everyone else, dressed in dull staff brown, with massive arms that spoke of a lifetime of labor. Unsmiling but reasonably friendly, he'd explained about weaning and why it had to be done. The foals would calm down, he said, and suggested she come back in a few days to see for herself.

Judah had been idle then, and lonely. Gavin was training and Theron was hiding and Elly had just begun to be sucked into the vortex of protocol that would prepare her for life as Lady of the City. Everybody had something to do except Judah, and she'd felt the loss of the others like she'd feel the loss of a limb, so yes: she came back to the stables a few days later, and yes, the foals were calmer. Her favorite, a pure black colt who shone like onyx in the sun, pranced around the paddock as if it belonged to him.

"Something, that one," Darid said when he noticed her watching the colt.

"He's beautiful," she'd said.

That time, he did smile—for all that he bit it back quickly. Then he clucked his tongue and patted the flat of his hand on the inside of the pasture fence. The colt came over to investigate. Darid handed Judah something small and wizened. It was an apple, or had been once. "Give him that, if you like. Hold your hand flat. Watch out for his teeth."

Now the colt was a yearling, as bold and glorious as ever, and she and Darid were friends. As much as they could be, anyway, since he was staff and she was…whatever she was.

But he smiled more easily now, and if the other stablemen found other places to be when she arrived, they were polite enough about it. Darid had told her about all the different shades of black a horse could be, in the sun and out of it: rusty black, coffee-colored, even faintly blue. The colt was jet black. Elban preferred jet blacks, for the impression they made with his white hair and black armor. (The Wraith Lord in the lowlands, the Ghost King across the sea, where it was said the Nali thought he was risen from the dead and wore charms against him.) The nimble little colt would someday carry Elban into battle, and he would probably die there, and so Judah tried not to care about him.

He made it hard. His ears pricked up at the sound of her boots crunching on the near-frozen ground and when he saw her, he trotted over to the fence, whickering. She'd brought him an apple, not one of the sad orchard rejects the stablemen were given but a firm, juicy one that she'd slipped into her coat at breakfast. "You only love me for my apples," she told the colt, as he ate it greedily and then pushed his warm nose against her hand, hoping for more. "It's okay. I'll take what I can get."

There were a lot of stablemen around that day: mending the pasture gate, hauling hay bales up to the loft, mucking out the stalls vacated that morning by Wilmerian horses. One of them had probably gone to find Darid as soon as she'd rounded the bend in the path, and sure enough, it wasn't long before he emerged from the stable and joined her at the fence. He was bareheaded but wore a heavy wool scarf against the chill. "Didn't expect you today," he said. "Figured you'd be sleeping in with the rest of them."

"Are you too busy?"

"Not at all. You want to help me mend tack?"

She did. She wanted to mend tack or clean out stalls or

oil leather or mix feed or do anything he suggested, as long as it was real work that he would have done anyway; as long as she was useful. The tack room was warmer, if not exactly balmy, and the air was fragrant with oil and leather and horse. There were stools but she preferred to sit against the wall on the floor. She wasn't very good at cutting leather, but she was good at stitching it—ironic, given how awful she'd always been at sewing. But this wasn't embroidering a handkerchief or a throw pillow. This was making something.

They worked in silence for a time. "I like your scarf," she said eventually.

The wool was rough-spun and undyed, but it looked warm. "My sister made it," Darid said, an unusual note of pride in his voice. He had several sisters. He wouldn't tell her exactly how many, or their names, or how old they were. He hadn't seen any of them since he'd come inside the Wall when he was ten. Once you came inside, you didn't leave. His family fascinated her. She was as persistent in asking about them as he was in refusing to answer.

"Which sister?" she said now.

"The one who knits."

"Did she send a letter with it?" Because he'd let slip that only one of his sisters could read and write well enough to send a letter.

He shook his head, amused. Not a *no*, but a refusal to respond. "How was the grand dinner last night?"

"Grand." She blinked away the image of the sweaty Wilmerian and focused, instead, on the bridle in her hand. "Dinnery. Did the Wilmerians notice that they got their horses back in better shape than they left them?"

He shook his head again. Staff members didn't get to decide where they worked, and some ended up in jobs they hated. But Darid loved horses—all horses—and he'd worked hard to bring the Wilmerian beasts back to something approaching health. Not that it would make a difference. Not that the Wilmerians would treat them any better on the long return to the guildhall than they had on the journey from it. But to speak ill of Elban's guests would be dangerous for staff and he wouldn't do it, even in front of her. Instead, he nodded at the bridle and said, "You're doing a good job."

She didn't press. "Thanks. What do the factories in the city make?" Questions about the city were her third-favorite kind to ask him, after those about his family and those about horses. As if someday he would mention some detail about life in the city and it would tug free an ancient memory of the people she'd come from. A child's fancy, she knew. But she still asked.

Gazing toward the ceiling—most of the ceilings in the stable were just the bottom of the hayloft above, but the tack room was lined in stucco so the leather would stay dry if the roof leaked—Darid said, "Different things. Iron goods. Paper. Toys and dolls and sewing needles, for all I know. I haven't been outside in—how old are you?"

"Twenty-two."

"Then that's how long it's been. I came inside the year you and Lord Gavin were born. So I don't know much about the city these days."

Out of the sun, his sandy hair could almost pass for brown and his eyes were a warm blue, almost green. "Was the Seneschal here, then?"

"Younger. He'd only been Seneschal a few years."

"I don't believe it. I think he's been here since they laid the foundations. They finished the gaslights in the House, by the way."

"What are they like?" he asked with interest.

"Purplish. Weird. Bright." She remembered the drunken Wilmerian and didn't want to talk about it anymore. She'd asked about the factories because the fires were pretty, from far away. Like stars fallen to earth, twinkling on the horizon. "We can see the city from some of the terraces. It's beautiful from here."

"I suppose it would be."

"I guess it's not, up close."

"I suppose not." His voice was neutral.

"Do you miss living there? Do you miss being outside?"

It was a dangerous question. "It was a long time ago. Another life," Darid said, and they continued to work.

CHAPTER TWO

On her way back up to the parlor, a muscle in her left thigh seized. The bloom of pain sent thorns bristling down the length of her leg and instantly, she froze. There was a wall close enough to touch but she didn't reach out to steady herself. Instead, she forced herself to examine the tapestry that hung there: a woman and a lion. The woman wore a stupid gauzy dress even though she was in the forest. A stupid thing to do. Stupid, stupid, stupid. Pain coursed through her leg. A dress like that would snag and rip and get in the way. She wished she were in the wilderness. She wished she could meet a lion.

In a few minutes, the pain faded enough for her to walk, and she did. Slowly, so she wouldn't limp. She had missed lunch but when she finally made it to the parlor, leftovers from last night's dinner sat on the table: slices of meat, bread, a pot of peppered cheese. If she spread the cheese thick, the bread wouldn't seem so dry. There was also an unopened bottle of wine. Characteristically, the Seneschal had not forgotten that he wanted Elly to build her tolerance. Characteristically, she had quietly ignored him.

Judah took the bottle and some bread and cheese with her to the sofa, where she hoisted her hurt leg onto the cushion with both hands, and began to eat.

The wine was decent. By the time Gavin showed up, limping worse than she had, Judah felt pleasantly warm. He gave her a sheepish grin; she scowled, and threw the wine cork at him. It hit him in the chest and bounced away harmlessly. "Be better at sword fighting," she said.

"That's the second time today you've thrown something at me." He dropped into a chair. "Sorry about the leg. I was distracted and I missed a parry. Those longswords are heavy. Where were you when it happened?"

"Alone in the corridor. Could have been worse."

His grin faded. "And it's going to be, I'm sorry to say. You have about ten minutes before the vulture gets here."

Judah's pleasant warmth evaporated. "They sent for Arkady? For a stupid bump on the leg?"

"Elban and the Seneschal were watching from the sidelines. Why do you think I was distracted?"

"I assumed there was a girl involved. Theron says you have a new one." She took another drink from the wine bottle, enjoying the way his cheeks flushed. "I want the Seneschal to evaporate. I want them all to evaporate. Do you think Theron has some weird thing in his workshop that will do that? An unpleasant-person evaporator?"

"You're the witch. Cast a spell." Gavin's blush had faded. He leaned over and took the bottle from her. "Where did you get this?"

"I cast a spell."

"If you can make bottles of wine appear by magic, I'll marry you instead of Elly."

"No, thank you. Three's a crowd and four's a bloodbath. Going to tell me about her?"

Gavin drank long, and passed the bottle back. He pushed himself to standing and crossed to the table, his left leg dragging. As he piled most of the food left on the tray into a massive sandwich, he said, "I saw your special courtier friend on the way up here, by the way. He said to send his regards, and he hopes you're well, all of that." Judah made a rude noise, and Gavin laughed. "Oh, the lady does not reciprocate his affections! Brutal."

"It does get so tedious, the constant stream of suitors humiliating themselves at my feet. And you're avoiding the question."

The door opened. Suddenly the room was full of people: the Seneschal, dressed as always in somber gray with an expression to match, and Arkady Magus, who they called the vulture because he was bony and hunched and they hated him. Accompanying the old man was a slender, bespectacled man Judah had never seen before. He wore his straw-blond hair back in a queue the way Arkady did, but the resulting tail wasn't very long. If he was a magus, he was new at it.

"Your Lordship," Arkady said in the fawning tone that was broken glass on Judah's nerves. The loose skin under his chin wobbled faintly with each word. "I came as soon as I heard."

"Heard what?" Gavin was curt. "I'm fine."

"Better to be safe," the Seneschal said calmly. The Seneschal was always calm.

"I walked here, up a hill and approximately forty flights of stairs. I'm fine."

"Nevertheless, my lord," Arkady said. "A minor injury can hold hidden dangers."

Meanwhile, the stranger hovered in the background, holding Arkady's satchel in addition to a second one that must have been his own. New apprentice, then. It was about time. Arkady had been ancient when they were children and he wasn't getting any younger. His skin was an unhealthy yellowish gray and his hair was thin and brittle-looking. The idea of him dying brought Judah great pleasure.

Gavin looked at her, grimly resigned. "I don't care," she said, although she did.

The Seneschal coughed meaningfully. How obscure this all must have seemed to Arkady's poor apprentice (who, in Judah's opinion, looked a bit dazed). They couldn't treat Gavin's leg without treating Judah's, because his leg would keep hurting as long as hers did. Treating Judah would require explanations, and explanations were most definitely not allowed. A fun corner they'd backed themselves into. She would enjoy watching them squirm in it.

Flinty-eyed, Arkady glanced at his apprentice. "I left my coat in the retiring room. Go fetch it."

"Have a page show you the way," the Seneschal said.

"I remember," the apprentice said, and left.

Then it was only Arkady and the Seneschal and Judah and Gavin. The two men were the only ones outside of the family who knew about the bond. Judah felt Gavin press a thumbnail against the pad of his first finger. The simplest and oldest of their signals: a nod, a wink, a hello. An acknowledgment that they both existed, that they were who they were, and nobody else was.

"Quickly," the Seneschal said. "Before he returns."

"Show me, girl," Arkady said.

Judah stood, hiked up her skirt, and unhooked the legging she wore beneath it. Gavin had seen her leg plenty of times; she didn't care if the Seneschal did, and she didn't want to be alone in a room with Arkady if she could help it. The sore place was on the side of her thigh, halfway to her knee, and edging toward spectacular, now that she got a look at it. The swollen, purple skin looked as if she were hatching an egg underneath it.

"You'll need a poultice for that," Arkady said.

"In the bedroom, please," the Seneschal said. "The apprentice will ask questions."

"No," Judah said.

"If we have to chloroform her, you'll lose the rest of the day, too, of course," the Seneschal told Gavin. "And there's the meeting with the generals in a few hours about the Nali campaign. Your father will be disappointed if you miss it."

"Treat us in the same room," Gavin said.

The Seneschal shook his head. "The apprentice will ask questions about that, too."

Gavin pressed his fingers against the edges of his eye sockets. Then, with an apologetic grimace toward Judah: "The door stays open."

Wordless, she dropped her skirt and stalked into the other room. Arkady followed her and closed the door halfway behind them.

Lying on her side on Elly's bed, Judah arranged her skirt so only the hurt leg showed. A quickstove sat on the table—a small one, and new. It burned vials of Wilmerian gas and could heat a kettle to boiling in minutes. Arkady filled the kettle at the tap, placed it in the bracket, and used a match to light the flame. Then he took out his mortar and began rifling through his herb box, pulling out one tiny cloth sack after another.

"Where'd you find the toady?" Judah said. Not because the silence was awkward—she loathed Arkady and knew the feeling was mutual—but because she actually wanted to know.

"My apprentice, you mean." Arkady began to grind herbs, gripping the pestle like it was a weapon and the herbs had offended him. An acrid smell filled the room. "You see, foundling, in the real world, people with no family or money must work to support themselves, or they starve." The kettle was steaming now. He closed the gas valve, poured hot water into the mortar, ground away at it a few more times, and dumped the whole mess into a towel. When he came to stand over her, the smell was strong and almost culinary, like food gone off. Arkady's fingers were bony and cold.

When she was younger, he'd occasionally taken liberties with those fingers. They'd put a stop to that, she and Gavin, and he had not taken liberties since. But she could not keep him from touching her, sometimes. He knew it, and let his fingers linger in a way she knew they would not have with Elly. Now he pushed aside her carefully-arranged skirt, prodding leisurely at the bruise and the flesh around it. "Lord Elban ought to make you hide that scab-colored hair, or shave it off," he said. "It's disturbing to look at."

"So are you," she said.

He slapped the poultice down on her leg hard. Aside from the bruise, the thing was hot and whatever herb he'd used was caustic. She couldn't hear her leg sizzling but it felt like it ought to be. He pressed the poultice tight to her skin, staring right at her. She stared right back. She didn't flinch.

"Inhuman thing," he said, and then the door banged all the way open and Gavin limped in, his face dark with anger. Elly followed behind him.

"What are you doing to her?" Gavin said at his most imperious. His glare was fixed on Arkady but Elly's eyes were on Judah.

"My apologies, Your Lordship," Arkady said as he slid a bandage under Judah's leg. Even through the pain she was disgusted by his touch on the inside of her thigh. "I'm afraid the water was a bit hot. It should be perfect for you if we hurry, Lord."

Elly was already there, taking the bandage from the vulture's thin hands, pushing him away from Judah. "Then hurry," she said, nearly as imperious as Gavin. "I'll do this."

Gavin looked at Judah, who said, "Go ahead. I'm fine."

When they were gone, Elly peeled back the poultice, sniffed at the soggy herbs and winced at the scalded skin beneath it. "I really hate that man. How are you not weeping right now?"

"Well-trained," Judah said. In the other room, she felt Arkady put a matching poultice on Gavin's leg. It was applied more gently, and not so hot, but the burn still flared anew. Since the door was closed now, and it was only Elly, she let herself wince, and close her eyes.

After Clorin died, they'd discussed sending Judah away—the Seneschal had told her so—but putting her in someone else's care was too uncertain, and Gavin cried and refused to eat when separated from her. Nobody ever mentioned if Judah had cried, too. But every winter, as soon as the first deep snow fell, they'd make her sit naked on a snowbank. She still remembered the feel of snow packed between her toes, of snowflakes hitting her bare shoulders. Watching through the glass-paned terrace doors as Gavin, inside by the fire, grew listless and blue.

They—Elban and the Seneschal—worried that someone might use her to hurt Gavin. Every choice made for them was made with that possibility in mind. At six years old, they'd never had a tutor, for fear of what their young tongues would let slip; other than Elban and the Seneschal, they saw only their illiterate nurses (who were sequestered from the rest of the staff, and who had a disturbing tendency to vanish after a year or so) and Theron. Who was only a second son, anyway, and with his cough that came and went, came and went, nobody had really expected him to survive his childhood. Judah supposed that if Theron had been as strong, handsome and charming as Gavin, she and Elban's older son would probably have suffered a tragic illness early on, and been mourned throughout the kingdom.

But Theron was Theron, shy and thin and not at all Lord of the City material, so Gavin and Judah lived. When Elban wasn't campaigning, the Lord even took a tiny bit of interest in his heir; he'd let the boy join him on guard inspection, or in the council chamber, or at executions. After Gavin's seventh birthday, Elban and the Seneschal scoured the distant—and less powerful—courtier families for the boy's future bride. Eventually they found her in Tiernan, a remote district known primarily for its sheep and secondarily for its blackwork embroidery; the girl's family was wealthy enough to be respectable, but poor enough to be glad of the brideprice, and willing to accept with it the condition that they'd never see the girl again. The child herself, the Seneschal had told Gavin on that long-ago afternoon, was pretty and obedient; smart enough to read and write, but not smart enough to be troublesome. Later, it made Judah laugh, all the ways that Elban and the Seneschal had misjudged Elly.

The marriage had been arranged earlier than usual, so that the bond between the two children would have time to strengthen, and any other bonds the girl came with had time to weaken. When hurting the Lord of the City was as easy as pushing Judah down the stairs, these things could not be left to chance. Even so—the Seneschal had explained—the secret must be kept. Judah and Gavin must learn to keep it.

They'd been eight. It was the first time Judah had ever been allowed in Elban's study. In her memory it was all warm yellow light from the oil lamps, shelves filled with books and strange weapons taken as trophies, and massive furniture that made Judah feel tiny. Elban himself, his white hair tied back like a magus and his eyes glittering in the lamplight, had held a glass of wine in his hand, the liquid a deep beautiful red like an overripe strawberry, like Judah's hair. He hadn't done anything but watch. It was Arkady who had brought the knives and the brands and the acid, and he and the Seneschal who had used them on her. Always her. The person who wasn't directly hurt healed faster and scarred less, and they wanted Gavin to stay perfect. He had tried to be perfect. He had tried to be brave, in the presence of his father. But even he had cried before long, and begged and pleaded.

We'll stop when you can keep quiet, the Seneschal had said. *You must learn to be quiet.*

When Judah passed out, they revived her and started again. She didn't know how long they spent in the study, if it was three nights or thirty. She remembered being forced to eat, to drink water. She remembered the Seneschal leaning over her, holding smelling salts beneath her nose. Saying, not entirely unkindly: *The only way out is through. You must learn to do this.*

She remembered the way Gavin had screamed when they hurt her. She remembered how she'd hated him for it: she remembered seeing, through blurry eyes, that hate reflected back from him. It was hard, in such a blinding storm of agony, not to hate the person that caused it, however unintentionally. It was hard to care about anything but stopping the pain.

In the end, the lesson took. Arkady cut a thin scarlet line across the width of Judah's thigh and neither of them so much as flinched.

"Good," Elban said, the first time he'd spoken. The Seneschal had nodded.

Very shortly thereafter, Elly had arrived from Tiernan.

Judah was still bandaged under her clothes. She still hurt. She and Gavin could barely speak to each other. They were in too much pain and the memories were still too fresh. Theron was little and scared and didn't understand. She felt utterly, completely alone, in a way she never had before.

And into the midst of this pain and confusion came Eleanor of Tiernan, wearing her nicest clothes (which still seemed old-fashioned and dowdy), her long hair braided into loops. Her thick-lashed eyes looked too big for her face and everyone who saw her was charmed by the quaint little thing from the provinces. Arkady examined the future Lady of the City and pronounced her healthy (and did not burn or cut or hit her, Judah could not help but notice); Elban came, too, his first visit to their rooms since Theron's birth and the last he would ever make. As he sat on the late Lady Clorin's pale rose-colored sofa, he'd taken the unprecedented step of bringing the new little girl onto his knee for a few minutes, asking questions in his cool, cultured voice. How had her trip been? *(Very lovely, thank you, Lord Elban, and the carriage you sent was extremely fine.)* Did she miss her mother and father, and all of her brothers? *(Only a very little bit, Lord Elban, because who could ever be sad in a place as grand as this?)* Would she behave herself, and work hard, and do everything she was told, so that one day she might be worthy of the honor of being Gavin's Lady? *(I could never be worthy, Lord Elban, but I will work very hard.)*

As they spoke, his icy eyes had moved from his oldest son, sitting impassive and stiff—there were bandages under Gavin's clothes, too—to Judah, skulking across the room. Judah felt the hate in those eyes, the contempt. Her life until the nights in the study had been relatively pleasant, but now she knew it didn't have to be. He wouldn't kill her, not until they were able to dissolve whatever it was that bound Gavin's health to hers, but he could hurt her, and he would. The lovely little country doll on his knee was acceptable; Judah herself, with her savage-colored hair and her awkward bandages and her offensive black irises, was not. The doll would be lauded—in fact, as Judah watched, Elban slid a ring with a pale pink stone onto Eleanor's finger—and Judah would be tolerated. Barely.

Judah didn't care about rings and she didn't want to sit on Elban's lap. She would rather have been touched by the burning brand Arkady had used on her than by those thin white fingers. But she clearly read Gavin's relief and greed as he watched his future bride, and it made her feel sick and unsteady. She realized later that this had all been deliberate. The men in the study hadn't broken the unnatural bond, but they'd torn Judah and Gavin apart just the same. They had made it hard for him to meet her eye and then given him someone else to look at: someone uncomplicated and beautiful; someone entirely his, who he was allowed to love, and who nobody would ever try to take away from him.

They'd given Judah nothing.

It would have made all the sense in the world for Judah to hate Eleanor. For a few minutes, she did. But then the adults left, and the four of them were alone: Gavin and Judah, injured and traumatized; Theron, perpetually a bit baffled but especially then (left alone for all those nights with only the silent nurse for company, and then Gavin and Judah came back sick and odd and none of them slept in the same room anymore, and now apparently this complete stranger lived with them); and the new girl herself, Eleanor of Tiernan. Elly, although she wasn't quite Elly to them yet. Who looked from one of them to the other. Smiled tentatively. Then dropped down on the rug where she stood, buried her face in her hands and wept.

Gavin and Judah both still found the sound of crying actively painful, so it was Theron, finally, who went to her, and slid a thin arm around her shoulders.

"He doesn't like me," she said, her teary blue eyes enormous. "He has to like me. If he doesn't like me he'll send me home and my father will have to give back the money and my brothers will be so angry, I don't even know what they'll do. He doesn't like me. But he's so *scary*. I'm so *scared*."

She was talking about Elban. The tiny perfect dolly was weeping with fear and terror of Elban. And yet she'd sat so sweetly on his knee and answered his questions so perfectly. Judah, who had recently learned a great deal about how difficult it was to feel one thing inside and another outside, found herself reluctantly impressed. That was her first glimpse of the steel in Elly. There would be more.

And then Judah thought again about the way Elban had watched her across the room as Elly sat on his lap: the frigid gleam of satisfaction in his eyes, the cruelest hint of a smile. It was the same expression he wore at solstice parties when two courtiers held one of their subtle, sniping arguments, competing for his favor. Although Judah was young, some prescient part of her realized that she was *supposed* to hate this girl. They had been set against each other like rats in a cage. The sense of rebellion she'd thought dead in the study flared back to life. Who, in this entire palace, should be more her friend than this girl, who no more belonged here than Judah did, for all her quaint braids and pretty manners?

She knelt down—stiffly—in front of the girl. "He doesn't like anybody. He hates me. He'd kill me, if he could. Oh, please stop crying." The girl's sobs were stabbing blades in Judah's skull, they made the cut on her thigh sting and burn. Judah reached out and touched Elly's hand. Theron laid his head on the pale girl's shoulder.

Elly peered up at her. Something about the angle of her head made Judah realize that her eyes looked so big because her face was too thin. "You're Lady Clorin's foundling."

"Judah," Judah said, and then—unexpectedly—felt Gavin's hand on her shoulder.

"My foster sister," he said.

Elly gazed up at him, her face tearstained and frightened. "I don't want to go back. They can't send me back."

"They won't," Gavin said.

"How do you know?"

"Because I won't let them," he said. For the first time ever, he sounded like his father. Judah remembered stifling a shudder, and being surprised, because it was harder than stifling a scream.

Arkady was a revolting person, but he was a good magus. His poultice worked well, and the person who wasn't actually hurt healed faster, and the next morning the egg on Judah's leg was barely a pebble. A summons from the Seneschal arrived for her with breakfast. Putting him off was pointless; he would send page after page, and eventually come to find her himself. So she made her way to his tiny office. It was poorly ventilated and his door was propped open with a brick to let in the fresher air from the corridor. Inside, he sat at his desk with his collar unbuttoned. The Seneschal's job—one of them—was to maintain protocol, but he only did so when it mattered. It was among his few redeeming qualities.

She tapped on the open door. He glanced up and beckoned her toward the only chair, which was straight-backed and hard. He was a solid man and in the tiny room he seemed like an extra wall behind his desk, unsmiling in his gray uniform, his hair cut so short that it was as colorless as the rest of him. "I'm surprised," he said. "I thought I'd have to send at least three messages before I saw you."

"Well, you didn't," she said. "What do you want?"

"One moment." He bent back over the ledger in front of him.

The desk was covered in clutter. From where Judah sat she could see three inkwells, two broken pens, countless piles of books and scrolls and papers; through the open window she could see the massive gate in the Wall, closed and barred today. The gate was opened one day a week, six men working each enormous winch, to let in the supplies that the House couldn't produce itself, and once a year for new staff. She and Gavin had stolen a glimpse of Staff Day once, the lines of ten-year-olds in worn city clothes trying not to be frightened. Darid had been one of those children once. She wondered if the Seneschal had.

There was only one other way through the Wall to the city: the Safe Passage, a twisting maze of switchbacks and locked doors, deliberately built to be confusing if you didn't know the way. Twice a year, when the Seneschal led the four of them, flanked fore and aft by House Guards, to the Lord's Balcony for Elban's speech, they had to pause every few yards so the Seneschal could unlock and relock the doors. The floor was covered in woven mats of oiled rushes to waterproof them, and their stench permeated the air. Every month, as Lady-to-be of the City, Elly had to oversee the replacement and oiling of the rushes while the Seneschal stood, keys in hand, and watched, wordless as stone.

He seemed just as stony now as Judah waited. She had spent too much of her life sitting in this chair; too many long, agonizing minutes staring out this window and biting back her words. Just being here made her tongue ache. Usually his summonses heralded some unpleasant new change in her life, like being banned from the library or expected to attend state dinners. She wondered what it would be today. His pen scratched. The window did not close tightly enough to block out the creak of cart wheels, the shuffle of feet on cobble-stone, the muffled voices of the courtyard staff. Life being lived. She sat. She waited.

Finally, he closed the ledger, put down his pen and looked at her. "Are you well?"

Judah shrugged.

He waited a moment, and when she still said nothing, leaned back in his chair. "So much for the pleasantries. We'll get to it, shall we? I was reminded this morning of a conversation I've been meaning to have with you. I've been putting it off, because it's not a particularly pleasant conversation."

In the study, when Judah was eight, the Seneschal had held a hot coal to her foot, over and over again, until Gavin could bite back the pain, and not cry. "I didn't know you had a preference for pleasant conversations," Judah said.

"I don't have a preference for unpleasant ones. At the Wilmerian dinner, you were seated next to a courtier. Firo of Cerrington."

"I sat where I was put."

"You were not put there with the expectation that you would be seen leaving the hall with him."

"I didn't leave the hall with him. Find one person who saw me leave the hall with him."

"It doesn't matter," he said patiently. "It is believed that you were seen leaving the hall with him. That's enough. Did he speak to you?"

"He may have complimented my dress." *Even if it is Lady Eleanor's winter solstice gown from two years past, it's been remade well*, he'd said. It wasn't true. The dress had been remade terribly. They always were.

"Your position here is—strange," the Seneschal said. "You have privileges, but no rank; a soft life, but no status. Your only purpose is to stay alive and healthy so that Lord Gavin stays alive and healthy."

"You say all of this like it's new to me."

He nodded. "We haven't given up, you know. We're still hunting for the midwife who brought you here. And one of the reasons Lord Elban is so interested in the Nali is that there are aspects of their culture that we would consider unnatural."

"Unnatural, like me?" Judah said.

"Well, you're not Nali, if that's what you're thinking. But the bond that keeps you here is unnatural, yes. The hope is that we can use Nali knowledge to understand how to break that bond."

"I'm not sure that would be to my benefit."

"Your concern isn't entirely unfounded. But Lord Gavin is very attached to you, as is Lady Eleanor. The closer they come to power, the more that matters."

"Elly gets power? She'll be delighted to hear it. We were all under the impression that she had nothing to do but oil the rushes and breed."

The Seneschal's eyebrows lifted, which was as close as he ever came to emotion. "And here we are. Arrived at the point."

"Which is?"

"No lovers," he said. "Not for you. Not ever."

Unexpectedly, she found herself wanting to laugh. "What?"

"Women die in childbirth, and in pregnancy, and trying to end pregnancy. Lovers driven mad by jealousy lash out in violent ways. We can't risk any of that."

Then she actually did laugh. "And where are they," she said, when she could speak again, "these lovers who'll be driven mad with jealousy over me? They sound unbalanced. I'd like to think I'd have better taste."

"Judah," he said.

"Maybe you should post a guard at my door."

"Hopefully it won't come to that."

Her laughter died. "There's a thing called a joke."

"I wasn't making one." He sighed. "We were hoping to find a solution before now. We should have done things differently, kept you hidden. But we didn't, and now, like it or not, people expect to see you. Like at the state dinner for the Wilmerians, or the betrothal ball next month. They're interested in you. Too interested, honestly. If they didn't see you, they'd talk. Ask questions. As it is, they spin all sorts of nonsensical tales about you and Lady Eleanor and the young lord. Particularly after Lord Gavin kicked out the last nurse."

The nurses had all been old, tongueless women who sat in the parlor between their bedrooms all night to prevent what the Seneschal called *impropriety*. When they were seventeen, Gavin had picked the last one up physically, put her in the hallway, and refused to allow another one back in.

"They are nonsense, I hope," the Seneschal continued.

For a moment Judah thought he meant the nurses. Then she caught up. "They must be, because I have no idea what you're talking about."

"People think your relationship with Lord Gavin has—transgressed. Inappropriately."

She blinked. "What, they think we're in love?"

"Something like that. I've never believed it, or we'd have had this conversation years ago."

"That's absurd. Gavin is—" She fumbled for the words. "We're not like that. He's not. I'm not."

The Seneschal picked up a stack of paper and moved it a few inches to the left. It occurred to Judah that the man was embarrassed. "I'm glad to hear it. Lord Gavin mostly favors his mother, you know, in both appearance and manner, which is to his benefit. But there does seem to be one way in which he favors his father. So it's natural, when his appetite for women is well known, that the women close to him would be scrutinized. After the wedding, most of the talk should die down."

Appetite for women. Judah didn't like that phrase, as if the women Gavin pursued were so many plates of food placed in front of him.

The Seneschal was still talking. "When we no longer need to have you and Lady Eleanor publicly not hating each other—"

"Elly and I don't hate each other."

"—then we'll arrange for you to miss one court event, and eventually another. In time—"

"I'll be in complete seclusion," Judah said grimly. "So why worry about my thousands of lovers?"

"You should be grateful. You could have been in complete seclusion all along. Anyway, don't be so pessimistic. Maybe we'll be able to arrange for you to be pledged to a celibate guild, eventually. One of the bookish ones; that would seem to suit you." He folded his hands on the desk, his eyes hard and cold. "In the meantime, we cannot risk even the suggestion of disloyalty. Therefore, you cannot mix with the courtiers. At all. They have spent their entire lives training in manipulation and intrigue and they will eat you alive."

Judah was picturing herself in some cold guildhall on a hill, all rocks and sackcloth and arcane rituals with no actual purpose. "You're the one who put me next to him at the damn table."

"I am deathly serious, Judah. You have a reputation for doing whatever you want, regardless of what's right or proper, and we have indulged Lord Gavin by indulging you. Frankly, what you do or don't do has never mattered, as long as you weren't physically hurt. But the time for indulgence is past, and now, in this matter, you will obey. I am deathly serious," he said again.

"How deathly serious can you be?" Judah said. "It's not like you can kill me."

"No. We can't kill you." Now, for the first time, he smiled: a sad smile, and weary. "How young you are. How little you know."

Exiting the Seneschal's office into a swirl of rushing pages and staff, Judah churned with fury. So she wasn't supposed to talk to the courtiers; who wanted to? But Gavin, Elly and Theron were too busy to talk much these days. Darid wasn't supposed to talk to her at all. One day he'd get tired of risking his head and very gently ask her not to come back. The life she saw stretching in front of her may have been soft and privileged, as the Seneschal had said, but it was also bleak and lonely. By the time they shipped her off to a guild, she might not mind leaving.

Meanwhile, she wasn't interested in lovers or courtiers, so she'd lost nothing. She didn't know why she was so angry. Her boots were on her feet and her work gloves were stuffed in her pocket; she would go to the stables while she still could.

The most direct route was the Promenade, a paved path that wound through the most charming parts of the garden. Normally Judah avoided it but today she resented having to go out of her way. The day was sunny and not too cold, and courtiers were gathered into stinging nosegays at every fountain and bench. They knew how to angle their bodies in morning light and afternoon, where to stand to ensure the vistas behind them made the loveliest backdrops; they knew, to a one, which plants and shrubs would complement the colors they wore. For the courtiers, self-awareness was an art. If one watched—if, say, one was forced to attend a state dinner—one could observe each courtier cycling through the poses and angles they believed most flattering. A tilted head here, a bent shoulder there. Over and over.

Now, like paintings, the courtiers stood frozen and silent in each gallery she passed. Unlike paintings, they erupted into bursts of laughter and chatter as soon as she was out of sight, which only stoked the fire inside her. She knew the picture she made in Gavin's old coat and Theron's old boots and Elly's old dress with the worn lines where the seams had been let out. Let them recoil. She was no business of theirs and they were no business of hers and it wouldn't hurt their pretty little eyes to see something ugly now and again. She held her head up. She took her time.

As she passed the last of the galleries, someone fell into step next to her. It was the courtier from the Wilmerian dinner. Not dressed as grandly as he had been that night, maybe, but his boots still shone and his aquamarine coat had been perfectly brushed. He wore less kohl around his eyes, and hadn't combed his hair quite as high, but he still wore the pea-sized diamonds in his ears. And his smell was the same. Lavender and something else, something sweet and cloying.

He bowed his head slightly without breaking pace. "Lady Judah."

"Leave me alone." She could be rude if she wanted. The Seneschal would approve of anything that drove him away.

"We met the other night, do you remember? That unfortunate incident with the Wilmerian." His features assembled themselves into a reasonable facsimile of sorrow. "One must be careful around guildfolk. The old ones are calculating and craven, and the young ones—well, they leave the world very young, some of them. No real life experience to speak of."

She didn't answer. He bowed again. "Firo of Cerrington, lady. Most pleased to meet you again under more genial circumstances."

"I'm not feeling genial," she said, "and I'm not a lady."

He raised his eyebrows, a sleek, practiced gesture. "Perhaps not. But Judah the Foundling makes it sound rather as if you're here to do magic tricks, doesn't it?"

"I might be. You never know."

"Stories they tell to scare staff children," he said dismissively. "Nobody of any caliber credits such talk. Believe me, if magic were real, every courtier in the House would be studying sorcery. I don't believe I've ever seen you on the Promenade before."

"I try to avoid it."

"Not unwise." She was walking quickly, to convey that she wasn't interested in a chat, but his long legs easily kept stride with her. "People talk about it as if it's a loop, but it's more of an—oh, an intricately beaded necklace, I suppose. Brilliantly designed. Lots of secret nooks one can duck into if one has the need. But of course secrecy works both ways; when you can't be seen, you also can't see. You never know who might be listening." She felt his hand touch her elbow, gently steering her toward a shadowed lane that ran long and straight beneath an arbor bristling with ancient wisteria. "Now, this walk, as you can see, has no such nooks: the House on one side, the reflecting pool on the other, with the arbor providing concealment from all directions. It's just as it appears to be. Straight and direct."

If the Seneschal hadn't just told her she was forbidden to talk to courtiers, she would have shaken him off. As it was, she let herself be guided. She was headed in that direction, anyway. "No surprise it's empty, then," she said.

"They call it the Discreet Walk. Although I'm afraid there's nothing discreet about being seen entering it with someone else."

"As you've just been."

"And you," he said.

The path below the arbor was cold and overgrown with

moss. Even now, bare as they were, the gnarled ropes of wisteria formed a decent cover, but Judah could see that in the summer the leaves would make an almost solid wall. The blossoms' perfume would be strong and the air would vibrate with the buzzing of bees and wasps. Someone walking under the arbor then would not be seen, or smelled, or—if they were careful—heard. She was impressed.

"May I, too, be straight and direct?" the courtier said.

"I doubt it." She liked moss, she decided.

"Don't be so negative." Firo sounded amused. "Think of us courtiers as traders from across the Barriers. We may speak a different language among ourselves, but that doesn't mean we can't speak yours, too."

Discreet the walk might be, but it was also short. The exit glared with white winter sun, barely fifty feet away. If Judah's mental map was accurate—and it was—this walk would spit them out not far from the walled-in east garden, which was out of fashion. He wouldn't follow her there, and on its far side were the kennels and stables. "So speak," she said.

"You need a friend," he said. "I'd like to submit myself for the position."

That surprised her so much that she stopped and stared at him. "You want to be my friend?"

"I do." The violent colors of his clothes were muted in the dappled shadows under the arbor.

"Why?"

"In my language, I would say that I treasure your unique perspective, that I am entranced by your rapier wit." His eyes flickered upward. "The stormy scarlet radiance of your hair, perhaps."

"Storms aren't radiant." She felt her cheeks burn nonetheless.

His kohled eyes crinkled. "Yes, well. I've realized recently that most of the compliments in my arsenal are sun-based. Comes from living in a country where everyone has golden hair, I suppose. You pose some interesting poetic challenges." Whatever those challenges were, he brushed them away with one well-manicured hand. "Anyway, mere convention. The words wouldn't matter. If you'd been raised in the court you'd already know the meaning behind them."

"Which would be?"

"You have power."

She laughed. "You've taken too many drops from your vial. Your brain is addled."

"This is why you need a friend," he said. "You're one of the most powerful people in the House, and you don't even realize it."

"I am the least powerful person in the House. I'm nobody. I barely even have a name." She began walking again.

He matched her pace. "You have unlimited access to the future Lord and Lady of the City. You have their ears, their friendship and their trust. You're unconstrained by any obligations of your own; you have no family to advocate for, no agenda to promote, no lands to protect. Also, you probably don't know this, but the cityfolk love you, to an absurd degree."

"They do not." Judah's teeth were clenched together but her stomach suddenly felt odd.

"Oh, but they do. Why do you think they work so hard to make all the staff scared of you? Because out in the city, toymakers sew sweet little blood-haired dollies for children to play with, and then those children come inside. And they are young and puny and weak, but there are so very many of them, the dirty little things, and you...you're a folk hero, to them. The nameless nobody foundling who gets to live among the highborn. Why, a word from you, and who knows what would happen?"

"You're lying," Judah said, not bothering to disguise her scorn. "The Seneschal would never allow dolls that look like me."

"To the contrary. The Seneschal encourages it, outside. Raising you with his heirs is the one moderately positive story anyone can tell about Lord Elban."

As he spoke, one of his eyebrows bent, his head tilted, and his mouth pursed: each gesture so subtle it was barely noticeable, and yet they all worked together to add a layer of nuance to everything he said. She was beginning to see what he meant about speaking another language, but she couldn't imagine how hard your brain would have to work to wring all the hidden meaning from every word and gesture. Even this tiny dose of it made her feel nervous about what she might be missing. She didn't like it. "Are there really seditionists in Highfall, then?" she said, deliberately blunt.

"Leading an empire is difficult," Firo said. "You can't please everyone. Suffice to say that at the moment, every courtier in the House is particularly alert for—opportunities, shall we say. The firmest of rocks on which to step."

"And I'm a firm rock?" She was bad at courtcraft, but she was excellent at derision, and she packed as much of it as possible into the words.

Firo didn't appear to notice. "Lord Gavin certainly thinks so, which makes you useful. Also, I suspect you're bored, which makes you vulnerable."

"What makes you think I'm bored?"

"If you weren't, you wouldn't be spending quite so many of your afternoons shoveling filth in the stables."

Involuntarily, Judah froze. Another one of those complex expressions rippled over his face: part pity, part amusement.

It made Judah feel tiny. "Nothing escapes notice here," he said. "You seem to think that because you choose not to notice the courtiers, they'll choose not to notice you. Or maybe you think their notice is limited to snickering at your clothes and hair? I assure you, it's not. Don't think there's a single courtier inside the Wall that hasn't thoroughly considered your position, and how it may be leveraged to support theirs. And not everyone will approach you as forthrightly as I do. We speak beautifully, when we want to, and we dress beautifully as a matter of course. But inside the silk and perfume, we're venomous."

"That's hardly news," Judah said, but privately, she was discomfited. She knew the kind of gamesmanship the courtiers engaged in, but Firo was right: she'd never considered that she might be considered a playing piece. She'd assumed that nobody had noticed her trips to the stables because she assumed nobody noticed her. "I suppose you're about to tell me there's nobody I can trust but you."

Firo shook his head. "Oh, no. I don't think I flatter myself if I say that generally, I'm one of the nastier specimens you'll find. But I find myself in an interesting position at the moment."

"Which is?"

"Lovely Cerrington suddenly finds itself poor." He waved a hand. On one of his fingers he wore a garnet ring, and in the shade the stone appeared almost black. "It's mostly agricultural, you know. There are fields, and the farmers grow things in them. We're particularly famous for our flowers. Beautiful, but useless. Our real value, for the last two decades or so, has been strategic."

"Flowers are strategic?"

"We've had problematic neighbors. One in particular that I'm sure you've heard of—no? Not up on the latest news from the provinces? Well, Cerrington borders Tevala, and for the last two decades, Tevala has been under the control of a man named Pimm. Have you met him?"

Judah shook her head.

"Would you like to? I'm afraid you won't find him much of a conversationalist. His head is on a spike in the kitchen yard. Third from left, I believe."

There were always heads on the spikes in the kitchen yard. "Elban does love a good beheading."

"And if you need any further indication of your power, my dear," Firo said with a lift of his plucked eyebrows, "consider that the words that just left your lips would leave my own lips, along with the head they're attached to, right next door to Pimm of Tevala. Who was an idiot, by the way. If you're going to attempt a coup, don't mumble about it for twenty years beforehand." He shook his head. "Anyway, Cerrington has historically been a very willing partner in Elban's efforts to keep Pimm under control. Now Pimm—and his sons, and his grandsons—are all dead, and Tevala is in the hands of his step-nephew-by-marriage-in-law or some such, whose name I can't remember but who's more than happy to stamp out dissent at home in exchange for a pretty room in the House and the pretty adventures that come with it. None of this is of any importance to anybody but me, of course—but it's very important to me. Suddenly, my beloved Cerrington has no purpose. Fields and fields of flowers, but no reason to exist."

"I don't see how I fit into this," Judah said.

"I don't, either. Not yet, anyway. But it's in my family's best interest to make Cerrington useful again, and if we can't make it useful, we need to make it liked. You see, I'm speaking very bluntly to you. If you were a courtier, you'd already know all of this, and the moment you saw me approaching you'd remember all the favors you owe me and all the favors

I owe you and all the favors we owe each other's friends, as well as any particularly nasty gossip you might have in your pocket about any of the above. But you'd also think, *Oh-ho, Cerrington is on a downswing, perhaps I can leverage away a few of those favors I owe him*, or *Perhaps he might be amenable to that scheme I was thinking about last week that nobody else is desperate enough to touch*. But you're not a courtier, so I have to do all the work myself. In the meantime, just know that I'm here among the spiders, keeping track of the webs. Should any of those webs come uncomfortably close to you, I can give you warning. Better yet, I can give you advice."

There was no urgency in his voice. There was hardly any emotion at all. Judah, on the other hand, found her head swimming. He was right: Gavin would become Lord of the City and Eleanor its Lady, and all the courtiers they'd spent their lives dodging and ignoring and feeling contempt for would suddenly become inescapable, even necessary. Which was bad enough, but to know that the courtiers watched from the wings, scuttling back and forth on their impractically-heeled shoes—that they were not just scorning her clothes and hair but waiting for an opportunity—

"You need me," Firo said. "You're not the only one with Lord Gavin's ear, you know. He has a particular friend among the courtiers. He's had several, of course; he's his father's son, after all, and although tradition may keep Elban from remarrying, the royal scepter hardly goes unpolished. Although I will say, his favorites always seem to lose their taste for court life. Inevitably, they move to the provinces as soon as his interest wanes." Then, offhandedly, "Lord Gavin's favorites haven't shown any particular preference for the provinces. But he's young yet. Give him time."

She didn't know what Firo meant, but she didn't like it.

"What Gavin does with his time is nobody's business but his. He's not Lord of the City yet."

"But he will be. So, in fact, what he does with his time and who he does it with is of great interest to—oh, pretty much everybody. But we were speaking of Lady Amie. She's a Porterfield; an old city family, although their money comes from the provinces. Mining, mostly. Metalfiber, iron ore, that kind of thing."

"So what?"

"So, she's clever, and not overwhelmed with scruples. And she'd be exceedingly difficult to drive off to the provinces." They had come to the end of the Discreet Walk. Firo stopped, looking back the way they'd come. Judah followed his gaze and saw two figures at the other end: women, judging by their skirts. One wore pink, the other violet. They were fluffy and unreal and she couldn't see their faces.

She thought of the Seneschal—*Here, in this matter, you will obey*—and found her stomach churning. "Gavin is in no danger from you, or any of your kind."

"Not danger, no. Not explicitly."

"I shouldn't be here," Judah said. More to herself than Firo.

Those eyebrows lifted in mocking curiosity. "Is that what you said to that common low-ranking Wilmerian guildsman after you agreed to go out into the corridor with him?"

Her anxiety became exasperation. "I did *not*—"

"It hardly matters. What matters is perception and opportunity." He raised a finger. "This is exactly the kind of valuable guidance I'll provide for you. Think of the rumors, Judah. Always think of the rumors." He bowed his head again and turned away: back toward the Promenade and the two fluffy shapes still silhouetted there, waiting and watching.

She had to pass the kennels to reach the stables. The hounds were as unlike the floppy, friendly kitchen dogs as Judah was unlike the courtiers. Not even Darid liked them, and he could love the meanest stallion or the moodiest mare. When she came near, the animals hurled themselves against the wooden kennel fence. She had never seen an entire hound, just glimpses through the slats: a mad eye here, a slavering tongue there. And all the while, the furious barking. She wanted to grab the slats and bark back. She wanted to bite and claw with frustration. Firo had spoken of the House as a web and it felt like one, sticky and confining. She couldn't pretend it wasn't there. She couldn't brush it away.

Later that night, lolling in front of the fire with his head in Elly's lap, Gavin asked what had made her so angry earlier in the day. "Nothing worth talking about," Judah said, sure that one of them would catch the odd note in her voice—but Gavin was playing with Elly's braid. She was slapping his hand away. Theron lifted his head from his notebook; gave her a long look, then dropped it again. Judah let it go.

CHAPTER THREE

On Nate Clare's second night in Highfall, the fog rolling up from the Brake was a half step away from being as wet as the river itself, and not much cleaner. It clung to the brim of Nate's hat, wormed its way inside his coat, stuck his shirt to his skin and collected on the lenses of his spectacles. More than once he nearly tripped over a beggar or a child or a begging child huddled for paltry shelter in the lee of a building. Elban's House Magus lived in Porterfield, one of the city's richest neighborhoods; beggars weren't allowed there. Nate didn't know about children.

Limley Square wasn't the grandest or biggest square in Porterfield, but it was still nicer than anything Nate had seen while staying across the city in Brakeside. The cruel blue spires of the guildhalls and manors stabbed at the sky here just as they did elsewhere in the city, but there was grass here, there were trees and trim iron fences and flower beds in front of the houses. Which were mostly freestanding—unlike in Brakeside, where people built on every square foot, squeezing shanties and half-shanties into the narrowest of closes and then squeezing entire families into them. Multiple families, even. The wagons he'd grown up in hadn't been much bigger, but they'd used the space better, and they'd never been parked in the grimmest part of Highfall, where the fog and stench of the Brake were thick enough to cut.

And over everything, the implacable Wall loomed like the end of the world. Here in Limley Square the sidewalks were paved in the same white stone that formed the Wall, so the featureless expanse felt more like an architectural feature and less like a prison. Seeing it made Nate's breath catch so he didn't look.

He found the magus's house easily. The door was painted blue, with an ostentatious brass knocker shaped like a hawk's head. Nate lifted the heavy ring and dropped it, three times. Belatedly it occurred to him that he had no idea if handshaking was the custom in Highfall or not. His fingers were wet from the fog that had condensed on the metal, and he wiped them on his coat, which wasn't much drier.

The door opened. The man behind it was dressed in neat but plain gray—servant's clothes—but the look he gave Nate seemed reserved for things just dredged up from the bottom of the Brake. "Magus doesn't see people off the street," he said, and started to close the door.

Quickly, Nate stuck his boot in it. "I've got a letter."

The servingman eyed him. "Let's have it."

So Nate reached into his coat and found the packet, which he'd been smart enough to wrap in waxed paper so it was more or less dry. He handed it over, then pulled back his foot. The servingman closed the door and that was that. Nate would either get in, and his mission could continue, or he wouldn't, and everything would be lost. While he waited to see which it would be, he stood on the step, in the fog. His wet hair made the back of his neck itch under his collar.

Just when he was becoming convinced that the door would never open again, it did. The servingman stepped back. "Come in," he said.

The dim hallway smelled like wood smoke and dried herbs. The floor was dark and glossy, but Nate couldn't tell by the light of the servingman's single candle if it was wood or stone. Before Nate set foot on it the servingman handed him a towel and told him to dry the soles of his boots. Nate had cleaned them as best he could before he came, but they were still coated in layers of dirt from the Barriers and beyond. Some of the dirt he wiped off in the hall had probably traveled all the way from the other side of the mountains with him. He dropped the filthy rag into a bowl held waiting by the servingman, who gave it the same dead-rat look he'd given Nate and whisked it away. In a moment he was back to lead Nate down the hall and through a set of double doors into a room warm with oil lamps, where the magus sat in one overstuffed armchair and another man, so lushly dressed he could only be a courtier, sat in another. There were plenty of other places to sit; the room was crammed with far too much furniture, all of it too opulent for the space. Nate remained standing.

The magus was aged and balding, the ponytail that marked his trade long and braided more intricately than was technically necessary. The packet of waxed paper lay open in his lap, the letter of introduction in his hand. "Nathaniel Clare," he said.

No handshake, then. Nate bowed instead. "Magus."

The courtier, whose curled hair gleamed like spun gold in the firelight, examined his painted fingernails, his legs in their violently-colored trousers stretched languidly out in front of him. The magus shook the letter. "I've never heard of any of these people, Nathaniel Clare."

"Pardon, magus. They've heard of you."

"So has the slopman who comes twice a week for the garbage. Shall I take him as an apprentice, too?" the old man said, one eye on the courtier for approval.

The courtier obliged him with a high, mannered titter, which the magus lapped up like a cat with a saucer of cream. "Now, Arkady. Don't torment the poor boy." The courtier's voice was deeper than the titter would have led Nate to believe. His thick-kohled eyes landed on Nate with only the most distant interest. "The magus doesn't know Lord Tensevery, but I do. And he, apparently, knows you."

"I grew up on his estate, in Duviel," Nate said.

The magus peered at the letter. "This says you saved his daughter's life."

Nate bowed again. "A fever. It might have broken anyway."

"The Tenseverys are in forestry," the courtier said, stroking the wood armrest of his overstuffed chair. "This very mahogany might have come from their mills." His eyelashes fluttered. "You know their son, Landon, boy?"

"I know of him, lord courtier. He's well known, and well liked."

The magus sat back. "What did you give the girl for her fever?"

"Willowbark."

"For rheumatism?"

A test, then. "The same."

"Convulsions?"

"Valerian."

"Pox?"

"Depends on the pox," Nate said. "For small blisters, a redfern poultice, but for flat pox, I'd use chokeweed."

The magus grunted. The courtier yawned. The fire crackled. Nate waited.

Eventually the magus leaned back in his chair. "You're fortunate that Lord Bothel happened to be here when you arrived, and that he knows the Tensevery family well enough to vouch for them." His eyes on Nate were cold. "I've never taken an apprentice before. I don't know how I'll like it."

"What's not to like?" Lord Bothel said with a languid wave of his hand. "The magus at my father's estate is never without one. Sorry wretches, most of them. But it's free labor. And good to have somebody to do the tedious tasks."

The magus grunted again. "Indeed." He considered a moment. Then he threw Nate's letter into the fire, where it instantly began to smolder around the edges. Nate's hopes flared with it. Ordinarily, the gesture would have been a threat and a demonstration: without a letter, he wouldn't be able to get an apprentice position with any other magus in the city, so he'd be stuck with Arkady. But Nate's circumstances weren't ordinary. No other magus in Highfall was of any use to him. It was Arkady or nobody.

"I won't pay you, but I'll feed you," the old man said. "You'll sleep in the kitchen. Vertus will show you the way."

Nate bowed one last time, low and grateful and completely sincere. "Thank you, magus. You won't be sorry."

"The more you speak, the sorrier I'll be," Arkady said, and Nate felt the servingman, who must be Vertus, at his side. Quickly, before the magus could change his mind, he bowed again and backed out of the room.

"The more fool you," Vertus said when they were well down the hallway and away from the parlor. "That man's so mean he shits stone."

"You'd know," Nate said.

Vertus grinned. "You'll eat well, so there's that. I'll bring blankets. You can make a pallet here by the stove."

The place Vertus pointed out was thick with coal dust. "And the laboratory?"

"Through there." Vertus nodded at a closed door. "It'll be locked now. He'll show you in the morning. Yard's through the other door, if you want a smoke or a piss. Just be sure to draw the bolt on your way back in."

When the pallet was made up and Vertus had gone upstairs to his own bed, Nate listened. No more voices could be heard in the parlor. The courtier must have left. Carefully, quietly, he slipped out into the yard. He couldn't see much in the darkness: some vague shapes that were probably bushes and other vague shapes that were probably trees, and in the back, a coffin-like shape that was probably the privy. The air smelled like mud and urine and, faintly, something spicy and herbal.

Mostly, though, it smelled like garbage. The bin in the back corner was overflowing. Nate picked his way through the garden to it; nearby, as he'd expected, a gate had been built into the high wood fence, so the slopman could grab the bin without bothering the household. The latch was simple and in a moment he was outside in the alley. It was barely wide enough for a single person, and Nate's fingers found waist-high scores in the wooden walls from the slopman shoving his cart through. He followed the scores to another alley, and another. Porterfield's broad squares and paved streets gave the impression that the neighborhood had been planned but the alleys told another story. It would be easy to get lost here, but Nate had been raised in the wilderness: he had a good sense of direction, and he knew that eventually the slopman's marks would lead him to the avenue. Soon, he found himself on the street, around the corner from Limley Square.

Ahead, he could see Lord Bothel, standing on the corner

and peering anxiously in the other direction. The streetlamps hid the lurid colors of his clothes and his curls were wilting slightly in the fog. Nate tapped him on the shoulder. Bothel— whose real name was Charles, and who wasn't a courtier any more than Nate was Lord Tensevery's former apprentice— started, and frowned. "I thought you'd come from that way."

"I didn't."

"You can almost see the old pig's yard from here, that's why." Charles lit a pipe and his wilted curls shone in the brief flare of brimstone. "All well?"

"All well. You'll tell Derie for me?"

"When I see her. Good luck to you. That old man is a nightmare."

"Thanks," Nate said. "Nice clothes, by the way."

Charles scowled, kohl wrinkling around his eyes. "Blow it out your ear," he said. Then he walked away, the quick clip of his heels on the whitestone pavement echoing through the empty square. They had been friends for nearly their entire lives. When they were ten years old they'd had a fight under one of the wagons, and Charles had broken Nate's nose. Nate watched him disappear into the fog. He had not asked where Charles would go; they were all safer if he didn't know. But he suspected that it was the last he would see of his friend for a long time.

For the first weeks, Arkady wouldn't let Nate do anything but wash herbs. He wouldn't even let him pick them from the garden. Which was ludicrous, because the herbs in Arkady's garden were spindly and sad, none of them truly useful. The old man wasn't quite what Nate thought of as a nightmare, but he was certainly unpleasant. He wasn't the worst healer Nate had ever seen—that honor went to a man on the other side of the Barriers, who rinsed out the nasal cavities of his patients with a mixture of powdered mouse bones and turpentine—but neither was he the best. Still, he never hit Nate, and Vertus had been right: they ate well, although not abundantly. Sharp cheese, well-cured meat, plenty of wine. And if there was sawdust in the bread, Nate couldn't taste it.

His tiny pallet in the kitchen was hard and the blankets smelled as if they'd been rained on and not allowed to dry properly. If the house had been his, he would have put the lab in what was now the front parlor, the room where he'd first met Arkady with Charles; it had the best light and the best ventilation. But the dim, stuffy lab was still the best equipped that Nate had ever seen. There was glassware beyond his wildest imaginings and cabinets upon cabinets upon drawers upon shelves of neatly labeled supplies. Even if the herbs were substandard, most healers Nate had known worked out of battered trunks or—more often—satchels. Arkady's counter space alone dazzled him.

It was a pleasure to work there, even at menial tasks. A month passed before Arkady permitted Nate to polish glass in the lab while Arkady himself mixed tonics and prepared salves; more weeks passed after that before Nate was allowed to actually watch. Nate kept quiet and tried to make himself indispensable. It wasn't hard for him to anticipate a few steps ahead as Arkady worked, so that he could be standing silently by with the necessary tool or herb or oil the moment Arkady realized he wanted it. The first few times this happened, the old man grunted with a grudging surprise, but after a while it just became the way of things, and Arkady would reach out his hand wordlessly and expect Nate to fill it with whatever was needed.

Mostly Nate was ignored, except for the dullest, nastiest tasks and the most tedious errands. That was fine. He was used to pleasing difficult, thankless people and it was what he'd expected. Vertus was mercurial, treating Nate like a brother on some days and his worst enemy on others. A friend would have been nice, but wasn't required; and Nate soon noticed that whenever Arkady left the house Vertus soon followed, on business of his own, and decided that it was better to keep his distance from the servingman. Eventually Arkady let him grind herbs and hang them to dry. Nate had forgotten more herblore than Arkady had ever known, but he did as he was told without complaint even when he knew there were better ways. So far, he hadn't seen Arkady do anything that would kill anyone. He was grateful for that. Storing herbs badly was one thing; Nate wasn't sure he could stand by while Arkady gave his patients poison.

Most of those patients were courtiers with petty, cosmetic complaints. Their water was clean, their manors weren't flea-infested, and they ate and slept too well to develop any real sickness. On occasion a rider would come from the palace, ringing a hand bell as he rode to warn pedestrians to clear the way; soon after, a phaeton would arrive, and Arkady would climb into it and disappear behind the Wall. In a day or two he'd be back, wine-stained and happy, with his pockets full of coins. Vertus said that when Arkady was done treating his highborn patients, he made off for the parlors and retiring rooms, and lived like a courtier until the Seneschal suggested he leave.

Whenever the phaeton came, Nate found somewhere else to be. He was afraid his eagerness shone like a beacon out of his eyes. He wanted to be in that phaeton like he wanted his next breath. More. He wanted it so much that the wanting was like a tumor in his chest. It took up space; it grew; it lived. It was of him and not of him.

All in good time, he told himself. Meanwhile, he learned about the city, which he'd arrived in for the first time less than forty-eight hours before presenting himself on Arkady's doorstep. Nate had grown up surrounded by quiet forests and verdant plains. He'd been in cities before, but he'd never spent so long in one. The gracious avenues of Porterfield, the desperation of Brakeside, all the gradations of grandeur and misery in between; Beggar's Market, where literal scraps of food sold for pennies, and the Grand Bazaar, where luxurious patrons browsed luxurious goods. A few foreign traders moved among the locals, with rich warm skin and varied features that made Nate think of his people in the caravans, who came from everywhere, but with eyes that carried the natural wariness of those far from home. But the people he saw in the streets here had been born and raised here. Nate hadn't, and he could not help but feel the unsteadiness and rot in Highfall's streets. The city was like a spoiled egg, a thin shell of respectability barely containing the foulness inside. He didn't like it, but it soon stopped feeling overwhelming and chaotic. (Except on feast days, when the gaiety quickly slipped into an almost deliberate danger, when brawls spilled out into the streets and you had to be careful where you stepped, or you'd be ankle-deep in blood.)

Arkady sent him on errands to the Grand Bazaar, because he wanted his apprentice to be seen buying goods there, but Nate found that most of the herb sellers at the Bazaar waterlogged or oiled their wares, to make them seem heavier or healthier. In the Beggar's Market the same herbs would be wizened and bruised but sometimes more potent, and the small market by the Harteswell Gate—just a few stalls—often had unusual things, because the foreign merchants on their way out unloaded unsold goods for cheap to stallkeepers who had no idea what they were buying. One day, near the Beggar's Market, he stopped a man with a rash on his cheek. "I can treat that," he said when the man glared at him. And he could.

It was simple enough, and he'd just bought the very herb he needed: a pathetic specimen, but once it was simmered in oil and the oil cooled to a solid, it would soothe away the rash in a matter of days. He told the man to come to Arkady's manor, to the back gate by the slop bin. Nate didn't expect that he would, but he made the salve anyway. He was pleased when the man showed up.

"Why do you do this?" the man said, still suspicious, as he took the salve.

Nate shrugged. "Because I can."

Word got around. People started to stop him on the street—the shabbier streets, anyway—to pull him aside. "You the magus?" they said, and he was always quick to say no, he was just an apprentice, but they called him magus all the same. (He would rather have been called healer or apothecary or even herbalist, but on this side of the Barriers it was always *magus*.) Sometimes he could help on the spot, telling the women to feed their babies goat's milk instead of cow's, or suggesting the men alternate their bundles between their left and right shoulders. Others, he told to come to the gate. They began to call him the Gate Magus. They paid in small goods, eggs from backyard chickens or bags of brown flour, or in services. One seamstress sat down cross-legged right in the alley to sew a button onto his coat. Another time, a shoemaker brought his tools and fixed the worn heel of Nate's boot.

More importantly, they paid him in goodwill. "You're a good man, magus," the weaver's husband told him once, when he gave the man a syrup for his son's colic. "You go all the way down." In Brakeside and Marketside, the original cottages that lined the narrow streets had been built up and out, with rooms propped unsteadily over the streets themselves. Collapses weren't uncommon. Nate had talked a young boy through a breathing spasm in one of these attaches, as they were called, barely able to breathe himself for fear while the floors bent and creaked perilously beneath him. Back on the hard cobbles, he finally understood what the weaver's husband had meant. All the way down, indeed.

Merchants in the Beggar's Market showed him better goods. Pickpockets left him alone. If the guards were raiding a specific street, a wink and a shake of the head would tell him to take another route. The fruitmonger would pass him an extra date. All of this was nice, and gave Nate some small sense of belonging to this strange place where pale people lived on top of each other. He had tried to be friendly to the foreign traders, but had soon discovered that they didn't trust him any more than they did any other Highfall citizen. Their reticence made him lonely but he could understand it. He supposed, even, that it was for the best.

Because what he valued more than anything else were the stories the locals told: of their lives, of Highfall, and (best of all) of the palace. No matter where he was or what he was doing—clipping herbs in the dim miasma of Arkady's yard, making his way through the Market with a loaf of bread under each arm—he could feel the palace, with her in it, pulsing quietly under his days like his own heartbeat. He had seen the whole thing once, from the crest of a hill outside the city. The land enclosed by the Wall was almost as big as the city outside it, the palace itself a patchwork tangle of colored roof tiles and mismatched towers, crenellated, peaked, brick or stone. The people he spoke to in the streets knew it only through stories. Inside were trees that grew any kind of fruit you could dream of; inside were herds of fat cows that gave milk all year round, and goats and lambs and pigs. Inside were medicinal gardens of strange herbs and aromatic plants from faraway lands, vegetable gardens that grew produce three times the size of anything in a city market (this, Nate could believe), and formal gardens full of rosebushes the size of carriages and plants that bloomed even in the dead of winter. Inside was a spring that never ran dry, and great kitchens where the fires never went out, and glass windows in every color a person could imagine. The tables were spread with delicacies from morning until night and if you were hungry you just ate, whatever and whenever you liked.

Nearly everybody had somebody inside, a daughter or son or cousin or sibling. People spoke of them the way Nate had heard people in other places speak of loved ones who had joined guilds or armies or taken berths on sailing ships: sometimes with pride, sometimes with loss, most often with a mix of the two. Some clearly preferred not to speak of the subject at all—or perhaps they had nothing to say. Nate doubted that many Highfall residents could read or write (most of the signs in Brakeside and Marketside had no words, only pictures) so letters home seemed unlikely. But even if they had no stories to tell of their own loved ones, they had a thousand stories about the palace's highborn residents. Funny stories, embarrassing stories, stories told with a twist of rancorous loathing. There were stories of the fearsome Lord Elban who—depending on who you talked to—may or may not have been quite so fearsome before he'd lost his poor Lady Clorin, and there were stories of Lady Clorin herself, so kind and generous and beautiful. There were even stories of the courtiers, which reminded Nate of trickster tales he'd heard all over the continent, wherein the unscrupulous either earned their comeuppance or dished it out.

Most of the stories, though, were about the Children, as they were called, even though they were well into adulthood. Actual children sang songs about them as they played and crowded around puppeteers in the market to watch their favorites come alive on strings. In skipping chants they went up, up, up the tree and counted all the apples that fell, fell, fell.

There were even dolls: Elban's heir Gavin always in red, his sickly brother Theron in blue, and Gavin's betrothed, Eleanor, in as much cheerful pink lace as the owner's parents could afford. And—most popular of all, which thrilled Nate's heart—the fourth, in drab gray with her mass of dark red ersatz hair, so striking in this land of milky blondes: Lord Gavin's foster sister, with him since birth although she had no name and no family and a background that was a complete mystery. The love child of Clorin's favorite maid, some said; a hostage from the Southern Kingdom, said others. Some even said she was just a common orphan from the city, brought in by a midwife. With her hair and eyes being what they were, this story was regarded as the most unlikely, but there were still those who clung to it, as proof that birth wasn't everything, that luck could befall even the smallest and most humble child of Highfall, and that maybe Lord Elban even had a heart, somewhere inside that bloodless skin of his.

The children loved her. The people loved her. They called her the foundling, which Nate thought too ordinary a name for her, and too small. The first time he'd seen a doll in her likeness at a toy stall he'd been so filled with something like awe and something like shame that he'd had to walk away, quickly. The second time he'd seen one—clutched in the arms of a tiny child, and obviously well-loved—he hadn't been able to tear his eyes from it. Was it a faithful likeness, he wondered? Was the doll's berry-colored wig determined by the real shade of the girl's hair, or by the ready availability of berries? Was the curved pink line of her smile real? Had they given her things to smile about in the palace? Was she a happy person? Nate had heard enough children's stories to know they came with roles to fill: in the puppet shows, Lord Gavin was noble and heroic, his brother a bumbling clown, Lady Eleanor nearly angelic. The foundling was always cast as the friendly troublemaker who came out on top. He wanted to believe the picture the puppeteers painted. He wanted it desperately.

He dreamed of seeing her with his own eyes. He thought of her as he fell asleep at night and when he woke up in the morning and as he shaved his chin in Arkady's dank backyard. Walking the streets of the city he practiced what he would say to her, when the time came. If he would be able to speak at all. It would be like speaking with the great John Slonim himself, the first Worker from the first caravan, like one of his childhood fantasies come to life. Years of hard work and careful planning had gone into getting Nate to Highfall, to that musty pallet in Arkady's kitchen; years to get her here, too, to give him a reason to come. Years spent and lives spent, and it was an honor for him to be chosen, an honor to wait. So he forced himself to be patient.

Once a week, at noon, he met Derie at the plague shrine outside the Harteswell Gate. It had been years since the last plague, but people still left offerings at the shrine for luck, cheap trinkets and stale buns. Nobody remembered which god the tokens were supposed to flatter; they left gifts because their parents had taught them to do so when they were young. And enough people still did that nobody noticed when Nate stopped and knelt next to the old woman for a minute, just long enough for her say, "News?" and him to say, "No." Then she'd cough or spit and he'd get up and walk away. One day, though, he passed her in the street, which he'd never done before, and as he did she muttered, "Midnight."

So out he crept through the dark yard. In Porterfield the gas lamps burned all night, but in Brakeside people still carried torches to light their way. Only the taverns were open at that hour, and even the shadows were full of shadows: moving shadows, writhing shadows, fighting shadows. Some of the noises the shadows made were ecstatic and others were gurgling and choked. The moon's reflection quivered in the thin stream of liquid that ran down the middle of the street, and he could hear the quiet lap of the river itself, one street over; he could smell it, ripe and unwholesome.

He wouldn't have been at all surprised if he'd been robbed on the way—he'd even brought a few small coins so a frustrated thief wouldn't kill him out of spite—but the few people he saw out in the open seemed uninterested in him, and he made it to the Harteswell Gate unmolested. The guards were dozing. He didn't see Derie anywhere; the plague shrine was deserted. Without the crowd around it, the shrine wasn't very impressive, just a stone pillar reaching up from a dry basin. The basin was half-full of offerings, indistinguishable in the darkness. He reached into his pocket, took out a coin, and dropped it in.

"Warding off the pox?" Derie said, almost in his ear.

Trying to pretend she hadn't startled him, Nate took off his glasses and cleaned them on his shirt. They probably needed it anyway. They usually did. "Can't hurt, since I'm here."

She grunted and, leaning heavily on her cane, dragged herself over to a nearby bench. He followed. She had hobbled all the way across the Barriers on that cane. Or maybe she hadn't needed it quite as much when they'd set out; he couldn't remember. "Best not to mess around with other people's gods," she said, and dropped heavily down to sit.

Derie had been old as long as Nate had known her. Her skin reminded Nate of the floured dumplings his mother had made to sell for extra money, except that beneath Derie's soft whiteness was hard, unyielding bone. You could see it jutting out at her elbows and her shoulders and in her eyes. "Too slow, Nathaniel," she said.

He sat down next to her. "I'm doing everything I can. The old man's stubborn. But I'm making myself useful."

"It's not enough. You need to make yourself indispensable."

"It takes time."

"You're not seeing this with big enough eyes, boy. Making yourself useful." Her voice mocked him. She shook her cane as if to hit him with it. "This is useful—unless you can walk unassisted, yeah? Then it's just another goddamned thing to carry around. Make him *need* you."

"He will."

"When?" Her eyes, fierce and frightening, burned with power. "The boy will be betrothed to that Tiernan girl by summer, and that's as good as married to these high-bloods. They don't wait for the vows to start working on an heir, here, and if they pass on Elban's blood to a child, your task's all the harder, don't you agree? And I hear that old walking corpse is planning another trip across the strait to harass the Nali in a month or two. Good time to make our move, when he's their problem and not ours. Things are bad in the city. The people are restless. That Seneschal'll have his hands full, too."

"I can't guarantee Arkady will bring me inside within a month or two."

"Your parents were both such clever people," she said. "I don't understand how they spawned such a stupid boy. Maybe the bleach from your hair got to your brain. You *can* guarantee it. He doesn't need you now because he's strong. Make him weak."

Nate frowned. "You mean—deliberately?"

"Why not? You know how."

Of course he did. There were as many herbs with negative effects as there were beneficial. Already a tiny voice was whispering their names in his head: turp root, bitterweed, milkscorn. "I didn't think we'd have to hurt him," he said.

Derie laughed. "Have a soft spot for the old crank, do you?

Think he's a kind old soul, sprinkling healing fairy dust everywhere he goes?"

"No, but—"

"He's a cruel man, your Arkady." She pointed her cane toward the plague shrine. "When the pox came, he holed up inside the Wall. After it was done, he went through the orphan halls with a tonic. To make them strong, he said. Wasn't a tonic at all, of course. The very strong ones, who hadn't been long on the streets—they survived it. Solved old Elban's orphan problem, certainly."

"Still, if we can get in without—"

"If we can get in without." Her bark of laughter was violent in the quiet night. "If only we could do any of this without. If only we could have just walked into Mad Martin's throne room and said, *Hello, old chum, there seems to have been an injustice here, what can we do to resolve it?* How much better would that have been, eh? How many of our lives saved?" She spat into the hard-packed dirt. "You and that Charles. You bleach your hair and steal some Eastern clothes and you think you're in the stew. I've spent my whole life in this, Nathaniel Clare, as did my mother before me and your mother before you. Too many good people, planning for a time they knew they'd never live to see. We watched them die. We buried them. And now you sit here and you whine and you whimper because dear, oh dear, a stone-hearted old man might have to die."

Under the steely force of Derie's regard Nate felt himself shriveling, as if he were still a small boy in bare feet standing shamefaced by her campfire. That gimlet stare of hers could sweep a quarter of a century away like nothing.

"Did we choose the wrong Worker for this job?" she said. "Because I'll tell you, Nathaniel, there were those that had their doubts."

"I know, Derie."

"I had some doubts, myself."

"I know."

"Arkady's vermin. Kill him. Make him sick first. A nice wasting illness. Not too long." She put both hands on top of her cane and pushed herself up to stand. "I'm told the orphans convulsed and spewed blood before they died. Conscious every minute, too. At least plague brings delirium."

"See you Friday, Derie," he said, and she said, "See you Friday, Nathaniel," and hobbled away.

The phaeton came for Arkady the next afternoon. When the old man read the note the messenger brought, he'd grunted. Sometimes Nate heard Arkady's grunts in his dreams. It was the kind of sound that made a person fantasize about pushing a knife through the grunter's throat: even if a person considered themselves a healer, even if a person had lain awake all night trying to figure out a way to avoid killing the grunter.

"Trouble in the House?" Nate said, his shears continuing to snip at a plant as if the question didn't particularly concern him. Nobody who actually had anything to do with the palace called it *the palace*; to those who spent time inside, it was always *the House*.

Arkady grunted. Nate's shears closed with particular ferocity. "The head Wilmerian has gut trouble. Stupid guildsmen," the old man said, beginning to pack brown glass vials and bags of powder into his satchel. "They ought to stay in their guildhalls. They leave all their senses behind when they leave the world."

"I've heard the Elenesians have a lot of knowledge," Nate said neutrally. "In the West, they're said to have refuges in almost every city."

"The Elenesians?" Arkady snorted. Better than grunting. "*We are but cogs in the plan of the divine*—ha! You notice there's no Elenesian refuge in Highfall. Elban's father drove them right out. No interest in having the city swarmed with parasites. Hobbling around on crutches, begging for alms." He snapped the satchel shut. "The Elenesians know things, all right, but they do not know when to quit, and that is the truth."

"Will you need help?" Nate said, as if he couldn't care less.

"Yes," Arkady said, and Nate's heart leapt. But the old man just pointed to the bench where Nate was working. "Finish those herbs and hang them to dry. When you're done, do the same to the catchberry in the back. Tell anyone who sends for me that I'm busy in the House."

Nate waited until the sound of the phaeton in the street had faded, and all he heard was the regular sepulchral silence of Limley Square: no shouted greetings, no merchants crying wares, no street musicians, no laughing children. He waited some more, until he heard Vertus's quick footsteps down the stairs and out the front door, as the servingman went wherever he went when Arkady was gone. Then he put down his scissors and went out into the yard, which wasn't quite as dank at midday, when the sun could reach down between the spires to touch the ground. He took a blue rag out of his pocket and tossed it over the slopman's gate. He might have been cleaning something, hung the rag up to dry and forgotten about it.

It was a signal. Sometimes Nate put it out and nothing happened; sometimes, like now, the quiet tapping on the gate came so quickly that his patients had clearly been hiding in wait. Where they hid, he didn't know, but he supposed that when you were from Brakeside—or even Marketside, which was slightly less dismal—you learned to disappear when necessary. A birdmonger with an infected tooth was easy to treat with a pair of pliers, and the eggs the man gave in payment were more than welcome. (Arkady didn't like eggs. Nate did, and so did Vertus, and Nate still considered it worthwhile to try to keep on the servingman's good side.) A pregnant woman seeking a tonic that would guarantee her a boy was a more difficult case. She was clearly within weeks of delivering; he explained several times that by now her baby was what it was, and even if such a tonic existed it would be too late to use it. She somehow took this as an admission that the tonic did exist, and he was refusing to give it to her. Nate could hear coughs and rustling in the alley and knew there were others waiting. Finally, he lost patience and told her she had to leave. He also told her she might give up hoping that the baby had inherited its father's sex and pray, instead, that it had inherited his brain. She put her nose in the air and said, "Pray? I'm no country peasant, sir," with such haughty conviction that he knew that was exactly what she was. After she was gone, he felt bad. She probably had her reasons for wanting a son. They might even be good ones.

It didn't worry him that she'd gone off in a huff. *There is a magus who will treat people from Brakeside* was of more interest to anyone in Highfall than *And he will not give me a magic potion*, and most people were smart enough to realize that a magic potion was what the woman had asked for. Most of his secret patients, in fact, were quite clever; until he'd come along, they'd had nobody to treat them at all, so they'd learned to get by on what they had, which was experience, guesswork and passed-down knowledge. More often than not they introduced themselves by telling him what they'd already done, and although he occasionally hastened to warn them never to do those things again, usually the things they'd already tried were the things he would have suggested first, anyway.

He saw a boy who'd dislocated his shoulder working in one of the factories. Nate popped it back into place. Another man, a builder, had what was probably a concussion; Nate asked him if he could go home and rest and the man laughed, wincingly, so he gave him an elixir to ease his pain. The elixir was one Nate had made himself. He'd considered stealing such things from Arkady as needed, replacing them later, but quickly realized that his own preparations were better than anything the old man made. If the hidden line of patients was close to its end, he'd have time to cook the eggs before Arkady was due back.

The last patient he saw that day was a girl, twelve or thirteen, holding a baby in her arms. The baby was about a year old and seemed happy enough, but the girl looked worried. "His head doesn't feel right," she said.

Nate felt the baby's skull. It was soft. "Is this your brother?" The girl nodded.

"Mother? Father?" Nate had learned to be brief about such questions, and accept whatever the answer was.

He was relieved when the girl said, "Ma works in the paper factory."

But only for an instant. "Let me guess. She works from dawn to dusk, and brings him with her."

The girl nodded again. "Is he okay?" she said anxiously.

"Sure." Nate spoke more cheerfully than he felt. He'd smelled the air near the paper factory. He wouldn't vouch for the health of any infant that spent its days there. "But he's sun-starved. It softens the bones. Is there anyone else who can take him during the day?"

The girl was still for a moment. Then her small chin jutted out. "I can."

Nate wondered what she was giving up. "All right. Try to keep him out in the sun as much as possible. And feed him pork and eggs. Can you get pork and eggs?"

"There's a pigmonger down the street from us." She sounded uncertain.

Nate took a measured breath in, let a measured breath out,

and gave her his eggs. Her eyes grew wide at the unexpected bounty and Nate was ashamed of his own pangs of loss. "You know how to cook those?" he said.

"Sure," she said happily. Then a shadow fell across her face. "You have anything needs cleaning? Or errands? I'm a fast runner. And I can write. For messages."

That last was said with no small amount of pride. "Owe me one," Nate said. The girl nodded; then she, the baby and the eggs all disappeared through the slop gate. It was his least satisfying interaction of the day. Pull a tooth, pop a shoulder back into place: those were easy. With a good diet, and a mother who didn't spend all of her daylight hours in a paper factory, both of the children would be fine. They didn't have either of those things. There was nothing he could do about it.

Nobody else came through the gate. He waited a few minutes, just to be sure. Then he took the rag down off the fence and went back inside.

"Guildsmen are savages," Arkady said when he returned a few hours later. He was drunk. When he was drunk, he liked to sit in the parlor and feed the fire obscene amounts of wood until it roared; then he liked to sit by the obscene roaring fire and expound on the state of the world, and he liked for someone to sit and listen. Before Nate had come along, Vertus had served as audience, but now Vertus was free to do as he wished as long as he kept bringing wine.

"The crazy guilds—the ones that spend their lives dancing in circles and singing—" the old man said now, "you expect them to be idiots. The craft guilds, though. You'd think, they can make a thing. They have a skill. But these Wilmerians. It's like they can't think about anything that's not a bloody pot or a bloody tank of gas. Even the Guildmaster. Man gets milk-sick and even as he cries and moans and shits himself half to death, there's a plate of cheese on the table."

"The Temple Argent used to deliberately leave their wounds untreated," Nate said. "They thought it was a sign of faith."

"The Temple Argent never bloody existed."

They had. Nate had been to the ruins of the great stronghold, perched on the cliff above the cold, raging sea. But he didn't see the point of saying so. "The stories exist."

Arkady grinned. "Ah, the tales of heroism. When the warrior priestesses of the Temple Argent battled the sorcerers of Pala to the end of the earth, and scorched the north with ice and fire. As if a bunch of women could form an army worth anything. Had an uncle who used to tell such stories when I was a child. A drunken idiot like the one I wasted my time on this afternoon. Of course, the wine wasn't a waste. I've been drinking Sevedran all afternoon. Makes this taste like cat piss. You ever had Sevedran?"

"It comes from the other side of the Barriers, doesn't it?"

"That it does." Arkady made a satisfied noise and settled deeper into his chair. "Even the courtiers hardly ever see it, but today this cunning young courtier creature convinced the wine steward to break a few bottles free. Twinkled her pretty blue eyes and purred at him that she loved it most specially and even that stingy old bastard couldn't tell her no." He shook his head. "Probably doesn't hurt that she's got young Lord Gavin in her pocket, if what I hear is true."

Nate felt a faint flare of alarm. The fewer pockets Elban's heir spent time in, the easier his task would be. "Is that an accomplishment?"

"Meh. He'll go after anything that sparkles at him. Lord Elban, too—although they never seem to like his attention much, once they've got it." Arkady's smile was unpleasant. "But this one's smart. Porterfield girl. They're all crafty."

"Her family is from this neighborhood?"

Arkady laughed. "They own this neighborhood, boy. It's bloody named for them. Quick as thieves, the lot of them. I remember this one's father, in the old days. Vicious. Wouldn't cross him." There was admiration in the old man's voice. "And his sister! Oh, the lady courtiers, boy. Particularly those with the coin to afford rooms inside. Nothing like what you see out here. Not that I could ever get under one of the Porterfield girls' skirts, but there were others. Less proud. There used to be this drug from over the Barriers. Nowadays, they use those drops, and they get hooked if they use enough, but I think half of them are just in it to show off their vials. *That* drug, though—oh, they would just tremble for it, those courtiers. An excellent cure for pride, that was."

"What was the drug?"

"Who knows? I had a man who brought it into the city for me, special. Lord Elban held most of it, but I always managed to keep a bit on me to grease the wheels. Then one day, my man was supposed to show up and didn't. Supply dried up. Had a lot of sick courtiers for a while. Sick and desperate. Couldn't be convinced that I didn't have any, some of them. Willing to do anything for it. An interesting time. That was back before Lady Clorin died, of course."

"You knew Lady Clorin?"

"That one." Arkady rolled his eyes. "Always crying, always sick." Then he seemed to realize what he was saying and hastily added, "Poor thing, with all her dead babies. Sad."

"Two of them lived, though. And the foundling."

A hard glint came into Arkady's eyes. "Indeed."

"Indeed?" Nate kept his voice neutral.

"That foundling doesn't belong inside. A place for everything and everything in its place." Arkady leaned forward. The smell of wine on his breath nearly made Nate's eyes water.

"I'll tell you something. Give you a piece of professional advice. You know why magi in Highfall only treat courtiers and merchants?"

"Because they can pay."

"Well, yes. That. But not just that." Arkady jerked his head toward the window. "All those people out there, the scrabblers and thieves and laborers. They're necessary. They're the bones that keep Highfall standing. But they're no use to us weak."

Nate blinked in surprise. "Yes. I've been thinking that. I see children in the streets with sun-starvation—it's easy to treat. There's an oil made of junk fish—"

But Arkady was shaking his head. "No, no, no. See here, boy. There's two things we, as magi, can do for the scrabblers. We can treat each and every one of them, like the Elenesians do, at our own expense, and keep them healthy and strong. We'd never do anything else, of course, and the healthier they are, the more they breed. Inside two generations we'd have more workforce than we have jobs. We'd also have more bodies than we have houses and more mouths than we have food."

"We could build more," Nate said. "Grow more."

"Not if the courtiers have any say in it, thank you. They've got the place divided up just the way they want it. All the right people are powerful and all the wrong ones aren't. No, better to let nature take care of the scrabblers. Let the weak ones die. Not all the children you see in the streets are sun-starved, are they?"

A chill came over Nate, despite the roaring fire. "No."

"There you go. The healthy ones, those are our factory workers, right there."

"The sun-starved ones can contribute, too."

"Maybe. If they live long enough. Better they don't, though. Otherwise they'll just spawn a bunch of children prone to sun-starvation, and everything starts all over again. We need the courtiers healthy. We need them smart, to run their provinces and factories, to manage trade. But the scrabblers are a crop that never stops growing."

"I see," Nate said.

"Just think of the plagues," Arkady said. "There's always those that survive a plague. Maybe a few men are left with seed that won't take, but for the most part, the strong ones live and the weak ones die. If you've ever been here after a plague—once it's run its course, I mean—what a sight, young Nathaniel. What a sight. The streets are so clean."

Except for the dead bodies, dying orphans and ashes from the pyres. "So you think the foundling should have been left to die? Is that what you're saying?"

"I think raising a rat in the stables doesn't make it a horse," Arkady said.

In the caravans, there were a thousand ways to make a living and none to make a fortune, but it was enough. Nate's mother had said that. The wisdom of Caterina Clare: you're born with your blood, but you earn the dust on your shoes. Judge a lie by the fruit it bears, but don't judge a man in a box for not noticing the stars. Rain falls where it will; keeping out of it is up to you. Have patience with drunks and little children, for we've all been one and we could easily end up the other.

He did not sleep well the night after Arkady's trip to the palace. Trying to figure out if there was a way to have patience with Arkady, to believe that the things he'd said were just drunkenness and spite. He didn't know where Arkady had been born, how he'd lived. Maybe he'd spent his entire life in Highfall. Maybe that life had been too easy, or not easy enough. Maybe he was the man in the box who never noticed the stars.

Or maybe he was a mean old shit who didn't care what happened to the world as long as he got his.

Nate racked his brain, trying to think of some herb he could give Arkady that would incapacitate him just enough to render him needy but not dead. And he came up with a few, but they were slow. Too slow. He did not have years to make Arkady clumsy and weak, not when Elban's heir was nearly betrothed, attractive courtiers were complicating matters, and Arkady thought of the foundling as a rat in the stable. If the young lord was careless with his seed, Nate needed to know that, and sooner rather than later. If *she* was in danger, he needed to know that, too. (The very idea made him feel half-suffocated.) He had months, and not many of them.

Books were rare in the caravans—they were heavy and took up space—so they kept only those with value. And the most precious of all were Caterina's journals. She hadn't written them all, but they were hers now, and if Nate ever made it back, someday they would be his. They held the life knowledge of a half-dozen traveling herbalists, going back five generations to the days of John Slonim himself: every scrap of knowledge, every theory or rumor or vision. He would have cut off his left arm for an hour with those books now.

In the morning, a sour, hungover Arkady sent him out for willowbark. Once Nate had it in his pocket, he wandered first the Grand Bazaar and then the Beggar's Market, searching for an answer to his other, greater problem. When he didn't find one, he tried a few of the smaller markets. There were no answers there, either. He was about to give up when he heard someone calling him.

It was the girl from the day before and her brother, who seemed absurdly huge, tied precariously as he was on her back. The girl's eyes were alert and interested and her forehead was beaded with sweat. "Gate Magus!" she said. "I was going to come see you later."

"How's your brother?" Nate said, although it was too early for the eggs to have done any good.

She cast a glance over her shoulder at the baby. "Oh, he's fine. Although he weighs a bloody ton."

"I can show you a way to tie him on that'll be easier on your back."

As he unwrapped the length of cloth she'd tied the boy with and then retied it—the baby gurgled delightedly, as if being juggled from one arm to another was a hilarious game—the girl said, "Ma gave me money to give you, for yesterday. You wouldn't have had to wait except she was working the long shift and she just came home. Oh, that is better!" She eyed him skeptically. "How do you know about babies? You have a little one somewhere?"

Nate blinked, and felt himself blush. He'd been matched, not long before he left—but he'd had no news of a child, although he wasn't sure Derie would tell him if there was one. "Where I grew up, there were always babies around."

But she wasn't listening. Digging in her pocket, she pulled out three copper coins, and held them out. "Will this do? For the eggs, too?"

"More than enough." He took it. "Thanks. I can't remember the last time somebody paid me in actual money. How long is the long shift?"

"Four days. It's why I had Cantor with me to start with. Good thing, though. Ma said she hadn't noticed about his head."

"You're a good sister," Nate said.

"Yep," she said proudly. "Anyway, now he can keep me company while I work, can't you, Canty?"

"What kind of work are you doing?"

"Running messages." She reached into her pocket again, this time producing a filthy piece of paper and a stub of pencil. "See? People tell me their messages and I write them down, then I read them back so they know I have it right. Then I take them to wherever and read them out again. Ma got me the paper from the factory."

Nate nodded. "That's right. You told me yesterday you could write."

"I can do more than that. I can read, write, do numbers, everything. My brother's inside. He paid for me to go to school." He caught a flicker of something sad and stoic in her then; at first Nate thought it was the brother, gone forever inside the Wall—there was no coming out to visit once you went in—but then the girl said, "I'd learned it all, anyway, by now," and Nate knew it was school she missed, and school she'd given up to take care of the baby. There was nothing he could do about that, but he felt her sadness like it was his own.

Then her head went up and she put the sadness away. Nate could see her do it, could feel her pulling good cheer out of the heart of her like a carrot out of hard, frozen ground. "Well, customers waiting. I should fly."

You should, Nate thought. You won't. Not in Highfall. Not in Brakeside. The sadness was crushing him. "Bring the baby back in a few weeks," he said. "We'll take a look at that head."

But she was already gone, calling her thanks over her shoulder.

On his way home he stopped at a tavern and bought a bottle of brandy with the coins the girl had given him. Sitting in the kitchen after Arkady had retired, he shared the bottle with Vertus, and if Vertus noticed that the sharing mostly consisted of Nate picking up the bottle and putting it down again without drinking, he didn't say anything. Soon enough the servingman, too, stumbled off to bed. His bedroom was directly above the lab. Ordinarily, he was a light sleeper. He wouldn't be that night.

Nate waited a reasonable amount of time, though his own eyes were scratchy and sore with exhaustion. Then he took down the box where Arkady kept his tea. Barefoot, he carried it into the lab, careful to step on only the most solid floorboards; he'd been taking note of those that creaked for weeks, now.

It didn't take him long to find what he needed. The calculations took longer: the weight of the tea, the potency of the dose. Nate kept a tiny journal of his own tucked away in a pocket—nothing incriminating, out of context, and easily burned. If he made it home, he would transpose it into a real journal and add it to Caterina's collection. For now, the scratch of his pen seemed very loud to him, and almost soothing. It made him think of being a child, lying in his bunk while his mother worked at her desk. The herb-and-resin smell of Arkady's lab wasn't entirely removed from the fragrant wood-and-incense smell of Caterina's wagon. He could remember quite clearly what it had been like to be that little boy, lying under a quilt, knowing only the dusty ease of playing outdoors, the familiar excitement of setting up stage and footlights in a new town, the smoky campfire warmth of being loved by everyone around him. He'd had no notion, then, that he would ever cross the Barriers to the blue and gray spires of this strange, sad city, or that he would grow into a man who sat alone in a gloomy lab after midnight, figuring out how much poison per smallweight of tea. Not to kill; not right away; but to bring on a slow decline, a suffering shamble toward death. No long life lived on sun-starved bones. No convulsions. No spewing blood.

Well, maybe at the end there would be.

When he finished, he crept back to his pallet. He hoped he'd fall asleep immediately—he was exhausted—but instead he lay awake until morning, staring up at the ceiling he couldn't see. Slowly, the light grew hazy around him. Then the sun rose, and he rose, too, and another day began.

CHAPTER FOUR

Judah found Gavin in the solarium. In a month's time, the entire House would attend his betrothal ball there. Now, the room under the vaulted glass ceiling was like the Promenade brought indoors. Careful arrangements of sofas, ferns and potted trees carved temporary rooms out of the marble-tiled space, and every one of them was full. Any courtier who could afford to keep rooms inside hadn't bothered going home for the few weeks until the ball. Even if Judah hadn't spotted Gavin by the fountain, she would have known where he was by the way the courtiers subtly gravitated toward him, like flowers following the sun.

But they wanted nothing at all do with Judah, and scattered before her like pigeons. Gavin stood with a tiny woman wearing a shade of fuchsia that barely escaped vulgar. She was young and her makeup was too heavy, but her hairstyle was relatively restrained and not too crowded with decorations.

The lady courtiers were all draping themselves in stuffed birds and enameled insects this season, but this one wore only a single iridescent beetle over her right ear, where its blue-green shell brought out the strawberry in her hair. Her dress was trimmed in white fur and she'd brushed opal powder on her cheeks to make them sparkle. She reminded Judah of an iced cake, the kind that looked better than it tasted. Her blue eyes were round as sugar rosettes and about as lively. Or maybe Judah just disliked her on sight because she was a courtier, and seeing her laughing so easily with Gavin brought back all of the things she could do and Judah could not.

Gavin felt Judah's presence, looked up and grinned; with a few words to the courtier and a slight incline of his head—her opal-frosted cheeks pinked at the honor—he came to Judah, and took her arm in his. Which would also have been an honor, had she been anyone else. Judah knew that was why he'd done it. She also knew that nobody else noticed how careful he'd been not to let his bare skin touch hers. The spun-sugar courtier's blue rosette eyes watched, her mouth curled; one delicate hand touched the beetle in her hair and Judah remembered Firo's words, and the Seneschal's. *I'm here, among the spiders, keeping track of the webs. They will eat you alive.*

"You," Gavin said, as they walked toward the door, "smell ever so faintly of cavalry."

She'd spent the morning in the pasture with Darid, hunting milkscorn and low ivy, both of which gave horses colic. "And you absolutely reek of courtier. Was that Lady Amie?"

They entered the hall outside the solarium just in time to see a courtier in green silk grab his page by the ear and deliver two swift kicks to the boy's leg. The page, his arms full of paper-wrapped bundles (clothes from the laundry, probably), didn't even try to dodge the sharp toes of the courtier's shoes. "On your way, lord courtier," Gavin said, and the courtier—eyes widening with shock and consternation—mumbled something servile and dragged the page into the nearest hallway. Where, Judah didn't doubt, he'd resume kicking the boy as soon as he was out of sight. Gavin turned to Judah. "Did you want something?"

"Theron got a note from Elban today," she said.

His shoulders stiffened slightly, but when he spoke his voice was oddly calm. "What's it say?"

"No idea. He's been in his workshop all day and hasn't seen it yet."

"I'm sure it's nothing to worry about."

Judah stared at him. "Really. After twenty years of completely ignoring Theron's existence, you think Elban just wrote to say hello?"

"The witchbred foundling's been seen strolling on the Promenade with Firo of Cerrington. Clearly, anything is possible." He spoke with unaccustomed sharpness. "What does he want from you, anyway?"

Thoroughly annoyed, Judah said, "Marriage, probably. No doubt he's madly in love with me."

"Not bloody likely." Then he saw her face, and had the decency to wince. "Come on, Jude. That's not what I meant, and you know it. You're not Firo's type, that's all." He reached one hand out, as if to touch her shoulder, but then let it drop. His face softened with a sympathy that surprised her as much as the sharpness had. "I'm just making this worse, aren't I? The Seneschal told me about his meeting with you. I'm sorry. I know you like to cross him whenever possible, but...the courtiers... You have to be careful, Jude." Again, his hand reached out. Again, it dropped. "I don't like them talking about you."

Judah found the possessiveness in his voice distasteful. "They talk about me, anyway. What about the note?"

He drew himself up, his eyes sliding away. "What about it? I get three a week."

"Theron doesn't."

"Maybe that's changing."

He sounded normal, but Judah sensed something strange from him, something slithery and uncomfortable. She reached for his hand to get a clearer picture—but just before her fingers touched his bare skin, he stepped away. "I have to go," he said. "Theron will be fine. I'll see you later."

Out of all of them, Gavin seemed to chafe the most at life in the shabby parlor. And why wouldn't he, since what waited for him outside of it was so much grander than anything the others could expect? Only Gavin would ever see a wider world. Only Gavin would lay eyes on the ocean, the steppes, the icy peaks of the Barriers; only he would ever travel outside the Wall, ride through the city on a warhorse like his father or travel the provinces with an army at his back. (Judah didn't expect Theron to ever command that army; she didn't think the army would accept him. Gavin had promised to guild him, which was a less horrible prospect for thoughtful, isolated Theron than it was for Judah.) He claimed that spending time with the courtiers was merely an obligation, but Judah could feel the prickling restlessness that drove him to the salons and retiring rooms. He'd come back drunk and happy, or drunk and impatient, or just drunk. If Elly was awake, he'd throw himself at her feet, making wild, embarrassing proclamations of devotion. If Elly was asleep, he would scratch at Judah until she came to find him. She was usually awake, anyway; when he drank, her head spun, too, whether she liked it or not. (She felt other sensations, too, when Gavin was with the courtiers; sensations she was fairly sure Gavin would not want spoken of to Elly, so she spoke of them to nobody. Not even Gavin himself.)

Other nights came the summonses. Then, as soon as dinner was over, Gavin would put on a clean shirt, oil his boots, and go to Elban's study. "What does he want?" Elly asked once, and with a carefree smile Gavin said, "To bore me to death, so he can stay in power forever." But Judah could feel how it truly was in the anxious knots in his muscles. She waited up for him, those nights, long after the others had gone to sleep. He never wanted to talk after, but he was always glad to see her. She could feel that, too.

Direct skin contact between them felt like setting two mirrors facing each other, every sensation reflecting and doubling endlessly. It could be overwhelming, even frightening, so they rarely touched. But after spending an evening with Elban, Gavin would drop his head to her shoulder, and she would lean her cheek against the soft flax of his hair. Waves of anger and revulsion would sweep over her from him. She would do what she always did when he was upset: close her eyes and think fixedly of water. Of the aquifer beneath the House, very deep and very old, hollowed out over eons by the gentle friction of liquid on bedrock. The earthy smell of wet stone, the lap of water so faint it was almost silence. She held that water in her head, let it wash over him to soothe the twisted feelings inside him. She asked no questions. She didn't want to know.

Theron found the letter when he came down for dinner. As he unfolded the thick paper, Judah watched with barely-suppressed anxiety. Despite what Gavin had said, she didn't like the letter. She didn't like the way Theron's eyebrows had shot up when he'd seen it, she didn't like the way Gavin felt after spending time with his father, and she hadn't liked the slithery feeling she'd sensed in him outside the solarium. She liked even less that Gavin knew about his brother's letter and still hadn't bothered to join them back in the parlor for dinner. Elly spread butter on a roll, humming; she'd made of herself a bright, glassy lake that not even the strongest wind could ruffle, but Judah could see the worry under the brightness.

As he read, one side of Theron's upper lip curled, the way it always did when he was puzzled. "He wants me to go hunting," he said. "This weekend, in the western woods. They're bringing in deer."

The words hung in the air. Neither Judah nor Elly knew quite what to do with them. It was Elly who said, finally, "Do you want to go?"

Carefully, Theron put the letter down on the table. "I don't really think I have a choice, when it comes right down to it. But the bow's the only weapon I'm not completely useless with. Maybe he heard about that." His eyes, behind his glasses, were wide and almost...hopeful. Theron was so thin and nervous that he seemed younger than his years. They coddled him, the three of them, which annoyed him, but meant he'd never lacked for affection. It had never occurred to Judah that his father's disinterest might bother him. "Elban's never wanted anything to do with me before," he said now, and the words were tinted with a fascination that worried Judah and scared her.

Where are you, she scratched to Gavin.

Home soon, he scratched back. An hour later, she began to feel the first swirling lurches of drunkenness. *Liar*, she scratched to him in angry red lines. She didn't expect a response, and she didn't receive one.

"I don't like this," Elly said the next morning.

There was porridge for breakfast, lumpy and not as hot as it should have been, and Judah's stomach, sour with Gavin's hangover, liked its smell no better than its looks. She lay on the sofa with her eyes closed. Through the open terrace door she could hear the dull *thok, thok* of practice arrows hitting the straw target Theron had set up; she'd woken to the sound and it had been chasing her ever since. Each *thok* made her wince, not just in her sore head but in every muscle of her body. There was no sign of Gavin. His bed hadn't been slept in. Nobody mentioned it.

"Elban's never been interested in Theron," Elly went on. "He has no reason to be interested in Theron. And now suddenly he wants to take him hunting? With courtiers?"

Thok. Thok. Judah threw an arm over her eyes. "Elban's insane."

"Maybe, but he doesn't do pointless things."

There was a moment of silence.

"You don't have anything else to say?" Elly sounded impatient, half-angry.

"I don't know what Elban's thinking," Judah said. "He hasn't told me."

She didn't mean the words to bite, but they did. Eyes still covered, she heard Elly's exasperated sigh, and felt bad. "Sorry, El. I'm sick."

"I know. Every time Gavin decides to drown in a bottle, I lose both of you. It's not your fault, but it's—" Elly's voice stopped short, as if snipped with scissors. Judah heard the swish of skirts. Finally, she said, "It's not that he's with that stupid woman. And it's not even that he's being so obvious about it. But Gavin's the only one who might have the remotest clue what Elban's up to, and the fact that he's hidden himself away somewhere—it worries me."

Judah had no counterargument. It worried her, too. Moving her arm a spare inch gave Judah a view of Elly standing at the mirror, doing something to her hair. She was wearing one of her courtier gowns, soft and pink with too much embroidery. "Are you going out?"

"Theron has decided to pick this morning to go to training," she said. "Since Gavin can't be bothered to make an appearance, I'm going down with him." Judah's thoughts must have shown on what little Elly could see of her face, because the other woman—stormy though her expression was—managed a semi-amused grin. "It's okay. Courtiers do it all the time—observe training. There are even benches."

"Will there be courtiers sitting on them?"

"Maybe." Elly was cool. "I don't really see how it matters."

She could afford to say that. Protocol would have kept Elly away from the courtiers even if the Seneschal hadn't wanted it that way; she was supposed to stay apart, to remain impartial. Judah took her arm away from her eyes, dropped it casually across the other one over her stomach. Trying to be subtle, so Elly couldn't see, she scratched a curlicue and twist on the inside of her arm. *Where are you?* There was no answer.

She planned to spend the day mucking out stalls with Darid to make the time go faster. Horses required the movement of astounding amounts of hay: from hayrick to loft, from loft to manger, from stall floor to manure pile. But every time she sat up the lurching came back. Gavin didn't answer her no matter how many times she scratched, which distracted and annoyed her. Finally, she made it to her feet and stumbled down to the bathing rooms above the kitchen, where the great fires below kept the water hot. The steam and the pungent smell of the herbs steeping in the water cleared her head, but didn't quiet her stomach. Individual bathing rooms were supposed to be single-gender but nobody paid attention to that and she could hear laughter from the room on one side of her and moaning from the other. None of the laughers or moaners was Gavin.

Feeling somewhat more human, she dressed, braided her hair. Gavin wasn't in the solarium or the gardens outside. By the time she made her way down the wooden path that led to the training fields, the morning session was nearing its end. On the grassless field, men ran at each other in heavy leather armor, foreheads dripping with sweat, hair tied back or shaved entirely. Dust hung over everything. It coated her mouth and her eyes and the sleeves of her dress with a thin haze, like pollen. The benches set up by the training field were located upwind from the cavalry stables, for the observers' comfort. On one end, they bloomed with courtiers holding fine scented handkerchiefs to their noses against the dust. On the other end sat Elly: back held straight, eyes fixed on the field.

Judah joined her. "Where's Theron?"

"Can't you tell?" Elly said, and Judah realized that she could. He was the smallest, and the scrawniest, and he spent most of his time standing pointlessly in the dust, flinching when one of the guards came too near.

"He doesn't belong here," she said.

"No," Elly said grimly. "He doesn't."

Whatever maneuver the guards were practicing was over. Swords were being sheathed, gauntlets removed. Again, Theron was ignored. He trudged toward the edge of the field, dreary and dejected. When he spotted the two of them, he seemed to gladden. Up close, he looked ludicrous in his leathers. The pieces of armor didn't fit him or each other, and the mismatch was so obvious that it couldn't be other than deliberate. Anger swelled inside Judah.

"Well?" he said, by way of greeting.

Elly gave him an encouraging smile. "You did well."

"No, I didn't. But at least I tried." To Judah, he said, "Hello. Elly came down to make sure I didn't accidentally stab myself in the throat, but why are you here?"

"I never thought you'd stab yourself in the throat," Elly said.

"Wanted to see what all the fuss was about," Judah said.

"You're not the only one." Theron sounded depressed again. Judah followed his gaze to the courtiers. Laughter drifted over the field, musical and cold. "They've been here all day, cackling. As if this wasn't hard enough."

"When you're Commander of the Army, have all their heads cut off," Judah said.

"I'd settle for having them turned in another direction."

"Ignore them," Elly said. "You did well. Really, you did."

Wearily, he said, "I'm nearsighted, not delusional, but thanks. Now I'm heading up the hill before anyone else notices me. You two coming?"

"Of course," Elly said.

Meanwhile, a lone blossom separated itself from the bouquet of courtiers, and floated graciously toward them. Firo. "I'll be up in a while," Judah said.

Theron blinked in surprise, but when Elly nudged him and gestured toward the approaching figure, the surprise crumbled to disgust. "Fine, then," he said, curt, and started up the hill.

"Ask if he's seen Gavin," Elly muttered, and followed him.

When he was close enough, Firo gave Judah a courtly bow. "A surprise to see you here."

"I wish I could say the same," she said.

He cocked his head. The gems in his ears were blue instead of white today. "While I admit to occasionally going out of my way to find you, today it's you who's found me. I had no idea you'd be here when I came to watch the training. Did you find it diverting?"

"Not especially." Her tone was flat.

"Nobody does. It's tedious and dusty. But the House is very excited about the hunt this weekend, and when word got around that Lord Theron was here—well, we couldn't very

124

well stay away, could we?" He leaned in close. His eyebrows were drawn in kohl, as well. "Odds are being taken."

"On what?" she said, suspicious.

"Why, the results of the hunt. We're all intensely curious about the outcome. I had to call in quite a few favors to get myself invited along. Naturally, it's a disappointment that Lord Gavin wasn't on the field today, but we've seen him at arms before. And watching Lord Theron is its own satisfaction."

Judah had seen nothing satisfying in Theron's performance on the field. "Hunting is different than combat."

"Is it?" Firo made a humming noise under his breath. He nodded toward the benches below, where a tiny figure in emerald green broke away from the cluster of blossoms. The blossoms followed after it like windblown petals. "That's Lady Amie, by the way."

"Was Gavin with her last night?" Judah said.

"Indeed. He's probably in her rooms right now."

"Then why is she here?"

With faint surprise, Firo said, "Letting him sleep, I imagine. And, as I said, watching Lord Theron." Firo stared out onto the field, though there was nothing to see. "Have you ever read the work of the Zeldish poets?"

Judah didn't care about poetry. "No."

"One of the wandering guilds. Lunatics to a one, of course. At least they were. Nobody's sure if they still exist. Their devotion is—was—poetry. Strange poetry, about the least poetic things. Dead leaves and barren fields. Things like that. And yet somehow rather appealing."

"I don't care."

"Beauty in death, or that which is about to die. The beauty of transience. Watching a flame, knowing it will burn out, and be gone forever." His eyes were level and unblinking. "It's a shame that Lord Theron is not, himself, more beautiful."

"What are you talking about?"

"What, indeed," he said. "Didn't I say I would warn you, if a warning was necessary?" On the benches, the courtiers rose en masse, and slowly began to climb the hill like one single, multi-hued creature. "Ah, lunch. I must go," he said, and did.

Cold sick heat flooded Judah. Her mind whirled. A warning.

Beauty in death. That which is about to die.

The hunt.

Theron.

Elly was in the parlor. A pile of armor sat discarded in the corner but there was no sign of either brother. Lunch waited on the table, bread and cheese and cold meat with vinegar sauce. A knife to cut it with. All untouched. "Theron went to the workshop," Elly told Judah. Frustration twisted the word, stretched it in Elly's mouth. "Gavin hasn't come back."

Judah crossed to the table. The meat was rimmed in a thick layer of fat but the cheese looked delicious. It reminded her that she hadn't eaten since the night before. She picked up the knife. Then she flattened her left hand against the table, and drove the blade through it.

Elly gasped. Judah didn't even flinch.

"He will now," she said.

Judah let Elly wrap her hurt hand in a towel, knife and all, to contain the blood. But she refused to let Elly remove the knife or dress the wound. Nor would she tell Elly what had upset her. (She knew nothing, anyway, she told herself; she had only Firo's unpleasant intimations.) Elly was furious. She paced, lips tight and silent. Judah watched with dull detachment as bright splotches of blood bloomed on the towel. Once it had been white, the towel, but now it was a dim sort of gray.

Somebody—Clorin, perhaps—had embroidered peonies on its edge. She had known that towel her whole life. It would probably have to be burned now.

The door flew open and Gavin stumbled in. He wore an unfamiliar shirt, his left hand wrapped in some filmy, garish material. The glower he gave Judah would have melted glass.

"You're out of your mind," he said, holding his hurt hand in his whole one.

Elly stopped in front of him. She was a full head shorter, but as she took in the silk shirt and the feminine scarf, something in the force of her made him look small. He withstood only a moment of that glare before his eyes slunk away and he collapsed into the chair where Judah normally sat. "Elly," he said.

"Don't," Elly said. "Just don't." She picked up the bandages, sat down next to Judah, and without much gentleness, tore away the towel and pulled the knife out. Judah didn't react; neither did Gavin. Each of them was watching the other, to see. Blood surged from the wound. Elly washed it away and smeared the holes with salve. She made two thick pads of bandages, sandwiched Judah's hand between them, and tied a third around to hold it all together. Then she stood and went to the table; dumped half of the bread out of the breadbasket and began to refill it with slices of meat and cheese.

"Elly," Gavin said again.

Elly held up a hand. The straightness of her fingers and the stiffness of her wrist was enough to stop him. "Theron missed lunch. I'm taking him some food." Throwing an acid look toward both of them, she added, "Try not to grievously injure yourselves again before I get back."

Then she left. As soon as the door shut behind her, Gavin scowled at Judah and said, "One minute I'm opening a bottle of wine, the next my hand is gushing blood. I thought I was hallucinating. What if someone had been there, Judah?"

"You shouldn't ignore me."

"So I'm learning." Gavin sounded exhausted. Tearing the scarf from his hand, he tossed it into the fire, where it smoldered and stank. His wound had stopped bleeding already, because it wasn't actually his; it would heal long before hers did. He moved to sit next to Judah, and began to wash his hand in the basin Elly had left. The water was red with Judah's blood and by the time he was done, it was even redder. Judah didn't offer to help as he dressed the wound, tearing the bandage off with his teeth. He did almost as good a job with one hand as Elly had with two.

"Well?" Judah said when he was done.

"Well, what?"

"Theron," she said. "The hunt."

Gavin leaned back and closed his eyes. Judah waited.

Eventually, eyes still closed, he said, "Second sons don't live." She could feel the words pushing out of him in a torrent. "That's why I've been trying to get Theron down to the fields to practice a little bit. So at least he has a chance of defending himself. I know you heard me; your heart is beating hard and your skin's gone all cold."

He was right. Her heart was beating hard. The rush of it filled her ears and made her hand throb. "The second son commands the army."

"They're supposed to, but they never actually do, because they all die. Go down to the crypts and see for yourself. The dates are all there. I can show you the records. Illnesses. Injuries. Whoops, my knife slipped and landed in his throat. We tried our hardest to pull him out of the aquifer, but his fingers kept getting caught under our boots."

The sick rush of his anger washed over her. "Hunting accidents?"

"I try to protect him," Gavin said. "I try on the field, and

I try off the field. I tell every guard and courtier I meet about my genius brother, how he's the only one who can figure out how the old things work, what an asset he'd be if someone gave him a chance. It doesn't do any good. Nobody cares. All anyone cares about is that Elban's army is strong enough to hold this mess of an empire together, and Theron's kind of cleverness won't do that. Do you think it's easy to sit in Elban's study and listen to him tell me all the different ways my brother could die?" His fists clenched. The pain in their hurt hands was searing, but he spoke with crisp, precise consonants: like Elban. "A true Lord thinks only of the city. A true Lord does not let himself be distracted by mere people. People are tools, and they are only useful if they work. Theron doesn't work."

She could feel white-hot fury inside him—but it was still his anger, not hers. She'd had years of practice telling the difference. She felt... How did she feel? Curiously blank. When she thought of Theron himself—trudging up the hill in his ill-fitting armor, for instance—there was a high flutter of panic and fear in her chest that snatched at her breathing and, yes, made her skin cold. But the rest was nothing. Vacancy. Emptiness. "So you'll keep an eye on him," she said. She felt no surprise at all, no shock. And why should she? Killing was nothing to Elban. Theron was nothing to Elban. The only one he cared about at all was Gavin. None of this was new information. She touched Gavin's arm. His bare skin. A casual gesture, except it wasn't at all. When her skin touched his she nearly recoiled. A deep well of worry ate at Gavin; something ominous and sick-making, huge and impossible.

"Keep an eye on him?" he said, incredulous. "Judah, I'm the one who's supposed to kill him."

Now she felt shock. Now she felt dizzy and sick. Even after

she pulled her hand away from him, the sickness remained. It was hers. All hers. "You wouldn't," she said.

Of course I wouldn't, he was supposed to say. Instead, he leaned his head back on the sofa again, as if he were too tired to hold it up. "If I don't, Elban's taking Elly."

Those words made no sense. "Taking her where? Back to Tiernan?"

"Judah." Gavin grabbed her bad hand with his and a wave of pain crested over her, echoing back and forth between the two of them. She could feel that the pain gave him a hard pleasure: like clenching a fist when you were angry, except he was clenching her fist, too. He thought he deserved his pain. He thought he deserved all of it. "He's going to marry her."

Her hand was on fire. "The Lord doesn't remarry. Not once there's an heir."

"He can, in special circumstances. Guess who decides what constitutes a special circumstance?"

"The people like us more than him. Firo told me."

"Of course they do." Bitterness, sticky and black, filled his voice. "We're a fairy tale. But how much do you think they'd love the prince if he cast the princess aside and refused to marry her? After all this time? Because that's the story Elban will tell. With him as the hero, swooping in and saving her from the shame his feckless heir thrust upon her."

"He'll—" Panic rose in Judah's throat. "You have to tell her. You have to tell both of them."

"Tell them what?" he said. "That if I don't kill Theron in cold blood in front of an audience of courtiers, Elly will spend the rest of her life chained to our monster of a father? What do you think the two of them will do with that knowledge?"

"If it's the truth—"

Gavin cut her off. "If it was my death—or even yours, Jude—Theron would be very sorry, and very sad, and disappear into the old wing where nobody would ever see him again. Children would tell stories about Mad Lord Theron just like we tell stories of Mad Martin the Lockmaker. But for Elly? He'd throw himself off the nearest tower before he'd let anything happen to her, and you know it." This was true. Elly was the kindest of them, and the most patient. Theron valued kindness and patience. Gavin went on. "The same goes for Elly. Tell her that marrying Elban means Theron lives, and she'll be in his study by sundown, making the deal. Neither of us could stop her." His face toppled with despair. "Hells, probably he'd jump at the same time she signed the marriage contract, and we'd lose both of them. If I could fall on my sword and save them I would, but if I kill myself—us—Theron and Elly are on their own. If he could have another child, he would have replaced me long ago—I'm sure he tried—but he won't accept Theron as his heir. He barely accepts Theron as human. If I die, Elban will kill him anyway, and adopt a courtier or something. I've thought it all through, Judah. Every possible angle. But my father has, too, and he's craftier than I am. I'm trapped."

"Why doesn't he just kill Theron, if he wants him dead?"

"Because *just killing him* wouldn't make me miserable. He says the Lord of the City has to make hard decisions, with no interest in mind other than the future of the city." Again, there was that eerie shift in diction, and the voice coming out of his mouth was Elban's. "We are born with soft hearts, but softness is the one luxury in which the Lord of the City cannot indulge."

Judah felt his defeat. She saw it in the way he slumped on the couch. And she knew, suddenly, why he'd fled from them the night before, why he'd taken refuge in his courtier and her bottle of wine. "You're going to do it," she said, numb.

His mouth opened, and closed, and opened again. Finally,

he said, "If I kill him, he'll suffer for a few seconds. Maybe less, if I'm good. If Elly marries Elban, she'll suffer for the rest of her life." He was haunted inside, hollow. "You don't know my father, Judah. You don't know what he's like."

"I know what you're like," she said. "You can't kill your brother."

He was silent.

"She'll hate you," Judah said desperately.

"I know." His voice was lifeless. "You will, too. But you'll both be alive and safe."

"You can't."

"I don't want to," he said, and there seemed to be nothing else to say.

It was ghastly, the way he switched himself back on when Elly and Theron came back. Not because he didn't mean it, when he apologized to both of them for missing Theron on the training field or when—off to the side, although Judah knew what was happening—he apologized to Elly for the spectacle he'd made with his courtier girl. No, it was ghastly because she could feel that he did mean it. He was sorry he'd left Theron on the field alone. He was sorry he'd embarrassed Elly. But the hollowness remained, the deep sick well of horror. When dinner came the food tasted like ash in Judah's mouth, but Gavin ate normally, and answered all of Theron's questions about the hunt: how many people would be there, the order in which they'd all ride, the trappings and protocol and unspoken rules. And all the while, inside, Gavin was wretched.

She was wretched, too. After dinner Elly brought out the cards and Judah tried to excuse herself, but Theron said they couldn't play three-handed and Elly insisted she needed a decent partner. Gavin simply said, "Stay with us, Jude," and it was that which swayed her. The hunt was in the morning.

For these last few hours, they were all safe together, and life was not a horror.

So she stayed, but she could not concentrate. She and Elly lost the game.

She slept uneasily and woke sometime in the early hours, her throat and lungs burning. As quietly as she could, she rose and crept out onto the terrace where Gavin was smoking. He was already dressed in his hunting clothes, tall boots and a quilted jacket. Judah's feet were bare and the stone terrace was cold. She sidled close to him, stood against the warmth of his arm, and felt him lean his weight against her.

"What if Theron doesn't go?" she said after a long time. "What if he's sick or something?"

"Postponing the inevitable."

"You can't," she said. "Not really."

Her hand rested on the terrace balustrade. He laid his on top of it. The fear and horror inside him joined with hers, and reflected back, and reflected back. It made her feel dizzy and ill. "I don't know what to do. I can't let Elban take Elly. But I can't kill Theron." He considered. "I could kill Elban. But I'm sure he's expecting that. He won't give me the opportunity." He squeezed her hand harder. "Help me, Jude. Help me figure out what to do."

Gavin's hand clutched hers, hard, and she clutched him back. She had no answer for him, no help to offer save that she always offered: so she tried to think of water. Still puddles of water reflecting clear blue sky. Cold water frozen over with a skin of ice. Dark water lapping gently at rocks. Fear swirled through all of it in hot streaks of red, but the weight of his body against hers grew heavier, and she felt his head rest on the top of hers.

Water, she thought. Calm.

★ ★ ★

Dawn came a few hours later. Judah noticed the tremble of Theron's hands as he poured his coffee. His stutter was so bad he'd hardly been able to ask for milk. Gavin had tried to be easy, but it didn't take an unnatural bond to sense the grimness still in him, despite all the calm she'd poured into him on the terrace. It took all Judah had to let go of Theron when she'd hugged him goodbye; to watch Elly kiss his thin cheek, and not tell her to hold on a bit longer.

Judah and Gavin didn't look at each other. It wasn't necessary.

After they left, Elly prepared for her day, her bustling too busy. She didn't normally chatter this much about her hair, her earrings. "I hate this dress. I hate the way it hangs. It won't necessarily be a disaster," Elly said, and it took Judah a moment to realize the subject had changed. "Maybe all he lacks is confidence. And forty pounds of muscle, and the ability to see past the end of his nose. Oh, it doesn't matter what I look like. I'm just oiling the stupid rushes."

Judah picked up an earring and put it down again. "Elly—"

"What?"

She'll be in his study by sundown, making the deal. Neither of us will be able to stop her.

"Your dress is fine," Judah said.

Elly sighed. "Come get me the moment you hear anything, okay?"

Judah wanted to be where she could be found, so she waited in the parlor, hyperaware of every sensation she picked up from Gavin. Burning muscles in her thighs and back: riding. Pain in her palms and fingers: were his fists clenched, or was she just feeling her own blisters? She'd forgotten her gloves when she'd gone to the stable the day before. A faint headache: that could be hers, too. It wasn't foolproof, this connection of theirs. When Gavin was on the training field, she felt every blow, but the aches and pains of daily life were harder to pin down. She wished they'd arranged a signal for when the moment came. It might have already come. Theron could be dead already.

She still couldn't believe he would do it.

She scratched him until the skin on the inside of her wrist grew raw. At first the answers came immediately, almost impatiently—*all right? All right*—but then they stopped coming at all. Anxiety wrapped her in a tight cold girdle, squeezing her stomach, making it hard to breathe.

Noon came. With it, a tray of bread and meat paste, along with a bowl of early tomatoes from the greenhouse. The tomatoes were as hard as apples. She didn't even bother trying to eat. The smell of the paste was thick like body sweat. It drove her into her boots—Theron's old boots—and out.

Down to the stables. Where else could she go?

"How long does a hunt take?" she asked Darid. He was scooping out warm mash, the earthy smell of which didn't bother Judah at all, and the low chomping of the horses who'd already been fed was as peaceful as Theron's shooting had been relentless, the day before.

"As long as they want it to. Or until they've killed everything there is to kill," he said placidly. Judah flinched. He noticed, frowned a bit with his eyes. "Or until the hounds are too tired to run anymore, I guess. Are you worried?"

There was no point lying about it. "Accidents happen all the time on hunts. People get shot, hit in the head, thrown from horses—"

"It's not the horses you have to worry about." He finished with the mash and headed into the tack room; she followed. A saddle lay over a sawhorse. He picked up a rag and a bottle of oil and began to rub it down. After each swipe the saddle leather went dark and glossy, then dull again. "If it were me, I'd be worried about courtiers who can't shoot. And the hounds, of course."

"The hounds?" She thought of the kennel: the high slatted walls, the barking and growling that emanated from beyond them at the slightest noise.

"I used to work with them." The steady motion of the rag didn't falter but his voice was hesitant, as if he were telling her something he shouldn't. "My first job inside. I was excited at first. I always liked dogs. But they're not dogs. They're—something else." His mouth tightened. "And they aren't trained for clean kills."

Judah felt like she'd stumbled into some deep pit of feeling in Darid, something secret and uncomfortable. He wouldn't look at her. Awkwardly, she said, "I'm shocked to learn that there's an animal you don't like."

Then he did look at her, sidelong. "Well, I didn't much like the kennel master, either. And he didn't like me."

"I can't imagine anyone not liking you," she said without thinking, because her mind was still in the western woods. Then she realized what she'd said and blushed. He turned away to hide a grin and she knew he was trying to be kind, which just made it worse. To be standing here, chatting about animals. She couldn't stay anymore. She left.

She had barely pushed open the parlor door before Elly snatched it away from her. Judah could smell the fumes from the rush oil clinging to her, and her blue eyes were bloodshot—after finishing the rushes, she must have spent the rest of the morning reading in the Lady's Library. "Oh," Elly said, disappointed. "I thought you were them. They should be back by now, shouldn't they?"

"I don't know."

Elly wrapped her arms around herself. "Did you eat? There

was food, but I made them take it away. The smell. I can get more."

"I'm fine."

"Judah." She sounded desperate. "Something is wrong."

Judah remembered Gavin the night before, laughing and smiling at all of them through the blackness growing inside. She forced a curious smile. "What makes you say that?"

"Oh, don't," Elly said, impatient. "Gavin can get away with that. You can't. You're bad at it. And I don't know. Everything. Theron on the hunt. You. The courtiers I see in the hall. The way the girl who came to get the lunch tray looked at me." Her lips pressed together. She grabbed Judah's hands and held them tight. "I feel like there's something everybody knows but me. Is it that stupid woman? Is she pregnant?"

"I don't think so." Judah had no idea.

"But there's something," Elly insisted.

Her eyes were intense, pleading. Judah wanted to tell her—it seemed only fair, since the rest of Elly's life was at stake, too— but what was the point? If the hunt went the way Elban wanted it to go, if it didn't, there was nothing either of them could do. They were powerless, Elly and Judah both. They could only wait. "Nobody tells me anything, Elly," Judah said wearily.

Elly let go of Judah's hands and sank down on the sofa. "Furniture," she muttered, and Judah said, "What?"

"Furniture." Elly's voice was dull, frustrated. "That's how my mother told me to think of myself when she sent me here. Furniture, to be moved from one place to another as it suited." She picked up the deck of cards. "Come on, Jude. There's no point in brooding. Let's play cards."

When the girl brought the dinner tray, Judah jumped up so quickly at the sound of the door that she was dizzy. The girl was nervous. Elly asked her if the hunt was back and she mumbled, "Don't know, Lady," and fled.

"Well, that was helpful," Elly said.

"They're back," Judah said.

"How do you know?"

The dizziness hadn't subsided. It was worse, even. Judah's hand went to the chair for support. "Because Gavin's getting drunk."

Elly cursed. Which almost never happened. "That idiot. Sit down before you fall down."

"No." Judah held up her bandaged hand. "He's not allowed to hide from us. He and I have been through this."

"I'll come with you."

"No," Judah said. "Stay here. What if Theron comes back?" And she left.

Outside, she wheeled around a corner and felt like her head was spinning on a different axis from the rest of the world. Being Gavin-drunk was different from being drunk herself: when her own body was drunk, numbness filled her like water. When Gavin was the one doing the drinking, the confusion only rose partway, and the clear, sober part of her tossed wildly like a boat on its surface. This was how she felt every night Gavin spent with the courtiers. When she knew to expect it, it could be sort of enjoyable. Tonight, it made her angry.

By the time she reached the stairs, something unfamiliar was edging out the haze of alcohol. She pushed open the door just enough to slip through. The door's latch clicked and the noise broke in her ears. Her steps felt too big. She was suddenly unsure of the floor. Putting a hand to the wall to steady herself, the stone felt soft under her fingers, almost luxurious.

In her tiny boat on top of the maelstrom, Judah saw, in her mind's eye, a crystal vial, passed from pale delicate hand to pale delicate hand. This was what the drops felt like, then. She marveled, dimly, that the courtiers managed to take them and do anything else.

Gavin. She was looking for Gavin.

She stumbled her way through the evening-dim corridors, the deep, lugubrious waters surging beneath her. The House wrapped around her, in all of its complicated vastness, binding her like the corsets she refused to wear. She had long ago stopped noticing the ancient paintings that hung in its halls but now the strange flat-faced people in their odd clothes seemed far more real than the living people she passed. The sober part of her knew they were nothing to be scared of, but the dull faded faces seemed filled with hate. Vicious. Worse than any courtier. The waves of Gavin-feeling were increasingly violent. Occasionally one swept over her and swamped the tiny boat that was all she had left of herself, making her clutch the walls for support.

No, she thought, furious, the third time this happened. I am not Gavin. I am not hiding in a room somewhere. I am Judah. I am *me*. Ferociously, she pushed the waves back. She had been pushing back his pain since she was eight years old. This was no different. Her tiny boat grew slightly larger, slightly more sure. She forced herself upright again, and kept going.

Into the solarium, gaudy with courtiers and weird purple gaslights. Too much light. Too many smells. There was music but it didn't make any sense. She tried to feel for Gavin, but to reach out for him she had to push him back and it was too much, too strange. A hand took her arm.

"Judah," Firo said in her ear. "What are you doing here, dear girl?"

With no little difficulty, she shook him off. "I'm not a girl. Not your dear."

He turned her toward him. The gems in his ears glittered black as eyes. She could feel his actual eyes peering closely at her, and when he spoke again his voice was yellow with laughter. "Why, you're drunk. At the very least. This is no place for you to be out of your head, Judah. Come along, now."

"No." The floor felt strange underfoot. Soft. Stretchy.

"Just for coffee." He sounded impatient. "Something to eat."

She should not go with him. She knew that. But he was already leading her out of the too-loud, too-bright room; down a purplish hallway to one of the retiring rooms, where food and coffee was always laid out, where the music was quieter and a conversation could be had. In the daytime they were all polished brass and white linen, but this one was firelit and choked with thick herbal smoke that burned her eyes. In a corner she thought she saw two figures twined together in a chair but in her altered state, the deep-colored drapes at the windows seemed to be twining and caressing each other, too, so she didn't trust what she saw.

Firo deposited her in an empty corner and told her to wait. Curious eyes seemed to glint at her from the two twining figures. She thought she heard *foundling*. She thought she heard *witchbred*. Then Firo was pressing a cup of coffee into her hands, delicate white china instead of the thick ceramic they used upstairs. He sat down next to her. She thought he touched her hair, pushed some of it behind her ear. She might have imagined it. She trusted nothing.

"The hunt," she said.

"Very disappointing. Drink your coffee."

"What happened?"

"Nothing. That's why it was disappointing."

"Theron?"

His smile rang off-key and discordant in her ears. "Lord Theron lives, foundling."

Her worry had been a knotted rope inside her and when she heard those words it snapped, it recoiled, it waved madly around inside her. "To your dismay," she managed to say.

"To the dismay of some," he corrected. "To the rejoicing of others."

"Who?"

"Guess."

Judah closed her eyes briefly. But her eyelids were lined with colorless shapes that she did not like so she opened them again, and said, "I don't speak courtier."

"Particularly not in your current state. Who in the world got you like this, and why didn't they stay to finish the job? Setting you free in the solarium like that is throwing a baby bunny to the hounds."

"Shut up. Tell me what you know."

"Well, which, dear?" He laughed, delighted with either the question or her muddled state. When she bristled—was she sprouting actual bristles?—he held up a jeweled hand. "Easy, foundling. Don't call any more attention to yourself than you must. It's considered poor taste to notice other people on a night like this, but I'm not sure you count as people. Also, I know nothing. I only hear things. There's a subtle but real difference."

"What," Judah said, "do you hear?"

He had full lips. It was obvious that he painted them. Now they curved faintly. "I hear that the young lord is not strong, and rather clumsy. Liable to suffer illness or accident at any moment. And I hear that the weak-minded Lord Gavin is so taken with Lady Amie of Porterfield that he's considering renouncing Lady Eleanor, and taking Amie as Lady, instead."

"Not true."

"Drink your coffee." This time there was no doubt; he pushed her unbound hair back behind her shoulder and let his fingers linger there. "I'm not concerned with what's true. Merely what I hear." He leaned forward and she felt those painted lips brush her ear. His consonants were sharp, almost painful. "If Lady Eleanor were renounced, of course, it would be a terrible shame for her. And I very much doubt that poor sheepish Tiernan can afford the repayment of her bride-price.

Come closer, foundling. You must seem like you're enjoying yourself."

Firo's body radiated heat next to hers and his perfume was velvet-heavy and dark brown. Judah felt like she was choking. "Elban wants to marry her."

"That's another rumor, yes." His lips were touching the skin under her ear now, making her skin crawl, making her want to writhe. "But if such a marriage were to come to pass, my ebony-eyed darling, you would want to be very careful with yourself. You would, in fact, want to make yourself as scarce as possible. Lady Amie will not share her prize with anyone. She will want Lord Gavin utterly to herself. I risk my own future even being seen with you, which is why we've suddenly become so intimate. I shall tell everyone that you, poor naive thing that you are, got foolishly drunk and threw yourself at me. I'll be disgustingly detailed and, of course, reject you brutally. The other courtiers will love it."

The tip of his nose, cold and smooth, touched the tender skin under her ear. For a moment he was a great snake wrapped around her, the hand on her arm a coil and the arm pressing her body to his another. For a moment she was afraid.

"I have to find Gavin." Her voice sounded too loud.

She wasn't talking to Firo. Not really. Voices in the corridor grew louder and she sensed somebody stepping into the door. Firo's eyes moved toward them. He grabbed the side of her head, pulled it toward his. "Vanish, little foundling. Right now." Suddenly he stood up, unbalancing her. She slid boneless to the floor and landed on her knees. From far away, she saw her coffee cup topple onto the rug, and heard distorted laughter. "Go," Firo said. "Get out. Thing."

She stumbled to her feet and ran.

The hallucinations were getting worse. She couldn't go back to Elly. Not empty-handed. Not in the state she was in.

And she felt a powerful urge to actually set eyes on Theron, to prove that at least some of the words that came out of Firo's mouth were true. So she made her way to the workshop. The floor oozed like lamp oil underfoot and made her queasy. The workshop door was closed. She pulled it open, not caring if she startled him, only caring that he was actually there.

And he was. Sitting at his workbench in his hunting clothes—although the quilted jacket lay puddled on the floor where it had been dropped—and staring blankly at the spidery device he was building, which seemed somehow more whole than the last time Judah had seen it. The relief that flooded her smelled like lemons. She could only lean against the wall and stare. He was safe. He was whole. He was safe.

But there was blood spattered on his cheek, and more on his shirt. A single drop marred one lens of his glasses; behind it, his eyes were swollen and lifeless. Doll's eyes, made of glass. For a moment, he seemed wooden and covered in cloth, like a minstrel's puppet. She closed her eyes and when she opened them he was real again.

"Tell me," she said.

He didn't answer. The silence tasted coppery, like the blood on his glasses, and it swirled, and Judah almost lost herself in it. Then he said, "They killed a deer," and his words were made of stone, like the walls and the floor. They had solidity and weight. The room filled with them.

In stories someone killed an animal and the animal died. *Then he drew his bow and did slay the beast. With his sword he struck a goodly blow and thus the beast was slain.* Theron's words were words like *fix* and *repair* and *assemble* and he knew the depths those words contained, how they were the stories of things: how you couldn't *fix* a thing without understanding what it was for, and how it was meant to work, and the sophistication of the mind that had created it; how *repairing* was not a task to be checked off a list but an act of devotion, a moment of communion between one human being and the world. How *assembling* was a miracle as deep and beautiful as the stars. The conception of a thing that did not exist, the drawing of a path toward existence. Think of gold, mined in streams and rivers and veins beneath the earth's surface. Think of cogs, and the perfect distance between the teeth. Think of one gem, perfectly cut. One piece of metal. One idea. One machine.

Fix. Repair. Assemble.

As he followed his father and brother through the woods, unfriendly smirking courtiers all around them, words like *hunt* and *kill* and *death* seemed simpler. Putting a fire out was less miraculous than starting one. Watching clockwork wind down was less incredible than winding it up. Firing an arrow was an action Theron understood; the bow was a machine like any other, one that channeled the strength of the arm, magnified by the force of the pull, into the tiny point at the head of the arrow. Everything else—the fletching, the balance of the projectile—was refinement. Making sure the arrowhead hit exactly where it would be most efficient. One of the big veins in the throat, probably. Or the heart. Or through the eye to the brain.

He thought he could fire the arrow, hit the target. When they saw the deer in the clearing, the eye was too small, so it would have to be the heart or the vein. He admired the way the deer's legs were put together, built for fleetness and silence. He saw in an instant how the tendons and muscles were connected. He found these things beautiful, like the horses they rode, like anything that was designed to do a thing as perfectly as possible. He had time to consider that the horses were bred the way they were, but the world had created the deer on its own. He had time to marvel.

Then his father raised his bow, and his black-fletched arrow flew.

It struck far from any vital target, in the big muscle of the deer's hind flank, and at first he thought the shot was bad. But from the smirking courtiers he heard a murmur of approval. "Excellent shot, Lord Elban," one said, even as the deer bolted and the hunting party—horses and men and fearsome grizzled hounds that stood almost to Theron's shoulder—took up the chase. Theron was confused. It hadn't been an excellent shot. It had been inefficient and wasteful.

His horse was well-bred and well-trained and needed no instruction from him. "Just hang on," Gavin had muttered when the horses were led in front of them and Theron had gulped at the size of them, and as the horses gave chase to the wounded deer, *just hang on* was exactly what Theron did. He'd had daydreams—childish fantasies, he now understood—that while riding he would draw his bow and fire, but there was no question of loosing his grip on the pommel long enough to reach into the quiver that hung over his back for an arrow, let alone setting the bow and firing it, let alone in motion. *Just hang on.* Ahead of him, he could see that Gavin wasn't *just hanging on.* Gavin rode the machine that was his horse as if he had been designed for it, as if they were two machines working toward one goal. He even had time to glance quickly back toward Theron, to make sure he was *just hanging on.* It had always been that way. If the human body was a machine, Theron knew his own had been poorly built from half-functional parts. Even now his lungs were tight and he had no peripheral vision, around the lenses of his glasses. Gavin was the perfected model, the very best plans and the very best parts. Theron was built from what was left over.

But his mind was quicker than Gavin's, his fingers more nimble, and ever since realizing the difference between them—ever since realizing that he was not going to mysteriously wake up one day in a strong, capable body like his

145

brother's—he had done everything possible to avoid putting himself in any position where those advantages were worthless. And yet, here he was. The horse under him ran. He tried to keep from flailing and falling. It was the best he could do.

The hounds barked. The deer, limping badly, wheeled on its good leg, and just as it did another arrow flew, this one fletched in red. It landed deep in the other flank. A cheer went up. Blood drops falling from the first wound were joined by drops from the second. The hounds were deranged, slavering and snapping at the deer. Theron was baffled. What was happening, what was going on? They had come to kill the deer, and he knew there must be depths to *kill* that he didn't understand, but why weren't they even trying? Why were they doing such a bad job?

"Run!" Elban cried, and bellowed something at the hounds, and the hunters roared. Up ahead, Gavin bent down low over his horse. Theron's own mount seemed to lift under him; suddenly the world flew past. The motion was smooth and terribly fast and he could see nothing, not even with his glasses.

He heard Elban's voice again, cold and severe: "Hold!" The horses in front of Theron reared and stopped and Theron's did, too, nearly throwing him in the process. *Just hang on.* He found himself next to Gavin, Elban on his brother's other side. Again, Gavin risked a quick glance in Theron's direction, the same old question in his eyes: *Okay?* Theron found himself in a tangle of reins and straps; they had seemed orderly enough in the beginning, but now they'd all come loose, and Theron felt like a fool, trying to assemble himself into the easy effortlessness his brother managed by nature. But he nodded. He was okay.

In front of them, the hounds had circled the deer, growling. The deer's injured back half trembled on legs oddly splayed. Theron saw that it was holding itself up on its bones because the muscles weren't working. It was a doe, or at least antler-less; her wide eyes were terror-stricken, her mouth open and panting.

The hounds would take it now. They would leap for the throat. It would be bloody. He must not flinch.

"Take it," Elban said.

The biggest hound leapt—but not for the throat. Instead, the sleek gray beast went for the deer's midsection, tearing loose a flap of skin. The deer squealed. Another hound went for one of the delicate forelimbs, and with a twist of the great head and an appalling snap, the deer went down to one knee. The courtiers cheered again.

"Mark the time, Seneschal," Elban said, a muted delight in his voice. The Seneschal took out a pocket watch and flipped it open. "Gentlemen, give your bets."

"Three minutes, Lord," a courtier called out.

"Five!" said another, and then all the men on horseback were shouting out numbers. Two. Three and a half. Seven. A dozen or so courtiers rode with them; every face matched Elban's, in excitement and pleasure. Only one courtier was silent, a tall man with glittering onyx earrings who kept to the back, and he seemed to be watching his fellow hunters rather than the deer.

"Heir," Elban said. *Heir* meant Gavin. Theron had no idea what word Elban would use to address him. "What's your bet?"

Staring at the deer—who still struggled to stand, on two wounded legs and one broken one—Gavin was made of stone. "Eight minutes," he said.

Theron, with revulsion, realized they were betting on how long the deer would live. "Fifteen minutes," Elban pro-nounced.

Minute after minute passed: hard, gory minutes; minutes

loud with horrendous animal screeching. Great spurts of blood shot toward the courtiers, making them crow with delight, as the hounds tore the deer apart, bit by bit. They ripped her legs out from under her and tore them off when she fell; they chewed off her ears and her tail, and Theron didn't understand why the deer didn't die of fear and pain, why no part of the deer's brain called the battle for the hounds and let her suffering end. He didn't understand how the courtiers could stand and laugh as the deer tried to put her least broken leg under her. His own mouth was dry, his skin cold. Gavin remained stony.

"Why—d-doesn't it die—" he finally muttered, drawing his horse close to his brother's.

"Because it wants to live," Gavin said, his voice dull. "Everything wants to live."

On the other side of Gavin, Elban pulled at his reins. His horse stomped. "Does the Commander of the Army find the blood distasteful?"

It was more words altogether than Theron's father had ever said to him at once. "No, Lord," Theron said. "I mean, I'm f-fine, Lord." Cursed stutter.

Elban's ice-blue eyes fixed on him. "Time, Seneschal?"

"Fourteen minutes," the gray man said.

"In one minute, Commander of the Army, I will have won the game. Do you think the beast can last one more minute?"

The deer had given up standing. Her head lay in the dried needles and leaves on the forest floor. The hounds were disemboweling her with excruciating slowness. As Theron watched, horrified, she blinked. He could feel his tongue wanting to stutter. "Yes, Lord," was all he dared say. Elban said nothing in response, and neither did anyone else. In a panic to fill the silence, Theron said, "What's the p-prize, Lord?"

"The p-prize?" Elban smiled. "Tell your brother what the p-prize is, heir."

"Anything he wants," Gavin said.

Theron felt sick.

"Anything I want. That's the p-prize. Anything, or anyone." The courtiers laughed, hooting lewdly. "So. Just another day, I suppose." He pulled his reins again. This time his animal backed up, took a few steps to the side. Now he was next to Theron. He wore black, as always. A silver dagger hung at his belt. He pulled it out and pointed it at Theron. "I'll tell you what, Commander of the Army. When I have won my p-prize, you, too, may have what you want." He flipped the dagger in his hand, extending it hilt-first. "You may kill the deer. End the p-poor thing's suffering."

The last words dripped with sarcasm. The courtiers laughed again.

Behind Elban, Gavin did not look up. Theron took the dagger.

"Time, Lord," the Seneschal said.

Elban's eyes glinted. Theron knew eyes didn't really do that, but some motion in the muscles around them made him understand how that expression came to be. "Well, then. Commander?"

Still no help from Gavin. Slowly, Theron slid off his horse. His legs hurt and he paused for a moment with both boots on the ground, so he wouldn't stumble. Elban made a noise in his throat that drew all of the hounds back from what was left of the deer, and Theron made himself watch to see if her chest still rose and fell. It did. The hounds had blank, all-black eyes. There were as many of them as there were men behind him, and he felt the weight of all their gazes equally. Blood spattered their gray hides, dripped from their jaws as they panted curious about this new thing on the ground, sensing that he was somehow neither master nor exactly prey.

They had torn the deer's chest open, exposing her ribs. I'll just put the dagger through her heart, Theron thought. She won't feel anything. She'll just die. Then we can go back to the House. This will be over.

The trees in the western woods were smooth-barked and still leafless, reaching skeletally up into the sky. Dead leaves crunched under Theron's boots. He was acutely aware of the hunting horses behind him, all strong and quick and tall, the men on them strong and quick and tall, as well. He was the smallest, weakest thing in this clearing, with the possible—and only the possible—exception of the deer.

He took another step. The deer's eye—brown, not black—rolled toward him in the socket, to see what new torture he brought. He could not believe he had ever looked forward to this. He did not ever want to do it again.

"Commander of the Army," he heard his father sneer, behind him, and it made him angry. Who else was he supposed to be, other than who he was? How was he supposed to have grown into this person his father wanted, when his father refused to even acknowledge his existence? He gripped the dagger tightly, and made himself take the three steps to the deer.

Oh, gods. The smell.

He heard a noise behind him and turned.

Gavin was off his horse. The noise he'd heard had been his brother's boots hitting the ground. He had a dagger at his belt, too, except it wasn't at his belt anymore. It was in his hand.

He's going to do it for me, Theron thought with a mixture of anger and relief. He doesn't think I can do it. He thinks I'm a coward. He thinks I'm useless. He's right. I am a coward. I am useless. Then Theron corrected himself, as he always did. No. I'm not useless at this. But I can help the deer. I will.

150

Gavin's lips were pressed tightly together, his face white. He was holding himself strangely. Everything about him seemed strange. The dagger in his hand, poised to strike, his eyes fixed—

On Theron.

Behind him, Elban watched. There was no sound. Even the panting of the dogs had stopped.

Gavin took two steps toward him.

"No." Theron didn't mean to speak. Even as the word escaped his lips—without even a hitch, and *n*s were hard—he was thinking: this is not happening. This would not happen. The machine doesn't work this way; this is not the plan; Gavin would not do this.

Just hang on.

Then Gavin moved. He had not seen his brother on the training field in so long. He had no idea how *fast* Gavin could be, and even now the part of his brain that appreciated a well-made machine was admiring the way all the parts of Gavin's body worked with all the other parts, the fluidity of his movement, the sureness of his steps and the practiced line of his arm as he drew back the dagger; the way his brother's torso and hips swiveled to deliver the maximum possible energy through the arm and wrist and hand to the weapon, focusing all of the strength and beauty that was the human body at its finest and best-trained into the fine-honed tip of the blade, sharpened beyond what the eye could see.

Theron closed his eyes.

A breeze. The warmth of his brother's body passing within a hairbreadth of his own. A grunt, a thud.

He opened his eyes. Gavin's dagger was buried at the base of the deer's skull. He had severed her spinal column. She was dead.

All pleasure and excitement vanished from Elban's face, replaced by anger and distrust. Gavin pulled his dagger from the deer's body and wiped it on his trousers. With an illogical sidestep he swiveled, put himself between Theron and Elban. He still held the dagger point down but there was something dangerous in the set of his shoulders, the stance of his legs. It was a fighter's stance. Gavin was waiting for an attack.

Elban made a noise. The hounds all stood as one and took a step closer. The courtiers were silent. In front of Theron, Gavin's shoulders flexed.

Their father was going to kill them both. He would have them torn apart. "Gavin," Theron said, low—meaning what? That he did not know what was going on, but he knew they were in danger. That he did not want to be torn apart by hounds.

"Quiet." Theron could barely hear him.

The moment lasted only a few seconds but it also lasted longer than the fifteen minutes it had taken the deer to die. The moment lasted forever. "Well, then," Elban said finally, as if they'd just finished a negotiation, although nobody else had spoken. He spun his horse and rode away. The courtiers followed. Gavin's and Theron's own horses, confused, stamped impatiently at the ground.

"Gavin," Theron said again.

Gavin didn't look at him. With the courtiers moving away, his whole body slumped, as if all of his bones had gone soft at once. Hoisting himself up onto his horse looked as if it took immense effort, and his posture in the saddle was grim. If posture could be grim. The human body was an amazing machine, not just effective but flexible and expressive. Even in defeat, Gavin was beautiful.

"Come on," he said over his shoulder. Theron came.

In the workshop, for the first time, Theron seemed to notice the spatter of dried blood on his glasses. Deer's blood. He chipped at it with a broken fingernail. Judah found it too fascinating, the slow erosion of the perfect circle of blood.

"He was supposed to kill me, wasn't he?" Theron said.

"He didn't kill you," Judah said. Her hallucinations were intense and the words came out a sideways purple color. She was glad Gavin had not killed Theron. She was glad of the fact of Theron, perched on his stool, warm and alive. But there was a reason she could not be happy. Something she was forgetting; something that was drowning with Gavin's mind in whatever chemicals he'd found.

Theron laughed. It was an ugly laugh. It huddled in a corner and brayed at them. "He thought about it, though. He seriously considered it." He turned away from her, back to his machine. Like a door shutting. "Never mind, Jude. I'm okay."

"You're not."

"It doesn't matter."

Judah's chest opened like a box and something vicious and scarlet escaped it. She watched it swoop around the room, hot and unsteady like a bird with a broken flight feather. Then it vanished through the tapestry that led to the broken staircase.

Her legs melted underneath her, and a soft gray nothing descended.

When she came to, she was sneezing. Gradually she realized she had been sneezing for some time. Apparently some part of her brain had been counting; she was at seven. By the time her eyes were fully open she was at fifteen. The light from the workshop's one window seemed overly thick, a glowing fog that permeated the room, and her first dismayed thought was that the drops hadn't worn off. But the fog was just sun hitting dust motes in the air. The edges of the room stayed where they were; the floor was solid. The world seemed to be behaving itself again.

Theron had stretched out on his code-breaking table to sleep, but now he was sitting up, rubbing his eyes. His legs dangled over the edge like a child's. Judah herself was still on the floor. Theron's hunting jacket lay rumpled around her waist, having evidently been draped over her at one point. A pile of books sat where her head would have rested. She guessed that Theron was responsible for both things, and was touched: he had propped her head up with the books in case she vomited in her sleep, and covered her with his jacket in case she got cold. The books were dusty. That explained the sneezing. "What time is it?" she said.

"Early," Theron said.

A bit unsteadily, she climbed to her feet. Every muscle in her back protested. As soon as she was upright, all of the previous forty-eight hours slid back down onto her, a curious mix of relief and horror. Gavin had not killed Theron: that was the relief, both the relief of Theron remaining alive and the joy of Gavin remaining the person she thought he was. The horror was that Elly would marry Elban now. Theron didn't know that, she realized, and on the heels of that realization came another. Theron must not know, not for the longest possible time. It could not be helped now. It would only cause him pain.

She made herself smile. It wasn't too difficult. She would have Theron to smile at for years to come. "Let's go find some coffee."

"No," Theron said.

"You'll feel better when you've eaten."

He didn't move.

"Oh, come on," she said. "You can't just stay up here."

"I'm not going to stay up here. I'm just not ready to come down yet." He picked up his glasses from the bench and rubbed them on his shirt. "What am I going to say to him? Hey, older brother, thanks so much for not killing me?"

"He would never have killed you." Judah could say that, now that Gavin hadn't.

"I don't even understand why. I don't want to be Commander of the Army. I'd be terrible at it. They don't have to kill me to keep me from doing it." His voice was rich with anger and bitterness, which Judah's brain processed properly, without adding taste or color. "Gavin knows I don't want to do it. He told me I don't have to."

Judah tried another smile. It was harder this time. "You don't. But you do have to come downstairs eventually. Elly will worry."

"I'll be down in a while," he said. "Once I figure out what to say. I don't want to tell her the truth. It will upset her."

It was too early for staff girls carrying breakfast trays, but late enough that a different, younger set of girls crouched next to piles of dirty shoes in the corridors outside the guest rooms, furiously brushing and polishing. None of the girls looked up when Judah passed. If anything, they tried to make themselves smaller. And shoes were one of the first tasks House staff were given when they came inside, so the girls were pretty small already. The courtiers' shoes, some high heeled and gaudy with embroidery and gems and some—Judah could not help but notice—tall mud-splattered hunting boots, seemed giant in their hands. In her younger years, when she'd come upon the newest staff members, Judah had been known to make her hair extra-wild and growl as she passed, to see them jump. Now she knew they'd been fed a steady diet of stories about the witchbred foundling from the moment they arrived, and felt sick at what she'd done.

Or maybe she just felt sick.

In the parlor she found Elly asleep on the sofa, sitting upright in the same dress she'd worn the day before, chin on her chest. Her sketchbook lay half off her lap, where it had slid when she'd drifted off, and a charcoal pencil had fallen to the floor by her bare feet. The sketchbook lay next to her where it had fallen, page filled with one of Elly's forests: she would spend hours on the trees, making sure every branch and leaf was perfect, and then she would fill in the spaces between with half-glimpsed beasts and fierce eyes. There was no sign of Gavin. No boots, no coat, no dirty gauntlets thrown onto the table or dropped on the floor. Judah picked up the sketchbook, closed it and put it back in Elly's lap.

Elly's head jerked. She winced, put a hand to her neck. Then she saw Judah. "Are you just coming home? Where have you been?"

"In Theron's workshop." Judah sat down in the armchair. "Gavin was out of his head. By the time I got up there, I couldn't make it back down again. I passed out on the floor."

Elly stared at her; deciding if she was lying, Judah knew. It was painful to see. Finally she said, "That explains the dust. What about the hunt?"

"Everyone lived except the deer."

"Was it bad?"

Stealthily, Judah scratched *come here now* on the inside of her wrist. Jagged and angular, which was its own message. There was no answer. "Yes. It was. But it's over. And he's not hurt. Just—"

"Humiliated."

Feeling unclean, Judah nodded.

"And Gavin?"

Judah lifted her shoulders. Let them drop.

Elly's hair was braided down her back. She reached up with both hands and yanked it ferociously, like a bell that wouldn't ring. "Of course," she said. "Because coming back here and actually dealing with us would be difficult, and Gavin doesn't like difficult. Gavin likes fighting and wine and pretty little courtier girls who follow him around like geese. Oh, how *strong* you are, Lord Gavin. How *handsome* and *manly*."

"To be fair," Judah said, "Theron's not here, either."

"Theron has reason not to be," Elly snapped, and pressed the heels of her hands against her eyes. When she dropped them again the anger was gone. "Tell me about the hunt, Jude."

So Judah did. A version of the hunt, anyway, in which there was a bit more mockery of Theron's stutter and a lot less of Gavin nearly killing him. Nothing she said was technically untrue, but it was all a lie, nevertheless. "Anyway, he survived," she finished. "And it wasn't easy for Gavin, either, so stable your warhorse, all right?"

"Gavin." Elly's lips pressed together. "Gavin will wake up with a headache and be just fine." She sat down and began putting on her shoes. "I'm going to try to talk Theron into coming down. He can't stay up there, his lungs will rot. If anyone asks for me, tell them to go jump in a well. And if you see Gavin, tell him to jump in a well, too," she added, head held high.

As soon as she left—as if he'd been waiting and watching around a corner somewhere—the door opened again, and Gavin came in: pale and unsteady, hair disheveled and coat missing. His shirt was only half-buttoned, and incorrectly, with some brownish stain down the front that could have been wine or blood or either or both. His eyes were red and bleary. "I didn't do it," he said.

"I know," Judah said.

Theron had said that when Gavin remounted his horse he had looked as though his bones were slumped and soft. She saw now what he meant. Gavin dropped onto the sofa, just where Elly had been sitting, and everything about him seemed defeated. "He doesn't want her," he said. He had a headache, a blurry throb over his eyes that Judah hadn't noticed until they were in the same room. "He'll take her to make me miserable. He wants Theron dead, so he has one less heir to worry about, and he wants to know I'll jump when he pulls my string."

It felt like Judah had been angry with him for days. She was tired of being angry with him. It was too hard. She sat down next to him. "We'll figure it out," she said, and took his hand. He let her. The headache flared; her queasiness and his folded together, doubled, redoubled, until she couldn't tell where she stopped and he began.

She pulled herself together and focused. Water. Ripples in the sun. Slowing; quieting; still.

CHAPTER FIVE

Gavin decided that the most logical course of action was to kill his father with a knife to the throat in the most public place possible. Judah thought this was absurd. Gavin informed her that patricide was practically a family tradition. "He'll be disappointed in me if I don't at least try," he said, flipping the dagger he'd taken to carrying. It was overly jeweled and too well polished, but the long blade was nasty. "All I need is a chance."

Forgetting, apparently, his earlier certainty that Elban would never give him one. "Are you liable to catch him here in the staff corridors?" Judah said. Because that was where they were, even though she was going to the stables and he was going to the training field, where he'd spent nearly every waking hour of the last forty-eight practicing with the dagger, and there were faster ways to get both places if you didn't care about being noticed. Judah used the staff routes fairly often, but Gavin almost never did. "Or are you just avoiding Amie and her friends?"

He slid the dagger back into its sheath. "She was incredibly attractive before I thought I might have to marry her."

"Has she been disfigured somehow?" Judah said, and he said, "Let's just say I see her differently."

They came to the intersection where he needed to go one way and Judah the other. Before he could walk away, Judah grabbed his arm. "Before you murder your father," she said, "you need to tell Elly what's going on." Because he hadn't; neither had Judah. Being kept in the dark made Elly extremely angry and being angry made her extremely polite, and when Elly was extremely polite, she was formidable. Every icy *please* and *thank you* stabbed at Judah, and she felt an uncertain lurch in Gavin's stomach, too, the moment she spoke Elly's name.

But all he said was, "Speaking of telling, Cerrington's telling all sorts of stories about you from the night of the hunt. Which makes you the first woman he's touched in decades. Congratulations."

"Tell Elly," Judah said doggedly, "or I will."

In the stables, Darid sat in the doorway, braiding rope. He greeted her as normal, but when she picked up the pitchfork and began mucking out the nearest stall, she became aware that he would not look directly at her. "Am I doing something wrong?" she said.

"No wrong way to muck out a stall." His attention remained fixed on his rope, but something in the tone of his voice told her the sentence wasn't over. She waited for the rest and finally it came. "Not sure you should be doing it at all, though."

The words weren't a surprise. She'd known he'd say them someday. But she hadn't expected them to come now, when the rest of her life was falling down around her ears. She stuck the tines of the fork in the old wood of the floor. Harder than she needed to; the sound of metal stabbing into the wood was louder than she'd intended. "I've been mucking out your stalls for almost a year. You've never said anything like that to me."

"Thought it."

"Sure. But you never said it. So what's changed?" Then the connection snapped together in her head, as unnatural as the gaslights. "You heard something about me, didn't you? What was it? That I was chasing some courtier?"

The strands of hemp wound in and out around his fingers, the long tail of completed rope coiled next to him on the ground. Darid's fingers could weave rope on their own while his brain did three other things but suddenly the process seemed to require all of his attention.

"More than that?"

His eyes flicked up to her. She had blushed when Gavin mentioned Firo, but she didn't now. She could feel him searching for either confirmation or denial. She didn't know how to give him either, but one of her eyebrows wanted to lift so she let it, and a slow smile touched Darid's face.

"As long as no lord from the provinces is going to show up here with a horsewhip," he said, and then, "Don't look at me like that. People do odd things."

"I do odd things all the time," she said, "but not that."

She went back to her muck. He went back to his rope. After a few minutes, he said, "I have people to protect. My men. My family."

She kept her eyes on her work. "Yes," she said. "I know."

Before she left, Darid said that he would show her the next time she came how to weave rope herself; he had tried to teach her before, but she'd been hopeless at it. Darid didn't have time to waste on hopeless tasks so she took the offer as the apology she suspected it was meant to be, and said she would be happy to learn. Then she went down to the baths. This early in the day, they were deserted. No noises came from behind any of the closed doors, and not a single page waited outside the bathing rooms for a courtier. Judah had no page, and clean clothes would have required a trip back upstairs, so she had none of those, either. The steam was scented so strongly with eucalyptus and lavender that her eyes stung. After, she put her dusty dress back on and it smelled like horse and hay, and as she tied the laces she thought, *Elly is going to marry Elban.*

It hit her like a slap. She felt like one of Theron's clock-work things, wound to its limit every morning so it would go through the motions all day, spinning and ticking away. Meanwhile, the world burned, and for the thousandth time, she pondered how strange life was, how easy it could be to let your feet carry you through the hours despite the fire.

On her way back upstairs, she met the Seneschal. He was talking to one of the kitchen stewards about wheat: how much the fields inside the Wall could be expected to yield, how much would be consumed, how much would have to be purchased or traded from the provinces, how much all of it would cost. When he saw Judah he did not pause, but held up one finger. She considered ignoring it, but knew she wouldn't be able to avoid him for long. So she stood, impatiently, until the conversation was over. As the steward slipped past her on his way out, he slashed at the air. Protecting against the evil eye—her eye. Judah slashed back.

The Seneschal appeared not to notice. "This way," he said, and led her two hallways over to an empty guest room. It was shabby enough that it was probably meant for tradesmen or visiting servants; the cot was narrow, there was no sink or running water and the washstand was chipped. The only window opened onto one of the light shafts. This far down, the light had a long way to travel, and what made it through the window was weak and halfhearted.

"If you're going to yell at me about Firo," she said, "don't bother. Nothing you've heard is true."

He shook his head. "Firo likes beautiful men. Neither word applies to you. While I'm curious about the conversations he's obviously covering for, I doubt very much that they contain anything I don't already know. And Firo might be useful to us down the road."

"I thought I was supposed to stay away from the courtiers."

"Circumstances have changed. If Lord Gavin marries Lady Amie, she'll want you dead," the Seneschal said matter-of-factly. "Marrying you to Firo and sequestering you in Cerrington might not be the worst thing. He'd follow instructions if he were paid well enough, and there'd be little risk of pregnancy."

Judah recoiled. "There will be no risk of pregnancy. I won't marry Firo."

"Perhaps you'd rather be walled into one of the unused towers for the rest of your life, or beheaded." His consonants were crisp, bitten-off. "Lady Amie doesn't know about your bond with Lord Gavin, and she can't find out. Unlike Lady Eleanor, she would have no qualms about using the information to her advantage." Judah could practically feel the man thinking. It was like standing next to a hot fire. "It would take a lot of money to buy Firo, though. He's well-connected in his own right, and he wouldn't go against Elban unless there was quite a lot in it for him. We might be able to blackmail him; they don't think very well of men with his preferences in the outer provinces. Why is Lord Gavin spending so much time on the training field?"

"He likes hitting things," Judah said.

The Seneschal slapped her, hard, and the world flashed

white. It was more startling than anything. Then came the heat, and only after that the pain, like something rising out of the deep. She put a hand to her cheek. She couldn't feel the touch of her fingers at all. "Like that?" he said calmly.

Whenever she or Gavin broke a rule as children, Judah had taken the blows for both of them, although they'd shared the pain. But there had been warning then. There had been reasons given. She had never bothered arguing because she was a child (and not an important one, as she was constantly reminded). She wasn't a child now, and she was filled with a prickling sense of anger and affront so huge that she could make no sound big enough to express it.

"I suspect that Gavin is planning an attempt on his father's life," the Seneschal said. "If he asks you about the blow I just gave you, tell him that an axe through the neck hurts a great deal more. I cannot protect him from a charge of treason."

Only when he was gone did words come to her. "How dare you," Judah said, but she was alone in the room, and speaking to nobody.

"He hit you because he didn't dare come after me," was all Gavin said when he saw Judah's bruise that night. "I'm sorry."

"It doesn't worry you that he knows?"

He shrugged. "What can he do about it?"

"Behead you?" she said. "Us?"

They were on the terrace, leaning on the balustrade. Elly had gone to see Theron, who still said—as he'd told Judah, when she visited him earlier that day—that he was not ready to come back down. Gavin had not been to see his brother at all since the hunt. Now he surveyed the greenhouses and oat fields and sucked his teeth. "I think we can call that bluff, for now."

"If it's not a bluff, I'll resent you as long as I live," Judah said with more bravado than she felt.

She didn't go to the stables the next day. She didn't want to explain the bruise to Darid. Instead, she went walking through the fallow fields where the sheep grazed on wild grasses. After spending so much time with the quick, strong horses, the sheep seemed placid and dull. The ewes hadn't been sheared for lambing yet and they barely moved; it was hard to believe they could, under the weight of all that wool. A few herding dogs loitered around the edges of the flock, long-nosed and intelligent. They watched Judah curiously but without malice. She wondered if the hounds had ever been dogs like these, or if they had started as some other animal entirely—something imported from the Southern Kingdom or Duviel, made of heat and jungle.

When she returned to the parlor, the door stood ajar, and she paused outside it. She could hear strange voices within. Through the opening she saw a pair of boots, well-made but plain. If she tilted her head she could see the back of a thin, shabbily-coated person, blond hair tied back in a leather thong at the nape of his neck.

She pushed the door open. The boots were the Seneschal's, extended before him where he sat in Judah's chair. The man in the shabby coat was Arkady's assistant, whatever his name was, the one who never spoke. And on the sofa, hunkered like a bird, limbs hanging limp around him as if he lacked the strength to compose them, sat Arkady himself. "What are you doing here?" she said to the three men, reserving her harshest glare for the Seneschal. "Get out. You're not wanted."

"You'd know what that feels like," Arkady said.

The Seneschal stood, one hand upraised. "We're not here for you, Judah. Come back in an hour, and we'll all be gone."

"I'm not leaving. I live here." She stepped inside. "Why are you here?"

Arkady eyed her dress and boots, mud-spattered from her walk. "Foul girl. Have you been rolling in dirt?" The apprentice merely stared, eyes wide behind his glasses. He always stared. Judah paid no attention to either of them.

"There are rumors in the city about Lord Theron's health," the Seneschal said. "Arkady needs to examine him so we can issue a statement and dispel those rumors. People are putting in orders for mourning," he added as an afterthought.

Rumors. Firo had mentioned rumors. *He wants Theron dead*, Gavin had said. Elban always got what he wanted. Judah's fingernails were already at the soft skin of her wrist. *Come, come home, emergency.* "Theron's not here," she said, managing to sound normal.

"We know. Lady Eleanor has gone to fetch him," the Seneschal said. "She was very reasonable about it, once I explained the situation."

Elly was very reasonable about the situation because nobody had told her about the situation. *Hurry. Hurry. Now.* They should have told Elly what was happening. Judah should have. She hadn't. "I won't allow this without Gavin here," Judah said fiercely. Hoping fierceness was enough, because if they wanted to take Theron into the bedroom sooner than that, she had no idea how she would stop them. *Hurry. Come now.*

"It's not for you to allow," the Seneschal said.

"What's that, girl, a rash on your arm?" Arkady said.

Judah felt like she was screaming, but the scream had nowhere to go so it reverberated inside her.

Gavin burst into the room, red-faced and hollow-eyed. He'd been on the field again and hadn't stopped to take off any of his armor when he'd come running. His helmet was in his hand and his hair, soaked through with sweat, stuck up at odd angles from his head. His gaze swept over the two men in the room before landing on Judah. "What's wrong?" he said, breathless. "Why are they here? Who's hurt?"

"Nobody's hurt," the Seneschal said. "Everything is fine." Gavin gave him a hard look at that, but the Seneschal seemed not to notice. "We're just here so Arkady Magus can examine Lord Theron and issue a statement saying that the rumors of his illness are unfounded. Your people are concerned, Lord Gavin. Lady Eleanor has been kind enough to go fetch your brother for us."

At *rumors* Gavin's eyes had widened. Now he took a step toward the Seneschal, his shoulders down and his jaw clenched. "Lady—" By habit, Judah put out a hand to stop him, although she wouldn't have minded in the least seeing the Seneschal go down under Gavin's fists. But then Elly and Theron entered through the open door, arms linked. Elly took in the scene before her and looked, questioning, at Judah.

But Judah was staring at Theron. In the thin grayish light of his workshop, she hadn't noticed how thin and grayish he'd become since the hunt. He was unshaven, his beard coming through in sparse patches, and he'd obviously been wearing the same clothes for days. She should have taken better care of him. Made sure he stopped working occasionally, and ate and rested.

"What's wrong?" Elly said.

Our fault, Judah thought. Elly didn't know. She didn't know because we didn't tell her. Theron's expression was grim, but not grim enough. He squared his narrow shoulders. "Let's get this over with, if we're going to do it," he said to Arkady, who nodded and—with some difficulty—stood up. His apprentice moved quickly to help him.

Theron thought the danger was over, that it had been left behind in the woods. Judah could feel Gavin's sweat on her skin, the race of his pulse in her veins. She watched him strip off his gauntlets and drop them on the table. "I'm coming in, too," he said.

Theron glared at his brother. "I'm not a child. I don't need to have my hand held," he said curtly, and marched into the bedroom. His back was straight, giving him a military bearing Judah was sure he'd never managed on the training field.

Arkady shook off his assistant, who still held him by the elbow. "Neither do I, boy. Wait out here." There was a peevish irritation in Arkady's voice. As he made his way after Theron, he walked as if his guts hurt him, or his back.

The door closed behind the two of them with a final maddening click.

"You shouldn't have brought him down," Gavin said to Elly.

"It was easier than arguing." Her eyes traveled over him, then moved to Judah, and narrowed. "You're a mess. You both are. What's going on?"

The Seneschal sat back down in Judah's chair, disinterested. Gavin said something angry, and Elly responded in kind, and as Judah dropped, helpless and numb, to the sofa, the words all fell away because Arkady was behind the closed bedroom door with Theron, and anything could be happening in there, anything.

"Your cheek is swollen," a soft voice said. Arkady's apprentice stood next to her. He didn't even give Judah a chance to lie about the bruise on her face; just opened the satchel he carried, and began to root around in it. "I have a salve for that. It's very effective. My own formulation." The rhythm of his speech was odd. He wasn't from Highfall.

She didn't really care. Theron was alone in the bedroom with Arkady. There were rumors that he was ill. People expected him to die. She tried to reassure herself: if Elban wanted

Theron dead, he would do it publicly, with lots of blood and lots of witnesses. Not behind a closed door. Not in secret.

"I apologize. I'm afraid I'm not very organized," the apprentice said. He put his satchel down on the narrow end table. It blocked her view of everybody else in the room.

But maybe somebody else wanted Theron dead, someone who did not want Amie of Porterfield to be Lady of the City or anything close to it. *To the dismay of some*, Firo had said about Theron being alive. *To the rejoicing of others.* Judah had no doubt Arkady could be bought. She had no doubt that he couldn't be trusted.

Without warning, something fell into Judah's lap: a tiny brown bottle, the length of her finger and twice as big around. "Hide that," the apprentice said in an undertone, and suddenly the apprentice had Judah's full attention. She moved her hand over the vial to cover it.

"Arkady Magus is always telling me how unprofessional it is, all this rummaging. And he's right. Ah, here it is," the apprentice said, speaking normally now. He bent down in front of her, a small ceramic pot in his hand. His eyelashes were the darkest she'd ever seen. "This will feel cold," he said, and with two shaking fingers—he almost seemed afraid to touch her—he began to spread the salve from the pot onto the part of her cheek that felt too thick. His eyes darted down to the vial in her lap and, in the same undertone he'd used before, he said, "Give that to Lord Theron. All of it. The moment we leave."

Her fingers curled around the vial. "What is it?"

"Antidote." His lips barely moved.

Antidote. Poison. Her lungs seized. She couldn't breathe.

Then, in his regular voice: "There, that wasn't so bad, was it? The swelling and bruising will be gone by morning. Your skin might feel a little irritated, but that will pass."

He was odd-looking, even beyond the eyelashes. It was

almost as if his skin was the wrong color for his hair—pale, but the wrong color pale, somehow. His eyes were blue, like everyone else in Highfall's, but intense. Like a sky brewing a storm. The way they were fixed on her was almost alarming. "Why are you giving this to me?" she said as quietly as she could.

"Because I'm a friend." Quiet, loud. "A magus heals." He snapped his satchel shut and walked back to his place by the bedroom door.

Judah clutched the bottle in her fist. Theron was being poisoned. But poison felt wrong for Elban, not brutal enough. Unless, maybe, it was a particularly ugly poison. Agonizing. Long.

Or—maybe the poison lay in her lap. Her brain spun. Maybe whatever filled the brown bottle wasn't even fatal. Maybe it was just dangerous enough to make Theron sick. If she gave it to him—if she were seen giving it to him—the House was already against her, as far as it cared about her at all, but she was popular in Highfall. Firo had told her so. She wouldn't be, if she were a suspected poisoner. She would be a traitor. Easy to get rid of. Easy to wall up in an unused tower. Easy to execute.

Amie wouldn't mind seeing her executed, or so she'd been told. And Amie had connections in the city. She could have started the rumors.

The bedroom door opened and out came Theron. Did he seem paler? She couldn't tell. He'd been so pale to start with. Was he breathing hard? Were his eyes unfocused?

"He's well enough," Arkady said to the Seneschal. Theron himself showed only vague interest. He knew Judah loved him, knew she respected the lightning-quick connections his mind made. But he knew she loved Gavin and Elly, as well, and he was all too accustomed to thinking of himself as less-than. If someone told him that Judah had tried to poison him, to make things easier for the others, would he believe it?

"His blood seems weak, though," the magus continued. "And I'm not happy with his lungs."

Would Gavin believe it? Remembering the study, knowing what his father was capable of, knowing that she also remembered and also knew—would he think her capable of making the choice he couldn't, to spare him the consequences? The bottle was cold despite the heat of her hand, as cold as if the apprentice had drawn it from the bottom of the aquifer instead of the bottom of his satchel.

"I gave him a tonic," Arkady said, and Theron muttered, "Tasted bloody awful."

Judah felt as if her heart had stopped.

The Seneschal stood up. "I'm glad you're well, Lord Theron. The people will be much relieved. Thank you for indulging us. Would you take some refreshment before you leave, Arkady Magus?"

Of course Arkady would take some refreshment before he left. He always did. He barked at his apprentice, who scurried to his side, taking up Arkady's satchel as well as his own—but was it Judah's imagination, or were all three men leaving faster than they usually did? Normally, Arkady took every opportunity to fawn over Gavin and Elly or be horrible to Judah. This seemed too simple. Too clean. The door closed and only the four of them were left in the room. Theron wanted to go back up to the workshop immediately. He'd figured his device out, he said; he'd had a breakthrough. Elly was pleading with him to stay and eat, or at least change clothes. Gavin was offering to go down to the baths with him.

The moment we leave.

Maybe the poison was already in Theron, working its way

through his body. Maybe she was letting him die by sitting here, frozen with indecision.

Maybe the poison was in her hand.

She stood up. She would tell them quickly. Theron could decide for himself, when he knew everything. Look how much trouble they'd created by not telling Elly everything.

Give it to Lord Theron. All of it.

Judah opened her mouth to speak.

"Oh," Elly said, sounding surprised. "Theron, your nose is bleeding."

And it was: a thin but steady stream of blood that grew even steadier as Theron reached up to touch it. He squinted at his bloody fingers in puzzlement. Then he collapsed.

Elly cried out. So did Gavin, maybe. Judah couldn't tell. Elly pulled Theron's head into her lap as his entire body began to shake. Gavin tried to take off his brother's glasses. Judah knelt next to him. Fumbling with the cold bottle and its impossibly tiny cork with fingers that felt huge and clumsy. *The moment we leave.* Theron's breathing was loud and frightening, as if he were being choked from the inside. His eyes were wide but unseeing. The whites showed all the way around the blue. Elly and Gavin were calling his name. The cork flew out. Judah said, "Hold his head," surprised at how cool she sounded. She grabbed his chin and forced his mouth open, emptying the bottle into it. The liquid was clear and thin, like water. Then she held his mouth closed again and he choked and gagged and she thought, what if I'm killing him, what if this is me killing him right now?

His spine arched. The heels of his boots slammed against the floor. His eyes rolled back in his head and then closed. He went limp.

In the absence of his terrible breathing the silence was nightmarish. Elly seemed to be holding her breath and Judah could not breathe, either. I've killed him, she thought, once again stunned by how easily she could think that.

Then Theron inhaled, a great ragged whoop. His next breath was easier, and the one after that. Soon he was breathing normally. His eyes remained closed.

"What just happened?" Elly turned to Judah. "What was that? Where did you get it?"

"The apprentice. He said to give it to him as soon as they left." Over Theron's inert body, still lying half in Elly's lap, Judah met Gavin's eyes. "He knew."

Elly brushed Theron's sweat-drenched hair away from his forehead. "Arkady tried to poison him." She seemed to be testing the idea, speaking it aloud to see if the words sounded true. "Why would he do that? Why would Arkady want Theron dead? The Seneschal said they wanted to make sure he was healthy, because—" Her eyes widened. No fool, Elly. "Because there are rumors in the city that he's ill. That he's dying."

It was awful, watching the pieces fall into place in Elly's mind. Judah found the tiny cork, and jammed it back into the mouth of the empty bottle. Which just felt like glass, now. Not cold at all.

"Who wants Theron dead?" Elly's voice was flat and furious. "Why?"

Judah didn't answer. Gavin's eyes were fixed on his unconscious brother. Parsing it out, as Judah had before Theron collapsed, trying to figure out how much to say. Tell her, Judah thought to him, even though that wasn't the way the bond worked. Tell her everything.

"Because he'll be a horrible commander," Gavin finally said.

Elly looked at Judah. Who, for all of her grand intentions, found that she could not say the words, now that Elly was waiting to hear them, and who had to watch as Elly's lips pressed together, as her eyes grew hard.

"You let me deliver him to them," she said softly. "Both of you." Then she leaned down, kissed Theron's forehead and stood up.

Gavin stood up, too. "Where are you going?" He sounded alarmed.

"We," Elly said, in a cold, furious tone Judah had never heard before, "all of us, are going to put Theron to bed, and not leave him lying on the floor like garbage nobody cares about. Then we are going to close the door, and we are going to come back out into this room, and the two of you will tell me absolutely everything." She looked at Judah. "Grab his legs."

They didn't tell her absolutely everything—Gavin did not mention Amie of Porterfield—but they told her enough. Elly didn't speak for hours afterward. She sat by the bed where Theron lay—Gavin's bed, not the hard little cot in the alcove—and watched his thin chest rise and fall. The light outside dwindled and died, and still she sat. When Judah or Gavin tried to speak to her, she only nodded or shook her head. Even those movements were remote.

A kitchen boy brought dinner. Nobody ate much. The boy came back for the trays. The House grew quiet.

Judah expected Arkady or the Seneschal to come to see what they'd wrought, but neither did. Gavin stretched out on the sofa. Judah tried to get Elly to sleep, too, but her efforts only produced the faraway shake of the head, so she herself lay down on Theron's cold, dusty bed. She wanted to be close if anything happened.

She didn't expect to sleep, but eventually she did.

In the morning, she awoke to see cobwebs in the corners of

Theron's alcove. She sat up, rubbed the sleep out of her eyes and went into Gavin's room. Elly sat where Judah had left her the night before. "No change," she said.

Theron lay exactly as Judah had last seen him. Even his head rested at the same angle. Grief filled Judah. "I gave it to him too late," she said. "I waited too long."

"Don't."

"I was afraid it was a trick. I was afraid he'd given me the poison instead of the cure. Because, why me? Why would he give it to me?"

"Because nobody ever notices you," Elly said. The words stung, but they were true. Elly stood up and shook out her skirt. "I heard breakfast come. We should eat."

Bread and greens and grapefruit and spun honey, but Judah couldn't eat, couldn't wrench herself out of those precious seconds she'd wasted, standing idle while the poison worked its way through Theron's body. If he died because of her, she'd never forgive herself. Elban's grip over Gavin would die with him and that thought was even more shameful; once she'd had it, Judah knew she didn't deserve to forgive herself, not ever. Elly, spreading honey on bread, seemed so serene. Even sleepless and wan, even furious, Elly's essential goodness shone through. Judah knew that shameful thought would never occur to her.

She cursed herself. She wished it were her life at stake, so she could end it.

Fingers laced through hers. Gavin's. He'd sat beside her and she'd been so trapped in her guilt that she hadn't noticed. He squeezed her hand and she felt the thorny tangle of his mind, as gnarled as her own. Elly was so good at wearing the face she needed to wear, and Judah no longer knew what was true. She knew she loved Theron. She knew she didn't want him to die.

Toward evening he began to stir. Small movements at first,

like watching a room being lit one tiny candle at a time. Gavin pulled the cot into the main bedroom and they took turns sleeping there. When Theron opened his eyes in the early hours of the morning, Elly was asleep on the cot, Gavin on the sofa out in the parlor. Judah was the one sitting next to Theron's bed and his eyelids had been fluttering for almost an hour, so she was watching when they opened. For a few frightening moments, as his gaze wandered the room aimlessly, she was afraid he was blind. But then their roaming stopped, and he seemed to see her.

"Theron." She spoke quietly, so she didn't wake Elly. "Can you hear me?"

For a few even more frightening moments, she thought he was deaf. Then he nodded. His lips moved and he said something. She couldn't hear, so she leaned closer, and he tried again.

"What happened?" he said.

They hadn't talked about this, about what they'd tell Theron. Judah didn't know what to say. "You've been sick," she said finally. It wasn't a lie.

Theron's eyes drifted, befuddled, to Elly's sleeping form. "Arkady was here."

"Yes."

"Wasn't sick then."

"No." Judah's eyes were hot.

Theron seemed to think about this for a moment. Normally, to watch Theron think was to be in the presence of a tightly-wound machine, whirring away behind his eyes. This felt different. This felt like watching water drip out of a leaky bucket. He just woke up, she thought. He's still half-asleep. He's still sick.

"Tonic," he said dreamily. "Poison."

Judah's eyes closed. She made herself open them. "Yes."

176

This didn't seem to bother him. "Alive."

She tried to smile. "It's a long story, love." But he was already asleep again. Judah felt cold and frightened. Just woke up, she told herself. Half-asleep. Sick.

But the shameful thing that crouched inside her whispering horrible truths knew better. Throughout the night, the cycle repeated: Theron would wake, ask what had happened, and go back to sleep. By morning he was sitting up, holding a cup of coffee Elly had made for him, pale with cream and thick with sugar. He didn't seem to be able to remember it existed long enough to drink it. Every time he noticed it in his hand, he seemed surprised all over again. He would answer a question if it was put to him, and he didn't seem unhappy. But neither did he seem like Theron. He was content to sit in bed, eat what they gave him, and listen when they talked, all while wearing the same pleasant, vaguely surprised expression. Theron would rather work than sleep, always, and he was restless when not actively busy. But now he didn't ask to get out of bed, or complain when they told him to rest. He didn't even ask for a book.

It was unsettling. Judah suspected that, like her, Elly and Gavin hoped he would fall asleep again so the three of them could confer. He didn't. And yet, on some level, it was as if he'd never woken up. When dinner arrived, Elly made him a plate and took it to him; Judah and Gavin stayed in the parlor, picking glumly at their own food. They were surprised when, only a few minutes after she'd gone into the bedroom, Elly came back out and closed the door behind her.

"I told him I'd be back after I'd eaten," she said. "He didn't seem to mind."

"Why is he like this?" Gavin said. The question came from the thorny place inside him, and wasn't directed at anybody in particular.

But Elly answered, her voice chilly. "I don't know. We could send for Arkady, if you like, and ask him." She crossed the room and poured herself a glass of wine. Then she sat down.

"I'll do it," she said. "I'll marry Elban."

Judah couldn't speak. "No," Gavin said. "I won't let you."

"It's not for you to let me do," Elly said. "But of course it wouldn't have occurred to you to ask my opinion on the subject, because nobody's ever asked my opinion about anything in my entire life. Why start now?"

"It's not going to happen," Gavin said doggedly.

"You would have gone straight to Elban if we'd told you, and you know it," Judah said.

"Which is what I'm still going to do, except now Theron's half-dead. Congratulations, both of you. Nice work, well done." Elly's tone was neutral, almost matter-of-fact. But her words couldn't have hurt Judah more if they'd been made of fire.

"What happened to Theron isn't my fault," Gavin said. "And it's certainly not Judah's. But it doesn't matter. You're not marrying Elban."

"I'm not, am I?" Still neutral. A bit curious, if anything. "How do you plan to stop me?"

"I'm going to kill him," Gavin said in almost the same tone.

Elly's eyebrows went up. "You're not serious."

"Competely."

Elly took a long, deliberate breath, and then let it out. "Doesn't that plan rather depend on the willingness of the guards, the courtiers, and the Seneschal to go along with it? That aside, have you even stopped to consider who exactly it is who doesn't want me to marry Elban?" She gestured toward the closed bedroom door. "Because clearly somebody feels rather strongly about it. And I suppose it's possible that they just think Theron would be—what did you call him? A lousy commander? But murder seems like a drastic choice to avoid something that might never happen. I doubt you've made any secret of your plan to guild him."

Gavin said nothing.

"If you don't marry me, Gavin, who will you marry? You need an heir. They won't just let you *play* forever." Elly's emphasis on the word was ugly.

Judah could feel in her muscles how much Gavin hated this conversation. She could feel his confusion; this Elly was not at all the tolerant friend he'd been paying lazy court to since they were eight years old. Judah herself was less surprised. "Porterfield," he said. "That'll be the public story, that I'm renouncing you for her." Then, too quickly, "Which I would never do of my own volition. Which I will never do."

"Instead, you'll kill Elban," Elly said.

"Yes." He sounded defiant. "I told you, Elly. None of this will happen."

"And has it occurred to you," Elly said dryly, "that there might be some anti-Porterfield faction that doesn't want it to happen? Considering that courtiers are courtiers, and that if Theron's dead he can't be the stick Elban is beating you with. No, there's no other answer. I'm marrying Elban. Unless you really do have the Seneschal on your side, Gavin."

Gavin's eyes slid uncertainly toward Judah, then away. "I don't. But I refuse—"

Elly laughed. "How long have you lived here? Anyone would think you're the one from the province full of sheep, not me." Her laughter melted into anger, liquid and caustic. "You don't get to refuse. I don't get to refuse. The stupid Porterfield girl doesn't get to refuse, although she might not know it. All I do is read family histories, Gavin. Generations of them. Nobody gets to refuse." Elly's voice had not wavered once in this entire horrible conversation, but it did now. Judah knew that the waver was not grief but rage.

Gavin was quiet, deflated. Wrestling with something. Finally he said, "Elly, he's a monster."

Her shoulders twitched. "I come from a long line of monsters. I'm not afraid." She stood up and held her hand out to him. The gesture was uncomfortably formal. "Thank you for not killing Theron."

"You would never have forgiven me." Gavin watched her hand as if it pained him, and made no move to take it.

"No," she said. "I wouldn't have."

She arranged an audience with Elban before it had even occurred to Judah that such a thing was possible. They had an hour to wait. Judah spent it with Theron. Every lethargic motion of his head felt like a reproach, a reminder that she'd done nothing while Theron's mind drained away. Elly was building her own pyre to throw herself on and save them all. Nothing Judah did could help her. Sitting with Theron was nothing compared to the price Elly had volunteered to pay. Judah swore privately that she would take care of Theron as long as he needed it. She had no other purpose; she would devote herself to him.

Still, when Elly asked her to come with her to see Elban, Judah said, "If you want me to," though it meant leaving Theron alone. Judah knew her presence in Elban's study would not improve his mood any, but it might draw fire away from Elly. To that end, she would have gone in wild and rumpled as she was, but Elly insisted that Judah put on a clean dress, and made her sit to have her hair rebraided, so she'd be as presentable as possible. Elly herself wore the same dress she'd worn all day, with her hair in one braid that she pinned up out of her way. Practical, but plain—as plain as someone as lovely as Elly could be. She would not dress up for Elban. He might marry her, but she wouldn't play bride for him.

"I'm sorry," Judah said while Elly did her hair. "We should have told you."

"Yes," Elly said. Then, unexpectedly, she leaned her head down on top of Judah's, and put her arms around Judah's shoulders. Judah put her hands over Elly's.

"I'm sorry," she whispered again, and neither of them said anything more.

When the two women emerged from the bedroom into the parlor, Gavin was waiting by the door. He'd changed his shirt and cleaned his boots. The set of his jaw was stubborn. "Theron's asleep. We'll lock the door. I'm not letting the two of you go alone."

Elly shrugged. "Do as you like."

They did not speak at all as they made their way through the corridors.

Judah hadn't been in Elban's study since she was eight years old. The smell of it hit her like a blow: fire, brandy, leather, sweat. The dark, wicked tobacco Elban smoked. The room looked different by gaslight; brighter, colder. The books in the library, back when Judah had been allowed in the library, felt like friends she hadn't met yet; Elban's books felt like guards at a fortress. A glass-fronted cabinet held the good Sevedran wine Elban drank, a carved stone medallion hanging from the neck of each bottle. One small, delicately paned window was set into the wall, but the hour was late and the window was black.

Elban sat at the huge desk, pen in hand, book open to a blank page in front of him. In the purplish lamplight, he seemed even more cadaverous than usual, his long white hair hanging over his shoulders like a shroud. At the sound of

Gavin closing the door, he looked up. "You're all here," he said. "I shouldn't be surprised. You always did travel in a pack."

A big leather sofa and two armchairs were arranged in front of the fireplace, where a hot fire burned. He gestured toward the sofa. Elly sat down, her movements as fluid and dignified as if she were at a state dinner. Gavin sat on one side of her, Judah the other. As if they could offer her some protection, merely by being there. "Not quite all of us," Elly said. "Theron is ill."

Closing the book and crossing the room to sit in one of the big armchairs, Elban said, "I heard. Will he live?"

"He's recovering."

An iron poker rested in the heart of the blazing fire. Elban took a neatly rolled cigarette from the tray on the table and, leaning over, picked up the glowing poker and touched the cigarette to its tip. "It would be like him, after all these years of coughing and stuttering around the place, to die just now when it was least convenient." He blew a cloud of smoke into the air. His pale eyes studied Elly. "Your value is dropping, Tiernan. I bought you from your father for six hundred pieces of gold, but my son traded you away to save a half-blind weakling who might die tomorrow, anyway."

On the other side of Elly, Judah felt Gavin's skin go hot. But Elly's tone was smooth and even, without a single ragged edge. "Theron is worth more than all of us put together. And I wasn't traded away this time. This is my decision."

"Banish the word *my* from your vocabulary, Tiernan. Nothing belongs to you." He flicked the ash of the cigarette onto the carpet. "Well, say what you came here to say."

Elly's chin lifted. Gavin's stomach was a sick void. "I'll marry you. But I want your word. Theron lives."

"If fate wills it."

"I hope fate does will it, then, because if anything happens to him, I'll throw myself off the solstice balcony. Right into the Lord's Square." It didn't sound like an idle threat.

"Really?" Elban looked at her with no more than mild interest. "The girl who has to be forcibly dragged onto that very balcony, threatening to plummet to her death from it? How gruesome. Wouldn't it be easier just to kill me?"

Every muscle in Gavin's body tensed. Judah's, too. Elly didn't move.

"In my sleep, perhaps, after a night of conjugal bliss? You wouldn't be the first to leave my bed with murderous intent, Tiernan. Of course, you could try it right now." Elban spoke cordially, as if he were offering them all tea. "There are three of you and only one of me. Only one of you has any combat training, and I've killed more men than I can count—but still."

"I don't imagine that would end well for us," Elly said.

"Very perceptive." Elban raised his cigarette toward her in salute. "My guards all come from Highfall Prison, you know. The Seneschal selects them. Most were under death sentences—petty offenses, theft or fighting. Occasionally worse. Occasionally much worse." He spoke like a tutor lecturing them on some subject he knew so well it no longer interested him. "All of them are clever enough to recognize that they've been rescued. All of them know they owe me their lives. They are fiercely loyal." The smoke from his cigarette circled his head. "I've assigned one to each of you. If I'm found dead tonight, or any night, none of you will see sunrise. If my House falls, you will all fall with it. And you'll die horrible deaths. Long. Painful. Degrading."

"Maybe it would be worth it," Gavin said, so low he was barely audible.

"Maybe so." Elban sounded pleased. He threw his cigarette into the fire and stood up. With two graceful, menacing steps—no movement wasted, his eyes never leaving his son—he stood in front of Gavin. Who was on his feet, now, too; awkward by comparison, but standing between Elly and his father. The two men were of a height. Gavin had Elban's jaw, and his mouth. That mouth, Judah thought illogically: the thin lips, the curl at the corner that could be amused or endearing or, like Elban's, cruel. Theron had it, too. It was in every portrait, on every carved sarcophagus in the crypt, all the way back to the beginning of Elban's line. Everyone always spoke of Gavin as resembling his mother but now Judah saw that with the passage of a certain number and quality of years, he would look very like the man standing in front of him.

"Come on, then." The taunt in Elban's voice was so light. It would be easy to miss. "Take that stupid dagger you carry and put it in my throat. Patricide is a noble enough death."

Judah could practically feel the knife in Gavin's hand, his desire was so strong.

"But when the deed is done," Elban said, "take the knife from my throat and put it in your own, so you won't have to watch what happens to these two. Because you will watch; that's part of my orders for you." The curl in the corner of his mouth deepened. "Unless you kill them, too. But after what I saw on the hunt, I very much doubt you can do that."

Gavin didn't move. Judah didn't even think Elly was breathing.

Elban snorted and sat down. "As I thought. Suicide would have the same result, Eleanor of Tiernan. After your suffering ends, that of those you leave behind will be long and luxurious. If I remain alive to enjoy it, it will last all the longer. As I said before, nothing belongs to you. Not even your life. You live at my indulgence and you will die that way. Please me, and I'll make your death quick."

"You know, Lord Elban," Elly said, "it is possible to rule without being an utter monster."

Elban blinked. Then he threw back his head and laughed. "Who's your model for that, Tiernan? Your father? He once burned a mill full of children to punish their parents for refusing to pay his taxes. It's a good story. Ask him to tell it to you, if you ever see him again." The faint taunt was back in his voice. "Perhaps we should invite him to the wedding. Your father, and all of your brothers."

Elly didn't answer. Her hands were carefully folded in her lap but her clenched knuckles were white. She spoke often of her mother, who'd died when she was fifteen, but rarely of her father. Never of her brothers.

The Lord of the City leaned back in his chair and eyed her speculatively, his pale eyes showing more interest than they had. "I'll give you this, heir. Your Tiernan has courage. Of course, she's not yours anymore. But Porterfield will suit you well enough. Just let her put a collar around your neck, and be a good dog, and she probably won't be too hard on you."

Gavin's jaw was clenched so hard that Judah's teeth hurt, but he still said nothing. "What about Theron?" Elly said.

"He lives. For now."

"'For now' wasn't the deal," Gavin said.

Elban smiled. It was a sleepy, slow smile, full of confidence and loathing. "Oh, it won't be me that kills him. A few years from now, when you love the city a little more and your childhood a little less, when you find yourself not sleeping so well, knowing there's another living claimant to the throne—you'll find yourself making plans, heir. Or, more likely, letting Porterfield make them for you. About your brother, and about that." He nodded toward Judah. The curl in his lip spoke of disgust, now.

Elly took Judah's hand, her grip fierce and protective. "She's not part of this," she said, just as Gavin said, "She's fine the way she is."

"She looks like a foreign whore," Elban said. "Not that I have any objection to foreign whores, as such, but I generally don't let them live in my House. And nor will your new bride, unless I'm mistaking the Porterfields to their very essence. So tell me: until we break that filthy bond, how do you intend to protect the little pet you've grown so fond of?"

Judah felt twin dull aches in her palms. Not a signal: Gavin's fists were clenched, his fingers digging brutally into his palms. Elly still held Judah's hand. Judah wished she would put it down. The contrast between Elly's soft fingers and Gavin's hard ones was distracting and difficult.

"I'll talk to Amie." Gavin's heart was pounding, and that was how Judah knew that talking to Amie would do no good. "Or I'll find somewhere safe, where Amie can't get to her. A guild, maybe." He didn't want to guild Judah out. She didn't want to be guilded.

"Difficult to protect her from so far away," Elban said. "And guilds get raided, particularly those that accept women. Yes, a guilded woman's life is—difficult." The word left Elban's lips like a breath. "What if she were injured? What if she sickened?"

Gavin's heart pounded harder. Judah found herself breathing fast. He sounded desperate. "An apartment in the House, then. Somewhere out of the way."

"And when she grows tired of being out of the way? When she wants to go for a stroll in the sunlight? How will Porterfield react, when they meet on the Promenade?"

Judah already knew the answer. The Seneschal had given it to her. Gavin, though, was just figuring it out. "Then—she won't—" He stopped. His face was stoic but fear and pain radiated from the rest of him.

"Won't what? Won't go for a walk? Surely you don't mean to imprison your devoted little pet, do you, heir?"

Walled into a tower. That's where she'd be. That's what he'd do; what he'd have to do, to keep them both alive.

"No." But Gavin swallowed hard enough to make Judah's throat hurt.

"What else would it be called, then, when you put her someplace where she won't ever be seen or heard from again? Because that's the only way to make your Lady forget her, and as long as she's not forgotten, she'll be in danger. And so will you."

"You forget." Elly's voice rang out, clear and cutting. "Amie won't be Lady of the City, not for a long time. I will be."

Clearly enjoying himself, Elban said, "You? Power comes from connections, and you have none. We've never let you make any. You'll look very pretty next to me on the dais, and I'm sure I'll enjoy the time we spend together, but you're nothing."

Elly's fingers gripped Judah's. Gavin said, "I will not let either of them be hurt."

"The Tiernan is mine, and I will do with her as I please, and you will have nothing to say about it. And as for the foundling, you will, indeed, let Amie hurt her, if that's what she wants. Because the more attachment you show to her, the more Porterfield will resent her, and the more pain you'll both have to bear. And the more pain you bear, the harder it will be to keep your secret, and if you fail to keep your secret, well—" Elban shrugged. "The Porterfields aren't known for their empathetic hearts. I would not count on Amie's love for protection, once she understands just how easy you are to kill." He stood up. "Come here, foundling."

Judah had no choice but to obey. The image of him next to Gavin was still in her head. Same height. Same jaw. Pain flickered on the ball of her thumb: the oldest of their signals, going back years. Going back, in fact, to this very study. *Here with you.*

Elban surveyed her. "What's that stupid name Clorin gave you, foundling?"

"Judah." She didn't believe for an instant that he didn't know it.

He snorted. "Do you know the judah vine, foundling? It grows in the north. It's a parasite. Pretty flowers, but it ruins everything it touches. So I suppose it's not a bad name for you, at that." He smelled like nothing. All Judah could smell was cigarette smoke and the fire. She might as well have been standing there alone. He picked up the poker resting in the coals. The end was shaped with a point, a hook and a barb. "My son thinks he loves you. He has not yet learned that there's no such thing. There is convenience, pleasure, utility and gain, and that's all. One day, he will realize that he doesn't love anyone at all. Not the Tiernan, not his scrawny, unsatisfying brother, and not you."

Here with you.

Elban grabbed Judah's wrist and, fingers like iron, wrenched it to expose the skin on her inner arm. Her dress had half sleeves and she could see the marks from Gavin's scratching. "Let's speed that day along," he said, and pressed the flat side of the poker against her skin.

The pain was instantaneous and brilliant and the rest of the room shrank to nothing, but her training held and she did not cry out. She heard Elly's horrified gasp and heard—smelled— the sizzle of her own skin cooking. Her vision refracted in her tear-filled eyes. Countless Elbans. Countless pokers. Countless arms, all of them burning.

"See how easy she is to hurt, heir. See how easy *you* are to hurt." All she could see clearly were Elban's eyes, the irises so pale they were almost white. He lifted the poker—it stuck to Judah's skin, pulling free with a disgusting tearing sound— and before Judah knew it was happening he held the other arm and the poker came down again and the searing doubled. "See how quietly you sit and watch, what a well-trained little dog you are, already. So much for love."

"I'll lock her away." Gavin's voice sounded strangled.

"Yes. You will. But we're not bargaining." He lifted the poker again and dropped Judah's arm. She fell to her knees, staring at her branded skin. He had flipped the poker so the two burns were mirror images of each other: the point, the hook, the barb, in wet, mottled gray and red. The smell coated her throat. She very much would have liked to pass out, or throw up, and tried very hard to do neither.

Elban bent over Judah, examining the marks. Sounding once again like the worst of their tutors, he said, "It's a delicate balance, you know. Leave the brand too long and the nerves are destroyed, so the pain stops. But lift it too soon, and the scars don't shine the way they should." Satisfied, he straightened. "I think I've gotten these exactly right. Her scars will be pretty, even if nothing else about her is." He stirred the fire with the poker. Judah stared, fascinated and feverish, at the logs in front of her, as they shifted and glittered. Her arms glittered, too, shining as intensely as the coals. Gavin, far away, was gray with shock and pain and misery, sweat dampening the edges of his hair.

"Keeping in mind, of course," Elban said, "that all of this is only happening because you *love* your brother too much to kill him."

Theron. Judah needed to take care of him. She had sworn it. She focused all of her self into her legs, and stood up.

"Amazing." Elban's voice, bright and interested, was growing distant. "A normal woman would have to be carried to bed after burns like that. She's barely human."

She was not human. She was pain in the shape of a human. She glittered like fire. She burned.

★ ★ ★

In the corridor, Gavin's arm instantly circled her, trying to hold her up despite his own pain. "Jude, my arms—I can't carry you—" he said, sounding desperate and scared, but then Elly had her other side. Her feet dragged as her head lolled on Gavin's shoulder, as his voice in her ear told her he was sorry, sorry.

Then she was lying on Elly's big soft bed and Elly's gentle hands were moving around her. "Get the scissors from my sewing basket," Elly said.

"I'm sorry. I'm so sorry."

"We need to cut these sleeves off. Maybe the whole dress."

"I'm so sorry."

"Gavin. *Help* me." Elly's voice was sharp and direct enough to even break through Judah's haze. Judah could see her hovering overhead, carved into hard white stone with the force of her anger. In a moment Gavin was there, too, equally white but sweaty and sick from his own burns; careful not to move her arm, he took Judah's hand, then dropped his head to it. Kissed it, lay his cheek against it. The waters inside him were stormy and rough. Judah could not try to soothe them.

Meanwhile, she could hear the low sliding snick of Elly's sewing scissors, and then water falling into a bowl somewhere, as a cloth was wrung out. More kindly than she'd spoken to Gavin, but with just as much firmness, Elly said, "Judah, I'm going to clean your arms. It'll hurt, love."

Elly was right. It did hurt, love.

She could not eat dinner that night but drank too much of the wine they forced on her. When she woke into a silent world, she was alone. The shutters were closed and the bedroom was dim. Somehow she dressed, sliding her coat gingerly over her bandages. The burns still seared and her arms were stiff, besides, but she managed her boots, too. The air in the bedroom felt dense, unbreathable. All of her skin hurt. She had to get outside.

The parlor was empty. Sun streamed in through the windows and the edges of everything glittered. In Gavin's room, Theron slept, his hands unnaturally idle on top of the blankets. Gavin, himself, was gone. Poor Gavin, out there somewhere hoisting a halberd. Swinging a sword. Bearing a bow. The pain was never quite as bad when it wasn't truly yours, but still. Poor her, too. Creeping a corridor, lurching a lawn. It didn't work as neatly. She needed more words. *Through. Across.* Words to carry her, to move her from one place to another. The crisp spring air was a cool balm on her face, but something was wrong with her mind. Was Gavin drunk again? No. There was no sober little boat bobbing on the tide. This was hers. When she passed courtiers and staff she made a special effort to stand up straight, and threw her feet out in front of her in something that maybe, perhaps, seemed like a purposeful stride. Nobody stopped her. Nobody spoke to her.

The palm of her hand itched.

The walled garden was empty and she spent some time resting on a bench. Then she spent some time resting on the ground next to the bench so that she could lay her cheek on its cool smooth surface. She wanted to crawl inside it, to wrap herself in the marble like a blanket. She wished she were made of marble: a cold, still, painless statue, withstanding the rain and snow, feeling only the slow scratchy embrace of ivy. The ivy was green and thick and glossy. She felt green and thick, but not particularly glossy. She wanted to be out in the open air, away from the walls and hedges, where the breeze could blow away the thickness in her head. The glitter. Because the thickness and glitter were strangling her, she was choking on them. Guttering like one of Elban's gas lamps, right before it went out.

Elban. Elly was going to marry Elban. Fact. True.

Later.

She pulled herself up, brushed halfheartedly at the dirt on her dress, and resumed walking. Boots on the hard-packed path, one, two. From somewhere far above she watched them with great interest. It was marvelous, the way boots just kept moving. How did they do that? One scuffed brown boot into the dirt, then another. Gravel scattering beneath them. The hounds howled, but the sound soon faded. She heard a human voice. The snuffle of a horse.

The boots stopped. Something was blocking them. Other boots, like hers but larger. She heard her name. It took a moment for her to connect the word with the stifled thing inside her. A hand touched her chin, brought her head up. Darid, his brow wrinkled with worry. Somebody said, "She okay?" and at first she wondered how he'd spoken without moving his lips.

But it must have been somebody else speaking, because Darid answered. "No." His fingers were as cool as the marble had been. "She's burning up. Go to the House, tell them we need the magus."

Magus. Arkady. Arkady had poisoned Theron. Fact. True.

Later.

The tiny stifled part of her forced air from her lungs into her throat, into words. "No," she said. "No magus."

"Judah, you're sick," Darid said.

Elban burned her. To prove he could. That nobody would stop him. Nobody had stopped him.

I'll lock her away.

Fact. True.

Later.

"Not sick," she said. "Hurt. No magus. Magus hates me."

Darid made a noise. It sounded like the noises his horses made. "At least come inside. Let me do something for the fever." He took her arm. She screamed. He jerked back as if she were made of fire. She felt like she was. He said something else, but she couldn't answer, the pain had finally engulfed her, she was falling. She hoped somebody caught her.

He did.

Fact. True.

He made her drink something bitter that tasted faintly of hay. Not long afterward the glitter started to recede. It felt like she was coming out of a hole. She found herself lying on the bench in the tack room. Her coat was gone and her bandaged arms lay carefully placed on her stomach.

Horses got sick. Horses needed to be treated. A dog could be replaced in six months; horses were expensive, horses took a long time to mature and a long time to train. Darid had a substantial collection of herbs and mixtures and potions and salves. They were meant for horses but most of the staff had never seen a magus—staff was replaceable, too—so he knew how to use them on humans.

Wherever Gavin was, he was in agony. She could feel his pain like a gauze veil as her own receded. She was surprised that he hadn't felt her fever. But, wait: the itch in the palm of her hand wasn't an itch. Now that the pain from the burns had ebbed, she could feel him scratching, incessantly. When Darid stepped away, she scratched back. Just once, deliberate and slow.

After a moment, Gavin sent it back to her. The itching eased.

By then, Darid was back. Holding the back of her hand, he gently pushed the sleeves of her dress up over Elly's bandages. A few snips with a pair of brutally sharp shears and the bandages were gone. The burns were both covered with sickly gray-yellow ooze, the skin around them swollen and hot. Judah preferred their looks to the one Darid wore on his face. She remembered: on the second day after the Wilmerians' arrival, Judah had found Darid working on one of their horses. They were shorter and sturdier than House horses, made for work and not war—but the poor mare Darid had been tending wouldn't be doing any work anytime soon. Every rib stood out, and her legs were impossibly thin. Her mane and tail hung limp and tangled and there were oozing welts on her dirty cream-colored hide where a harness had been strapped too tightly and left too long. But her hind flanks were the worst, because the horse had been whipped, and viciously. Her dingy hide was stained with an ugly brown that could only be blood.

Normally Darid carried a lightness with him, but there had been no lightness that night. His face as he'd cleaned the little mare's wounds, as he'd shown Judah how to coax her to eat—it was the same face she saw now. She found herself afraid. Ashamed. She didn't want him to look at her that way.

After what seemed like an eternity, he did exactly that. "This was not an accident."

Mutely, she shook her head.

"And even if I knew who did this to you, there's nothing I could do about it." He seemed to be telling himself, more than her. "If it was someone on staff, I could. But it wasn't. Was it?"

She shook her head again.

His eyes were fixed on her arms, but for a second his pleasant stablemaster's mask slipped and she saw the rage beneath it. Tightly bound, deeply controlled. For her. He was angry for her—not because he felt the pain she felt, or someone had judged him responsible, but at the simple fact of her suffering. She wrapped herself in that anger the way she'd wanted to

wrap herself in marble, except the anger was warm and protective instead of cold and dead. It filled her with awe.

Darid's chest swelled and his nostrils flared as he took a
long breath in and let it out again. "I can heal this. Get rid
of the infection. That, I can do." He still held her hand in
his. She thought she felt his fingers tighten, ever so slightly.
Then he let go.

CHAPTER SIX

In retrospect, Nate probably should have given Derie more warning. He'd been too excited, almost drunk with it, and when he saw her at the plague shrine the news exploded out of him. "I was inside," he said, his voice high and giddy. "I saw her. She's alive, Derie. She's real."

The old woman's knuckles went white on her cane and for a moment Nate saw two Deries: the short round woman hunched in front of him, and the bonfire of Work that raged inside her. It knocked him backward as surely as if she'd put her two hands in the middle of his chest and pushed. He barely managed to keep his feet. Derie was so very powerful, and they'd been Working together since he was a child, but she'd never lost control like that before. It felt like falling off a cliff—balance gone, arms pinwheeling, brain too full of *no no no* to think rationally. Icy wind whistling around you, great emptiness waiting below.

Nate had almost fallen off a cliff once, in the Barriers.

So, after his next trip inside, he was more careful. Before meeting Derie he cut open the heel of his thumb, letting out just enough blood to draw her sigil on his shaving mirror. He didn't know where she was living in Highfall—or where Charles was living either—but it didn't matter. She would feel his Work, and know he had something to tell her.

It worked. When they met again in the midnight quiet of the plague shrine, she was able to sit patiently—as patient as Derie ever was, anyway—while he told her the story: how he'd walked into the lab, smelled the poisonous herb Arkady was distilling, and known immediately what it was and how it would be used, if not on who; how, when the phaeton came for them that afternoon, Nate had brought along one of the precious few vials of medicine he'd carried with him over the Barriers, prepared by his mother and labeled in her hand; how, after Arkady took Elban's younger son into the bedroom, he'd passed the vial to the girl herself, and how clever and troubled her eyes had been. He did not tell Derie he'd touched her. He didn't tell her how that had felt.

When the story was done, she stroked the cane between her knees. There was nothing special about it. It was just a plain wooden stick, worn smooth with use. "Quick thinking, bringing the antidote," she said finally. "You want her trusting you. You want her confiding in you." This last she said with no small amount of distaste. As if the act of confession was inherently weak.

"Why do you think Elban wants the young lord dead?"

"Who's to say it was Elban?"

"The Seneschal came to the manor a few days before," Nate said. "He does Elban's bidding, doesn't he?"

She brushed the topic away. He could see it didn't interest

her. "More likely he's doing some courtier's, this time. Poison isn't Elban's style."

"Wasn't he the one who told Arkady to poison the children in the orphanage?"

"That was expedience." Her cane tapped the hard-packed dirt. "No, if Elban had been behind this, he would have made more of a show. Elban likes a show. Poison's a courtier's game." She smiled wickedly. "Courtiers, and us. You saw her with the boy? How did they seem?"

When Derie said *the boy*, she meant Elban's heir. They'd always spoken of him that way, and although intellectually Nate knew how old he was, he'd still been surprised by the tall, broad-shouldered man he met inside, golden and handsome. At first glance, the younger son—bony and pale—seemed to have more of Elban in him; but the more Nate had looked at the older, the more he'd seen the hard lines of the father's face under the glowing warmth on the surface. "I don't know," he said truthfully. "He was concerned about his brother. They were both uneasy."

Dissatisfaction came off her in waves. He didn't need any particular skill to feel it. She spat into the dust. "Bah. Give me your hand, boy. I need to know."

He slipped his coat off, let it fall to the bench behind him and pushed up his sleeve. "Use my arm." Derie was not always kind with her cuts. "I need my hands."

"Guess you do." Derie pulled a small folding knife from her pocket. In the wavering light from the shrine torches, the metal of the blade barely shone at all. He saw a fat crust of blood on the heel of her thumb, just where he'd cut himself to signal her earlier. She reopened the wound before he could ask about it. Knife still wet, she carved a line in the meat of Nate's arm, then pressed the cuts together so she could draw their two sigils in the mixed blood. Derie was powerful and she'd been doing the Work for a long time. She was confident and formidably skilled. When she reached into him, he could feel the Work behind every cut she'd ever made, for good or ill; all of those people, through all of those years, and each one rummaging in Nate's head like a hand in a pocket. He even felt the echo of his mother's touch, faint among all those invisible groping hands.

It was all a little horrible. But he'd learned to push the horror aside, and focus on the wonder of it. And wonderful it was. With Derie in his head he saw the girl as if she were standing in front of him again, that moment when he'd dropped the antidote into her lap—more clearly than the first time, even, because Derie pulled his eyes to parts of her he hadn't had time to notice. Her muddy boots, her ill-fitting dress. Her dark eyes. Her hair, wild with running her fingers through it. Not at all the color of berries—what a spurious comparison that had been—but a dark cool red, almost black in its depths. Like the last embers of a cooling fire, like the darkest wine. Her cheekbones were broad, her chin round. He couldn't see her ears but he imagined them small, like a forest creature's.

Derie was already pulling the eyes of his memory away from her to the boy. Elban's heir. Who, he saw now, would not look at Judah, who barely looked at the woman he stood next to (delicately built but steely-eyed; except for the steel and the fine clothes she seemed like a nice girl, the sort Nate might once have asked to dance a creel around a bonfire without hope of much more, just to enjoy the sight of her). Elban's heir was not merely worried, Nate saw now. He was being eaten alive. There were shadows beneath his eyes and he could not stop clenching his fists.

Distantly, Nate was aware of an increase in the warm flow of blood on his arm. At the plague shrine, Derie grunted; back in his mind's eye, she unfolded the picture before them. Like a napkin wrapped around a morsel of food, like a rose with a bee at its heart. Like nothing Nate had ever seen before. He'd once seen a human arm dissected, skin sliced open, muscles and tendons and ligaments all on display, and it was a little like that, but it was also completely different. It was nothing he could have drawn in ink, not if his life depended on it.

In the center of everything, exactly where it was but also everywhere else, like wind or smoke or music, he *saw* the Work, like a thick purple rope that led from the young lord's chest to the girl's. But the words *thick purple rope* were too small, too limited. He had never *seen* the Work before, and like the spots that danced on the inside of his eyelids, he could not quite manage to focus on it. He knew that *thick purple rope* was the only way his mind could process the strength of it, because it was immense. It was everything. The people in the room were half-real by comparison. Nate himself barely existed.

Then Derie dropped his arm and, like that, it was over. The memory, the power, the invading hands: all gone. Nate found himself blinking into the darkness, feeling empty and disarrayed. Real again. Real enough that he was nearly sick. Hard Working did that to the inexperienced—while Derie was training him, their Workings had often left him puking and reeling in the dirt—but it had not happened to him for a long time.

Derie merely said, "More Maia's side than Tobin's. Comely enough. Wish I could see if she has enough power to break the binding, but—she must, with that blood in her. And the boy's well bound to her, at least." She took a scrap of cloth from her pocket, wrapped it around her hand and used her cane to hoist herself to standing. Only then did she squint down at Nate. "Pull yourself together, boy." She sounded faintly disgusted.

He did so, as well as he could. Although he couldn't stop the great whoops of air forcing their way into and out of his lungs, and couldn't stop the way the world lurched around him. He didn't have anything to wrap his bleeding arm with so he would just have to hope it wasn't noticed. He wasn't the only one to ever walk around Brakeside bloody. "This isn't your first Work today," he said, making his voice as neutral as he could.

"Caterina sends vague feelings of pride," Derie said. "Try to earn them."

As he made his way back to Arkady's manor he had a headache, and the smell of the Brake seemed worse than usual. The Work Derie had done on Nate shouldn't have left him feeling so bad; it was small, specific, and over no great distance. But the Work Derie had done *inside* the Work—exposing the bond between the heir and the girl—was a feat on another order. It was as if, having been assured all his life that his body contained a heart and lungs and a liver and two kidneys, someone had actually unzipped his skin and taken them out, one by one. It was unnerving and fearsome and magnificent, so bright he could barely think of it. Also bright was the memory itself. Which happened: when someone fooled around in your head, the things they touched never quite went back to the way they'd been. Sometimes the memories were left detached, almost faded, like they'd happened to somebody else. Sometimes only the shape of them remained, like a glass empty of water. In very rare cases, this was done deliberately, as a punishment or a healing; an unskilled or malicious Worker could leave them burning more fiercely than ever. Spreading them out like sketches on a table, and not bothering to put them away.

This was what Derie had done to Nate—not out of any deliberate choice, but because she simply hadn't cared enough to undo what she'd done. It wasn't the first time she'd left him this way. When he and Charles were together they could fix each other, but Nate hadn't seen Charles in weeks, and when he reached for the sense of his friend in his head, the other man was there, but also…distant. Like there was smoke between them.

So as he stumbled home through Brakeside, as he stopped twice to retch in the dirt, his head was full of the girl, clear as crystal. He had the time and luxury now to notice her without the press of the other people in the room, without Derie dragging his gaze around. The girl's hands were strong; their movements were quick and determined, not languid and ornamental like those of the courtiers. They were hands that wanted to grab, to hold tight. Her mouth seemed full of words bitten back. She was a torch waiting to burn; she was a Working, the moment before it ripped the world open.

Ever since he was nine years old, the idea of the girl had been the center of his existence, his reason for training and learning and being. Comely, not comely—who cared? She was real. He had heard tales of her his entire life, for half a decade before she was even born, and she was *real*. He had seen her, spoken to her, *touched* her. He soaked himself in her Work-brightened image like a drunk in a keg of whiskey. Nate had lusted; he'd loved, even. This was neither. This was—bigger. This was like the first Working he'd ever done as a child, the quick painful flick of Derie's knife opening a world that was so much deeper, so much more possible than he'd ever considered. He'd been frightened beforehand, but never again. That vast stretching possibility that he only ever felt under the knife was worth any pain. It had changed him. It had changed everything. And now, he found everything changed again. The girl was real. The bond between the girl and the heir was real. Once he'd helped her untie old Mad Martin's knot, he could have that sense of possibility anytime he wanted, no knife, no bloodshed. Anybody could.

She could. He'd never seen her when she wasn't hurt or

worried; the Work would make her happy. To be the one to make her happy, to be the one she confided in: yes, that would be nice, to have those dark liquid eyes trusting him to listen, to help. He sometimes indulged in ridiculous private fantasies wherein he entered the shabby parlor and her face lit up because now, finally, here was somebody who truly understood her. In his smaller moments, he indulged in even more ridiculous fantasies in which he came upon her being mistreated somehow, at the mercy of those poisonous lady courtiers who peopled the House like beribboned vipers or—and these fantasies were *very* secret—at the mercy of one of the men. Sometimes the imaginary man he rescued her from was the heir himself. Even in his fantasies he knew better than to think he could physically best the tall, strong young lord, who'd been training in combat since he was half-grown, so in these fantasies Nate's tongue became as acerbic as Derie's, his wit as quick as Charles's, his sense of justice as stalwart as Caterina's. It was one of these fantasies into which he slipped, with the preternatural clarity of his Worked memory, as he crossed the deserted cobbles of Limley Square. His imaginings carried him up the steps of Arkady's manor and through the front door—he no longer bothered to sneak out of the gate—and only when he met Vertus in the hall, and the servingman scowled and said, "What's got you so bloody happy?" did Nate realize he was smiling.

"Nothing." Quickly, he wiped the smile away, and nodded at the covered chamber pot Vertus carried. "How is he tonight?"

"Leaking blood from every hole." Vertus lifted the lid and showed him.

Nate waved the pot away, recoiling a bit from the smell. "I'll give him something to put him to sleep."

"Please. Just our luck the old lizard didn't get one of the

wasting-quietly-away diseases, huh? Something that takes the lungs out first?"

"Healthy people shouldn't complain about their luck."

"Whatever he's got, it's not wasting any time. Ever seen a cure for someone as far gone as he is?"

Nate shook his head.

"I have," Vertus said. "It's called death."

He took the pot out into the back to empty. Nate followed him as far as the lab, where he mixed a sleeping draught. It was one of the first things Caterina had taught him to make as a child. He made this one strong, and added a few extra things. They were the same extra things he added to almost everything Arkady ate or drank now. After smelling what was in the tonic the old man had fed the heir's unsuspecting brother the previous week, Nate had found his own qualms about poison significantly eased.

Upstairs, in the front bedroom, a fire blazed on the hearth and the room was prickly with heat. Arkady lay on top of the bedclothes, wearing only a thin nightgown, his limbs covered in slack flesh and the sheet beneath him brown with sweat. His eyes rolled toward Nate when he heard the door open. "Freezing to death," he said, his voice dry and cracked. "More wood."

"No more wood. You can have a blanket." Nate crossed to the table and checked the pitcher. There was just enough water in it to dilute the draught.

Arkady called him a foul name. Nate took a dirty glass from the table, poured the rest of the water into it, and added the draught. Arkady eyed it suspiciously. "What is that?" His voice was thin and querulous.

"Valerian, mostly. A lot of it. So you'll sleep."

Arkady snatched at the glass with a palsied hand. "Paltry kindness."

"It's self-serving. If you sleep, we sleep." Nate watched

as the old man greedily sucked down the draught. Then he picked up Arkady's wrist and felt for a pulse.

"More water," Arkady said, but he didn't show any actual signs of dehydration, so Nate shook his head.

"In the morning. Unless you want to wake up in your own piss again." He went to the chest at the foot of the bed and took out a blanket. "I'll leave this here for when the fire burns down. But I'd put it on now, if I were you. That draught will work quickly."

Arkady pulled the blanket over himself. Nate helped him, pulling it down to cover the knobbed, yellowing toes. The old man complained, said it was too heavy and too rough, but left it where it was. "You're a shitty nurse, boy," he said, "but you make good sleeping draughts." His words were slurred and his eyes unfocused. Nate wondered how much he could still see.

"Glad you approve," Nate said coldly.

"I don't know what's wrong with me." Arkady sounded as if his failing health were an intellectual puzzle that only vaguely interested him. "My mind feels wet. Like paper. Falling apart in my fingers." The old head rolled toward Nate like a fruit about to fall. "You're good, boy. You figure it out."

But Nate didn't have to figure it out. Nate knew. There were rotting black holes burning their way through Arkady: his stomach, his bowels, his lungs, his brain. His blood was separating inside his veins and his heart was struggling to pump the resulting sludge. He would not last much longer. Nate no longer felt even remotely bad about it. "I'll bring water in the morning," he said.

He didn't exactly forget the water, but neither did he go out of his way to remember. When Arkady's cracked shouts began to drift downstairs, Vertus knocked at the open door of the lab. "Should I bring him water?" he said.

Nate glanced at him. There had been a subtle change between them since Arkady had grown ill; they had gone from being equals to being—something else. Arkady's courtier clients still came to the manor for medicine and Vertus couldn't provide it, so Nate did. Slowly, without fanfare, he had moved more fully into the manor. He still slept on his pallet in the kitchen, and Arkady's chair in the parlor was always left respectfully empty, but it was a token gesture. Nate had taken over the lab, the parlor and the garden as if they were his by right. When there were decisions to be made, Nate made them. Vertus, for the most part, appeared to accept the change in their relationship with equanimity, but Nate felt something unsaid between them, and suspected that when it emerged it would be nothing pleasant. Even as Vertus asked advice about Arkady—*should I bring him water, should I open the window, should I give him brandy*—Nate could feel the servingman watching, calculating. Vertus was not stupid. Nate suspected that he knew more about Arkady's illness than he let on. Sewn into the lining of Nate's battered satchel was a cloth pocket that held, among other things Nate would rather keep secret, a leather wrist cuff with a tension-released blade attached: his springknife. Nate hadn't worn it since arriving in Highfall, but he often found himself thinking of the knife when he was alone with Vertus, thinking he might feel better with it strapped inside his sleeve. Vertus was a big, solid man, and *wiry* was the kindest word ever used to describe Nate. He wasn't sure wiry would be enough, if it came to a fight. He wasn't sure the springknife would be, either.

So he stepped lightly around Vertus, even as he rearranged the contents of Arkady's lab and replaced the sorrier plants in the garden with more useful ones. Arkady's courtier patients mostly wanted headache powders and contraceptive sachets, which took barely any effort. It wasn't hard for Nate to keep up his Gate Magus work, which he considered more important. His secret patients still came to the back gate, but without the need to hide from Arkady, anyone who needed help could come right through the garden and knock at the kitchen door. No messenger had come from the palace since Lord Theron had been poisoned (which was troubling, because no news of the boy's death had come; either the antidote had worked, or the boy was dying as slowly as Arkady) but Nate hoped to take over those duties, too, tending to courtiers inside with brains stirred by drops or stomachs burned with alcohol.

In short: Nate was busy. He no longer had time to run this way and that, from the Beggar's Market to the Grand Bazaar, seeking ingredients and information. He missed being out in the city, seeing the people who had become friendly and familiar, but there simply weren't enough hours in the day. He needed to be available when people needed him, particularly courtiers and most particularly the riders from the House, should one come. He dared not ask Vertus to run errands for him, but he needed help. When he'd chanced upon the messenger girl in the Market again a few weeks before, still wearing her brother on her back, Nate had felt the baby's head, pronounced it a bit firmer, and asked her if she wanted to work for him. "Regular work," he said. "Every day. As much as you want."

Her eyes had lit up. "Can I bring Canty?"

He'd said she could; of course he had. Bindy—that was what she called herself, although he doubted it was her given name—was irrepressibly cheerful, quick and smart and ready to laugh. While she waited for him to finish a preparation, she would play with Cantor on the floor of the lab. Highfall babies, he noticed, enjoyed the same games Slonimi babies did—*peekaboo, where's your nose, look what's on my head, look what's on your head*—and a giggling Highfall baby was as irresistible as any other. Nate liked having them around.

After a few days, when they were comfortable with each other, Bindy asked him shyly to tell her what it was like inside the House. At first, remembering that she had a brother inside, he told her reassuring stories about the plentiful food and beautiful gardens. But she'd heard all that before. "Tell me about the Children," she said, her voice eager. "Especially the foundling."

He hesitated. He didn't know if he could speak casually about the girl she called the foundling. "What do you want to know?" he finally said.

She laughed. "I don't know. Everything. She's always been my favorite. Is she nice? Does she seem like she'd be good to be friends with?"

He remembered of the girl inside, the wary reserve with which she carried herself, her obvious anger. Arkady had told him he always tried to separate the four to treat them: *The Seneschal made a mistake. Let them be raised in a pack like dogs. Best not to get yourself surrounded.*

"Yes, she does," he said.

Bindy was thrilled. "I knew it! I could tell."

When he sent her off to Brakeside or Marketside or even to the Bazaar, she'd strap Canty onto her back, grin cheerfully, and come back the same way. The first time he sent her to one of the manors in Porterfield, though, she came back with hard eyes, and her smile seemed forced. The third time this happened, Vertus confronted him. "You can't do that," he said. "Send her around town, saying she's from the House Magus. Dressed the way she is, with that baby on her back."

"Are you volunteering for errand duty? Because somebody has to do it until Arkady Magus gets well."

"She's a street rat. Any respectable courtier would drive her off with a stick, rather than be seen with her at their door."

"She's been doing fine."

Vertus made a contemptuous noise. "She's been giving your packages to the bloody kitchen maids, and probably getting quite a lording-over as she does it, too. Get rid of her."

Nate let his voice go cool. "Bindy stays."

"Then find another way," Vertus said. "This one's bad all around."

Vertus was right. Nate couldn't believe it hadn't occurred to him before. Bindy was Marketside born and raised; which wasn't as rough as Brakeside, maybe, but her experience with courtiers probably started and stopped at jumping out of the way of their carriages. She was always clean, her hair neatly braided; but her dress was obviously—if skillfully—mended, many times over, and her boots had been worn by many other feet before hers. The day Derie had wrenched his memory at the plague shrine, he'd given the girl a few coins from Arkady's chest upstairs, and told her to buy herself new clothes. Dress, boots, leggings and coat. Very plain, he was careful to say, not because he was afraid that she would come back with something gaudy, but because he wanted her to know this was a work uniform, not charity. "Picture an old lady you don't like, and buy something she'd wear," he'd said, and Bindy had laughed and said she knew just the one.

But whoever Bindy had in mind, it wasn't the woman who rapped at the kitchen door the day after Nate saw Derie. This woman's eyes were dark-ringed with fatigue, her forehead creased with worry lines, but she wasn't old and she didn't seem unlikeable. He could smell the paper factory fumes that clung to her clothes: this was Bindy's mother.

Nate still felt a bit weak, but he invited her inside. She would not sit down. Unbending and severe, she held out her hand. In her outstretched palm he saw too-smooth skin left by a nasty burn, or many nasty burns. On top of it rested the coins he'd given Bindy. "Take them back," she said without preamble. "You'll not buy clothes for my child, magus or no."

"I'm just an apprentice," Nate said automatically. He made no move to take the coins.

"I know what you are." Her tone was bristling and rigid. "Everyone says you're a good man. They say, oh, Nora, Gate Magus wouldn't do anything bad. Gate Magus goes all the way down. But I know people like you. I know how the world is. I do honest work. My two oldest girls do honest work and my son does, too inside. We don't do it so Belinda can be bought dresses by the likes of you."

Nate realized what she thought. He took a step back, lifting his hands up as if to show that there were no weapons in them; but he wasn't being accused of hurting Bindy with a weapon. "You've got me wrong. She's running errands for me, that's all. Making deliveries. If she's better dressed—"

"She's dressed just fine for Marketside." The woman—Nora—dropped the coins on the table. "Anywhere wants her dressed better is somewhere she doesn't need to be." She turned to leave.

"Then take her to work at the factory with you," he said.

She stopped. All Nate could see of her was her back. The thin fabric of her dress was worn gray over her shoulder blades. One shoulder in particular; she probably wore something slung over it while she worked. A tool belt or a bag of supplies. He'd seen factory workers who walked with a permanent list from years spent that way. "You won't," he said, talking fast. "You wouldn't. You sent your son inside, where you'll never see him again, to keep him out of that factory. I've heard what they're like. Working through the night, grabbing a few hours' sleep before the foreman wakes you up—no breaks, no food, no clean water. You didn't want that life for him."

She didn't answer.

"Is he smart, too?" Nate said. "Because Bindy is. And you know it."

Then, finally, she swiveled. Her face was proud. "All of my children are smart."

"Smart enough to know where they're safe and where they're not?"

"Smart enough to know who decides when they're safe," she snapped back.

"And who will that be, when she's back and forth across Brakeside, running messages for anyone with a coin?" he said. "When I send her out on an errand, she's under my protection. Which may not be much, but it's better than nothing."

Teeth clenched, she said, "And who protects her from you?"

"She doesn't need protection from me," he said. "I would never harm her."

"You say that now. Then later it'll be, 'Well, now, that wasn't *harm*, exactly.' But it's my Belinda who has to live with what you don't call harm." She spoke flatly, but with absolute conviction, and Nate knew that as far as she was concerned, every word she spoke was the unconditional truth. But it was not his truth, and in that moment, he determined that it would not be Bindy's, either.

"I swear to you," he said, "I intend her no harm and no ill, by anyone's definition. Not yours and not my own."

Nora's eyes narrowed. "Swear it on your blood, magus. And I warn you, I may be poor, but I am not friendless."

He understood the threat in the words. In all of the cities and towns and villages he'd visited, those who had no recourse to official justice made their own. "On my blood," he said, which was a direr oath for him than it was for her, because blood was everything to the Slonimi, and they did not waste it.

Nora watched him, considering. "She comes home every night," she said finally. "Even when I'm working, there's those who'll watch for her, and I'll know."

"Of course."

"And you don't feed her. She eats at home. Not here." She looked pointedly at the shelves visible through the open lab door, with their jars of herbs and powders. Nate nodded. She said, "Where's the old one, whose manor this is?"

"Upstairs. He's ill."

"That one wouldn't notice Bindy long enough to kick her out of his way. What happens when he gets better?"

He won't. But the words that came out of his mouth were Caterina's. "Wood'll burn when the match strikes."

Her chest twitched in a silent laugh. "You're no courtier, magus or no. Why waste your time here, with them?"

"It's not the courtiers I care about," he said truthfully.

"So I hear." She gave him a long, measuring look. "You keep your word to me, Gate Magus. I lost one child to those people. I won't lose another."

The next day Bindy was back, in a dour black dress and a pair of reassuringly solid-looking boots. She also wore a happy grin, though, and for a moment he imagined Bindy as she might have been in the caravans, where life wasn't perfect but at least there was sunshine most of the time. "Magus, you're magic," she said, and grinned with delight. "Magic Magus. That's what we'll call you from now on, won't we, Canty?" She bounced her brother on her hip.

"What have I done that's so magical?" he said.

She widened her eyes at him in mock awe. "Only crossed swords with Ma and won, that's all. Ask around about Nora Dovetail, and see how many people can say the same!"

"She was just worried about her daughter," Nate said. "I pointed out that the daughter in question was sharp as a tack and plenty smart enough to take care of herself." Not that the conversation had been about Bindy's intelligence, which would not necessarily have protected her from the harm Nora feared—but close enough.

"The daughter in question." Bindy laughed. "Well, the daughter in question would like to know if the Magic Magus likes her dress?" She made a passable curtsy.

"Not especially. I think the courtiers will, though."

"Only because it makes me look like I don't ever have any fun at all, and they don't think poor people have a right to any fun." But the somber fabric was thick and well-woven, and Bindy's eyes shone with satisfaction. "Won't give them a thing to sneer at, though."

"I'm sorry if people have been sneering at you," Nate said softly. "I didn't think."

"They're courtiers. Sneering is what they do. I'd rather they sneer than—anyway, I wouldn't be one if I could, would you? Not for all their pretty clothes."

"Not if you paid me. Bindy, how many brothers and sisters do you have?"

"Four sisters, two brothers. Counting the one inside. I never met him, but he sends letters."

"How many are—" He tried to think of a gentle way to say it, but then decided that kind of gentleness probably wasn't needed, with Bindy. "How many are alive?"

"Those are the ones who are alive," she said cheerfully. "All the others were just wee little babies. So where am I off to today, Magic Magus?"

Arkady was ill enough to die. One last, slightly larger dose of poison would push him over the edge. Nate even had the large dose prepared, in a vial in the lab, but he couldn't quite bring himself to administer it. Which was illogical; it wasn't any less murder if he drew it out. But somehow there was a difference between giving the old man small doses of poison that would kill him eventually and one large dose of poison that would kill him in an hour. Also, the dose was too large to hide in a cup of tea—there wouldn't be enough volume to mask the taste—so it would have to go in the soup, and Bindy brought the soup. She bought it from a woman by Harteswell Gate who boiled it down thick. Nate paid for it (well, Arkady did) but it had been Bindy's idea; the brothmaker was apparently legendary in Marketside, and Bindy's faith in the restorative powers of the golden liquid was obvious. She was proud that she'd thought to suggest the soup, and even prouder that Nate had taken her advice.

Nate couldn't bring himself to use Bindy's soup to kill Arkady. He also hoped it wouldn't be necessary. The old man was fading fast. Each day, he spoke less and less. On a night when he was feeling talkative, he said, "I hear you downstairs. Treating rabble. And that girl. Courtiers are where the money is. Don't neglect them. They need to be fussed over. Call on them, if they don't call on you." Then, plaintively, "Surely they ask after me."

"Not really." Nate shoved a spoonful of broth into Arkady's mouth. "The old men, sometimes, but the young ones, almost never. And none of the women." Another spoonful. "The women really seem to hate you."

The old man made an unpleasant noise. Maybe it was supposed to be a laugh. "They need me. They know it. They resent it. Magus has power, boy. He can give help, or he can withhold it."

Nate put the spoon down. "What do you mean, withhold help?"

"Little minxes want to play." Arkady's eyes glittered. "Don't necessarily want the get that comes of it, though. So they come to me. Some, I help. Others, maybe not. Maybe it's the Seneschal's say-so. Make their life not so easy for a while. Stop a marriage, push a divorce. Or maybe he wants me to give them something different, so they'll never catch—a family getting a little too powerful, say. Or maybe they're just brats who deserve to be dropped down a peg." Arkady drew in a long, wheezing breath. "They get desperate, you know. Desperate can be very interesting in a lady courtier. So they hate me. So what. Doesn't stop them begging when they need my help. Good for them to beg. Keeps them in their places."

Nate picked up the spoon again. "You're a terrible person," he said, and slid more broth into the old man's mouth.

Arkady swallowed most of it. A dribble ran down his chin. "Disapprove all you like, but when the Seneschal comes, you do as he says. Lord Elban might choose the road, but it's the Seneschal at the reins. When I'm up and well again—"

"You're not going to be up and well again," Nate said. "You're dying."

"Bah."

Nate stood up. The bowl was still half-full but he was suddenly sick of the room, of the smells of medicine and piss and the labored sound of the old man's breathing. "I don't think the world will find it much of a loss."

Downstairs, Vertus sat at the kitchen table. "How is he?" he said.

"Dying."

Vertus didn't say anything. Nate washed the bowl and spoon in the basin, conscious of the servingman's eyes following him and hoping he wouldn't notice the careful way Nate used his right hand, to keep the springknife dry. The room was filled with the kind of silence where every breath and movement felt magnified, momentous. He felt like he was onstage. It was always that way before trouble, in a field or a tavern or a kitchen off Limley Square. Caterina said it was a gift passed down from generations long dead, from ancestors who'd survived nights full of teeth.

He dried the bowl and put it back on the shelf. Not to let himself be knocked down: that was important. He put his back to the counter, bracing himself against it. He waited.

Finally, Vertus said, "How long?"

"A day or two. Maybe more. It's hard to know."

"Easier some times than others, I'd guess."

"Well, yes," Nate said dryly. Considering what Vertus might know. "I could predict his time of death with amazing accuracy if he had a knife in his throat."

Vertus smiled. "Doesn't he?"

"Not last time I saw him, no."

Vertus stared at Nate, and Nate pretended not to be unnerved. "I just think it's strange," Vertus said. "He's old as rocks, but he's always been healthy, as long as I've known him. Until you show up. Then suddenly, he's dying."

"Old men die."

"Guess so. Guess nobody's safe. Not even the most successful magus in the city, with a manor in Porterfield and the trust of the Seneschal himself. Not even Elban's House Magus, huh?"

"You die in the skin you wear when you're born," Nate said, shrugging.

Vertus nodded. "Must be tough, being a young magus just in from the provinces. Hard to make a name for yourself. You might have to treat street people, in secret, just to get your name out. And getting in with the courtiers—that'd be damn near impossible." The teeth were showing, now. Vertus leaned forward, his huge bulk shifting toward Nate. "Guess that's why you apprentice yourself out. Find an old man with a solid name. Let him introduce you to the courtiers, get you inside the Wall. Then—" he spread out his hands, either of which could cover Nate's entire face with room left over "—who knows? Maybe he'll get sick. Maybe he'll die. Maybe you can step into his place. The courtiers, the Seneschal, the nice manor."

Too late, Nate tried to remember when he'd last oiled the catch on his springknife. There'd been that blizzard in Butantown; they'd been trapped in the tavern for a week with nothing to do but go over and over their plan, over and over their supplies. Charles had oiled his knife then. Nate couldn't remember if he'd done the same, or just watched.

Vertus stood up. "Think I'll go check on him," he said, and began to climb the stairs.

Nate flexed his wrist. The steel blade popped out smoothly, with a faint click. He slid it back into place and followed after Vertus.

Upstairs, in the sickroom, Arkady was as Nate had left him: motionless, breathing loudly. When the two men entered the room, he barely moved. In a thin, creaky voice, he said, "What?"

Vertus stood by the bed. Nate tried to read his face but there was nothing there. "You're dying."

Arkady's lip curled. He said something obscene.

"I don't believe in ghosts and such," Vertus said. "I think dead's dead. But you never know, do you?" He jerked his head toward Nate. "This one's poisoning you. I fed some of your tea to a stray dog and, well, there you go."

Arkady's eyes went wide. He began struggling, futilely, to sit up.

Vertus picked up a pillow. "Never liked poison much myself. Cowardly. But I thought you should know, just in case dead's not dead. He's the murderer, not me. I'm the one doing you a kindness." Then he pressed the pillow down over Arkady's face.

Arkady kicked desperately at the bed, fighting for leverage. The old hands clawed at his wrist; the thin body bucked. But even healthy, Arkady could not have fought back against a man Vertus's size. Vertus, holding him down, wasn't even breathing hard. The air in Nate's own lungs was suddenly as useless as if it were his face the pillow covered. Fists jammed tightly in the pockets of his coat, he stood and watched Vertus kill the old man, and was he glad? Was he relieved not to have the death completely on his own conscience? Was he, as Vertus had suggested, a coward?

He made himself watch every moment, every kick and every flail, until they slowed, and finally stopped.

Vertus stayed where he was, bent over the bed, his full weight on the pillow.

Nate leaned against the wall, his knees weak. "Is he gone?"

"Not yet. It takes longer than you'd think."

They waited. This silence, too, was all-consuming; but it was companionable, shared between them.

Finally, Vertus stood up and tossed the pillow aside. "He'll have fouled himself. They always do," he said. Then he went downstairs. Arkady's open eyes were fixed on the ceiling. His face was slack, as if he were asleep, except that he was very clearly dead. Nate drew down the eyelids and pushed the old man's jaw up to close his mouth; it instantly fell open again. A moment later Vertus returned with a small prybar. Nate watched as the servingman—former servingman, he corrected—broke open the chest in the corner. Inside were half a dozen or so small bags, sewn out of thick dun-colored cloth. Nate knew each one was full of gold. They vanished into Vertus's pockets, one by one. The last one wouldn't fit so Vertus tied it onto his belt.

"Would you have done it anyway?" Nate said.

Vertus shrugged. "I'm not a murderer, but I'm not a fool, either. I know an opportunity when it comes knocking. This way, I get my share."

"I didn't do it for the money."

Vertus took Arkady's watch from the nightstand and slipped it into his pocket. "Not my business what you did it for. I'm glad to have known you these past few months, magus." There was an unpleasant stress on the title that Nate didn't like. "Seems to me we'll keep friendly in the future. A thing like this—it binds men together, doesn't it?" He glanced at the dead man on the bed and left.

So that would be the way of it. Well, it couldn't be helped. Nate left the dead man gaping at the ceiling and went downstairs to the parlor. Vertus had taken Arkady's brandy, but left the goblets and the silver tray that sat underneath—valuable, doubtless, but also bulky. Nate brought the tray and his satchel out into the garden. He took a small knife out of the satchel; the springknife was for stabbing and slashing, not the delicate cuts of the Work. The night was clear and moonless. In the spectral light from the stars he could barely see the knife's edge. He reopened the wound Derie had left on his arm by feel and collected the blood in a black pool on the tray. He didn't need much, just enough to spread into a thin layer with the heel of his good hand. Quickly, before it got sticky, he drew Derie's sigil; hesitated a moment, then added Charles's.

The Work would have been easier in moonlight. Something about the moon and blood and the ocean: if a full moon shone on the blood, the Work was clearer, just as the rest of the world was. Everybody Nate had ever known described the Work in a different way—although these were uncomfortable conversations, never easy, like talking about sex; despite its communal nature the Work felt very private—and to Nate it felt like moving stacks of books to find the one he wanted. He even got a dull ache at the base of his spine sometimes, the way he had when he'd helped Caterina empty out their wagon for cleaning. He found Derie instantly; Charles came more slowly, as if he'd been asleep. Derie was rustling around in his head, as crude as Vertus in Arkady's wardrobe. Bringing out Arkady's graying face, his blueish lips.

Then the blood was dry, and they were gone. Nate was alone in the garden. In the manor. He was alone.

Derie came so quickly that at first Nate thought the slow, steady drag of her cane on the Porterfield cobbles was just an afterimage of the Work. Then she rapped on the back gate. He let her in, leaving the gate unbolted for Charles. He'd been sitting in Arkady's chair in the parlor (nobody's chair, now), feeling increasingly clammy despite the roaring fire, and with some reluctance asked her if she wanted to go upstairs.

"Not these old bones," she said. "I can feel he's dead from here."

She probably could, too, for all that Arkady had never seemed to have the dimmest glimmer of power about him. The Work gave you a feel for life, for the ebb and flow of blood and tides. They had to wait a long time for Charles. The log in the fire had almost burned down and Nate had started to worry that his old friend had left Highfall, or been taken by the guards, when there came a low knock at the back door. Nate let him in and nearly gasped. Charles had been well-muscled when they'd arrived in Highfall, even after the long trip across the Barriers. Now he was skeletally thin. His skin was patchy, his eyes bloodshot and deep-ringed with purple. The hair that Nate had last seen perfectly combed into golden curls hung ratty and limp. His dark roots weren't showing, so at least he'd managed to keep up with the bleach, but the luxurious courtier's clothes they'd worked so hard to steal were rumpled and soiled, the boots scuffed.

"You look awful," Nate said. "Are you all right?"

"Fine. Let's get this over with." His words sounded dull around the edges. His Highfall accent slipped and slid; behind it, Nate could hear the broad vowels of the Slonimi.

In the parlor, Derie, sitting by the fire with her hands propped on top of her cane, stared at Charles with hard, suspicious eyes. "Charles Whelan, is your head clear?"

"Yes." Charles's voice was curt. Without another word, he began to climb the stairs.

Nate followed. They wrapped Arkady's body in the soiled sheets and blankets from his bed and used three of the old man's plainest belts to bind it. As they carried him downstairs, Nate told himself that it was a bundle of wood they carried, that the thin bones of Arkady's ankles weren't bones at all, but twigs in cloth. Derie had them bring down the dirty featherbed next, so she could remake it. Then they dragged Arkady out into the garden, where Charles had brought a wheelbarrow.

"Fold him," Charles said. But Arkady was beginning to stiffen and bending him to fit in the barrow took much massaging and coaxing of the dead muscles. When he was finally inside, and Charles moved to pick up the barrow handles, Nate stopped him.

"I'll do it. I'm dressed more like a laborer than you are." He paused, and then added, "If we get stopped, you should run. I hear things about the guards."

"We both look disreputable enough," Charles said. "And the guards won't stop us if we keep to the alleys."

They did just that, pushing Arkady all the way through Porterfield and Marketside to Brakeside. The manors gave way to row houses and attaches; the row houses and attaches gave way to warehouses, with taverns and rooming houses and eel shops squeezed between them. Their first night in Highfall, before they'd separated, Nate, Charles and Derie had stayed in just such a rooming house, in a clammy basement common room, sleeping draped over their packs to keep away thieves. It was almost midnight now but barges were still unloading on the Brake by lantern light, the shouts and directions of the stevedores drifting disembodied through the darkness. Nate and Charles carried their dead cargo long past the barges to a disused landing near the charred rubble of a burned-out warehouse. The embankment wall had crumbled low there. They weighed Arkady down with rocks and slipped him into the water that lapped gently at the broken stone; watched, together, as the pale color of the once-rich bedding they'd used as a shroud disappeared.

Nate looked at ragged, bony Charles, staring down after the corpse, and was filled with a sudden certainty that his friend would try to follow it. He found the thought alarming. The Work forged connections between its users—everyone you touched, everyone they touched—and the connection between Nate and Charles was old and clear and strong. But before Nate could speak, Charles pivoted away from the water on one scuffed heel and said, "Let's go."

They didn't speak on their way back to the manor, where they found that Derie had finished sewing the new feather-bed. The parlor reeked of burned feathers; she had ripped open a pillow to replace the fetid ones she'd destroyed. "Going to report this to the Seneschal? What are you going to say happened?" she said to Nate.

"In the morning," Nate said.

"What do these people do for their dead?"

"Not a lot. Crematories outside of the city, if you can afford them. Lime pits if you can't."

"Some of the courtiers keep private crypts in the provinces," Charles said.

"I'll say I sent him to family," Nate said. "I'll say they came and got him."

"He has family?" Derie said.

"A brother." This was true. It was also true that Arkady had told Nate the two hadn't spoken in decades.

"Will there be trouble about the manor? Worth a lot, in this neighborhood."

"I have no idea."

Derie nodded. "I'll hire a deadcoach, and livery for you, Charles. You'll come for him tomorrow. Put on a show." Too late, it occurred to Nate that it would have been both easier and safer to actually send Arkady out in the hired deadcoach. He felt a bubble of frustration but before he could say anything, Derie said, "Better he's in the Brake, Nathaniel. A real deadcoach would keep records, and the Brake has more dead bodies than fish in it. Nobody'll think twice if he washes up."

Nate nodded. He'd grown used to the way Derie pulled thoughts out of his brain, but he still didn't like it.

"Give me the money. I'll take care of the deadcoach myself," Charles sounded a little too eager.

"I think not," Derie said and left.

Charles called her a few choice names. She was no longer there to hear, but Nate still flinched; Charles saw, and laughed bitterly. "We're not children anymore, Nate, for all she treats us like we are. Did the old man have a wine cellar?"

He did. Vertus had taken the best bottles, but there were still several bottles of ordinary wine and one bottle of brandy. Charles chose the wine. They drank it in the parlor. Charles raised a glass.

"To Nathaniel Magus," he said. "The master of the manor."

His voice was faintly mocking. Nate ignored it. "Where have you been living?"

"Around."

"You could stay here now, you know. There's a guest bedroom upstairs. Three of them."

"I'd be a terrible servingman."

Nate was appalled. "You wouldn't have to serve."

"Oh, but we all serve." The mockery was out in the open now. It twisted Charles's mouth; it stained the air. "What purpose do we have, save slavish devotion to unbinding old Mad Martin's evil work?"

"None," Nate said.

Silence fell. Charles drank freely and blinked at the fire; Nate sipped his first glass and watched as Charles's spine sank lower and lower into the chair. It was the same chair he'd occupied that first night, as the foppish Lord Bothel. He'd chosen the alias because it sounded like *bother*, as they sat around a campfire on a hill overlooking the city. They'd seen all of Highfall stretched below, that night: the white stone of the Wall slicing the city as surely as the Brake did, the palace hunkered beyond.

As if he could read Nate's thoughts as well as Derie did, Charles said, "What's it like inside?"

Nate chose his words carefully. "Elaborate. Why have a plain, functional doorknob when you can cover it in gilt filigree? But also run-down, in places courtiers don't go."

"Sounds fitting."

"Is that where you've been? With the courtiers?"

"I was supposed to maintain my identity, remember? In case we needed it again." Charles gestured wryly to himself. "I don't think Derie likes the way I did it, though."

"What way was that?"

Charles reached into his pocket and pulled out a battered metal vial. He tossed it to Nate. The surface was badly scratched and there was a dent in one side, as if it had been stepped on. Nate opened it carefully and found a thin rod attached to the inside of the cap, just big enough to extract one drop of the fluid inside. It was clear, but smelled odd, acrid and medicinal. Slippery; almost familiar. He thought he could figure out what was in it, given enough time, but he still asked, "What is it?"

"I have no idea," Charles said, "but it feels amazing. Like someone wrapping half your brain in the softest blanket imaginable. I get it from Lady Maryle's youngest, plainest daughter, Gainell. We drop together and fuck like cats, it's delightful."

Lady Maryle was a minor courtier; so minor, in fact, that Arkady had put her treatment off to a lesser magus. Her manor was near, but not technically in, Fountain Hill. Nate couldn't remember the family industry, but it had something to do with manufacturing. "She buys drops for you, looking the way you do?"

Charles smiled a slow, sleepy smile and said, in Lord Bothel's bored, condescending drawl, "These days, all the best courtiers are hopeless addicts, Nathaniel." Then, in his own voice, he added, "Not that Gainell's family are the best courtiers. I picked the wrong family. They're barely courtiers at all. Anyway, when I met her, I was prettier. I don't think she's noticed the change. She drops more than I do, which is saying something."

Nate recapped the vial and tossed it back to Charles. "I think you should stop taking them."

"I think you're right, but I like them too much." Charles twisted the vial in his fingers. The firelight played on the dull surface. "You've seen her. The girl."

Not Gainell. "Yes."

"And do her feet float half an inch above the ground? Does a faint aura of unearthly light surround her wherever she goes?"

Nate felt oddly hurt. "Of course not. She's a person. Like you and me."

Charles shook his head. "No. Not like you and me." Then he seemed to reconsider. "Although all three of us had our lives mapped out long before we were born, so there's that. I hear she's strange."

"So would you be, in her circumstances."

"So I am. So are you, for that matter. At least in Highfall, we are." Still fingering the vial, Charles said, "It's funny, you know. Gainell's mother can't pay her own daughter's way inside, let alone mine, but even if she could—I don't think I'd want to see the girl. I thought I would, after everything. But I think I'm afraid to." He opened the vial and shook a drop from the thin rod onto his tongue. The motion had such ease, such practice, that he might as well have been taking a sip of wine. "To be honest, I don't even like being in the same city as her."

Nate wondered how long the drops took to kick in. "What are you afraid of? She's a girl."

"That's what I'm afraid of. That she's a girl. An ordinary girl. Ten fingers, ten toes. Feet on the ground. No faint aura of unearthly light." His eyes began to drift, as if he were having trouble focusing them. "I'm afraid that she'll be nothing. That we'll all be nothing. That it will be a waste." Charles saw Nate's face, then, and laughed. It was a high-pitched, giddy laugh. Lord Bothel's laugh. "Oh, come on. It must have occurred to you, too."

Hot with indignation, Nate said, "How can you say that? How can you even think it?"

"You said it yourself." Charles's words were slurred and thick. "She's a girl."

"She's not just a girl," Nate said. "She's everything."

But Charles's head was sagging. His eyelids drooped and his mouth hung as slack as Arkady's had. As Nate watched, breathing deeply to quell the anger inside himself, a thin rivulet of drool dropped from Charles's lower lip. If his friend hadn't blinked, just then—slowly, with great effort—Nate would have thought he was dead.

CHAPTER SEVEN

A shattered cup could be glued back together, but it would never hold liquid again; its shape might remain but its essence was gone, its purpose annihilated. That was how the four of them felt to Judah now: broken into shards. They hardly talked. There was nothing to say. Sometimes she saw Gavin watching Theron with shielded eyes and guessed that he was thinking about killing his brother—his odd, half-present brother, who seemed so much less than he used to be. But she knew, and Gavin knew, that killing Theron would not fix what was broken. It would not rescue any of them; it would merely lock them in a different kind of prison. Later, she'd see how gentle Gavin could be with Theron, helping him shave or cutting his food for him, and she knew that the murder was idle daydreaming. The gentleness was real.

It didn't matter. Nothing changed.

Every afternoon, the gates creaked open to let in a long train of supply carts and carriages and entertainers for the betrothal ball: acrobats and jugglers and musicians, arriving sometimes on foot and sometimes in gaudy wagons with their names and talents painted on the side. Some were from Highfall, some from elsewhere, and they had skin and hair and eyes in every color Judah could imagine. It wasn't Staff Day but by special dispensation, two dozen new children were brought in to serve as pages. They wandered the halls, wide-eyed and afraid; usually lost, often weeping, and trying to hide both. A person couldn't pass the kitchen or the laundry or the tailor's suite without hearing one of them being berated.

The three dresses Elly would wear for the actual wedding, on the summer solstice, were still in pieces in the tailoring suite. Her betrothal gown, though, already hung on Elly's bedroom wall, the scarlet and gold wrapped in fine gauze to keep off the dust. Elly had endured the fittings stoically. She'd seemed much more interested in the green gown being made for Judah, and the ferocity she devoted to that one was almost frightening. Elly had insisted for months that this once, at least, Judah would have her own dress, made just for her. Since Judah had been burned, Elly had put all of her energy into making sure that dress was perfect, with the result that the gown hanging in Judah's little alcove actually fit her. It was even flattering, and—Judah grudgingly admitted—quite beautiful, with an embroidered silver vine crawling up from the hem and down from the neckline. The dress had long sleeves to hide her burns, which were crusted but healing (thanks, in large part, to Darid's skill in tending them). Elly even had something planned for Judah's hair. She refused to say what it was, but hinting about it was the only thing that made Elly smile.

Judah didn't see why her appearance mattered, but would not deny Elly any pleasure she could find these days. Everything was suspended: there was no studying, no training. Only the oiling of the rushes happened on schedule, and that probably would have been put off too had Elly not been grimly determined that it should happen. Too often an assertive tap at the door brought a summons from the Seneschal, ordering Elly and Gavin to meet with some important courtier—people familiar to Gavin, though Elly knew them only by name. Inevitably they came back drained, as if smiling their way through the formalities of introduction had taken all they had. And why wouldn't it? Judah had to assume that, at this point, all the courtiers knew Gavin and Elly's betrothal would never happen. At the ball, Elban would make the announcement: Amie of Porterfield would step into Elly's place, and everyone would pretend to be surprised—or not—but in the meantime, the fiction had to be maintained. The courtiers were probably enjoying it immensely.

In private, Elly ignored Gavin. Gavin knew better than to try to mend the breach. He spent hours on the terrace, attacking the target Theron had set up before the hunt. He shot arrows. He threw knives. From the way his heart beat, Judah guessed that he was imagining them landing in vital parts of his father's body. Sometimes Judah watched, sometimes she didn't. She tried to spend time away from the House, in the stables or the pastures or even the orchard. Every time she saw a guard wearing Elban's scarlet badge, she wondered if she were looking at the guard who'd been assigned to murder her, or Elly or Theron.

Theron, as it turned out, was the only one of the four of them who remained untroubled. He had reclaimed the music box he'd fixed for Elly, and he spent hours sitting in Gavin's room listening to the uncomfortable little tune. If he was asked to get up or move or eat or wash, he did so, occasionally with help, but a part of him seemed never to have woken up. When he was spoken to, he answered, and when she could think of enough questions to ask in a row it was almost like talking to the old Theron. He still gave off a faint sense that he was waiting for you to finish talking instead of actually listening, but where the old Theron's waiting had been colored with impatience, in the new Theron there was just…nothing. It was as if he were waiting for a clock to finish chiming. As soon as she ran out of questions, he would go back to the music box. Once, when Judah brought him coffee, she found that he'd opened the side of the box, and felt a thrill of hope. But he watched the gears spinning inside with the same vague interest he applied to the shadows moving across the wall, or the coffee she brought him.

She hated Gavin's hurt; she hated Elly's self-isolation. But it was Theron who filled Judah with hopelessness. Sometimes she thought she would welcome the walled tower, when it came, if it meant she didn't have to see those distant eyes anymore, and know they were her fault.

Two days before the ball, someone knocked on the door. Theron was listening to his music box in the bedroom while the other three sat in the parlor like broken dolls. None of them rose. Gavin called out to whoever it was to come in.

It was the Seneschal. Arkady's apprentice was with him, but Arkady wasn't. The Seneschal took in the motionless room, the odd tune of the music box, and said, "I'm sure you've all noticed that Arkady has not been well recently. I'm sorry to tell you that he has succumbed to his illness and died."

He paused, as if expecting a reaction. There was none, although Judah felt a faint lifting that could almost be described as pleasure: the first she'd felt in weeks. The Seneschal continued. "You've all met his former apprentice, Nathaniel Magus. He was with Arkady at the end, and he'll be taking over Arkady's duties for now. We are here to see Lord Theron."

At the *for now*, the apprentice's eyes darted a bit. Although Judah supposed she should start thinking of him as the magus, instead of the apprentice. The lifting was growing, swelling, as the words sank in, those glorious words: *Arkady Magus has succumbed to his illness and died.* Never to hear his sneering voice again, never to smell the tobacco and tooth-rot smell of his breath. Never to feel his cold fingers probing at her. Never to hear his snide insinuations, his nasty hinted threats.

Elly stood up and held her hand out to the magus. "Thank you for coming," she said with a reasonable attempt at friendliness.

"Of course." The magus took her hand—a bit uncertainly, Judah thought—and bowed. "I'm sorry to hear that Lord Theron is ill."

Elly's lips thinned. "Yes, well. *Ill* isn't exactly the word for it." She gave the Seneschal a pointed look. He didn't react.

"I'll try to help," the magus said. "Is he in the bedroom?"

"I think we'd rather you examine him out here, where we can see you," Gavin said coolly, and called out toward the open door, "Theron!"

A moment later, Theron drifted through the doorway. There was no other word for it. His shirt and trousers were clean enough—Elly made sure of that—but he wore no vest or coat over them; his collar stood open, his cuffs dangled unfastened, and his feet were bare. His face was clean, too, and Gavin kept him well-shaved, but it had been a while since his hair had seen a comb. As always, he looked at his brother and the two women with faint surprise. His reaction to the Seneschal and the magus was no different. He might have been standing in a garden, watching a flock of birds. "Hello," he said.

Elly, still standing with the magus, put out a hand. Theron came to her like a dog. "Theron, love, you remember Arkady's apprentice, Nathaniel Magus. He's here to check you over."

"Oh," Theron said. "Am I still sick? I thought I was better."

"You are." Elly sounded more reassuring than Judah could have. "I'm sure they just want to make absolutely sure, before the ball."

"Lord Theron," the magus said. "It's a pleasure to see you again." Then he asked Theron to sit on the sofa. Elly sat with him. The Seneschal stared fixedly out the window, apparently wishing he were elsewhere. Theron, of course, seemed to actually be elsewhere, but the rest of them watched closely as the new magus peered in Theron's eyes and throat and listened to his heart, as he asked Theron to follow the finger he moved from side to side, forward and backward. Gavin's hands were deep in his coat pockets and Elly's expression was one Judah remembered seeing across the table at lessons, when Elly knew the answer and Judah didn't. As if, through sheer force of will, Elly could put it into Judah's brain.

Now that will was directed at Theron. Who obediently moved his eyes back and forth and up and down, who pushed and pulled against the magus's outstretched arm, but who somehow wasn't giving the right answers. Behind the magus's glasses, his eyes were thoughtful.

Finally, Judah could stand it no longer. "I waited too long, didn't I?"

The magus tilted his head, and opened his mouth. If his face was any indicator, the next words out of his mouth should have been, *Oh, no, that's not it at all.* "Well," he said.

"Waited too long for what?" The Seneschal was frowning.

"To call for help," the magus answered, before Judah could say anything at all. "And I don't know that you did, really. This sort of thing—it's complicated."

"What sort of thing?" Elly said.

"Illness in the brain. We don't understand it very well, I mean."

"He'll get better, though," Gavin said. "He'll be himself again."

Theron watched all of this as if the birds he'd found in the room had begun to sing. The Seneschal, smooth and controlled once more, said, "Perhaps we can have this conversation another time."

"I don't think that's necessary." To Theron, the magus said, "Lord Theron, I don't know if you're aware of this, but you came very close to dying."

Judah felt the flinch that passed through the room as much as she saw it. Theron only nodded. "Yes. I think I did know that."

"It will take you some time to recover from the shock," the magus said. "How do you feel?"

Theron gazed around at all of them. Slowly—fumbling for the answer—he said, "I feel...unlocated." Then he shook his head. For the first time since he'd been poisoned, he seemed genuinely distressed. "No. That's not right. I'm sorry."

The magus put a hand on Theron's shoulder with a warm smile. "Don't worry. It will get better."

"Will it?" Judah said.

The magus's smile faded. He stood up.

Elly stood, too. "Thank you," she said, extending her hand again.

The magus took it more confidently this time. "You're welcome. I'm sorry I can't be of more immediate help."

"Arkady's death was very sudden, wasn't it? I hope it wasn't a difficult one."

"There's a certain kind of person," the magus said gravely, "for whom death is never easy. There's something in them that refuses to let go."

"It would not surprise me to hear that Arkady Magus was one of those people. But I'm glad it's you that's replaced him. You seem very kind," Elly said.

He bowed. "My mother used to say: when you look into the night, count all the stars you can."

"Does that mean something?" Gavin said rudely.

"That no single good act will ever be enough, but every good act is important," the magus replied. "I do my best."

When he and the Seneschal were gone, Gavin shook his head. "He's a strange one. Doesn't seem to mind too much that Arkady's dead."

"Do you?" Elly said in her new sharp voice. Gavin didn't answer and she turned to Judah. "I think he likes you."

Startled, Judah said, "Why?"

"Because he wouldn't look at you." Elly smiled. It seemed like a real smile, or something close to it. "Maybe he'll marry you, and you'll end up the happiest of all of us."

"I'm not allowed to marry," Judah said, keeping to herself the new amendment the Seneschal had proposed, which was that she was allowed to marry anyone who was completely disinterested in her, and whose allegiance could be bought. "Not that I would want to, if I were."

"You could do better than some foreign-born magus, anyway," Gavin said.

Who was to say she herself wasn't foreign-born, or at least that her parents weren't? Judah bore more physical resemblance to the entertainers filing through the gate than she did anyone else in Highfall. Before she could say so, Elly said, "I think marriage should be abolished. No alliance marriages, no marriage-leaving tax. No way to keep anyone with you except by treating them well. No way to ensure trade but by being a good neighbor. Maybe when I'm Lady of the City—" words she'd said thousands of times, now filled with bitterness "—I'll make it a law."

"Wouldn't work," Gavin said.

"Why not?" Elly sounded almost belligerent, and for a moment all the reasons why not hung in the air like smoke: because the Lady of the City didn't make laws, because marriages were all that kept the courtiers from killing each other, because no tax would ever be abolished, because Elban would never allow it.

"Because people aren't like that," Gavin said. "Offer them freedom on the condition that they take responsibility for using it wisely, and they'll take the chains."

"Maybe men would," Elly said. "Ask the women."

"I'm just telling you what history teaches."

"Whose version of history?" she snapped. "Elban's?"

It was the longest conversation they'd had in days. "Theron," Judah said, to break the tension, "would you like to go up to your workshop? See what you were working on before you got sick?"

Theron gave her the same puzzled look he always gave her, and oh, how tempting it was to grab him and shake him until it rattled clear (even if his befuddled state was her fault, even if she had waited too long). But before he could say anything, Elly said, "No."

Judah was surprised. "What do you mean, no?"

"I mean no." Elly stood up. "The air is bad up there and it's cold, and he's not well enough. I'm not throwing my life away so he can get sick and die anyway."

Pain razored through Judah. She didn't know if it was Gavin's or her own. Elly didn't seem to know, either; her eyes darted back and forth between them. Then she left the room abruptly, closing the bedroom door firmly behind her.

Contemplating the closed door, Theron said, "What did she mean, throwing away her life away?"

"Nothing," Gavin said. "She didn't mean anything."

"Oh," Theron said.

Elly was giving up the most, and she had the right to insist that what little remained of Theron be kept healthy. But his vagueness and puzzlement were driving Judah mad. Intelligent, acerbic Theron: this was not the way he was supposed to be, and so she went to the workshop herself. It felt strange to be there alone. The cluttered workbench and damp stone walls felt expectant, as if waiting for their usual occupant; the air smelled like Theron, char and sweat and metal. She sat down on the high stool, just where Theron would, with all of his tools and bits of brass spread out in front of her. His notebook was open to two pages filled with narrow, precise writing, but nothing she could understand. She flipped back a few pages and found sketches matching the half-built thing on the bench: a compact sort of box, with a cavity in the middle. The sketches showed the thing from each side and pulled apart and even in slices like bread. This was how Theron's brain had once worked: he found a thing, took it apart, and saw what was missing. Tucked to the side, Judah found a misshapen rectangle made out of clay that matched the cavity in the device's center. The edges crumbled at her touch.

Theron, too, had been taken apart and put back together. Theron, too, was missing something central. She had waited too long and it had slipped away.

Nearly immobilized with sadness, she stared at the wall curving in front of her. A strip of wood circled the wall just above the level of the workbench, marks carved along the bottom of it like the minutes of a clock, with other marks above in some script she didn't recognize. The door leading to the stairway was propped open; she could almost sense the tower lying in wait above the cobwebbed darkness, as empty as Theron. She had a sudden urge to climb the stairs, broken or not: to get away from all of this, up into the unknown. Nobody would bother her there. Nobody would even know where she was. She would be safe. All she had to do was slide down off the stool, let her feet carry her upward—

She heard a noise behind her and knew instantly who it

was. "Are you going to take over for him? Judah the Foundling, Rebuilder of Lost Objects." Gavin pointed to the device. "We had the same idea, you and I. Think it will help?"

Judah tore her thoughts away from the tower. "I don't know if anything will help," she said, "but it's worth a try."

They found a box filled with broken glass in one of the cupboards. After they emptied it carefully onto a shelf (the glass was probably garbage, but might be important) they loaded it with everything from the workbench except the clay shape, which Judah carried in her hand so it wouldn't break. Down in the parlor, Elly was gone; Theron stood on the terrace, gazing at the top of the Wall. They let him be and cleared off the dressing table in Gavin's room. Pushing it in front of the window, where the light would be good, the two of them laid out all of Theron's things, as near as they could remember to where they'd been in the workshop. It felt good to do all of this. It felt good to have a project, to work together, to feel like they were accomplishing something. For the few minutes it took, Judah felt an ease she had almost forgotten.

Gavin led Theron in, and they showed him what they'd done. Judah didn't know what she'd expected. She knew it was too much to hope that whatever was missing in Theron would suddenly find itself; more likely, he would merely say, "Oh," and drift away.

Instead, he said nothing. His hands dropped, limp, to his sides, and for a moment Judah was afraid that her instincts had been utterly wrong, and she'd somehow managed to break Theron even more.

Then, moving as if his joints didn't quite fit together, he pulled out the chair they'd put at the table, and sat down. He didn't speak. His eyes were vacant. He was like a fire that had gone out.

He sat there until Gavin could bear it no longer, and went to throw knives at the target on the terrace. Judah, too, fled.

"Busy weekend," Darid said mildly as he dressed her arms the next day, and she was so tired of people speaking mildly to her when all inside her was upheaval that she almost screamed. "The House must be buzzing."

"Like a hive of wasps." The curlicue scars disappeared under the clean white bandages Darid used to wrap them. She was always glad when they were covered again. "At least the stables feel sort of normal."

As soon as she spoke, she realized she was wrong. The stables didn't feel normal. As usual, the stablehands had found somewhere else to be when she appeared, but unusually, she could still hear them: talking, laughing. Even whistling. Darid finished with her arms and she followed him into the storage barn to help arrange the tack that had come in with the courtiers' teams. There was a lot of it already, splendid with brass and obnoxious with color even in the dim light from the open door. Farther back, she could see the vague shapes of carriages and phaetons. Outside the barn, somebody sang out. Just one line, something about a tavern, before they were quickly hushed—reminded that she was there, probably. "No," she said. "Things don't feel normal here. Why not?"

Darid grinned. "We'll have a party, too, once the gates are closed and we're not needed. The stablemen, some of the other grounds staff. The orchardkeepers. The dairymen."

A party. For most of the House, that was all the betrothal ball would be. "Well, that's nice, that you can do that."

"The Seneschal turns a blind eye. Balls are a lot of extra work for us."

"Lucky you have me to pick up the slack," she said, and Darid laughed.

When she was finished with the tack, Judah still didn't want to go back to the House. She stood with Darid by the paddock, watching the horses. Her favorite, the gleaming black colt, crept up behind one of his year-mates, nipped his flank and sprang away. She could almost hear him laughing.

Darid followed her gaze. "That one's a troublemaker. His sire was, too."

"Who's his sire?" The stallions were kept in the cavalry stables—their war training made them vicious—but she knew them a little, by sight.

"Gone now. Elban's last campaign."

Judah remembered Elban's speech, the night of the Wilmerian dinner. It seemed like years ago. *Were lives lost? Yes. Such is the nature of war.* "The Nali Strait?"

Darid nodded. "Lots of horses lost there."

"How many is a lot?"

"The whole regiment."

"I never knew that. Nobody ever told us that." But why would they? "How does that happen? A whole regiment lost?"

"I only know what I hear. The ships landed—it's only a day's passage—and Elban split his forces, planned an ambush. But the Nali ambushed them first. No way to send a message. No way to warn the others what was coming."

"I thought they used smoke. Or pigeons."

"I don't know. I only heard there was no time. It's a shame." His eyes were fixed on the colts, sad and resigned. "Men sign up for the army. Horses don't."

Judah was watching the colts, too, but her mind was racing. "If there were a way of sending messages, it wouldn't have happened? Elban would have won?"

"Who can say?" Darid said. "Maybe."

The rest of the day would be a blank to her: what she did, what she ate, any other conversation she had. Except for that one word.

Maybe.

She found Elban after breakfast the next day, in his council chamber. Not that there had ever been a council, not as long as she could remember. The guards outside the massive door eyed her distastefully, but didn't stop her. Inside, Elban sat in his grand chair, the Seneschal standing at his side. One of the older courtiers stood before him, shoulders hunched and submissive. He was in the middle of a speech that sounded entreating. Judah didn't recognize him. She wasn't sure how to announce herself. Queasy with nerves, she hesitated.

The Seneschal saw her an instant before Elban did, his mouth tightening. Before he could say anything, Elban noticed her, too. The Lord's pale eyebrows lifted, and he held up a hand.

Instantly, the courtier went silent. "Let her stay," Elban told the guards, who had moved close, in case he wanted them to eject her. Then, to the courtier: "You're boring me, anyway. You know what I'm going to say; assume I've said it, and we'll all save ourselves a lot of time."

The courtier scurried away, glowering at Judah. He was overdressed, and his eye makeup was running. The Seneschal cleared his throat. "Lord Elban—"

"You, too," Elban said to him.

The Seneschal glanced at Judah. "I would advise against that, Lord Elban."

Elban waved a hand. "The foundling will behave herself. Won't you, foundling?"

Judah didn't answer. The Seneschal bowed. On his way

out, he paused next to her, for the merest breath. "Whatever you're doing," he said quietly, "be careful."

Then he was gone. On the throne, Elban laughed.

"Such looks you give me, foundling. It's extremely entertaining." The room was vast, gleaming with polished wood. For a long moment, Elban watched her expectantly, enjoying her discomfiture. She tried to show as little of it as possible.

"Show me your arms," he said, but when she held them out—trying not to tremble—he shook his head. "No, no. Take all that off. I want to see your scars."

So she undid all of Darid's careful bandages, stuffing them in her pockets. Maybe Elly could use them again. "Closer," Elban said, and she inched toward him. He leaned over to inspect the two curlicues. Then he reached out with one long finger and scraped off some of the thick salve covering them. He wasn't gentle and the motion sent a shudder of pain through her. "What's this?"

"Just salve."

He rubbed the salve between two fingers. "What's it do?"

"Helps them heal."

"Those scars are mine, foundling. If I don't like how they turn out, we'll do them again until I do." He wiped the salve from his finger onto the front of her dress. She was better prepared this time and did not shudder. "Did you want something, or did you just come to quiver before me? Because I do like that. It's the least disgusting I've ever found you."

She stepped back, well out of striking distance. The place on her arm where he'd scraped her throbbed. "I want to make a deal." Her voice sounded stronger than she'd expected. "You like deals, don't you? Bargains, and trades?"

"I do." Slowly, deliberately, his eyes moved up and down her body. She had often seen courtiers do that to each other, or to staff girls, but she'd never been on the receiving end, and it made her want to peel off her own skin. "But you have nothing to offer me."

She hadn't fainted when he burned her. She wouldn't falter now. "Actually, I do. And it's something you'll want."

He slouched down in his chair, leaning his chin on one long arm. "All right, foundling. Impress me."

"Deal first. If you accept my offer, Elly marries Gavin and Theron lives."

"We're still on that, are we?" He yawned. "If you plan to offer yourself in the Tiernan's place, I'm not interested."

"You're not interested in Elly, either. You're only marrying her to hurt Gavin."

"I don't want to *hurt* Gavin." But he was smiling now. "I want to break Gavin. He'll be stronger for it, and he'll need to be strong to keep my empire. I can't think of anything you could possibly offer that I want more than that."

Judah took a deep breath. "You lost an entire regiment on your last campaign. Surely you want to avoid that happening again."

He was up and striding toward her before the words were all the way out of her mouth, teeth bared in a snarl. She forced herself to keep speaking. "Your soldiers were ambushed. Mowed down like grass. No way to warn them."

Now his long white fingers were manacle-tight on her upper arm. One of his incisors was missing, making the canine next to it seem particularly long and sharp, and she found herself suddenly scared that he'd bite her. "Who told you that?" he said, shaking her hard enough to rattle her own teeth. "Speak of such things again and I will rip your tongue out."

"If you'd had then what I'm offering now, it wouldn't have happened. None of those men would be dead, and I know you don't care about dead men, but you hate taking the time to train new ones, don't you?"

He shook her again. "Lying, witchbred—"

"You could have won," she said.

Elban stopped. His fingers still dug painfully into her arm but he was no longer shaking her. "If you're wasting my time," he said, his voice low and dangerous, "I will knock all of your teeth out and beat you unconscious."

"Deal first."

He hit her. White flashes filled her vision, then cleared.

"Deal first," she said again.

He hit her a second time and stunned her—but the Seneschal had hit her harder the week before. If Elban had been hitting her as hard as he could she would be unconscious already, or at least on the floor. This beating was for effect. Which meant that he wanted to hear what she had to say. An ugly hope surged inside her.

"Everyone else gets left alone," she said through thick, clumsy lips.

He raised his hand again. She didn't flinch. He grunted and let the hand fall. "Fine. If your offer is sound, my heir can keep the Tiernan. We'll pay Porterfield off. She was getting too arrogant, anyway. I hate an arrogant woman."

"And Theron lives."

He shrugged. "Whatever." Dropping her arm, he folded both of his own across his chest and waited.

She took a deep breath. "Gavin and I feel the same things," she said. "Wherever he is, wherever I am."

"Wasting my time, foundling. Telling me things I already know."

Judah held out her left arm. Where her palm met her wrist, just above where her bandages had been a moment before, a fresh scratch stood out, raised and red. "Do you see this scratch? Gavin did that when you hit me."

As they watched, the scratch redrew itself, deeper. Wherever Gavin was, he had suddenly found himself dazed and in pain, and he wanted to know why. Elban's eyes narrowed. Judah pointed to a curl on the end of the new scratch. "This means he's worried." She drew a finger down the curve. "He wants to know where I am."

Elban's eyes grew wide. "A code."

"Since we were children."

"You use pain to communicate." Slowly, a smile blossomed on his face: full of fascination and pleasure, it was the first genuine smile she had ever seen there. "Oh, that is very beautiful, foundling."

She pushed down the sick feeling that smile gave her. "You're taking Gavin on campaign as soon as Elly is pregnant, aren't you? Take me, too. Put me with a different regiment. You'll never be caught unaware again."

She could see his mind at work on the idea. Unfolding it; examining every facet, all of its possibilities.

"How should I respond?" she said. "I can tell him I'm fine. I can tell him where I am. I can tell him you hit me. Or I can tell him you're about to knock all my teeth out and beat me unconscious."

"I'm still deciding about that." But he licked his lips. "Tell him you're fine."

Holding up her arm so Elban could see, she drew the quick crosshatch that meant *all well*—although she didn't believe it, not at all, not the way Elban was looking at her. Her cheek throbbed and her burned arms were on fire.

Elban reached out and touched the scratch. It was gentle, that touch. Almost a caress. It was also revolting. "Do we have a deal?" she said.

"I could just take you, now that I know," he said. His nostrils flared. She realized that his breathing was fast and ragged. His fists clenched and unclenched at his sides. "But yes. We have a deal. Now get out of here. Go to the kitchen and tell them to give you some ice for your face, so you're no uglier than usual for the ball." He licked his lips again, his eyes still fixed on the scratch. "Go quickly. Before I do something I regret."

She didn't have to be told twice. As she fled the room, she wondered, uncomfortably, what kind of thing would make Elban, monster that he was, feel regret. She didn't want to know. She suspected she would probably learn.

But Elly never would, and Theron would be safe.

For the ball, great chandeliers had been hung from the wrought-iron roof of the solarium, glittering crystal that refracted the light of the candles inside them until they blazed like miniature suns. The mezzanine balconies were filled with musicians. The glass panels in the walls had been opened and outside them, the garden, too, was lit; the paved walks were strung with colored lanterns, and the galleries were filled with acrobats, illusionists and every kind of dancer Judah had ever heard of. Dancers with swords, dancers with fire, dancers wearing nothing but scraps of gauze that swirled around them like smoke. Near the open doors, tables were laid with sweets and roasts and ices and warm creamy drinks that were almost syrupy at the bottom. A rainbow of wine, another of cheese. To cover the smells of the food, incense burned in vented cavities beneath the floor, and greenhouse roses crowded every surface not intended for reclining or dancing.

On the parquet floor, the courtiers whirled in vivid silks and satins, hair in every shade of gold combed and teased into elaborate shapes and dressed with gems and feathers and the enameled insects that were still in style. Standing on the edge of the floor was like standing at the edge of one of Theron's machines writ large as the courtiers spun and revolved and spun again. Every step was choreographed. The slightest deviation sent ripples of discord through the engine. Theron himself would have found it fascinating, if Theron had still been himself. And maybe he was still fascinated, a bit. His eyes were fixed on the dancers, at least. Drained of his nervousness and acuity—drained of his Theron-ness—and dressed in a drab version of Gavin's finery, he seemed more than ever like a badly molded imitation of his brother: all the same features, dulled and misplaced by the hairbreadth that made the difference between ordinary and beautiful. He'd been carrying a small cake in his hand for most of the night. From time to time he noticed it, and lifted it to his mouth, but before it got there he'd inevitably forget it again and his hand would slowly drift back down. The cake was beginning to disintegrate around the edges and the icing was grubby.

He and Judah stood away from the food and away from the doors. They were nowhere anyone else would need to be, the foundling and the unimportant son, and they would not be forced into the dance. Judah's arm looped loosely through Theron's, mostly so he wouldn't drift away—but also so she could feel him next to her, vacant as he was, and relish the notion that he might be safe. She had not been quick enough or brave enough to save him from the poison, but maybe, just maybe, she had saved him from the rest. She didn't trust Elban, but she was more certain than ever now that he didn't actually care about marrying Elly, and poor damaged Theron wasn't a threat to anyone's throne. But Elban did want the scratch code. No; he *desired* it. What Judah wanted and what Elban wanted seemed to align. She wasn't sure her plan would work, but she thought so.

Because she couldn't be sure, and because she knew they would object (probably rather strenuously) she hadn't mentioned anything about the deal to Gavin or Elly, who danced together in the center of the machine, faces frozen in polite emptiness. The merest possibility that they might be safe, though, let Judah enjoy watching them, in their coordinating scarlet and gold. They were beautiful together. Elly was summer, her sky-blue eyes and hair so vibrant the gold pins she wore in it dulled by comparison; Gavin was autumn, warm and burnished. His eyebrows wanted to frown but somehow, on him, that cruel mouth of Elban's wanted to laugh. The idea that he might soon have something to laugh about gave Judah immense pleasure. They would make lovely children, and they would be kind parents.

Occasionally she caught a glimpse of Amie, whose dress was a deep indigo that had doubtless been chosen to complement Gavin's scarlet coat when she was called up on the dais, and whose hair was surrounded by tiny enamel butterflies on wires that bobbed and flitted as she moved. Judah would not let herself look directly at the woman, as if refusing to see her would somehow keep her away, and make Elban do what he'd promised (although she allowed herself to picture that smug little forehead creased with disappointment, those perfect bird hands clapping politely while the lady courtier's plans fell around her). Judah would not look at the Seneschal, either, because he seemed to be trying to catch her eye. His job at this affair was to keep everything running smoothly, to stand by Elban's side and make sure that all was as he wished it. Later—as long as Elban kept his word, and did not claim Elly for himself—the Seneschal might be dispatched into the crowd to collect someone the Lord of the City wished to take back to his chambers. The someone would be beautiful and blushing and he would probably destroy them, and that was sad. But the someone would not be Elly, and that was not sad.

The Seneschal was definitely watching her, his face hard, almost angry. The emotion seemed out of place among the light music and the elegant courtiers. He was down off the dais now, moving around the edges of the crowd; toward her.

She didn't want to talk to him. She didn't know what he knew but she suspected. Her arm was still hooked through Theron's; she let it drop, ignoring the pain as the burns inside her silk-lined sleeves (the bandages had not fit) pressed against the rough braid of his coat, and took his hand instead. "Come on," she said, and led him in the other direction. As she did, the music changed, and the dance did, too. This one was a social dance, the kind where partners were traded back and forth. Judah scanned the crowd for Elly and saw that she had withdrawn to her seat next to Elban on the dais, pale and flat-eyed. It was taking everything Elly had just to dance with Gavin tonight, and she would not be willing to make conversation with whatever courtier happened to be next to her when the figure changed. Elly thought she was going to spend the night with Elban. Sitting next to him, Judah knew, was her being strong, and proving she was brave.

There was a moment of chaos in the new dance as partners were found, figures formed. The Seneschal took advantage of the pause to cut across the floor. He was close now, and Judah saw that she'd trapped herself in a corner. Just like with the Wilmerian. When the dance started in earnest, there would be no escape.

Through the crowd, she saw Firo, resplendent in copper-traced teal. A table of cakes like the one Theron carried stood nearby; Judah pushed him gently toward it. "Theron," she said. "Go eat."

He stumbled a bit. She must have pushed him harder than she'd meant to. He stared at the cake in his hand, and its fellows on the table. "Eat?"

"Or wait. Whatever." His slowness exasperated her (and would that there were some part of herself she could trade to fix that, too; she would happily give an arm or a leg or a foot to have quick snappish Theron back). He frowned but obeyed, as she'd known he would, and Judah scanned again for Firo's teal coat. If he'd found a partner—but, no, he was working his way out, too. She pushed rudely through the crowd and set herself in front of him. His purple sash was also edged in copper and perfectly matched the amethysts in his ears. His hair was very high, his kohl very thick. "Dance with me," she ordered, and pushed herself into his arms; then the figure started in earnest and he had no choice, if he didn't want to disrupt the dance and call attention to himself. To both of them.

He frowned, muttering, "This will not serve me well," but one of his hands found hers, the other going to her waist. The Seneschal, at the edge of the crowd, watched stone-faced as Firo led her into the dance. Judah took a deep breath. She could feel Gavin, his curiosity breaking through his misery when he felt her pounding heart, her sudden nerves.

"Relax," Judah said. "Soon nobody's even going to remember I was here, much less you." Elly had left the dais after all, and was leading Theron into the dance.

"Is that so?" All at once Firo's grip on her waist was hard, his long fingernails pressing her hand. Not digging in, but threatening, all the same. His eyes were narrow, calculating. "What do you know, foundling?"

A flutter of high, giddy excitement coursed through her. Elly and Theron were dancing, and Elly was even managing to smile. "What I've said," Judah said airily. "You aren't the only one who can spin webs."

Firo cocked an eyebrow. Across the whirling, rotating dancers she saw Gavin. His current partner wore indigo. Amie. As they revolved Judah saw her lips moving. Whatever she said was dragging Gavin down: his eyes, his spirit. Inappropriately,

Judah found herself stifling a laugh. You, too, you silly sugar flower, she thought at Amie. You might be surprised, too.

Firo, meanwhile, was watching her carefully. "You know, you're unexpectedly lovely tonight. Have they brought in a new seamstress who doesn't know you're always to be shabby and a bit misshapen?"

Judah flinched. She was suddenly very conscious of the green fabric draped around her and—worse—the grand mass of her hair, which was marginally contained in a delicate web of silver and sparkling crystals but still very much its unruly self. In the soft flattering light of the solarium, the red of Judah's hair was almost black, and Elly said the headdress looked like stars peeking out at sunset. Judah thought it looked like her hair, with some metal and rock wrapped around it. "Elly did it."

Across the room, still with Theron, Elly caught Judah's eye, winked.

They heard the small flourish in the music that meant a switch in partners. The courtier who should have been Judah's new partner, a tall, handsome young man in lavender, ignored her and held tight to his original partner's hand. A wave of dysfunction rippled through the dance. "You're murdering me," Firo said through gritted teeth, but he kept her in his arms.

Elly and Theron had managed to stay together, too. "No," Judah said. "Just embarrassing you."

"They're the same thing."

The Seneschal was back at the dais now, speaking with Elban. "Then get me to the edge and let me go."

"That's not the way this dance works," Firo said. "You've already called enough attention to us."

Gavin was dancing with somebody Judah didn't know, a courtier in yellow with huge red ladybugs nested in her hair. She didn't even notice that Firo was carefully moving her to the edge, like she'd asked, until their two bodies revolved and she found herself at the foot of the dais, staring up into Elban's eyes. He regarded her hungrily; the Seneschal stood next to him, stern and forbidding.

She clutched at Firo. "No. Don't let me go."

"Make up your mind." But he spun her away, back toward the middle of the circle. Then there was another flourish and suddenly Judah was standing in front of Gavin. With a cool nod toward Firo, he took her hand, and she let herself be pulled back into the dance. She was glad he was wearing gloves. She didn't know what he would have been able to tell if he touched her bare skin.

"You're dancing," he said with a mirth that went nowhere near his eyes. "Your courtier beau actually convinced you to dance."

"Not exactly." Over her shoulder, she saw Firo standing alone, trapped awkwardly among the dancers but with an expression that said it didn't matter at all; then somebody stepped up to him, too. Somebody in blue. Amie.

Gavin's grip on Judah tightened—sensing, perhaps, the sudden tension in her body. "What's wrong?"

"I'm avoiding the Seneschal. I think he wants to talk to me." Elly and Theron were still together, still dancing. Elly seemed almost to be enjoying herself. Theron looked, as always, dazed.

Gavin's eyes went to the dais behind her. "He certainly does. Did you do something to piss him off? I've seen friendlier-looking torturers."

"You have not," she said.

A little of the mirth in his voice touched his face, like a candle flame that wasn't quite dead. "You don't know what I've seen. But don't worry, we can keep you away from him. This is the last dance before Elban's speech."

As he said the words, the flame guttered and died. "Don't lose hope," she said to him gently. Elban was watching the two of them like they were food now.

"Too late. Amie's already trading favors in my name." Gavin sounded morose. "Look at her, working your courtier. I hope he tells you about it later." Then she felt his breath freeze in his chest. Something had just occurred to him. He glanced back at the Seneschal and when his eyes came back to Judah they were full of panic. "He can't take you away," he said. "It's too soon."

With the grandest flourish of all, the music stopped. Judah felt cold fingers lace through hers: Theron, who was creeping close like a scared puppy even though Elly held his other hand. The four of them stood in a tight group, almost a circle.

And then the Seneschal was there, too. He glared at Judah, but it was to Gavin that he spoke. "It's time."

His words sent pain like ice through Gavin's body. In front of Judah, Elly's hand found his. Her fingers were squeezing Gavin's as tightly as she could, and a wave of—something—coursed through Judah. Grief. Nerves. Hope. They were all linked, she saw. All together.

Then Elly dropped Gavin's hand. And, more gently, Theron's. "I'll stay down here."

"As you like," the Seneschal said, not unkindly. He glared one last burst of venom at Judah and followed Gavin up to the dais.

Somebody came by with a tray of silvery crystal glasses. Elly took one and drained it. "I don't know what will happen after. Stay with me, Jude? For as long as you can?" She was ghastly pale, almost gray.

"Elban's talking," Theron said unexpectedly.

And he was. His voice filled the air, as clear and cold as the crystal in Elly's hand. "Gathered here, we are, to celebrate the betrothal of my son and heir, Gavin of Highfall. Gathered here, in the eyes of my court and the eyes of my kingdom. As the power of the words I speak tonight extends beyond this room, so do the actions we take here extend beyond our time: into history, into the lives of our children and their children and all who come after." The ceremonial words rang hollow, almost mocking. Everyone knew Elban had no intention of yielding power. The time he spoke of, the time of their children and their children's children, existed—to him—deep in an impossible future that he never truly believed would come. "The choosing of a mate to continue the line of our House is of profound consequence. Would that I'd had the counsel of my lost Lady to guide me in this choice, but it was not to be."

Judah suspected that he would no sooner have consulted Clorin than he would have Darid.

"Upon the Lady of the City rests the trust and well-being of our empire, and upon her rests the trust and well-being of the Lord of the City himself. She will be the mother of our future. As my lost Lady served, comforted and counseled me, so will my heir's Lady serve, comfort and counsel him. She must be humble and wise, pliant but unbreaking."

Out of the corner of her eye and above the heads of the crowd, Judah saw a cloud of tiny indigo butterflies move slowly toward the dais. The room held its breath. All of these words weren't necessary; Elban was dragging this out, enjoying it. The watching courtiers were starving, avid. More than one painted mouth hung open, panting for the drama they expected any minute.

"We stand on the cusp of a great time in our history. Our enemies underestimate our power." Elban's eye fell on her. On Judah. "I promise all of you: they will not do so for long."

Elly's hand was in Judah's, damp and cold. Somebody was trembling but Judah didn't know if it was Elly or herself or

Gavin, up on the dais. He was almost as pale as Elly but his face was expressionless, as if he were a portrait of himself. His eyes were focused somewhere above the crowd, so perhaps he did not see the last of the courtiers step aside to allow Amie through. She was very pretty. Her face was innocent and interested.

If Elban broke his word, Judah would run to the tower above Theron's workshop. They would find her but it would take time. They would not hurt Gavin to find her, Judah thought, and then amended: they would not hurt him too much.

"In this spirit," Elban said, "I present to you the betrothed of my son, the mother-to-be of his heir, and your future Lady of the City." His eyes found her again and she glared at him with all of her fury, as if the sheer force of her will could make him obey. His smile seemed all for Judah, as he threw an arm out toward the crowd, jutted his chin toward the massive chandelier, and roared, "Eleanor of Tiernan!"

The gasps from the courtiers hit Judah like a wave of ice water. There was a horrible moment of stillness where cheering and applause should have been; in front of the dais, Amie was a marble statue. Judah heard a brittle snap as some part of the fan the lady courtier held broke. Then she let it drop and dangle on the bracelet that bound it to her wrist, like a bird's wing that would no longer fly.

Her chin went up. She began to clap.

The silence broke. All of the courtiers around them, poised for drama, finally had it. It wasn't the dish they'd been expecting, but Judah could tell from the cheering that—with the exception of a few pockets of silence that must have held Amie's coterie—most of them relished it, nonetheless. Judah's knees felt weak. Elly was clinging to her arm, both hands clammy, her cheeks pink now and her eyes filled with tears.

"Judah. Judah! Why?" she was saying, her voice high and thin. "What's happening? Theron, oh gods, Theron." Her eyes darted around the room, perhaps for guards moving menacingly toward them, and she grabbed Theron protectively by the sleeve. Her whole weight rested on Judah's arm as if she, too, were afraid she'd fall, and it was almost enough to pull Judah down. Gavin was still on the dais but his heart, too, was pounding, his vision gray.

"It's okay, Elly," Judah said. "He's okay."

Then the Seneschal was at Elly's side, and now that it was all done Judah felt only gratitude as he took Elly's arm, and her weight, and led her forward. Elban said her name again. This time it was a command and cheers swelled around them. On the dais, Gavin was recovering; the Seneschal tried to deliver Elly up to him but Elly shook both of them off, her back ramrod straight, and climbed to the dais herself. Beautiful; regal. Judah had trouble seeing because her eyes were filled with unaccustomed tears. No guards were coming for Theron—Theron was safe. Gavin held out a hand. Elly took it, and then her place next to him. The despair that had shadowed them blew away like fog and the two of them shone like gold.

Judah wanted to dance. Not the tightly wound performance the courtiers called dancing but something wild, passionate: she wanted to whirl and leap, to throw her head back and crow. She had saved them. She had saved them all.

A hand grabbed her arm. Strong. The Seneschal. He pulled her through the open solarium doors into the cool night and there was no resisting him. As they left behind the light and cheering she could barely keep up, she almost tripped over her skirts. Through the garden, away from the acrobats, down the Promenade he dragged her, until they came to the Discreet Walk, where he almost hurled her into the darkness under the arbor. Clusters of wisteria in bloom hung heavy and spectral in the night air and so did their fragrance.

Gripping her arm, drawing her close, he hissed, "What have you done?"

"I saved them," she said boldly, not caring what he did to her. Saying the words aloud was magnificent. She started to laugh. "I saved all of them."

"Saved them." He dropped her arm, disgusted. "Saved them? Who have you saved? Have you even thought about this, you stupid girl?"

"Elly and Theron and Gavin," she said, still shaking with laughter. "Everyone who matters. I saved them."

"Judah. *Judah*. At what cost?"

His words emerged ragged with frustration, almost a wail. She had never heard the Seneschal sound like that. Her laughter died. "None that matters."

"None that matters," he said wonderingly. "None that matters. Oh, you stupid, stupid girl."

The laughter left an empty place in her, and now anger rushed in and filled it. "How am I stupid? I saved them. What did you do? Nothing. I saved them!"

"You keep saying that." He was angry, too. She thought he would probably hit her again. "All right, fine. Lady Eleanor will marry Lord Gavin, as planned. Lord Theron will live. Amie will go plot revenge somewhere. But you—*you*—"

She heard excited laughter. The ceremony must be over. Courtiers were beginning to filter out into the garden again. He took her arm and pulled her deeper under the wisteria, dropping his voice to a whisper. "Tomorrow Lord Elban leaves to attack the Nali again. His hope is to capture one of their chieftains, and make them break the bond that makes it necessary to keep you alive. Two hours ago, your fate was either a quick death, if he succeeded, or a life spent here if he failed.

Imprisoned, but alive. Well cared for. If Lord Gavin came to heel for no other reason, he would have done so to keep you safe. You would be bored, and you would be lonely, but you would live." He put up his hands. "Now? Now, Judah…you are equipment. He will take you on every campaign he wages for the rest of his life and yours. He will never let you out of his sight, no matter how much he hates you. And he does hate you, Judah. He hates you with every fiber of his being."

"I don't care," she said defiantly.

"Was it just too terrible to think of Eleanor at his mercy?" The Seneschal stood very close to her now. "Because Eleanor's life with Elban would have been afternoon tea compared to what yours will be. You will sleep in his tent at night, if he allows you to sleep. He will write his messages on your skin in blood and he will not care how much it hurts. He will chain you like a dog and he will do anything he wants to you, and everything he does, Lord Gavin will know. Everything he does, Lord Gavin will feel. Did you consult with him before you took your clever little plan to Elban? Did you ask him which outcome he'd prefer? Because at least when Eleanor suffers, Gavin doesn't have to feel it."

Judah couldn't speak. She had no breath.

"Stupid girl," he said, for what seemed like the thousandth time, and this time she understood. He was right. She had been stupid.

It was worth it! something in her cried. *I saved them!*

But the Seneschal wasn't done. "He wants to break Gavin to his will, and you have given him a better way to do that than anything Lady Amie could offer. How long do you think it will be, once Elban has you, before Gavin is willing to give his father anything he wants, do anything he says—not even to stop it, but just to make it not quite so bad? A week? A day? An hour?" He shook his head. "The campaign tomorrow is a pleasure excursion, now. He has no reason to break the bond, since you've shown him how useful it can be, but if the stars are with you, he'll find someone who can do it anyway. That way, when every inch of your body is covered with scars; when he's driven you insane and killed everything inside you; when dragging your carcass around becomes more trouble than he deems it worth, he can kill you. That is the only peace you will ever know again."

"I don't care." She was barely able to hear her own voice. "I don't care."

He stared at her for a long moment. Then: "You have no idea what you've done," he said, then turned around and walked away.

Her shoes dissolved in the walled garden, halfway to the stable. They literally came apart: with one step she was wearing shoes and with the next step she wasn't. She saw the pale leather soles half-sunk in the earth between the broken paving stones, surrounded by scraps of embroidered green felt. She kept walking. The stones felt so smooth they were almost soft under her feet; where there were no stones, the soil felt as thick and lush as the richest carpets in the House. Her mind had gone blank. It was true that she had saved them and it was true that it was worth it and everything the Seneschal said was probably true, too, and it was also true that she was scared. She felt as if she were perched on the edge of a yawning void and she wanted to selflessly believe that it was better she fall than any of the others. But the Seneschal was wrong; she wasn't stupid. She knew Gavin would be furious when he discovered what she'd done. She'd done it to both of them but she hadn't let herself think about that—she had only let herself think that he would be on campaign anyway. He might even hate her, and she couldn't let herself think about that, either; couldn't imagine a world where Gavin hated her.

Her mind kept going back to the new pages, hunched over courtiers' shoes on the corridor floors, small hands scrubbing furiously.

The stablemen's barracks, a long building tucked behind the stable itself, glowed with the warm light of oil lanterns. She could hear a chaotic hum of voices, too many for the stablemen alone. A woman laughed. Somebody played a violin, the music high and giddy. She stopped, suddenly aware of how she would look in her fine clothes, barefoot and muddied though she was. She didn't belong here. The haven she was hoping for was somewhere else, was nowhere. She should go back to her room. Wipe the mud from her feet so she didn't leave a mark on the fine marble floors.

A figure stumbled out of the barracks. Drunk, by the looks of it. Somebody from the brewery staff must have brought a barrel of beer. As she came closer she recognized his long hair and bowlegged gait. One of Darid's youngest stablemen, she didn't know his name. He didn't see her as he lurched to the pasture fence, put one arm out to steady himself, and opened his trousers. Moving now would only call attention to herself; Judah stayed still and silent and hoped he didn't see her.

But he did. Fell backward and cried out an oath she didn't know, scrambling to close his pants again as he fled—as well as he could—back into the barracks. Calling for Darid.

She took one step backward, then another. But Darid had already heard the call. His curly-haired bulk was outlined in the doorway, unmistakable.

She could have run anyway. She didn't.

He didn't stumble the way the stableman had, but something in the loose way he carried himself and the broad smile he wore told her that Darid was a bit drunk, too. "You've made young Con ruin his boots," he said, his voice musical with amusement.

"I can try to find him some new ones," she said.

He saw her face and the amusement was replaced by concern. "Oh, now. Don't worry about it. It'll teach him a lesson. He's too old to be thinking he's seeing ghosts." He glanced down. "Besides, you ought to find some for yourself, first."

"I was wearing shoes. They fell apart. Not actually intended for walking in, as it turns out."

"That'll teach you a lesson, then. You're too well-dressed to be tromping through pasture mud."

He took off his coat as he spoke. She said, "I'm not cold," but he held it out to her anyway, and there didn't seem to be anything to do but put it on. The material was thick and coarse. It smelled like horse and wood smoke and sweat. Like him.

"Why aren't you at the ball?" he said.

"I was. It was lovely. Gavin and Elly are going to get married and make one, or at most two, adorable blond children together, and Theron will live a long life staring blankly at walls, and I—I will—"

She couldn't finish. "Do your arms hurt you?" he said finally to fill the silence. "Is that why you're here?" He picked up the arm that had taken the most damage, the one Elban had burned first. The sleeve of his coat was far too big for her arm and pushed up easily. Carefully, he undid the buttons that held her sleeve closed, then pushed that up, too. In the darkness she could hardly see the curlicue branded onto her skin, but his fingers found it. Tracing it lightly, a touch she could barely feel—and she could not feel *him*, she realized, with amazement. The only sensations she felt were her own. And he was careful. Even the pain from the burn was faint.

"You should go back to the House," he said. "You shouldn't

be here." His fingers loosened on her arm, and she surprised herself by putting her other hand over his, so he couldn't take it back. The pressure made the burn hurt more but she didn't care. For a moment they both stood, stock-still, and stared at the simple, impossible thing between them: his hand on her bare arm, her hand over his. And why shouldn't her hand be there; why not, when soon enough—but she couldn't think about that, that was a place she did not want to go. And it came into her brain that she wanted to kiss him, which was even more impossible, but this was a night for impossible things, a night for the unthinkable, and so she did. Her lips touched his, and pressed.

He jerked back.

Then his arm was around her shoulders. Not affectionately. This seemed to be her night for being grabbed and shaken and dragged from place to place, because he was pushing her into the stable. The horses whickered softly at the intrusion.

"What are you doing?" His voice was as angry as the Seneschal's had been. Her night for making people angry, too. But she heard fear mixed with the anger now. She didn't want Darid to be scared of her. She wanted him to stop talking. She put her hands on his face and held it. His breathing came fast and alarmed.

But he didn't pull away. She felt him—sink. Like something in him had collapsed under its own weight.

"You're going to get me killed," he said.

"I'm sorry," she said. "You should send me away."

He didn't send her away. She didn't leave. The horses stamped; blew; calmed.

CHAPTER EIGHT

The morning after the ball, in the warm blue light that presaged the coming dawn, the massive drums started up. The Lord's Guard assembled in the courtyard, helmets and spear-points hovering ghostly above their armor; the House Guard lined up in ranks to see them off, the Seneschal at their head. The Lord's Guard wore scarlet badges; the House Guard wore white. The cavalry horses stomped and champed but no human spoke. The drumbeats filled the courtyard like mist. Even the raucous dawn chorus drifting into the courtyard from the gardens was buried under the throb.

The rest of the House was sleeping, except for those who hadn't slept at all. The sleepers included the courtiers, half of the kitchen staff, and most of the outdoor staff: shepherds and kennelmen, orchardkeepers and gardeners. The still-awake included the other half of the kitchen staff—busy with breakfast before the shift changed at lunch—the stablemen, and the new pages, who already scurried through the halls cleaning shoes and creeping through unlocked doors to silently lay fires, empty night pots, and brush discarded finery. Also awake were the entertainers from outside. Most of them had already loaded their supplies back into whatever conveyance they'd arrived in, and stood yawning and waiting for the campaign forces to march so they could leave.

Not far from the entertainers, Judah waited, too. She was one of the ones who hadn't slept. She still wore her gown from the night before, although the green silk was dulled by a thin sheen of dust and littered with bits of straw. The silver-and-diamond headdress had been first removed and laid carefully aside with gentle fingers, and then carried into the parlor in a damp palm and dumped into an unceremonious heap on the table. It lay there still, tangled beyond recovery for all Judah cared. She had taken the time to jam her dirty feet into boots and put her coat on. Catching a glimpse of the unruly mess of her hair in the mirror, she had picked up a hairbrush; then decided that she liked the unruliness, and put the brush down.

Now she stood in a corner where she wouldn't be noticed. Her mind felt thick with exhaustion and her eyes were hot with it, but for the first time in weeks, she was at peace. Gavin and Elly were officially and publicly betrothed, and nobody could hurt them. Theron, too, was safe. Across the courtyard a stableman appeared, holding the rein of a giant black warhorse with silver metalwork on its black leather tack. The stableman had broad shoulders and curly hair, and she felt no tension when she looked at him, either; only a memory of ease and warmth.

Darid didn't normally deal with the warhorses once they were transferred to the cavalry stable. But when the Lord's Guard marched, all the stablemen worked. The horse he held was Elban's. It would not be long now. And, yes: the doors were opening, the honor guard forming a neat gauntlet, banners aloft. There he was, white hair flowing loose over his black armor and the pommel of his sword rising over his shoulder like a second head, gnarled and silver and deadly.

Elban was the last thing she feared. He was leaving in minutes but she would belong to him eventually. The steady beat of the drums—their skins the size of tables, the mallet heads larger than her own—drove deep into her, jangled her nerves, throbbed in her eardrums. They were so loud she couldn't hear her own heartbeat. Surely nobody was sleeping now. Surely that was the point. Everyone in the House, and probably beyond, was being pulled roughly from sleep. They could yank blankets over their heads, muffle the pounding with pillows, sip from the bottles or vials they'd gone to bed with; but when they woke, they would know. Elban's army had marched. His embarkation would not be ignored.

Gavin and Elly, Judah knew, waited on the balcony above the Lord's Square, so they could raise their hands in farewell as Elban rode out of the city. She had not seen them led to the Safe Passage but she could imagine their progress through the locked doors and switchbacks that twisted through the Wall, the fumes from the oiled rushes on the floor and the metallic smell of the guards themselves. The closer Elly came to the spiral staircase and the tiny chamber at its top—the closer she came to the narrow balcony so high above the Square—the more her feet would drag, the more her hands would shake. She would force herself out onto that balcony but she would cling to Gavin. She would be terrified and embarrassed. He would be thrilled.

At the solstice, Judah would be with them, but this time she hadn't been invited. She could have been in bed or having breakfast or washing her feet. But she had wanted to see for herself as Elban strode down the aisle his guard made for him, as he leapt onto the back of the warhorse. When it felt his weight in the saddle, the horse tossed its head, hooves restless on the cobblestones. It was eager to go. Judah was eager to see it, and its rider, gone. From the saddle, Elban scanned the crowd. She didn't think he could see her in her shadowed corner. He paid no attention to Darid. "The gate!" he cried, and each guard began to stomp one heavy boot down on the cobbles, in perfect time with the drums. The two ancient winches groaned to life, six men at each, and the enormous wooden gates, thicker than a human being was long, began to part as the great House opened its mouth to speak the army into the world. Judah had never seen the Lord's Square from the ground before. Now, if not for the guard, she could walk out into it; stand on its surface and wave to Gavin and Elly. The cobblestones in the courtyard were the same as those in the Square. For some reason, that was what she found most startling: the cobblestones continued.

Gates fully open, the House held its breath. Then Elban gave a mighty cry; the drums quickened; the guard began to move, boots still keeping time with the drums. The drums themselves began to move, pulled on wagons by small tough ponies that, Judah knew, would be the first to be eaten, if it came to hunger. The mass of men and weapons that moved through the gates, slow and relentless, would rumble through the city to the bivouac outside Highfall, where another hundred men waited. Then they would move on to the next town, and the next bivouac, and between collected forces and conscriptions picked up along the way, the guard that seemed so fearsome inside the Wall would be but the smallest, deadliest portion of the army that eventually boarded the ships and sailed across the strait to Nali territory. A smaller portion still would return. For all their training and weaponry, they were nothing but rocks thrown at the enemy, and some of the rocks would break through and some would fly wild and some would simply shatter, because even a rock could break. Particularly when it was made of flesh and bone and blood.

For now, though, they were fearsome. Judah didn't look at the faces beneath the helmets. Because she understood, seeing the guard on the march, what Elban had said—that people were simply tools—and found it horrible. Their willingness to follow him, their acceptance of their fate. Prisoners, he'd said. Men with death sentences, given a chance to live again. They belonged to Elban, too, and perhaps she found that most frightening of all, because the next time this featureless mass marched, she would be among them. As would Gavin. Tools, waiting to be used.

Gavin's father spurred his horse and rode, as the drum carts began to roll and the army with it. Judah observed Elban's white hair, the bony shoulders, the perfect straight line of his back. He would chain her like a dog and do whatever he wanted with her. She added this knowledge to the long list of things she could not bear and could not help: like the long days in his study so long ago; like Arkady's cold hands poking and prodding before that last afternoon, when Gavin had felt her fear and revulsion and come in with a knife; like the mother she'd surely had but knew nothing about. There was nothing to do but endure. So she merely stood—apart from the acrobats and musicians and those few courtiers who'd managed an early start, apart from the remaining guards and the Seneschal at their head—and waited for the last marcher to pass under the arch, for the great drums to follow them. By then the sun was rising. The cobbles in the Lord's Square were touched with pink and gold as the entertainers began to trail after the army. Across the courtyard, Darid waited to be dismissed. Maybe he saw her; maybe he knew to scan the shadows for her.

She thought of his hands in her hair. The sweet smell of hay.

★ ★ ★

"I don't understand," Elly said later that day. "I could believe he was only being cruel, if it was just us. But that courtier was involved, too. And all the courtiers who followed her." *That courtier* was the only way Elly would refer to Amie. She shook her head. "I'm not complaining, and I'm certainly not about to ask anybody for an explanation. But I don't understand."

She and Judah were walking in the orchard. None of the courtiers ever went there; the soft ground was littered with dead leaves and dropped fruit, and the cidery smell of ferment clashed with their perfume. But Elly had good boots and so did Judah, and neither of them minded the smell. They'd played there when they were children. It was a happy place for them. Elly, Judah knew, wanted to be happy today. After Judah had left the ball, she and Gavin had danced late into the night, their steps light with reprieve, and not even Elban's smug amusement had spoiled it. Nor had it kept them from slipping upstairs to their rooms when the ball began to break up. They had brought Theron with them, and Elly had put tea in a pot to steep. But only Theron had still been in the room when the tea was ready: sitting where they'd left him, watching the steam rise.

Elly's cheeks had reddened as she told Judah that last part, and Judah knew she felt bad for leaving Theron there to fall asleep upright, still wearing his glasses, with the tea cooling in the pot because it hadn't occurred to him to pour it. "Oh, Jude," she said with weary amusement. "It's all so preposterous."

Judah hadn't asked what, exactly, she'd found so preposterous. Elly didn't seem amused at all now. "I asked Gavin what he thought that courtier would do next. He said—well, first he told me not to worry my pretty little head and let the big strong man take care of it, but then I pointed out that the big strong man was mostly why we'd ended up in this mess to begin with, and then we yelled at each other for a while."

"I would have liked to see that," Judah said sincerely.

"It's nothing you haven't seen before. Although he did almost seem surprised, as if now that we'd spent the night together I wouldn't ever argue with him again. I think he's still a little angry, actually. Anyway, he saw the Seneschal this morning after Elban left, and apparently *he* said that courtier left the House. Gavin said he thinks she'll be too humiliated to show her face for a while. Which—honestly, I don't know how much of this is even her fault. She might have found herself stuck in a mess just like we were. But still—" She hesitated for a moment, and then said, "Do you think you could ask Lord Firo what he thinks? I spoke to him last night, for a minute. He seemed kind enough. And Gavin says his courtcraft is impeccable."

"When did Gavin say that?"

"When he was following you around after that guild dinner. Will you ask him?"

"If I see him."

Elly smiled. It was a significant smile.

"What?" Judah said.

"Nothing," Elly said merrily. "You danced with him for quite a while, that's all. Also, I noticed that he seemed to disappear right around the same time you did, and I'm not in a position to swear to it but I'm fairly sure you didn't spend the night in our rooms last night. Oh, don't scowl, Jude. I like him well enough, for a courtier. He's not young, but the young ones are all such pompous little jays. I can't see you with one of them, anyway. And I know Gavin says he usually goes with men, but just because he usually does doesn't mean he always does."

Judah was silent: first, because she was biting back a burst of indignation, and then—with a flash of inspiration that instantly cooled the indignation—because she realized that if Elly thought she was having an affair with Firo, she wouldn't comment if Judah disappeared, from time to time. "Think what you want," she finally said, guessing that Elly would take a lack of denial as a confession, and when Elly's eyes lit up, she saw that she was right.

"Whatever I think, I promise I'll keep it to myself. You deserve some happiness. And it won't hurt to have a prominent courtier like him on your side." Elly stepped over a root. "I'm still not convinced that Elban doesn't have some horrible new trick up his sleeve. You don't go from *I'll have you all killed horribly* to *oh wait never mind* without something happening in between."

Judah chose not to hear that. She pretended Elly's words were birdsong that filled the air with pretty, meaningless sound, and required no response.

Late that night, after everyone else was asleep—Elly had insisted on not changing the sleeping arrangements, privately telling Judah that it was good for Gavin not to get absolutely everything he wanted whenever he wanted it—Judah crept out through the quiet parlor. The House was quiet, too; the few courtiers who remained inside were mostly those who had not yet emerged from the ocean of wine and drops they'd sunk into at the ball. The gas lamps were low. One of the retiring rooms spilled over with warm light and the smell of burned coffee; Judah paused at the door to let a staff girl hurry in with a tray of something savory-smelling, but didn't look inside. The corridor doubled back and then she was passing guest rooms. Another staff girl tapped timidly on a closed door, looking uncertain; when she saw Judah coming she turned the knob, almost silently, and slipped inside. Before the door closed behind her Judah saw two bodies draped motionless over a couch. Judah didn't know what the girl's job might be, but she doubted the passed-out courtiers would notice if she did it or not.

Outside, the moon was high but the gardeners were hard at work by the light of lanterns that ran on Wilmerian gas like Elly's quickstove, trimming hedges and clipping away dead leaves so that all would be beautiful in the morning when the House woke up. They went predictably quiet as she passed. The dry fountains and broken statues in the walled garden glowed eerily in the moonlight, and the path was easy to pick out. The hounds in the kennels barked ferociously. Judah was a thing they didn't know and so they wanted to kill her. She could not imagine Darid working among them.

Another lantern hung from the hook outside the stable door, but the light it shed was so feeble that it barely penetrated. All seemed deserted. Judah lifted the bar on the door and went in. The horses murmured softly, but unlike the hounds, they knew her, and so weren't alarmed. She could feel them more than she could see them, huge and warm and breathing in the darkness.

Motion at the other end of the stalls. The sound of footsteps, coming toward her. Darid.

"You came," he said and kissed her. It was strange to be kissed by somebody she couldn't see. It was strange to be kissed at all. Kissing was a thing courtiers did, devouring each other's mouths as emotionlessly as they did cakes or canapés. But here she was, her mouth on his, his body solid in front of her like a friendly wall. She'd never stood this close to anyone by choice except Elly and Gavin and Theron. She'd certainly never felt anyone else's body pressed against hers, the way Darid's was now. His hands moved across her collarbones, which she liked, and then slid backward into her hair. Which she might have liked had it not been for the drunk Wilmerian, all those weeks ago. Her hair had been the first part of her Darid had touched, tentatively, the night before. Lips still pressed against his, she wondered, a bit dispirited, if men would always want to touch her hair. Maybe she'd cut it off before Elban took her on campaign.

But further than that, she refused to think. Tonight she'd tied her hair back with one of Elly's ribbons; now Darid pulled it loose. He was less tentative than he'd been the night before. She put her hands on his chest, and pushed him gently back. "Hello," she said.

"I wasn't sure you'd come." He was taller than she was. Who wasn't? His mouth was somewhere far above her forehead, which was made evident when he leaned down to kiss her there, too.

"I said I would."

"You might have thought better of it."

"Because you're a lowly stableman?" She knew he couldn't see her any better than she could see him, so made sure her voice was light and friendly.

"Yes."

"You're head stableman," she said. "I'm just the witchbred foundling. It should be you who thinks better of me, really."

"Is that what this is?" His voice was filled with fascination. "Have you put a spell on me?"

"I hope you're joking." This time she didn't care if it sounded friendly or not.

"Put a spell on me," he said. Suddenly she found herself swept up into the air, one of his massive arms under her knees and one behind her back. Her stomach lurched nervously as he carried her through the dark to some unknown place. Instinctively, she clutched at his neck. "Put a thousand spells on me."

"Put me down, or I will," she said.

But he was already putting her down, somewhere soft and prickly with hay. She felt him drop next to her. Then he was kissing her neck and collarbone urgently. The urgency was sweet and the hand stroking her side was not entirely unwelcome, but—

"Darid," she said. Not sighed, not breathed, not moaned, but said, in a normal tone of voice. As if she were about to ask him to pass the bread.

The stroking hand paused, and the kisses stopped. She felt him looming over her, waiting. And since he was waiting, she had to speak. She didn't know half the words for what she needed to say. They were things that nobody had ever talked about to her. "I don't think," she said carefully, "that I want to—" She felt him freeze, and so, quickly, she said, "No, no. I want to be here. I thought about you all day. I saw you in the courtyard this morning and I couldn't stop seeing you." She reached up, then, and touched *his* hair. Which was only fair. It was soft and very silky and the curls clung to the tips of her fingers.

He pressed his head against her hand like a cat. "I saw you, too. What don't you want to do?"

"The thing that everybody does. The thing the courtiers do, and the thing that Gavin and Elly have to do—"

"*Have* to do?"

She wasn't sure, but she thought he might be laughing. "For the heir," she said a bit stiffly.

"Oh. That thing." He bent his head down and she felt his forehead touch her shoulder. There was no doubt now: he was laughing. His breath came in quick puffs against her neck.

She was hurt. "Don't laugh at me. Hardly anybody ever talks to me about it and when they do, they use words that don't actually mean anything. The Seneschal told me I wasn't allowed to take a lover; should I have said that I wanted to be here and I wanted to kiss you but I didn't want to be your lover? Would that be better?"

"Why would he say that?" he said in surprise.

"Because if I got pregnant, it would be—complicated. It's hard to explain."

She felt him touch her cheek. The laughter was gone. "I think there are probably a lot of things about your life that are complicated and hard to explain."

"Only a small library's worth."

"Lucky for me, I don't read that well," he said. "All right, witchbred foundling. We won't do that thing. You're not the first person who's told me that, you know."

No, she wouldn't be, would she? Because staff girls had as much to lose as she did. Maybe more. "What words did they use?"

He chuckled and put on a thick Highfall accent, the kind staff children all had beaten out of them in their first month, so Judah had hardly ever heard it. Every word seemed to have an extra vowel thrown in. "I'll not be having sex with ye, ye greet hulking lummox," he said. "Put it right out of your filthy heed, aye?"

Judah was delighted. "Oh, that's amazing. Do more."

"It's been a long time," he said, in his normal voice. Which probably wasn't his normal voice at all, she realized, as he slipped fluidly back into Highfall. "But sure, girl, if it give you a chuckle, I'll oblige ye."

"I love it." Then, greedily, "And I want to hear about all these other women who wouldn't have sex with you, too."

"Do you?" He was laughing again, but this time she didn't mind. "Why?"

She couldn't say. It had something to do with the courtiers, and the way they carried themselves, like the world was a performance; it had something to do with Gavin and Elly, who were expected to produce an heir as soon as possible, and it had something to do with the black void where her own life experiences should have been. "Never mind why. Just tell me." She kissed him. "I want to hear about the ones who didn't say no, too. Tell me everything."

"Everything?" he asked, a bit querulously.

"Everything."

He groaned. "Aye, girl, it's a hard heart ye've geet," he said, but still, he was obliging.

Any courtier who had an estate in the provinces sobered up, packed their things and went there. The staff relaxed; some of the new pages brought in for the ball were even heard to laugh occasionally, when they thought nobody could hear. The horses had more exercise and grazing and less unnecessary grooming. With fewer people to feed, the food brought up to their rooms was fresher. So was the air, since the laundresses from the fabric rooms had time to wash the drapes and tapestries, to drag the carpets and cushions outside and beat the dust out of them.

Elly and Gavin still had responsibilities, but their days started later and ended earlier. Since there were fewer courtiers around to meet in person, the Seneschal set Elly to memorize the ancestral lines of the most prominent highborn families, and Judah spent more than one pleasant hour sitting in the parlor with the terrace doors thrown open wide, drinking iced tea and checking Elly's notes as the Tiernan recited generation upon generation of dead sycophants. The terrace itself would have been nicer, but Elly refused.

"Lepfield...ugh, they're a city family, they go back forever. Temper, Joren, Evett, Robert the Greater, Robert the Lesser, Robert the Bad—those three are easy—and then Caber, and—

oh, a bunch of others—and then that poor, desperate woman. What's her name. Maryle."

"I'm not sure 'bunch of others' is an acceptable answer. Why poor and desperate?"

"Because she has six daughters and a district with nothing to offer. At least Tiernan has sheep." Elly shook her head. "Maryle's husband actually joined the army, they were so poor. He died on that last Nali campaign, the rout. She cornered me at the betrothal ball after you left. Wanted to sell us one of her daughters, for Theron. I told her the second son never married and she said, 'Oh, they wouldn't have to *marry*.' I didn't know what to say. At least my mother held out for a marriage contract." Elly looked genuinely pained. "The poor thing."

Judah didn't know if the poor thing was Lady Maryle, or her daughter, or Theron. Who still lived as in a dream, and rarely spoke. Sometimes Judah found him blandly studying the device that still sat in pieces on Gavin's dressing table, but now that he was less likely to meet anyone who mattered, he spent most of his time wandering the halls. The staff skittered away for fear of offending him, not knowing that if Theron had ever had the capacity to be offended by staff—which was debatable—he'd lost it. Gavin didn't think he'd come to any harm, so they let him wander. Like a cat, they trusted he'd come back. Like a cat, he generally did. Sometimes Judah had trouble remembering when he'd been any way other than unfocused and vague. She still thought it was her fault, the way he was now, but the pangs of guilt were less acute. A person could adjust to anything, given time.

Elly was reciting more names. Judah hadn't been checking them off. She scanned Elly's notes, trying to find her place, but then something slammed into her left arm. Rather, into Gavin's left arm: with Elban's guard gone, the House Guard was spending their training time wrestling, mostly for fun.

Gavin wasn't very good at it but he came home happy. The men in the House Guard liked him. He felt good when he was with them. He felt good in general, these days. Judah had not fully appreciated how eaten alive he'd been by anxiety until the anxiety vanished; he felt easy and relaxed, and as long as she kept all thoughts of Elban tucked away, she could be easy and relaxed, too. Except now her arm was numb, and half of her iced tea had spilled on Elly's notes. The ink was running.

Elly handed her a napkin from the table. "He'll be sore tonight."

"I'll take wrestling over practice swords any day. Those things sting." Judah mopped tea from her dress.

"Speaking of swords," Elly said cheerfully, "I saw Lord Firo yesterday."

Puzzled, Judah said, "Why are you blushing?" but then she figured out what kind of sword Elly meant, and made a face. "Oh, Elly."

Elly laughed. "Sorry. It's hard to bring the subject up, since you refuse to talk about it. Which is incredibly unsatisfying for me, personally, by the way."

"There's nothing to talk about."

"So you say. Gavin says otherwise. He also says it's not spying if he can't help it, so don't get annoyed with him. Ha! Now you're the one who's blushing."

Which was true, but it had nothing to do with Firo. Judah hadn't even seen the courtier since the ball, and had no desire to. It occurred to her now that it might be worthwhile to seek him out, and find out if he planned to stay inside. He was a convenient alibi for the time she spent with Darid.

"I didn't know you felt—that sort of thing, too," Elly said. "I thought it was just pain."

"It's not the sort of thing a person talks about," Judah said. She found herself a little angry at Gavin, for chatting so casually about things that were privately hers. He should have at least had the decency not to mention it. Judah never had; not since the first time she'd woken in a sweat, yanked from sleep by sensations that weren't hers. But then again, nothing was truly hers, was it?

"Well, I know, but you could have said something to me. You really feel it every time he—" Elly stopped. She didn't have the words for this conversation, either.

"Did you want me to tell you," Judah said, "every time he?"

Elly grimaced. "Gods, no. In fact, let's never talk about it again. Anyway, what I really wanted to say—well, here." From her pocket she produced a handkerchief wadded around something, and dropped it in Judah's lap.

Judah unwrapped it and found a small sachet made of some kind of thin silk. It appeared to be full of herbs. "What is it?"

"It'll keep you from having a baby," Elly said bluntly. "Put it inside. First. You know what I mean?" Not trusting herself to speak, Judah nodded. Elly looked relieved. "Don't tell Gavin. He doesn't know I use them. He said that Arkady used to make them, too, and the courtiers didn't think they were all that reliable. But Nathaniel Magus says his are better. And I know the Seneschal would be angry with you if you got pregnant. So." Businesslike. "If you don't want to ask him for more, I'll get them for you. But he's not hard to talk to. The magus, I mean."

"Noted." Judah wrapped the sachet in the handkerchief again, and put it in her pocket. The breath whooshed out of her as someone threw Gavin on his back. When she'd recovered, she said, "Speaking of Firo, Cerrington's next."

"Founded by Lord Cerring, then it's Cerring after Cerring until the last six: Cantor, Oren, Yan, Hubert, Cantor again—then Firo. Who has one son, still a child. The mother died," she added, significantly. "Anna. Generally, the women aren't considered important enough to bother learning, of course, but I made an exception."

"Wait," Judah said. "Why are you trying not to get pregnant? Isn't that what you're supposed to do? Wouldn't everyone be thrilled?"

"Oh, they'd be ecstatic." Elly's voice was cool. "The sooner I make an heir, the sooner Gavin can go fight a war like a real City Lord. The wedding's only a formality, you know that. They'd almost prefer it happen on childbed, so they know you're a proven breeder before the papers are signed." Then, less archly, "And Gavin would rest easier."

"So do it."

"Not yet."

"Why not?"

"Because I don't know what Elban is planning," Elly said. Then she smiled, a cold, satisfied smile. "Speaking of not having Gavin's babies, let's do the Porterfields next."

That night Gavin took a great deal of teasing from Judah, who felt like she'd spent her whole day being thrown against the ground, and from Elly, who'd spent her whole day watching. He bore it good-naturedly. "I like wrestling," he said. "It's honest. Two men, no weapons. And I'm not half-bad at it, either."

"That's what you say about everything," Elly said.

"It's true about everything, I'm sorry to say." He didn't sound sorry. "I am not half-bad at pretty much every kind of combat I've tried. Fortunately, *not half-bad* seems to be all they want of me. The training master says he thinks I'll rise to the occasion once I see actual battle."

"An optimist," Judah suggested.

"I guess we'll see," Gavin said.

Theron drifted in. There were large damp patches on the backs of his thighs. "Where have you been?" Judah asked him.

As always, he seemed surprised to learn that other people occasionally spoke. "I was down by the aquifer. It's quiet there."

The parlor fell quiet, too, as it always did when Theron made one of his observations. "Yes, it is," Gavin said.

Chicken pie, that night. Despite Elly's initial attempts, the sleeping arrangements were more or less permanently altered: Theron slept in Gavin's bed, and Judah took his dusty little cot, which wasn't that much different from her own dusty little cot so she didn't see that it mattered much. Most nights she managed to slip away herself, anyway. The thing she and Darid had together was strange, not like the love affairs she'd read about in stories. She liked being with him. She liked feeling his arms around her, being close to him; she had never felt that close to anyone except Gavin, which was so entirely different that it hardly compared, except she had nothing else so she compared it anyway. They did not use Elly's sachet, although Judah kept it in her pocket. If her reluctance frustrated Darid, he didn't show it. The world wasn't perfect, he said. Some nights, they barely spoke. Some nights, they just lay together and watched the stars move across the sky. But sometimes they also moved across each other and those times, it was her body that felt like it was full of stars, the sachet felt like a second sun ablaze in her pocket and the next step seemed so obvious, so clear.

Then she would catch sight of the curlicue scars Elban had left on her arms, and she would remember that she didn't belong to herself anymore. All the more reason, she would think, resentfully, but she always pushed that thought away. The bargain with Elban had been her idea. Knowing that didn't keep her brain from drifting toward the future she didn't have, for all she scolded and berated it. If she couldn't berate the gloomy mood into submission, she would kiss Darid goodbye and go back to the House. There was no point wasting what little time they had together sulking.

On one such night, she returned to the parlor and smelled tobacco smoke. The bedroom doors were closed, but the terrace door stood open; Judah barely had a chance to slip out of her boots before Gavin appeared there. "Caught you," he said. She put a finger to her lips, and he shrugged. "Theron's gone, Elly's asleep. Come sit with me while I finish this cigarette?"

So she slipped her boots back on against the chill—in Highfall, the nights were only truly warm for a few weeks in summer—and joined him, leaning against the terrace railing.

Then, the words practically bursting out of him, he said, "You know I feel everything you do, right?"

His voice was merry but she didn't feel like laughing. "Turnabout is fair play."

He grinned. "We should be careful about our timing, though. I mean, there are distractions, and there are distractions. And some of us can't hide it as easily as others of us can. Now, Jude, don't make that face. I'm glad you're enjoying yourself. I admit to being a little surprised at how much you're enjoying yourself, though. Who would have thought Firo had it in him?"

"Stop," she said, irritated. She didn't feel like being teased.

"Sorry." He lifted his cigarette, and examined the orange coal of it. "Can we talk about Firo, actually? Just for a moment? I know it's none of my business. Elly only tells me so sixty thousand times a day. And I am really glad you're happy."

"But?"

"But he's a courtier. And not a neophyte, either. He's been around for years."

"People do like to remind me that he's old."

"It's not that at all. Don't tell Elly, but the first woman I was ever with? Was there the night we were born. In an honorary capacity, not a hands-covered-with-blood capacity." He shook his head. "The world is weird. You never know who's going to catch your eye, or whose eye you're going to catch. And I know the Seneschal doesn't want you to be with anybody, but—"

He stopped. "But," Judah said. Again.

"But." There was a note of reluctance in his voice, in the tilt of his head. "I may not have to lock you in a prison anymore, but I don't know how much joy your life is going to bring you. It's not my fault, but it also is." He reached over and put his hand on hers. It wasn't the sickening experience it would have been before the ball, but she could feel sadness in him like a toothache. It was for her, this sadness. She didn't think he'd feel so bad for her if he knew what she'd signed him up for. "I promise you, I will do everything I can to make you happy, forever. And I hate that I can't just tell you to go forth and rejoice. But you can't trust Firo. You know you can't. I can feel it in you every time I say his name."

She didn't say anything.

"None of the courtiers are trustworthy. They all have agendas. But I can list any number of dumb, good-looking boys who'd throw themselves at your feet if they thought it would get them in good with me. And if I were to make a list of courtiers I'd recommend you avoid, Firo would be at the top of it. He's lost a lot of power, politically, since the whole mess with Tevala, but he's still got a hook in every fish inside the Wall." He sounded like a tutor, explaining something to a recalcitrant child, and she could not help bristling. "And frankly, he's spent the last twenty years going after every young lord with a pretty face. So for him to suddenly become interested in you—"

She yanked her hand back. "Go hang."

"I don't mean it's surprising for somebody to be interested in you, you know I don't mean that. But he's *only* been with men, Jude, and lots of them. He did marry that woman back in Cerrington, because he's obligated to have an heir, but he didn't stay long enough to actually meet his son. He didn't even go back when she died."

"Maybe I know all this," she said. "Maybe I'm quick enough to realize that there's only one reason somebody like Firo would be interested in me. Maybe I don't care."

"So maybe you'll tell me what you think that reason is."

"You already said it. He wants to go through me to get to you." Then she pretended to consider. "But not for sex, I don't think. At least, he's never mentioned you that way."

"You're teasing," Gavin said. "That's fine. Tease me all you want. Just promise me you'll keep your eyes open."

"Fine. I'll keep my eyes open." It would be an easy enough promise to keep, since her relationship with Firo was entirely fictional.

"You have to be careful." He took her hand again. "Elban let us go once, but—" He didn't finish the sentence. Probably because he thought he didn't need to, and he didn't, but not for the reasons he had in mind. Elban hadn't let them go at all. By the time the city was Gavin's, he would be scarred inside and out. It would be Judah's fault. Probably he would hate her for it. She knew this. He didn't.

Gavin's obvious concern, though, was enough to make her spend the next morning searching, single-mindedly and methodically, for Firo. She found him in the solarium, a letter open on his lap. "Hello, foundling," he said, unreadable as always. "How lovely to see you."

"We need to talk."

"Do we?" He lifted an eyebrow. "I hope you're not ending things. I've so enjoyed our dalliance."

The rumors had reached him, too, then. Every courtier left in the House seemed to be in the solarium; she assumed they were watching without bothering to check. "As you like."

"Any way I like?" His voice was mocking. Then, more quietly, "Smile, darling. This is a lover's meeting."

She didn't respond. He folded the letter and slid it into an inner pocket of his coat. Then he stood up. "I was about to visit the baths. Join me?"

He extended an arm. She suppressed her distaste and took it, allowing herself to be led out of the solarium, through the corridors and main hall, down to the bathing rooms. People they passed watched them curiously, even those who pretended not to. When they came to an empty bathing room, he opened the heavy wooden door for her, and locked it behind them. The air inside was damp and fragrant. Firo dropped her arm unceremoniously, took off his coat and began to unfasten his boots.

Alarmed, Judah said, "You're actually bathing."

"I am. I enjoy baths." There was a wardrobe in each bathing room. He put his boots in the bottom of it, and began unbuttoning his shirt. "Also, there are signs, you know. Pink cheeks. Shriveled fingers. A freshly-pressed look to clothes that have been hanging, unoccupied, in the steam. And if you think that nobody is going to be watching for those signs, you're more naïve than I thought. Turn around."

She took a step backward. "Why?"

"So I can help with the lacing on that horrible garment you're pretending is a gown." He continued to undress. "Really, Judah, if we're going to continue this affair, you need to do something about your attire. Telling people I'm in it for the power will only go so far."

"I'm not taking my dress off," she said.

"Then nobody will believe we're having sex right now. It's nothing to me, but since you've come this far, I assume it's not nothing to you. The choice is yours."

A sick feeling filled her stomach. He was taking his trousers off. "They say you prefer men," she said. Nervously, stupidly.

"I do. Vastly. Which makes our torrid affair all the more interesting for the casual observer." He was naked now. His body was ropy and thin, if a bit soft in the middle. His shoulders were narrow and his chest slightly hollow; the few hairs there, unlike the ones on his head, were mostly gray. Embarrassed, Judah looked down—but that was even worse.

"Now, dearest." His voice was quiet and poisonous. "Does it look like you're in any danger from me?"

She had to admit that it didn't. "I can undo my laces myself."

"Then do so." He crossed to the sunken stone bathing pool, and lowered himself in. Then he leaned his head back and closed his eyes.

Quickly, Judah undressed and hung her clothes in the wardrobe next to his. Then she, too, immersed herself in the pool. The water was very hot and the smell of lavender and eucalyptus was so strong that her skin tingled and her eyes watered. The pools, ringed inside with stone benches at sitting height, were big enough to accommodate half a dozen bodies; she stayed as far away from Firo as possible. She was sore all over from Gavin's wrestling adventures. Under different circumstances, the water would have felt good.

He lifted his head up and opened his eyes. He wore lash-blackener, she saw. "Well, my darling love," he said, "whatever you want, you've convinced me that you want it very badly.

But a bit of advice, dearest. When you're naked in a bathing pool with someone you barely know and aren't entirely sure of, it's worth getting in first so you can ensure you're closest to the door. Just in case." With one finger, he pointed over his shoulder to the bolted door.

She gritted her teeth. "It's not a position I commonly find myself in."

"And yet, here we are," he said. "Why are we here, my moon and stars? Why does the entire House think I'm fucking you?"

"Didn't you tell them so? Weren't you disgustingly detailed about it?"

He laughed. The tendons in his neck stood out and the flesh under his chin was loose. He favored high collars, and now she knew why. "I told them you threw yourself at me, and that I threw you some paltry attention for novelty's sake. The speed with which our affair has progressed is news to me. Are you pregnant?"

"No."

"Good. It would be highly inadvisable to try and pass a child off as mine."

"Because you already have an heir back in Cerrington?"

His eyes went hard. "Do not speak of what you don't know, foundling."

"I'm not pregnant. I'm not planning to be. We danced at the ball and you left right after I did, and that started rumors. Which you knew it would."

Nodding, he said, "We all expected Lady Amie to win, of course."

"Lady Amie," Judah said acidly, "was never in the race. None of it was ever about her."

"Really? Interesting. I'd like to hear more about that, in the future. But for now: when poor Lady Amie was so cruelly rejected, you suddenly became potentially useful again, so yes, I expected the rumors. I did not expect Lord Gavin to act as if he believed them. And that, my ebony-eyed paramour, is what I'd like to hear more about now."

Judah sank lower into the water. "What do you mean, act as if he believed them?"

"He's been antisocial since the ball. Waiting for the dust to settle after the Amie debacle, I imagine, although officially, he's been too busy enjoying the company of his betrothed. There's a rather rude word for it, but I'll spare you. When he does appear, all he seems to want to talk about is me. My character, my habits, my proclivities. Do my friends like me. Do I have any friends. That sort of thing." He tilted his head. "It's almost as if somebody close to him, somebody he trusts, has given him reason to act the protective brother. It's quite sweet, really."

"I never told him there was anything between us."

"But you let him think it. I assume you have reasons." He stretched his thin arms out along the edge of the pool. "My darling love, are you untrue, so soon? Do we need to revisit the pregnancy discussion? If you're relying on those sachets, I wouldn't. Of course I don't have much personal experience with them, but I've known ladies who swore they actually got pregnant faster while using them."

"None of that is any of your business."

"Oh," he said, "but when the Seneschal has let it be generally known that any courtier caught unawares with you—as I might be, at this very moment—will experience the immediate removal of most of themselves back to their home provinces, it is, indeed, my business. The parts of me that he would keep—well, I would miss them, even if you would not."

Startled, she said, "They'd do that?"

"They do it quite regularly to the staff. Not as a matter of course, but it happens—particularly if there's a valuable skill worth preserving. If I remember correctly, the last one was a carpenter. Apparently quite good with his tools, as it were. The laundry girl he got pregnant wasn't so lucky, of course, but they rarely are. Now, a courtier—that hasn't happened in many years, but it *has* happened. The House Magus does it, in that case. They'll usually take the fruit but leave the tree, which is something, I suppose. Still, not an experience I'd like to have." His tone made her feel cold despite the hot water. "If I'm at risk, I expect to be compensated, in the only coin you have worth spending. Bare your soul, my love. You've bared everything else, after all."

She felt a flutter of panic and pushed it down. She needed Firo on her side. "There is someone."

"And this someone is inappropriate."

"For me," she said bitterly, "everyone is inappropriate."

He rolled his eyes back toward the ceiling. "That's a situation I'm familiar with," he muttered. Then, more normally, "Well, if it were a courtier, I'd know. The young lord isn't clever enough to carry off the subterfuge, and he's too obvious, anyway. The other young lord is too—oblivious. So it must be staff, or one of the guards." An unfamiliar expression came over his face. It took her a moment to recognize it as puzzlement.

Before the question she saw there could make it to his mouth, she said, "Will you warn me if you plan to leave the city?"

"Why? So you can write me love letters?" Suddenly, with a swoosh and swirl of water, he was directly in front of her, one arm on either side of her body, pinning her against the edge of the bath. He wasn't touching her but if she moved at all—even to curl her body into itself—he would be. She froze. The steam had smudged the kohl and lash-black around his eyes and left him looking haunted, and very fierce, as he gave her a hard, piercing look.

"Before the ball, the Seneschal asked me if I'd ever considered marrying again," he said. "Was he thinking of you?"

"Not anymore." Her voice sounded tough, she was glad to hear. Inside, she was horrified: by his proximity, by his nudity, by her own.

"Why are you so confident about that?"

"He told me so."

"He told me he wouldn't give you to me, specifically? Or anyone?" She didn't answer. Firo's eyes narrowed. "Is he the one you're fucking? Does he intend to keep you for himself?" She managed a disdainful glare and he said, as if thinking aloud, "No. He's stone, through and through. So he's staff, your secret lover—or she is. But why does it matter?" He still looked fierce, but now the ferocity was tempered with fascination. "Courtiers go through staff like kindling. Nobody cares. You're not a courtier, but—"

Suddenly she'd had enough. "Get away."

He didn't move. "Why can't you fuck staff, dear? What's so special about you?"

She put both hands on his chest—cringing at the feel of his wet skin and the sparse crisp hair under her palms—and pushed with all the force of her arms, pressing her back against the stone edge of the pool for leverage. The water churned dramatically, but he only pivoted, settling down on the bench more or less next to her. Far enough away that her skin no longer crawled, at least. "Intriguing," he said. "All right, foundling. I'll warn you if I go, so you can find some other excuse for your tryst. But there will be conditions."

"I would never imagine otherwise," she said, still alight with anger.

"Tell Lord Gavin and Lady Eleanor how much you love

me. At great length, with particular emphasis on my intelligence, knowledge and trustworthiness. Within two weeks, I want to be seen publicly with them. Lunch in the solarium, perhaps. By their invitation." As an afterthought, he added, "You needn't be there. In fact, it might be better if you weren't."

Judah didn't like it, but she said, "I'll see what I can do."

"Please do. I'm not exactly welcome in Cerrington, but occasionally business does draw me out of the city, sometimes with very little notice. I'll expect to be asked to your rooms, as well. Again, publicly. An invitation from Lord Gavin himself would be ideal." The idea of Firo sitting in the parlor made her feel greasy. He pointed a long, thin finger at her. "I'm going to figure you out, foundling. And when I do, I'm going to plant a hook so deep in you that you'll think you were born with it."

Gavin had used the same metaphor. She almost laughed. As if the hook she'd begged Elban to sink into her left room for anyone else. "Good luck with that."

"Don't underestimate me, my precious love. Now, I would bet any money that as soon as we leave this room, some curious soul is going to duck in to see if it smells like sex. They needn't be disappointed, but if you don't want to help, you should probably leave now."

"That's all I want to hear about that, thanks," she said. "Turn around."

"I'll close my eyes," he said and did just that. She turned around and pulled herself out of the water. With her back to him she dried off and dressed as quickly as she could. When she glanced back, his eyes were still closed. His fancy purple coat hung next to the hook where her dress had been, and she considered dumping it in the bath. But, loathsome as he was, she needed him, and so she left him.

★ ★ ★

That night, as they sat on one of the big rocks in the pasture, she asked Darid if Firo's story about the carpenter was true. "Most likely," he said. "It was before my time, though. Elban's father tried gelding all of the staff boys when they came in, but too many of them died, and the ones that lived didn't ever reach their full strength. Not worth it. Now it's just a punishment. Or a solution to a problem, if a man has a skill too valuable to lose."

"That's terrible," she said.

"Beats hanging. And they've gotten better at it. They hardly ever kill anyone anymore."

Sick with horror, Judah said, "I thought it wasn't common."

"It isn't. But it happens." Darid hesitated. Then, "When I came inside, one of the kennel boys I worked with, he…well, I think he'd been—damaged. Worked hard enough, and did what he was told, but he had trouble controlling himself." He shook his head. "Jon never meant to hurt anybody. He just didn't understand. Which didn't help the people he went after. So they gelded him. It was a mercy. They could have killed him."

"He's still alive?"

"Works in the midden yard."

"And does he still—have trouble?"

"Different trouble. One of the reasons he works in the midden yard. I know what you're thinking, by the way."

One of his arms was underneath her, cushioning her head from the hard rock. The hand attached to that arm was lazily stroking her hair. The motion didn't falter, didn't even slow. "What am I thinking?"

"You're worried that if they catch us, they'll do the same to me."

"Aren't you?"

291

He shrugged. "Not really. Lots of people are good with horses. They'd probably just kill me."

She sat bolt upright. "Don't say that."

"I'm not going to die of old age, Judah." His smile was amused. "Every day I wake up and there's no way of knowing: is this the day a courtier gets kicked by one of my horses, or falls because their tack breaks? Or I say the wrong thing, or do the wrong thing? Every month, my mother waits for the coin that means I'm still alive. One day, it won't come." Suddenly he sat up, too. "Wait. You're not a courtier."

"So?"

"I've been thinking of you as if you were. Courtiers can do whatever they please, but—" He took her hand. "I know what I'm risking. Do you?"

"I'm risking nothing. They can make my life unpleasant, but they won't take it away."

"Why not?"

He looked so open, so unguarded, that she almost told him. Instead she said, "I have a skill that's too valuable to lose. At least, Elban thinks so."

The openness slammed shut. Disgust, resentment, righteous anger—at least, he probably felt it was righteous—all flipped across his face like pages in a book. "Of course you do. Nothing around here gets kept without a purpose." His voice was bitter. "Elban takes staff girls sometimes, you know. They don't come back."

"It's not like that," Judah said.

"Good," he said. "Because you're meant for more than that."

And the staff girls aren't? she almost said, but didn't. "None of us are meant for anything. We're tools in a box, that's all. Pieces of wood carved like stablemen and courtiers and—and foundlings." She heard the words come out of her mouth and was grimly satisfied to realize that she believed them. It was easier to feel that way, to think that the course of her life couldn't be changed. Elban would have figured out how to use the connection anyway, eventually. Or—and this realization came so clear that she knew it must be true—Gavin himself would have, the first time he lost a regiment or a province because there was no way to deliver messages as quickly as he needed them.

But Darid was shaking his head vehemently. "Maybe most of us are tools in a box—for sure, I am—but not you."

She tried not to roll her eyes. "Why, because you like me?"

"No." He dropped her hands, afraid he'd said something he shouldn't have. A pained expression came over him.

She was suddenly angry. "Fine." She stood up.

"I was there when you were born," he said.

"When I was brought in, you mean," she said. "I wasn't born here."

His eyes closed, and then opened again. Still scared, but there was something determined in the set of his jaw now. "Yes, you were. I was there. I saw it happen."

Judah's lips and her chest and her fingers all went numb. Suddenly, she felt afraid, too. "You saw my mother," she said.

"I was there," he said again.

He told her.

He'd been new, and barely ten. The Seneschal—younger himself, then, but not new; he'd risen early on talent and ambition—had looked him over, deemed him too rough for the House and sent him to the outbuildings, where he'd been assigned to the kennels. He'd been relieved at first, because he liked dogs, but then he met the hounds and they weren't dogs. They were enormous slavering beasts, coats as thick and coarse as the wolf pelt he'd once seen a trader wearing in the Beggar's Market. Cold eyes, flat faces. Flapless ears to provide small targets, not much more than bare holes in their skulls. Standing, the biggest of the hounds could look him in the eye. One glimpse of those dead yellow eyes, and Darid knew he was less than nothing to an animal like that.

Barr, the kennelmaster, spoke to them in grunts and growls that were almost barks, themselves. He carried a knobbed length of wood as big around as Darid's arm and used it to beat the hounds when they didn't obey immediately; he beat Darid with it, too, and for the same reason. Once he'd beaten Darid so badly that the boy thought his ribs would never stop hurting. (One of them never did; even when he was an adult, he could still feel the place where the stick had landed.) Another time, Barr had beaten one of the hounds to death, right there in the kennel. A young male, an upstart. It had snapped at Barr's leg. Ten minutes later it was dead. The other hounds lolled, and panted and watched.

"Why don't they attack him?" Darid asked the older kennel boy, Jon, afterward.

"Because Barr runs the pack," Jon had said.

Barr left the dead hound in the kennel yard for the others to eat. When the meat was gone, he told Darid to throw the bones in the midden yard, but leave the skull. There were two ways to be with the hounds, Jon had told him: you could take Barr's route, and try to brutalize them into obedience, or you could cower, let them tackle you and bite at your neck and go limp, to show submission, and hope that would be enough. When he went in for the bones, Darid took the latter route, and Barr and the others laughed heartily, seeing him down on his back like a puppy. As they'd laughed, the three biggest males sniffed and nipped at Darid, their muzzles still spotted with their pack mate's blood. One put its jaws around his neck and shook its head—lightly, almost experimentally, but it was enough to make Darid's heart pound in his sore chest. With one grunt from Barr, he knew, the jaws would clamp down, the nips and buffets turn brutal. In a few days, another kennel boy would creep in to get his bones.

One night, Darid, asleep in the corner under a blanket, heard voices out in the kennel yard. The noise in itself wasn't enough to wake him; Lady Clorin's birthing time had come, and the House and grounds were full of strange people come inside to see if she'd finally have a baby that lived. People he'd never seen the likes of, even in Highfall: people who teetered on high wooden heels carved like flowers and whose arms were so thickly hung with gold bracelets that it was a wonder they could move their arms. And some of these people came to peek at the hounds through the fence, to squeal and laugh and exclaim about the stink. They often came late at night, when they were drunk. Over the last few weeks of Lady Clorin's lying-in, Darid had grown used to ignoring them.

These voices were different. There was laughter, but there was also crying and pleading. That combination didn't mean anything good. Sometimes Barr and his men would catch an unlucky staff girl, a dairymaid or even a House girl running an errand, and tease and threaten her with the hounds until she promised to do whatever they wanted. Sometimes it was a boy they caught, which made Darid very grateful—and very ashamed at being grateful—for his broad, plain face that nobody seemed to think much of. The older kennel boy, Jon, was pretty. Darid knew he had it worse.

Darid closed his eyes tight, trying to will himself back to sleep. But he couldn't close his ears. The hounds snarled. He could hear excitement in their voices, and in the voices of the kennelmen, too. When the screams started he gave up pretending to be asleep and tried, instead, to pretend he was in his mother's kitchen with his sisters. It was the baby who was screaming, he told himself, with hunger or tiredness or who even knew with babies, and anyway the baby would not be hungry now because he was here, and a messenger would bring his mother a shiny coin every month. He did not want to but he could pick out two screaming voices, one female and one male. That was Nell, then; Frederick from next door had taken her doll again, her one and only doll, her most special special. Darid had trounced Fred for that, the last time he'd done it, and then he'd shown Nellie how to do a little trouncing of her own. That was all he was hearing. Nell and Fred.

But the screams rose. They were beyond pain now. They were beyond anything Darid had ever heard. His imagination snapped and broke on that terrifying animal noise. He could only clutch his hands over his ears and wait for it to be over. Eventually it was. The screams trailed away, became whimpers. Then they stopped.

Jon came in and dropped down next to Darid, breathing hard and ragged.

"What's happening?" Darid said.

"Two people snuck in past the Wall. Man and a woman. Lord Elban said to feed them to the hounds. So we did. Awful. Awful." Darid felt Jon move up close against him. The other boy's skin was clammy and he, too, was shaking. Jon's thin arms slid around Darid's middle and his nose pressed to the back of Darid's neck. "Awful."

Darid stayed quiet and still. Some people adapted to life inside better than others, an undercook had told him. Jon— who, to tell the truth, had probably always been a bit simple— had not adjusted well, for all that he'd been here three years longer than Darid. Living at the mercy of Barr and the others probably hadn't helped. During the day Jon was all bluster but at night, sometimes, he was like this: clingy, needy. His hands wandered. Out in Marketside, where survival in pairs was easier, Darid had known men who lived with men and women who lived with women. But what Jon wanted was different. After three years under Barr and the rest, the line inside him that should have divided what was okay to do from what wasn't had started to blur. Darid was learning how to handle him, to put him off gently enough that the older boy still thought they were friends. But Jon was getting bigger and officially he was in charge of Darid, and Darid knew there would be a time when Darid would say no, and Jon would simply ignore it.

But the night of the screams wasn't that night. Jon tried to bring Darid's hand to his crotch, but when Darid feigned a yawn and pulled his hand away, Jon let go and rolled away to take care of his own business. In a few minutes there came a soft grunt, and then Jon rolled back, pulled Darid close again, and went to sleep. As Darid lay in the dark and the filth, Jon's body twined over his like the ivy that climbed the Wall, the other boy's soft breath in his ear didn't drive out the memory of the screaming, not at all. The knowledge that this was now Darid's life made him so weary he could barely gather the strength to breathe himself.

He still heard voices outside the kennel but soon they, too, were gone. Barr would be too keyed up after the slaughter; he and the others would want to find other staff, share the story. Darid waited for silence to descend over the kennel.

But it didn't. There was a noise. An unsteady, gurgling noise. He closed his eyes and pretended it wasn't there. Then he told himself it was none of his business, and there was nothing he could do, and it was better not to see, anyway.

None of this worked.

Finally, carefully, he extricated himself from Jon's grasp and crept out of the kennel. Inside the yard itself, several lumpy piles of various sizes were discernable in the moonlight. Most of the hounds had retreated to the corners, chewing objects that Darid didn't like to think about, but one still hunched in the middle worrying at the largest of the piles. Darid had good ears that hadn't been boxed too many times and he knew, as much as he didn't want to, that the large pile was the source of the gurgling; the pile was a person, and the person was still alive.

Barr had his own special beating stick, but for lesser members of the kennel staff, there was a communal bucket of similar weapons just inside the door. For the first time ever, Darid picked one up. Slowly, he unchained the gate and slipped through. Avoiding the piles, and ignoring the new gruesome smells that threaded their way through the ordinary ones, he walked to the hound in the middle. It paid him no mind. He wasn't a threat. He was barely even worth noticing.

As quietly as he could, Darid made a noise in his throat that he hoped sounded like Barr's *leave-it* noise.

The hound growled faintly.

Darid lifted the stick, not sure if he could use it. He had never hit an animal before and his hands shook. But then the person took in a deep, rattling breath, and twitched all over, and Darid brought the stick down as hard as he could, right between the hound's eyes. It yelped, startled and jumped back. The growl deepened.

"Back," Darid said under his breath, and hit it again. The feeling of the stick hitting living flesh was extremely unpleasant.

The hound shook off the blow, confused. It made a motion toward the dying person in front of it again, and Darid hit it one more time. "No." His voice sounded stronger this time. "Mine."

The hound glared at him. Then it picked something up— unfortunately, Darid got a good enough look to identify it as a hand, with a decent bit of arm attached—and wandered off, as if that had been its intention all along. Quickly, before it could change its mind, Darid dropped the stick and hooked his hands beneath the shoulders of the mauled body in front of him. He dragged it out of the kennel yard, locked the gate behind him, and then crouched down next to the body, feeling sick. The head had been partially scalped, but the hair that was left was dark, possibly with blood, and tightly braided. A woman. She was still breathing, but not for long. He glanced around quickly; if Barr caught him, he would be in serious trouble. A tiny voice inside asked him why he'd even bothered risking it.

Because he couldn't let the woman be eaten alive like her companion had been, that was why. There wasn't much left of her face and nothing left of her ears. He doubted she could even still hear him. Both hands were gone. She should not have still been alive. He put a hand on her shoulder. "It's okay," he said, although it wasn't.

Out of the corner of his eye: motion. Then again.

The hounds had torn open her abdomen. He didn't want to see it. But there was the movement again—was it her breathing? No, he could hear that. The movement didn't match. He steeled himself, and looked closer.

Then he stifled a cry and scuttled back from the woman. He didn't want to believe what he'd seen. It was unbelievable. It was unthinkable. But then the movement came again and suddenly he was running. Toward the House, toward people. He was new enough, inside, that the only thought in his head was to find his mother, that she would know what to do. Because he didn't. He didn't know. He couldn't even think straight.

He found himself in the courtyard. Bizarrely, it was empty—the courtyard was never empty—except for a single woman. A city woman, by her clothes, about the same age as his mother. Her blond hair was luminous in the moonlight, her head cocked as if she were listening for something. He didn't know why she was standing there doing nothing. He didn't know why there was nobody else around.

Then, as if she'd known he would be there, she turned toward him. "Help," he said, panting. She was not his mother but she would do. "I need help." He grabbed her hand.

And found himself lying on the cobbles. He hadn't seen her push him down but she must have. Or had he fallen? A big satchel hung across her body, the biggest he'd ever seen. She towered over him, pale and fierce, and for a moment he thought she was going to kick him. Instead, she said, "Sorry. I'm edgy. Show me where."

When it was over he would marvel that she'd managed to keep up with him with such a big satchel, because he had run as fast as he could. The gardens would have been quicker but staff weren't allowed there unless they were working, so he led her down the rough service path by the Wall. Miraculously, he didn't trip and neither did she. The trip back to the kennel seemed to take only a fraction of the time it had taken him to run to the courtyard, but trips back always felt shorter. It seemed only moments before the blonde woman knelt next to the mauled body outside the kennels. There was still nobody else around. Incredibly, the thing was still breathing.

Not *thing*. Woman.

He expected the blonde woman to react to the wreck of flesh before her, but she only made a small pitying noise. She laid a hand on the woman's bloodied breastbone—her fingers twitched over it for a second first—and closed her eyes, as if praying.

Darid had not brought her here to pray. "But—she's—"

"I know," the strange woman said, eyes still closed. Then, to Darid's relief, she opened them; nodded briskly, opened the enormous satchel, and began digging through it. A moment later, her hand emerged with a short, fat knife. Like her hair, it seemed to glow.

Unceremoniously, she bent over the dying woman's abdomen, and cut. The sound was like fabric tearing. Darid squeezed his eyes shut and oh, lords, he would rather be anywhere else than here right now, he would rather be back in the kennel with Jon or fighting the hounds or being kicked to death by Barr.

"There," the woman with the knife said. Gently, almost crooning. "There, brave girl. Almost done." In a normal voice: "There's a towel in my satchel. Get it for me."

Still managing not to look, he opened his eyes a slit. Just enough to see the bag. Inside, he did, indeed, see towels, and soft blankets, and a metal tool he remembered from the night his second sister was born. Forceps.

"You're a midwife," he said, startled. "How are you a midwife?" The coincidence—the impossibility—of having stumbled upon exactly the person he needed, in exactly the place he needed her, with no impediments and no difficulties, was so huge and overwhelming that he forgot to be scared, forgot to keep his eyes closed. So he was watching the midwife, stunned, as she reached inside the body of the dying woman, and brought out an impossibly small baby, long cord still attached.

It would be dead, he thought fuzzily. Surely it would be dead. But then one miniature fist moved, and the head, and he heard a thin, weak wail.

"Towel, please," the midwife said.

He had been unable to look. Now he was unable to look away. He fumbled blindly in the satchel for a towel and thrust it toward the midwife with both hands, like a shield. He could not have been more shocked when, rather than take it, the midwife put the new creature down on top of it. In his hands. It was a girl. That was unsurprising. In Darid's experience, all babies were girls.

The midwife was rooting through the satchel again, this time for a ball of twine. She tied off the baby's cord and then cut it with another flick of the knife (as black as night now). Instinctively, Darid wrapped the towel around the baby and clutched her gently to his body. She had an alarming shock of dark hair, he noticed. Like her mother, maybe. He found himself filled with a deep, gentle joy. He hadn't felt anything like this in months, not since he'd come inside, and maybe he hadn't felt it ever. That something so new, so full of potential, could escape unscathed from the horror that the hounds had left—that life could persist through such depravity—it was as if he had a hearth full of embers inside him, and as the tiny face frowned and yawned a gentle breeze caressed them, and they came to life.

Then he saw the midwife, sitting back on her heels, watching him with a faint, sad smile. "Was going to tell you how to hold her," she said, "but you're doing fine, aren't you?" Then she turned back to the ruined body of the baby's mother, who no longer seemed quite so horrifying to Darid. She put a hand back on the woman's breastbone—which, Darid saw now, was nearly the only unscathed part of her—and, as if in answer, the dying woman let out one last rattle and was still.

"Well, that's that." Slowly, the midwife climbed to her feet. She shook the dust off her skirts and held out her arms. Darid found that he didn't want to give the baby up, which made no sense. "Give her to me," she said impatiently. "I've got a good hold around us but it won't last forever." And that didn't make any sense, either, but the authority in her voice was undeniable. He let her take the baby, then stood and watched as she unwrapped the tiny body, rewrapped it in an expert swaddle, and then placed her carefully in the big satchel. Making sure, he saw, that the forceps and other sharp cold things were well buried, and that the bundle of blankets and toweling was tucked firmly down so it wouldn't cover the baby's face. Then she brought the opening of the satchel together, leaving a space of an inch or so.

"You're a good boy," she said to Darid. "You did well."

He felt himself blush. "What about—" he said, and couldn't finish. He nodded toward the mother's body.

"She's gone. You can put her back where you found her. She won't mind now." With that, she started back toward the courtyard. Darid stood where he was and watched until the white glow of her hair disappeared, feeling a confusing combination of joy and loss. Then he looked down at the body.

"I'm sorry," he said, although she wasn't there to hear him. But it made him feel better as he dragged the body back into the kennel and kicked dirt over the place where she'd been, obscuring the puddle of blood.

By morning the hounds had stripped most of the bones clean. In a few days, when they'd lost interest altogether, Darid and Jon carried what was left to the midden yard behind the kitchen. During the day Darid continued to endure Barr's kicks and cruelty, and at night he endured Jon's feeble—but increasingly insistent—attentions. He had one free hour a day, one hour that was his own; in the past, he'd used it to crawl off into a corner and sleep, but now he found himself wandering the grounds. Watching the orchardmen, the dairymen, the shepherds. Eventually he discovered the horses. They drew him back day after day. The head stableman let him get close to them. When, eventually, he let Darid touch them, Darid felt it again: that same joy he'd felt on the night of the baby. He didn't know the word *serenity*, but he knew serenity itself.

He found that he could reach for it when he needed it; he found that it never entirely left him.

Darid finally stopped speaking. Judah felt fevered and sick. Weak, somehow, all the strong and hard inside her dissolved by the story. The pasture looked different. Darid looked different. The House spreading out in the distance looked different. The Wall looked the same.

"When word got around that Lady Clorin had adopted a little girl, I knew it was you. I always listened when people spoke of you, no matter what they said. When you came, that day we were weaning the colts, I was glad to see you. But I wasn't surprised. Not that I ever expected this." He gestured at her, at himself, at their proximity. Somewhere she heard a night bird chirping out its incessant, repetitive song: *I am here, I am here.* "I've never been the wander-and-wonder type. I have a job and I do the job and I'm good at the job. But everything about you makes me feel like—always, even that night, when you were just a tiny baby in a towel—like there's something I've forgotten. Something as basic as my own name, something I should know and don't. Like one of those dreams where you can't find your own house, when you walk and walk and walk down the street and it's not where it should be." He shook his head. "I'm not making sense. None of it makes sense."

No. It didn't make sense. "I suppose I should thank you." Her voice sounded flat and lifeless.

Puzzled, Darid said, "Why?"

For finding someone to cut her free of her dying mother. For carrying that mother's bones to the midden yard when they were picked clean. The two thoughts existed on top of each other, like layers of silk over the world. He had held her when she was a baby. He had seen her mother. He had seen her born.

Instead, she stood up, a little unsteadily. Her legs didn't seem entirely connected to her body. "I have to go."

"Should I not have told you?" The wondrous look was gone now. He looked sad. "I just wanted— It was amazing, don't you see? That I was there, and the midwife—just at the right time—and the courtyard is never deserted, there's always someone around—"

"Yes," she said, hearing the chill in her voice. "I'm a miracle, aren't I?"

He shook his head. "I don't know. But being there that night was the best thing I've ever done. It was the best thing I imagine I'll ever do. It led to you, being here. And so I know I can do good things. I know the good things I do make a difference. Maybe that's just the world. But—it's a better world than it could be. Isn't it?"

"I have to go," she said again.

Outside she stumbled up the path that led from the pasture to the House. By the time she reached the stables, she felt like she might be walking instead of stumbling. She had been cut free of her dying mother. The hounds ate her mother alive and the kennel boys threw her bones in the midden yard. The boy who threw them (the boy who had saved both of them, the boy who had no choice, the boy who sold his choices long ago) became the man who kissed Judah. Who *chose* to kiss Judah. Who would choose to, still.

She'd had a mother.

She found herself at the kennel. It was inevitable. There was nowhere else she could have gone but here, to stand on this patch of dust, a few feet from the gate. Was this the spot? Ten-year-old Darid, dragging her mother's body (her mother's body, she'd had a mother, her mother was dead, Elban had ordered her killed)—had he made it this far? If she dug down far enough, would she find traces of the blood he'd kicked dirt over?

Her mother's blood. Her mother had stood here, died here. She'd had a mother.

Then, another thought: this is where she'd been born. All those years of staring off at the lights of the city, and it was here. There was no family waiting outside, no home to find. Nobody like her.

In the kennel, the hounds bayed and howled at her presence, as they always did. Did they know? Did they smell her mother's blood in her? (She'd had a mother, her mother was dead, she stood in the place where her mother had died as she was born.) She stepped up to the fence. There were gaps between the wide wooden slats. She hooked her fingers into one of them, and on the other side a hound rammed against it, slavering. Its single visible eye was enraged, as cold and yellow as Darid had described.

How long do you live? she thought coldly at the beast. Did your mother eat my mother? Did you?

She'd had a mother. This is where her mother died.

Two people had climbed the Wall. Man and woman. Who was the man? Was it her father? Had both of her parents died here in this terrible place?

The kennel door slammed open. It had to be the kennelmaster; nobody else would have the nerve to approach her so directly. People feared her.

"I'd step back if I were you, girl. Anything you stick through that fence you're likely to lose." His voice was nasty. Of course it was. Nastiness would be a requirement for the job. She didn't know why the Seneschal had ever thought Darid suited for it. Then, if possible, the kennelmaster's voice got even nastier. "Now, if you want to pet a puppy, come on inside. We got lots of puppies for you to pet."

The hounds howled. Judah wasn't afraid. She turned toward the man.

He was older than Darid: solid and balding, an oozing pustule on his chin. Whatever he saw in her made him go pale. He stepped backward, slashing at the air frantically, almost compulsively. "Witch, slut witch," he said, stumbling in his haste to get back inside. Behind him, she caught a glimpse of a thin, dirty body with a thin, dirty face, one cheek badly bruised. The current kennel boy: wary, fearful. Warmth surged in her for the boy, as brief and searing as Elban's poker. She found that she forgave the boy (who darted away almost as soon as she saw him). She found that she loved the boy. It was a strange love but she was strange, she had been born in the dust of a kennel doorstep, cut from the body of her dying mother by a midwife who should not have been there to help.

She realized: the first kindness she had ever known had been Darid.

The fence shook again. She gripped the slat harder and felt the scar on her arm tug and pull.

He will chain you like a dog.

Maybe that's just the world.

From inside the kennel, she heard a thud and a muffled cry; then another thud, and the soft sound of a child weeping.

CHAPTER NINE

There were more guards on the streets of Highfall than Nate had ever seen before. Bindy said they were just City Guards, not the Lord's Guard; the Lord's Guard, she said, would have marched with the army. Nate asked what the difference was. "The City Guards have a white thing on their uniform. The Lord's Guard has red," she said, so he knew that what she called the City Guard was what he thought of as the House Guard. "None of them are what you'd want to meet on a dark street, but the Lord's Guard is the worst."

"Why?"

"City Guards take people all the time. Beat them up a bit, throw them in the cells for a while, then let them go. The Lord's Guard hardly ever takes people, but when they do, nobody ever sees them again. It's bad luck to talk about them," she said with an air of finality. "Where am I off to today?"

Nate sent her to Lady Maryle's with a health tonic and his

compliments—exactly the sort of thing Arkady had encouraged him to do, before the old man died. It was one of the few situations when Nate had come to agree with Arkady; the deliveries kept him on the courtiers' minds, and the bit of opium syrup Nate slipped into his tonics ensured that at least some of them would seek him out again. They paid him in coins, which were nice to have, and—unknowingly—in gossip, which he filed away carefully in his memory. Sometimes he thought he was stepping into Arkady's shoes in more ways than one. Sometimes it worried him.

But the tonic for Lady Maryle was less about money and more about finding out if Charles was still at her manor, glomming onto her youngest daughter and taking those vile drops. He sent Bindy over once a week or so to check. Lady Maryle, whose fortune was waning, was flattered by the attention, and Bindy—as always—managed to come home with exactly the information Nate needed. In her new clothes, with her hair neatly braided and a little coaching from Nate to smooth out the Marketside edges in her speech, she'd become a bit of a pet to some of the courtiers. More of a pet than she liked, sometimes, and he quickly learned to tell from her bearing which courtiers he should keep her away from.

The tonic for Lady Maryle had used the last of his opium syrup, so he was in the lab preparing more when someone pounded on the front door. It was the House messenger. His face was grim. "Nathaniel Magus," he said. "You're needed. The phaeton is coming."

And come it did, bare seconds after Nate had managed to grab his coat and satchel. The usual driver was at the reins, but his forehead was damp with sweat and he, too, looked unhappy. "What's happened?" Nate said, climbing in.

"Lord Gavin is unconscious," the driver said, and then they were rattling over the cobbles and it was too loud to speak.

Inside, the Seneschal awaited him in the young people's parlor. Lord Theron stood by the window, and Lady Eleanor—pale and beautiful, wearing an unreadable mask of cordiality, as always—stood with him. Both bedroom doors were closed and a guard stood by each. Their badges were white. City guards, then. He had never seen guards in the parlor before.

Elban and the Seneschal had kept the bond a secret, Derie had told him, so he wasn't supposed to know—but if the boy was unconscious, so was the girl. He wanted to see her, but knew he couldn't ask, so he said, "Where is he?" If a note of impatience colored his voice, he assumed the Seneschal would ascribe it to the emergency, and nothing else.

"In the bedroom." The Seneschal opened the door himself. Nate followed him inside, where the young lord lay still and pale on the bed.

"What happened?" he said as he peeled back the boy's eyelids.

"A training accident. His head hit a rock," the Seneschal said.

Nate didn't care. He cared about the girl. He choked back his impatience and felt for Elban's son's pulse, checked his reflexes, listened to his breathing. He was not examining the boy; he was examining her, through the boy. No broken ribs. A nasty contusion on the back of the head. He noticed a bizarre scar on the inside of each of the boy's arms: delicate, almost graceful curlicues, perfectly matched mirror images of each other in smooth raised flesh. They looked like very old burns, on their way to vanishing. Probably some ridiculous House fashion. He disliked touching the boy. Elban's flesh, Elban's blood. In the caravans, Nate would have done a quick Work to make sure the boy's mind was intact, but he was revolted at the very idea. There was no way the boy was anything other than corrupt inside.

Finally, he sat back. "He's lucky. His skull isn't broken. If he'd hit it a few inches lower, his neck would be. If he doesn't awaken within the day, I'll give him a stimulant, but I don't think it'll be a problem."

The Seneschal nodded, but didn't move. "I hear you're doing well in the city. The courtiers speak highly of you."

"I'm glad to hear that."

"We need to speak frankly," the Seneschal said.

If Elban's son was fine, the girl would be. The Seneschal must know that, after all these years, so this was something else. Internally, Nate was jumping with nerves. Calmly, he snapped his satchel closed. "About what?"

If Nate thought himself cool, the Seneschal was a block of ice. "The House Magus is an honored and illustrious position. In Elban's father's day, the holder of that title spent his entire life inside the Wall. Arkady was the first to live in the city."

"Why the change?"

"By the time he was called to the post, he had a wife and child. Lord Elban found them annoying."

Nate felt a bit queasy. "Arkady never mentioned a family."

"They died," the Seneschal said dismissively. "My point is this: it is time for me to officially offer you the position of House Magus, and for you to officially accept it. You have served us well, but we would not usually have appointed someone so young and of such unknown origins to the post."

"Lord Tensevery—"

"Has never heard of you."

Nate's chest seized up. The Seneschal continued. "You chose your cover story well. It took me weeks to get word to him in Duviel, and weeks more to get an answer. I assume you got your hands on one of the directories of courtiers, and picked the most remote one." He waved a hand. "Oh, I don't care. You're a better magus than Arkady was. And our system is too tightly controlled, sometimes. I'm glad to have a fresh perspective."

Nate swallowed hard. He couldn't speak. All he could do was nod.

"If you accept the position, you may continue to live in the manor on Limley Square, which is owned by the House. You will have reasonable lines of credit at the better merchants in town; other funds are available to you on request. If you desire rooms in the House, you will be given them. Although I would encourage you not to abuse that particular privilege."

Nate recovered his voice. "As Arkady did, you mean."

"Yes," the Seneschal said bluntly. "The post is a prestigious one. It is also complicated, and involves a great deal of discretion and unquestioning obedience. There will be times when you will be told to do things you do not like. You must do them anyway. To do otherwise would be treason, and the penalties for treason are severe."

"Death?"

"If you're lucky. Understand, magus: I am offering you the post, but I am also offering you a chance to leave. Say the word and the phaeton will take you back to Limley Square. You may pack your things and leave the manor. But you will never come back inside the Wall, or speak of anything that happened here."

"I accept the position," Nate said. Four words, so simple; and yet, they were the most important words he'd ever spoken. It was odd that such a momentous occasion took place in a dingy room with unswept corners, the only witness an unconscious boy full of Elban's foul, poisonous blood.

"Are you sure? It is a lifetime appointment, one way or another. If you do not leave now, I will have to tell you things that are...irrevocable. Once you hear them, you will belong to the House. You will not leave Highfall. You will not marry.

If you have children, you will neither acknowledge them nor pay for their rearing. When Lord Elban returns, he might revoke the edict allowing you to live outside. He might also disapprove of my choice, and have you put to death. Do you understand?"

Nate nodded.

"Do you still accept the position?" The Seneschal's voice was always formal, but now it was somehow more so.

"I do," Nate said, just as solemnly.

The corner of the Seneschal's mouth curled with something like relief. Nate realized this was the answer the man had hoped for. "Good. I'm glad to have someone with experience of the world beyond Highfall. Of course, I'm the only one who knows you've deceived us. Should anyone else find out, things will go badly for you."

A threat. No; a leash. But if Nate accomplished what he'd come here to do, and unbound the power beneath the House, things would go badly for Elban and anyone associated with him. So the Seneschal's words didn't matter. "I understand."

The Seneschal nodded. "Then we must speak even more frankly," he said, "but not here."

Outside, Lady Eleanor waited expectantly. The Seneschal said, "Lord Gavin will be fine. Nathaniel Magus believes he will awaken within the day. I have offered him the position of House Magus, and he has accepted. Now, he and I have some business to attend to."

Lady Eleanor's mouth fell open and her face came alive with indignation and anger. "Seneschal—" she said, and Nate was glad that fierce, implacable tone wasn't addressed to him.

The Seneschal barely appeared to notice. In fact, he cut her off. "Later, Lady Eleanor. We will be back shortly."

He bowed politely—Nate following his lead—and then

walked out. Nate followed him there, too. As the door closed behind them, he heard a strangled female cry of indignation.

"She is emotional," the Seneschal said. "It has been a difficult day."

"I'm sure she's worried for Lord Gavin."

"It has been a difficult day," the Seneschal repeated.

He led Nate down one corridor and up another, until finally they stopped at a heavy wooden door. It felt central, but after so many turns, Nate couldn't be sure. Before opening it, the Seneschal stopped. "One more chance to turn back."

No, there were no chances to turn back. Not for Nate. But he did wonder uneasily exactly what the Seneschal had in mind, that he felt the need for such repeated warnings. "Forward," he said.

The Seneschal nodded and produced a heavy set of keys. Effortlessly, he found the one that fit the keyhole in the wooden door and pushed it open. The room beyond was the grandest Nate had ever been in. The walls were lined with red silk and bookshelves. Inside a glass-fronted cabinet were bottles of what appeared to be Sevedran wine; for the price of just one of those bottles, the entire caravan could have eaten for months, and skipped the hokey, obligatory medicine shows and entertainment. An enormous settee and two armchairs, all of the same rich leather, were arranged before an enormous fireplace, and if the fireplace wasn't made of Ophenian marble then Nate himself was. The air smelled of expensive tobacco and paper and wine—but it also smelled stale and unused. Under that smell was another, dusty and metallic. Old blood, Nate realized, with some surprise. Derie could smell blood years after it had been spilled. He'd never been able to before.

"This is a beautiful room," he said, although suddenly the blood was all he could smell and he would have liked to leave. "Your office?"

"Lord Elban's study," the Seneschal said. "Generally, nobody is allowed inside when he's gone, but it's extremely private." He did not move to sit down, nor did he offer a seat to Nate. "What I have to tell you is extremely private, as well. If you were anything less than the House Magus, you would have your tongue cut out before you heard it. It involves the foundling, Judah. You've seen her. I believe you've even spoken with her."

Nate's breath caught, but "A time or two," was all he said, as if it mattered so little he couldn't quite remember. He considered shrugging, but thought better of it. "I found her pleasant enough."

The Seneschal's eyebrows went up. "*Pleasant* is not exactly the word I'd use. What do you know of her story?"

"I've heard all the rumors," Nate said carefully, "but I wasn't aware that anybody actually knew her story."

"Indeed. She was brought in by the midwife who delivered Lady Clorin of Lord Gavin. In her satchel, with the rest of her supplies. When Lady Clorin heard the crying, the old woman said the baby was the result of her earlier night's work, that the mother had died, and that she had not had time to dispose of the infant before receiving the summons and rushing to the House. Lady Clorin had lost several children by then. She could not bear the thought of the child being thrown into the river, so she begged Lord Elban to let her keep it. He agreed."

"Because he loved her?" It was a real question. If Arkady had taken a wife, anything was possible.

"Because he didn't care. He had his heir. Once that heir was proven healthy, I don't believe he had any intention of seeing Lady Clorin again." He shook his head. "He has come to think of it as his greatest mistake, taking in the foundling."

"Why?" This story was one that Nate had heard all his

life—but this version was different. Inside-out. He was fascinated.

"There is something unnatural about Judah. He hates her for it, but I don't believe it's her fault. I don't believe there's anything she can do to change it."

He was right enough about that, Nate thought.

The Seneschal shook his head. "There is no easy way to say it. What Lord Gavin suffers—illness, injury—Judah does, and vice versa. It has been that way all their lives. We have tested the bond in every way we can think of, and we have not been able to break or even lessen it."

Nate had practiced for this moment. His mouth fell open. His eyes grew wide. "That's—"

"Complicated?" The Seneschal nodded. "It is. Lord Elban did try to produce a new heir when the problem was discovered; thus Lord Theron, who I'm afraid was unacceptable even before his illness. I think Lord Elban would have gone against tradition to marry again if any of his other women had fallen pregnant, but none of them ever did. The last plague left some men sterile, and Lord Elban seems to be one of them." The Seneschal shrugged. "At any rate, he hopes that the Nali chieftains will be able to break the bond. They are supposed to have some knowledge of such things. Along with a great deal of gold, of course."

Nate had been basking in the knowledge that Elban's line really did end with the two boys, but suddenly his mouth went dry, and his feigned shock became all too genuine. He didn't know anything about the Nali. He hoped Derie did. "What would happen to Judah if the bond was broken?"

"That's not our concern today."

The Seneschal's tone was final. Nate closed his eyes briefly, took a deep breath, and tried to compose himself. At least his discomfiture would seem genuine, he thought wryly. "So she's in the same condition as Lord Gavin?"

"Yes, but if he will recover, so will she. That's not the problem."

"What is, then?"

The Seneschal picked up the poker from the cold fireplace and put it down again. "Judah is...well, she's clever, and she's bored. When they were children that led to mischief. Now it leads to actual trouble." His mouth went thin. "She's had an affair with a staff member. Against my explicit orders, I might add. I knew all about it, although I'm sure she thought she was being very secretive. Nothing in this city happens without my knowledge." Nate caught a hint of smugness in the man's tone. "I figured that once she was caught, it would serve as a relatively harmless way to demonstrate to her that my prohibition was serious. But that's also not the problem."

Nate went cold. "Is she pregnant?"

"Unclear, as of yet. But that's not the problem, either. The problem is that she was with the man when Lord Gavin was injured. She collapsed. The man was understandably alarmed, as anyone would be. He picked her up and ran with her to the House. Burst into the great hall calling for help." He shook his head. "Considering that it will cost him his life, it was actually very brave of him."

Nate thought of Judah with a man: after all the years of sacrifice, the generations of planning, to be pawed at like a common *girl*. "He'll be killed?" Nate said, and realized that he took a savage pleasure in the idea.

"He'll have to be. We can't have a repeat of this incident. The man's punishment must be severe, so that even if Judah would disobey me again—and she might, she's willful—none of the staff will have her. It's a shame; he's head stableman, and I understand that he's quite good at his job. It'll be relatively

quick. Not too quick, of course, or it won't be a deterrent."
The Seneschal rubbed his eyes. "She might at least have chosen a courtier. I wouldn't have to kill a courtier. And she'll
be punished as well, of course."

"How?"

"She'll be caned." Nate's face must have revealed his horror, because the gray man smiled a tight, unpleasant smile.
"Yes, it's unfortunate. But the damned fool stableman ran
right through the gardens with her in his arms. There aren't
many courtiers inside right now, but there are enough to make
sure Lord Elban hears of it. And if I can't assure him that she
was suitably punished, he'll want to know why. We won't do
it publicly, of course, but the rumors will spread. When the
courtiers hear that she was whipped bloody for sleeping with
a staff member—which they never would be—it will rein-
force the idea that she's not one of them, and perhaps they'll
be less inclined to involve her in their little games."

"But if Judah is...whipped bloody..." Nate almost couldn't
speak.

"Yes," the Seneschal said again. "Lord Gavin will suffer, as
well. Which is why we need to do it now, while the House
still thinks he's recovering from his head wound."

Head wound. "I would not recommend this while she's
still injured," Nate said.

"I agree, but I don't have a choice. I'm telling you all of
this because you will need to be here, and I want you to understand exactly why what you see is happening. It may seem
cruel, but it's actually the kindest possible scenario. As I said,
Lord Elban will hear about all of this. If he deems the punishment not severe enough, he will order one he finds more
suitable. Shall I give you some examples of the sort of thing
Lord Elban might consider a suitable punishment, or will you
believe me when I say that none of us want that?"

His voice was hard. "I'll take your word for it," Nate said. "I assume I'll need to be here to tend Lord Gavin?"

The Seneschal nodded. "And Judah, as well. But you'll be with Lord Gavin during the caning. You can treat his wounds as they occur. He can't be drugged, because the guards will no doubt report what they see to Lord Elban, and Judah must seem aware of what's happening. We'll do it as soon as Lord Gavin begins to awaken. That's another reason we have to do it today; he will do whatever he can to stop the caning, so he'll need to be restrained, and I don't think he'll let that happen if he's fully conscious. You and I will bind him ourselves. I can see that you find this situation distasteful. Rest assured that I do, as well. If there were another option, I would take it." Then, as if to himself, he added, "A few more weeks and it might not have mattered."

"The shock might kill her," Nate said coldly. "It might kill both of them."

"You're here to prevent that."

No. That wasn't why he was here at all. He was there to take care of Judah, to help her find her power and untie the knot Mad Martin had wrought. "How will Lord Gavin react when he's put through all this pain because of her?"

"It will remind him of lessons he learned as a child, which he would do well to remember, anyway. But that's none of your concern. Do you want to examine her before she's caned?"

Nate gritted his teeth and said that he did, and they went back to the rooms where they'd started. The girl lay on a tiny cot in a dusty, windowless room off the grand state bedroom where the Tiernan slept—surely with the young lord, now that they were betrothed, and what must that be like for Judah, to lie alone in a cold bare room meant for a servant, while mere feet away the two more fortunate highborns took as much

pleasure in each other as they liked. The bond would trans-
fer pleasure as well as pain, but secondhand pleasure would
not be the same. No wonder she had been driven to find her
own. He hoped she had found it.

He still hated the stableman, though.

He checked Judah's eyes, pulse and reflexes, just as he had
Elban's son's. Aware of how he handled her more gently;
aware, too, of the smoothness of her skin, the warmth of it.
Whatever she and the stableman had been doing when she was
stricken, she was fully dressed now, if barefoot, so he could
not find out for sure if she was pregnant. He could feel her
abdomen, and did; but the Seneschal was watching, and unconscious as the girl was, Nate didn't want to undress her in
front of him. He hoped she wasn't—Derie wouldn't like it—
but even if she was, she might not be for long after the caning. Nate had seen it happen before.

When he had done all he could for her, the Tiernan pale
with worry and wringing her hands in the doorway, the Seneschal said, "Do you have everything you'll need, or do you
need to return to the manor?"

"I can make do with what I have now, but it would be better if I could get a few things."

"Then do so," the Seneschal said. "But be fast." With a nod
to the Tiernan, he left the parlor. Nate moved to follow, but
before he could, Lady Eleanor stopped him.

"Magus," she said. "A word, please?"

Her voice held the faintest unsteadiness. Nate liked the girl
well enough but found himself impatient; she probably just
wanted more of the contraceptive sachets. He filled his voice
with a deference he did not feel. "Lady, I'm sorry. I did not
bring—"

Her blue eyes went to the door the Seneschal had so recently passed through, and she stepped close to him. "Never

mind that." The unsteadiness was gone. Her words fell quick and sharp. "There's a courtier named Firo. He's a friend—sort of—of Judah's, and of mine. When you leave our rooms, turn right instead of left. There's a staircase halfway down the corridor. He'll be waiting for you on the landing."

"Lady," Nate said, "time is of the essence, for your betrothed and for Judah."

"This is for Judah," she said, insistent. "Please."

Something in her face was urgent and human, so he nodded. Outside, the corridor was empty. He turned right instead of left and found the courtier as she'd promised, lounging indifferently on the landing. Before Nate had come to Highfall, he'd had a picture in his head of what one of Lord Elban's courtiers would look like, and it might have been painted after the man in front of him: overstyled hair gleaming with oil, garish clothes, gaudy jewels on every available appendage. No doubt the jewels had been mined by slaves in the Barriers. No doubt this courtier, this Firo, knew that, and didn't care.

"Well, magus," he said. "I see Lady Eleanor has convinced you to join in her little subterfuge, as well. What has she offered you in payment? Arkady could be bought for a few glasses of wine and an hour or two with a willing woman. Do you come so cheaply? I might require your services one day."

"She offered me nothing," Nate said curtly. "And I don't have much time. What do you need?"

The courtier's eyebrows lifted. "I need nothing, good magus. We are on a mission of mercy. Would you care to see my rooms?"

"As you wish."

The courtier looked him up and down in a way that Nate was not entirely comfortable with, and rolled his eyes dramatically. "What I wish is that this was a different kind of story entirely, my lovely young magus, but oh, well. Maybe another time." Then he smiled. "You look shocked, magus. Do you disapprove of my predilections?"

"They're...unproductive," Nate said.

"How quaint. Have you been visiting with my father?" Firo laughed. "I assume that you mean un-reproductive. There's no shortage of babies in the world, magus, but there is a distinct shortage of delight."

"I'm not here for your delight, and I'm not here for you."

Firo drew himself up. "All business, then? Fair enough. Onward, good sir. To the guest rooms." Picking up a large bundle that Nate hadn't noticed from the floor—a bundle which clanked softly—Firo led Nate downstairs, through a rather utilitarian corridor to a grander, more sumptuously appointed one, studded with highly polished doors. Nate guessed that they led to the rooms the courtiers paid handsomely to keep. The door Firo opened was halfway down; the room behind it was a riot of color, lushly carpeted and sparkling with glass, although the narrow bed seemed at odds with Firo's licentious manner. In the middle of the room, holding himself stiffly without touching anything, stood a huge man wearing drab staff clothes. His hugeness was mostly in his arms and shoulders, which told the story of a lifetime of hard work; his curly hair was damp with sweat, and his broad, ordinary face was twisted with worry and sadness and an exhausted sort of resignation. There was a smell in the room that did not match the furnishings, a smell of horse and manure and leather. Add in wood smoke and the creaking sound of wagon wheels, and with his eyes closed, Nate could have been convinced he was home.

"Do they not teach you to sit in the stables?" Firo said once the door was closed, letting his bundle clatter to the ground.

Glancing uncertainly between the two men, the stable-man—for that was who he must be—said, "I did not know if I was allowed to sit, my lord. This is the nicest room I've ever been in."

Nate felt a pang, remembering his own reaction to Lord Elban's study. Firo merely said coolly, "I'm glad you like it. I had to pay a great deal of money to have you brought here. If we're caught, I imagine the price will increase dramatically."

Even more confused, the man said, "Then…why—"

"I suppose I like the idea of Lady Eleanor owing me a favor more than I fear death. Now." He kicked the bundle open with one polished, high-heeled shoe, revealing a leather cuirass with a white badge. Nate could see other pieces of armor underneath it. "This should fit, for all that you're freakishly large. Fortunately, most of the guards are also freakishly large." To Nate, he said, "Our Judah has interesting taste in men, does she not?"

Nate scowled, but he had imagined someone more handsome, someone confident and predatory, like the young Slonimi men who caused trouble with village girls. The stableman went scarlet. "Please, my lord," he said. "Is she—"

Firo pointed at Nate, who said, "She's fine. Nasty bump on the head."

The scarlet drained away, leaving the stableman deathly pale. "I swear to you, I would never hurt her."

"No need to explain," Firo said. "As I was just telling the good magus here, we take our pleasure where we find it in this ugly old world. Now—" picking up the cuirass "—how do we put this thing on you?"

"The straps buckle." The stableman's voice was barely audible. He shook his curly head. "My lord, forgive me, but this won't work. They'll come looking for me."

"They'll get their blood. You're being replaced."

Warily, the stableman asked, "By who?"

"By somebody replaceable," Firo said impatiently, "which

Lady Eleanor, for some reason, seems to believe you're not."
He shoved the armor at the stableman, who took it rather
than drop it—through years of having things shoved at him,
Nate suspected—but did not move to put it on. "Stupid man.
You're being given your life."

He stared at the cuirass. "They'll go to my mother's house.
They'll burn it down. My sisters—"

"Then go somewhere else. I swear, whatever she saw in
you, it eludes me." Firo shook his head. When he spoke again,
his words came slowly and with precise enunciation, as if he
really did think the stableman was stupid. "Here is the situation. Lady Eleanor wants you rescued, so rescued you will
be. You have no choice in the matter. After you're outside the
Wall, I don't care what happens to you. But I would not advise getting caught."

Showing a spark of nerve, the stableman said, "If I am,
they'll find out who helped me."

"They will," Firo said. "But it'll take time. I can make that
time very unpleasant for you. And for your mother and sisters, too, I suppose." He frowned at the stableman with genuine confusion. "Is there anyone else I should be threatening
to convince you to let us save your life? A beloved cousin,
perhaps?"

The stableman's muddy blue eyes went to Nate, who gave
him nothing. Then, slowly, he began to put the cuirass on.

In cuirass, helmet and greaves, the stableman made a reasonably believable guard, but it soon became clear that he was
utterly lost in the House. Fortunately, Nate was able to find
the courtyard where the phaeton waited, even if he made a
few mistakes on the way; even more fortunately, nobody they
passed seemed to notice that both he and the guard accompanying him were out of place and lost. Before he climbed into

the two-person carriage, Nate muttered, "Stand on the side rail," to the stableman, so he'd know what to do. Nate didn't usually have a guard, but it wasn't unheard of, and the phaeton driver glanced at the helmeted stableman pulling himself up onto the rail without much interest. Then his eyes widened. Despite his instinctive dislike of the man responsible for Judah's situation, Nate felt a surge of panic. If they were caught, it wouldn't be good for him, either.

"Onward," he barked at the driver. "Hurry."

The driver looked from Nate to the stableman and back. Then, eyes still wide, he said, "Sir," a new note in his voice—was it respect?—and cracked the reins.

It took scarcely ten minutes to travel back to the manor. As befitted a guard, the stableman hopped down first. He accompanied Nate up the front walk. "Come in, I guess," Nate said. This was not his plan and nobody had told him what happened next. Inside, he called, "Hello?" and was relieved when Bindy didn't answer. She'd gone out on an errand that morning and must not be back yet. He went to his lab and began gathering supplies: surgical thread for stitching tattered skin; the opium syrup he'd been preparing for numbing away agony; a few other, less potent things to ease pain and encourage healing. When he came back into the kitchen, the stableman had peeled off the armor. He was holding it awkwardly, and didn't seem to know what to do with it.

"Just put it on the table," Nate said. He would find Charles later, and see if the armor could be sold. "What you're wearing will work in most of the city."

The stableman placed the armor in a neat pile, clearly used to keeping things tidy. "Is Judah really all right?"

"She will be. Eventually." He considered asking the man outright if Judah could be pregnant, but decided it was a stupid question. Of course she could be; the question was whether or not she was. "There's a gate in the garden. You can leave that way."

"She just collapsed." The stableman didn't move. "I've never been so— What will they do to her?"

"She'll be caned." Nate found callous gratification in the way the massive man's giant body crumpled into itself. Let him be hurt. Judah would be.

But then the stableman said, "People die from caning," and the pain in his voice was so bare that Nate's pleasure evaporated. His fists hurt, he realized. He'd been clenching them ever since he left the courtier's room. This man, this stupid man, who'd meddled with things so far above him, who'd risked everything Nate had ever held important—and for what? For a few moments spent rutting in the stable.

But that was unfair, and Nate knew it. It was unfair because she was guilty, too, and because this man had run with her to the House when she collapsed, knowing that it meant his death. He forced his fists to relax. "She won't die. The Seneschal doesn't want her dead, and neither do I."

A spark of hope lit the stableman's face. "Can you keep her alive?"

"I can. She'll be all right in the end." And she would be, if Nate had to burn out his own mind as fuel to make it so. "Where will you go?"

The stableman shook his head, as lost as he had been inside the House. "I haven't been outside since I was ten years old. Brakeside, I guess. Find a barge to take me out of the city." He looked at Nate. "Can I give you a letter for my sister?"

"I don't think that's a good idea."

"No. I guess not." He sighed. "I'm so stupid to have got us in this mess."

With an attempt at levity, Nate said, "You're not the first man brought low by a beautiful woman."

The stableman shook his head fondly. "Beautiful, she's not. But she is…" His voice trailed off.

"Yes," Nate said. "She is that."

When Nate emerged back into Limley Square, satchel over his shoulder, the phaeton driver was waiting. He greeted Nate with a bow so low that his forehead nearly touched his knees. "What's that for?" Nate said, surprised, but the driver didn't answer.

Back in the House, he was taken to the parlor, where the Seneschal waited with the Tiernan and the younger boy. The Tiernan didn't look at Nate and so he avoided looking at her. "They're stirring," the Seneschal said. "Do you have what you need?"

Nate nodded. "I still advise against this."

"Will it kill her?" the Seneschal asked seriously.

The Tiernan made a strangled noise.

"You're piling two serious injuries on top of each other," Nate said.

The Seneschal dismissed that. "The caning won't be that serious. It will be unpleasant and humiliating, and it will leave her with a few scars and a renewed sense of obedience."

"Ordinarily, maybe. But with the head injury—"

"Perhaps you didn't understand me earlier." The Seneschal's gaze was as hard and cold as the stone floor they stood upon. "If she dies, Lord Gavin dies."

"Then don't cane her. Let her heal."

"For how long?"

On the sofa, the Tiernan stared up at Nate as if he were the hero in a campfire story, desperate and fragile with hope. "A few weeks," he said.

The Seneschal shook his head. "Lord Elban might return within a few weeks. So she will be caned now, with whatever mercy she can have, and she will not die. The first is my responsibility, Nathaniel Magus. The second is yours. Now, you and I must tend to Lord Gavin."

Elban's son was barely conscious. With a clever knot the Seneschal knew, Nate and the Seneschal looped the ropes loosely around the bedposts and then his wrists and ankles, leaving one end long. Then, one on either side of the bed, they each took up the two long ends nearest them and pulled all the knots tight at once. The moment the ropes touched his skin, the boy burst to life, and fought savagely, spitting curses as coarse as Nate had heard in any Barrier tavern. But the knots were very clever indeed, and the young lord's struggles only tightened them. When he finally gave up, and lay panting and heaving with rage, the Seneschal said, "She risked your life, Lord Gavin. I am sorry for the pain you must suffer, but it's on her shoulders." He turned to Nate. "Gag him before it begins."

In the other room, Judah was awake, but only just. Gavin's struggles had agitated her and the guards had to pin her so that Nate could examine her again. Then, sick to his stomach, he stood back and let the guards hoist her to standing, pained to see the limp way she dangled between them. They tied one of each of her arms to the tall bedposts of the Tiernan's bed, holding her upright. "She doesn't even know what's happening," he said angrily.

"She will soon enough," the Seneschal said.

Another guard entered with the cane itself, dripping with moisture—it had been soaked, to keep it from splintering. The Tiernan followed him. Her eyes were red but she wasn't crying. "I'm staying," she said.

"I would rather you didn't, Lady Eleanor," the Seneschal said, as if discouraging her from attending a particularly dull party.

Lady Eleanor's chin went up. "You have no say in it. If Gavin won't go through this alone, neither will Jude. I'll be here, and I'll be where she can see me."

She and the Seneschal locked eyes, a contest of wills so fierce that Nate could almost feel it, for all that there was no Work involved: the solid gray man on one side, the fair willowy girl on the other. But the fair willowy girl's feet were planted, her mouth a thin line. The Seneschal would order the guards to remove her; they would handle her as easily as they'd handled Judah. The memory twisted his gut, made the sick pang already lurking there worse, and for a moment he thought he might throw up.

But the Seneschal didn't order her moved. He merely nodded. "As you like."

"Stay away from her lower back," Nate said to the guard holding the cane. "If you break her spine or rupture her kidneys, she'll die, and there'll be nothing I can do." The guard nodded. His bluish eyes kept going to Judah, hanging limply between the bedposts.

In the other bedroom, the young lord lay bound facedown on his bed. When he heard the door open, he twisted to see who'd entered the room; his bonds were tight and he couldn't turn very far, but when he saw Nate, he cursed him, called him things that would get all his teeth knocked out in the caravans. Nate didn't react. He stripped the boy to the waist, as Judah would be in the other room. The well-muscled arms and shoulders already bore a few scars, but not from caning. Training scars, probably. And the weird curlicues. Which Nate suddenly recognized: a fireplace poker, like the one the Seneschal had picked up in Elban's study.

When the highborn finally quit cursing him long enough for Nate to get a word in, he said—laying out what he'd need, the threaded needles and salve and opium syrup—"You'll be

able to hear her scream. Do you want me to stop your ears?"
He spoke with no great sympathy. Elban's son, he thought,
staring at the boy's skin, touched with gold from hours training in the sun. Elban's blood. His legacy.

The boy made a frustrated, inarticulate sound. "She won't
scream." His torso rose and fell, rose and fell. He was breathing quickly, his arms and legs flexing against the ropes that
held them, testing their strength. A high thin tremor of panic
and fear colored his voice. "They trained us not to scream."

Nate would have liked to hear more about that. "I have a
salve that will numb the pain. Yours and hers."

Through clenched teeth, the young lord said, "Do you have
one that'll make it worse?"

"Why?"

"Because the more she screams, the faster it will be over."

Nate shook his head. "There's no need to be selfless."

"I'm not." His lips curled like an angry animal's. "I am
being absolutely fucking selfish. Make it worse."

Nate sometimes used lemon juice in poultices and he had
a bottle in his satchel. He soaked a cloth with it. The smell
was as pleasant and normal as a summer's day and as the room
filled with it, strange laughter began to bubble up from the
young man on the bed. Also in Nate's satchel was a padded
leather strap; he used it to gag the boy, fitting it between his
teeth and over his tongue. It would keep him from breaking
the former or biting through the latter, but it didn't stop the
thin sound of his laughter. A few layers of bandage bound
over it did, mostly.

He knew how the bond worked, probably better than anyone else in Highfall except Derie. Even so, he was shocked
when the first wound appeared out of nowhere on the smooth
sun-kissed skin, a heavy violet streak like a swipe from a paint-
brush. That one didn't break the skin but the second one did.

As each bloody welt appeared, the skin splitting apart like smiling mouths where no mouths should be, Nate pressed the lemon-soaked rag against them. He was impressed that his hands did not shake. The ropes that held Elban's son to the bed were soon as bloody as the rag. The muffled screams that escaped the gag were harrowing.

Judah's, from the other room, were worse.

By the time Nate made his way back across the parlor to Judah, she lay as if lifeless across the Tiernan's bed. She wasn't lifeless; she'd passed out. Nate had seen to that. The boy in the other room was in the same condition. She had bled more, though. Someone had thrown a towel across her to absorb the blood.

Lady Eleanor sat next to the bed, her face greenish but her eyes dry. "I told them to leave her here, on my bed," she said. "She's actually been sleeping in Theron's room since the betrothal, but—"

The Seneschal, standing over the unconscious girl, said, "Have you tended Lord Gavin?"

Nate peeled the towel away. It was ruined, sodden with blood. "He's fine," he said. Seeing her blood spilled like this gave him a pang. The only consolation was that none of the idiots in this city were smart enough to know what they were wasting. He looked for somewhere to put the towel.

Two pale white hands took it from him. He looked up at Lady Eleanor. "Leave it by the door. I'll take care of it," he said.

She nodded. On her way into the parlor, she glared at the Seneschal. "You've had your show," she said. There was nothing quiet about her now. "Let him tend to the wounds you caused."

"Lady," the Seneschal said.

"Without you here," she snapped.

He inclined his head and left.

The marks on Judah's back were gruesomely familiar. After watching them drawn in blood on Elban's son, they were like a map he could almost read. The Seneschal was right; there would be scars. But at least Nate already knew which wounds needed stitching. By the time he had the needle threaded, Lady Eleanor was back.

"I checked on Gavin. He's asleep, too. I assume—his back—" All the fierceness was drained from her voice.

"Like hers," Nate said, indicating Judah's mangled back. Then he remembered that this girl would be married to the young lord eventually. "There'll be scarring, but it shouldn't be too horrible."

"Oh, I'm not concerned about that." She managed a thin smile. "Don't think I'm callous. I assume they told you about the two of them. You saw the scars on his arms?" She was holding Judah's hand, although the girl couldn't have felt it, and when Nate nodded, she gently turned the limp arm over. Judah's wrists were bloody from her bindings, too, but beneath the bracelets of blood were the same fireplace-poker curlicues he'd seen on the highborn. His had seemed years old; hers were mere weeks healed, still a livid pink. "The one who's not actually hurt scars the least. Judah has all the best scars, of course." Her voice almost broke, but she held it back, and her face grew hard. She nodded toward Judah's bare feet.

Nate looked, then looked away. Oh, how he hated these people, he thought, as he sewed the bloody mouths on Judah's back shut. He hated all of them. All of them that had ever lived. He would hate them even if their ancestor hadn't strangled the world, all those generations ago. He hated them for this girl, whose soles were crosshatched with scars and whose back would be, too, now. When the whole point had been to keep her alive, to keep her from being hurt. They found reasons to hurt her anyway. Because they could.

"You're taking all of this very much in stride," Lady Eleanor said, wiping a wet cloth across Judah's forehead.

"So are you," he said.

"My father liked public canings," she said curtly. She dipped the rag in water again, wrung it out and began dabbing the blood away from Judah's wrists. He would have to bandage those, too. "But I meant—the thing between them. Elban says it's unnatural. Most people are afraid of unnatural things."

Nate tied off the last stitch on the worst split, then began on the next one. "The natural world is very big."

"You're kind. I suppose it's awful to say this, but I'm glad Arkady is dead." She picked up the girl's hand again. "Poor Judah. Her one happiness. Did he make it out?"

"He did," Nate said, and Lady Eleanor said, "Good."

The Seneschal was waiting for Nate outside the parlor door. Standing straight upright, not even leaning against the wall. "We can have a room made ready for you, if you'd like to stay the night," he said. "Dinner will be served in an hour."

Nate stared at him, dumbfounded. Sewing together tattered flesh wasn't the sort of thing that built up an appetite. Then he remembered that this had been Arkady's habit: to treat his patients, and then spend as much time as possible living like a courtier. "No, thank you. I have matters to attend to in the city. But I'll be back tomorrow to check their wounds, if you'll send the phaeton first thing."

"I will. Is Judah pregnant?"

"I didn't check." He'd been too busy keeping her from bleeding to death. "If she is, it'll keep a few days."

"Are you familiar with Lady Amie of Porterfield?" the Seneschal said.

"I think I treated her mother for a headache." The headache had been caused by the violent green dye the woman favored, for dresses and everything else. Nate had warned her against it but she'd scoffed and dismissed him.

"Please arrange to see her. There's a chance that she's pregnant, too. I need you to make sure that she isn't."

"Even if she is, you mean?"

"You can do it, I assume."

"Of course I can do it. But why does it matter if a courtier is pregnant or not?" He heard the rudeness in his voice and was distantly surprised by it. Apparently his patience stores were drained for the day.

"This empire is a machine. All the cogs must spin without impediment. She can have another child later, if she wants," the Seneschal added offhandedly, and then Nate understood: she could have someone else's child later, if she wanted. Would the maybe-child in question be Elban's or his son's—and which son, for that matter? He would not have suspected Theron, since the poisoning, but he supposed it was technically possible.

"I'll pay her a visit," Nate said.

"I'll let her know to expect you. By the way, I understand that you provide some of the courtiers with preventative measures. You're not to do the same with Lady Eleanor. If she asks, give her something fake. And harmless, of course." He ran a hand over his thinning hair and suddenly looked very tired. "Judah's timing really is spectacular. I hope Lord Gavin won't be ill long; it would be good for Lady Eleanor if she were pregnant by the time Gavin's father returns. It would be good for both of them, really."

They had been walking all this time, and now they came to the door leading to the main corridor. There would be no guarantee of privacy on the other side. "So, that's two possibly pregnant who shouldn't be, and one who should be and isn't," Nate said.

"As our day's work shows," the Seneschal said, as if he and Nate had spent the day building a stone wall together, "people don't always know what's best for them."

True enough. But Nate had no intention of letting Eleanor get pregnant. Not with Elban's grandchild. Elban's line would die with his sons; she, too, could have someone else's baby later, as far as he was concerned. She seemed nice enough. He hoped she did.

He found Derie waiting in Arkady's parlor, shoes propped in front of a blazing fire, tumbler of wine in her hand. She cackled when she saw Nate's surprise. "Read you like a book," she said. "Not that it was hard. You were practically shouting."

Nate dropped his things on the floor and himself into the other chair. "I'm tired, Derie," he said, and then, "She still lives."

"I know that, boy. Tell me everything else."

So he did. When he was done she said, "I hope you got everything her blood touched."

"It's in there," Nate said, nodding wearily at the bundle he'd carried.

Derie crouched on the floor next to the bundle and untied it eagerly. It fell apart: the rags, the destroyed towel, even the silk quilt from Lady Eleanor's bed. He'd told Lady Eleanor he would burn it all. Nate was not squeamish but when he thought of Judah bleeding on that quilt, he felt queasy. Derie pressed her face into it like it was a perfumed handkerchief.

"Good boy," Derie said, and stuffed the quilt into a big rough-spun bag like the one laundry women used. Nate hadn't noticed it before now, but she'd had it waiting. "Help me."

So he knelt and helped her, choking with revulsion as she

exclaimed with delight over every bloodstained scrap. Nate was no innocent but normally, when he'd dealt with blood in these quantities, it had been willingly given. It felt different. It smelled different. He didn't know what Derie planned to do with the stuff but he knew that anything marked with Judah's blood was too valuable to burn or toss away.

As she worked, she said, "The courtier can't be pregnant by Elban's line. I don't care which of them stuck it in her."

"You and the Seneschal are in agreement, there." Nate wondered if he would ever get the smell of blood out of his nose.

Her cane lay against the chair she'd been sitting in. She picked it up and used it to haul herself up. "Neither can our girl. Her babies will be too precious to waste on some stablehand. You'll deal with it tomorrow."

All this talk about pregnancies, those that should be and those that shouldn't, shuffled and passed around like cards in a game, and it was one thing to have those conversations with the women themselves but this way made Nate think too much of old dead Arkady. *Magus has power, he can give help or he can withhold it.* He much preferred the former. "Can I give her a chance to recover from being beaten bloody before I force a miscarriage on her?" he said wearily.

"Stupid boy. Of course not. You don't know how long that stableman's been having at her. Soonest broken, soonest mended."

The exasperation swelled into anger and he said, "That stableman is a person. The courtier and the young lord and Judah—they're people. Real, actual people."

Without warning, she switched her grip on her cane and hit him with it. Hard, on the side of his head. His glasses flew off and he collapsed to his hands and knees. "Maia and Tobin were people," she spat, and hit him again. In the side this time. He felt one of his ribs crack. "They gave up their lives for her, and you're going to lay on the ground like the weak-willed little worm you are and whine to me about Elban's foul blood?" The cane came down again. He felt a blaze of pain in one of his kidneys, exactly where he'd told the guard not to hit Judah. "I grow weary of dragging you along by the ear, Nathaniel," Derie said conversationally. "If you weren't Jasper and Caterina's son I'd drown you in the Brake like a runt kitten. I'd drain every thought out of your head and dance you like a puppet." Spasms racked him as the cane came down again and again. Punctuating her words like breaths. He curled into a ball to protect himself. "You were born to do a job just as *she* was and you will *do* your job and you will see that she does hers, and you will not whimper about her being a person, and I will do my job and refrain from beating you to death, as much as you deserve it, because we have come too—"

Whack. The old woman grunted.

"—far—"

His eyes were open and through a haze of pain and near-sightedness he could see Derie's pointed shoes in front of him.

"—to start—"

He would have sworn the shoes lifted from the floor with the force of each blow.

"—over!"

Then the beating itself was over. At least, it seemed to be. Distantly, he heard her stomp away and then stomp back and he used the time to survey his battered body, to guess which of the painful places would be enduringly painful, and which were merely bruises. "I'm sorry," he gasped, even though apologizing never helped.

"You're more than sorry. You're pathetic." Something clattered in front of him and she kicked him in the thigh. Not as hard as she might have. "You're a disgrace to your entire line. Sit up."

He tried. On the third attempt, he managed it. The clattering thing was his knife. "Draw your blood," she said coldly. "Right there in the dirt on the floor, because dirt on the floor is what you are."

He fumbled for the knife. One of the blows had landed on his wrist and his fingers were numb. Derie kicked him again and he managed to force them around the hilt. Then, awkwardly—he was afraid to put the knife down again—he unfastened his cuff, pushed up his sleeve and cut his arm, deeply and unevenly. The blood dripped onto the dusty floorboards and he watched it form drops, then bigger drops, then a puddle.

"Sigils," she said. "All the way back."

Shakily, he dipped his finger into the puddle. The warm, thick feel of it was familiar but drawing his sigil on rough wood instead of slick cool silver or warm skin felt debasing, shameful. As it was meant to.

"Nathaniel Clare," he said.

Next to his sigil he drew his mother's and his father's.

"Caterina Clare. Jasper Arasgain."

Then his grandparents, on both sides. His mother's mother had not been born Slonimi so that line ended with her, but Jasper's went all the way back to John Slonim. With each name, he drew a new sigil, right next to the one that came before. The sigils marched around in a circle like dancers around a campfire. With each sigil came the lightest touch inside his mind. When he could not remember the name of his great-great-grandfather, Derie kicked him until he did, and when he reached the end, he had to begin again, with the girl—with Judah. And Maia, and Tobin. He had to cut himself four more times to finish them all. The circles were as big as his arms could reach, all of those sigils and all of those lives spiraling out from John Slonim himself. By the last one the world was graying around him, but his mother's sigil still shone, distinct, near the end of the shortest line. He had never been much good at reaching across distances but he thought he felt her, not a stinging bee but a hand on his head, stroking his hair. Like she'd done when, as a child, he'd come home from lessons with Derie, weeping and beaten. Her soft, warm voice: *next time you'll do better, my child. My Nathaniel.*

When he heard Bindy moving around in the kitchen the next morning, he dragged himself from his pallet, which he'd moved to the lab. Thankfully, Arkady had arranged for running water to be piped into the sink there. It was cold, but it woke him up and cleaned off the worst of the blood. He'd kept bleeding during the night, and his bed looked like somebody had died there, or been born. He tossed the thin sheet into a corner along with his ruined clothes from the night before. He'd burn it all later. It would be unpleasant; that was part of the punishment.

Waves of light-headedness swept over him and, as always when he'd overdone it with the Work, things were a bit blurry: not just shapes—his glasses were still on the floor in the parlor—but colors and sounds and smells. He wanted to go back to bed but Bindy was here, and the phaeton would be coming. He hoped that Derie had found something worthy to do with Judah's blood. He hoped Judah felt better than he did.

And she might, for all that, because he felt like death. He was surprised and a little hurt that Charles hadn't felt him suffering and come to help, but with the amount of Work he and Charles had together over the years, Charles might not be feeling that good, either. Or he might be deep in a vial.

For the first time, the vial didn't sound like a terrible idea.

No. The phaeton was coming. He had work to do, for the

Seneschal and Derie and all the names he'd drawn in blood on the floor. Next time he would do better; next time he would not falter, would not fail.

How many times had he made that exact vow to himself, and how many times had he broken it?

He managed to put on a clean shirt and a clean waistcoat, and to tie his hair back like a real magus—on another day, the length of the resulting tail might have pleased him—before stumbling out into the kitchen. He had to grab at the door frame for support.

He didn't remember cleaning up the blood on the floor but he must have, or Derie had, because it was gone. Bindy stood at the stove, staring blankly at the teakettle, which was whistling. Nate had heard the noise but assumed it was inside his head. "Morning, Bin," he said.

She jumped, startled. He expected her to be horrified by his appearance—although Derie had not hit him anywhere it would show; she never did—but she hardly seemed to notice. "Oh," she said, "are you unwell, magus? I'm making tea." She pulled a cup and the tea box down from the shelf, then looked around. "I think there's bread somewhere." It was on the counter, next to her elbow. She saw it before Nate could point it out. "Oh." Then she picked up a knife, and seemed to forget what to do with it.

"Bindy, what's wrong?" Nate dragged himself to a chair. Fortunately, it was already pulled out from under the table. "Where's Canty?"

"Ma kept him today."

"Is he unwell, too?"

She seemed to have to think about this. Bindy was quick as lightning, fleet as a fox. She never had to stop and think about anything. "No," she said. "It's just, my brother is dead. The one inside. A guard came this morning and told us."

He slumped down in his chair. This city. This city. These *people*. Too weak to be angry, once again he wanted to kill all of them. What a full schedule the Seneschal must have had yesterday, with the whipping and two executions: whatever unfortunate soul had been swapped in for Judah's stableman, and now Bindy's—

Wait. "Where did he work?"

"Darid? He was head stableman."

Oh, no. Nate's face felt slack and the world telescoped down, shrinking to the size of Bindy's tearstained face. But she was still speaking, her voice bitter. "They don't even tell you how they die, magus. They just say, he's dead, no more money. Then they ask if you've got anyone else to send in." Suddenly, she sat down on the floor, legs splayed out like a baby's, like Canty. She started to cry. "Oh, this is stupid," she said through her tears. "I never even met him. He was inside before I was born. But we wrote letters. I made him a scarf. And Ma is so upset. She won't let Canty out of her sight. I had to beg her to let me come here."

He wanted to fix it. He wanted to tell her that her brother was still alive. But she would no doubt tell their mother, and perhaps Nora would tell somebody else, and soon enough the word would get back to the Seneschal. *Nothing in this city happens without my knowledge.*

"You didn't have to come," he said numbly, and then realized what *no more money* would mean, to Bindy's family, and knew that she did. And he hated the city even more, and he hated himself, too.

CHAPTER TEN

There was a time when there was pain and the world was soft and white and something kept her from moving her arms. She didn't understand and she didn't try to. When a straw was held to her lips she drank, and the fluid was bitter.

That time passed.

There was a time when there was pain and her eyes were closed but she saw, as if in a memory, Elly standing among a group of guards. The sound of ripping fabric. Tears on Elly's cheeks. Wrong, all wrong. Elly didn't need to cry. Judah had saved her.

Hadn't she?

That time passed.

There was a time when there was pain and the Seneschal's voice filled the room like stone and she could not breathe.

The magus, she could not remember his name, but his voice was there, too, and it said, he said, *I warned you*, and there was anger in his voice and a tiny cramped place where she could grab the tiniest sips of air.

But the Seneschal was the one who had warned her. Nothing made sense.

That time passed.

There was a time when there was pain and she fled from it, went somewhere else, and in that somewhere else she lay barefoot on warm grass while the sun sparked gold in Darid's hair and his face was happy, but something was wrong, there was danger, she wanted to warn him, but her mouth would not do anything but smile, she could not make it stop.

That time passed.

There was a time when there was pain and somebody in the room was singing, a high thin voice that cracked on its way up and cracked on its way down.

That time passed.

Time passed.

The pain stayed.

CHAPTER ELEVEN

Then there was less pain. She drifted up through the soft sea of white into consciousness, and she still could not move her arms or legs. She waited to drift away again but the current seemed to have stopped. All she could do was lie—yes, her cheek lay against something, that was the softness—and wait. Each rise and fall of her body was searing agony so she breathed shallowly. She blinked, and realized she could blink, that there was a difference between closed eyes and open ones, and also that blinking helped the blur around her coalesce and separate into specific forms. A bright blur became a window full of light. A brown blur became a wooden table, holding small blurs that sharpened into bottles and a large blur that was a pitcher and a pile of white blurs—bandages? Maybe.

She was in Elly's room, facedown on the bed. Some of her hair was in her eyes, blood-colored streaks across her vision like bars, and when she tried to lift a hand to brush it back her hand wouldn't come. She could lift her head, though, and did. Pain rippled down her back like burning water but she saw soft strips of cloth tied around her wrists, holding her down.

So she was *tied* facedown on Elly's bed.

She took further inventory. She was naked, but covered up to her waist by a thin sheet. Her scalp itched and she could feel a thick layer of grease on her skin although the sheets she lay on were clean. There was a stale smell in the room. Her hands were sticky with old sweat. The pain in her back was constant, blazing. Her head hurt. The muscles in her neck ached. Her mouth was dry. She wished that somebody would bring her water.

Her back hurt like the burns on her arms had hurt, but worse. Had she fallen into a fire?

She had been with Darid, in the far pasture. He had pulled her boots off and she had laughed, and then he'd run his hand up the outside of her leg, fingertips barely touching the bare skin above her legging. She had teased him: *Am I a horse you're thinking of buying?*

Then nothing.

Then Elly, tearstained.

Then the magus. *I warned you.* He had never warned her of anything. He wasn't talking to her.

A fluttering, sick panic surged in her and she realized that she was scared. She squeezed her eyes shut and willed herself to drift away. Willed it and willed it and willed it, but when she opened her eyes there were the bottles, there was the pitcher, there were the bandages.

Her back hurt so much.

There was a new sound. The door opening; whispering footsteps coming toward her, she could not bend her head enough to see their owner. She could only lie there and wait for them to enter her field of vision.

Dark trousers, a white shirt. With a flood of relief she recognized Gavin, his shirt loose and unbuttoned, his jaw bristling with golden stubble. "You're awake."

Something was wrong with his voice, or possibly her ears. She licked her lips as well as she could. "What happened?"

His unshaven face twisted into a smile. There was something wrong with that, too. "Where would you like me to start?"

"I don't remember," she said.

An empty armchair waited next to the bed; somebody had been sitting with her. He lowered himself into it. The way he moved wasn't right, either. He was stiff. Slow. "I was on the training field, wrestling. I got thrown; hit my head on a rock and knocked myself unconscious. You, too, apparently."

His voice was cold. That was what was wrong with it. He sounded like Elban.

"The head stableman ran into the House carrying you in his arms. Right through the garden into the great hall, with your hair down and your feet bare." He smiled that ghastly smile again. "We still haven't found your boots."

Carried her. Into the House. The panic came back, stronger than ever. "Darid."

"Was that his name?" Icy. Freezing.

Was. "Where is he?"

"I haven't gotten to that part yet." Oh, he did sound like Elban, he sounded exactly like Elban. Mocking and heartless and poisonously friendly. "Don't you want to know why your back hurts?"

Elly's face. "No."

"You were caned," Gavin said. "Right here, tied to the bedposts. Half-naked, with guards watching."

Ripping fabric. The top of her dress torn to her waist. A sea of helmets. The Seneschal, flat-eyed. Elly, crying. She did not know what she really remembered and what she could only imagine.

Gavin's glare was hard. "I wasn't there, of course. I was tied to the bed in the other room, much like you are now. Would you like me to take off my shirt and show you what your back looks like?"

She remembered that cold hard look. From when they were children, in the study. When they would not stop hurting her because she would not stop screaming and his face had hurt her, too: long past love, wanting only for her to shut up because he, too, was hurting. Blaming her, hating her. As he hated her now.

But they were both still here and they were both still alive and once Elban returned, Gavin would have hated her anyway, she remembered.

Was that his name?

Was. "Darid," she said again.

"Was not very smart. If he'd had the sense to send a stable boy with a message, instead of making a spectacle of himself, you and I wouldn't have spent the last week drowning in opium syrup. By the way, if you were pregnant, you aren't now. The magus saw to that."

"Gavin," she said, helpless, desperate.

"Were you pregnant?"

"My back hurts," she said.

He leaned forward. She sensed his scathing fury and for a moment was afraid he was going to hurt her. Then he spoke, and his voice was so frostbitten, so black and blistered with barely-controlled violence, that she almost wished he had. "So does mine."

Her eyes filled with tears. She didn't want them to spill over onto her cheeks, but they did. Gavin leaned back again, his anger touched with satisfaction, now.

"Tell me what happened to Darid," she said. Pleading.

"I'm very sorry, Judah." He didn't sound sorry at all. "I'm sorry your life is the way it is. I'm sorry you won't get to see everything you want to see and do everything you want to do, get married and have a sweet little cottage somewhere and lots of purple-haired babies. But it's not my fault any more than it is yours. Fucking a courtier would have been bad enough, but at least a courtier would have been smart enough not to get caught. But staff, Jude?" A bitter laugh escaped him. "How many lectures did you give me on that very topic? Don't fuck the serving girls, Gavin. They have too much to lose, Gavin. You're being selfish, Gavin. Selfish!" He pointed at her. "You never get to call me selfish again. Ever."

She couldn't even wipe the tears away. They ran unchecked.

Ticking off each point on his fingers, he continued. "Elly's upset. I've spent the last week in agony for something I didn't even do—and in case you're too *selfish* for that to bother you, did you miss the part where they stripped you half-naked in front of a room full of guards?"

"Why are you being so mean?" The question came out sounding so childlike, so powerless, that it only made her weep harder.

"Because I have spent the last twenty-two years defending you," Gavin said, "and this is how you repay me."

She was stunned into silence. Even her crying stopped. She had thought of Gavin in many ways over the years: as brother and playmate, as a cad and a spoiled child and a silly boy playing soldier. Her confidant, her conspirator; a glorious hope made flesh, because someday when he was Lord of the City her life would be better and so would everyone else's. Her love. Her burden. Her responsibility. Her friend. Never had she thought of him in terms of debt, or repayment, or owing. "You sound like Elban," she said.

She meant it to sting, but he didn't even flinch. Not even inside. "Maybe he's right. Maybe I do need to lock you up, if you're going to keep doing such stupid things." But then, maybe, the barb went home, because suddenly he looked exhausted. "Why did you do it, Jude? Were you that lonely? I do everything I can for you, you know that. Why?"

Now he was the one who sounded like a child. Dry-eyed, she said, "Tell me what happened to Darid. Did they let the hounds have him?"

She felt a sick burst of something from him. She didn't know what it was. The sadness vanished and he went cold again. "First they castrated him. Then they cut him open. Then they cut his throat. When they were done, they threw him on the trash heap. Whatever the crows haven't eaten is probably still there."

She couldn't talk. He stood and walked to the door. Then he stopped.

"They didn't spike his head," he said. "I did that much for you."

She didn't know how long she lay there after that. Darid was dead and it was her fault and Gavin hadn't even untied her hands. When she heard the door open again she didn't bother to lift her head. These footsteps were heavier, and the chair creaked as someone sat down. She counted her heartbeats in silence. Ten. Twenty.

"Well," the Seneschal said finally, "I did warn you."

Had it been him, and not the magus, who she'd heard speaking those words through a cloud of opium? Either way, she saw no reason to respond.

"I hope you realize how lucky you are that this didn't happen when Lord Elban was here. Your little arrangement with him would actually have made this worse, you know. You're not just the disobedient foundling anymore. You're his property, just like his horse or his soldiers or his sword. He might still have something to say about it, when he comes back."

No point responding to that, either. When the Seneschal spoke again, he sounded weary. "You must begin to think before you act, Judah. Elban might not be willing to kill you, but surely you realize now that killing is not the worst he can do. What happened here was the bare minimum that I could order, and still have a chance of satisfying him. I'm doing everything that I can to help you, but I can't promise that it will be enough."

She opened her eyes. "This is helping me?"

"Right now, this is the best help I can give you."

No point. She let her eyes close again.

She heard the Seneschal stand. "Nathaniel Magus is here to see to your wounds. If he thinks it's safe, he'll untie you. The restraints aren't a punishment. You were delirious, and we didn't want to risk you rolling onto your back." Apparently, she was supposed to say something to that because he paused, and after the pause he sounded stern and disappointed. "The magus has made sure you aren't pregnant, but he'll need to examine you again to make sure the bleeding has stopped. Do what he tells you. We won't speak of the stableman again. Maybe the House will forget and Elban will never hear of it."

Footsteps. Receding.

Darid was dead and it was her fault.

As the magus untied her, he said, "I'm very sorry for everything that's happened to you. I did what I could to help."

He had to help her move her arms down to her side. It hurt, a stabbing pain through the joints of her shoulders. Unlike the fire in her back it was a good pain, or would be, but she almost cried out. The shock of it opened her eyes; the magus crouched next to the bed, where he could meet her gaze with his own, which was concerned and genuinely sad. His glasses had been broken, she noticed; a thin crack marred the lens, and the frames were clumsily mended with a piece of wire.

"Everyone keeps telling me how much they've done for me." She relished the bitterness in her own voice. "And yet somehow I don't feel helped."

"I don't blame you. I need to see your back. I'm sorry, I can't give you any more opium syrup. But I'll be as gentle as I can." She closed her eyes. A stretchy pain was added to the burning one. "The bandages stick a little. I have a salve that will help, but in a few days, it would be good if we left the bandages off and let the wounds air. There are some stitches here that have to come out. It might pinch." Whatever the magus was doing now hurt, but not unbearably. He took a bandage from the table. "You'll have some scars, but I've seen worse. And you have some scars already, I see."

"They told you about Gavin and me."

"They did. It's very interesting. Lord Gavin really has healed quite a bit faster than you have. He woke up earlier, too, by several hours." There was an audible snip, and a tiny, almost insulting pinch. "What caused the scars on your feet?"

"Different things. Nobody ever sees feet." Darid had seen her feet. The last day had not been the first time. He had never said a word about her scars.

Pinch. "Lord Gavin said you were taught not to scream."

Darid was dead and it was her fault. Through gritted teeth: "Couldn't have me saying ouch when he stubbed his royal toe."

The magus's scissors snipped, snipped. "Whatever the source of the bond between you, I don't think it was intended to be used that way. To hurt you."

She opened her eyes. "Oh? Then how do you think it was intended to be used?"

Either missing her sarcasm or ignoring it, he said, "Maybe someone was trying to protect you." He put the scissors on the table next to the bed, and then laid something across her back, something cool and damp that quenched the fire.

"Then someone underestimated Lord Elban," she said. "Someone underestimated this whole horrible place."

"Perhaps they had a reason."

"Perhaps they had a sick sense of humor."

The cool damp thing came away. "Have you ever been out in the city?"

"No."

"Lord Elban is not beloved there," he said. "You are."

"Until they come inside, and everyone tells them I'm a witch."

"Well," he said, and then again. "Well. You're not like them. They sense that. This is just salve. It shouldn't hurt." His fingers moved across her back in long straight lines. The touch only stung a little. "The Seneschal said I don't need to explain this, but I'm going to anyway. While you were unconscious, I gave you an elixir that would end a pregnancy, if one existed. It...did what it was supposed to do."

Darid was dead. It was her fault.

"If you were pregnant, it was too early to tell. But you bled more than I liked, and you had a seizure. Only a small one." As if that helped. "I'm sorry. I wanted to wait, and see if it was even necessary, but the Seneschal—wouldn't wait." He sounded pained, almost embarrassed. "You can still have children. I'm as sure as I can be about that."

"I don't want children."

"You might change your mind."

"No. I was born, once, and look how I ended up. Look

how—" Her mouth snapped shut. She had been about to say, *Look how my mother ended up*, and it was the first time she'd thought of her mother since awakening, and the anger and grief slid back onto her with the weight of the entire House.

"I think the bleeding has stopped," he said very gently. "But I need to check again."

Again. He had done this before, while she was unconscious. The idea disturbed her, but what was the point of arguing? What was the point of anything?

"Roll onto your side, please," he said. "I will be as quick as I can."

He was true to his word. Where Arkady had been crude and gleeful, this magus was quiet and efficient. She even thought his hands might be shaking, but she felt so thoroughly dulled that she trusted nothing her body told her except the pain in her back. When he was done he said everything seemed fine and he would check on her back again soon. Then he left. As soon as he opened the door Elly burst through it, hurried to Judah's side and kissed her forehead.

"I wanted to come in with the magus, but the Seneschal wouldn't let me. I thought it would be okay, anyway. He's not like Arkady." Her voice was low, but her words tumbled all over each other on their way out of her mouth. Her blue eyes were wide and anxious. "It was okay, wasn't it?"

Judah wanted to reassure her, but she could not seem to do it. "I'm not pregnant."

"I know. Thank the gods, neither am I." Elly stood up and began poking through the wardrobe. Finally, she held up a white cotton nightgown. "This is loose. It shouldn't hurt you. Lords, Jude, what did I say?" Because Judah's eyes were filling with tears again. Judah could see Elly, eyes wide and startled, running through the past few seconds in her mind. Then her face crumpled. "Oh, no. I'm so stupid. I'm sorry.

They've just been—well, never mind. I'm sorry, that's all. Please forgive me."

Judah nodded. She swiped angrily at the tears, tried to sit up and failed. The motion made her sick to her stomach and her back howled.

"Let me help you," Elly said, and she did. Neither of them spoke. The dressing process drained what little energy Judah had and her back protested every movement, no matter how small. When she finally lay down on her stomach again, queasy and damp with sweat, Elly crawled into bed next to her and took her hand.

"Jude." Her voice was gentle, almost a whisper. "Did Gavin tell you about—the person we're not supposed to mention?"

Judah nodded. Relief filled Elly's face, but only for an instant, because Judah was crying again. She didn't seem to be able to control it.

"Oh," Elly said. "Judah, my love, I'm sorry. I'm so sorry for all of this."

"You were there," Judah said. "You were with me."

"I will always be there." Elly was crying, too. Her words were choked but fierce. "I will always be with you."

After another day in bed Judah was able to stand up and hobble around the room; the day after that she made it out into the parlor, and sat gingerly in her chair. By the time she could twist her head enough to see her back in the mirror, the shallowest welts were well on their way to healing. There were four wounds that would scar: three across her upper back, in an X with one double bar, and one lower down. She did not spend long looking at them.

Gavin was still furious with her. When she entered the parlor, he left it. His healing was further along than hers, and he was back to training; she even saw the sweat marks on his shirt that meant he'd been able to wear his cuirass. Judah wore one of his other shirts—Elly brought it to her—that flowed loose over her back, and her lightest skirt. The others, in their boots and tunics and summer coats, came in like creatures from a different world, smelling of other rooms, of outside. Guards stood watch over the parlor door in the corridor. They allowed Gavin and Elly and Theron to pass, but Judah knew they wouldn't do the same for her. Not by the Seneschal's orders; by Gavin's.

"I obviously can't trust you," he said in the only conversation they'd had since she left her bed.

Elly, scarlet, with clenched fists, told him, "You're being a petulant child."

"You're not the one who suffers for what she does," he said, stern. This new Gavin, the one who made firm decisions about everyone else's lives, seemed to have replaced the old one entirely. Maybe the cane had stripped away the last of the person, and left only the lord.

Elly wasn't cowed. "She didn't do anything you haven't done a dozen times over. And don't even try to tell me that's not true."

"It's different and you know it," Gavin argued.

Elly drew herself up and seemed about to say something else, but Judah said, "Let it go, Elly. It doesn't matter. I don't mind."

She didn't. She had nowhere to go anyway, and no boots to wear there. The dull feeling that had come over her when she'd heard Darid was dead had not left her. She suffered physical pain and the occasional burst of weeping, but both felt disconnected from the core of her. Everything important inside her was dead. She was like an unlit stove, except that she wasn't even engaged enough to be cold. She was just—there. Inert.

Theron sat with her sometimes. Which she knew would

have warmed her, if she'd been able to feel warmth: the new Theron came and went like weather, with little notice of those around him. But when he came into the parlor and found Judah sitting alone, he would stop and sit, too. He still didn't speak much. But he only sat in the parlor when she was there. Something in him seemed to think she needed company. She didn't think she did.

Once she asked him how things were in the House. He pondered for several seconds before answering: "There are more guards than usual. The ones with white badges."

"Really," Judah said, unsurprised. The Lord's Guard, with their red badges, had all marched with Elban.

He nodded. "And more cats."

She stared. "Cats?"

"Cats," he said, and that was the end of the conversation.

One day when the magus came to check on Judah, Theron was with her. The magus's glasses were still broken. Judah had stopped noticing the crack, but Theron immediately said, "Your glasses are broken."

Judah realized that sometime since his illness, Theron had stopped wearing his own glasses. "Yes, Lord Theron," the magus said with a bow. He'd grown marginally less servile around Judah and Elly, but still seemed nervous around the two young lords. "I really must make time to find a spectaclist."

"Give them to me," Theron said.

The magus frowned, but said, "Of course, my lord," and handed them over. Theron took them, then stood up and wandered to the door and through it and out.

"What was that about?" the magus asked.

Judah shrugged, as well as she was able: sort of a twitch of her elbows. "Theron doesn't really do things for reasons anymore." She turned her back to the magus and unbuttoned

Gavin's shirt, letting it fall down her back. As he began to peel away the bandages, something occurred to her. "How well do you see without those things, anyway?"

She heard a faint exhalation that might almost have been a laugh. "Well enough, up close. You're healing."

She twitched her arms again. Then there was the salve, and the bandaging. The magus was gentle but she could not help tensing as he touched her. Hands on her bare skin brought to mind either Darid or Arkady, and neither memory was welcome. Elly slept next to Judah every night—"Until you're better and Gavin stops being a child"—but actually being touched was different. The magus seemed to sense her discomfort, and, as always, was quick.

As she buttoned the shirt and he washed his hands, he said, "Have you been outside? Fresh air might do you good."

Wordless, she pointed at the open terrace doors.

"Exercise, then," he said. "I'll accompany you, if you like. You could show me the House."

"I lost my boots." She leaned back carefully, tucking her legs up under her skirt. "And I assume you noticed the guards at the door."

The magus nodded. He seemed very young without his glasses. Theron had been the same way. When you were used to seeing a face with glasses, seeing it without them was like catching a glimpse of a private room. "Are they there for you?"

"Gavin's angry."

"Because of the caning?" He began to pack his supplies into his satchel, a process she liked watching as much as she liked anything. Everything had its place. A leather case for the silver scissors. A rubber-lined pocket for the salve, another lined in silk for the bandages. The day Theron was poisoned, he'd called himself disorganized. He'd lied. "Or because you kept a secret from him?"

"It's complicated," she said.

He shook his head. "I can't imagine what it must be like, being Lord Elban's son."

"Gavin is nothing like his father," Judah said automatically.

"They were both born knowing they would eventually rule everything they saw." He took the old bandages and stuffed them into a cotton bag. "My mother is a healer. I spent my whole childhood muddling grass into water, doing what I'd seen her do. Experimenting, to see what was possible."

"Women aren't healers."

"Things were different where I grew up. Anyway, I imagine it's strange for you, too. He feels everything you feel physically, but he'll never see the world the way you do. His experience of life is too different from yours."

He seemed to expect an answer so she told him what Elly told her, every night. "He's a child throwing a tantrum. He'll get over it."

The magus lifted an eyebrow ever so slightly. Judah wasn't even sure she wouldn't have noticed it if he'd been wearing glasses. "On my way to Highfall, I passed a village where Lord Elban had thrown a tantrum. The ashes were still warm."

"Gavin is nothing like his father," she said again.

The door opened and Theron wandered back in, the magus's glasses in his hand. He laid them absentmindedly on the table. They were perfectly mended. Even the crack in the glass had disappeared. Something twisted in Judah's heart, a piercing stab that died as quickly as it was born. Theron had not fixed anything since the poisoning.

The magus picked them up. "Thank you," he said, surprised. But Theron had already drifted away.

Dinner came. Judah cut her food mechanically into pieces and ate it, though it was sand in her mouth. Gavin ignored

Judah and so Elly ignored him. Judah could feel Gavin's itchy, uncomfortable anger coming off him like an odor. All of them were eating as quickly as possible. Mealtimes were bleak, these days.

Suddenly, Theron put down his fork. "I feel," he said, "like there are conversations going on, and I can't hear them."

There was a silence.

"Nobody is talking, Theron," Elly said.

"No. Not here," he answered. "Everywhere else."

There was another silence.

Then Judah said, "Do you mean that people are talking, but they stop when they see you?" People did that to her. It could make a person feel crazy.

"No. I feel there's always a conversation happening." Theron frowned. "Conversation isn't the right word. Not talking. But..." He shook his head, mouth tightening in a rare display of frustration. "Things were easier to explain before I got sick. Maybe I knew more words, then."

Theron had never before mentioned the difference between what he was once and what he was now. The moment felt delicate, dangerous. Judah thought Gavin's gaze darted to her, the way it always had when something puzzled or disturbed him. She kept her eyes on Theron.

Very gently, Elly said, "Perhaps you should talk to the new magus, love. He's not like Arkady. He's a good man."

"He's not a bad man," Theron said. "But it's worst when he's here." His face brightened with inspiration. "It's like everybody is wearing clothes under their clothes. Layers and layers, all the way down. It's always been that way, but it's louder, now. Do you think the magus could fix my head?"

This time, Judah couldn't help looking at Gavin. "What does your head feel like?" he asked his brother.

"Distant," Theron answered, after a long time. "Like my thoughts are happening somewhere else."

"Where?"

Gavin was being too pushy. Too stern. Judah remembered what the magus had said, that Gavin was experimenting with ruling. He would drive Theron away; he would break the moment.

Sure enough, Theron only shook his head, and wouldn't or couldn't say more.

"Can you help Theron?" Judah asked the magus the next time he came.

"Lord Gavin just asked me the same thing downstairs," he said.

"What did you say?"

"I told him that his brother was alive, and clever enough to fix my glasses, and I didn't see a problem with him."

Judah cocked an eyebrow. "You did not, either, say that."

His cheeks turned pink, and he laughed; the same half-swallowed exhalation she'd heard from him before, as if he were afraid to laugh out loud in front of her. "No, I didn't. Lord Gavin scares me."

Now it was Judah who half laughed. "Gavin's not scary."

"Perhaps not to you." The magus spoke very seriously. "Although I would point out that he's had you locked in this room for nearly three weeks."

Being locked away didn't frighten her, though. Being locked away felt inevitable. She didn't say that. Instead, she said, "Theron isn't the way he used to be."

"Life changes all of us."

The cold stove in Judah flared. "Life didn't change Theron. Arkady's poison did."

"Like the Seneschal's cane changed you?"

The flare died. The stove went cold. "No. Theron used to be a genius. He still would be, if not for me." She sank back in her chair and took a bitter satisfaction in the wails of pain that rose from the rent skin of her back. They were less than she deserved. (Darid dead, Theron changed. All her fault.) And they were growing quieter, day by day; soon she wouldn't even have that. In a perverse way, she looked forward to Elban returning, and the new pain that would come with him.

The magus cocked his head, puzzled. Then comprehension dawned. "You're talking about the antidote."

"I didn't give it to him fast enough. I was a coward."

The magus's bare shock surprised her, but she didn't trust it. "Have you been blaming yourself for Lord Theron being the way he is?"

"You said give it to him immediately. I didn't."

"And I knew what Arkady planned before we even left the manor. Blame me, if you have to blame someone." He was sitting in the armchair and now he leaned forward, elbows on knees and fingers laced tightly together as if to control them. "How long did you actually delay, Judah? Ten seconds? Thirty? Maybe it would have made a difference, maybe not. The poison Arkady used was vicious. Even if you'd given it to him the moment we left, there was still a good chance that Theron wouldn't be the same. He—" he hesitated "—well, where I come from, we would have said that he'd dipped a toe in the black water."

Judah thought of the aquifer beneath the House, the vast expanse of silent water that bloomed through the living rock below. "What does that even mean?" she said, her voice harsh.

"It comes from old stories my family tells." He stumbled over the word *family*, like it wasn't quite what he meant.

"Tell me?" Her interest wasn't feigned. When she was a child, and still allowed to visit the library, her favorite books had been the oldest ones, with edges that crumbled in her fingers: old nonsense stories about talking animals and magic wells. When it was discovered that she liked them, they disappeared. What remained were mostly war histories, occasionally exciting and often bloody, but not the same. By the time Gavin had started training, even these had been forbidden her. She envied the magus his family stories. She had only the one Darid had given her about her mother, and she did not like to think of it.

His face was fond and sad, as though he were thinking of people and places that were dear to him, and lost. "They say the world used to be different. That a great power ran through everything: the sap in the trees and the dew on the plants, and the soil and the rocks and the grass. And the water: not just actual water, but also all the blood, inside the foxes and rabbits and great cats and—and us, of course. Blood is mostly water, did you know that?"

"So what was it, this power?"

His mouth twisted. "It was…power. Imagine that the world we live in now is frozen over, all ice and snow, and I'm telling you about a time when the sun was warm and everything bloomed. Cold and dead versus warm and alive. In this world, the power is invisible, but in the next world—the one we go to after we die—it's an actual river. And like any river, it flows to a sea. When we're born, we're made from the waters of that sea. When we die, we follow the river and make our way back." He still wore that half fond, half sad look. "When I was a child, I used to picture it black as ink, running across a great plain where it was always midnight. No trees. Just giant rocks and scraggly weeds. We followed a river into the north for a few weeks when I was very young, up where it's dead. I think that's where the idea came from."

"Followed a river into the north?" There was nothing in

the north but wasteland and ruins. "Where exactly did you grow up, magus?"

She meant it as a gentle rib, but he jumped as if something had bitten him, and said too quickly, "Nowhere special. One of the outer provinces. Anyway, that's what I mean when I say that Lord Theron dipped a toe into the black water. It's an overly poetic way of saying that he came too close to dying. I don't think you could have done anything to stop that." Suddenly, unexpectedly, the magus reached out and laid a hand over hers. "What they did to your back was horrific. What they did to the man you loved was horrific. They wanted to make sure you never dared love anyone again, but there are different kinds of love, Judah, and there are more kinds of people in the world than you can possibly dream of. They are not all like Lord Elban."

She looked at the hand covering hers, and then up to his washed-out blue eyes ringed by too-dark eyelashes. "Nathaniel Magus," she said, "are you flirting with me?"

He jerked away. "Of course not! No, never. I apologize if it seemed that way. I just— You seem sad, and I—"

She let him fumble, feeling only the faintest flutter of amusement: like a courtier must feel, burning people with words. Then she realized the amusement was the fond variety, and an instant after that she realized she was being cruel. She held up both hands in a placating gesture. "Peace, magus. I was joking. I'm sorry. It wasn't funny."

His lips snapped shut, and he exhaled with relief. "I was afraid I'd offended you."

"Difficult, but not impossible," she said. "Keep trying. Or don't, actually. Right now I think you're the closest thing I have to a friend."

"You have Lady Eleanor." But his cheeks were pink again.

"She feels sorry for me. You don't, do you?"

"No." He couldn't meet her eyes as she said it. She wasn't sure if that was a good sign or a bad one.

Two days later, she sat alone in the parlor. It was late afternoon, that time when the sun shone its goldest. Her back was the kind of sore that made her want to stretch, but she didn't know what state of healing her skin was in. Nathaniel Magus would come again soon—tomorrow, possibly—and she would ask him about stretching. Meanwhile she sat on the sofa, itching a bit from the bandages, playing solitaire on the empty cushion next to her. Relishing the silence and loneliness and hating it and anticipating its end, which was an interesting, queer mix of feelings.

Unexpectedly, the door opened and Gavin entered. He was sweating, covered with dust, and he seemed startled to see her. Which was absurd, because hadn't he been the one to give the order that she be prohibited from leaving? Where else did he expect her to be? His eyes darted around the room for Theron or Elly. But there was nobody. Only the two of them.

She made him nervous. He was almost as depressed as she was. She could feel it.

Wordless, he went into his bedroom. Judah went back to her game. Through the open door, she heard him run water into the basin and splash the dust off his face. She heard the wardrobe opening and closing.

In a few minutes he was back in clean clothes—courtier clothes, red trousers and a shirt with a ruffled collar—and wet, freshly combed hair. His boots were the high-polished ones he always wore in the House, and he carried his brown coat over one arm. He looked very handsome. Judah expected she would feel very drunk later.

But meanwhile, she could feel his indecision, the way seeing her twisted his stomach. Then he disappeared back into the bedroom. She heard the clipped sound of his hard leather soles cross the floor and the creak of the wardrobe hinges; then the clipped footsteps came back into the parlor and stopped in front of her. She flipped over three cards.

Something fell to the floor with a thick double thud. She lifted her head the barest fraction, to see a pair of boots, the leather smooth and new, the buckles dull steel. Too small for him. Just right for her.

"Elly's right," he said. "I'm being a child."

She didn't speak, but she picked up her cards so he could sit down, and felt something ease in him.

He took the empty seat and she caught a faint hint of cologne. "I shouldn't have let this happen."

Then she did look at him. His eyes were on her, frank and direct and relieved. She wondered if he meant Darid, or everything that came after. "How could you have stopped it?"

"I don't know. The House Guard does what the Seneschal says. Even the ones I'm friendly with—sometimes I get this sense from them that it's nothing personal, they like me okay, but they'd still love to take my head off if they had the chance. Today on the field they were all over me." He sounded and felt exhausted. "I could have tried to stop it. I didn't."

The caning, then. Something the magus had said came to Judah's mind. "Were you angry because of the beating, or because I kept a secret from you?"

"Both, probably."

"You keep secrets from me." She shuffled the cards, reshuffled them, tapped them into a nice, tidy deck. "You didn't tell me about Amie, or that Elban wanted you to kill Theron. At least, not until I dragged it out of you."

"That's different."

"Why?"

"It just is."

She bridged the cards. They came together with a swift, deadly-fast flutter. "You said that to Elly, too. What's the difference? Why are your rules different from everybody else's?"

"Because I'm not everybody else," he said curtly.

She became aware that she was angry. It was a slow anger, all in her head where he couldn't feel it. Its roots ran deep into the most fundamental parts of her: she was left-handed, she was blood-haired, she was angry. There was none of the surging heat she normally felt. She could sit, coolly, and consider her words. "Darid wasn't the only secret I've kept from you," she said.

Gavin frowned. "Don't say his name."

She could feel the small, shameful pain it caused him. "Why not?"

"I just don't want to hear it." He shook his head with disgust. "None of this would have happened if not for him. Elban was gone. We were happy."

"You weren't bothered when you thought it was Firo."

"Because Firo made sense," he said. Snapped, almost. "Courtiers talk and wheedle and convince. How a stableman could convince you to—"

She made another bridge. This one broke. "There was no convincing." He didn't respond, but she could see that he didn't believe her, which only fueled her anger. "I'm not a stupid little sheep to be herded this way and that. I have my own mind."

"I never said you didn't." He took a deep breath, trying to regain control. "When Elban said that eventually I'd see things his way and lock you up, it's not true. This—" he gestured to the door, and presumably to the guards beyond "—was a weakness. A temper tantrum. It won't happen again, I promise." He reached out and touched her shoulder. "It wasn't about me. It was about you. When you're here, in this room—I know exactly where you are, Jude. I know you're safe."

She did not remind him that he had agreed to lock her up the night Elban had burned her. Instead she said, "When I'm safe, you're safe."

He winced, then scowled. "Maybe. Gods, I don't know. It makes my head hurt, this thing between us. Part of me hates it. The rest of me can't imagine how other people don't all kill themselves from sheer loneliness." He took her hand, and suddenly she was inside him: a dozen small hurts from the training field, the still-tender skin of his back. A sick nausea unfolded into limp relief as he laced his fingers between hers. He was glad they were talking. He did love her. He was sorry for everything. He was also angry, and resentful and confused. She could even feel the sharper pain of her own back through him. The bits of herself scattered through her sense of him were like flat notes in an orchestra, and she realized that the dullness she'd been laboring under was actually a loneliness so keen it would have brought tears to her eyes, if she'd let it.

Gavin's hand tightened on hers. "Your back still hurts," he said. She was baffled—was that really all he'd felt in her?—but before she could say anything, he smiled. "Guess what I'm going to do tonight, as soon as Elly's done with the rushes?"

She managed one of her truncated shrugs.

"Have dinner with Firo." He laughed. "Elly insists. He wants me to talk Elban into keeping a garrison in Cerrington, and I guess I don't have a reason to be suspicious of him anymore. Do you want to come? We're having that duck you like."

She shook her head. She didn't trust herself to speak.

"This other secret of yours," he said. "Am I going to find out eventually?"

She nodded.

"Well, then, I won't bother you about it." He pulled on her hand and slid his other arm around her shoulder, pulled her over to him and kissed her forehead. "I'll never let anybody hurt you again, Judah. I promise." Then he let her go. Standing up, he put on his coat, winked at her and left the room. The confidence was back in his walk, and his steps were light and comfortable again.

"I traded us to Elban," she said to the empty room. "So he'd let Elly go. He's going to use us to send messages. He's going to cut us to pieces."

CHAPTER TWELVE

Seven days later, the four of them stood together on the balcony over the Lord's Square, even though the summer solstice was still weeks away. The Seneschal stood with them, a row of guards stony behind him. A sizeable crowd had gathered among the linden trees in the Square. Someone had taken the time to set up the courtiers' dais in front, where they were protected by more guards and soft scarlet ropes; many of them were already there, glittering and resplendent. Behind them stood the higher-class commoners—wealthy but landless merchants, well-regarded clothiers, factory managers—and there were a great many of them, too. Around the edges were the true commoners. The markets had been closed but the factory fires still burned, so there weren't as many commoners as usual. Most were still working.

No banners flew. People wore what they'd had on when they'd heard the drums. Judah had never seen the city in its normal dress before. The white-badged guards were a heavy presence in the Square. On her first tentative forays out of the parlor Judah had seen that Theron was right: there were more guards than usual in the House. Now, though, her eyes slid over the guards, barely noticing them. She realized that she no longer wondered about her mother when she looked out over the city; she knew where her mother was. But she couldn't help thinking of Darid's mother and his sisters: the one who could knit, the one who wrote letters.

The Seneschal had come shortly after dawn. His face had been somber but Judah had seen—or imagined—a faint glimmer of mania in his eyes. "A messenger arrived this morning," he'd said. "Lord Gavin, your father has been injured."

Nobody reacted. "How?" Gavin finally said.

The Seneschal shook his head. "It's war, Lord Gavin. This is what happens in a war. People are injured. Even City Lords." He told them that the army was marching back now. It would reach the barracks outside the city within the hour; an hour after that, Elban's own guard would enter the city itself, bringing the Lord with them. They should wait on the Lord's Square balcony, he said. It was only proper.

So they waited. The drums grew louder. Gavin stood in front, noble and somber despite the queasy excitement Judah could feel coursing through him, elated one minute and nervous the next. Elly was next to him, equally composed despite the fact that—as always—she'd had to be dragged up the stairs and onto the balcony, and now clung tightly to Judah's hand. They'd found Theron and put him in some clean clothes. Most of his attention seemed to be on a flock of birds that soared and swooped over the manors on the Square.

Judah felt like a bird herself, straining at the end of a tether. If Elban was injured—if he was seriously injured…oh, if he _died_—there would be no next campaign. There would be no life on the end of Elban's chain, no blood spilled for the sake of a troop movement. Gavin would be Lord of the City. Elly would be Lady. Judah didn't know what her own future held, but with Elban dead, it would have to be better than anything she'd expected.

And on top of it all: to see Elban die. To stand over his corpse. That would be sweet. Perhaps she would steal the corpse from his crypt and throw it to the hounds.

The drums were very loud. The day promised to be clear and lovely. Ten minutes after Judah caught the glint of sun on armor down the broad avenue at the end of the Square, she caught the flutter of Elban's banner, and ten minutes after that she could discern upon it the red-and-gold dagger that was his emblem. Below the balcony, Judah heard the grinding of the winches as the gates in the Wall began to roll open.

The officers marching at the front of the column weren't as battered as Judah had expected. Those who were courtiers— and only those from very poor or very large families joined the army—wore armor enameled with the colors of their individual lineages, and their horses' skirts and head plumes were still clean and fluffy. Here and there, she spotted a bandaged arm in a sling. Only a handful of horses rode empty, and most of those were clearly nothing Darid had bred. On the battlefield, the living horses of dead officers were usually appropriated by the living officers of dead horses, but because it was tradition to lead a fallen officer's horse riderless back into the city, the army would pick up any horse they could on their way home to make up the difference: buying them, trading them, or—more often—just taking them in Elban's name. The new horses would be dressed in the colors of the fallen and led as if they belonged. If they were worth breeding, Darid had always kept them. If not, he was supposed to kill them, but he'd confessed to Judah that he usually put them to work, or quietly let them out to pasture until they died on their own.

Thinking of him hurt. She didn't know who ran the stables now, or what they would do with the outside horses.

After the officers, half of the Lord's Guard marched on foot: first the spearmen, then the archers. Here, too, it was traditional to leave a space empty for a fallen comrade. A few gaps showed in the ranks like missing teeth but, again, not as many as Judah would have expected. It seemed to her that the ranks seemed smaller overall, but she'd never paid much attention.

"There should be more of them," she heard Gavin mutter on the other side of Elly. She could feel his dismay. Something was off, besides the numbers. Her brain sensed it, but she couldn't pin it down.

Next came the prisoners. There was only one this time. Instead of being marched in chains ahead of Elban himself, he stood in a barred iron cage on wheels, pulled by two outside horses. His arms were bound over his head to the top of the cage; he winced with every cobble, and Judah's own shoulders ached in sympathy, remembering full well how much being bound that way hurt. She had expected some sort of elaborate costume but his clothes were ordinary, brown trousers and a sleeveless tunic and boots. He could have been any man from Highfall, except for his coloring: his short-cropped hair was as black as Darid's colt's, his bruised, dirty skin white as skimmed milk. At least, she thought it was. His arms were covered in tattoos. Nobody in Highfall wore tattoos. Fashions changed too quickly and tattoos couldn't be undone.

After the prisoner and the guards surrounding him came Elban's riderless horse. A glorious black, huge and proud and so very clearly Darid's work—so like the colt she'd loved—that Judah's heart ached. The horse didn't seem to mind that his saddle was empty. His steps were proud and his coat gleamed. Even the silverwork on his saddle seemed recently polished.

Behind him, surrounded by a phalanx of guards, was the palanquin.

Where had they found these things, Judah wondered—the palanquin, the cage? Did armies ride out with such things as a matter of course? She hadn't noticed them when the troops had marched. They seemed too sturdy to have been put together on the road. The palanquin was hung with thick curtains and carried by eight guardsmen, stepping carefully to avoid jostling the injured man inside. Past them Judah could see the rest of the guards, more archers, more spearmen (although too few of those, again), with the supply carts and drummers bringing up the rear. Her eye kept returning to the palanquin. Something was wrong there, too. It nagged at her. She could feel it nagging at Gavin, as well.

The crowds in the Square were already thinning as the Seneschal ushered the four of them back into the small antechamber. In the rush-lined passage, the lamps were lit, the air thick with the smell of oil. A larger-than-usual group of guards escorted them through the passage, out the courtyard door and into chaos. As the great doors slowly creaked shut behind the procession, the new-returned guards split off into groups, calling orders, arranging for the disposition of the horses and goods and the prisoner and the fallen Lord, but the guards surrounding their own small group hustled them across the cobbles and into the House. As the door closed, Judah thought she heard a cry—of celebration or pain, she couldn't tell.

They were escorted all the way up to their own rooms, where the Seneschal was waiting. Once they were inside, he bowed and said only, "I will send for you when he's settled." The words hardly seemed worth climbing the stairs for. The door closed. Judah listened as his footsteps moved away, and then realized that his were the only ones that had.

"He left the guards," she said matter-of-factly.

"Just security," Gavin said, but he was chewing his lip.

Elly, meanwhile, had sunk down on the sofa, her hands in her lap. Her voice was tuneless. "I feel like I should be relieved, but I'm not."

"Colors," Theron said.

They all looked at him. He was so quiet these days that they often forgot he was there. "What?" Gavin said impatiently.

"The colors were wrong."

"Nothing is wrong." Gavin's tone was almost belligerent. Judah knew he was reassuring himself as much as the rest of them. "Everything will be fine."

"You sound certain," Elly said.

"I guess the old monster could pull through," Gavin said.

They waited. A page brought food: soft cheese covered in pepper and sliced meat that none of them could eat. When they let the page in, Judah saw all eight guards still standing in the corridor. An hour later, another guard came; simply but politely, he said the Seneschal had sent him to fetch them, so they left the food uneaten and went.

The door guards came with them, four before and four behind in a disconcertingly formal procession through the House. They saw nobody else: no pages, no stewards, no staff of any kind. Not a single courtier. From a distance Judah heard another cry, like the one she'd heard in the courtyard. The procession ended in Elban's parlor. Judah had never been there before. It was surprisingly austere, with only a simple wooden desk and chair, and one sofa which was well-brushed and not at all worn. There was a door in one wall, and another in the wall facing it.

With a bow, the guard who'd come to fetch them left. The other eight remained.

"He doesn't use this room much." Gavin spoke nervously, to fill the silence. "Just the bedroom, and—" His voice trailed off, and he nodded at one of the doors.

"And what?" Judah said.

Gavin glared at her. "And the other bedroom."

In a moment, the door opposite the other bedroom opened, and the Seneschal emerged. "A head wound," he said. "Serious, I'm afraid."

"What happened?" Gavin said, although Judah didn't see why it mattered. "Who's the prisoner? Is he the one who dealt the blow?"

The Seneschal shook his head. "He's a Nali chieftain. Apparently after our army captured him, his people tried to take him back. That was when Lord Elban was injured. Come in; I think you should all see."

The bedroom was large and grandly appointed. All of the fabrics were new, rich and saturated with color, and every surface that could be gilded had been. Elban lay on the bed in a plain white nightgown, a stark contrast to the rest of the room. The side of his head was completely caved in. Nathaniel Magus, who sat at his side, had covered the wound in bandages and padding, but the dressing didn't disguise the concave shape of Elban's skull. The magus looked up at Judah. His expression was grave, but—as with the Seneschal—she saw a faint excitement there, buried deep. The same excitement lurked on the guards' faces. For all she knew, it showed in hers, too.

Her voice soft with horror, Elly said, "Can you help him, magus?"

"Do you want him to?" Judah said without any horror at all.

"Treason, Judah," the Seneschal said, but without much conviction.

The magus shook his head. "No, I can't help him. His skull is shattered. But I've made him comfortable."

And Elban did seem comfortable. The rise and fall of his chest was slow but steady, and what was visible of his face was calm. He looked more like Gavin than ever. "If it's not treason to ask," Judah said, "what do we do now?"

"There's nothing to do but wait." Reluctantly, the magus added, "I can hurry things along a little."

"No." The Seneschal was firm. "Let death come when it will."

So they waited. Food was brought into the parlor: more cheese and meat, but also sweet pastries, fruit and soft bread. Gavin felt that someone should stay in the bedroom with Elban, but clearly neither Judah nor Theron was suited to the task, so it fell to Elly and Gavin. They took turns: one would sit and watch while the other sat and ate. The Seneschal came and went; he didn't eat or drink, and it occurred to Judah that he never had, in her sight. When he was in the parlor, he received a steady stream of messages delivered not by pages but by guards, who whispered them in his ear or passed them to him on slips of paper. He didn't share their contents.

Judah gorged herself on the pastries, which were fresher than she was used to. Then she grew bored with eating, and bored in general. The second door was locked; a moment after Judah tried it, Theron did. Five minutes later, he tried again. And five minutes after that. She expected him to try to pick the lock and was disappointed when he didn't.

So they passed the day, Theron alternating between the window and the locked door and Judah restless, pacing or sitting or making strained conversation with whoever wasn't with Elban. "You'd almost think we loved the old monster," she said at one point to Elly.

"He can't hurt us anymore," Elly said grimly. "And death is death. It deserves respect."

The longer Judah sat, the more surreal the situation seemed. All of the evil Elban had wrought in their lives over the last few months was simply…ending. Drifting down the black river to the sea, as the magus would say. She felt strangely cheated. When the magus went away to rest and the Seneschal was drawn out of the room by one of his many messages, Judah drifted into the death room. Elban would not want her, so she took a petty pleasure in being there.

Gavin sat next to the bed. The bandages covering the Lord's skull showed faint blooms of blood, but he remained quiescent, his long snowy hair lying gracefully on the pillow. From a certain angle, Elban might open his eyes at any moment and smile his cruel smile. As Judah watched, one of the long pale hands on the quilt twitched, as if it wanted to hit her.

"He was a monster and I hated him," Gavin said, "and now he's dying."

"Not very satisfying."

Gavin's head fell, limp, against the thickly upholstered chair. "He's my father, Jude."

Technically true. But all she felt was a wish that the body on the bed was not so quiet, that it was racked with pain. He should suffer more. He deserved to suffer more. But there was no point in saying any of that to Gavin, who already either knew it or wouldn't want to hear it. So instead, she said, "You're going to be Lord of the City."

Gavin took a deep breath and looked at her. "Yes, I am. Do you think I'll be good at it?"

She didn't know what to say to that. Once she would have said yes, unequivocally, but she was no longer sure. "If you do what Elly tells you."

"And what you tell me."

"No. Not me." Because Elly would want to do what was best for Highfall. Judah wasn't sure that she did. She wasn't sure what she wanted at all, if Elban was dead. Then she said, "I made a deal with him." Because there was no point in keeping it a secret. Maybe there wasn't any point in speaking, either, but she had been holding the bargain poised like a weapon in her mind for so long that she couldn't put it down without at least showing someone she had it.

Gavin's eyes snapped alert, which she found satisfying. "What deal?"

"So he'd leave Elly and Theron alone. He was going to take us both with him, next time he went on campaign, and use us to send messages. So there wouldn't be another ambush."

A series of complicated emotions cycled through Gavin. Judah waited, like she'd just spun a wheel, to see which would win; but when his face settled, it was into a calm as deep as that of the body on the bed. "Your other secret," he said, and she nodded. "You know what he would have done to you."

His tone was casual, passionless but pleasantly interested, and she saw that this was something he was trying on, for when he was Lord of the City. "I do," she said.

"To both of us, really," the almost-Lord said.

She nodded again. "It seemed worth it."

"I feel like I should be angry with you. Maybe I will be, later."

"That's fair," she said. "I knew there was a chance it would make you hate me."

Then, with a crooked smile, he was himself again. "I don't hate you." He paused. "It's a good idea. I hadn't thought of it." Judah felt very tired.

Elly was with Elban. Theron sat on the sofa, staring into space. Occasionally he stood up and tried to drift out the door, but was patiently rebuffed by the guards. Meanwhile, Gavin paced the room's perimeter, edgy with waiting, and after a while Judah could almost tell time by the two of them. It became a game to her; every time Gavin completed three full circuits of the room, more or less, Theron would try to leave. She felt dull and exhausted and intensely bored and her mind latched onto the pattern: satisfied when it completed itself, disappointed when it failed. She could almost forget that Gavin was Gavin and Theron was Theron; she could almost see them as gears and springs, spinning around inside a great clock keeping irrelevant time.

The Seneschal entered and her reverie broke. With him came a tight clot of guards, bristling with weaponry and accompanied by the clinking of chains. In the middle of the clot, surrounded on all sides and hooded, was a tall, thin figure with shackled arms. The arms were milk-skinned and tattooed.

The Seneschal crossed to the locked door. With no ceremony whatsoever he pulled a ring of keys from his pocket, selected one and opened the door. Then he beckoned the guards and their prisoner inside. "Lord Gavin," he said. "Judah. A moment, if I may."

Judah glanced at Theron. His eyes were fixed on the prisoner with a keener interest than usual, but no alarm. He made no movement to rise, and the Seneschal ignored him. Unexpectedly, Gavin held out a hand to Judah.

In the strangeness that surrounded Elban's return, she had forgotten why he'd left. But here was the Nali chieftain he'd sought, to try and break the bond, and although the great Lord lay dying in the other room, the Seneschal clearly intended to continue his mission. It made sense—if Gavin was to be Lord, it was better that he be unencumbered by unnatural attachments—but suddenly she remembered something Gavin had said, only days before, that he sometimes wondered how other people kept from killing themselves from loneliness. The prospect of being alone in her head, free to think or feel or hurt or love or even kill herself (if she wanted, which she didn't)—now that it was real, it was alarming. When she took Gavin's hand she was glad of it, glad of him. Glad of what might be the last few minutes truly together.

They followed the others into the room. It was another bedroom, as Gavin had said, but a strange one. The floor was hard and bare and the cot in the corner, a bare, rough bedstead, made Judah's seem lushly appointed. The windows were bricked over except for small gaps at the top, through which nothing was visible but sky; a wooden shutter hung above each, so even the gaps could be blocked entirely. The room also held a trunk and a wardrobe, both fastened with heavy locks, and one armchair with black upholstery. In such coarse surroundings, its gleaming wood and soft cushions seemed luxurious, regal.

Strangest of all, the walls of the room were filled with mirrors. Several hung on every wall and there was one in each corner, including one high up near the ceiling. The chieftain stood in the middle of the room, facing Judah, but in the various mirrors she could also see his shackled hands, the backs of his tattooed shoulders, and the top of his burlap-covered head.

"Leave," the Seneschal ordered, and Judah realized he was talking to the guards, who rustled, but didn't move.

"Seneschal—" one of them said.

The gray man cut him off. "Lord Gavin and I both have knives and the prisoner's shackled hand and foot. If you're needed, I'll call."

The guard who'd spoken didn't look happy, but he obeyed. The rest of the guards followed with ominous scowls and shuffling boots. None of them spoke to Gavin or even acknowledged him, which seemed strange.

But the Nali chieftain was stranger. As soon as the guards were gone, the Seneschal pulled away the hood. The prisoner's thin chest swelled as he took a deep breath. His eyes—as dark as Judah's, although that was where the similarity ended—blinked; what remained of the windows didn't let in much light, but the mirrors reflected it until the room was as bright as outdoors. His well-defined features were all planes and angles, his lips thin. Delicate silver earrings looped through his ears, two in one and three in the other, and his eyes were thickly lined with some deep emerald substance that looked like kohl but couldn't be—she'd never seen kohl that color.

He surveyed the room as if he'd been invited for dinner instead of dragged in blindfolded. There was a glamour about him, despite the shorn hair and plain clothes. The tattoos, some crisp and some gone soft and blurry with time, added to the effect. She was willing to bet that if a courtier ever got a glimpse of him, green kohl and shackle bracelets would be all the rage inside a week. But they would never be able to replicate the way he held himself. His eyes were bleak without being hopeless as they took in the hard furniture, the mirrors, the ostentatious chair; the Seneschal, still holding the burlap bag, and Judah and Gavin themselves, hand in hand like scared children.

He took another breath, long and savoring. His upper lip twitched as if he smelled something unpleasant. His gaze lingered on Gavin and Judah, but then—clearly knowing who was in charge—he looked at the Seneschal, and waited.

The Seneschal cleared his throat. "I'm told you're a chieftain."

The chieftain's dark eyes slid up at an angle and back again in an impressively economical gesture that said everything there was to say about the situation in which he found himself. "If that's the word you like." He spoke with a strong burr and a stronger disinterest.

"Do you prefer another?"

The thin shoulders moved in the barest of shrugs. "It'll do. Your language is limited."

"You speak it well."

"My people value knowledge for its own sake." It was clear from his tone that he believed Highfall didn't. Judah felt Gavin bristle.

The Seneschal didn't seem to take offense. "We're in need of your knowledge, as it happens. In exchange for your assistance, I offer you amnesty in Highfall, or an escort back to your own country, if you'd prefer that."

"If help was all you needed, you could have just said so, and left fewer bodies in your wake."

"Would you have helped us if we'd just said so?"

At that the chieftain smiled, brittle and brilliant. "No."

Gavin stepped forward, dropping Judah's hand. "I'm Lord Gavin. Lord Elban's heir." Imperious and unflappable, Lord of the City. "When he's dead, I'll rule Highfall. I guarantee you amnesty." He said the words, but Judah knew he was anxious, too.

The chieftain shook his head. The movement spoke of great fatigue. "It doesn't matter. I can't help you," he said to Gavin. Somehow the words included Judah and excluded the Seneschal. A twinge of something she couldn't identify ran through her like a shudder.

"We haven't even told you what we want." Some of the imperiousness in Gavin's tone was replaced by surprise.

"You haven't told me you've got a nose in the middle of your face, either, and yet there it is." His eyes were so black that it was disconcerting, but people probably felt the same way about her. There was something strange about the way those eyes rested on Gavin and Judah, as though the two Highfallers were misshapen, or oddities to be pitied—

No. As though they were *an* oddity to be pitied. The chieftain looked at Judah and Gavin like they were a single creature, and all at once Judah was certain that he knew about the bond. Quickly, she scratched *he knows* to Gavin. A cross with a hook. A warning.

The chieftain watched. He knew exactly what she was doing, she could see it. But all he said was, "It's impressive. And—" The word he used was a knotted tangle that Judah didn't understand.

Gavin had frozen the moment she scratched him and was still locked in a stunned silence. The Seneschal said, "What does that mean?"

"Evil," the chieftain said. Then he tilted his head and appeared to reconsider. "Well. Ill-intended. Poorly conceived, let's say. It adds up to the same thing."

"But you can sense the bond." The Seneschal's expression was urgent, almost desperate.

"I'm surprised you can't," the chieftain said carelessly. "Maybe living in this place has left you dull-witted."

"What's wrong with this place?" Gavin would not hear Highfall slighted when it was so close to being his.

"This place," the chieftain said, as if the word barely applied, "is the very heart of all that's wrong with the world. Being here is like being sealed in a grave." He looked at Judah. Now his words were softer, almost sorrowful. "You, I would help if I could. You don't belong here."

In one motion, Gavin grabbed her hand, pulled her close and stepped in front of her. She nearly stumbled with the force of his grip. "She belongs here more than you do," he said, and the words came out in a snarl worthy of one of the kennelmaster's hounds.

"And yet neither of us asked to come," the chieftain said.

The Seneschal ignored both of them. His voice rough with urgency, he said, "Do you know how the bond works? Do you understand it?"

"Do you understand why each beat of your heart is followed by another?" The chieftain gave him a withering look. "Stupid man."

"Can you manipulate it?"

"I'd rather be roasted over hot coals."

The Seneschal's face hardened. "That can be arranged," he said, and then, "Take him away," and somehow, suddenly, the room was full of guards. The burlap hood was yanked back down over the chieftain's head. Until the last moment his black eyes bored into Judah and she was glad when they were hidden. They terrified her. He terrified her. In the scarcest of moments the guards and the chieftain and the Seneschal were all gone and Gavin and Judah were left alone in the strange, empty room.

He wrapped his arms around her, which he almost never did, and she fell into a cataract of fear and agitation. His strength was ferocious. "I won't let them do it," he said. "I won't let them take you away from me."

Judah couldn't answer. She could barely breathe.

All of a sudden he let go and stepped back. Theron had entered the room, drifting silently through the open door the way he always did. His eyes floated their way across the cot, the shutters, the locked chest, the chair.

"This is a bad room," he said. "Bad things happened here."

Gavin took his brother by one arm and Judah by the other. "Come on then," he said furiously. "Get out. Go."

As evening fell on the second day, the Seneschal called them all into the death room. The magus, worn from his long vigil, stood at the Lord's bedside, his hands clasped neatly in front of him. His eyes were fixed on Lord Elban's inert body, his lips faintly parted. Nobody had lit the gaslights but two oil lamps filled the room with a diffused glow that seemed steadily warmer as the sun outside fell beyond the Wall.

Two guards waited in the room. Judah hadn't noticed them come in, but she'd been dozing. The Seneschal's face was grave. "It's time," he said.

Theron looked mildly interested. Elly moved closer to Gavin and took his arm. Then, for good measure, she laced the fingers of her free hand through his. Her eyes were very wide, her forehead damp. Judah felt ragged, out of control. The world past Elban's death was a yawning chasm of possibility, exhilarating and unnerving. She found herself wanting to take Gavin's other hand, to move close to him the way Elly had, but forced herself to stay still. This was their moment. Gavin and Elly. Lord and Lady of the City.

Elban's breath rattled. Then, as they all waited, it stopped altogether. In the silence left by its absence, nobody else seemed to breathe, either. For a bizarre moment, Judah found herself nearly panicking. That couldn't be it. That couldn't be the end of him. It was too simple, too quick.

Moving slowly, as if through heavy liquid, the magus leaned over and touched the long, pale neck. When he looked up, his eyes practically glowed. For some reason, they were fixed on Judah. "He's dead."

The Seneschal stepped forward, his eyes darting from the magus to the guards to the four young people. "You're witnesses," he said. "I did everything I could. I spared no effort. Is that true? Magus?"

The magus looked faintly puzzled, but said, "It's true."

The Seneschal turned to Gavin. "Lord Gavin? Lady Eleanor?"

"Yes," Gavin said. For all Judah knew, this was some formality that had to be dispensed with.

Next to him, Elly nodded mutely. Then she seemed to gather herself. "Of course, Seneschal. Nobody would doubt your dedication."

The Seneschal looked at the guards, who nodded.

"I'm Lord of the City," Gavin said softly. Something new was filling his face, just as the light from the oil lamps was filling the room. A warmth, a flush. He was smiling, faintly.

Transfixed by the changes in Gavin—the subtle squaring of his shoulders, the relaxation of something tight that had been there so long it had become natural to him—Judah barely noticed the Seneschal motioning to the guards.

"No." His voice was clear and firm and oddly gentle. "I'm sorry, Lord Gavin, but there will be no more Lords of the City. No more courtiers. In time, maybe no more House."

The world froze. Receded. Judah could not have moved even if she'd known where to go, and she didn't. Gavin and Elly, too, seemed locked into place, shock breaking over them.

But it was the magus who broke the silence with a strangled sound from deep in his throat. As if this were all normal, Theron said, "I told you, wrong colors," and tapped his chest.

And it was true: all the guards in the room wore House white. She could not remember seeing a red badge since Elban's return. If they'd bothered to ask Theron what he'd meant—if they hadn't grown so used to ignoring him—

Then they probably still wouldn't have been able to do anything. Judah was not at all sure how she felt. Gavin stood stock-still, naked with disbelief. Elly looked—hurt. The Seneschal's expression was one of pity, even sympathy. "Take them to their rooms," he said.

Two guards stepped forward and took Gavin in hand, one at each arm. He stared numbly at them and she wondered if they were men he'd trained with, men he knew. The room was suddenly full of guards and Judah found herself similarly surrounded, although the guards didn't quite seem to want to touch her. Theron looked at the guards who held him as though not entirely sure where they'd come from.

Then they tried to take Elly. She shook them off. Her hurt feelings had evidently morphed into anger. "What happens next?" she asked, furious. "Are you going to kill us?"

The Seneschal did not answer. The guards did take Judah's arms, then, and Elly's, and all of them were dragged away.

PART II

CHAPTER THIRTEEN

The first night was chaos. Nate, bewildered, didn't even try to sleep as Limley Square filled with the sounds of panic. The courtiers had been given twenty-four hours to leave the city with whatever they could carry, but based on snatches of conversation Nate overheard through the drafty windows, most of the servants dispatched to fetch horses from the city stables were returning empty-handed or not at all. Those courtiers who actually managed to find their horses didn't fare much better. Near midnight Nate heard cries; peering through the front window, he saw a man in fine clothes lying in the street near a stopped carriage, being kicked by a guard. Other guards were emptying the carriage, while the man's wife and daughters stood by and wailed. When the goods were gone, the carriage itself was driven away; the wife and daughters fled into the night. The man's body lay where he had fallen. When all was silent, Nate took his satchel and opened the front door.

Two guards stood on his front step, well-armed and wearing the Seneschal's white badge. They nodded politely at him. "Best you go back inside, magus," one said. "Bit risky out here tonight."

The Square looked eerily normal except for the man in the street. Standing on the manor doorstep, pulled equally by his urge to see to the beaten man's health and to protect his own, Nate could hear desperate cries and a steady percussion of splintering wood and breaking glass. The smoke in the air was denser than usual. In the distance, something exploded.

The guard who'd spoken followed Nate's gaze to the fallen man. "Don't worry about that. Someone will be along to get that eventually."

"Is he dead?" Nate said.

The guard laughed. "Oh, yes." Then, reassuringly, "You just go back inside, magus. Seneschal sent us to stand guard. You'll be safe enough."

"What's happening inside the Wall?" he said.

"Nothing for you to be concerned about," the guard said.

If the courtier was dead, there was nothing for him to do. If Judah was—

Nate went back inside.

Around three, he heard a faint but insistent tapping on the back door, and opened it to find Bindy, wearing Canty on her back and surrounded by three other girls who looked very like her: one a few years older, and the other two considerably younger. Their eyes were all wide and exhausted. He hustled them into the kitchen. "Oh, magus, the city's gone mad!" Bindy burst out before he could even say hello. "Things are burning and people are killing courtiers, and—"

"They deserve it," the older girl said with bitter satisfaction.

Bindy ignored her. "We stayed in the house but none of us could sleep. And there's a moneylender near us, they hung him. Right from a lamppost. And he wasn't a courtier at all, he just did business with some, and Rina and me started to think that people might—because I run errands to courtiers—" She glanced at the little one holding her hand, and clearly amended what she had been about to say. "Well, anyway, Ma's at work. And I figured you'd be safe. So we came here."

"I'm glad you did." Nate discovered that he meant it. His throat felt tight and his eyes burned. "Is your mother working the long shift?"

"She's all right. I ran to check," said the older one, who Nate guessed was Rina. Her face was rounder than Bindy's, her eyes wider, and her hair fiercely curly. Different father, probably. "They're taking the factories back from the court-iers. The managers are going to run them now. The managers are going to run everything. And they're appointing workers' committees and they asked Ma to be on one and I want to be on one, too. Isn't it exciting?"

The young girl clinging to Bindy's hand started to cry. "It will be, maybe," Nate said. Then he crouched down to the crying girl. She didn't seem to be hurt. In her arms she clutched a grubby doll with a matted thatch of badly-dyed red hair. Nate's heart hurt to see it. "What about you?" he asked the girl as gently as he could. "Are you all right?"

"She's fine," Rina said, but Bindy gave the girl an encour-aging nudge and said, "Say hi to the magus, Kate."

"Your name is Kate?" Nate said to the little girl, who nod-ded. "Well, Kate, I'm Nate. Our names sound the same, isn't that funny?" He pulled his face into an exaggerated beam of surprise and delight. "Nate and Kate! We'll have to be friends, with names like that."

Some of the fear melted out of Kate. She smiled. Then she yawned.

"Are you sleepy, Kate?" he said, and she nodded.

With Bindy's help, he got them all settled in the three guest bedrooms upstairs. Rina caught sight of the dead man in the Square and kept going back to the window with a regretful expression, as if she were sorry she'd missed the murder itself. "Ignore her," Bindy said quietly when Nate frowned. "She worked for a courtier for a while. He was nasty to her. She's a good person inside." Then, fatigued as she was, her face broke into a grin and she covered her mouth to hide a giggle.

"What's funny?" he said.

"Nate," she said. "I knew you had another name besides Gate Magus, but—*Nate*." She giggled again. "Sounds like a little boy with a slingshot."

"Once upon a time, I was a little boy with a slingshot." He bowed low, like he'd seen the courtiers do. "Nathaniel Clare, at your service."

"Belinda Dovetail, at yours," she said with a small, merry curtsy, "but I'm still going to call you magus."

When she and the others were all breathing quietly in their beds, Nate still didn't go to his. The manor full of sleeping children was soothing and daunting all at once; he no longer felt quite so lonely, but the weight of responsibility was heavy. At least it weighed down the sick feeling inside him, and stifled some of his fear. He wondered where Derie and Charles were, how they were faring in the pandemonium. This was not a part of the plan. He did not know what to do next.

The Wall was very high. Anything could be happening beyond it. Anything.

The children stayed through the next day. Taking turns with Canty, the older girls each marshaled one of the younger ones and began cleaning the manor from top to bottom. Nate told them, repeatedly, that they didn't have to do it—in fact, it made him uncomfortable, having them poking innocently into the corners of Arkady's decadent old life—but Bindy ignored his protests. "Gives the littles something to do," she said. "Better than having them sit around fretting." In truth, he was glad of the distraction. Retying aprons and cutting slices of bread and butter kept him busy, too. The idea that Judah might be dead, and he wouldn't know, was nearly driving him mad.

Charles arrived just after nightfall on the second night, barefoot and bedraggled. The guards were still on duty in front so he came to the back door, like Bindy's family had. Nate hadn't seen him in weeks. He was shocked at the change in his old friend: the hollow cheeks, the sunken eyes. Charles's chin was covered with a bronze haze of stubble and there was a sizeable bruise under his left eye. He carried nothing with him, not even the satchel he'd brought over the Barriers. "Lady Maryle's dead," he said.

Rina, who had been spooning potato soup into Canty's mouth, froze when she heard this, her face bright and vengeful. "Wait, Charles," Nate said, and pulled him into the parlor.

Charles barely seemed to notice the interruption. "Set fire to the manor, with everyone in it. Said she couldn't bear to lose a single thing more, not one thread of tapestry. Gainell and her sister and I made it out. But they couldn't get the old woman to move." Charles's eyes were haunted. "I couldn't help her. Her own daughters couldn't help her. She was too big for us to carry out. We barely made it ourselves. There was a crowd outside and I ran. We all did."

"Maybe you should have run faster," Nate said, nodding toward the bruise on Charles's face.

Charles blinked without comprehension. Then, remembering, he touched the bruise. "Oh. That. I cut through the Bazaar. Stupid. Of course they were looting it. Fortunately for me, a better courtier came along. Not fortunate for him, poor bastard. Although if he were poor, and a bastard, he might have had better luck." A high, nervous giggle escaped him. "The Seneschal's arrested the heads of all the best families, you know. It's the ones in the middle they're stringing up. Figures, doesn't it? We worked for five generations to bring Elban down, and practically the moment we get here, he's deposed."

"The power is still bound," Nate said. "We're not done yet."

"You might not be, but I am," Charles said. He pulled a vial out of his pocket and disappeared into Arkady's bedroom. Nate bit back his anger—Charles had abandoned his satchel and Lady Maryle, but saved his drug—and let him go.

The rest of that night was no quieter than the one before. The dead courtier still lay where he'd fallen across the Square. The weather was warm. Nate knew the body would soon start to rot.

On the third day, Nora came to get her children, walking confidently past the guards to the front door as if she'd done so a thousand times before. She wore a white sash across her chest, bound in brown embroidery that looked hastily done. Nate made tea.

"I thank you for taking in my children, but they'll be safe enough now," she said, and pointed to her sash. "I'm on the worker's committee for Paper. Nobody will bother us."

"Rina mentioned the committee," Nate said. "What does it do?"

"Everything. Factories always ran this city, you know. Only difference will be that now the money's actually going to the people who work in them, instead of some courtier's pocket. Managers know the running of the factories better than the courtiers ever did, anyway." She called out to the children, and the manor was suddenly full of the sounds of running feet as the littles blasted through the kitchen door to leap on her. Bindy and Rina followed at a slower pace, with Canty on Bindy's hip. Something in Nora's eyes released when she saw them, and her voice was brighter than Nate had ever heard it when she said, "Hello, my lovelies! You've not been making trouble for the magus, I hope?"

"They've been a huge help," Nate said.

"They always are." Nora took Canty from Bindy; delighted, he wove his little fists into her hair, and she kissed his soft cheek. "And I'll tell you all, the first thing the committee's changing is the schedule. No more long shifts. No more days spent at one task, never seeing sunlight, no time to rest or breathe or have your own thoughts, begging for privy breaks and eating while you work."

"It's a new world," Rina said, her eyes glowing, and Nora said, "We'll see."

"Have you heard anything about what's to happen to Lord Gavin and the other Children?" Nate said.

"No *lord* anyone, anymore, magus," Rina said.

"They haven't been children for years, now," Nora said. "Seneschal put Elban's corpse in the Lord's Square so we could all see it and know the old bastard was dead. But he hasn't announced what's to become of Elban's House, or his family." She shrugged, resigned. "Not their fault where they were born, I suppose. But neither was it my Darid's, nor any of the other children who've disappeared inside the Wall over the years."

"Magus knows the Children, Ma," Bindy said. "He goes inside, remember?"

"So he does." Nora gave Nate a measuring look. "What do you say of them, then, magus? Since you know them so well. Should they live?"

His mouth dry, Nate said, "I would hate to see anyone die who didn't deserve it."

"Deserve it?" Nora's eyebrows went fierce. "I watched them grow up same as anyone. Made my own children dolls of them, took them to see the puppet shows. But don't you talk to me about *deserving*. Did my Darid deserve to be sold like a side of beef into that House, to be mistreated however they like and hung when they felt like it? All the House staff are out now, you know. The stories I'm hearing would curl your hair. Told us they'd be well fed and well cared for, they did, but they cut my Darid into pieces and threw him on the trash heap. *Deserve it*, indeed." Bindy put a hand on Nora's shoulder. Nora leaned her head against it and then gathered the littles closer around her, reaching out for Rina's arm; holding everything she had left in a death grip to make up for her vanished son.

Her son wasn't gone, not the way she thought. The sadness in her eyes made Nate's heart ache, but if word got back to the Seneschal that the head stableman hadn't been executed after all, he was going to want to know how Darid had escaped. Nate couldn't risk that. He wondered who was making sure the four young people had food and wood for their fire, if the staff was gone; he wondered if Judah was hungry and cold in this amazing new world where the managers ran the factories and corpses rotted in the streets. He wondered if she was already dead.

And then he felt bad, because of course Nora was right. He wouldn't be here if Highfall had ever been fair, and when there was unfairness on the table, the weakest were always served the biggest helping. Which made him think again of Judah, and the cane-marks on her back, and he was sick and conflicted and wished the Seneschal would send word. He wished he knew something. Anything. He had been so close. She almost trusted him.

When all of the children were gone, the manor seemed

painfully quiet and painfully empty. The next morning, the courtier's body had vanished.

Worry chewed on the edges of Nate like a dog with a shoe. He signaled Derie, but received no answer. To make up for the food they were eating, Bindy and her sisters had made loaf after loaf of bread. Nate didn't have much appetite and Charles barely ate—as the drops wore off, he began to weep, constantly and uncontrollably—but by the fifth day after the coup, even the most misshapen and oddly-textured loaves were gone. Finally, Nate ventured outside.

The streets were quiet. People walked quickly, heads down to avoid seeing anything around them. Guards watched from the corners of every square, every major thoroughfare; on the lesser streets, Nate noticed more than one person wearing a white sash like Nora's. The colors of the embroidery varied. Different factory committees, Nate guessed. They held themselves with an air of grim importance, and Nate found himself walking quickly, too. He found that he didn't want these people to look at him for long.

The Grand Bazaar was closed, the stalls inside shuttered tight. Some of the locks had been broken. Ruined goods were scattered over the wooden floor. The air in the empty aisles smelled the same as it always had, like nutmeg and wine. A poster had been tacked up next to the entrance: a map of the city, divided into uneven slices like a badly cut cake. Nate stopped: the old neighborhood names were gone. Each wedge was labeled with the name of a factory. *Paper. Textiles. Steel.*

The managers are going to run everything.

The slices were uneven because sometimes there were two factories close together, and of course none of them were anywhere near the better parts of the city. It was clear that a lot of deal-making had taken place as the map was drawn. Limley Square was probably closer, as the crow flew, to Textiles, but for some reason it was included in a lump growing off the eastern edge of Paper. The map had been made on a press, quickly and not very neatly. The letters across the bottom—*Know your factory district! Please cooperate with resource inventories! Your New Life in New Highfall!*—were blurred.

Your New Life in New Highfall. As revolutionary slogans went, Nate found it a bit vague. It didn't even have a verb. He didn't know what the resource inventory was, but assumed he would find out.

He skirted the Lord's Square, not knowing if Elban's body was still on display there and not caring to see it if it was. Not far away, a crowd gathered in what had once been a lovely garden. A decorative statue—something graceful and lithe—had toppled off its plinth; it lay in pieces in the mud, and a man with wild eyes stood in its place. "They cut out their tongues!" he cried. "They cut off their fingers! When a courtier was barren and needed an heir, they chose one of your daughters or sons, anyone they liked the looks of—and why not, since it was what they did anyway, aye? But woe betide the girl who came down with a child unwanted. Did your daughters not come home? Like as not, they lie in the great trash heap, holding the tiny bones of a courtier's lust!"

Nate kept walking.

The Beggar's Market had fared better than the Bazaar. It still seemed mostly the same, although the piles of food were a bit smaller, the carrots a bit spindlier. But there was still milk, and butter and lamb; Nate bought some of each, and a bit of cheese. He wanted coffee, too, but the prices were ridiculous. Everything was more expensive than it had been. The vendors all told him that his House account was no longer good. They were polite about it; he knew them all, and they seemed happy to see him. But something was missing, something was off. It took him a moment to realize what it was. The traders, the ones from outside Highfall or across the Barriers: they were gone. All the people he saw were pale and golden-haired, with round blue eyes.

"Where are all the traders?" Nate asked the dried fruit man.

"Gone." The man threw a few more apricots on Nate's pile. "With the courtiers?"

He shook his head. "On their own. By sundown the day Elban died, wasn't a single foreign trader left in the city. I had friends among them. Folk I've known for years."

Nate wasn't surprised. No matter how big the city or small the village, when trouble came and people were scared, their eyes fell on the outsiders. No better way to learn that lesson than to grow up in a caravan. Nate, Caterina and the others had been run out of more places than he could even count. The makeshift market by Harteswell Gate might never have existed; the plague shrine was still there, but the offerings—like everything else in the city—seemed a bit paltry. Nate waited there for an hour, long enough for the guard keeping watch over the shrine to begin eyeing him curiously, but Derie didn't show up.

When he came back to the manor, Charles—wiping the still-uncontrollable tears from his cheeks—met him at the door with a summons from the Seneschal.

The Seneschal's new headquarters were in one of the big manors on the Lord's Square. The courtiers who had surely lived there before were gone now, either fled or ejected. A guard at the door directed Nate to a dim hall full of closed doors and a sense of harried activity. A low hum of indistinct voices underlay all of the normal noises, as if every room held a busy meeting, and a constant stream of guards flowed through the front door, up the polished wooden staircase and back down. People wearing white sashes bustled from room to room. They carried water jugs or stacks of paper or baskets full of food; they opened doors and slipped through on waves of animated conversation that cut off as soon as the doors shut. For all he knew, Nora was behind one of the doors, but he didn't see her. Finally, one of the sashed people—a woman around Caterina's age—asked him what he wanted. When he showed her the summons from the Seneschal she led him upstairs, down a bare corridor to a door flanked by white-badged guards. Neither of them spoke or moved to stop her as she knocked; a voice called, "Come in," and she gestured to Nate, so he did exactly that.

The massive wooden desk where the Seneschal sat gleamed with hours of hard polishing, but the surface was covered with loosely stacked paper, flat and rolled. A half-eaten sandwich on a plate was wedged in among the mess, along with three empty mugs. The room smelled like meat and old coffee. It wasn't a particularly pleasant smell, but the presence of old coffee hinted at the presence of new coffee. Nate hoped he would be offered some.

"Magus," the Seneschal said, sounding genuinely pleased to see him. "Delighted that you could come. I'm sorry I wasn't able to send for you earlier, but—" he gestured to the piles "—I've been busy." He pointed to a chair.

Nate sat down. "I would think so. Congratulations."

The gray man lifted an eyebrow. He still wore the same clothes he'd worn under Elban, but he seemed more relaxed. "I don't think congratulations are in order. All things come to an end, do they not? And new things emerge." He sat back in his chair. "If you want to congratulate someone, congratulate the people of New Highfall. They're the ones doing the work."

"And the factory managers, from what I hear."

"Who better? Now that they're no longer hampered by the

outdated mindsets of their former owners, New Highfall's factories will be more prosperous than ever."

"And who will benefit, now that the courtiers are gone?"

"If the factories prosper, everyone prospers. Higher profit means higher pay. And the courtiers aren't gone. They've merely returned to their own provinces to manage their own industries. Under the watchful eyes of their new ministers, of course." The Seneschal smiled with satisfaction. "I have such amazing plans, magus. You'll see. This city will be the vanguard of a new world."

"Very exciting," Nate said, and then could restrain himself no longer. "How are the Children?"

"Well into adulthood, as you're aware. Confined to their rooms while my resource assessors finish with the House, and perfectly safe."

A dizzy rush of relief washed over Nate. He wasn't sure how well he hid it, so he said, "I'm glad to hear it. I've grown rather fond of them."

"They're not unlikeable," the Seneschal evenly. "Much like yourself. You're a striver, magus. I was a striver, when I was young. Also, you're a good magus, and worldly. I thought about asking you to represent the magi on the leadership committee, but it turns out that the other magi in the city don't particularly like you. Apparently they felt it was a bit presumptuous of me to appoint you House Magus."

"I don't have time for politics."

"Not while treating all of Marketside and Brakeside for free, you don't." The Seneschal waved a hand. "It's fine. It's your time and your herbs. Elban didn't want to bother treating the poor when they got sick, but Elban's dead. I say if they have the wherewithal to find medicine, they're welcome to it. We need a working class. Just don't neglect your official duties."

"I'm still House Magus, then?" Nate said warily. "For how long?"

The Seneschal stared at him, then said, "Oh. You're wondering if I'm going to kill the Children. It would be the usual course of action after a coup, wouldn't it? My guards risked a great deal, turning on Elban and taking down the Lord's Guard, and now they have to risk even more, fending off delusional loyalists who want to put Gavin on the throne, gods help us all. The boy may look like Clorin, but what little he knows about governance he learned at Elban's knee."

"The story about Elban's death was a lie, then," Nate said. "The Nali didn't try to retake their chieftain."

"Oh, they did. They just didn't get very far. My men were on the lookout for an opportunity. They killed Elban, they killed his guard—now, I think, nothing would make them happier than to kill his heirs, and end the empire once and for all." The Seneschal seemed to notice the sandwich, then, and pulled it closer. "But I have bigger plans. And as you know, killing Gavin is no simple matter."

"So Judah dies, too." Just speaking the words made Nate's skin crawl. "Why do you care?"

"Well, for one thing, I'm not a monster. I do like the girl." He lifted the top piece of bread from the sandwich, contemplated the meat inside and pushed it away. "But it's the bond I'm interested in. I doubt I can figure it out by cutting into their dead bodies. You haven't seen anything like it before, have you?"

"No." At least, not exactly like. "I thought that was Elban's great quest, to figure it out."

"Elban's great quest was to destroy it," the Seneschal said. "Oh, before he died he started to develop some broader ideas, but ultimately, he had no vision."

"You're different, of course."

Amused, the Seneschal said, "Do you know what I see at night, when I close my eyes?"

Nate didn't answer.

"I see the House," he said. "Not the building; the entity. The machine. So much material in, food and goods and bodies; so much material out, influence and power and wealth. And what did the City Lords do with that influence and power and wealth? Wasted it. Gorged themselves on it, and accomplished nothing. The courtiers liked to play at politics, but for the last few generations it's been the trade ministers and factory managers who've been Highfall's real motive power. They're the engine. Elban and the others were—" his mouth twisted with distaste "—a pretty gold casing that hid the real work. What I've done is strip the casing away. Give the provinces to the ministers and the factories to their managers. Let the engine run as fast and far as it's capable of going—but now, instead of wasting energy fueling the House, it will power itself. Do you know what hampered Elban most, magus?"

Nate was impatient. He wanted to know what would happen to Judah; he didn't care what happened to Elban's empire. "A profound lack of humanity?"

That got a smile, albeit a cold one. "Time. It takes a man on a fast horse three weeks to ride from here to the farthest reaches of Elban's empire. A carriage, with any kind of burden, half that much again. His forebears made court life attractive specifically so the families that controlled the provinces would keep a member or two inside. So instead of a sending an envoy who'd be gone for months, the Lords could send a page for the appropriate courtier. Whatever decisions needed to be made could be dispensed with in a matter of minutes, once the courtier sobered up and put their clothes back on. The courtier could choose to send an envoy home, on their own coin, or not. Most of the time they went with *not*."

"I'm told you've abolished the courtiers," Nate said.

"The city courtiers, sure. We took their factories and manors, and so forth; that makes for a good show and fills the coffers without doing any actual damage. But the provincial courtiers, whose home provinces have something useful to trade—iron or metalfiber or food—we sent them home, as long as they were willing to sign new trade agreements, and abide by the decisions of my ministers. I even sent guards with them to protect them along the way. Unlike Elban, I don't actually enjoy the idea of slaughtering people I've known for years. Which is not to say I won't do it, if necessary—I will, obviously—but my hope is to hold the empire together by mutual benefit, not force. Which brings us back to time. As it stands, it takes weeks for me to hear about problems in the provinces, and weeks more to respond. The delay isn't acceptable."

"And what do you propose to do about that?" Although Nate knew. Of course he did.

"Gavin and Judah," the Seneschal said. "Elban went after the Nali because the way the Nali fight—it's like fighting a hive of bees, or a flock of sparrows. They move as one, silently, without any apparent means of communication. They can still think for themselves, but it's said that each fighter knows at all times not just where every other fighter is, but what they're seeing. They have a rather poetic name for it, which doesn't quite translate, but which means something like seeing from inside the reflection on the water. Not quite what Judah and Gavin can do, but not entirely unlike it, either, don't you think?"

Water and blood and tide and the moon. He had never seen such a Work done, and he wasn't anywhere near knowledgeable enough to know how to perform one himself, but it seemed possible. It surprised him that none of the Slonimi had ever tried it—but they hadn't needed it, had they? They never fought organized battles; if they ran into trouble on the road, they fled. Perhaps it would have been useful to them now, in Highfall, but he could practically hear Derie scoff. *Waste of good Work. We've got mouths to talk with, don't we?*

Everything the Seneschal was saying terrified him.

"But Judah and Gavin can't actually communicate, can they?" he said calmly.

"Not in words. But over the years, they've developed a code. Scratches on their skin, specific patterns that mean specific things. Judah's idea, I'm sure. Gavin's not nearly clever enough. We never knew about it, all these years, although I suspected they had something. Anyway, Judah told Elban about it right before he left on his final campaign."

Nate couldn't hide his horror. "Why would she do that?"

"As a bargaining chip. Elban was playing one of his games with the four of them. Setting them on fire to watch them run in circles—pushing Gavin, primarily. Most people have no idea how cruel the old bastard could be." The Seneschal's distaste for Elban was clear. "She's very lucky things happened the way they did. I was quite angry with her when I heard about it. If she'd just been patient—anyway, the point is that the chieftain the army brought back could sense the bond between them. He wasn't willing to do anything about it, then, but after further reflection, and a few weeks in High-fall Prison, he's beginning to change his mind."

Something about the Seneschal's tone suggested that the chieftain's so-called *reflection* was both involuntary and painful. Distantly, Nate thought he should care, but he didn't. "You think he can break it?"

The Seneschal looked surprised. "I don't want to break the bond, magus. I want to replicate it." He considered. "Well, I want to break it, then replicate it. I want to be able to break it or forge it at will. What I really want—" and his face was alive now, like an unlit torch bursting into flame "—is to build a new Guild. The Communicators. Or perhaps we'll call them after Judah. The Judanese, maybe, or the Judanians. The Nali bond only works in relatively close proximity, you know, but we haven't found a physical limit with Judah and Gavin. I took him two weeks' travel out of the city when he was a baby— when Arkady cut Judah's heel back in the nursery, the cut on Gavin's foot appeared instantaneously." The Seneschal's eyes were alight with fervor. "Imagine: instantaneous communication. Pairs of communicators, sent throughout the empire. Bond them when they're children, raise them together if that seems to be important. Maybe we could even bond more than one person together, like the Nali. Or maybe it can be passed down to offspring. You've seen the bond, magus. You know it works. Why shouldn't we use it to our advantage?"

Because to do so would be a perversion of the Work and a crime against all that makes us human, and the invalidation of my entire life. "No reason, I suppose. But why tell me all of this now?"

"Because I need your help. According to the chieftain, the formation of the Nali bond is difficult; not everyone lives. They've never deliberately tried to break it, but of course people do die in battle. The rest of the group survives—it wouldn't be much use, strategically, if you could take out the whole unit by killing one member—but sometimes one of the survivors goes mad. I'd prefer that Judah and Gavin not go mad, and obviously, I'd rather they not die. From what the chieftain says, the entire process will go more smoothly if they're willing participants. Which is where you come in."

Hope fluttered in Nate's chest. "Where I come in?"

"Judah trusts you. Convince her to consent to the chieftain's experiments. Once she's on board, Gavin will follow, weak-willed as he is. You'll have your work cut out for you. She doesn't like me at all, and the chieftain predicted that the process will be painful. But she's strong. She can withstand quite a bit of pain." He spoke casually, as if discussing Judah's favorite kind of cake.

"I don't know how I'd do that." Nate forced himself to sound reluctant, but the flutter of hope was growing, unfolding. *Convince.* That sounded like the sort of thing that had to happen inside the Wall, in person.

"Just carry on the way you have. My men are taking the crops and livestock and anything else of value from the House; it's a bit absurd to leave all the fertile land inside the wall unfarmed, but right now the managers are focused on the city, and they'll accept house arrest for the Children. That place wasn't built to be lived in unstaffed, though. Just getting water will be an ordeal, particularly once we strip the pipes from the aquifer. The four of them have lived comfortable lives; after a month or two of hardship, I expect they'll be very receptive to an alternate arrangement." He leaned forward. "Ultimately, I'd like to move them all out of the city—which is another reason it would be better if they were willing, so Gavin could give a speech before they left. Leaving for the good of New Highfall, or something. The place I have in mind is very remote, and we could work on the project in earnest, without distractions."

That was unacceptable. Gavin and Judah had to be in the House. The power could only be unbound in the place where it was bound. Nate realized that everything would have to move faster now. Stalling, he said, "What about Eleanor and Theron?"

"Gavin and Judah are attached to them. I didn't particularly enjoy Elban's games, but they did demonstrate the usefulness of love, as either carrot or stick." He shrugged. "If an opportunity arises to get one or both of them out of the way, cleanly, I wouldn't refuse. Eleanor has an independent streak, and Theron is impossible to keep locked up. I swear, that boy can pick a lock just by looking at it, addled brains or no." There was something close to admiration in his voice. "At this point, the guards are just there to keep him from letting the others out."

"Judah has an independent streak, too."

"I'm counting on it. That girl has spent her entire life being reminded at every moment how little she matters except as a body with a pulse. It was always the others who were important, not her."

"She's important now," Nate said, which at least felt true; and the Seneschal said, "Magus, as far as you're concerned, she's the most important person in the city."

On his way home, he felt like he must be glowing with panic and frustration, but none of the passersby seemed to notice. There was no time. He checked the Harteswell gate but found no sign of Derie. Back at the manor in Limley he signaled her again, but she didn't respond. There was nothing to do but wait.

Two days passed. Charles wept, and moaned and—once—drove his head against the floor, over and over, begging Nate to make it stop. Nate did not want to give him opium and exchange one addiction for another; there was nothing he could do. He barely slept. The coup had been chaos and screaming, but it had fallen on the residents of Highfall—sorry, New Highfall—like an ice storm in summer: something entirely unnatural and out of their control. They were left dazed, unseated. Some of them, like Bindy's sister, had latched onto their New Lives in New Highfall with ferocious enthusiasm, but most of the people Nate saw in the streets were merely trying to get through their days, to sell their bread or weave their cloth, to brew their beer or drink it. Those patients who came to the front door did so with an almost childish daring, as if racing through a burial yard at midnight. Those who came to the gate wouldn't discuss the coup. They seemed to feel that even speaking of it was dangerous, and it was best to ignore the entire thing.

New people moved into the manors on Limley Square. Rina told him that factory managers and employees were being moved into the districts the managers controlled "because they'll care more for their own neighborhoods, of course." She was at Arkady's manor for the resource inventory, which turned out to be a half-dozen workers from Paper going over the manor from top to bottom, writing down everything they found and taking any goods they deemed valuable or luxurious. Once it was established that the lab—and Charles, huddling on Nate's pallet inside it—would be left alone, the inventory didn't bother Nate at all. The search committee could take what they wanted; nothing in the manor was his. Rina, in a white and brown sash like her mother's, had clearly found herself in a position of some power. Eagle-eyed and efficient, she followed the workers from room to room, making sure they didn't miss anything. She could not be less like Bindy; there was no merriment in her, no music.

"What will they do with it all?" he asked her, as Arkady's favorite chair left the manor feet-first.

"Sell it," she said promptly. "Reinvest the profits in the factory."

"Sell it? To who? Nobody has any money anymore. It's all been confiscated."

He spoke without thinking. Rina's eyes turned to flint. "Surely, even where you're from, farmers expect to be paid for their crops, and miners their ore. For once, they'll be getting a fair price."

Nate almost asked how those farmers and miners would feel about being paid in confiscated furniture, but Rina's glower told him he'd better not. Every citizen over the age of fourteen had to work now, and each position had to be approved by the factory committee. Bindy was just fourteen. Nate had applied to the New Highfall Productivity Board for her to be named his apprentice, officially, but he hadn't received confirmation yet. Rina and Nora had argued over the apprenticeship; Rina had wanted Bindy in the factory, where she'd have more opportunity for advancement. Nora said Bindy was just fine where she was. He didn't know why Bindy's mother had intervened, but he was grateful. Also, and more worrisomely, Rina had warned him that even Charles would need to find work, and soon. He didn't know if Rina could make either process more difficult, but he knew that he didn't want more trouble to fall on people he cared about, so all he said was, "I'm glad to hear it."

Rina gave him an arch look. "A lot of outsiders have been sent back where they came from, you know, magus. But you needn't worry. Seneschal has you on his list of indispensables."

"I'm glad to hear that, too."

"Yes," Rina said. "You should be."

Three days after his visit to the Seneschal, Derie came. As he let her in the garden gate, he said, "Where have you been?" and the question was part anger, part curiosity. He didn't know where she was living or how she was surviving, but she seemed no worse for the wear.

"None of your business," she said harshly, "and don't grouse at me, boy. I couldn't answer, and that's all you need to know. Get inside."

"Charles is here," he said as he closed the kitchen door.

"I know. I don't care." She reached into her skirt pocket, took out a knife. "Now shut up and sit still. Let's see what's going on."

So he had to endure it again: having her inside his head, tossing his memories the way Rina's crew had tossed the manor. It was worse this time, and he hadn't thought that was possible. When it was over he lay on the floor and discovered that his words were gone. He wanted to communicate, and knew that he'd once known a way to do it, but the means simply weren't there anymore. He couldn't think of her name. He couldn't think of his own, either. She seemed very tall, perched above him on a sort of frame that he'd once known the name of, made of something he could no longer identify. A long piece of the same stuff was in the nameless one's hand. It made small noises on the floor. He'd once known the name for those, too. The sounds. The long thing.

"Nasty piece of work, that Seneschal," the nameless one said. "Well, we'll just have to be nastier, that's all. No more dancing around." There were brown things at the end of her body nearest to him. One of them moved and he felt a pain. "No more wasting time, you, boy."

You, boy. Was that him? It felt familiar. The nameless one made a sort of grunt that he knew meant she wasn't happy with him. He curled around himself in case she hurt him again. She took a soft, floppy thing from the flat thing next to her and tossed it toward him. It hit the part of him that saw and breathed. He flinched.

The nameless one cackled. "Sick on yourself. Oh, a mess, you are. Well, we'll put you back together again." He did not want that. He did not want her touching him. He tried to push her hands away. "Fine, we'll do this the hard way," she said, and *did* something, and he found himself frozen. Her Work wrapped around him, tied him down, held him. He could barely breathe.

It was not pleasant this time, either, but when she was done, he had snapped back into himself like a dislocated shoulder going back into joint. The hand holding him vanished. All the elusive words came back in a rush. *Derie, table, chair, towel, cane. Boot.* He picked up his glasses where they'd fallen to the floor—not broken this time—and slipped them on. The world around him came into crystalline focus and his brain was crystalline, too. He saw more clearly than he had in days: what was coming, what he would have to do, how best to do it.

Derie watched him. "Better?"

"Yes, thank you," he said.

"I suppose I could have been a bit more careful. But I put things back neater than I found them."

"I guess you did." There was vomit on the floor. On his shirt, too. He stood up—only a bit unsteadily—and went to the lab, where his things were; leaving the door open, he stripped off the filthy shirt and put a clean one in its place. At the washstand, he splashed his face and cleaned his glasses. He could hear Derie stomping around the kitchen. Making tea, probably.

Sure enough, two steaming cups waited on the table when he returned. He wiped up the vomit on the floor, then took his cup and settled himself into the chair across from her. That nudge in the ribs she'd given him with her boot had been within a hairbreadth of a kick. He could still feel it.

"What was that you did to me?" he said eventually.

"Needed you still, so I made you still," she said. "I'll show you how later. You can try it out on that wastrel Charles, he might as well serve some purpose. You're infatuated, you know."

He stifled the urge to flinch again. The new clarity she'd left in his brain didn't let him lie, not even to himself. "With Judah? A little, I suppose. Can you neaten that up, too?"

"I could. I left it be for now. Might work in our favor." She put a soft, cold hand over his. "You're a good boy, Nathaniel. You know what you need to do, and you'll do it." Kind touches from Derie had always been rare, even when he was a child. She patted his hand and stood up. "We can always fix you up afterward. Whatever needs to be done."

"Of course you can," he said, and there was no doubt in him whatsoever. She could, and would. Whatever needed to be done.

The crystalline clarity lasted through that day and into the next. Late that afternoon, Nate heard the rattle of the phaeton outside his door. His whole body came alive, like a wild creature sensing prey. He met the guard at the door, already holding his satchel. "Am I needed inside?" he said.

"No, it's the prison," the guard said. "Seneschal said you could be trusted, if a magus was needed," and, still sharp-edged and hard with the force of his new clarity, Nate answered, "Yes. I can."

The phaeton had been denuded of all Elban's insignia. Only ghosts remained: bare silhouettes, cleaner than the rest of the phaeton's surface but marred by careless prybar work and empty bolt holes. The bell was still there, and the driver rang it aggressively as he drove through the city, yanking hard on the chain so the bell clanged harsh and tuneless, a vicious pleasure visible in his face as people scattered before the phaeton like dried leaves. The guard hanging on the foot rail said nothing. Empty storefronts with broken windows gaped like missing teeth in each street. Some of them had been burned. There were blackened places on the cobblestones, too, and at the bases of some of the lampposts: bonfires, or worse. Whatever had been burned had already been cleared away. He saw lots of white sashes, embroidered with different symbols and different colors, but he also saw a number of matching white caps. He asked the guard what they were.

"Work enforcement. Making sure everyone who can work, does. No work, no scrip."

"Scrip?"

"Companies keep their own stores now. Scrip's what they take. Stops the price gouging at the markets."

It made perfect sense. But Nate found himself asking, "What about the old and the sick?"

"Most people can do something, if they try hard enough," the guard said.

Highfall Prison was a crumbling brick tower crammed onto a lump of land in the Brake that could barely be called an island. It wasn't a large building; Elban hadn't favored lengthy prison sentences. The same guard who'd hung off the phaeton rowed Nate over in a tiny boat, greasy green water splitting sluggishly around the prow. At the best of times, a person didn't want to look too closely at things floating in the Brake. These were not the best of times. Nate kept his eyes straight ahead.

The guard led Nate into a dingy hallway. Through open doors on either side, he could see two reception rooms, one fairly nice and the other less so; they were meant for important visitors, which Nate wasn't. He was taken instead to a dank staircase at the end of the hall. The walls of the staircase wept and the stone steps were slick with dampness. At the bottom was a similarly damp corridor, or rather, a wet corridor. As they walked, the guard directed Nate around puddles of standing water that had seeped up through the floor. Occasionally, these were deep enough to warrant planks of moldy wood lying across them as bridges.

The cell doors were solid, with hinged slots permitting the passage of food. There was no way to tell if a cell was inhabited or not, but as Nate passed one cell in particular, the back of his neck broke out in prickles. Power, but an unfamiliar sort. He paused by the door. The guard stopped, too.

"Hear something? That's where they keep that Nali they

brought back." A smile crept over the guard's face. "Doesn't say much. He cries a lot, though."

Reflection, the Seneschal had called it. Nate nodded, and resumed walking.

Eventually they came to a room that was more or less dry, which held a table, a chair and a small, hard cot. Yet another door in the far wall bristled with locks, to which the guard applied keys from a large ring until it swung open. The room beyond stank of many unpleasant things—all the fluids that could be taken or expelled from the human body, as well as char and meat—but they all added up to suffering. Iron-barred cells lined both sides, and the large space in the middle was full of devices that Nate chose not to consider. A man greeted them, clothed in a heavy apron of stained leather. Nate chose not to consider the stains, either.

"Here's the magus, Interrogator," the guard said.

"Pleased to meet you, magus. This way." The Interrogator spoke pleasantly enough, but Nate could feel invisible blades of malevolence radiating from him. He couldn't tell if the blades or the job had come first, but he supposed it didn't matter. The aproned man led Nate to one of the cells. The door was open and unlocked; inside, Nate understood why. The man who lay on the floor had two brutally broken legs. His toes, knees and hips all pointed in contrary directions. He was extremely unlikely to stand up and walk away.

Nate knelt next to the prisoner and saw that his hands were mutilated, too. The man's breathing was loud and ragged. Both of his ears had been cut off, the wounds crudely cauterized to black char. Nate found a bit of uninjured skin on the man's throat. It felt cold and clammy, the pulse erratic.

Nate stood up, grateful for whatever it was that Derie had numbed in his brain. "Where would you like me to start?"

The Interrogator seemed vaguely embarrassed. "Well, magus, I'm not exactly used to this sort of thing."

"It looks like you're used to it."

"Trying to get information, I mean. Under Lord—under Elban, rather—we just killed 'em, however slow he wanted. But this one, he's got a mouth on him. Said the crudest things. Not the things we wanted him to say, of course. Courtiers have filthy minds, the lot of them. And this morning—well, I'd just had enough." He wore a look of mixed distaste and affront. The man he'd been torturing had offended him, Nate realized, and in his new icy state almost wanted to laugh. "It's not as if I didn't warn him. I told him a dozen times, he'd better watch that tongue if he didn't want to lose it. He wouldn't listen, so out it came."

Forgetting that without a tongue or a hand that worked, the smashed heap of human being on the floor would find it difficult to share any information at all. "I can't sew his tongue back in, you know."

The interrogator chuckled. "Not after I threw it on the fire, you can't." Then, more anxiously: "I was thinking about his hands, maybe."

Nate bent back down. He didn't recognize the courtier, but he wasn't sure he would have, anyway. Most of the bones in the man's face had been broken, including his jaw—probably when he lost his tongue. He put a hand on the courtier's shoulder. The man cringed and shuddered.

"Which hand do you write with?" Nate asked him.

After a moment the right elbow twitched. Nate examined that hand. Evidently, the Interrogator had started by pulling out the fingernails and then worked his way up, smashing each bone individually.

"He's got jewels hidden in his manor," the Interrogator said over Nate's shoulder. "He was famous for them, wasn't he?

But those jewels belong to the city, now, and this selfish pig won't tell us where they are." His voice grew strident. "The managers could trade those jewels to the provinces for food to feed the city this winter. But that ain't good enough reason for him. He's holding out. Don't know why. After we're done with him, it'll take more than jewels to make him pretty."

For money. They had done this for money, and on the strength of hearsay. Nate laid the man's hand down gently. "This man is in shock. He might be dead by morning no matter what I do. But I can fix his hand well enough for him to write, eventually, if you'll leave it alone to heal."

The Interrogator nodded eagerly. Nate opened his satchel. He preferred to lay out what he needed before he began to work, but he didn't want any of his supplies to touch the mucky floor of the cell, so he worked directly out of the bag. He had a salve that would help the man's bloody lips, which were as dry as paper (and of course he couldn't lick them). But before Nate did anything else, the man needed opium syrup. Nate took out the bottle; then stopped and considered.

The courtier was perched on the very edge of death, his bloodshot eyeballs staring right into the depths of the black river—but he might survive. It wasn't likely, but it was possible. The injuries to the man's face would not heal cleanly, though. Even with the best of care, any life Nate could help him back to would be misshapen and colored with agony. Nate's thumb traced the edge of the cork in the syrup bottle. It would be a simple thing to empty it between the man's cracked lips. He would be unconscious in minutes and dead in hours. Caterina would have considered it a kindness. But Caterina would also have checked the man's lineage, to make sure his line would survive him, and conferred with the rest of the caravan. She might even have reached inside the man's mind to ask his own opinion. Nate could do none of those things; he had nobody to confer with, and he wasn't talented enough to read the man's thoughts. But he could end his pain.

Behind him, the Interrogator laughed at something the guard said. Nate glanced toward them, to make sure they weren't watching—and as he did, he heard again the words of the guard: *Seneschal said you could be trusted.*

With his new hardness, Nate knew he needed that trust. He had no choice but to leave the courtier here to suffer and—with any luck—die on his own. This hideous room with its hideous smells must be part of his life, now. He would set bones so they could be smashed again, stitch wounds so they could be opened anew. He would pump water from the lungs of the half-drowned while the bucket waited, amputate one charred limb while the fire was stoked for the other. He would loathe every second and he would loathe himself, but that didn't matter. He had to stay in the Seneschal's good graces. He had to have access to Judah.

One of the man's eyes opened as much as it could. All Nate could see was a tiny slit of blue and black and bloodred. The man must have been in incredible pain. Nate didn't even know if he understood what was going on. Reflexively, he gave the man a reassuring smile. The opium bottle was still cool in his hand.

He turned back to the Interrogator. "Can I give him anything for the pain?"

"Not much point," the Interrogator said.

Nate nodded, and put the syrup away. He carefully cleaned and bound the oozing sores where the man's fingernails had once been. The bones in the hand were not broken so much as obliterated. Judging by the bruising, the damage was several days old. He splinted and bandaged the fingers as well as he could. The courtier moaned at first, low and ragged, but soon the moans stopped and Nate knew he'd passed out.

Finished, he closed his satchel and went back to the Interrogator. "Leave that hand alone from now on. And let him rest until morning."

The Interrogator eyed the courtier with distaste. "Will he live that long?"

"I think so. But call me earlier next time."

"Thanks, magus," the Interrogator said, clearly relieved. "Without your help, might be me in his place next."

And then it would be the Interrogator that Nate put back together. He didn't think that would bother him; but he said he was happy to help, and followed the guard out.

At the manor, all was quiet. Charles, thankfully, was asleep in Arkady's room. Bindy had left Nate a piece of roasted meat, which he ate between two pieces of bread. He drank a beer that might as well have been water. He washed and shaved, and took the dirty water out into the garden to dump it.

Night had fallen. The moon was full and the garden was silvery and unreal. Carefully, he poured the water at the roots of some ferns that needed it. The air was warm and soft and damp, and it made Nate think of planting, and burial and renewal. It made him think of his mother.

Suddenly the ice inside him broke, and all the walled-away horror of the prison flooded through him. He smelled again the fetid cell and the courtier's wounds and saw every single torture device in bitter, detailed clarity; and he was appalled. Who am I, he thought numbly. What have I done; what will I do? The memory of the courtier suffering in the Interrogator's cell hurt him, ached in him like a bad tooth; like the worst tooth, like a tooth you would knock out with a rock rather than suffer with it for one second more. The Work Derie had done on him had not lasted. It happened sometimes. Things reordered themselves. He could go to her and tell her; he could ask her to redo it.

But he remembered, with a shudder, the feel of that uncon-
querable paralysis she'd put him under, his complete powerlessness in her grip, and something in him rebelled. He would
go to the prison when summoned, and he would do the Seneschal's disgusting bidding, because that was what he needed
to do. Derie would do what she wanted to him, whenever
she wanted, because that was what she'd always done. And he
would let her, because that was what he'd always done—just
as Charles let Nate practice the paralyzing Work on him, because Derie had ordered it—but he would not invite her attention, and he would not beg for it.

Still, without the numbness she'd Worked on him to shield
him from what he'd done, sleep would be impossible. He went
into the lab and mixed a strong draught: valerian, opium,
anything that might wall the dying courtier away for a few
hours. It tasted like acid and burned going down. By the time
he made it to his pallet he was already stumbling, but it took
several minutes of lying there, clenching and unclenching his
fists, for oblivion to come.

He woke early. His brain felt a little tender, as if it had
stumbled into a tavern brawl the night before, but the sky was
clear, one of Highfall's rare cloudless days. As Nate made tea,
he knew he could go on.

Charles still slept, so Nate took his tea out onto the front
step to wait for Bindy to save her knocking on the door. Normally if he wanted fresh air, he took it in the garden—which
was considerably less dank and a healthier place in general since
Nate had taken over—but today he wanted to see the trees in
the Square, to feel a bit of space around him. The morning
was brilliant with color: the gold-green of the light filtering
through the leaves, the glimmers of blue from the sky above,
the gray shadows on the white stone. The spires reaching up

in the distance, which could seem cruel under overcast skies, seemed almost elegant. The sun warmed his feet in his boots, and he heard the tiny *chip chip* of the sparrows pecking the ground for crumbs. The air smelled of smoke and the faint stale must of the Brake.

He heard footsteps. They slowed, and stopped. Nate looked up.

Vertus stood at the end of the walk. His clothes were nicer than they'd been when Nate had known him; not the violent colors the courtiers had favored, but not drab servingman's gray, either. The rich fabrics hung well on him. His eyes were as intent as ever.

"Good morning, magus," he said in a knowing, amused tone. Like he saw a joke that Nate wasn't quite clever enough to get. "Made it through the coup, I see."

His Highfall accent was broader than it had been. "As did you," Nate said.

"Indeed." Vertus put his hands in his pockets and rocked back on his heels. "Indeed, I did."

There was a long, evaluating silence. Nate was thinking about that last grim night with Arkady, aware that Vertus knew everything Nate had done. He was also considering the Seneschal, if his belief in Nate's utility would outweigh his years' acquaintance with Arkady. He was wondering, in short, how much damage Vertus could do. He would have been willing to bet that the former servingman's thinking ran along the same lines.

"Well," Vertus said finally, "just thought I'd see how you were getting on."

"Good to see you." It hadn't been, but it was what one said.

"Don't worry, magus," Vertus said. "You'll see me again soon."

CHAPTER FOURTEEN

Judah was walking back from the orchard when she came upon the Seneschal in the courtyard. Summer was ending and she wore one of Gavin's old coats against the chill in the air. Until she met the Seneschal, she'd been feeling lucky, because she'd found six unripe apples in an out-of-the-way corner of the orchard. An unexpected bounty, since the Seneschal's plunderers had stripped the grounds pretty thoroughly. She'd left three apples to ripen and marked the tree with a piece of cording that had once held back the drapes in Elly's bedroom. The plunderers had taken all the rope, too.

When they were first let out of their rooms—a month after the coup, that was, and a month ago, now—she would have run back to the House instead of walk. During those bizarre early days she'd found a destructive glory in hurtling through spaces that had once belonged to the courtiers: to hell with them, to hell with anything they'd ever thought or said about her. The Seneschal's men had taken everything of use or value during their month-long imprisonment, and as far as Judah was concerned, the rest belonged to the four of them. If she wanted to scuff the floors and spatter the marble with mud, she would, and she felt no remorse. The garden paths made for delicate silk shoes were already furred with moss, the carefully groomed galleries on the Promenade blurry with overgrowth. There were broken windows in the solarium and carpenter bees had eaten perfect round holes in the armory. In another year, the Discreet Walk would be impassable, the wisteria thick and tangled after the wet summer. Anything destructive Judah did was merely helping along the entropy of neglect.

Today, she felt too dull to run. She hadn't eaten anything since morning, and not much then. When she saw the Seneschal standing on the wide marble step that led to the grand foyer her feet grew even heavier, but she thrust her chin out at an angle she hoped read as arrogant, and said, "Come to visit?"

The Seneschal lifted a heavy-looking burlap bag. "I brought food. I took it up to the parlor, but nobody was there."

She gave the bag a critical glare. Her mouth was already watering, though. The food in the Seneschal's bags was never luxurious, but it wasn't boiled oats with winter squash, which was most of what they ate now. The oatmeal came from a huge bag the Seneschal had brought; the squash grew from seeds thrown in the midden yard. "Gavin's in Elban's study. Gavin's always in Elban's study. You know that."

"Yes. But Gavin wants to kill me."

With an affectionate smile, Judah said, "He really does. You should probably bring a guard with you when you come."

"I don't want to bring a guard. I'm not his enemy."

"He disagrees."

"The four of you are as much Elban's victims as anyone in Highfall." The Seneschal's gray eyes had new lines around them. "Surely, after everything that's happened, none of you can disagree with that."

"Elban didn't have me caned. Elban didn't kill my friend."

"Neither of which I would have had to do if you'd taken my advice."

"Advice? Are you referring to when you told me I wasn't allowed to take—what was your word—lovers? Because that felt more like an order."

"And is it so hard for you to believe that occasionally, my orders were in your best interest, and not merely designed to make your life horrible?" The Seneschal sounded as tired as Judah felt.

She didn't care. "Are you going give me the food or not?" He handed her the bag. She peeked inside: bread, a small bottle of what was probably oil, a bundle of greasy paper that held either meat or cheese. Not quite enough to get them through the week to his next visit.

Reading her expression, he said, "Things are still unsettled in the city. Goods are scarce."

Judah closed the bag. "That's disgraceful. You should find whoever's in charge and complain."

His lips twitched. "It'll get better."

"Doubtless," she said and walked away.

He didn't want to kill them. That was what he'd told them a week after the coup: *I watched you all grow up from children. I don't want to see any of you dead.* But he'd also told them that Highfall—or rather, New Highfall—was his top priority. He had other things on his mind than them at the moment; they would be allowed to stay in the House through the winter, and beyond that, they would see.

"He can't leave me alive," Gavin said as soon as he left. "Or

Theron. We'd be rallying points for Elban's loyalists. And he can't leave the House just standing here empty."

But the Seneschal had done exactly that, and none of them knew if Elban even had any loyalists. For four sleepless weeks, they'd listened through the locked door as the House was torn to pieces around them. They hadn't been given enough water to wash with, and soon their rooms reeked with stale linen and bodies and stress. Judah had started a mental list of tips for being put under house arrest: at the first sign of trouble, make sure you have clean clothes and clean linen. Lay in stocks of water, firewood, nicely perfumed soap, tooth powder; gather foods high in fat and sugar, alcohol and coffee. You will have trouble sleeping and you will have trouble staying awake. Find a deck of cards. Make sure none are missing. You will be bored; you will be very, very bored.

By the time they were released, Judah would have willingly walked to her own execution, as long as she could do it through fresh air, alone. They were on each other's nerves, all of them. Gavin had lost his father and his empire and had become fixated on Elly, on whether or not the Seneschal would still allow them to marry; she tolerated it as well as she could, but by the time it occurred to him to ask her opinion, her patience was gone. She'd told him that she really didn't see the point; he had looked stunned, then angry, and snapped that perhaps the point was that they loved each other.

Elly—who, with little else to do, had been drawing as Gavin talked—had put down her pen. "Gavin." Her blue eyes were hard and the word sounded less like an address than a call to attention. "Your father bought me for you when I was eight years old, just like he'd buy you a pony or a fancy new sword. My father wanted the money, and my mother wanted me away from my brothers, so they sold me like a useless plot of land, and ever since then you've worked your way through staff girls and courtiers and anyone else who'd have you. Love was never what our marriage was going to be about and it's childish and stupid of you to suddenly want me to pretend that it is."

Gavin's skin seemed to shrink on his body. Judah felt it. Elly shook her head. "I know you feel like everything's been taken from you, and I'm sorry. Truly, I am. But I'm not the last coin in your treasury and I'm not the last piece of your great lost empire. I'm a human being."

They hadn't spoken since. That afternoon, the Seneschal had unlocked the door, and Gavin more or less disappeared.

The rest of them went to work. The guards had taken their belt knives, but Elly had begged to keep hers, on the grounds that it was the smallest and least lethal and they needed some sort of blade to prepare food. They didn't bother looking for a way out; the Safe Passage was locked, as always, and the gate winches took six large men to work. They were one small-ish, addled man and two women, and they had enough to do. A handful of chickens had managed to evade the plunderers. Judah, out foraging, found a wily ewe that had absconded into the thick hedges at the foot of the Wall, spring lamb in tow. The stables were closer to the House than the sheepfold, so Elly had tied a drapery cord around the ewe's neck and led her there. (Judah had wanted to name the two sheep Current Mutton and Future Mutton, but Elly had preferred Cheese and Warm Socks, and since she was the only one who knew how to milk a sheep, she won.) On top of that, the plunderers, who were guards and not farmers, had missed a good bit of actual food in the kitchen garden, so they'd had greens and would eventually have tubers to eat. Some of the dustier shelves of preserved goods in the pantry had escaped notice, too.

But the tubers still weren't ready and the spinach was long gone. Elly was saving the jars of jam and pickled peaches to eat when the snow came, when there would be nothing fresh at all. The squash from the midden yard seemed a boon at first (Judah forced herself not to think about Darid, or her mother, or any of the other bodies buried there) but they'd long since grown sick of it. Past the kitchen garden were fields of rye, oats and wheat—which were how the sheep had survived—and at first the Seneschal had suggested they make use of those for food. But Elly remembered the scything-threshing-winnowing process from her childhood in Tiernan, and had resisted this, on the grounds that it was impossible. Two women, one smallish addled man.

"And what do you think small families do in the countryside?" the Seneschal had said.

"They don't grow oats as their primary food crop, and when they do grow oats, at harvest time they either hire help or trade for it," Elly said. "Are you offering me a field full of farmhands?"

"What would you pay them?"

"How about quarried stone? This whole place is built of it. They can take it away rock by rock for all I care."

The Seneschal had brought the twenty-pound sack of oats the next day, and after that Elly was in charge. She was the only one of the four of them who had ever seen bread baked or wheat ground, and it quickly became apparent that she was the only one of them who knew anything useful. In addition to milking the sheep, she could tell which of the plants in the ruined garden were weeds and which were beets and potatoes. She'd dispatched Judah and Theron to search the pillaged storerooms and pantries and guest rooms for anything forgotten, and she'd brought a pile of ancient, moldering herbals and cookery books from the Lady's Library. In addition to the oats, the Seneschal provided them with paltry amounts of oil, stringy meat, a wizened vegetable or two (never soap, coffee, butter or wine), and Elly was the only one who could make the packages into actual food.

The coup had made all of them more of whatever they'd been before. Elly had always been pragmatic and difficult to ruffle, and now she kept them all alive. Theron had been half-insane, and now he muttered to himself about cats nobody else could see and twitched at imagined noises; but he had also always been an ingenious problem-solver. When Elly sent him to the aquifer for water (the pipes had been ripped from the walls for their metal) he returned faster than anyone else, because he knew the quickest route, and the best way to distribute the weight of the waterskins on his body. After watching Elly try and fail to cook oatmeal first on the big stove in the kitchen and then in their small ornamental fireplace—she still had the little Wilmerian quickstove and one precious canister of gas for it, but she wanted to save that for an emergency—he had somehow found the scraps necessary to build an inelegant but efficient cookstove in the parlor, complete with ductwork to carry the smoke to the chimney. When Elly mentioned that the berries growing on the edges of the orchard would go bad quickly once picked (they had no sugar for jam), he'd appeared two hours later with a shiny square contraption that, when placed in the sun, dried the fruit in days. He built a winch to replace the one taken from the well in the stableyard, which made watering the sheep infinitely easier, and when Judah said, "How about a new pump for the water trough?" he didn't even seem to consider that she might be joking.

"The gasket would be the hard part," he'd said, and wandered off. He hadn't reappeared with a pump, not then or in the weeks since. But Judah had no doubt that one day he would.

As for Gavin—Gavin had always been vaguely selfish, and

now he'd done away with the *vaguely*. He showed up for meals because he had no other source of food, and would grudgingly do something specific if Judah or Elly told him he had to. They left the brute-strength tasks to him: because brute strength was what he brought to the table, but also because Elly was clever enough to see that chopping firewood was not unlike hacking at a practice dummy. It was difficult, and physical, and took just enough exactitude to distract him from his moods. But as soon as the firebox was full, he'd disappear again. Sometimes, in the evenings, the ground felt unsteady under Judah's feet. Trust Gavin to find a secret stash of alcohol somewhere in the House. He didn't invite her to drink with him, and she didn't invite herself. He'd lost his father, his kingdom and, effectively, his wife. She supposed he was entitled to his grief—for a while, anyway.

And Judah? She scavenged, she mended, she stirred a pot when Elly asked her. She scratched for Gavin when they needed him, and tried to cajole him into working a bit more than he wanted, but half the time when she set out to convince him to do something helpful he ended up convincing her to do nothing instead. "One hand of cards, Jude," he'd say—luckily, the deck of cards they'd had in their room when the coup came was complete—and the one hand would become ten and she'd end up slinking back shamefaced from Elban's study or the armory or the chapel (the plundered House suffered from a dramatic lack of seating), helpful task undone. She would vow to be more responsible next time. And then next time would come, and she wouldn't be any more responsible at all.

She could feel enough of what was inside him to know she didn't want any more of it, and avoided touching him. Her own feelings were bad enough; as busy as she was, she felt dazed, detached, always faintly angry. She missed food with flavor and she missed fires laid by unseen hands; she missed not ever having to consider that the food and firewood had been prepared and lugged and arranged by people whose childhoods had ended at ten so that people like her wouldn't get splinters. She resented having to work so hard, and felt guilty about resenting it, and resented the guilt. Judah had never felt like a courtier but their system had benefited her, as well, and her new firsthand knowledge of how hard staff jobs must actually have been waged constant war against her memories of pain and powerlessness. When she drew water for the sheep from the well by the stable she knew that lugging a few buckets of water was nothing compared to the work Darid had done every day; how unknowing she'd been, back then, and how kind he'd been about it. Then again, Darid had had underlings and a trough with a working pump—but how dare she think of Darid as lucky and herself as unlucky? Darid, who was buried somewhere in the very midden yard where their squash grew, who had died suffering, and done it for her. Her mother was buried there, too, somewhere deep in the layers of vegetable peelings and fireplace ashes—but she had seen Darid, held his hand, known his smell. If he could see her now, he would laugh at her, at the slipshod, half-capable way she did her chores.

No. Darid wouldn't laugh at her. He would be proud of her. *They didn't spike his head. I did that much for you.*

It had seemed a hollow gesture at the time. But three spiked skulls still stared over the kitchen yard, and every morning, while Judah gathered eggs under their empty eyes, she was resentfully grateful that none of them were Darid's.

As she moved from chore to chore she often found herself in places that had once been enemy territory. The grand foyer, the council chamber, the solarium: all empty and echoing, the life that had been lived there as faraway as an old story. Sometimes she dreamed that she was a ghost, that she'd slipped an hour ahead or an hour behind the rest of the world: she could feel the life that had been, hemming her in on all sides, but she couldn't see it or catch up or get further away and she didn't know which she'd choose, if she'd been able. Worse still were the bleak moments when she found herself at some mundane task that she'd done in exactly the same way the day before and would do in exactly the same way the next day—filling waterskin after waterskin at the edge of the aquifer, for instance, cold hands in the dark water and only the light of her lantern in all of the huge damp blackness yawning around her, knowing with all her being that she couldn't, she simply could *not*, load those skins onto her back and make the long, brutal trek upstairs under the weight of them. It was impossible. She would scream. She would lose her mind. She would do it anyway. Moments like that came a dozen times a day, moments when she considered whatever she had to do, thought, *I can't*, and then did. Instead of making her feel triumphant it made her exhausted and angry and frustrated.

The first time the magus had tapped on the open parlor door, a few days after they'd been freed, she was glad to see him. His was a different face to look at, and nothing about him made her feel guilty. "The Seneschal sent me to make sure you're all still healthy. And I brought food," he added.

But it wasn't just food, it was *good* food: butter and ripe cheese and bread, real bread, yeasty and crusty and sometimes even still warm. And candy. Dear gods, the candy. Of all the things Judah missed, she craved sugar the most: not soap or meat or even coffee but *sweets*, cream cakes and fruit tarts and smooth chocolates with bursts of liqueur in the middle that exploded like kisses in her mouth. She could stand the grime that covered every surface, the clothes that never quite felt clean and the constant feeling of being slightly colder than she'd like to be; she could even stand the drudgery (or had so far) but the idea that she might never again taste caramel made her want to burn down the world. That first time, he'd brought candied orange peel. Not even one of her favorites but the feel of the sparkling crust of sugar on her tongue had nearly made her cry. She'd intended to save some for the others but she'd eaten every bite, her throat aching with unshed tears.

He came every week after that, and proposed an exchange of goods for services: he would bring them food if they would let him check in on them. And maybe, he suggested, Judah could show him the House. Despite all the time he'd spent inside the Wall since Arkady's death, treating courtiers and the four of them, he knew only the corridors, their parlor, the Seneschal's office, and a few of the guest rooms.

"That's funny," she said. "I always had the impression that Arkady had to be forcibly removed from the premises."

With a sourness that she wasn't accustomed to in him, he said, "I'm not Arkady."

So she took him everywhere: the deserted solarium and the council chamber, the great hall and the kitchens. She'd shown him the retiring rooms and described to him the vanished tables of pastries and cheeses, the silver samovars of coffee and tea and drinking chocolate, the plush chairs and polished tables. She'd even shown him the tailor's suite and the cold, moldering baths. Soon she looked forward to his visits. She knew he was spying for the Seneschal to some end she would probably regret, but the food was precious and he wanted so little in return. He asked her to call him Nate, but that—oddly—she found that she couldn't do, so she called him nothing at all and he didn't seem bothered.

He was the one person she knew who didn't seem at all changed by the coup. When she met him in the courtyard the day after she found the apples, his clothes were neat and plain, his hair in its tidy queue. The glasses Theron had mended still sat on his nose. The eyes behind those glasses lit up when they saw her, as they always did, with an intensity that she didn't take personally.

He held out a small white paper bag. "Toffee almonds. How are the others?"

Chocolate-covered toffee almonds, actually. They were sweet and salty and rich and perfect. She ate three immediately and slipped the rest of the bag into the inside pocket of her coat so she wouldn't be tempted to eat the rest. "They're fine. Thanks for the candy. What shall we see today?"

One of the buttons on his shirt didn't match the others, and the thread wasn't exactly the right shade, either. Like the rest of him. She'd never been able to put her finger on the off thing, but it didn't bother her. "How about the outbuildings?" he said. "The stables, maybe?"

Fine. The shortest way to the stables was through the walled garden. During the wet summer it had sprouted a truly impressive crop of ferns that bent and swayed over the path; these and the other plants drew the magus's interest and she waited while he wandered around, peeking at mosses and, once, pulling up a root, which he brushed clean and pocketed. The toffee almonds called to her: the smooth chocolate coating, the crisp toffee jacket beneath it, the meaty almonds themselves. She tried not to think about them.

"Find something useful?" she said when he returned, and was surprised when he blushed.

"I think it's a sort of wild turnip. Good for lightening black moods."

"Do you suffer from black moods?"

He laughed. "I suffer the aftereffects of being raised by Caterina Clare. My mother can no more pass by a useful plant than she can fly."

"I forget that there are female magi where you come from."
She didn't know where that was, but she knew it was far away.

"There are no magi at all where I come from. We call ourselves healers or herbalists. My mother prefers herbalist. I prefer healer. If she'd called herself a healer, I'd probably want to be an herbalist." He grinned. "I guess it's always that way with mothers."

"I wouldn't know."

His expression softened. "Surely someone was there for you."

"Elban was all the father a girl could want," she said with a flat smile.

"Oh, well, fathers," he said dismissively, and then laughed. "Sorry. It's not an important relationship where I'm from. I always found it bizarre how obsessed with paternity the courtiers were here."

Judah thought of Firo, with his showy makeup, his embroidered coats, his absent son's dead mother. "What happened to the courtiers?"

He blinked, surprised by the change of subject. "Most of them left, at least the ones who had somewhere to go outside the city, and a way to get there. The heads of the richest families were…encouraged, I guess you'd say, to sign new trade agreements with the Seneschal, and then they left, too."

That wouldn't have been Firo. She remembered him telling her how poor Cerrington was. "What about the ones who weren't rich?"

Reluctantly, he said, "Not all of them made it. There was a lot of anger."

"They were killed?" Even as she said the words, Judah didn't know how they made her feel.

"Not necessarily. I know one woman who burned herself alive rather than give up her manor, since they aren't allowed to own property anymore. Some people would rather die than change." His jaw went tight. "Others went underground. Occasionally the guards catch one of them and make a big show of sending them to prison for hoarding. What's this?"

They had come to a burned black square in the grass. The air still reeked of ash, but a few green sprigs were already fighting their way up through the char. "The kennels," Judah said with the same surge of satisfaction she always felt. "Elban's hunting hounds were kept here."

Surveying the ruins, the magus said, "The guards burned it down?"

"No, I did," Judah said cheerfully. "Of course, Elly took the rest of my matches away afterward, but it was worth it. My only regret is that the hounds weren't actually inside at the time."

The magus's eyes widened. "You must really hate dogs."

"They weren't dogs." There was no reason for her to tell the story, but there was no reason not to. "And they killed my mother."

The magus froze. His cheeks went pale. "The hounds did?"

"Death by hound: one of Elban's favorites. The guards locked her in with them and they tore her apart. She was pregnant with me at the time. The hounds would have torn me apart, too, except—" Except that Darid had found her, and saved her, and twenty-two years later been executed for trying to save her again. Darid was a step too far. Darid was none of the magus's business. "Except they didn't."

He swallowed hard. "That's—that's horrific," he said, and his voice was rough with emotion.

"I don't remember it." She didn't know why she'd brought it up in the first place. "Obviously. So, the stables?"

The sheep were grazing in the paddock where the colts had been weaned. When Judah and the magus approached, they made their way to the fence to see if the humans had brought anything interesting. The magus let them sniff his hand.

"The big one's Cheese. The little one's Warm Socks," Judah said.

Scratching Cheese behind the ears, he said, "Clever. I'm guessing the stable looks like a stable inside, stalls and mangers and so forth. Smells strongly of horse."

No, the stable smelled like Darid. Or it had, the first time she'd been there after the coup. She'd had to step outside, then, and lean against the wall until she found her strength. Now the stable smelled different, and she minded it less. "More like sheep these days. But if we go in, these two will expect to be fed."

Cheese butted him firmly through the fence. "They already expect to be fed. What's the building in the back?"

It was the barracks, where Judah had never been. The magus wanted to see where the stablemen had lived, so she took him into the long building with its low ceiling and rows of hard narrow beds. Over every bed, a single nail had been hammered into the whitewashed wall; the day of the coup had been warm but only one coat hung there, too threadbare to bother stealing. Darid would never have allowed one of his men to wear something so tattered, but Darid hadn't been in charge by then.

"The staff must be out in the city now, too, aren't they?" Judah said, stepping over one of the small wooden chests staff were given for their few possessions, which had been emptied when the stablemen vacated and left where it lay.

The magus nodded. "The Returned. Most of them went back to their families. Any of them who wants a job in a factory can get one for the asking. In some ways, they're better off than anyone else, because the Seneschal is determined to make a big show of treating them well. Don't tell him I said that."

"Don't tell him about Cheese and Warm Socks. Elly's afraid he'll take them away if he finds out about them."

"He probably would." He gazed around the dingy room, where nothing remained to say anything at all about the men who had lived and died there. Then he shook his head and sighed. "Maybe you should burn this one down, too," he said.

"Maybe I will," she said.

She and the magus parted ways in the courtyard. The huge doors leading into the grand foyer were heavy, and she had to strain to push them closed. Turning then, she saw Gavin sitting on the broad marble staircase, watching her with amusement. His hair grown long and his shirt half-buttoned, he had never looked quite so much like a courtier to her. A little kohl, some ostentatious jewelry, and he wouldn't have looked even a bit out of place stumbling into one of the retiring rooms for coffee in the morning.

She wasn't surprised to see him. Since the coup, whenever they were together she'd noticed a weird doubling in her perceptions, as if she were seeing and hearing everything twice. She assumed the sensation had always been there, and she'd just been used to it because she'd seen so much of him. Now she saw him an hour a day, if that. "Catch," she said and tossed him the almonds.

He caught the bag and opened it greedily. "I thought I smelled the magus. The scent of lovesick puppy is hard to miss. What else did he bring?"

She dropped the bigger bag from the magus on the floor, and sat down next to him. "That's for Elly. You want a share, ask her for it."

"I'll pass. She hates me," he said cheerfully, and threw a handful of almonds into his mouth.

The profligate gluttony of it made Judah feel twitchy. "Give me some of those."

"Didn't you eat yours already?"

"I ate exactly a fourth. But if we're being selfish, I want my full half."

He grinned and handed the bag back. "Since we're being selfish, want to get drunk?"

Judah felt her eyes narrowing. "Why are you being so social all of a sudden?"

"I'm always social with you," he said, but that wasn't enough and they both knew it. He sighed. "Because every week, the magus comes, and he makes you look at things you don't want to look at and think about things you don't want to think about, and it hurts you and makes you sad, and that hurts me, and makes me sad. Plus, I knew you'd have candy." He stood and held out a hand to help her up.

She stared at it. It was not a gesture he would offer casually, not anymore. Finally, reluctantly, she slid her hand into his dry palm. In the time it took him to pull her to standing she saw everything inside him. Less of it was anger than she'd expected; most of it was grief mixed with a flat, colorless despair. Then she was standing next to him, his face full of curiosity and a faint surprise. Because of course he would have been able to read her as clearly as she read him. What she'd seen in him felt slippery and she worried about her losing her footing there; if Gavin had questions about what he'd seen, he kept them to himself.

"Come on," he said, dropping her hand. "You'll like this."

She left the magus's bag in the foyer and followed him to the kitchen. The massive worktable, worn smooth by generations of scrubbing, was covered in dust. Gavin picked up a lantern, one of the old ones with a candle inside, and lit it. Apparently, he still had matches. "This way," he said, and led her through the pantry to the steep staircase that wound down to the cellars. The lantern she used when she came down for water was one Theron had made, with a reflector to cast the light wide.

The circle of light picked out by Gavin's lantern was small and milky by comparison. They passed the root cellar, the wine cellar, the door that led to the catacombs and crypts; the air grew cooler and damper, the ground changing from smooth stone to brick. After Gavin passed the archway that led to the aquifer, the passageway—such as it was—narrowed. Soon she could touch either wall just by putting out an arm. Finally, they came to a small wooden door. Gavin ushered her through it.

If the circle of lantern light seemed small in the passage, inside the aquifer's cave it was minuscule. They stood on a stone ledge. The aquifer stretched out in front of them, silent and massive, and the cavern smelled of damp rock and cold. A rowboat lay upended next to the water. She hoped Gavin didn't intend to use it.

But Gavin was, indeed, flipping the boat over and pushing it into the water. The wood scraped uncomfortably on the stone, but then there was a swallowing sort of splash and the boat floated. He stepped into it and, steadying it against the ledge, said, "Get in."

"You're kidding." The thought of her tiny self floating in a flimsy wooden shell above those unknowable depths made her queasy.

"Not at all." He'd hung the lantern from a hook at the prow behind him, and was backlit. But she could hear the grin in his voice. "Come on, Jude. If I was planning to drown us, you'd already know."

Yes, she would. Gritting her teeth, she climbed into the boat, which rocked wildly. The ledge she'd just stepped off gleamed slick with moisture. There would be no climbing back up that way if she fell in.

When she was settled, he did something to the oars, and started to pull the boat out across the water. She could feel the faint burn of exertion in his shoulders and she could feel him enjoying it. If he did this on a regular basis, she should have felt it before; but she was so achy in her own right from lugging water and fodder for the sheep that she probably wouldn't have noticed. They spent so little time together now. They hadn't had one of their clandestine card games in—she had to think—nearly a week. She realized that she missed him. "Where are we going?" she said.

"Not far. You should be more impressed. This is a state secret, you know."

"Then how do you know about it?"

"Elban's journal."

"He wrote state secrets in his journal?"

"A few. Mostly they're about people he killed." She still couldn't see his face. Over his shoulder, the wan circle of light suddenly illuminated a damp stone wall and there was a soft thud as the boat knocked against something. Gavin shipped the oars and threw the rope over something Judah couldn't see. "Here, watch."

Carefully, she leaned over the side until she saw it: a small wooden platform, floating low in the water. A short length of chain tethered it to the wall, and a dozen ropes, thick and glistening with oil, snaked down from it into the water. Gavin chose one and began to haul, making the boat rock uncomfortably. The rope was dark and wet where it had been submerged and as Gavin pulled it out of the water it lay coiled in the bottom of the boat like a serpent. When the ghost of something appeared at the end of it, floating up from the depths, it wavered in a way that seemed almost alive. Judah shivered.

The something was only a wooden box. It was bound with a rusty iron bolt, but not locked. Gavin opened it and Judah was surprised to see that the straw inside was dry, or at least dryish. He set a handful of it aside, revealing nine small circular objects, poking out of the straw like seedlings: corked wine bottles. Gavin pulled one out. It was sealed with red wax; the metal chain around its neck was corroded but the stone tag that hung from it, carved with an elaborate S, was still legible.

"Elban's best Sevedran," Gavin said. "Apparently there's something about aging it in water. The only person who knew it was here was Elban's favorite guard, and he's one of the ones who died in the coup."

"The Seneschal doesn't know?" Judah had a hard time conceiving of anything happening in the House without the Seneschal's knowledge.

"Seneschal's an ascetic. No wine, no women, no song. Anyway, I'm sure he knew at one point, but he seems to have forgotten. By the time he remembers, I plan to have drunk it all." He took a second bottle out and handed them both to her; then he tossed the straw back into the box, closed it, and let it back down into the water. "I'll show you my new favorite drinking spot. It's hilarious."

After they dragged the boat out of the water, he led her through the catacombs to the crypts. Each tomb was marked by a bust of its occupant. The first tombs were very old ones, before Gavin's family had taken power. The busts were utterly unfamiliar, the clothes and hairstyles quaint. It wasn't until the third corner that Judah began to see familiar features: Gavin's jaw, Elban's cheekbones, that particular mouth they all shared. Carved stone eyes, blank and dead. They passed Mad Martin the Lockmaker; Gavin's grandfather; a few younger men that were probably second sons, the ones who didn't live. Eventually they came to Clorin, whose stone visage was beautiful and sad. Beyond her, the ledges were empty. Elban's corpse had been burned, eventually, the ashes tossed in the midden yard like countless staff before him.

Gavin pulled himself up to sit on one of the empty ledges and began rummaging through his pockets. Judah looked at the place he'd chosen, and back at Clorin's tomb, and did a quick calculation. The ledge he sat on was his own. "That's morbid," she said.

"But funny." He nodded at the other end of the ledge, which was wide enough to accommodate a stone sarcophagus and would be plenty comfortable for two. "Sit down."

Reluctantly, she sat. He had a corkscrew. Where had he found a corkscrew? The wine was cool and creamy, thick as suede on her tongue. "That's good," she said, voluptuous warmth spreading through her.

"Yes." Gavin took the bottle back from her. "It is."

He sat against one end of the ledge and she sat against the other, their legs slotted next to each other like books on a shelf. The crypt wasn't unpleasant. It was cool but not cold or damp. The presence of his mind at the edge of hers felt companionable and easy as they traded the bottle back and forth. Somewhere above them, Elly was probably stoking the fire in the stove, putting on a pot of water to boil whatever mess they were going to eat that night. It seemed irrelevant. Everything Gavin drank layered on everything Judah drank and they didn't feel the same but they didn't feel entirely different.

"The magus isn't a lovesick puppy," she said. Her tongue was thick in her mouth. So drunk, so fast. "And he doesn't make me sad. He brings me candy."

"Something made you sad today."

She thought of the way the kennel had burned, the long gray column of smoke. The flames had seemed as depthless as the aquifer and they'd crackled happily as they ate the building from inside. It had collapsed with a mighty *whoosh* that had felt like a piece falling out of the world. The empty space felt clean, unencumbered. But that was too hard to explain. "We went to the stables."

"Ah," Gavin said. He moved his legs so they pressed against

hers in a warm, comforting sort of way. "That seems like another lifetime, doesn't it?"

Darid's capable hands, thick and scarred with work but so deft at tying a knot, soothing a horse. "Not really."

"That was back when I was going to marry Elly. I guess we've both lost love."

"Yours wasn't eviscerated," Judah said. "Yours is upstairs cooking, and if you'd try being reasonable for once, you might still be able to fix things."

Her tone was acid, but he only laughed. The bottle glinted in the lantern light as he took another drink. "What would be the point? The Seneschal's not going to let us live. Elly, maybe; Theron and me, no way. Can't have stray heirs for people to rally around."

"Glad to hear I have such a long and healthy future ahead of me."

She expected to feel the heat of a blush, but he only said, "If you want to duck out early, I'm game. You're the only reason I'm still around." His voice was offhand and terrible. "Well, you and a lack of sharp objects. I've never heard of anyone dying by falling on their axe, and I don't think Elly would let me use her knife."

A crawling chill ran over Judah. "I don't want to die."

"Then we live," he said simply. "As long as the Seneschal lets us."

"He hasn't killed us yet."

"I'll bet he's got a very good and nasty reason for that."

"The people like us. The stableman—" she couldn't say his name to Gavin "—said his sisters had dolls of us, even."

"Yes, I'm sure when we die of mysterious illnesses, they'll all mourn deeply and profoundly for about a week."

He sounded relaxed and pleasant. Posturing even now. Judah found it annoying. "Stop."

"Stop what? I know how these things work, Judah. I've been reading Elban's journals. I know how *everything* works. He was an obsessive journaler, did you know that? Multiple volumes, private and extra-private. The ones I've been reading lately are the extra-private ones." He half laughed. "And you used to scold me for flirting with the staff girls. You want to know what Elban used to do to the staff girls? And boys, occasionally. Even a lesser courtier or two. That extra bedroom of his—you want to hear about that?"

"You're not like him," Judah said.

"I wasn't going to be. I was going to be better." He was twisting the corkscrew in his hand, pressing his thumb against the pointed tip. Judah could feel it, a tiny sting that threatened more pain than it delivered. "But maybe I wouldn't have been. Maybe it's too much power for one person to have and still stay...sane. Human. Maybe it's a good thing that all of this is ending. Maybe—"

Suddenly Gavin stopped; cocked his head, listening. All at once he was crouched next to her. The sarcophagus for which the shelf had been built would have been huge, grand; there was more than enough room for him to press her back into the corner. Both of his arms were around her. It was more contact than she'd had with anyone since Darid, and more contact than she'd ever had with Gavin. His smell filled her nostrils, wood smoke and wine and the same stale smell they all had, because they could never get clean, and his slippery, treacherous despair filled her mind. It was frightening. Her spine arched against him in resistance and a gasp of horror escaped her.

Quickly, he clamped a hand over her mouth. Which was worse: bare skin. His strength was too much and the despair was too much and she went limp.

Then she heard it, as if from underwater. Footsteps. Slow,

steady. There was nobody it could be, nobody it *should* be, down here. No light came; only the steps. The walker was passing Gavin's grandfather's tomb. Clorin's. The walker was in sight: Theron. Moving through the darkness with no light of his own, he didn't even seem to notice as he entered the wan flicker of their lantern. His eyes were fixed on the ground, his expression blank.

Gavin's arms tightened around Judah, his hand pressed more firmly against her mouth. She could barely breathe. She could barely have breathed, anyway. As Theron passed them, he shuddered; his steps quickened; but he didn't speak to them. In a moment he'd disappeared farther into the crypt, where nobody had bothered to carve niches yet. Maybe even down to the natural rock, the caves worn by the aquifer eons ago: before the crypt, before the House, before any of them.

When Theron was gone, Gavin's arm around her loosened, but didn't let go. He took his hand away from her mouth, but it was too late. She'd seen inside him. The courtiers had pretended not to care, wearing apathy like a veil to shield their private desires and agendas. Gavin truly didn't care about anything. His inner self was a yawning pit of grief and frustration. There was a flicker of warmth for her, pangs of longing for Elly and Theron. That was all.

"You don't want to talk to him when he looks like that," he said quietly. "I've tried. The things he says—" The words trailed away and she felt his cheek press against the top of her head. Another flood of despondency washed over her. It felt like the drug the magus had given her after she'd been caned. It dragged her down, emptied her. In desperation, she did what she had always done when he was upset, and filled her mind with water: the aquifer, with its permanence and patience. The feeling of drift on the boat. She had hated the boat but for Gavin she made it easy and restful.

The knot inside him loosened. She felt his body ease, too. He let out a long breath of air, and his arms around her went lax. "I'd forgotten how good it feels to be around you."

She squirmed away from him, suddenly angry. "Because I make you feel good, you idiot." He'd grabbed her, held her, covered her mouth so she couldn't even object. She was angry about that, but she was also angry about the despair. Who was he to despair at the loss of his future when she'd never had a future at all?

"What?" He sounded puzzled, and she realized: they never talked about the bond. Even the scratch code had evolved without an actual conversation. The only time they'd ever discussed the bond had been in the study, when they'd been forced to.

Tell me when you feel the knife. Tell me when it begins to hurt. Do you feel the warmth of the coal, or just the burn?

"When you're angry, or upset, I—touch you and I think about water." She felt exposed, vulnerable. "To calm you down. Just now it was the aquifer."

"I was thinking about the aquifer," he said, wondering. "I didn't even realize. Do you always use that?"

"No. It could be a puddle, or the reflecting pool. Anywhere calm. It's as much for me as you," she added. "Your head's not exactly a pleasure garden, you know."

"Like you're any better." He took her hand. "Do it again."

Appalled, she pulled away. "No."

"Just for a minute. So I can see what it's like, now that I know you're doing it."

She hesitated, reluctant—but her reluctance didn't make any sense, did it? She'd done the water thing hundreds of times, thousands even. She didn't know why it should feel different now, but it did. "It doesn't feel right."

"It doesn't feel right." He leaned back against the ledge, his voice cold. "So it's fine for you to play around in my head as long as I don't know about it, is that how it works? What else have you been doing in there all these years?"

"Gavin," she said, exasperated.

"Can you make me do things? Pull my strings like a little puppet?"

"Our lives would be a hell of a lot easier if I could," she snapped. The anger she felt in him was petulant, manipulative and—unlike the despair—entirely for show. "Oh, for gods' sake. You impossible, whining child. Sit down, give me your stupid hands. I'll show you."

She sat on the ledge next to him and took his hands. The petulance, as she'd expected, vanished instantly now that he had what he wanted; his fingers curled eagerly around hers, his face interested and expectant. For a moment, through all of her exasperation with him, she felt a twinge of pleasure, of comfort. He needed her. So much had changed, but this one thing hadn't.

She thought about water. Not the aquifer; the crypts were cold and the despair in him was cold, too, frustrated and impotent. So she gave him the baths. At evening, the best time, when the light was soft and the bathing rooms quiet. The smells of herbs and wet wood. The water itself, steaming and fragrant, surrounding cold toes, legs, everything, soothing away the chill like an embrace. The gentle motion of the ripples from the pumps that kept the water clean, the soft laps like kisses at the edges of the pool. Movements slow and languid. Gentle resistance on fingers. She had done this so many times. She could do it without trying.

Slowly, she became aware that something was different: a sense of unfamiliarity that swelled into unease, and then ripened into fear. Something new was happening. The water was the same, and the sense of being doubled, herself and notherself. But there was also…something… She felt like she was slipping away. Being drained. He was reaching into her, she realized; reaching into her and *taking*.

She yanked her hands back. Curled them protectively against her. "Don't do that."

"Don't do what?" His voice was thick, his words almost slurred. In the dim light from the lantern he gave her a dazed, delighted grin. "Judah," he said, and put his hands on her knees. "That was amazing. You've been doing that for me? All this time?"

Not like that, she wanted to say.

"It's wonderful." For the first time since the coup he seemed quick and lively and full of happiness. "How did I not know? No wonder the world's felt so bleak lately." Before she could speak he grabbed her head in his hands and kissed her on the forehead. "Oh, Judah, I love you. You beautiful, devious sorceress, you. I love you more than anything. You're my life, you know that? You're my entire life."

And because his hands were still on her, because he was pressing his forehead to hers, she could feel that it was true. His love for her was as strong as his depression had been, warmer than the water in her imagination, softer and more fragrant. The last time she'd felt so unequivocally, comfortably loved, she had been lying in a sunny field with Darid as he unlaced her boots and peeled down her leggings. But she'd had to judge Darid by his words and aspect; Gavin, she could *feel*.

"Do it again," he said. "Gods, let's never stop."

"Just—easy, okay?" Feeling like she needed to say something, not sure what words she should use. "Be patient. Just let me do it."

"I will let you do whatever you want," he said, and took her hands again.

Oh, Gavin. Her Gavin. He was dying inside, and she was

the only one who could help him. She steeled herself, because she knew that he would not be patient; steeled herself, and thought of water.

After, he held her hand all the way upstairs. It no longer seemed to matter. He felt placid and smooth, all his thorns pulled. If something still flowed through their clasped hands, she was numb to it. She was more exhausted than she had ever been. She could not have pointed to the place where she hurt but she felt scraped raw. If he dropped her hand she knew her arm would fall like a dead thing, and in fact there was a good chance that all of her would fall like a dead thing, so perhaps it was good he kept her hand in his until they reached the parlor door. When he did let go—reluctantly? Was it her imagination? He gave her a wry, almost secretive smile, and kissed her forehead again. She accepted the kiss as she would a passing moth. Then he pushed the door open.

The parlor smelled blandly of whatever was in the porridge Elly had simmering on the stove. Theron was already eating, bent low over a bowl. Whatever state he'd been in down in the catacombs, he was back now; when Judah and Gavin entered he frowned, but kept eating. Judah was too tired to worry much about the frown.

On the settee, Elly focused on her own bowl of sludge as if she could will it into being something more palatable. She looked up, saw Judah and Gavin, and said, "Hello," with only the vaguest interest.

Gavin held out the bag the magus had brought; Judah herself had almost forgotten it. "Look what we have," he said, and dropped the bag into Elly's lap. Then he leaned down and kissed her lightly on the cheek, which made her jaw drop; took a bowl, filled it, and began to eat.

CHAPTER FIFTEEN

After that, wherever Judah was, Gavin was never far. At night she went to tend the sheep—Elly was trying to make bread, some process involving a frothy bowl of flour and water that smelled musty and alcoholic—and Gavin came along. Walking to the stable with him, working together to separate the lamb from the ewe and filling the mangers with whatever fodder they had to offer, Judah found herself reminded of all the reasons she loved Gavin. His sense of humor bit and surprised, and it was fun to bat words back and forth with him. What she didn't like was what inevitably came after the night's chores, when the bucket of milk was secured in the wagon Theron had built and Gavin reached expectantly for her hands. He made her feel emptied out, like a discarded wine bottle. And she couldn't say exactly what he took from her, but she knew what she got in return: anger, depression, hurt. When Gavin was in her head, Judah herself seemed trivial and unimportant, nothing worth bothering with. She tried to hold on as long as she could, but there always came a moment when she could feel nothing that wasn't him and think nothing that wasn't him and know nothing that wasn't him. A part of her liked the oblivion, even craved it: the absence of that tangled snarly thing she felt herself to be, neither here nor there, neither this nor that. Her Judah-ness was sand in the water that was Gavin, ashes swirling in his wind. Every time, it was easier to disappear into him. Every time, it was harder to find herself again.

One morning, when she met the magus in the courtyard, she was feeling particularly lethargic, particularly not-herself. As she took the bag from him, she said, "I don't suppose you brought any coffee, did you?"

He shook his head. "There's no coffee to bring. Coffee comes from the Southern Kingdom, along with green dye, oranges and about half a dozen herbs I'd love to get my hands on before people start dying this winter. Even the black market hasn't been able to get coffee through yet."

"There's a black market?"

"Of course. You don't expect the factory managers to live on the same overpriced trash they sell to the rest of the city, do you?" His tone was caustic, needle-sharp. Then he smiled a tense, weary smile. "I'm sorry. Things are difficult in the city right now. Yes, there's a black market. The courtiers who stayed—all they have to sell are their contacts."

She thought again of Firo, and that horrible girl who'd had her hooks in Gavin—funny, Judah had hated her so much, but now she couldn't remember her name. "Gavin says the Seneschal will kill him eventually. That he can't let Elban's heirs run around with a claim to the throne, because the courtiers might try to put him back on it."

"I suppose they could," the magus said, as if it didn't matter. "Can we see the old wing today?"

So she led him through the dusty corridors to Theron's workshop. His tools were still in the parlor where Judah and Gavin had left them, so the workbench was bare, but other than that the place was unchanged: notebooks piled on the shelves, the cloth over the window. The smell was the same, smoke and lamp oil and metal. She felt a pang of sadness, of longing for the days when Theron could be found hiding away here, too busy tinkering to talk.

A moment passed before she noticed the magus standing stock-still in the doorway. As she watched, he moved like a sleepwalker to the tapestry that covered the stairs; pushed it aside, and peered up into the gloom.

"It's a tower," she said, "but the stairs are broken."

"Impassable?"

"Unless you can fly." She understood the tower's appeal. The last time she'd been here, it had called to her, as well: the idea of getting away, rising above the toil and the grimness.

The magus gave her a quick, fierce look—it reminded her of the way Theron had looked, when most of his mind was engaged in a problem and he wanted to be left alone to figure it out—and then stepped through the door. By the time Judah followed him he was already climbing the winding stone stairs. He wouldn't get far; she remembered the collapsed place, the steps nothing but broken teeth jutting out of the wall. She remembered watching Gavin test one with a foot, and hearing the short, startled scream from Elly, waiting below, as the tooth broke and fell clattering to the ground. They'd been twelve then, and in her memory Gavin's body was still child-slight, all long limbs and narrow shoulders. Remembered him calling down to Elly, teasing: *You sure you won't come see, El?* They'd teased her mercilessly about her fear of heights. At the time it had felt harmless, but now it seemed cruel. They'd all been so young.

Above her, she heard the soft shuffle of the magus's boots slow, stop, and—after a moment—descend. When he reached the bottom, he said, "There are gaps, but they'd be passable if a person was really determined."

"Nobody is."

"Aren't you curious? Don't you wonder what happened here?"

"I don't have the energy for curiosity anymore."

They were back out in the workshop now. "You do look tired."

"Oh, I'm fine," Judah said with a breeziness she didn't feel. "If you're going to be concerned about someone, be concerned about Theron. He's still seeing imaginary cats."

She meant to distract him, but he surprised her. "Just because you can't see something doesn't mean it's not there. Some people would call the link between you and Gavin imaginary."

"That's different. That's real. We were born with it."

"I doubt that. You aren't related. You weren't born in the same room. How would you be linked from birth? The real question, though, is not when, but why you were linked."

"I've always assumed it was a bad joke."

He raised an eyebrow. "Your mother was torn apart by dogs getting you in here. Seems like a lot of trouble for a bad joke." She didn't respond. Patiently, he said, "Think about it. If your health wasn't linked to Elban's heir's, they probably still would have let Lady Clorin keep you—for a while. But as soon as you could be taken away and put to work, you would have been. Somebody didn't want that for you. Somebody wanted you to live, and they wanted you to live here. As close to Elban's blood as you could possibly get."

Nobody had ever said things like this to Judah. All at once

she was filled with a cold, prickling suspicion of this man, with his spectacles and odd coloring. Who she didn't know, really, any more than she'd known Arkady. She felt her eyes narrow. "Why does the Seneschal send you to spy on us?"

Evenly, and without hesitation, he said, "He wants to know if you're getting desperate. And *spy* is a harsh word. It's not as if you don't know he's sending me."

The prickling suspicion faded into a faint unease. "Is he paying you?"

"I get to keep my manor and my apprentice. I don't care about the manor, but my apprentice is special." He hesitated. "So are you."

She ignored that, although his murky blue eyes were sincere enough behind his glasses. "What happens when we get desperate?"

"Gavin abdicates. The empire falls. For what it's worth, I don't think the Seneschal has any intention of killing you."

"That doesn't make sense," she said, and he said, "Nothing here makes sense."

In the parlor, Elly was scrubbing midden dirt off a squash; when she saw the bag from the magus, she said, "Theron, love, come do this for me, please," and took it eagerly, wiping her hands on her skirt. "Butter. Real cheese! Oh, smell that, Jude." She thrust a chunk of ripe cheese under Judah's nose. "Whatever you're doing, keep doing it. I love that weird little man, I really do."

"The Seneschal makes him come," Judah said.

"Who cares?" Elly said cheerfully. She pulled a paper sack out of the parcel, peered inside and sighed with pleasure. "Chocolate. Ask him if he can get more gas flasks for my quickstove."

They ate the squash roasted, with rice and wild onions.

Thanks to the magus's butter, it tasted better than usual, but if Judah never saw another squash again, it would be too soon. No matter how much Elly scrubbed them, Judah could never entirely get the sight or smell of the midden yard out of her mind. When they were done, Elly took the scraps and pulp and seeds and added them to a pot she kept on the stove, full of a bland dirty-orange stock. She used it for cooking rice, or oatmeal, or whatever she had; once she'd said that if they had nothing else, they could always drink it. It had been a joke, but if the Seneschal ever stopped bringing supplies, Judah knew they'd end up there eventually.

Afterward Gavin offered to help Elly with the sheep. While they were gone, Judah sat with a book, but the oil the Seneschal brought them was cheap and gave off a wan, blurry light that was hard to read by. The book was a history of some province she'd never heard of; it was old and dull. All of the books left in the library were old. Sometimes the pages fell out at the gentlest touch, because the glue was so desiccated. She wondered if anyone was writing new books anymore. She wondered how long it had been since anyone had.

A frantic scratching started on Judah's wrist. *Need you. Find me.* He was digging deep. It burned. A few moments later, Elly came back in alone. She hung up the shawl she'd worn, which was too delicate for the weather, and said, "I wish the coup had happened before shearing time. We could really use the wool. Can't shear now. They'll need their fleece to get through the winter." She sat down and began to unlace her boots.

Now? Please?

"What happened?" Judah said, and Elly said, "Why do you think anything happened?"

Wordlessly, Judah pulled up her sleeve and showed Elly the angry red scratches. "Oh." Elly seemed to deflate, her spine bending and her shoulders sinking. "Well."

Need you.

Judah sighed. He'd drawn blood, she could feel it. She stood up.

"Don't go," Elly said suddenly. "Let him deal with it himself."

"I'll be back soon," Judah said.

She could feel him pulling on her, drawing her to him. He was in Elban's study; of course he was. The room hadn't changed. Nothing had been taken during the coup. A fire crackled in the fireplace, and Gavin dug at the logs with a poker. The same poker she'd been burned with, probably. Relief flooded his face when he saw her. "Finally," he said. He stood up and reached for her hands.

She put them behind her. "How are you, Judah? Anything new in your life, Judah?"

"I know how you are." His voice was lifeless. "I know everything you feel. There's nothing new in any of our lives, and there never will be. Unless something's happened with your scrawny little magus." She thought he meant the words to come out teasing, but instead they were nasty and cold. "Which would mean he's not very good at it, because I never felt a damn thing. He'll have to work harder than that to compete with your stableman."

Hearing him mention Darid in such a crude way made her anger flare. "Keep being unpleasant and I'll fill your head with fire instead of water," she snapped.

For an instant his face was ugly and belligerent. Then he winced, and collapsed onto the sofa. "You're right. I'm sorry." He shook his head. "I shouldn't have said that. I should never say anything again."

Warily, she sat down next to him. "Why? What else have you said?"

"I asked Elly tonight if she still loved me. She said she didn't

458

know. That she thought she had, all those years, but maybe she'd just been relieved that I wasn't awful." He looked miserable. "I lost my temper. Asked her if that was all it took to get her into a man's bed. Him not being awful."

Which was Gavin all over. Why be content with a mere insult when you could go to the most unpleasant place possible? "Oh, Gavin," Judah said.

"She said that 'not awful' was a step above what I'd always looked for in a woman. Which—" The fire snapped. He stared at his closed fists. "Everything used to be so simple. We were just…together. It worked. I went with other women, sure. But not seriously, and she never seemed to care. Now there's nobody else—literally, nobody else—and suddenly she's not sure she ever loved me. She said to me, we can make our own decisions now. Like there are any decisions to make, except die now or die later. And even that's more the Seneschal's choice than ours." He pressed his hands to his eyes, digging at the sockets with the heels of his hands. "Gods, Judah, I can't go on like this. Nothing is the way it was supposed to be. Why am I the only one who seems to notice that? Why am I the only one who cares about anything other than food?"

The inside of him was all twisting and agony. "Because food is important," she said. "The rest of us are just surviving, Gavin, the same as we've ever done. But I know it's different for you, and I'm sorry."

"I don't want your pity. I want your help." He didn't open his eyes, but his sadness and anger radiated. "You're the only one who can actually help me. So help me, Judah."

"I'm trying," she said, and he said, "Not with words," and put his hand out toward where he knew she would be. And because he didn't open his eyes, he didn't see her flinch; he didn't see her hesitation, or her doubt, before she took his hand, anyway.

★ ★ ★

Theron's fruit-drying contraption was clever but it took two people to take it apart so the drying trays could be brought in. Judah was helping him in the damp, fading evening, although her fingers felt stupid. Theron frowned as they worked. Judah knew he was probably thinking about the contraption, trying to figure out a better way. She was of no use; her mind felt stupid, too.

So when, out of nowhere, he said, "You shouldn't let Gavin do what he does to you," her stomach lurched, like she'd tripped and almost fallen. It was on the tip of her tongue to say *Gavin doesn't do anything to me*, but Theron's face was open and frank and so she didn't bother. Instead, she said, "What do you know about that?"

"I know it makes you feel wrong. The magus feels wrong, too. He's not what he says he is. He's a pot with a lid, you know? You don't see what's under."

"Everyone's like that."

"No," he said. "You are, and Gavin is, and he is."

His eyes did that thing she found so disconcerting, tracking nothing across the floor. But not mindlessly, not thinking of something else. Watching. "What about your cats?" she said. "Are they what they seem to be?"

He gave her a surprised look. "You can't see the cats."

"Theron," she said as her eyes filled with tears, "there are no cats."

It felt—to use his word—*wrong*. Like waking a sleepwalker. Theron only nodded. "I know. They're not really cats. I think my brain just sees them as cats." He considered. "I'm not sure they're anything. I think they're extra. Left over. Like when I used to take something apart and put it back together, sometimes it looked right and worked right, but there would be a piece left." His eyes were wide and guileless. "I make you feel guilty."

The tears were spilling over now. She dashed at them roughly. "I gave you the antidote too late. The magus said to give it to you as soon as he left. I waited too long. And now—" She stopped. She couldn't say what Theron was now. She didn't know.

"I'm not the same," he said. "But I'm not unhappy. You are."

He spoke so gently. She touched his hand. Sweet Theron—no, he had never been sweet. But he had been perceptive and honest. The hallucinations were new, but he had always seen what others hadn't.

"I'm fine," she said.

The next morning, she met the Seneschal in the courtyard. He gave her a hard look. "Have you seen the magus lately?"

She had. Was it the workshop? Was that the last time? She couldn't think. "A few days ago, I guess."

"You look tired."

Judah no longer felt the need to be polite, and was tired of hearing about how tired she looked. "I've eaten nothing but squash and oatmeal for weeks. How should I look?"

"I know life in here isn't easy for the four of you." He was always so placid. "And I'm sorry about that. It was the only way I could keep you alive: to tell the people that you were undergoing some of the same hardships they always have."

"Yes, I'm sure this is all very satisfying for them. Can I have the food now?" Breakfast had been slim that morning: Elly's latest bread experiment, which was rock-hard and flat-tasting, and—of course—squash. She knew the bulging bag held the drabbest and cheapest of foodstuffs, but she wanted it anyway. The last bag the magus had brought was already empty. Had it really been only a few days? Or longer? She reached for the bag.

The Seneschal held it away. Grabbing for it would mean dodging around him like a child and she didn't have much pride left, but she had too much for that. Just the faintest awareness of it, like a limb about to go numb.

"Marry me," he said.

She froze. "You're joking."

"Not at all. You're the only one everyone in the city unequivocally likes or sympathizes with. Seeing you throw in with New Highfall would raise morale." He considered, then added, "There needn't be anything physical between us, but you'd be treated well. And you'd get to leave the House. You wouldn't have complete freedom, of course—you know nothing about the city, and you wouldn't be safe without a guard—but life would be easier for the others while they remain inside. Food goes further split three ways than four, doesn't it?" He held up the bag. Still not giving it to her. "They'd be better fed. Healthier. So would you. Also, the Nali chieftain is still in the city. What if we can figure out how the bond between you and Gavin works? You've spent your entire life subject to him, haven't you? When he misbehaved, you were punished. When he got drunk, you ended up with the headache. Wouldn't you like to be your own person? Completely independent, beholden to nobody?"

"Except you," she said.

He dismissed that. "You've always been beholden to me. I've protected you your entire life. When you were a baby, and Clorin wanted to keep you, I convinced Elban it would do no harm. Later, when we discovered the bond...you might not realize it, but I protected you then, too, just as I'm protecting you now."

"You held a hot coal to my foot," she said.

He nodded. "And put you in the snow, and bled you. Elban was for killing the both of you and starting over entirely. Once again, I convinced him otherwise. I told him I thought the bond could be managed with the proper training. Elban enjoyed seeing you hurt. I didn't."

At last, he offered her the bag. She still wanted what was inside, but she didn't want to take it from his hand. She didn't want to take anything from his hand. But she needed the food. They all did. Humiliated, furious, she snatched the bag from him. "Go away."

For the first time, he stepped toward her. She automatically stepped back, but his gray eyes were serious, not amorous. "You have known me in unkind circumstances. I am not an unkind person. I will not force you to do anything, but this is your best choice. Surely you see that."

Her best choice. She had spent all her life watching Elly prepare to be Lady of the City and listening to the Tiernan talk about how it could always be worse, how wives in Highfall had only the rights their husbands gave them. What rights would the Seneschal give her? A life outside the Wall, in the city, but under guard. As much a prisoner as she'd ever been. Brought out occasionally, perhaps, to make the Seneschal look good. On the balcony over the Lord's Square, say. Twice a year. On the solstices.

No. With every weary shred of her being: no. The Seneschal wasn't even *not awful*; he was merely not as awful as he could have been. He had deliberately tortured her when she was a child, every year, for all the years of her life. And now he expected her to marry him because he hadn't enjoyed it.

She didn't mean to tell anyone, but that night, watching Elly milk, the words came out of her mouth, anyway. And she'd known they would, hadn't she? She'd felt the weight of them pressing inside her like a sneeze or a laugh, and she'd known from the moment they'd left the parlor that she wouldn't be able to keep them to herself.

"The Seneschal asked me to marry him," she said.

Milk squirted sideways as the ewe's teat slipped out of Elly's hand. Hands still at the sheep's udder, she gaped at Judah for a moment. Then suddenly, wryly, she laughed; took the ewe in hand again, and went back to work. "Well, that's a surprise. Are you going to do it?"

"When I was eight years old, he held a hot coal to my foot." *And put me in the snow, and bled me.* She didn't know why the coal held precedence, except that its glow had been so bright and lovely, and Elban had burned her, too. "So, no. I don't understand why all of their plans involve us marrying or not marrying, anyway. First Elban, and then Gavin, and now him."

Elly's mouth twitched. "You should marry Theron and upend everything."

"At least Theron wouldn't put me under constant guard." Judah wanted to kick something, but everything around her— the bucket, the wagon, Elly's stool—was scarce and valuable. Savagely, she said, "Do we exist only to be married?"

"I do. Or at least, I did. It was the justification of my entire existence." Elly's hands still worked at the sheep's udder. "I hate to say it, Jude, but...hot coal aside, it's not a bad idea."

Judah let that sink in. Finally, she said, "He hinted that the Nali chieftain could break the bond, but...if I can keep that from happening, and I marry him, he won't kill Gavin. Which means he probably won't kill the rest of you, either."

"That has nothing to do with why I think it's a good idea."

"Should I not take into account the fact that you might be executed?"

"Oh, please. As if I haven't known since I came here, practically, that there was a better than average chance of that happening." Elly's hands flexed and pulled, flexed and pulled.

Milk squirted angrily into the pail. "Gavin's grandmother was hung in the kitchen yard because the courtiers stopped liking her. I've read her diary, you know. The last entry says, *Thank the gods this is almost over.*" She shook her head. "I've read all of their diaries, the Ladies. The ones that weren't callous and stupid were miserable, to a one. I might be cold and half-starved and constantly on the verge of execution, but I'd rather live this life for six months than that life for sixty years."

"This is your argument *for* getting married?" Judah said.

"No." Elly's dress was patched and now she was the one wearing a pair of Theron's old boots; her hair was pulled into a no-nonsense braid that hung down her back. She had never used much cosmetic but even the pale pink lacquer she'd once painted on her nails was gone. Nor did she bother with the gliding gait she'd been trained to use, which was meant to look effortless but took so much time and practice to perfect. The Lady's head was supposed to float above her shoulders. The Lady's face should be a careful mask, so perfect and unchanging that it might as well have been made of porcelain and tied behind her ears every morning. When Judah thought of Elly now, she thought of work, unending chores and ceaseless, grueling effort. Somehow she had missed that Elly, even hungry and overworked, was more naturally herself now than she had ever been. "No," Elly said again. "My argument for getting married is this: get out of here. Get that chieftain to break the bond and go far away. Get away from Gavin. He has a good heart, but he'll never stand on his own when he can stand on you."

"He's not standing on me." But the words seemed small in the growing gloom. They sounded like a lie.

Elly stood up. The ewe bleated. "Yes," she said. "He is. My mother sent me away forever to get me away from my brothers. And Gavin isn't dangerous or loathsome the way they were, but I'd happily send you away forever if it meant you'd be free of him. He'll never deliberately hurt you, and he'll be sorry when it happens, but he'll hurt you all the same, and he'll keep on hurting you, because somewhere deep inside where he doesn't have to look at it, he thinks you can't walk away from him." She grabbed Judah's hands with her own, warm and damp from milking. Her grip was ferocious. "Prove him wrong. Marry the Seneschal. Grit your teeth and give him a baby and make him buy you an estate in the country, and then live your life. Get away from here. Get away from Highfall."

Judah's throat hurt. Her eyes did, too. "I don't know if I can."

Elly didn't release her hands or her gaze. The sheep moved to the manger and began to eat. Low, rhythmic chomping filled the stable. "I don't know what Gavin's doing to you," Elly said finally, "but I know he's doing something, and I know it's bad. I can see it in the way he looks at you. Maybe he's angry at me, and taking it out on you—"

"Elly, stop." Judah was desperate.

"I don't care what it is," Elly said harshly. "I don't know if I love Gavin or not, but if I do, it's because I never had a choice. You, I love for your own sake. I want you to be happy, for your own sake." Her voice grew thick, as if she was fighting back tears. "So you'll have a guard. Guards can be bribed, or befriended. You could meet people, maybe even find your stableman. He probably left the city, but—oh, no, Jude, what? What's wrong?"

Because Judah had yanked her hands back and was pressing them protectively to her chest. She felt cracked, suddenly. Unwhole. It was a cruel thing for Elly to say. Elly was never cruel. The two things could not reconcile in her head. "He's dead," she said. "They killed him."

Elly's brow furrowed. "No, they didn't."

The ground bucked under Judah's feet. "What?"

"That was somebody else, some man from the midden yard who wouldn't quit groping the kitchen maids. I felt bad about that, but—no, Jude. Firo helped us. I made Gavin have actual dinner with him, he hated it. Oh, gods, have you been thinking he was dead all this time?" She stared at Judah, baffled. "We got him out, Jude. Gavin said he told you."

Judah pressed her hands closer to her body. "Gavin told me he was dead."

Elly's lips pressed together with cold fury, and all at once Judah knew the truth, and found herself filled with rage.

Back in the study. Gavin lay on the sofa, reading a book with an unmarked binding. When he saw her he sat upright in surprise, letting the book fall closed. "Is Darid dead?" she said, with no preamble.

"Who?"

"Darid!" Her voice was shaking. "The stableman. *My* stableman."

"Oh." His confusion vanished, replaced by a resigned impatience. "Him."

"Him." She was on the other side of the couch now. She didn't remember walking around it. He stood up to meet her. If he hadn't, she would have pulled him up by his throat. "Don't lie to me, Gavin."

"I don't know why you're bringing this up now." His tone was cool. "He was executed. You know that. You know why, too."

Lies and more lies. Enough. She grabbed his head in both of her hands and reached into him, deliberately. She hadn't known she could do that, but it wasn't hard, it was easy. He gasped. His shoulders snapped back and his eyelids fluttered. Maybe she was hurting him. She didn't know. She didn't care.

The inside of his head was like a book and she ruffled the pages until she found what she wanted: his bedroom, pain, sun streaking in long knives to the floor. The cool white of his pillow. Elly's voice, urgent. All blurry, all underwater. But there.

—we got him out, but Firo will expect something in return. Dinner, lunch—some sign of favor—

Gavin. *I gave my blood to help her. Why should I do any more than that?*

Elly. *Because it is a good thing and you can do it and you will. For once in your life, you will not be selfish.*

And worst of all was that Judah was on the inside of him, not the outside, and so she felt the resentment, the anger, the petty, unreasonable betrayal that cycled through Gavin's mind. It wasn't just the caning; Gavin felt as if Darid had tracked mud on Gavin's favorite rug, or lamed his favorite horse. His. Judah was *his*. Just because he, himself, wasn't fucking her—

She let go. She didn't want to know any more. Gavin stumbled, put a hand to his head. Gagged once or twice, but didn't vomit. When he managed to pull himself upright, his face was filled with defiance. "I did it, didn't I?" His voice was low and furious. "I let the world see me with Cerrington, let them see me treat him like he mattered."

"Did it cost you so much?" Judah felt strangely calm.

Gavin recoiled as if she'd slapped him. "Forgive me if I didn't want to watch you waste your life fucking some staff boy."

"Then who shall I fuck, Gavin?" It sounded so normal. Just a question. "Who do I have your permission to fuck? Oh, yes. I remember: any number of dumb, good-looking courtiers who only want me so they can get close to you. That's what you said, isn't it? Back when you thought I was fucking Firo."

"Quit talking like that," he said. "Quit using that word."

"Which word? Fucking?" She wanted to bite him. She

wanted to tear his throat out. "You used it. Or is that something else you're allowed to do and I'm not?"

He ran his hands violently through his hair, and his voice shook with an obvious effort to retain control. "Look, dead or alive, it's not like you're going to see him again, so I'm not sure why we're arguing."

"We are arguing," she said, "because you seem to think that all of my decisions should be made with your best interest in mind. You seem to think that I should just stand quietly off to the side until you're bored and need entertaining, or upset and need soothing, and then come running to serve you, because of course I should never want anything for myself. I shouldn't even want to live except through you. I should just let you use me and use me and use me until we both die of it!"

She was screaming now, the sound luminous and resonant. Like she had opened a door inside herself and discovered an aquifer's worth of grand hot rage, as precious as gold. She had thought Darid was dead. She had thought it was her fault.

Gavin grabbed her upper arms. She tried to pull back, but he wouldn't let go. "You're hysterical," he said, furious. "You need to calm down." He pulled her close, fingers digging deep into the meat of her arms, and pressed his head roughly against hers. The more she struggled the more fiercely he held her. When she felt him push into her mind she was not surprised—she'd expected that—but she hadn't expected the implacable cold that spread through her. Her rage dulled and then faded entirely. What was left was still and stony as marble. She watched from far away as her legs collapsed under her and both of their bodies slid to the floor, his head still against hers. The feeling didn't have the gentle flow of water, the soft ripple of reflected light. It was dry. Her eyes closed and then everything was still. A shared stillness: theirs, nobody else's. Together.

And then, like the crate of wine emerging from the depths of the aquifer, something began to take shape, there in the quiet. A face. Another. They drifted behind her eyelids, carved and pale—all different, all somehow the same, so many with the same particular mouth—

And then, his face. Hers.

Horror bloomed in her. He was thinking of the crypts. Instead of living water he was imagining them both as stone effigies of themselves, unending and unalive. She tried to pull away, but she was too heavy to move or even breathe. The stone pushed everything else out. Motion was a faded memory that belonged to somebody else. She could feel nothing but cold, could hear nothing but the sound of the increasingly thick air fighting its way into her lungs. Somewhere, her heart beat. But slowly. Slower. It wasn't that she couldn't breathe. It was that she couldn't remember why she'd ever wanted to.

No.

With incredible effort, she pushed him away. Inside her head and out of it. The two of them were slumped against the sofa. Gavin's skin looked bloodless and cold. His head lolled to the side as if he didn't have the strength to hold it up. Then his eyes focused on her, and he seemed to gather himself. "Please, Jude. Let's end this. I can't stand it anymore." He reached for her again.

This time she fought, lashing out with everything she had. On the floor, scrabbling and clawing at him like an animal. She felt the give of flesh under her nails and four long scratches appeared on his cheek, one welling up with blood. She felt the sear of them on her own face, too. Fighting him was hard. She could feel the emptiness inside him, yawning like hunger. He was weak, hurting. He needed her. She could help him. Nobody else could. It would be the easiest thing in the world. It would be like falling asleep. She was so tired.

Then she was up on her feet. Standing over him. "No," she said.

His fists clenched. His head dropped. The void inside her ached and it would be so simple to fill it, but then there would be nothing, she would be nothing. She would never be apart from him. She could not be near him. There was no choice, except to flee.

And so Judah fled. She didn't know where she was going. She only knew that she was going away.

CHAPTER SIXTEEN

When Eleanor was a child, somebody told her a story about a woman who unraveled her husband's wool scarf to knit socks for her children. There had been some twist that she couldn't remember; somehow it had been funny, that she was unraveling the scarf. Eleanor had loved the story about the charming mother who made socks for all of her happy children. Her own mother had been wary and grim and watchful, and as Lady of Tiernan, she hadn't knitted. Embroidered, yes, the famous Tiernan blackwork; miles of that, and the occasional piece of tatted lace. But knitting was for peasants and shepherds and people who were concerned about staying warm. The mere sight of a pair of knitting needles in her mother's hands would send her father into a frenzy, *No wife of mine*, and all that. It had been Eleanor's grandmother who had taught her to knit, hidden away with the old people and children where her father couldn't see. Knitting was secret, illicit. Arcane.

The knowledge had turned out to be useful, along with several bits about sheep that Eleanor never thought she'd need. The coup had happened at the beginning of summer and their winter clothes, in storage, had been taken. Now the weather was growing cold. Theron made needles for her, and she'd started to unravel an old knitted blanket she'd found under the quilts in her linen chest. She couldn't get the story of the mother and the scarf and the socks out of her head, but the actual work soon lost its charm. The washing and untangling and laying-out-to-dry was awkward and tedious, and too often the strand broke in her hands as she wound it. But when winter came they would need warm feet and warm hands, and to get warm feet and warm hands they would need socks and mittens. Sweaters, maybe. She'd never made anything but doll scarves. She hoped there was a book in the Lady's Library.

Wake up each day and figure out how to survive it: that was something else her grandmother had taught her.

She was swishing a mess of dirty yarn in the washtub on the terrace, as far from the edge as possible, when the Seneschal emerged from the parlor and told her that her father was dead. There was a bench on the terrace, but the Seneschal remained standing. He was an oddly formal man, even now, and would not sit without being invited. "It happened around the same time Elban died," he said. "The message just came through. I'm sorry for your loss, Eleanor."

"Are you?" she said. She had never particularly cared about being called *lady;* when the magus called her Eleanor, it was just her name. But every time the Seneschal did it, she felt like he was relieving himself in front of her. "I'm not. I haven't seen the man in fourteen years. Who's ruling Tiernan?"

"Your oldest brother, Angen."

Her oldest *surviving* brother. The actual oldest, Millar, had been thrown from his horse when Eleanor was four. The paper in the Seneschal's hand was battered, but she recognized the white wax seal: a ram's head, lowered to charge. "There was a second message, as well," he said. "A newer one. Angen has asked me to extend to you an invitation to return, given the circumstances."

"The circumstances?" She pulled two handfuls of sodden wool from the dingy water.

"You were contracted to marry the Lord of the City. Now there is no Lord of the City. You have no children with Gavin. Nothing holds you here."

The wool had to be wrapped in an old towel and squeezed gently. "What about the money Elban paid for me? Is Angen giving it back? Or are you offering him more to take me off your hands?"

A grudging humor came into the Seneschal's eyes. "Neither. He has merely offered to accept you back, if you want to go."

She sat back and wiped her hands on her apron. "Is it really my choice?"

"It is. May I make a suggestion?"

"Is there any way I can stop you?"

"Don't refuse immediately. Consider the offer. You might not relish the idea of life in Tiernan, but at least you know what it'll be like."

She raised an eyebrow. "I know what life here is like. Unless you're not planning on keeping us here indefinitely, perched on the edge of starvation."

"Nothing is indefinite," he said. "Take my advice. Consider your options."

Then he left. Eleanor squeezed the rest of the water out of the yarn, then laid it out to dry, winding the damp, dull-colored strand into parallel ranks like soldiers in formation. Her brother. Angen of Tiernan. He would surely be married by now, possibly for the second or third time. There would be children. She wondered if any of them were girls, and pitied them if they were.

"Judah's gone up to the tower," Theron said.

Elly was boiling oats for dinner. The heat on the stove was uneven and she had to stir the pot constantly or risk it burning. As Theron spoke, all at once the porridge thickened. Quickly, she took it off the stove. "What tower?"

"The one above the workshop."

Impossible. Salt; a handful of wild onion. She wished she had pepper. There'd been a cheese she'd used to like, its thick rind studded with whole peppercorns. The pepper permeated the creamy inside, giving each bite had a satisfying sting. She missed that cheese.

Wait.

Theron was already wandering away, his flitting moth of a mind having found another light. She grabbed his arm. "Tell me again, Theron."

"Judah went up to the tower above the workshop."

Creeping doubt began to fill her. "But the stairs are broken."

"Not for me." His cloudy blue eyes slid away from her. "And not for Judah. I'm not sure about you or Gavin."

What did you do now, Gavin? she thought wearily. She had so much to do. She always had so much to do.

Gavin was in Elban's study with a bottle of wine. He sprang up when the door opened, his face earnest and exposed in a way it rarely was; but, seeing her, his mask slammed down. The Grand High Lord, thwarted by his stubborn Lady-that-should-have-been, proudly hurt by her lack of consideration for his feelings. "What do you want?" he said curtly. Four long scratches marred his cheek, one crusted with blood.

"If Judah did that to your face," Elly said, "you deserved it."

"Did I?" he said.

"You lied to her about the stableman. All this time she's been thinking she killed him, and now Theron says she's gone to the tower above the workshop, so what happened?"

For a moment, guilt drew his mouth tight, but when he spoke his voice was petulant and cross. "That's nonsense. There's nothing in the tower above the workshop."

"According to Theron, Judah is, and I trust him more than I trust you," she said.

His brow furrowed. "She's really up there?"

"Yes. Why did you lie to her about the stableman?"

"I was angry," he said, his voice colored with a mix of contrition and frustration. Yet another thing gone wrong for him, another obstacle in the way of the young lord's happiness. "What does it matter? I'll go up and bring her down. That's what you came here to tell me to do, isn't it?"

It was. It had been. But then he'd said, *What does it matter*, and it did matter. It mattered very much. If he couldn't see that, she couldn't blame Judah for leaving. "Wrong," she said. "I came here to find out what you'd done. And to tell you to leave her alone." Then she walked out of the room and left him there. She hated that room, anyway. It smelled like Elban and misery.

Theron helped her with the sheep. They ate porridge in silence and Elly wound the newly-dried yarn. When the fire burned low she banked the coals, so she wouldn't have to use one of her few precious matches to relight it the next morning, and retired to her bedroom. It would have been warmer to sleep in the parlor with Theron. But she liked to have two doors between her room and Gavin's, these days. In her big, cold, stale-smelling bed, she worried about Judah, and missed her warmth and company, and it took her a long time to sleep.

When she opened her eyes in the morning, the bed was warm and for one delicious minute the chill on the tip of her nose was less a hardship than a pleasant reminder of how warm the rest of her was. Then it all came crashing back down again: the fire to be stirred to life, some sort of food put in their stomachs. Judah in the tower. They'd tried to climb it once, when they were twelve. Judah and Gavin had gone ahead. Elly, frozen with fear, had managed only the first step when a crumbled piece of stone crashed down past her. Above, Judah and Gavin had laughed, but the pieces of the cracked stone were still there and Elly would have still been there, too, if the others hadn't come to unfreeze her. She'd been unable to make her legs move, unable to keep from feeling like she was balanced on the branch of a tree. Angen's voice echoing in her head: *silly little kitten, stuck up a tree. However will the kitten get down? What if the wind starts to blow, and the tree begins to shake? Like this—*

Quickly, she climbed out of bed and pulled on her clothes. The cold drove away the comfortable warmth and most of the uncomfortable memories. In the parlor, the fire had already been stoked, the pot of oatmeal from last night set to warm over it. Theron huddled next to the stove, a bird in a rainstorm. "You did the fire," she said.

"No. Gavin."

He must have felt guilty. Good; he should feel guilty. "Theron, can you get up the tower steps?" He nodded. "Will you take Judah some food today?"

He shuddered. She didn't think it was from the chill. "I don't like the way it feels up there."

"She took you food," Elly said. "She took you food all the time."

The shudder stilled. His eyes were blank. "I didn't say I wouldn't do it."

She wrapped up the last of the bread and cheese from the Seneschal's visit. The bread was tasteless and gritty, the cheese greasy and dried-out. She wished she had something comforting and loving and good to add, but there was nothing but medium-cold oatmeal and boiled squash. So she wrote a note instead, on the crumbling flyleaf of a cookery book.

Judah: I love you and I miss you. Come down.

The ink in the bottle—her last—had been watered down nearly as much as it would stand. She regarded the note for a moment, then put her pen over the period at the end of the sentence, so the mark would disappear into the ink, and added: *when you are ready.*

By then, Theron had disappeared. Oh, well; the package would keep an hour or two. The parlor door opened, and she looked up quickly, hoping it was Judah—but it was the magus, his battered leather satchel slung over one shoulder and the burlap bag over the other. Heavy laden as he was, and with the ineffable alien air that always clung to him, he reminded her of one of the peddlers that sometimes knocked at her father's door. "Eleanor," he said, no small amount of alarm in his voice. "Is Judah ill? I waited in the courtyard but she didn't come."

Eleanor hesitated, and then said, "She's fine. She's just busy." He was disappointed, she could tell. Maybe Gavin was right, and the magus had feelings for Judah. Marrying him might hold more appeal for Judah than marrying the Seneschal had, she thought, and then remembered Judah in the stables, saying, *Do we exist to be married?*

I do, she'd answered, just as she'd realized it was no longer true.

"The Seneschal told me about your father," the magus said. "I'm sorry."

"I'm not. My father was a terrible person who sold me to the highest bidder, and the world is better off without him."

She expected the words to shock him, but he only nodded. "My mother used to say that my father had one service to do the world, and it was over and done with nine months before I was born."

Elly smiled. "I like your mother."

"I like her, too." His voice was wistful, which Elly found fascinating. She didn't know anyone who was wistful about their parents. "Although I think she didn't give my father enough credit. I met him once or twice. He seemed decent enough." He handed her the bag. "Here. I wish it were fuller."

She opened it: good bread, some fruit, a tiny pot of something. Candy, he always brought candy. Gavin was definitely right; the magus had a soft spot for Judah. The things he brought were chosen with her in mind.

Which gave her an idea. She passed the bag back to him. "Take it to Judah for me, will you? She's in the tower above Theron's workshop. Do you know the way?"

He seemed disproportionately startled. "I can find it. But why—"

"She and Gavin had an argument."

The magus had gone very still, but his eyes were wild. "What about?"

"Remember the stableman? The one we helped, when she—" She stopped, not wanting to say it. "Gavin said he told her we got him out. But he lied—he told her nothing of the kind. She's been thinking he was dead, and assuming it was her fault. Just like she thinks Theron is her fault, as if she could have done anything to stop Elban poisoning him. Anyway, the truth came out, and she and Gavin had words about it." She chose not to mention the scratches. "Now she's in the tower. Why the tower, I don't know. The stairs are treacherous, but Theron said he could climb them, and you're not that much bigger than he is. No offense," she added hastily.

"None taken. Brawn isn't much of an asset in my line of work."

"I can't go, I don't like high places," she said, knowing her worry and frustration were showing. "Will you go? Try, at least? Take her that—" she indicated his bag "—and some things from me?"

He nodded. She added the food from her bag to his, gave him the note she'd written, and he left. But the worry and frustration stayed with her and she knew that dull, repetitive work like unraveling yarn or picking squash seeds out of pulp would be maddening. Hard labor was what she needed, something physical and distracting. So she took the waterskins down to the aquifer to fill them. It was strange, the things that bothered people: Judah didn't like the aquifer. The water was too big and too dark, she said. Elly had no problem with that, but she didn't relish the idea of the House above her, crouched like an animal waiting to drop.

That had been another favorite trick of Angen's, to drop out of trees and scare her.

She met Gavin on her return trip. His scratches were healing, but only at normal speed. They'd been his to begin with, then. In the tower, she knew, Judah's would already be pink with new skin. Wordlessly, he took the waterskins from her, and they made their silent way to the parlor. As she transferred the water into the ewer—it went stale faster in the skins—he finally said, "I'm sorry."

"Don't apologize to me," Elly said. "I'm not the one you hurt."

"Well, I'd apologize to Judah, but you told me to stay away from her." He'd grown leaner since the coup, like the rest of them. His face was more angular, more like Elban's—but he could never truly look like his father. He had too much of his mother in him, and too much humanity. "And for the record, I didn't hurt her. I would never hurt her."

"Does lying about the stableman not count as hurting?" He said nothing. Elly went on: "Anyway, you've done something to her. You've been doing it for weeks."

Something in his eyes flickered. Not quite guilt but... awareness. She wasn't wrong, she saw. There had been something, all these weeks. At first she'd suspected it was sex, because the wariness in Judah's eyes had reminded her of her mother, or the way Eleanor herself had felt around Angen. But there was a difference: Judah had seemed wary, but not afraid. Not trampled. "I wouldn't hurt her," he said.

"You would not deliberately hurt her," she said quietly. "And you would be very sorry afterward. Just like now."

Silence dropped, heavy and thick, and Elly let it lie where it fell.

So many hours passed before she saw the magus again that she decided he'd left without stopping back in to see her. It surprised her when he appeared in the open parlor door, still holding the bag. He was pale and the skin under his eyes was an alarming grayish-purple. She put down the spoon she'd been holding and went to him. "Are you all right?"

"I'm fine," he said with a weak smile, and held out the bag to her.

It felt too heavy in her hands. "I hope she kept some of this."

"She did. But I bring it for all of you." One of his hands drifted toward the doorjamb for support.

"Please, magus. Sit down."

He sank gratefully into the nearest chair. "I'm sorry. It's the stairs, that's all."

"You made it up?"

"Oh," he said, and his eyes slid away. "No, that part's fine. It's just a lot of climbing. I shouldn't get winded, walking around the city as much as I do."

"Maybe you're coming down with something."

"Maybe I am." His gaze drifted in a way that tugged at her memory, but before she could follow the thread to its source, he said, "I'll go home to bed. But I wanted to bring you the food. I told her I'd be back tomorrow, but I'm not sure I can get you more supplies by then."

"Tomorrow?" She blinked, surprised. "Oh, of course not. We appreciate everything you do for us. Judah's all right?"

"Fine." He squeezed his eyes shut, then opened them again. "Eleanor, there was something I wanted to say earlier, and didn't. I'm here on sufferance, because the Seneschal allows it, and it's a bit—sticky. Sometimes I have to think carefully before I speak. But I'm on your side, as much as I can be."

"We know you are."

"I don't think Elban poisoned Theron. I think it was the Seneschal. He came to Arkady's manor a week or so before. It was the only time I ever knew him to do that. I can't imagine Arkady taking any action the Seneschal didn't approve. He always said the Seneschal held the reins." The magus had a bandage wrapped around one arm. She hadn't noticed it before. His hand went to it now. "Don't trust him."

The Seneschal had known Theron since he was a baby. Eleanor stood frozen in her own empty shell; as sweat beaded on the magus's forehead, and he paled even more; as he said, "I must go," and did. Still she stood, the bag limp in her hands. The sun began to sink behind the Wall and the parlor grew cold, and she did not stoke the fire and she did not put anything on for dinner.

The light in the room faded from gold to gray.

Wake up. Find a way to survive.

She hadn't been to the workshop since she'd brought Theron food after the hunt, and not for years before that. She and Gavin had been so busy training with their respective weapons, axes for him and protocol for her, and what good was any of it now, Eleanor thought, as she made her way through the old wing in her patched, dingy dress. She didn't care that the dress was patched and dingy. The dress had come by its wear honestly. She liked her own competence, she liked finding solutions to problems, she liked building their paltry winter store. She had deluded herself, perhaps, into thinking that she was happier now, that she had more freedom. But they lived at the Seneschal's mercy, all of them, and he'd tried to kill Theron and marry Judah and he wanted to send her away, back to Tiernan and Angen. She could do nothing about any of it. Judah could do nothing about any of it. But they could do nothing together. They could...not be alone.

In the base of the tower, the staircase wound up and up. The magus had been right. There were a lot of stairs. Carefully, she stepped onto the first one. Instantly, she became aware of the empty space next to her. Instantly, the solid stone under her foot felt like slender wood and bark. Her head began to spin and her skin broke out in cold sweat and she heard Angen's voice calling up from the bottom of the tree, sweet and musical and cruel.

What will you do for me if I let you down, little kitten?

Angen was far, far away. Angen could not hurt her. It didn't matter.

Will you play nicely, and not whine like last time?

She pushed his voice away and called up into the growing gloom, "Judah? Can you hear me?"

The words echoed and died, and there was only silence.

The last time she'd stood here, she'd worn lovely embroidered slippers with ice-slick soles, just the thing for careful gliding steps over flat marble floors. Now she wore Theron's old boots, like Judah always had. They were sturdy and strong and she could climb anything in them. She forced herself to put one of them on the next step. One step at a time, just like storing food: one dried fruit, one bag of oats, one bundle of dried onions. Don't think about the long cold winter ahead, and how full the shelves will need to be before it begins, and how empty your stomach will be before it ends. Wake up each day and figure out how to survive it. One fruit. One bag. One bundle.

One step. Then one more. She would climb a thousand staircases, each only one step high. At the top of the last one, she would find Judah. One step, over and over. She would do it. She was doing it. She had found the strength to feed them and keep them alive and she would find the strength to do this, too. She didn't dare turn to see how far she'd come, but soon it seemed she had climbed a hundred steps, two hundred, and her heart began to flutter with victory.

Then she made a mistake. She looked up.

There it was, mere feet ahead of her: the broken place. The one that had kept the others from climbing to the top, all those years ago—but Judah had done it the day before, and the magus had done it today. Broken steps jutted out from the wall, crumbling and rotten. Like a game of checkers, she could see how she would have to move from one to the next, but she could also see the places where she would have to stretch and leap, and she knew there was no hope. She couldn't breathe water and she couldn't drink fire and she couldn't climb those stairs, and if she had hated Angen (and Edouard and Grey, but Angen was the worst) before, she hated them doubly and triply now. She had not thought of them for years, she had decided they no longer mattered. But they had broken something in her, all those years ago, and now Judah needed her and she needed Judah and she *still* couldn't go. The steps were broken. She was broken. She couldn't even move.

Stop crying. Bad kittens who cry get punished.

Angen had only yelled at her for crying because he liked yelling at her. He liked it when she cried. Just like Elban would have liked it when she cried, and oh, dear gods, she had almost married him. Most of the time she could keep the long view, most of the time she could be strong inside. But right now the panic was so close to the surface that all its sources blended together and she felt sick.

"Judah!" she called again, desperate.

This time, there was an answer. Her own name: but from below, not above, and it wasn't Judah's voice but a man's. Gavin's. She was envious of the quick thud of his boots on the steps, and then his body was between her own and the edge, and his arm was around her shoulder, and she was grateful for him. She hated that she was grateful for him.

"You made it a long way," he said, his voice kind. Not at all mocking. Last time he'd mocked. Last time he'd been twelve. "You did really well."

"It isn't fair," she said. "None of it is fair. I want to go see her and I can't."

She expected him to say something bland and reassuring. *It's all right. It will all be fine.* But instead, he surveyed the staircase winding above them, eyeing the gap. His legs were longer, but he was heavier. "Shall we try it together? If I go with you?"

"No," she said, and she hated—again—that there was not even a second when it seemed possible. "Not now."

"She'll come down when she's ready," he said gently. Then he helped her turn around, and she counted the steps that she'd climbed and saw that there were only eight of them, and almost wept.

She met the Seneschal in the courtyard, because Judah wasn't there to do it. Surprise painted plain on his face, he said, "Is Judah ill?"

"No," Eleanor said, although it had been four days and she had no way of knowing, truly. The magus came every day, went all the way up to the tower. He assured them all that Judah was fine, warm, eating. As Elly took the bag from the Seneschal, it felt lighter than it should have, and she glanced inside: a bottle of oil, a bag of oats, some dried meat of uncertain origin. All things that would make their life possible while sending a very clear message that it would never be pleasant.

But it was a lovely fall day, crisp and not at all damp. Around her neck Eleanor wore a scarf made of pale wool, plainly knit and as clean as it would ever get. She had made it herself, and her neck was warm. She didn't know what game the Seneschal was playing; it didn't matter. She would wake up each day and figure out how to survive and she would make sure the others survived, too. If the Seneschal wanted to kill them, he would have to use a knife.

"Have you thought about what you want to do?" he said.

"Actually, I've been thinking about the day Theron was poisoned." The words were carefully chosen. If she accused the Seneschal outright, the magus might pay for it.

Neutrally, he said, "The day he fell ill, you mean."

"The day Arkady poisoned him," she said. "He was healthy, and Arkady made him drink something, and he nearly died. I'm not stupid, Seneschal."

"I never thought you were." But there was something new in his voice.

"Elban wouldn't have poisoned Theron, not without being there to see. He liked to watch the suffering he caused. But somebody gave Arkady the order; he never did anything without an order. And when I think about who that somebody could have been, the only person I can think of is you."

The Seneschal's flat gray eyes studied her carefully. Finally he said, "It wasn't a decision I made lightly. At the time, it seemed the best way to protect the rest of you. And I wasn't happy with the result, if it matters. Arkady told me it would be painless."

"You did it for us." Eleanor's tone was aloof and cool, exactly the way her protocol tutors had taught her that a Lady of the City spoke.

He nodded. "Elban was pushing Gavin too hard, and Gavin was weak. He was going to break. I needed him not to break. I needed more time."

"To arrange your coup."

"Yes. Not enough of the guards were on my side yet. Gavin would have killed Theron if Elban had kept pushing him, and I think murdering his brother would have driven Gavin insane, don't you? I didn't want him insane. I still don't. Will you go back to Tiernan?"

"Why should I?"

"Because you can. You can be with your family."

"My family is here," Elly said. "Until you try to kill them again. And maybe even afterward; your success rate isn't great."

"If I wanted you dead, you would be." He smiled as he said it. It was an appreciative smile, almost friendly. Eleanor said nothing; merely stood, icy, and watched. The longer they stood, the more his smile withered. Eventually, it died. In its place was something suspicious and hard.

"Where is Judah?" he said.

She didn't quail. She had trained for this; her whole life had been training for this. And the moment was supposed to take place in a throne room or at a state dinner instead of a deserted courtyard, and she was supposed to be wearing velvet and silks instead of a plain dress and old boots. But it was the same, it was all the same. The Seneschal stared at her, a new awareness dawning. His lip curled in a snarl.

She was not afraid.

CHAPTER SEVENTEEN

Judah was tired of fighting. The scratches on her cheek were fresh and bleeding and she was tired of impossible decisions that benefited everybody but her. She wanted *away*. She didn't want to be sought and found the way they were always seeking and finding each other. She didn't want the nagging awareness of Gavin at the edge of her mind and she didn't want the nagging knowledge that Elly was toiling away at some menial chore, and she didn't want the nagging guilt of knowing that Theron was what he was because of what she'd failed to be. Darid was alive and that was impossibly wonderful, but Gavin had lied to her about it and that enraged her, and she could not think of one without the other, and the mixture made her feel sick. She didn't want the Seneschal. She didn't want the magus. She didn't want any of it.

She went to the old wing, but that wasn't *away* enough. She could easily be found there. Only one place existed in the

House where she could not be pursued, could not be sought out. So she pushed aside the tapestry, like the magus had done; gazed up at the staircase, spiraling into the dim reaches of the tower; hesitated only a moment, and began to climb.

The slit windows let in just enough light for her to see her feet and the edge. When she came to the crumbled place, the stones protruding from the wall seemed barely wide enough to hold a foot. The last time she'd been here, she and Gavin had stood on the edge and he'd said, *Dare you*, and she'd said, *No, thanks, I plan to live to see adulthood.* Then a rock had fallen. He'd laughed. She'd laughed. The truth was that neither of them particularly wanted to climb the tower; they'd climbed other towers, and found nothing but old furniture and dust. They'd been looking for an adventure, and towers were boring. Not an adventure at all.

Now, though: now, she wanted to. Because nobody else would. Gavin was too heavy and Elly was too scared and Theron never came to the workshop anymore. She would be left alone. She would be *away*.

She put one foot out, and then another, balancing across the gap with each foot on a stub of stone. The gap was smaller than she'd thought. The stone held her weight without even a wobble. She reached out for the next stub with her toe and tested, as careful as she had ever been in her life, to see if it would break and clatter to the floor below. It didn't. Neither did the next one. The step after that was across an uncomfortable-looking span, onto a triangular stone with its bottom half flaked off. If it broke she would fall. There was nothing to hold on to, nothing to grab. She shifted her weight. Lifted her back foot. Swung her leg carefully—ever so carefully—forward.

But either the piece wasn't as small as she thought, or wasn't as far away as she thought, because the uncomfortable span was not so uncomfortable at all. Neither was the next. Her hand clung to the tower's curved inner wall, finding nooks and holes to curl her fingers into, and each step was easier than the one before that. The magus had said the stairs would be passable, if someone were determined enough, and she was: determined enough to keep climbing as the stairs wound up and up, around and around, higher than seemed possible. There were more broken places, but she navigated them as easily as she had the first. The teeth always turned out to be larger and more secure than they first appeared, the spaces between them easily crossed. Up and up, around and around. The air changed; it became fresher and colder, as if a window were open. She didn't even feel tired. In fact, she felt—was it elated? Was that the word?

Then, suddenly, there were no more steps. She stood on a small stone landing, facing a wooden door. The lock had been broken—annihilated, really, there was nothing but a jagged hole in the wood—and the door hung open. She frowned; the stairs would probably be enough of a deterrent, but she wished the lock worked, too. The door pushed open stiffly on corroded hinges. She stepped through.

And immediately understood why the air felt so fresh and cold. Half the tower looked like the workshop below, lined with shelves and cupboards. Several small tables dotted the room, none upright; a high stool and a settee seemed to have fared better, although the settee had one broken foot and listed at an awkward angle. Scraps of brown paper crumbled amid piles of dead leaves and bundles of feathers, twigs and egg-shells that might once have been birds' nests. Spiderwebs and wasp hives, abandoned for winter, sprouted from the shelves. Against one toppled-over table, the leaves and detritus had broken down enough that a small tree had managed to take root. It was frail, but surviving. Nobody had been up here in a very long time.

The other half of the tower was…gone. There was no rubble, no debris; it was as if an enormous mouth had bitten the top of it away, leaving neat, smooth edges. The floor was mostly intact, a nearly perfect circle, but only half of the roof remained and at least a third of the wall was missing. Beyond was open air, the ripe gold that presaged sunset.

She walked to the edge of the broken place. The parti-colored roof of the House spread out below her; off to the left, the sun glinted on what was surely the glass roof of the solarium, and above it she could just see the treetops of the wood where Elban had taken Gavin and Theron hunting. In the distance, of course, was the Wall. What she couldn't see, in any direction, was the ground itself, which meant that someone standing there would not be able to see her, either. This tower wasn't secret, but forgotten. The smoke and spires of the city were behind her. She didn't know what lay over the Wall in the direction she was looking. Nobody had ever told her, she'd never thought to ask, and all she could see was sky.

Something in her eased. *Away*, she thought. *I'm away.*

An undamaged colored glass window was set into the wall opposite the demolished one. On the floor beneath it, broken metal pieces lay on the floor—gears, tubes—and a small round panel set into the window looked as if it were meant to slide, or maybe even open. She couldn't get it to move and lost interest quickly. Under the thick mat of leaves on the floor were the same overlapping circles that decorated the chapel windows, inlaid in colored stone. She opened a few of the books on the shelves, but the writing inside them wasn't any language she recognized. Since she couldn't read the books, she used three of them to prop up the broken corner of the settee. In a chest in the corner she found a long piece of dark fabric, not too mildewed; she wrapped it around herself and curled up on the settee.

The sun was setting, and the break in the tower wall spread open before her like a stage. Pale rose deepened; became orange, gold, even a ferocious fuchsia that would have rivaled the gaudiest courtier's gown. Judah leaned her head against the high carved back of the settee and watched. The colors melted, changed, darkened. A seemingly impossible number of stars flared to life. The air was cold. She was not. The moon crept into view, wide and gleaming. Her eyes grew heavy, and closed.

When she woke, Theron sat hunched on the floor, ankles crossed and arms wrapped tightly around his knees. The sky outside was new-dawn blue. She had slept through the night and into the morning, later than she'd slept in months. Poor Elly would have to milk the ewe alone.

She sat up, which set off a cascade of protesting muscles in her back and neck from the unfamiliar settee. "Here," Theron said, and handed her a flask. She felt the warmth of the contents through the thick ceramic, and was grateful. "It's just water, but it's hot. I used Elly's quickstove."

"She'll be mad at you for wasting the gas," Judah said, and Theron said, "She wasn't there."

The water tasted stale but the warmth was good. "How did you find me?"

"The cats told me," he said as if it were a perfectly reasonable answer. "But I don't think Elly will believe that." His throat worked as he swallowed hard. His eyes darted nervously around the room. "I can't stay here, Jude. I'm not sure I can come back, even. It feels…tangled. Like being stuck in a thornbush. And the air—" His thin shoulders twitched. "I can't stay here," he said again.

Judah could feel nothing wrong with the air. It was damp and crisp and fresh. "I'm not ready to go back. Tell Elly—" she hesitated "—I'll be down soon."

But she didn't go down. Toward noon she felt a tentative scratch on her wrist: *Sorry. Please. Come. Talk.* She ignored it.

When she heard footsteps the next morning, she was lying on the floor, watching the clouds. *Theron again*, she thought, and didn't even feel inspired to call out. The ruined door opened and the footsteps crossed the floor. They didn't sound like Theron. She looked up just as the magus sat down next to her, breathing hard.

"That's a lot of steps. Here." He dropped a bag in front of her. All sorts of delicious smells emanated from it. Judah realized she was starving. She fell greedily on the food inside: real bread—she tore off a piece immediately and stuffed it into her mouth—a small jar of shredded meat, two juicy-looking red fruits, and chocolate. Slightly grainy, less sweet than she liked it. But chocolate all the same.

The magus watched her eat with as much pleasure as if he'd been eating the food himself. Then he said, "Eleanor sent me. Has she always been afraid of heights?"

Judah's mouth was stuffed with bread and chocolate. The combination was divine. "One of her brothers used to chase her up trees," she said through the food. "And then shake them until she was so terrified that she'd do anything he said if he let her down."

"I thought it might be something like that."

Judah swallowed. She had eaten exactly half of the chocolate and exactly half of the bread. Opening the jar of meat, she sniffed. Vinegar and pepper; underneath, the carnal smells of blood and flesh. "Did you bring a fork?"

"Spoon. In the bag."

Good enough. The meat tasted better than it smelled. Some spice in it reminded her of state dinners. "Are you here to talk me into coming down?" she said.

"Not in the least," he said. "But I think the Seneschal is still expecting an answer to his proposal."

"Ha." Now she had eaten half of the meat, too. She found the lid, screwed it back on.

"Being Lady Seneschal doesn't appeal?"

"I would rather die," she said, and knew it was true.

The magus nodded. "Wise choice. Don't trust him."

"Theron says the same about you." She lay back down on the cold stone, enjoying her full stomach. The Seneschal seemed a thousand miles away, trustworthy or not. "Of course, Theron also says that being in this tower feels like being stuck in a thornbush, and he gets messages from invisible cats, so probably Theron's insane."

The magus lay down next to her. "Theron's not insane. He's not normal. But he's not insane. He's...complicated. He said the tower feels like a thornbush?"

"Something like that." Suddenly, she didn't want to talk about Theron. She didn't want to think about him. Theron made her sad.

He hesitated, and then said, "Eleanor told me about the stableman. I'm sorry. I thought they'd told you."

"Were you in on that, too?"

He nodded. "He seemed like a decent person, which is more than I can say for the courtier Eleanor enlisted to help."

"Firo?" She smiled. "He's no worse than most courtiers. Better than some, I think. Have you seen Darid? Since then, I mean."

"No," the magus said. "Last I heard, he was planning on leaving the city."

Judah turned back to the clouds. Darid, alive. Darid, out of the city. She pictured him, walking down a dusty road. Passing a green field. The field might be full of horses. The horses might be in foal. "Good," she finally said.

"You know," the magus said, "the city wasn't always the way it is now."

"I'm sure under Elban, it was much better," Judah said.

"I'm not talking about Elban." There was distaste in his voice. "What Elban called his empire was nothing but a group of greedy thugs that more or less agreed not to kill each other. And the Seneschal might think he's different, but he's not. I'm talking about before Elban. There were laws, then. Courts. There had to be, to hold together an empire that big. People aren't all the same, you know. They have different feelings, wants, perspectives. But they're all people."

"You weren't alive before Elban," she said.

"No, but my ancestors were," the magus said. "And they passed the stories down to me. Do you want to hear this, or don't you?"

"Sure," she said. "Why not? I like stories."

"Well, years ago, the Lords of Highfall held everything from the Barriers to the eastern sea. Then one of them decided he wanted more. You know about the wasteland in the north?"

"I know there is one."

"I've been there. Nothing grows. It doesn't rain, it doesn't snow—most of the time when people say *wasteland*, they mean *desert*, but deserts aren't wastelands at all. Deserts are filled with life. The north isn't like that. There was a war, a thousand years ago, between Pala and the Temple Argent—"

"They fought a war and destroyed themselves in the process. Everybody lost." Some tutor had told them about it years ago.

"Yes. Lord Martin—"

"Wait," Judah said. "Mad Martin? The Lockmaker? Gavin's however-many-times-great-grandfather?"

"Five. Five times great. Yes. Although he was more like Theron than Gavin, which probably won't surprise you to hear. He was very interested in history, and he became obsessed with the northern war. Specifically with Pala." She heard him take a deep breath. "There was a power in the world then. Nobody quite knows what it was, but it was everywhere. Like water, or air. Some used it, some didn't. They used it to make their lives better; to free time and energy. To give themselves choices. Most rulers don't like choices. And, of course, the easiest way to control a populace is to keep them tired. Tired, hungry, drunk.

"And the more obsessed with Pala Lord Martin became, the more afraid he became that this power—this simple power that simple people had, to keep a fire burning or a well flowing— would be used against him somehow. His people were beginning to question his own power, after all. They always do, after a while. So he gathered together his most loyal scholars and told them to study the problem, the power and the questioning and how they were connected. They sequestered themselves for months, and when they finally emerged, they told him that they'd devised a way to bind the power, and restrict its use to only those who would use it according to the Lord of Highfall's wishes. We don't know how they planned to do it, if it was a ritual or a machine. Whatever it was, it took all of them working together."

Judah broke off another piece of chocolate and let it melt on her tongue. "Did they succeed?"

"They did." Now his voice was soft. "But they erased themselves from existence in the process. Like a wet rag on chalk-covered slate. The scholars, the tools they used—even part of the tower where they worked."

Judah looked at the neatly sheared edges of the gap, the smooth gray slices of exposed wood where the shelves ended. "This tower?" she said. "Is this story true? Is that what happened here?"

"I believe it is," he said, and smiled at her. It was a sad smile. "That's why I'm here. And I believe that's why you're here."

A funny feeling spread inside her, a shivery something she couldn't quite identify. The remnants of chocolate were sickly in her mouth. "Magic power and secret rituals. You're as crazy as Theron is."

"Why is it so crazy?" he said. "If I go downstairs and stab Elban's son in the throat, you'll bleed to death as sure as he will. Is it any stranger than that?"

Something about the way he said *Elban's son* struck her oddly. "That's different."

"Why? Because you've experienced it firsthand? I was with him while you were caned, you know. I watched the marks appear on his back. If I tell somebody else about it, should they assume I'm a liar, because they didn't experience it firsthand?"

"I don't think you're a liar. I think you're insane."

"Like Theron is insane."

"Yes."

"Theron's not insane." The magus's eyes glittered, his voice cold and sure. "I know the poison Arkady gave him. People use it because they think it's painless, but they only think that because they don't know what it really does. There is something inside us that makes us *us*, Judah. Individual and unique in all the world, a song sung only once and never again. Call it conscience, call it essence, call it soul. That poison drives it out of the body. Sends it *away*—" Judah shivered "—to wherever we go when we die, the river of black water or the waiting place or the roots of the great tree. Whatever you believe.

By the time you gave him the antidote, most of Theron was already there. Not all of him came back."

"Stop it." Tears pricked at Judah's eyes. That long moment of indecision. Her fault.

"Why?" the magus said rudely. "I'm only telling you about it. You have no proof that it's true, no firsthand experience. Arkady wanted Theron dead, that's all. That he wasn't a good enough magus to know what he was really doing, that nobody in this wreck of a city could know—that's probably just a story. Probably part of Theron's brain got too much or too little blood, and that's why he is the way he is."

"I was scared." The tears were falling now, leaking from her eyes and running down her cheeks. "For all I knew, the poison was in what you gave me. For all I knew, you wanted me to kill him myself."

The hardness melted out of the magus. "I'm sorry." His voice was tired. "I had no way of proving myself to you. You did the best you could under the circumstances."

And it hadn't been good enough. "Theron wouldn't agree. He would hate the way he is now."

She expected the magus to argue, but he only nodded. "Theron is half in this world and half out of it. In a way, he's far more unnatural than you and Gavin. He shouldn't exist. He can sense things that most people can't, though, like the cats." He looked thoughtful. "What's wrong with him—I can see it, but I can't fix it."

Judah sat straight up, tears drying. "What do you mean, you can see it?"

The tower was quiet. The only sound was the gentle rush of the room's broken edges carving away the breeze. The magus was pale, his lips slightly parted; there was something wild in his eyes. But when he spoke, his voice was calm. "It's easier if I show you," he said.

★ ★ ★

From his satchel, he took a bundle of soft leather. Inside was a folding knife, a small mirror and a square of cloth. As he spread the cloth on the floor and laid the knife and mirror on top of it, his movements were deliberate, almost reverent. He glanced at the sky, which was the same cheerful blue it had been all day. Out of nowhere, Judah wondered what she would do if there were a storm. Be cold and wet, she supposed.

"It would be easier at night. Something about the moon; I never really understood it." He hesitated, then said, "Honestly, I'm a little nervous about this. I think the reason that Theron doesn't like this tower—the reason this part of the House was abandoned—was because the ritual that happened here made it an uncomfortable place to be. But you say you don't feel anything."

"Why does that make you nervous?"

"Because you should feel it. I do, and by rights, you should be…well, a lot more sensitive than I am. You must have developed some fairly strong defenses is what I'm trying to say, and since nobody ever taught you how, they won't be the kind I understand. I'm not sure what's going to happen if we breach them." He gave her a wry smile. "I'm actually not the world's most talented Worker. I'm only here because I'm pale enough to not look completely bizarre with blond hair, and healing is a useful enough skill to get me in anywhere I needed to be."

"Worker," Judah said.

He took up the knife and, without flinching, made a small cut on the inside of his arm. Not for the first time, Judah noticed: his skin was ridged with old scars, most neat and cleanly healed. The blood dripped down his arm and pooled on the surface of the mirror. He drew a symbol in it with one finger: like a letter, but not any letter she knew. "This is Work," he said. "And that's a sigil. It's like…what you see when you close your eyes, only most people can't make sense of it. Everyone has one, all unique."

Disgusted and transfixed, Judah said, "A song sung only once and never again."

He smiled. "I guess you could say sigils are the sheet music. This is my teacher, Derie's. And this—" he drew a second symbol next to the first "—is my mother's. She's very strong too, but farther away. When I do this, it's like calling their names. Asking for help. They're not actually here, but you can communicate with them."

"Like Gavin and me," she said.

"Exactly. It's Work that binds you. A very powerful Work, done by a very powerful Worker who died long ago." The blood on the tray was beginning to clot. The magus hesitated, then drew a third sigil.

This one felt different from the others. There was life there, in the swirls and hashes, and…personality. The sigil pricked at her, caught her and held her. "That one feels different," she said carefully. "Why does it feel different?"

"Because it's your mother's," he said. "You have her blood."

Judah felt dazed. "My mother?"

"She was one of us. Not from my caravan, but I did see her once, when I was a child. I knew your father better." Carefully, the magus wiped the third sigil out. Judah felt as if a piece of her was being torn away. He must have seen, because he gave her a kind smile. "Some people can Work with the sigils of the dead. But I'm sorry, I'm not that strong."

"My father," she said.

"His name was Tobin," the magus said. "Your mother was Maia. They were both incredibly powerful, but…especially Maia. That story you told me. To survive that, for you—"

Something in his tone reminded her of the creepy Wilmerian, all those months ago: when he'd talked about eating clay, when he'd gawked at her hair. But it didn't matter. *Maia and Tobin.* Her parents were people. Her parents had names. A thought occurred to her, so huge and marvelous and fearsome that it drove the Wilmerian from her mind. "Your people." The words had to be forced out, they didn't want to come. "Your people are my people."

"The Slonimi," he said, and a brilliant, beatific smile spread across his face. "Yes. You're Slonimi, like me. Oh, how I've wanted to tell you, Judah. But I couldn't. Not until we were here. Not until I could show you."

"I have people," she said. Then, "We look nothing alike."

He laughed. "None of the Slonimi look anything alike. We come from all over." He took her wrist carefully, as if it were blown glass, and poised the knife over her skin. "It's polite to ask permission before I do this. Do I have your permission?"

She stared down at the arm he held, which was scratched and raw from Gavin's incessant attempts to lure her downstairs. The curlicue scar was just visible at the edge of her sleeve, raised and pink and smooth. Probably she was insane. Probably this was all as imaginary as Theron's cats.

Maia. Tobin.

Why not? she thought, almost belligerently. At least he'd asked first, which was more than Gavin or his father had ever done. "Go ahead," she said.

He was quick, the knife was sharp, and there was hardly any pain. Then her blood joined his on the mirror, thinner and brighter. It ran into the marks he'd made—the sigils—filling them in. Below them, like lines of words on a page, he drew two more. "Mine and yours," he said. The mark he called hers was graceful and strong. It didn't feel like something that would come from her.

"How do you know my...sigil?" Now there was pain, a slow warm burn.

His own cut was still oozing blood and all it took was a flex of his wrist to reopen it fully. "Because it shines out of you like a bonfire. This will be strange," he said, and pressed her cut to his.

The world opened. Split like an overripe fruit, the rind falling away. It hurt, but it was a relieved kind of hurt: lancing an abscess, pulling a splinter. The room—which she could still see faintly—was full of purple membrane, impossibly knotted and nearly the same color as her hair. She could feel it as much as she could see it, growing through the House like ivy, tree-trunk-sized ropes of it winding up staircases and tendrils working their way into the tiniest of cracks. But the tower was the root of the Work, the source.

The sigils on the mirror glowed now, and she could feel the people who belonged to them: nothing as unimportant as their faces, but their very essences. The person the magus had called his teacher was ferociously smart, determined, cruel. The long years she'd lived piled inside her like bricks. His mother was just as smart and determined, with fewer years stacked up behind her—but oh, the love between her and the magus made Judah's heart ache, and the ache was so sharp that she reflexively pushed away.

Downstairs, in the catacombs—the walls of the House were irrelevant, her body was irrelevant, distance was irrelevant; wherever the Work was, she could be, and the Work was everywhere—she could feel Theron, but wispy, only half-there. Scattered, somehow, like a page torn free of its book. Other, smaller wisps floated through the House, pieces of the purple membranous stuff that split off and fused again, or drifted across the floor like leaves. Theron's cats. He had figured it exactly right: his brain was turning the wisps into something it could understand. Her brain, she suspected, was doing the same thing; Theron saw cats that nobody else could see, and she saw purple rope. What would an observer standing in the tower see now, she wondered? Just her body and the magus's, lying among the leaves on the dirty floor, blood trickling down their arms?

She looked down and was unsurprised, in this strange lifted world, to see a thick purple rope sprouting from the middle of her chest and disappearing through the floor. Judah could feel it reaching through layers of rock and plaster and wood like she could feel her arm inside her sleeve, down through the House to Gavin. Who stood in Elban's parlor, at the open door of the room where they'd met with the chieftain. The pulsing tether that sprouted from her chest ended in his. But while the rest of the membrane felt organic, like cobwebs or moss, the rope between her chest and Gavin's appeared almost woven, like the ropes Darid had made. There was pattern to it, and rhythm. She could feel Gavin through it. Not like a nagging doubt in the back of her head, but really *feel* him. If she wanted to, she could slip inside him like a suit of clothes. She didn't want to. The empty room was a terrible place. The membrane there was sickly and blackened.

That extra bedroom of his—you want to hear about that?

Elban had killed people here, she suddenly knew. Tortured them, made them suffer, watched them die. What she saw was the remnants of their pain and fear and death. She didn't think Gavin could feel it the way she could—or at least, she didn't think he *knew* he was feeling it—but he knew the place was awful and he feared that he was awful and some part of him was making himself stand there and feel the horror as a punishment or a penance. For her? For Darid? He was a mess inside, Gavin. Knotted and snarled, packed with feelings that clashed like soldiers on a field.

She could fix him. Untangle him like a necklace. He would feel better. She reached out.

And felt herself restrained. *Don't.*

It was the magus. Nate. In the ordinary world she had resisted calling him that, but thinking of him any other way in the Work would be like thinking of a chair as a dog. Without thinking, she slipped inside him, and he opened like a warm bed to let her in. In the tower she heard his body make a noise, but it was only his body, it was unimportant. She was radiant, hyper-alive. She was the center of his being. He was a hallway full of doors and she threw them open with reckless abandon; behind each one was a memory. She remembered flipping through the pages of Gavin's mind, back in the study, to find the lie he'd told her about Darid; that had been nothing to this, that was peering into a shadowy room through half-closed eyes. In Nate's memory, she heard the creaking wheels of a wagon in the sun, smelled green grass and horses and childhood and joy. His eyes showed her a woman with copper hair, braiding long fronds of some plant; a handsome young man with a bloody nose laughing and splashing his face with creek water; a girl with closed eyes and skin the color of sand after a rainstorm lying in the grass. When her eyes opened they were full of passion, and it was night. The air was clear and sweet and Nate had been young and full of mad soaring energy. He could remember. She remembered with him.

The memory made him sad. She could feel that, too. She tried another door. Behind this one was a towering woman with steel-gray hair, impossibly tall—no, it was Nate who was small, and Judah inside him. The woman was beating him. As blows rained down from her cane, he wept with pain and humiliation. The woman's sigil shone from her like light from a lantern: Nate's teacher. Judah didn't understand her cruelty, but she understood beatings. She fled.

Another door. A village, dusty and worn, but somewhere in it gleamed someone who carried with them a power as bright as a star. Older now, more thoughtful, Nate was searching for that someone. It wasn't a competition, but he wanted to be the one, he'd never been the one, and when he rounded a corner and saw that he'd found source of the power—a plain girl with a missing front tooth—triumph exploded out of him in a broad smile. Surprised, the plain girl smiled back.

Another. A narrow path carved into the edge of a cliff, hoary with ice, the howling wind tearing at his body.

A campfire, surrounded by singing and dancing and clapping. A drum, a flute. Comfort. Home.

A dingy kitchen, walls black with soot. A sad pile of blankets that didn't keep the floor from being cold and hard. He didn't want her to see that, for some reason.

Door after door, each one holding a moment of Nate's life: she had lived her whole life inside the Wall and she was greedy for experience, starving for it. Perhaps there were more noises in her body's ears and perhaps they were coming from his body, but she ignored them, throwing open one memory after another. Crowded taverns, singing musicians and bantering jugglers, groups of children chasing each other. Somebody's baby. A drunken fight. A less drunken one.

Then she came to a door that was locked. She pushed it, rattled it, and finally threw herself against it, filled with disproportionate annoyance that something was being kept from her, there was a place he wouldn't let her—

She found herself back in the tower, lying flat on her back. She was dazed. Her arm hurt. The membranous stuff was gone. The magus lay in a tight, protective ball next to her, both hands clutching his head. She heard a funny noise—how strange to hear only with her ears again, what limited things her five senses were—and realized that he was retching.

The locked door. Her insistent, frustrated pounding on it. She'd hurt him. She pulled herself up to her hands and knees and crawled to his side. His hair was drenched with sweat and he'd bitten his lip hard enough to draw blood. His eyes, red like he'd been crying, rolled and pitched in his head, but then found her.

"Water," he croaked, and she scrabbled across the floor for the skin he'd brought. She had to hold it for him at first, watching anxiously as he drank. Eventually his ragged breathing slowed and he managed, slowly, to push himself up.

"I'm so sorry," she said.

"So am I." His voice was rough. "I should have told you to be careful. But you shouldn't have been able to go that deep inside my head, not on your first—" He seemed to be having trouble finding his words. Pulling his satchel close, he took out bandages and a pot of salve. "Let me dress your arm," he said, and reached for her.

But she recoiled, holding the arm stiff against her body where he couldn't reach it. The pain wasn't bad—she'd suffered far worse—and she felt like she deserved it. Even now he was too pale. His lip was still oozing blood and every time he sucked it clean she felt worse.

Gently, he said, "It's all right. You didn't know." She let him take her arm. Moistening a cloth, he dabbed at the crusted blood. "You're...very talented."

A blush heated her cheeks. But even through the blush, even through her guilt over what she'd done to him, she couldn't help asking, "Could we undo what's between Gavin and me? By moving that purple stuff?"

The salve was clear and smelled faintly of lavender. "Look at me," he said. She did; he looked fragile, as if he'd just recovered from a long illness. "You didn't even try to change anything, and I can barely stand up. Meddling inside other people's heads is dangerous. I'm not strong enough to do that kind of Work and you haven't been trained for it. You could end up with your brains addled worse than Theron's."

She knew it was true. Her hands still shook; she felt blistered inside and out by what she'd seen, what she could do. Even so, she said, "But it must be possible. What about the Nali chieftain?"

The magus shook his head. "What the Nali do is very different. And the chieftain isn't in the city; he's in prison. He's been there for months. I suspect he's been tortured. If he didn't deliberately scramble your brain for revenge, he might be so weak and out of practice that he'd do it accidentally." He finished bandaging her arm, and then patted the bandage lightly. There was something insensate about the way his hand moved, like it wasn't entirely under his control. "I'll come back tomorrow. We'll keep practicing. Get to where you don't feel like a volcano erupting inside my head. Then we'll talk again, I promise. Is it so awful, the bond between you?" he added wistfully. "Do you want so badly to end it?"

Was it? Did she? Sometimes she had pitied other people who were alone in their heads. But she had seen that kind of life from the inside, now: the magus's life, the good and the bad of it. And she supposed that, with what he could do, his head was different than Elly's or Darid's would be, but still. There had been so much *magus* in it. So much space for him to fill, with thoughts and feelings and sensations that were his and his alone, love and hate and pain and sadness. And no uncertainty if a feeling was really his own, no trying to ignore the nagging pressure of someone else's desires, motivations, rages. "It's not awful," she said finally. "But I'm not free."

The magus wrapped the bloody mirror carefully in the cloth. She wondered that he didn't clean it, but assumed he knew what he was doing. "None of us are free," he said.

CHAPTER EIGHTEEN

Two weeks later, Nate stumbled into the Seneschal on the front steps. Literally. He'd been in the tower nearly every day; Judah was starving for the experiences she found in his memories, insatiable. The blood loss he could deal with, but untrained as she was, she left his head such a wreck that he could barely find his way back to the manor, where Derie waited to put him back together. "Making progress?" the Seneschal said.

Years ago, Nate had slept with a village girl named Anneka beneath a wagon, lying on soft grass sprinkled with tiny ugly flowers that released all the perfume of heaven when crushed by their bodies. Had his life not already been spoken for he might have stayed with her, married her, spent his life raising goats and chickens and lovely children with his eyes and her beautiful skin; but he belonged to the Slonimi, so he'd had only that one sublime night. Judah loved his memories of Anneka. She returned to them over and over again. Now the smell of the flowers was strong in Nate's nostrils and he could feel the wagon above him, comforting and familiar. Both were more real than the man standing in front of him. With great effort, he said, "Enough."

"Is she coming down?" the Seneschal persisted.

Nate's lips were dry. He resisted the urge to lick them. "Eventually."

"Sooner rather than later." It was a command.

Nate flexed his wrist so his springknife leapt out of its casing and buried the blade in the man's eye. Just like that bandit on the road, after they'd passed through the Barriers. Blood and fluid running warm over his hand.

He closed his eyes. Gathered himself. Opened them again. The real Seneschal stood in front of him, eyes intact. Nate wasn't even wearing his springknife. He never did when he went to see Judah, because flashes like that hit him not infrequently on his way home, and he couldn't risk trouble.

"This tower situation is very frustrating," the Seneschal said. Nate had shown him the broken place in the stairs. None of the Seneschal's guards, who were all great hulking men, could have navigated the narrow chunks of protruding rock without planks and ropes and a great deal of effort. The Seneschal's proposal to Judah had been a calculated move, not a romantic one; when winter came, the man had explained to Nate, the House would grow cold, and Judah would remember that he had offered her kindness and a choice. Both false, of course—all of the Seneschal's plans ended with Judah in a guildhall, being experimented on by the Nali chieftain— but having his men build ramps up the tower to drag Judah down by force would show the Seneschal's cards long before the gray man intended.

They had come to the door of the Safe Passage. "I wish

I understood how you make it up those stairs so easily," the Seneschal said, pausing to take out the huge ring of keys that would unlock the Passage's maze of doors. "You must have been raised by mountain goats."

"I'm just careful," Nate said.

It was a lie. Nate lied to the Seneschal a great deal—he would have said anything to get inside the Wall to Judah— but even if he was in the habit of telling the man the truth, he didn't think he would have told this truth: that the forces bound into the tower *knew* him, recognized him, and let him pass; that the broken stone steps grew to meet his feet, and the spaces between them shrank to match his stride. He hadn't known what would happen when the Seneschal insisted on seeing the broken place for himself, and watching Nate cross the gap. From Nate's view, the stones had swelled, the spaces had shrunk. From the Seneschal's view, apparently, everything had looked utterly normal.

"I want her out of that tower, magus," the Seneschal said, unlocking another door, standing aside to let Nate pass, and locking it behind him. "Out of the tower and cooperative. That's why I let you in and out, because you told me you could get her to come willingly, and do as I tell her for once in her life."

Another of Nate's lies. Nobody could ever make Judah do what she didn't want to do. The oiled rushes were unpleasant under his feet and the smell made his already-queasy stomach feel even worse. "You have to give me more time," he said. "She's not ready yet."

They had come to the other side of the passage. As always, the Seneschal's guards clustered around it. The man himself turned stony eyes on Nate. "Lure her, magus," he said, a touch of impatience coloring his voice. "You're a traveled man. Tell her everything she's missing. Make the world sound amazing."

And if only the Seneschal knew the ferocity of Judah's craving for life and experience and beauty, the depths of her talent. Nobody in the Slonimi bred for love. Every child resulted from the careful consideration of bloodlines, of similar and complementary talents. Reproduction was a responsibility, a calling. Nate himself had even been paired off, not long before he and Charles and Derie had left for Highfall, in case he died and his bloodline was lost. As was tradition, the first time, Nate had been very drunk, so he remembered the woman's smell and her name but not her face. Derie had given him to understand that the pairing had failed, anyway.

But there was no failure in Judah. Talented parents sometimes produced a dud, but Judah fairly shimmered with power. She Worked as easily as she breathed. Not that she knew it; as far as she knew, every child with a bleeding arm could walk through defenses like they were paper and rummage through memories like a trunk of old clothes. It had taken him a year of hard training with Derie before he could hear her thoughts in his head; another two before he could send her his own. Derie's powers dwarfed Nate's, and Judah's made Derie's look like a child's. It was all he could do when he Worked with her to keep that one door locked, so she would not know absolutely everything he knew and be frightened by it. It was all he could do to put her to sleep before he left so he could weave the threads of Work through her without her knowing, swaddling her in it like an infant. Someday she would understand, he told himself, and forgive him.

The walk to Limley Square seemed long and he remembered wistfully how quick Elban's phaeton had been. Nate felt weak and nauseated; he slept late every day, and often came out of unconsciousness to find himself being carried around the lab between Bindy and Charles like a passed-out drunk. He had trouble focusing his eyes, and had finally traded some herbal remedies to a decent spectaclist in exchange for new lenses in his glasses. His appetite was gone, which was fortunate because his guts had crawled to a stop. His mouth was dry all the time and he had developed sores on the underside of his tongue; he drank more water and applied a very light solution of opium syrup to dull the pain.

His dreams, though, were amazing. In his dreams he made love to Anneka again; he waded through the knee-high prairie grass outside Tagusville, skin warm with sun, as fat little rodents darted and chittered unseen at his feet. He stood on the pier at Black Lake, watched the boats unload their catch into waiting wagons, smelled fish and water and tar. He dozed in an opium den in Carietta, watching half-asleep as a girl so pale she might have come from Highfall crawled on top of Charles and pulled aside his clothes. Best of all, in his dreams, he saw his mother again. He worked beside her in the caravan, stood by a makeshift stage where she sold her tonics; drove the horses as she sang for him and him alone, his hands on the reins browner, younger and less scarred than now.

In Highfall, he passed the Beggar's Market. One of the factory gangs drilled in the space where the stalls had been. Their heavy boots all hit the floor in perfect time as they marched, pivoted, marched some more. He didn't know which factory wore green embroidery but the marchers were uniformly young, with the rabid light of conviction in their eyes. All the older workers had already settled back into torpor as, one by one, the managers' promises had withered and died. He'd even heard that the long shifts were beginning again. But the young ones, the ones who hadn't been beaten down before the coup—they still believed. Belief could be dangerous. Nate altered course as if he'd never intended to go that way.

He thought he saw Anneka in the road ahead of him, then

Judah, then his mother: hallucinating again. It didn't matter. Derie would fix it.

When the old woman met him at Arkady's door, she laughed. Her glee sounded brittle, jagged. "She's draining you like a boil, isn't she? Good and strong."

"Very strong," he said.

Derie laughed again and clapped her hands. Then she caught at his elbow, because he was falling. "I hope you've eaten something, boy. It'll take a lot of blood to clean up the mess in your head. What a force she is!"

The blood was the least of Nate's misery. Derie treated his memories like junk in a dead man's wagon. Anneka and the dead bandit in the Barriers: thrust aside, old news. The woman Nate had been paired with, the child she probably wasn't carrying because he was useless, lame, pathetic: nobody cared. His mother: irrelevant.

She snatched greedily at everything involving Judah, though—her face, the touch of her mind, every thought Nate had had about her, every bit of her he'd seen. Like the Seneschal, they needed her to do as she was told; unlike the Seneschal's, their plan was righteous. Derie's questions pried through his mind like fingers. Was she biddable enough to do what was needed? Was Nate? Was he weak enough to love her? Was he strong enough to control her?

Derie's voice cut through the chaos like a beam of light. *Quiet, stupid boy.* And she twisted something inside his mind. A noise that he'd not realized he was making cut off abruptly. Inside, he still screamed.

He woke up and the light was different. Gradually, he realized this was because he lay in Arkady's guest bed, the sheets around him clean and cool. His clothes were gone, his arms neatly bandaged. The world was blurry. He put his hand out to the small table next to the bed, found his glasses. Everything slipped into focus. Slowly, he forced himself to sit up. His stomach swung violently. A groan escaped him, and he hunched over.

The door opened and Charles entered. Drawn by the groan, Nate supposed. He carried a glass of clear, pale green liquid. "Drink," he said, passing it to Nate. Nate drank. The draught was faintly herbal and very gingery. He had brewed it himself before going inside yesterday; he'd known he would need it. As he sipped, his nausea eased and he felt stronger.

"You know," he said, "you don't have to keep putting me to bed every time."

"You piss yourself, and that's not all. Not that Derie cares. She'd happily leave you lying in your own blood and filth all night." Charles spoke without much expression. After weeks away from the drops, his weeping had finally dried up, which was a relief; but the way Charles was now, wan and listless, was even harder to take. "Besides, you put me to bed, didn't you?"

Nate—who was wondering what Charles meant by *that's not all*—had indeed put Charles to bed, but didn't want to embarrass his friend by talking about it. "Is Bindy downstairs?"

Charles nodded. "She has a list of calls for you to make from yesterday." He hesitated. "Her sister came to walk her home last night. The pretty one with the chip on her shoulder, the Paper stooge."

"Rina." Nora's tenure on the committee had been brief—she was too old and worn-out, she said—but Rina had risen quickly in the ranks. She wore her Paper sash with pride and wielded it like a sword, her fervent eyes always on the watch for shirkers, hoarders, violators of any kind. People on the street ducked away when they saw her coming.

"She asked if I'd been issued working papers yet," Charles said.

That was worrisome. People without working papers were

sometimes ejected from the city. But Nate kept his voice light. "I'll talk to the Seneschal. Tell him you're my ailing cousin or something. He'll call her off. The Unbinding will be done soon. You'll feel different after. Everything won't seem so... hopeless."

"It's not hope that I'm missing. I had hope. We had nothing but hope, you and I. Do you need to practice that paralyzing thing on me today?"

Charles might as well have been reciting the shopping list. "No," Nate said. "Not today."

One of the calls was an address in a narrow street in Brakeside where the buildings channeled the wind into a cold, gritty blade. The house was so overgrown with attaches that it seemed about to topple; climbing the rickety stairs, Nate hoped the number on his list would match one of the doors in the main part of the building, where the floors would be more stable, but no such luck.

The door was opened by a boy so thin he was almost gaunt. "No!" he cried, the moment he saw Nate. "No, I told you not to send for him!"

"Calm down, Georgy," somebody else said. The door was opened the rest of the way by an elderly woman. Nate recognized her; she was a seamstress, arthritic in both hands, and one of Nate's first patients in Highfall. He kept her in ointments, one with capsaicin and camphor that she could use whenever she wanted, and another with opium that she was to use sparingly. In exchange, she kept him more or less tatter free. As she let him in, she looked him over, head to toe, and said, "Give me that coat, magus. I can see the lining's torn from here."

Nate gave it to her. "It's good to see you."

Meanwhile, Georgy hovered protectively by the room's

lone bed, where a young man lay. "Not good to see you. Go away," he said to Nate.

"Hush," the seamstress said and nodded at the man on the bed. "See what you can do for my boy's leg while I sew, eh?"

Georgy scuttled over to a corner, still scowling. The man's eyes were clouded with pain, his breath short. Understandably, since his leg was broken in at least two places. As Nate measured out a dose of opium syrup—he would have to set the bone, and it would hurt—the injured man said, "Don't mind Georgy. He's just scared."

"Of what?" Nate said.

The seamstress, sitting on a stool next to a table piled high with clothes, snorted. "I don't have my independent's license yet, that's all. They cost the earth, those things!"

"The factory magus took away my papers when I got hurt," the man on the bed said quietly.

Taking his papers meant the other magus thought the hurt man wouldn't ever work again. The company stores wouldn't sell to anyone without work papers or an independent's license, but the seamstress was right: the licenses were exorbitantly expensive. Nate found the whole process infuriating. At least Elban's system had left enough cracks for the people it broke to survive. Before the coup, the man's coworkers would have taken up a collection to pay an outside magus, but all anyone had now was company credit. He wondered how the tiny family was finding the money to feed themselves. "I don't see anything to report," Nate said, passing the man on the bed the opium and rolling up his sleeves.

The man nodded at Nate's springknife. "That's a pretty thing. How's it work?" So while they waited for the syrup to take effect, Nate showed him. The man seemed particularly fascinated by the spring. "Never seen metal like that before," he said, and then his eyes glazed over and Nate got to work setting the bones.

He needed both the woman's help and the boy's, which they gave with nary a wince, even when the bones snapped back into place with a loud, uncomfortable jolt. After, as he wrapped clean bandages around the splint, the woman picked up her needle again. "When the Seneschal took over, I thought I'd be paying you in coin," she said ruefully as they both worked, "but here I am still doing your mending, except my needle's duller and my thread is garbage. The more things change, eh?"

The boy, who had retreated to the corner, hissed. His bitterness was startling in one so young. "Now, George," the woman said. "Gate Magus and I are old friends. Gate Magus won't rat on me." Her tone was admonishing but Nate saw a flicker of fear in her eyes.

"Sure he won't," George said, sullen. "Cozy in the Seneschal's pocket as he is, with his own apprentice's sister the third-lieutenant from Paper."

"Which only means I can help more people. You've nothing to fear from me." Nate hoped he was telling the truth. He couldn't be sure; he could never be sure. He tried to do what he could. He knew he was distracted, though. Each time he went to the House, it became harder and harder to focus, even after Derie was done fixing him. A broken leg was simple, mechanical, more a matter of brute force than reasoning or insight, but more than once he'd caught himself making a potentially dire mistake with ingredients or dosages, and he was loath to think how many he'd made and not caught. He'd started teaching Bindy some elementary herblore (she was his apprentice, after all) and she drank it in like a starving cat with a saucer of milk. She caught his mistakes now. And nagged at him all the time to take better care of himself, to eat or sleep or have some brandy. Her efforts brought tears to his eyes.

The mood swings: elation, tears. That was the Work showing itself, too.

The boy, George, skulked out of the room. "Grandson?" Nate said.

"Just a stray."

"It's a hard time to be taking in strays. You're good to do it."

She sniffed. "Wouldn't let a dog go to one of those orphan halls. The factories will get him eventually, anyway."

On his way home, he stopped at the Grand Bazaar. The awnings were dusty and faded, and rat droppings collected in the corners. The few merchants who still bothered to set up sold goods too frivolous to be stocked by the company stores: cheap jewelry, bolts of grubby viscose, acrid perfumes. Leda, one of Nate's favorite herb sellers from before the coup, had moved from a large fragrant stall in the center to a chair behind a rickety table. She sat with her arms folded and groused at the guards, a few sad sprigs of spindly oregano and basil laid out before her. "Afternoon, Leda," he said. "How's your grandson? Headache any better?"

Leda gave him a huge, too-white smile. She'd been very grand before the coup, and still used acid to whiten her teeth even though Nate had promised her the habit would lead to her losing them. "Aren't you kind to ask," she said. "Seems to bother him most in the morning. Probably something to do with the damp." Meanwhile, her foot crept out, independent from the rest of her body, and pressed down on the end of one of the wide wooden planks. The other end lifted up, revealing a cavity under the floor. Now they were carrying on two conversations: one in their normal voices, in case anyone passed by, and the other under their breath. "My sister used to be like that. *Willowbark?* Took funny in the damp."

"Some people do," Nate said. "*Opium.* Has she ever tried camphor tea?"

"*On the left.* Camphor, you say? Sounds awful."

"It is. Tastes hideous. *Looks dry.* You can add honey, but I can't decide if that makes it better or worse."

"*Fresh as it comes.* Perhaps I'll try that with the boy, then. That something you can make, the camphor tea?"

She was a strong negotiator. She was also one of the few herbmongers in New Highfall who managed to bring in opium, along with valerian, pennyroyal and basically any other herb with an actual use. Bartering care had never worked with Leda, and Nate couldn't sew, so he ended up parting with most of his weeks' credit vouchers. Which were valuable, because they came from the Seneschal and were good anywhere. As he slipped the small wrapped package into a hidden pocket in his satchel, she winked and said, "For all his headaches, he's a clever little thing, my grandson. Stay and hear the clever thing he said?"

Nate wasn't sure the grandson even existed. "I always like a clever story," he said.

Without missing a beat the foot pressed a different board, Leda prattling all the while. Something about a puppy. Inside the revealed compartment, a handful of dull metal vials gleamed against black fabric, carefully arranged to catch the light. Not that they wouldn't shine on their own, for anyone who really wanted them.

"Hilarious," Nate said, when she paused, "but I have to move on."

The foot slid away from the board. The vials disappeared. "Good day then, magus."

"Good day, Leda," he said.

He heard Bindy talking in the kitchen as he opened the front door of the manor. She sounded animated and cheerful in a way he hadn't heard in weeks. A male voice answered. As he hung up his coat and hat, Nate wondered, surprised, if she was speaking to Charles, who generally avoided her like she was contagious. But the man's voice was too deep, and the accent was wrong. Charles, like Nate, hadn't entirely been able to shake the Slonimi lilt in his voice, and his consonants were courtier-sharp. The voice in the kitchen was pure Highfall.

No. It was pure House. Nate went tense.

In the kitchen, a fragrant pot of cinnamon tea simmered. Bindy sat at the table with a man whose face made Nate's brain spin in alarmed circles. That broad face, those sandy curls—his first instinct was to bury the springknife in the man's throat. Bindy leapt up.

"Magus!" Her voice was as warm as the cinnamon in the air. "Look! It's my brother, the one from inside, that they told us was dead! But they were wrong, isn't it amazing? I didn't even know who he was when I found him with Ma in the house. I almost ran for the guards." She laughed. "He was kneading the bread."

The stableman grinned at her. The mug of tea seemed tiny in his giant hands. "Not your fault. You'd never met me in person, for all the letters you wrote."

The fondness in his voice was unmistakable. The stableman loved Bindy and Nate still wanted to kill him. Joyously, Bindy said, "Want tea, magus? There's lots. Darid says you two knew each other, inside."

"We met." Warily, Nate joined them at the table, not taking his eyes off the stableman.

"My brother and my magus, and none of us even knew! What a funny old world," Bindy said, and went on to elucidate all of the ways in which the world was both funny and old. Darid's eyes bored into Nate, as if trying to tell him something, but Nate couldn't understand what it was. Nor could he explain his nearly uncontrollable desire to see the man dead. But he was sane enough to recognize the murderous thoughts as insane, so he sat with a fixed smile and let Bindy pour tea as she chattered on about (seemingly) every letter she and her brother had ever exchanged. There had to be some errand he could send her on, some way to get her out of the House so he could—

kill.

—talk to her brother. Finally, she paused for breath, and Nate said, "I'm sorry to disrupt your reunion, Bindy, but I need you to take some headache powder to the magus in Archertown. You know where he lives?"

Bindy wrinkled her nose. "Yes, but he smells funny."

"So does the headache powder." Nate was surprised by how easy he sounded. "He'll give you some herbs to bring back, and some agar for clotting poultices."

She looked from Nate to her brother, clearly reluctant to leave. "You'll show me how to make them?"

"I will," Nate said, and the stableman said, "Go do your work, Bin. I'll be around. You haven't seen the last of me."

When she was gone—almost the moment the door closed behind her, as if the words were ready to jump off his tongue— the stableman said, "How is Judah?"

He wasn't being polite. There was urgency in his voice, and pain. "She's fine," Nate said. "They're all fine."

Darid visibly relaxed. "I don't care about all of them. I just care about her." He carried a hardness that Nate didn't remember; but then again, the only other time Nate had spent with him, he'd just been snatched from certain death. Which would leave a person somewhat less than themselves, perhaps, and why did Nate want to kill him so badly? He should excuse himself. Take off the springknife, leave it in the lab where he wouldn't be tempted to use it.

"I thought you left the city," he said, instead.

"I came back when I heard about the coup. Wanted to see my mother."

The slightest flex of the wrist was all it would take. The blade would leap out like a bird startled from a bush. "You don't look anything like Bindy."

"Different fathers. Me and my first two sisters, Nell and Connie—our father died in the plague. Con died, too, right before I went inside. Ma's sent a lot of people off on the dead-cart."

"What are you going to do now?" Nate asked.

With a shrug of one massive shoulder, Darid said, "Not sure. I can't work. Don't have papers."

"I'm sure you could get them. Other Returned have."

"How many of them are supposed to be dead?" Darid's tone was cold.

"I could speak to the Seneschal for you. I don't think he has anything against you personally. He needed to do what he did." The words struck Nate as ridiculous even as he spoke them. The stableman's mouth tightened and his eyes went hard and Nate wanted so very badly to kill him. Because Judah had loved him, he realized; because she'd been grievously in-jured, in more ways than one, and Nate had been made to be party to it, and oh, it would feel good to stab him. "He'd find you a job."

"Thanks," Darid said drily, "but I think I've had enough of being assigned work by the Seneschal." He shook his head. "I thought things would be different now. I heard about people inside coming out. But nobody's out, you know. They just moved the Wall. Made it invisible, so nobody would notice. Bindy told me what you did to keep her. Why? Why put your-self on the line for some Marketside factory worker's girl?"

"I wouldn't call it putting myself on the line," Nate said. "I filled out a form. Anyway, Bindy's smart and I like her.

Are you going to accuse me of evil intentions? Because your mother and I already covered that."

"Why me, then? Why'd you put yourself on the line for me?"

"To be honest, I have no idea." Now it was Nate that was cold. "I didn't have a lot of time to think about it. Eleanor asked me to, and it seemed like Judah would have wanted it. By the way, you haven't asked, but I'll tell you anyway. If she was pregnant, it was undone shortly after the caning. I saw to it myself."

He expected the stableman to flinch; had wanted him to. But Darid only shook his head. "Then you added to her pain for nothing. We never had sex."

It was Nate who flinched, then. The stableman leaned forward. He really didn't look anything like Bindy; Bindy's hair was strawberry, almost red, and her eyes a clear sky-blue. Everything about Darid was plain and drab, but his dull blue eyes were intense as he said, "Why'd the Seneschal let her live?"

Nate couldn't speak.

"Elban's sons, I get. The Seneschal doesn't want to let them go rally up an army but he doesn't want to make them martyrs, either, so he tucks them out of sight and mind, lets the hope die slowly so nobody even notices it's gone. In the meantime, he gets to pretend he's not as cruel as Elban. Plus, maybe sometime he'll need somebody to blame for something, and there they'll be." The fate of the two men clearly didn't bother him. "But why keep Judah? Kill her or let her go, sure. But keep her?"

With unaccountable malice, Nate said, "Maybe he's in love with her."

The stableman dismissed that idea quickly with a curl of the lip. The gesture spoke volumes of a life where opinions were pared down to their slimmest possible expression. "The people who've come out keep talking about the orchards and pastureland and fields. There's talk of taking the House by force."

Nate felt the color drain from his face.

"Nobody's taking it seriously yet," Darid went on, "but come winter, they will. And when they do—people still have warm feelings for the Children, but they've got warmer ones for their own. If it comes to violence there's no way to guarantee she'd be safe." Then, all in a burst, "She shouldn't have to live or die with them. She's none of Elban's get. She deserves a life."

"With you?"

The man withered at the contempt in Nate's voice. "No. I can't imagine she'd want that. I'm not sure I want it for her." He hesitated. "Does she know I'm alive?"

"You want me to tell her?"

Darid shook his head. "Let her believe I'm dead for now. I might as well be, until I think of a way to help her." He sucked at his lower lip. "Who'd they kill instead of me?"

"I don't know," Nate said. "I wasn't involved."

Later, when Nate told Derie about the stableman's visit, the old woman was alarmed. "Oh, no," she said. "No, no, no. We can't have her losing focus now. That won't do at all," and made Nate let her into his head again, where she shoved the memory of Darid's visit so far behind the locked door that when she was done, it felt like something he'd dreamed, or dreamed of dreaming, deep in a fever or on the edge of death. It made him uncomfortable, itchy. He didn't like to think of it again.

Why can't I do anything in the real world? Judah asked, petulant, the next time he was in the tower. They were in the Work, but she had not yet immersed herself in his memories and the tower was still visible around them, with the purple membrane strung across every surface. She had her fingers in it and was playing with it like clay. The sight made Nate shiver. *All this stuff is everywhere and you say it's powerful. Why can't I walk on it, or build a fire with it, or use it to fly?*

Because that's not the nature of it. You might as well ask why you can't walk on water, or build a fire with water or use water to fly.

Water can't tell me that Gavin stubbed his toe this morning. It couldn't tell me every time he snuck off with some staff girl.

Nate forced down his alarm. *Did he do that a lot? Did any of them ever get pregnant?* If there was another heir somewhere—more of Elban's foul blood—

If they did, they ended up in the midden yard. The membrane between Judah's fingers blazed scarlet. *That's what Darid said would happen.*

Even the mention of the stableman's name was enough to make Nate feel faintly queasy. And he didn't like the way her hands moved to the tether in her chest, the thick rope of membrane that bound her to Gavin—the way her fingers began to tease, and dig—

No! Nate leapt for her, took her hands in his. Although they weren't his real hands and they weren't hers either, their real hands were in the real tower lying limp beside their real bodies. *No. Not yet.*

Why not?

It's too dangerous. It might hurt you. You have to be patient.

A burst of stubbornness, like a flapping bat. *Sick of being trapped*, she said.

He made his thoughts gentle. *Look in my memories. Can you find the Temple Argent? Can you take me there?*

It's real? she said.

Look and see, he said.

He felt her inside him. She was gentler now. Suddenly they stood together on the edge of a cliff. Hundreds of feet below, the raging ocean threw itself on the rocks, over and over. The ruined Temple was a massive tumble of stone scattered behind them. Tiny succulents crawled quietly over the surface, giving no hint of the force that had torn the citadel apart. She had seen many things through Nate's eyes over the past weeks, mountains and plains and cities, but he had deliberately kept the ocean in reserve. He was stunned by how real the waves were, when her Work unfolded them from his mind: salt spray landed like needles of ice on their cheeks, and a cold breeze pulled at the hem of her dress. The horizon was not merely two lines meeting, but a reality that went on and on, infinitely. He would suffer for this later, he thought, feeling his own strength draining away—but he had drawn Derie's sigil and Caterina's before he'd even entered the tower, and he could feel them feeding him threads of their own power. These he sucked at greedily, not caring that they coursed through him and melted him the way lightning did sand. Judah's depthless eyes were wide, transfixed. She had no idea how amazing she was, how terrifying her power. He wanted to hurl himself at her feet, to worship her; to evaporate so she could inhale him, to tear himself apart.

Good, he said. *Let's try something else.*

"Make her come down," the Seneschal said. "The managers want this land and I want my guild." Frustration burned in the gray man's face. He was not a man who was accustomed to being frustrated, not anymore.

Nate wobbled back and forth in reality like a loose tooth. The empty courtyard around them was simultaneously desolate and alive with carriages, and thick with the trees that had been felled to clear space for it. The rush of the Argent Sea was loud in his ears. The oil-soaked air of the Safe Passage was empty and packed with shouting bodies and on fire. It was all incredibly distracting. "I'm trying."

"Try harder," the Seneschal said. "And I will try not to think about how much easier it would be to throw some boards on the damn stairs and drag her out in chains."

"Do that, and she'll chew your throat out with her teeth if she can't find a knife."

"Yes, yes, it must be done willingly," the Seneschal said. "So says the chieftain. He's had a good bit of time to consider the problem in his prison cell. Perhaps you would find that setting equally productive."

Prison cell. In Nate's unreal state, thinking of the prison was as good as actually being there. He'd felt the chieftain's power outside the man's cell: like the old days, going village to village searching for unaware Workers, sensing power like music. The song in the prison had been playing in a key he'd never heard before. "You need me," he said. "I'm the only one she trusts."

Which was true and also ironic, because Nate no longer trusted himself. On the way home from the House he saw John Slonim, the man who'd driven the first Slonimi caravan, back before the Slonimi *were* the Slonimi, before the first Work: a rail-thin man with dark skin and a heavy beard, standing on a box doing sleight-of-hand for petty coins. He saw a tall woman with enormous horns that curled behind her head, a knitted scarf wrapped around her neck and carefully tucked under the tips of the horns. He saw a mother holding a crying baby in the crook of one arm. The mother brought a dull silver vial to the baby's mouth. The crying stopped.

Nate looked away. It is not real, he told himself. None of it is real.

"Better work faster, boy," Derie said at the manor. "You're

like a pot that's more glue than clay." Then, as Charles held Nate down, she cut his arm, and put him back together.

When Nate woke the next morning, Charles had cleaned him up and put him to bed again, but was nowhere to be seen. It took some time but eventually Nate rose, and dressed and went downstairs. The last of the bread sat, stale and hard, on the counter; when Bindy arrived, she warmed a slab of it in a pan on the stove until it was soft again and stood over him while he ate it, frowning like a concerned mother. Then she wrapped herself in her shawl and went to the Seneschal's manor to pick up Nate's credit vouchers for the week.

The errand would take hours. As soon as she was gone, Nate went into the garden and threw up everything he'd eaten. Then he hung a rag over the gate in the garden: not blue, but white. Or at least it had been white, once. Inside, he fetched the box he'd prepared earlier that week, and put it on the table.

A moment later, he heard a tap at the garden door, and opened it. "Firo," he said.

The former courtier was transformed. The crinkles around his eyes were free of kohl; instead of being combed high with pomade, his hair hung long, and instead of the gems he'd once favored he wore plain steel earrings, like a dockworker. His coat was as battered and drab as any factory worker's, but the shirt under it was spotless. Behind him in the garden, a lumpy sack thrown over one shoulder, lurked a heavily muscled young man whose good looks hadn't yet been worn away by work and privation. Soon enough.

In the House, Firo's predilections had been permitted but not generally spoken of, which Nate could almost bear. Now, though, Firo went about shamelessly with his new pet, as if there were nothing unnatural at all about the relationship. To the Slonimi, passing on your power was everything. For a man to waste his time in a dalliance where there was no chance of a child was seen as selfish, even traitorous. Persistence of such pursuits was one of the few crimes that merited expulsion, and the stripping of power. "You can come in. He stays out," he said to Firo.

The young man made a face. Firo rolled his eyes and gave his companion a conspiratorial, pitying look: *What can you even do with these people?* It did not endear him to Nate, but the young man grinned and handed over the sack.

"Really, magus," Firo said when the door was firmly closed, "I don't know what isolated little backwater bred you, but it's long since time you left it behind."

Nate gestured to the box on the table.

Firo's slouch vanished. The two steps it took him to reach the kitchen table were full of courtier insouciance and swagger. Opening the box, he examined the three dozen vials packed inside it. They were identical to the ones hidden beneath the plank in Leda's stall, identical to the one Nate had hallucinated the mother holding to her baby's mouth (it must have been a hallucination—he was more glue than clay, his brain could not be trusted). Nate had made them all, after taking a few days to figure out the formula. It had been Vertus's idea, although the former servingman preferred to use Firo as go-between. Nate hadn't actually spoken with him in weeks.

"What are the odds," Nate had said to the courtier the first time, "that I've had dealings with both of you, and now you have dealings with each other?"

Firo had only laughed his horrible courtier's laugh. "Fairly good, since Vertus runs three quarters of the black market in New Highfall. A better question is how a judgmental prude like you has made two such interesting friends," and Nate had said, pointedly, that they were not friends, and never would be.

As Firo inspected the vials, Nate emptied the sack. Inside he found a supply of empty vials, as well as good, soft flour, butter, cheese, some meat that looked like goat, and a pile of decent-looking root vegetables. There were also three smaller, very well-wrapped packages: one sugar, the other two candy. Chocolate caramels and glazed cherries. Cherries were long out of season. They smelled like sunlight and open air and freedom.

Firo watched Nate's deep inhalation with some amusement. "A funny world we live in now, magus. The confectioner's trade is as illicit as yours. Speaking of secrets, how is our little dark horse these days?"

Nate, feeling like he'd been caught doing something salacious—Firo made him feel that way about almost everything—rewrapped the candy. "Not that it's any of your business, but she's fine."

"I'll take your word for it. At least somebody's been eating all those lovely sweets, and it's clearly not you." Firo surveyed Nate critically. Nate knew he was thinner—every day his bones seemed to emerge further from his flesh—but he didn't like being looked at by Firo, no matter the motivation. Suddenly, Firo laughed. "Dark horse! To think, all the time and lovely talk I wasted on her, and all I needed to do was offer her a sugar cube."

Nate scowled, but said nothing. Firo shrugged. "Speaking of treats, I ought to be getting on. The longer Vertus waits, the smaller our cut gets. Poverty makes my William cranky," he added fondly.

"So treats work on him, as well?" Nate didn't bother to keep the nastiness from his voice.

"Loving somebody who loves you back isn't such a terrible thing, magus. You ought to try it sometime," Firo said, his voice full of cool pity. Then he left.

* * *

Nate tried to get Bindy to take some of the black market food. "Some candy, if nothing else. For Canty, and the other littles," he said.

At the mention of her brother's name, Bindy looked wistful. Canty spent his days in the factory crèche now, being cared for by women too old or pregnant to work. Nate knew she missed him. He did, too. "I ought not to," she said. "If Rina found out, she'd turn you in. Anyway, magus, we don't need food. We're okay. But I'll take some for Darid, if you don't mind."

As always, Nate felt an irrational stab of fury on hearing her brother's name, but he was careful not to let it show. "What does Rina think of Darid, then?"

"He's not staying with us. Ma says it's best not to talk about him when she's around. Rina's done really well on the factory committee. She's got a talent for it," she added loyally. Then, "Sign my papers, magus?" The crèche wouldn't let Bindy pick Canty up unless Nate signed her off as having worked a full day. Once, when he'd lost track of time inside and Nora had been working the long shift, Canty had spent nearly two days there. Now Nate signed a few days in advance.

After Bindy took food for her brother, and some was put aside for Judah and the others inside, there was still enough for Nate and Charles. They'd have to manage somewhat carefully, since he'd surely end up trading away the new vouchers like he had the old, but neither of them had much appetite these days. While the goat stewed, Nate made a Slonimi pan bread that baked up warm and pillowy in an iron pan on the stove. For flavor he used the last of his supply of a particular spice that he'd brought with him across the Barriers, and not seen since. The smell of it brought Charles downstairs to the table. When he tore open his share of the bread, steam rose from the soft interior. Charles inhaled deeply. But then, instead of eating, he put the two torn pieces back on his plate with exaggerated care.

"I'm leaving, Nate," he said.

"Because I make the drops?" He knew Charles didn't like what he did for Vertus, but he hadn't thought it was so bad.

"No. The drops don't bother me. I mean, I want them like I want my next breath, but I prefer to be in my right mind." Charles shook his head. "No, the committee came knocking yesterday while you were inside. Left a summons for me and my nonexistent working papers." With a glint of humor, he added, "I've been ignoring it, but that strikes me as rather a short-term solution, wouldn't you say?"

Nate's mouth was suddenly dry, the bread turning to sand in his mouth. "We'll get you papers. You can be my apprentice."

"Bindy is your apprentice. Do you want to choose between us?"

There was nothing Nate could say to that. "My porter, then."

"I think the Company of Porters would object."

There was nothing Nate could say to that, either. "You're my friend," he said finally.

"You're mine, too. And that's why I'm telling you: I'm leaving." He leaned forward, his face filled with an earnest intensity Nate hadn't seen there in a long time. He felt struck nearly dumb by the force of it. And of course, this was why Charles had been chosen to come along, wasn't it? His persuasiveness, his charm. "Come with me," Charles said now. "Don't stay here. It's killing you. You know it is."

"The world needs—"

"No." Charles was stern now. "I don't believe it anymore, Nate. Oh, I know, the Work seems real. But everything I felt when I was dropping seemed real, too, and it all came out of a bottle. We've both been told since we were children that if we cut holes in ourselves we can work wonders, but what wonders have we actually seen?"

Nate shook his head. "You haven't been in the tower. You haven't met—"

"The girl?" Charles's expression twisted. "The girl is a girl and the world is the world and it's always been like this, Nate, it's never been any other way. There's nothing to unbind. There are only our lives to live. Be in love with her if you want, but don't delude yourself, don't think of her as some sort of miracle—"

From the front of the manor came the distinct and impossible sound of the locked front door opening. Both men froze as an irregular *thump-thump-tap* made slow and steady progress down the hall, past the parlor and stairs. Two feet and a cane.

Charles was wide-eyed, frozen in fear. Nate imagined he looked much the same. They were both children again, waiting for Derie to come *beat some brain into them*, as she called it.

"Run," Nate whispered, barely able to hear himself.

Charles shook his head with a fearsome resolution.

The kitchen door opened. Derie hobbled in. "Dinner, boys? And poor old Derie not invited."

For a moment, neither man said anything. Then Nate pushed a third chair out with his foot. The legs screeched on the wooden floor. Derie sat down; she took up Charles's forgotten bread and bit into it. With grudging approval, she said, "Not bad, Nathaniel. Not as good as Caterina's. It's the water that makes the difference, you know. Water's dead here. Like everything else." She tossed the bread down. Then she looked at Charles.

"Leaving, are we?" she said. "Or just talking about it endlessly, like a jay?"

Nate found his voice. "Just talking, Derie. Not endlessly."

She barked a laugh. "Says you. This one's been chewing

on it in that parboiled mind of his for days now." To Charles, she said, "You've got no defenses anymore, boy. You burned them all out with that poison you put in yourself, and now, you don't take a shit without me knowing about it."

Charles raised his chin. "I did my part. I got Nate inside."

Derie made a scornful noise. "Would have been nice to have had a courtier on the inside, too, wouldn't it? One that hadn't stewed his own brain like tea leaves so it'd feel nicer while he wasted his seed in some third-rate courtier girl."

"It wouldn't have mattered," Charles said, unfazed. "Shame the Work can't show you the future, old woman. Never occurred to you that anyone else might have designs on Elban's empire, did it?"

"This is not about his empire, you stupid boy. This is about the entire world." Derie's voice was a vicious hiss.

"I'm not a boy," Charles said.

Nate felt the antagonism burning between the two of them, and fear began to burgeon into panic inside him. "Derie," he said, and went silent. There was no balm for this wound, no salve for this betrayal. Because that was how Derie saw it, he knew: a betrayal not just of her, but of everything generations had worked for. Lives and blood, vanished like water into dry dust.

Part of Nate agreed with her.

Suddenly Derie smiled, brilliant and hard. "Well, what to do about this? Can't let you go feral, with all that Work in you."

"Send him home," Nate said.

"Where he'll do what?" she said, as if Charles wasn't even there. "All he's ever been trained for is pretending to be a courtier. I can doubt he can even hitch up a horse anymore." She picked up the bread knife. "And of course, he won't have the Work anymore."

Sometimes an ordinary person was born powerful. Away from the caravan, without planning, without interference. You could feel them, your first day in a new village, like a campfire in winter or water in the desert. It was easy to pick them out of a crowd, because they were the ones everyone else either gravitated toward or edged away from; they were the only ones who seemed real.

And sometimes the opposite happened. Sometimes, a person born with power grew up unworthy; wanted to leave, or was expelled. But they couldn't take their power with them—it couldn't be allowed to spread unchecked. So it was removed. Nate had been thinking of expulsion just that day, with Firo, but he had never actually seen one happen. When he was a child, Caterina had never let him watch, and when he grew older he didn't want to.

Now he sat frozen as Derie sliced into her hand and drew quick sigils in the spilled blood. Nate felt the Work rasp over his mind, where it had touched Charles's. Like an insect, Derie began to strip away Charles's power like leaves from a tree, unweaving every bit of Work he'd ever done. It was brutal, ugly. Nate ached with empty places where Charles had been, where he was torn away. Charles himself gasped for breath, gray-skinned, lips bluing. Sweat beaded his forehead. The sounds coming from him, small and helpless, were worse than Judah's screams during the caning. Nate knew he could do nothing to stop this.

"Stop," he said anyway. "Stop, Derie."

"I think not," she said.

Charles was a dwindling flame, then a spark. Nate reached out to lend some of his own fire, and felt himself slapped back, the sting of it reverberating through his entire body.

The spark sputtered. Died. Charles's writhing stopped. He

slumped dull-eyed in his chair. "You've killed me." His voice was a void.

"Not at all." Derie stood up. "You can live like that as long as you like. Of course, most find they don't like to for very long. But that's not my problem." Leaning on her cane, she stomped to the counter and picked up a basin that Bindy had left to dry on the shelf. Then she stomped back. Dropped it on the table in front of the living husk that had once been Charles. "There. So you don't leave a mess if you do decide to do the decent thing."

She left. Charles was uninjured physically, and looked exactly as he had before Derie had arrived, but everything was wrong. His friendly presence in Nate's head was gone. Nate's heart broke for him. He tried to imagine living like that, stripped of all power, all connection. Cut off from the world, from all the people he'd ever loved. The loneliness of it. The misery.

Charles closed his eyes. His head moved ever so faintly back and forth, and Nate remembered him saying, a lifetime and mere minutes ago: *I prefer to be in my right mind.* "Knife," he said. His voice sounded like it was three rooms away.

Nate brought his knife. He laid the weapon down on the table in front of Charles. "You don't have to do this," he said. "You could—" But even as he spoke, he knew better. Nobody ever survived having their power taken away. Nobody ever wanted to.

It took Charles some time to get the knife into his hand. It took more time, and effort, to bring the knife's edge to the vein in his arm. It was excruciating to watch but it was unthinkable to Nate to do anything other than stay, and wait, and witness as, finally, Charles mustered the strength to open the skin, as his blood started to flow into the basin. It was as dead and lifeless as the rest of him, no more alive than the sludge at the bottom of the Brake.

And although it took longer than either of them would have liked, Charles began to grow pale. "Nate," he said eventually, and Nate said, "I'm here." They had to speak the words aloud, because neither of them could feel each other anymore.

The next morning, Nate still sat there, motionless at the table with three bowls of clotting blood and the dead body of his oldest friend. When Bindy walked in and gasped, Nate only blinked. He felt like he'd just woken up, but knew he hadn't slept. "Bindy," he said calmly, "will you please go find a guard? Charles has killed himself."

By the time the deadcart arrived—nothing so grand as a deadcoach, not for somebody like Charles—Nate had dumped the bowls of blood in the garden. Even inert blood made good fertilizer. It didn't bother him. He'd watched the stuff drain out of Charles, but could feel nothing of his friend in it. Even the body itself felt meaningless, and it did not disturb him overmuch to watch the two workers dump it unceremoniously into the back of the cart, where several bodies already lay jumbled on top of each other. Nate stood silently with the guard as the two workers pulled a soiled piece of canvas over the bodies to cover them, and cracked the whip over the decrepit mule who began to ploddingly carry them all away.

"Where are they taking him?" Nate said.

"Pits outside the city," the guard said. "Sorry about your friend, magus. Was he a dropper?"

"He used to be."

"Once a dropper, always a dropper." The guard nodded at the disappearing cart, then spat into the dust. "Two of those others were, too. Stuff turns a man into a parasite. Wish they'd all do like your friend. No disrespect meant, of course."

"None taken," Nate said.

★ ★ ★

As the Seneschal let him into the courtyard the next day, the gray man said, "You have one more week to convince her to come down on her own. Then I'll bring her down, one way or another." His voice was flat. "You might suggest to her— subtly, of course—that the broken stairs don't protect Gavin."

"I thought you didn't approve of the way Elban used them against each other," Nate said.

"I don't. It will be clean, my way. Fair." One gray shoulder twitched in a shrug. "I'll only hurt him until she comes down. No tricks."

Judah would certainly come down if Gavin were being tortured. Nate needed to finish his work soon. As he navigated the corridors to the parlor, he felt dull surprise that the end was finally so near: he had spent his entire life building a house, and now there were only the curtains to hang and the horse to hitch up. Although generally one didn't hitch horses up to houses. His metaphors were mixing. Charles was dead. Soon Judah would be wreaking her usual careless havoc in his head. Not knowing who he was would almost be a relief.

He found Eleanor sitting on the parlor floor in a tangle of dingy gray yarn like a bird in a nest, and gave her the flour. Her thanks was halfhearted. "Put it on the table, will you? Sorry, I can't get up. If I lose my place in this I'll never find it again. I had it outside drying, and the wind picked up." She shook her head once, as if she had no movements to spare. Then, looking more closely at him, her eyes narrowed. "Magus, are you feeling all right?"

"I was about to ask the same of you."

"I'm just tired. Of this yarn, mostly. We really are grateful for the flour, magus. It means a lot. Will you bring that flask on the table up to Judah when you go? It's squash soup."

"She'll like that."

"She'll hate it, actually," Eleanor said, "but it's food. There's a letter, too."

He took the flask. He burned the letter in the workshop, as he did all of Eleanor's letters. They would only remind Judah of Eleanor and the outside world. They would only hurt her. And he needed her focused.

You seem sad today.

They stood on a windy mountain, thick soft cloud obscuring everything beneath them. The snow never melted there, but in Judah's Work, it was only cold, not freezing. For her, the glittering crystals of ice in the air were beautiful, not piercing; for her, the crunch of snow underfoot did not carry a fear of crevasse, collapse, death. Around them the peaks of the Barriers reached majestically skyward, blue-gray and frosted with white. In reality, by this point, Nate had not been able to open his windburned eyes enough to see through them; Charles had lost a toe, and for all of them, remembering the sensation of being merely *cold* had been like remembering summer. But Nate had hidden those darker memories behind the locked door, because to explain why the three travelers were willing to suffer so would require explaining why they were here, and Judah wasn't ready to hear that yet. To her, the Barriers were merely dark and lovely and wild.

I suppose I am, he said. *A friend died.*

The snow settled on her hair like diamonds and didn't melt. *I know how that feels.*

You do, don't you? Nate changed the scene: showed her the stableman as he'd seen him that first time, in Firo's room. Wary and pale, but unafraid. Like a cow going to slaughter was unafraid. He could feel the stab of pain the dull face brought her. The empty spaces the stableman had left in her were the empty spaces Charles had left in him. It was dreadful to lose someone. *He's not dead, though.*

He might as well be, she said curtly. He could feel her sadness as keenly as he felt his own.

Watch the snow, he told Judah, and set the silver crystals of snow spinning and whirling in the air. Her eyes grew wide, as he'd known they would. Snow never danced that way in reality. While she was distracted, he reached into her, felt for the jagged places the stableman's absence had left. He pressed the broken edges together and smoothed the seam over. It was complicated Work and he was almost frightened by how quickly and easily he could do it. It was true that the more you Worked in someone's mind, the more malleable that mind became, but this was something he'd never been able to do before. He knew he wouldn't be able to do it now were they not in the tower.

Even so, she gasped, and pressed a hand to her chest. *What did you do?*

A kind of Work. The faintest smugness colored his voice. The smoothing was the sort of talent he had long envied in Caterina, who did it as a treatment for grief or anger. But now Judah's lips were pressed tight together, her eyes flinty.

Undo it.

But I took away your pain.

It's my pain. The ice crystals near her seemed to darken from diamond to onyx and the wind began to snatch at Nate—nowhere near as cold as reality had been, but worrisome, nonetheless. *I want to feel it.*

The sky was beginning to tilt sideways and slide away. He wasn't even sure she knew she was doing it. Unsettled, he said, *I've given you a gift. You're better off without him.*

With a sound like shattering glass, the crystals of black ice snapped together into a long, sharp wedge. For a bare instant it hovered in the air between them—then it flew straight toward his heart. He felt the merciless point tearing into his skin, splintering his ribs like kindling—

And he lay on the floor of the tower, out of the Work, gritty stone beneath his hands. He tried to take a breath, but something was wrong with his lungs. Something was wrong with all of him. His arms and legs flailed against the floor, his back straining in an agonizing arc, but his mind was clear—as clear as it ever was, anyway—watching his body twist and spasm. The pain was very real, the pain was brutal. The back of his skull rammed three times, hard, against the stone floor, and the world was full of flinty ice again and everything went gray.

When he became aware of himself once more, his body was mercifully still. The side of his face pressed against cold stone. A pebble dug into his cheek. Faintly, he heard somebody gasping. He didn't think it was him. Carefully, he moved one arm, then another. Braced them beneath his body and pushed himself upright.

Judah sat a few feet away, her back pressed against the curved wall. She was only inches from the place the floor stopped. It terrified him to see her so close to the edge. Her arms were wrapped tight around her body. She was the one who was gasping. Her eyes were wild, like a panicked horse. "I'm sorry," she said.

"It's all right. I'm all right," he said, although something in his head was damaged. He saw everything in multiples: Judah here, Judah on the mountain, Judah a year from now. Infinite Judahs observed by infinite Nathaniels. The ends of himself flapped loose and he knew that Derie would not be able to put him back together this time. He tried to gather as much of himself as he could.

He must have done a decent job because her breathing slowed, and the terror faded from her eyes. "I saw your friend in your head," she said. "I saw him kill himself. You just sat and watched. How could you just sit and watch?"

"Derie took his power away. He was already dead."

He could smell her puzzlement like smoke. Then she understood, and the smoke vanished. To Nate's great relief she came forward, onto her knees, and slid away from the terrifying drop—came close to him, and took his hand. Her hand felt dry and cold, her touch tentative. "I'm sorry I hurt you, magus. And I'm sorry for your friend. You loved him."

"I did," he said. Her eyes were as black as the icy dagger she'd sent into his chest, and all of the many fractured parts of him were sure that if he kissed her now she would let him, if he did anything she would let him. Some of the fragments inside his head were already kissing her, already doing much more, but the lump of his real body in the tower was sluggish and hard to control. And wouldn't Derie be angry. Wouldn't she use her cane on him then.

As if in answer, he heard his old teacher's voice—real or imagined, he didn't know, those lines were fractured, too—as cutting as the mountain wind. *She's not yours, boy.*

He flinched away. Judah frowned. Before he could say anything she reached out one of her cool, dry hands and touched his cheek. He would have flinched back from that, too—but the coolness spread over him, like floating in a pond in the warm sun. It was better than a kiss. It was better than anything he'd ever felt. The pieces of him weren't joined, but they were soothed. He was a great tree surrounded by a pond and all the fluttering leaves of him were useful, all grew from the same place. He could stay like this forever. He never wanted to move again. And she hadn't even cut him first—even that faint delicious pain was absent—

She hadn't even cut him first. His eyes flew open in amazement. "What are you doing? How are you—"

Judah pulled her hand back. He was still cracked and broken, but the lovely peace remained. "I do it for Gavin when he's upset. You seemed so miserable."

"You can just…do that," he said.

She shrugged. "It's not the same as what you do."

No, it wasn't. It was much, much stronger. This was why it had to be her, Nate realized. This was the Work the Slonimi had wrought, all of them together, over all these years. She wasn't like him or Caterina or Derie; she wasn't even like Maia or Tobin. She was something else entirely. He could see her slipping already back into the docility that he and the tower wove around her. Her jaw and cheekbones stood out more now. She wasn't eating enough and she probably didn't even know it, the Work he and the tower did on her when she was asleep kept her from feeling hungry. Or cold—he had felt her touch, he knew her body was cold. She was dying in this barren tower, isolated from everyone she knew, and it all probably felt completely normal to her. It probably seemed a perfectly reasonable way to live.

Sometimes, as the Slonimi traveled, they found a villager so powerful they could not be left behind, whether the villager would come willingly or not. It was hard. They always yelled and fought, and had to be chained until they accepted their new life. Caterina hated it. *It's for the best*, she'd say, though, and she was right. Caterina's own mother had been one of the Unwilling. Charles's father, too. What the Seneschal had told Nate in Elban's study was true: people didn't always know what was good for them, and they rarely considered what was good for the world. Sometimes you had to force them. Sometimes they had to be tricked.

"You're getting very good," he said.

"Yes," Judah said. Her voice sounded drowsy. She pushed

his knife toward him. "If there were a contest for the person who was the very best at digging through your head, I'd win."

No, he thought, wryly. Derie would. "You're finding truths that I don't even know are inside me. Soon you'll be able to manipulate them."

"Like you just did? With Darid?" She blinked, her face slack with the effort of thinking. "I didn't like that."

"But it helped you. You trust me to help you, don't you?"

"I trust you," she said so dreamily that his fragmented heart broke into a few more pieces, just for her.

"Good." He took her hand in his. "Because you'll need to trust me, if you're going to unbind yourself from Gavin."

Some emotion broke through her complacency like a lantern through fog: excitement and dread and fear and trepidation, all at once. "Could I do that?" she whispered finally.

"It won't be easy," he said. He kept his voice neutral. Just in case she had some tendrils inside him, he thought fixedly of the locked door inside his head. "You'd have to do exactly as I say. Even if it's hard. Even if it hurts."

With a glimmer of her old cheek, she said, "Are you seriously asking me if I'm afraid of pain?"

"I mean it," he said. "You have to trust me."

She rolled her eyes as if the answer was obvious. "I trust you."

And she did. He could feel it with all of his selves. He very much doubted that she had much choice—the tower did its own kind of Work—but still. It overwhelmed him. He still held her hand; now he pressed the back of it to his lips, which was all he dared to do. Perhaps after. Perhaps there would be time.

But then he realized how limp her hand was in his, and—mouth still pressed to her cool skin—he looked up. Saw the dazed distaste in her eyes, the wariness.

Well. Maybe not.

He let her hand fall. Then he picked up his knife. It was spotted with old blood and grit from the floor, but he didn't think it mattered, any more than her distaste mattered. After, when she was asleep, the tower would smooth everything over.

CHAPTER NINETEEN

Something was wrong. Like a word on the tip of Judah's tongue, or a dream—she knew the wrongness was there, but when she tried to grab for it, it slipped away.

It wasn't the Work; she loved the Work. The Work was alive. The blood, which she'd initially found gory, hardly bothered her anymore. The purplish membrane didn't particularly interest her, but the world Nate showed her inside his head was dazzling. There was so much of it. Forests of vine-shrouded trees with tops that pierced the clouds; giant rust-colored rocks littered across a plain like discarded toys; wide meadows greener and more fragrant than anything she'd ever seen or smelled. The Work was all that was real; the tower was the dream. She watched the magus's fine, pale hands cleaning crusted blood away from her cuts and remembered Darid's hands, big and callused, dabbing salve over her burns; those big hands had seemed the only solid thing in a world that slipped and slid with fever, but now the memory seemed empty, meaningless.

In another language, another world, around a corner, under a bed, some hidden part of her knew: something was wrong. Something was missing. No matter how she searched, she couldn't find it.

She thought she had searched.

She was sure she had.

A thin crust of snow appeared in a perfect semicircle near the broken edge of the tower. Elly sent up a blanket, but Judah wasn't cold. The magus's visits were brilliantly clear, but she had no idea how she passed her time in between. She devoured the food he brought, but was never aware of being hungry. She had nothing to do, but was never bored; she must have slept, but remembered neither falling asleep nor waking, and was never drowsy. Through the purple membrane she could feel Theron drifting around the house, but he meant nothing to her. Scratches from Gavin marred her skin, around the old curlicue scars and the tidy cuts the magus made, but they didn't seem important.

In the Work she felt everything. Every touch of breeze, every flake of snow. Her body felt hyper-alive and the world felt hyper-real even though she knew it wasn't real at all. Her memories of the places the magus took her weren't even really hers. They were secondhand, with the shape of his identity still in them. But they felt like hers.

Why does the inside of your head look like the old part of the House? she asked once. Because when they weren't working with specific memories, he let her explore, opening closed door after closed door. And it did look like the old wing. *You had never been here before I brought you.*

You had, he said. A bit wry, even in the Work. Having her wandering the halls of his brain was uncomfortable for him but he let her do it anyway. He said it was fine, that what mattered was that she was learning—and she was. She could open his memories, unfold them to see things in them that he'd never noticed and couldn't consciously remember. She could even change them, if she wanted. There was a girl he'd been with, Anneka, his memory of her strong because—Judah thought— she had been his first and they had been young and it had happened during the time the magus thought of as Before, When Things Were Easy. The memory was easy to manipulate. Her changes were subtle at first, the weather or the smells or the feel of the ground under Nate's hands. Then she changed the color of Anneka's dress, made her older, gave her a scar. The young magus still kissed her throat and told her she was beautiful. The memory seemed to rest not just in the girl, but in his younger self with the girl: Did his feelings for Anneka stay the same no matter what Judah changed, or was he simply unable to remember himself acting any way other than he actually had?

Then one day, she went back to Nate's memory of his night with Anneka, and—it didn't feel right. Was it like a piece of paper that had been folded? A pillow that smelled like somebody else's head? Eventually she decided that it was like the patch of silk on the parlor wall that they'd scraped off accidentally. Elly had brought out her paints and tried her hardest to match the color, and they'd all agreed that she'd come very close, but Judah knew the spot was there, and her eye was always drawn to it. The inside of Nate's head felt like that: patched. And as soon as she realized it, she suddenly saw patches everywhere inside Nate. Patches, and seams, and places where memories were just sort of...crammed together, awkwardly, in no particular order. All of the things that he'd said to her about how the Work could damage a person's mind came back to her: somebody had been Working in Nate's mind, and the somebody had been very powerful and very careless. She wondered if she could fix the tattered places, but she didn't quite dare try.

Then one day, he brought her to a Slonimi campfire, a circle of wooden wagons on a great soft plain that smelled of lavender. Somebody played a pipe, someone else played a harp. All sorts of faces gathered around the fire, different skins and eyes and hair, more difference than Judah had ever seen in her life; and as strange as they were to her, they were also familiar, because this was the magus's caravan. These were people he'd known all his life. He didn't think of them as *cousin* or *aunt* or *sister.* They were simply his family.

Except for his mother, Caterina. Who was a beautiful woman, still, for all that she must easily have been Elban's age, her long hair in its many braids shot through with gray. There were lines at the corners of her eyes, and more next to her mouth, but her smile was easy. Judah particularly liked the way she moved. She seemed entirely comfortable in herself. Her expressions were sometimes comical or odd because she felt comical or odd, and she had clearly never seen a reason for her face and feelings not to match.

You must love her very much, Judah said the first time he'd shown Caterina to her. *She's ten times brighter than everyone else.*

Nate had laughed. *I do love her, but that's just the way she is.*

And maybe it was. In Nate's memory of the bonfire, she watched Caterina pulled to her feet by a brawny man with a beard. They danced for a scant three bars and all eyes were on her, not because she was beautiful, but because she was herself. They enjoyed seeing her dance, all the people around the fire. They laughed when she swatted playfully at the bearded man and sat back down. She seemed wise, unflappable. Watching her, Judah wished she could talk to the woman, to ask her about the tattered places. Then she thought, well, why not; found a soft place in Nate's memory of Caterina, and slipped inside it.

Suddenly she stood inside one of the tiny wooden wagons. Both walls were lined with tiny drawers and bookshelves, with slabs of wood like desks set under sunlit windows of rippled glass. Dried twigs, candles and cloth sacks filled every available surface. A small door was set into one end of the wagon; on the other was a bunk topped with a thin mattress and a colorful scrap quilt. A tiny body slept there. The wagon swayed gently, pulled along by the horses hitched to the front.

Caterina sat on a stool at one of the desks, gazing bemusedly up at Judah. Her voice was low music as she said, *Oh. Oh, my. You're her. You're Maia's daughter.* The woman's eyes were filled with tears, her voice filled with wonder.

Is this real? Judah said. *Are you actually talking to me?*

Caterina laughed and wiped away her tears. *Apparently. A minute ago I was picking wood oak, and now I'm back in my wagon and three decades in the past.* Judah must have looked confused, because Caterina smiled and pointed to the small body on the bed. *That's Nathaniel, napping. And he quit napping when he was three.*

Judah didn't feel any less confused. *I was in his memory. You were there. I wanted to talk to you.* Defensively, she added, *I didn't know it would work.*

I've never heard of anything like this. But then again, you're not like anyone else, are you? Before Judah could ask what she meant, Caterina sighed. *Something tells me I am going to be wicked sick after this.*

I'm sorry, Judah said, instantly contrite. *I always make the magus sick, too.*

The magus, Caterina said, and a wide grin lit her face. *My little boy, the magus. He's all right?*

Yes.

Caterina's grin died. *It's very hard to lie while Working. For all your talent, you don't seem to have the knack.*

He doesn't…look good.

Show me.

Judah thought of the magus. Nothing happened. Caterina watched, her eyes the same muddy blue as Nate's. *Try this*, she said, and a muscle flexed in a limb Judah hadn't known she had. Nate's image appeared before them, as if he were standing in the room. He looked just as Judah had first seen him, with Arkady.

Oh, Judah said. *I see. Let me try.*

Flesh melted off his body, color drained from his cheeks. The queue of blond hair grew longer, coarser. Dark circles appeared under his eyes and lines drew themselves around his mouth.

My boy. His path isn't easy. Now Caterina sounded soft and sad. She drew in a long breath and let it out again. *Well—* more cheerful now—*since I'll probably wake up in my own vomit anyway, watch this.*

Nate's image morphed again: his back unhunched, his chin lifted. His skin ripened to a sun-burnished gold. His clothes changed; the cut of his shirt was more flamboyant, and an indigo vest bloomed out of it like liquid seeping through the fabric. A riveted leather cuff appeared on one of his wrists, and his hair shortened and browned to copper. This, Judah knew, was Caterina's Nate. He was not exactly handsome, but there was something appealing in him, something open and laughing. Judah could see why he had so many memories involving attractive young women. *He bleaches his hair*, Judah said. *That's why it looks so odd.*

I think it looks ridiculous, Caterina said. *But he had to blend in.*

Why?

To get to you.

Why?

Caterina stood up. She took Judah's hand—carefully, as if

it might hurt. *Let Nathaniel worry about that, dear. Why did you want to talk to me?*

I think somebody is doing things to his mind, Judah said, and told Caterina about the tattered places. Caterina listened, and then shook her head.

Derie, she said. *She's never been kind. I tried to keep him away from her. With that pale skin of his, I knew she'd choose him, and I saw the way poor Charles was around her. Skittish as a kicked dog.* She tried to smile, but Judah could see the strain in her. It was hard to lie in the Work. *I'm glad you care enough about him to worry, but it will be okay. It's like I said: Nate's path isn't easy. But from the looks of things, he'll be done soon. And then he'll come home, and I can fix him.* An urgent note came into Caterina's voice. *He's a good man, my son. Please, whatever happens, try to remember that.*

Why? Judah said, instantly wary. *Is something bad going to happen?*

Bad, good. Nothing is black and white. That's what that evil old Martin was doing: trying to erase the gray from the world, to make all the answers simple. And look at the damage he did. With a weary smile, she said, *Has Nate told you about us? How all of this began?*

No.

Tell him to show you John Slonim. And tell him I love him, and that I'm proud of him. I've asked Derie a thousand times, but she won't do it. It's not her way. Caterina gave Judah a long, thoughtful look. *My, but you are amazing.*

I'm not amazing.

My dear, Caterina said, *you're a miracle. Now let me go, please.*

Like falling down a hole, the gentle sway of the wagon becoming the heat of the fire becoming the cold tower floor. The magus moaned next to her, clutching his stomach and head in turn, tongue bitten hard between his teeth. Judah's arm hurt. She traced the source of the pain to a red welt on the inside of her wrist. For an instant, she could feel Gavin's presence. Then the importance drained out of him like water from a punctured bucket.

"Something is wrong," she said. She didn't think the magus could hear her.

Who's John Slonim? she asked.

His eyes widened in surprise. *How do you know about John Slonim?*

You mentioned him, Judah said, although she didn't know if he had or not. *You said you'd show me sometime.*

I did? Nate looked confused. *I suppose I must have.*

So show me now.

He seemed to think about it for a long moment. He looked better in the Work, too; more the way his mother had seen him. *Yes. Yes, why not?*

He brought her to a poor village in the woods. She saw hollow cheeks, sunken eyes, thin shirts piled on top of each other instead of warm coats, and sickly, too-serious children huddled against their mothers. But the torches stuck on the sides of the now-familiar Slonimi wagons around the clearing were cheerful and beckoning. The Slonimi were thin, too, but their clothes were a colorful hodgepodge of styles and fabrics that spoke of long journeys and distant origins. The air smelled of fire and roasting nuts and snow. This memory felt different than the others Nate had shown her, something in the way the torchlight picked out the hollow faces and the contrast of the saturated caravan colors with the drab clothes of the villagers. This wasn't a scene Nate had seen; this was a scene that had been shown to him. She was seeing it not just through his eyes, but through all of the eyes it had passed through on its way to him. She knew things she couldn't have known: the way the villagers had been drawn to the clearing like water drawn downhill, the bleakness of their lives stretching out beyond it. She knew the empty storerooms without having to see them, just as she knew the shed in the woods, full of tiny dead bodies and old thin ones, stacked like cordwood, waiting for the thaw.

A few planks stretched between the two grandest wagons for a stage, a piece of scarlet cloth tacked overhead for a canopy. The edge of the stage was lit with a dozen candles in reflecting lanterns so the man onstage seemed to glow. His skin was a warm brown, his cravat a brilliant red, and in the candlelight none of the people on the ground could see the stains that dotted it, or the worn places in his coat. His coppery eyes sparkled and his face was alive with excitement. You, that face said to every single person in the audience. I am talking to you. You are special. You are important.

I bring you magic! he cried. *I bring you blossoms in the dead of winter!* Judah heard him in all of herself, the music in his voice, the practiced warmth. With a showman's flourish, he reached into the battered silk hat he held.

The performer's grin lifted away, rising with the smoke. Confusion spilled across his face. Then: astonishment.

His hand emerged from the hat holding a fistful of flowers. Not the folded paper that Judah (somehow) knew he expected, but real flowers, vivid and luminous: irises, orchids, lilies, flowers nobody knew the names of, flowers nobody had ever seen. Out of the hat spilled more flowers, and more, and with them came leafy vines, growing at an alarming pace, reaching across the planking, down to the ground. The man dropped the hat and backed away from it. The faded black silk undulated as it gave birth to a torrent of plant life, more green and more color than this faded village had seen in the last ten summers. Somebody cried out, but there was no fear in the sound; only power, and life and magic.

A vine as thick as a human arm detached itself from the mass, reaching up toward the man. Its glossy leaves unfurled like fingers. The man reached out, tentatively; the vine twined around his arm, as gentle and friendly as a cat. The dazzled man wept. Then, all at once, he began to laugh. He lifted his arms, and the plants exploded out in a mighty wave.

That was John Slonim, Nate said, *and that was the first Work. Everything we do is descended from him. Everything we know, he helped us learn. He figured out how to do the Work at will, how to find people with talent. His blood flows through you. Me, too, on my father's side.* There was pride in his voice. *Now there are a dozen caravans, hundreds of people, from all over the continent. Hundreds of Workers.*

They were standing on a white-sanded beach, next to an ocean the impossible color of one of Firo's coats. *I thought you said the Work didn't affect the real world. That it wasn't that kind of thing*, Judah said. Who was Firo?

Not since John Slonim, the magus said. *Although if it could happen anywhere, it would be in this tower.*

Oh. Firo. Garish clothes, flamboyant hair, perfume, leering insinuations. His fish-belly pale body, exposed in the bathing room. How long had it been since she'd thought of him? And the rest of the world. The purplish gaslights. The ball. The Discreet Walk, the Wilmerian dinner, the life she'd lived before the coup. The coup.

Why had she forgotten her whole life?

In the Work she wore the same clothes she did in reality. They were cleaner here because she didn't think of herself as dirty. Her left sleeve was pushed up. Her arm was smooth and unmarked. No cuts from the magus's knife, no burn from Elban's poker. A warmer sun than Judah had ever known seemed to make her skin glow from within. The arm was beautiful. It was also wrong.

Watch, Nate, in what passed for her present, said, and pointed out to sea.

For a moment, there was nothing. Then the water exploded upward and a great gray beast rose out of the water, leaping into the air with a stately exuberance. Like a fish but not a fish, its lines so graceful and sleek that by comparison the colts seemed clumsy, too leggy. Impossibly high it leapt, and then fell back into the water, the enormous flukes of its tail hitting the surface with a splash so loud that Judah blinked to protect her eyes from spray.

They breathe air, Nate said, satisfied. *Like us*.

She saw the colts in her memory, running across the pasture, nipping and playing with each other. Not clumsy. Perfect.

Is something wrong?

Yes, she wanted to say.

Back in the tower, the dullness persisted, but uneasiness ran through it like veins through marble. Those moments when she was in herself—those fleeting moments when she stood on her own feet and saw the world with her own eyes—were tangled and difficult. She felt caught. When she closed her eyes she saw vines pouring from the brown man's hat. Some of them were green. Some of them were purple.

The something-that-was-wrong felt closer than ever. It was at the tips of her fingers. If she stretched, she could touch it.

You'll need to trust me if you're going to unbind yourself from Gavin.

She looked down at her arm. In the Work it was unmarked, perfect. Now, for the first time in weeks, she saw it as it really was. Scratches on scratches, like leaves fallen on top of each other: *please come need you sorry worried are you okay answer please worried need you please sorry.*

She felt nothing. Gavin's face, in her memory, was a cold fire, a dry well. Something was wrong and the something that was wrong was that nothing was wrong. The places inside her that used to feel were dull and silent.

She thought of other faces: Theron. Elly. Elban. The Seneschal. Darid.

Nothing. They were all nothing.

Had the magus done that? She doubted it. She remembered when he'd drained Darid away from her, on that path in the Barriers. The act was not one he'd taken lightly; he was proud of himself, and a little surprised. He hadn't been sure he'd been able to do it until it was done. And afterward, in the tower, when she'd reached out without thinking and soothed him like she'd always soothed Gavin—he'd been surprised, then, too. *You can just...do that,* he'd said, astonishment at war with envy in his voice.

If it could happen anywhere, it would be in this tower.

A memory came to her, as clear and sharp as Work: climbing the stairs. The stairs were broken, impassable—but the gaps between the stones had been smaller than she'd expected, the stones themselves bigger. Like she would in the Work, she held the memory, unfolded it, watched as Memory-Judah lifted a foot.

The stone of the step stretched of its own accord to meet her.

The magus hadn't been there, then. The tower had moved the steps, or the power bound inside it had. And if her mind was dull—if her memories were empty—maybe the tower was doing that, too.

The tower. She needed to leave the tower.

But the moment she stepped through the door, the stone

steps spiraling down in front of her, a crushing sense of anxiety welled up in her chest and she couldn't breathe. She would fall. The stairs would collapse beneath her. The staircase itself would come to life and swallow her like a snake. Stupid. So stupid. Descending stairs was not a complicated skill and staircases never ate people and all she had to do was keep moving, but the animal part of her was convinced that downstairs lay mortal peril. Even if she didn't fall and wasn't eaten by the tower, even if she made it all the way down, she would die. There was no air down there. There was fire down there and flood down there and the earth would open up and swallow her *if she didn't get back where she belonged*, and that part made her angriest of all because alongside this irrational nonsense was the equally irrational certainty that the only safe place for Judah in the entire world was a tower with half its roof blown off. She could feel it behind her, waiting to hold her and protect her and never let anything hurt her, ever.

She fled backward, slamming the door closed and pressing her back against it, staring out at the wide expanse of sky. She couldn't leave. She wasn't brave enough. Her lungs were open again and every breath was delicious, but she could not physically leave the tower and as her pulse slowed, as her mind calmed, she felt herself sinking back down, into that dull place where she knew she would no longer want to leave.

All right. If she couldn't leave physically, there were other ways. After all, hadn't the magus been teaching her, for who knew how long, to do this very thing? All she had to do was close her eyes, fight tooth and claw against the tower's dullness, and slip away into the Work.

It was surprisingly easy. And the easiest path of all was the one that led out of the middle of her chest, straight to Gavin. He was in the kitchen yard: overgrown, now, with their chickens pecking in the tall grass. In front of her was the stump of a tree, its surface scarred with countless axe cuts, where a block of wood stood on end. As she watched, a pitted axe blade swooped down from somewhere over her right shoulder and she thought, *Right through your neck, Seneschal, you scheming bastard.*

Or rather, Gavin did. Then he sensed her and the blade went wild, knocking an awkward splinter off the top of the wood and sending the rest flying. The world tilted wildly as he jumped out of the way of his own axe and Judah slid quickly sideways, so that she was beside him instead of in him. When he saw her, his eyes widened. He dropped the axe with a clatter. Not on his foot, luckily.

She looked down. Her body seemed solid; her feet rested on the ground, the wind moved in her hair. She cast no shadow, but neither did Gavin. The sky was gray.

"Jude." Gavin's face—thinner now—bloomed with joy and relief. "You're back."

I did it, she said, amazed.

But the words came out of her head, the way they did in the Work. Gavin's relief died. "You're not back. You're a hallucination. I'm finally going insane."

You're not going insane.

"Obviously, the hallucination would say that. It's okay. It's sort of a relief, actually."

Gavin, she said, exasperated, and threw her arms around him. She was delighted to find that she could feel him. He wore a thick sweater she'd never seen before, sort of a dull gray, a bit misshapen. When she pressed against it, the wool felt scratchy on her cheek.

Slowly, his arms circled her—tentatively at first, as if she might evaporate; then, as he became convinced of her solidity, almost painfully tight. But when he pulled back, he was frowning. "Strange. I can touch you, but—"

You can't feel me in your head. I know. I can't feel you, either.
Instead of sensations from his body, it was her own body she
felt, back in the tower. Which, she became aware, was pulling
at her. *I think it's because I'm already in your head. I came through
your head to get here.*

"So you are a hallucination."

Sort of. Not really. It's complicated.

"Of course it is," he said with faint, deadened amusement.
"It's you. It's us. We're always complicated." He began to walk
away. She found herself pulled along.

Where are we going?

"Anywhere Elly isn't going to catch me talking to myself
like a courtier with a vial problem," he said. They passed the
stands of hops, dry and dead, and the empty but still fragrant
piggery, and then came to the pasture. Judah had never come
this way before. She'd always come around by the stables, even
before Darid. Kitchen staff swatted and shooed; stablemen and
dairymaids didn't care.

Gavin stopped. "All right, hallucination or no: I'm sorry
about the stableman, Judah. And everything else. I should have
told you the truth. I don't blame you for being angry with me."

Gavin—

He held up a hand. "But it's not fair to Elly, the way you've
been ignoring her notes. Without you, all she has is me and
Theron, and neither of us is much use."

What notes? She hasn't sent any notes.

"She gives them to the magus for you."

And oh, gods, her memory was such garbage, she didn't
know. If she'd been given notes from Elly, would she have
bothered to read them or cared what they said? Was there a
pile of them sitting in the tower somewhere, ignored, buried
in the leaves?

She tried to picture the magus handing her a slip of paper.

The image didn't feel true at all. The anger she felt: now, that felt true.

He hasn't been giving them to me, she said.

Gavin frowned. "Jude, what's going on?" He pushed up one sleeve of the rough sweater and held out his arm. "Does it have anything to do with this?"

The inside of his arm was covered—as hers was, in the tower—with the magus's tidy, careful cuts. They were more healed than hers; his were a healthy pink. Judah felt even worse. Of course her cuts made him bleed, too. It hadn't occurred to her. *Yes*, she said.

Gavin put a hand on her arm, his jaw set with worry. "Come down. We'll figure it out."

Tears pricked at Judah's eyes. *I want to.*

"So do it."

I want to right now. I think in a minute, I won't want to anymore. The tower—makes me not care about things. She was sure now. Out of the tower, all of the dead places were alive again. Not getting the notes Elly had sent her made her angry. Seeing Gavin made her want to slap him, or hug him, or both. Darid was still gone, though. Where the bitter ache of his absence should have been, she felt nothing. Meanwhile, her body—or the tower? Or her body in the tower?—pulled even harder at her. The world was becoming shimmery and unreal, and the place in her chest where the rope connected felt tense and stretched.

Gavin, oblivious, was shaking his head. "I'll come get you."

The stairs—

"I'll be careful. If that lying sneak of a magus can make it—"

I think the tower helps him. I think it helped me.

"Do you want me to try or not?" Now it was Gavin who sounded angry.

She hesitated. The magus had told her he could teach her how to unbind herself from Gavin; she remembered that very clearly. He'd seemed certain. He'd *felt* certain. She had been inside his head; she'd seen his most dearly-held and shameful memories. Anneka. Caterina. The blond man dying at the table. She didn't think he could lie to her.

But he hadn't delivered Elly's notes. He kept a locked place in his head. With everything she'd seen, what could possibly be left to hide? The only answer: something he didn't want her to see. Specifically. She remembered him kissing her hand, how wrong that had felt. She would have to trust him, he'd said. She didn't. It hurt her to realize, but she didn't.

She took Gavin's hands. They already felt less real in hers and she knew she didn't have much time. *Try. I'll try, too.*

Frustrated, confused, he said, "You'll try what? Judah, what's going on?"

I love you, she said, and slipped away again.

Back to the tower, and into the Work. The blood was stupid. The blood was a crutch, a silly, disgusting tradition passed down through generations of people too timid to use what they knew. Caterina had said Judah was special—*amazing*—but if she was, it was only because she was unhampered by all the magus's years of lessons and training and worship at the altar of the Work. It was *there*, like water; no point in singing to it when you could dive in and swim. But what if she wasn't swimming? What if she was only splashing around in the shallows? Everything she saw around her in the tower was exactly what she'd expected—luminous purple lace draping everything, each strand coursing with life and power—but that didn't mean it was all there was. Like standing at the edge of the aquifer and sensing the vast caverns in front of her, she stood in the Work and sensed that there was more to see.

So she opened her eyes.

This, she was surprised to find, wasn't easy. There was a general feel of reluctance around her. Like Theron as a child, watching cautiously from the ground as she climbed up to the thinnest branches in the apple trees, saying, *Ugh, Judah, please don't, you're going to fall.* A soft voice whispering, *Unsafe, unsafe.* She ignored the voice. She was determined. There was an ineffable tearing sensation around her eyes—

And suddenly the room was clogged with Work, choked with it. The membranous purple filled the very air; it drifted like smoke, and she realized with horror that she had been breathing it in all this time. She looked down at herself.

The great rope wound out of her chest; that was familiar. But peeking out of her collar, just at the edge of her vision, she saw something else: a thread, a taut bit of Work. She pulled the collar down and saw that her body—what she could see of it—was nearly covered in purple stuff, threads of it disappearing into her and emerging in the perfect precise stitches of an expert seamstress.

Or a magus.

It was so easy, now that she knew how. She only had to look inside one of the stitches, and there it was. There *he* was; there they both were. Her own self, asleep—looking not at all the way she did in her head, her face smudged and too thin, her fingernails dirty and broken, her dress spotted with blood. Half of her hair had come free of her braids and stood out around her head like a greasy, tangled crown. But her eyes were closed and her face looked somehow mindless, like Gavin when he'd passed out drunk, or Theron anytime.

The magus was bent over her, bandaging her arm with unsteady hands. He kept squeezing his eyes shut behind his dirty spectacles, as if trying to clear them. He didn't look much better than she did. Cleaner, maybe; his hair was neatly tied back, but she didn't see how he could have done it the way his hands shook. Did he live with someone who loved him enough to tie back his hair for him? Was there a lover in his Highfall life, some latter-day Anneka who trembled at his touch? She could hardly imagine. The kiss he'd pressed on her hand had been familiar and intimate—and why shouldn't it be, since she'd lived through most of his memories?—but the moment his lips touched her skin she had known with crystalline clarity that she would never want him to kiss any other part of her.

And that had been when she'd still trusted him. She felt sorry for him, and she felt sorry for the loss of him, but the faint sway of his shoulders made her uneasy. He was singing some simple up-and-down-again tune, like something one of the dairymen would whistle. She moved so she could see his face and he was further gone than Theron, with slack mouth and half-lidded eyes. He managed to finish bandaging her arm, to put the unused bandages, scissors and salve back into his satchel. Then he took out a needle. It was long and curved.

Still singing, he plucked a strand of membrane out of the air. She had asked him once why she couldn't use the Work in reality, and he'd said it simply wasn't that kind of thing—and yet here he was, threading the membrane through the eye of the needle like purple silk. It went agreeably, stretching and thinning to slip easily in. As he bent over her sleeping body, the needle fell from his fingers. He didn't seem to notice it was gone. His thumb and first finger were still pinched together as though he held it, and she understood that the needle was like the blood: a crutch. A way in. A method of activating the Work so he could do what he was doing now, as Judah watched with growing horror: humming his stupid song and sewing the membrane into Judah's body like he was embroidering a pillowcase. Sometimes he pushed the thread all the way through her, catching it on the other side and sending it back. Sometimes he actually reached into her to retrieve it.

Her unconscious self didn't wake but moaned and writhed. He made small soothing noises, but almost to himself; stroked her filthy hair, but didn't stop. Everything about him said that he felt he had every right to do what he was doing. The drifting gaze he cast down at her was affectionate, almost loving. The body on the floor was only a memory; but watching the magus Work made her arms twitch to cover herself. She was revolted, but she had to see what had happened to her. She had to know.

As she watched, the pitch and volume of his humming increased. His breath grew ragged and his pale cheeks flushed. Still his hands moved, weaving the stuff of the tower in and out of her, and if they had seemed unsteady before, they were smooth and confident now. His eyes closed. His hand sewed.

Then, all at once, his shoulders hunched and he let out a cry, small and shuddering. His hands slowed and stopped. He was still.

If Judah had been repulsed before, now she felt sick and furious. She wanted to reach into him and tear him apart. She couldn't do that; he wasn't actually there. This wasn't her memory or his, but the memory of the tower itself. The Work, the *tra la la* song, his shabby climax—all were in the past. All she could do was observe as he put her dirty blanket over her, as he wrapped up the food he'd brought so it would stay fresh. He made no effort to clean himself. As he moved around the tower, he mindlessly picked up the fallen needle, and when he stood again Judah caught a glimpse of his eyes and they, too, unfolded, just like the stitch had.

And then she was inside the magus, and she didn't know if she had slipped into the real magus, as she had the real Caterina, or if this was some half-formed tower-memory, so she was cautious. He had no idea what had happened. He knew about the weaving, but he didn't know he'd dropped the needle before he'd started and he didn't know he'd come as he'd finished. She wondered what he'd thought when he'd undressed at home, what story he told himself to explain the mess.

Very carefully, she found the locked door and discovered that it stood open. Not all the way open; not enough for her to step through, but enough for her to peek through the crack.

A terrifying-looking old woman with white hair and cruel eyes. His teacher. The one who wouldn't tell him his mother loved him.

The tower must have more of a hold on her than the boy does when the Unbinding comes.

I think the weaving hurts her, the magus-memory said, and a white flash of pain filled his eyes. The old woman cackled.

Did that hurt you, *Nathaniel? Don't be pathetic. It doesn't matter if it hurts her.*

That was it. That was all she could see. She slammed the whole scene shut like a book. With a flash of anger she made her dress go away—she would have torn it off, but in the Work she had only to will it gone—and looked down at her own body as if she'd never seen it before. Which she supposed she hadn't. She had certainly never seen the purple seams that traversed it, so much uglier than the scars that marred her real body. When she ran her hands over her stomach she felt the ripple of the stitches beneath them. The sheer number of them took her breath away. He must have been doing this since the first day. All this time, the Work had seemed miraculous, and all this time it had been…infecting her.

The boy. The boy must be Gavin, but somehow she doubted that *the Unbinding* was the unbinding the magus had promised her. They had another plan, the magus and his nasty old teacher, and she didn't know what it was, but she knew it involved her and Gavin.

Her pain didn't matter, did it? Well, that was familiar.

She found a stitch just above her left breast that was nearly an inch long. Slid a finger under the purple thread. Ripped it out.

She screamed. The world went black.

She came to on her knees, sobbing. It was the worst pain she'd ever known. Worse than the poker, worse than the caning, worse than thinking Darid was dead. But she was still in the Work, and the stitch had vanished.

She found another stitch and tried again.

The world went black again.

Hundreds of purple stitches marred her body. She pulled out four of them before the pain kicked her out of the Work entirely and she found herself lying on the cold stone floor of the tower. Night had fallen. She crawled to the sheared-away edge and was sick over the edge of it. Her whole body hurt. She told herself that she would rest for just a minute. Maybe two. The floor was so nice and cool on her aching body and the fresh air felt good.

When she woke, she was shivering. Her arm dangled over the edge. Lifting her head, the first thing she saw was the drop. All at once fully awake, heart pounding and breath short, she crawled away, not trusting her legs to carry her. Only after she was safe did she realize: something was different.

She was hungry. She was cold. She was lonely.

And she was furious.

CHAPTER TWENTY

Nate didn't dare treat patients anymore. He was afraid he'd kill someone. Word had gotten around Marketside and Brakeside that his friend had died and people seemed content to leave him in what they judged to be grief. On the street, he was the recipient of many a pitying smile and kind pat on the shoulder. Waiting at Leda's, he lost track of the world and when he found it again, he was holding a wizened sprig of mint. Based on Leda's expression, he guessed he'd been standing there quite a while. "You'll find someone else, magus," she said. "No heart dies forever." Confused, Nate only nodded. It wasn't until later that he realized that Leda had assumed Charles was his lover. Once, that would have humiliated and infuriated him, but it no longer seemed to matter.

Bindy took care of him in a quiet way that he found almost intolerable. He suspected that she was filling and delivering simple orders so she didn't have to bother him with them, but her apprenticeship had withered and died on the vine. When she decided he needed something—food, water, a shave—she put bread or a cup or his razor in front of him, so unobtrusively that they might always have been there. When she started to bring soup again he knew she was truly worried for him. He wasn't hungry, but he ate to please her. The soup tasted different. He doubted the broth lady could get her hands on chicken anymore. He didn't like to think what she'd found to use instead.

A week passed like this. It was the week the Seneschal had given Nate to get Judah down from the tower. On what he knew would be his last morning in the manor, he woke to find Derie sitting in the kitchen. "Locked the door in case your little wenchlet shows up early," she said, and nodded at a cup on the table. "Might as well drink that."

It was broth, but cold. He drank it anyway.

Derie watched. "Today, then."

"Today." He frowned into the broth. "Derie, if we ever go home, I want to bring Bindy. If she wants to come."

"Her?" Derie's voice dripped with contempt. "She's got nothing in her at all."

"Still. I'd like to ask her," Nate said, dogged.

Derie huffed. "I'll consider it. But I'm not making you any sort of deathbed promise about it, boy."

"Deathbed?" Nate swallowed. "Do you think I'm going to die?"

"Doesn't matter."

"It does to me."

She shook her head. "God, you're stupid, Nathaniel Clare," she said. "Not that you had any hope of turning out otherwise, with Caterina fawning all over you like some precious little prince instead of the disappointing cross of two lines that weren't more than decent to begin with. Tried like hell to beat it out of you, but small hope of that when she was always there to pat your little head afterward and tell you how special you were." She thumped the end of her cane on the floor. "Hear me now, Nathaniel: you are not special. You are not important. Live or die, you don't matter. All that matters is the Unbinding."

Nate's mouth was dry. "I'm not going to fail."

Derie rolled her eyes. "Oh, for—give me your arm, you sad little wretch."

He wanted to say no, but there was no point. He had never said no to Derie. He wasn't sure he could. He gave her his arm. She no longer made any attempt to be gentle, but the knife didn't bother him. What did bother him was the way she shuffled his brain, pushing everything in it further away than she ever had. Normally, things that mattered reasserted themselves after a while, but this was different. Nate could only watch as she tore at his most precious memories one by one, shoving them behind a veil where he could barely even see them. Caterina, Anneka, everything. Charles. His whole history. The stars over the Barriers, the sea by the Temple Argent. The dirty skin of Judah's hand pressed against his lips. All meant nothing. He clung to Bindy for as long as he could, but Derie snatched her away like everything else, and soon after that nothing bothered him anymore. It was all gone.

When it was over, he didn't feel sick. There was a pounding in his head, but he felt clearer than he had in a long time. The great city around him had been pared away; only one wide avenue led forward, lit to daylight.

Across the table, Derie wound a cloth around her bleeding arm. "Well, Nathaniel Clare," she said, "what are you, now?"

"Nothing," he said.

"And you know what to do."

"Yes." The pounding wasn't in his head, but outside of it. The door.

"You fail," Derie said, "come back here. I'll send you off like I did Charles." He could feel her contempt as clearly as he could hear it. "Now go open the door before the wench-let breaks it down."

So, as Derie left out the back, he went to the front door and unlocked it. Bindy burst in breathless, eyes scanning the front hall as if expecting it to be full of bandits. "Magus," she said, "are you all right? I heard screaming."

"Did you? Must have been somebody next door."

"But you're bleeding."

She pointed to his arm. Her concern was meaningless. "I cut myself," he said. "It's nothing."

He found the Seneschal outside the Wall, waiting with a half-dozen guards. Some carried bundles of wood and rope; others, knives and swords. "She comes down today," the Seneschal said.

The tower wasn't visible through the Wall—it wouldn't be from the inside, either—but Nate could feel it even if he couldn't see it. The avenue in his head led there. "Give me two hours," he said.

"No."

"One, then."

The Seneschal shook his head. "I expect the builders in less than an hour," he said. "You have until they arrive."

Only one guard accompanied them through the Passage; the others remained outside. To go from the relative clamor of the Square to the silence of the courtyard was like entering a tomb, it always was, but this time Nate barely noticed. He noticed his failure to notice, but it meant nothing.

At the last door, the Seneschal said, "See you soon, magus," and went back through to the Square, locking the doors behind him. Nate followed the glowing path. It led down to the mildewed kitchen, and from there to the pantry, where he found a lantern. He lit it with a match and continued down, along the damp stone passages to the aquifer. He had never been there before, but whatever Derie had done to his head, whatever she'd cleared away… He no longer remembered what was missing, but its absence left a great deal of space. He could feel things he had never felt before. The tower; Judah within it, like the heart of a candle flame; and the object of his current search, a mess that offended his sense of order and must be tidied before he could proceed. If only he had been like this from the beginning. If his brain had been this cool and uncluttered, perhaps he could have developed some real skill. Perhaps he wouldn't have been quite so *nothing*. He would have liked to be powerful like Derie. To be smart like her, capable; to make decisions, to make things happen. To be of consequence. To matter.

No point thinking about it now. Everyone was what they were meant to be and he was nothing. He was not sure if that was his thought or Derie's, because he knew she was with him; he couldn't be trusted alone. When he came to the aquifer, he could feel all that water, reaching into the caverns, filling deep wells of rock that no human had ever seen. He stood at its edge for a moment and then turned toward a particular dark place. Where the mess was.

The darkness moved. Theron stepped into the light.

For a breath, he and Nate stood in silence. The boy really was mangled inside, Nate saw. A hopeless, disordered jumble. "How did you know I was down here?" the boy said. Even his voice was only half there.

"Eleanor told me."

"You're lying." Theron didn't sound like it mattered much.

"All right, then. I could feel you." Nate paused, and then added, "I'm not going to hurt you."

Theron sighed. "More lies. It's now, isn't it?"

Nate could feel his own heartbeat, hear his own breath. "Yes. I'm sorry," he said, and he was. But it was a distant sort of sorry, like a memory of sorry. He could feel Derie scoff at it all the same.

In the dim lantern light, the boy's gaze drifted. Maybe Nate was boring him. "Don't be. It's frustrating not to be—whole. I used to be—" He stopped, let out a long breath. "I'd actually rather you get it over with. Is Judah going to die, too?"

"I hope not," Nate said, and realized that he did. Faintly. Derie had left him that; just a touch of it. "But I don't know."

"If it could be me, I'd do it. But you need him, don't you?"

"I need Elban's heir."

Theron nodded. "That's Gavin. I was always an afterthought." His eyes were bright with clarity. "You don't have to do this, you know. You believe you do, but you don't. Nothing you've been told is true."

"All of this was drawn long before you or I were even born."

Theron shook his head. He seemed as unafraid as Nate himself. "I'm not strong enough to stop you. I'm sad for Elly, though. I've tried to help her as much as I can. It doesn't feel as though there's much of me here these days." Thoughtfully, he added, "There's not much of you, either."

Nate stepped close to him. "I have opium. For the pain."

"Oh," Theron said, "I don't think it will hurt. You know how to get to the tower from here?"

"I can find it," Nate said. Then he took a fistful of Theron's hair, flicked out his springknife and plunged it into the big vein in the boy's throat. Theron's eyes went wide, but he didn't make a sound. Nate had a vial in his pocket and he filled it at the wound with blood, like water from a spigot. When the blood slowed, he let go. The body slumped to the ground and Nate kicked it into the aquifer. No bubbles rose from the boy's white face. It blurred and wavered; sank into the depths and was gone.

Judah lay on the tower floor, motionless.

Every part of her hurt. Her arms and legs might as well have been fused to the floor, for all that she could move them. The light playing on the arched stone was the limpid blue of morning, which meant she'd slept. Which meant it was time to start over: force herself to move, to eat, to go back into the Work and rip out the stitches the magus had woven into her. Pass out. Wake up. Do it again. She had lost count of how many times the cycle had repeated. Every stitch she destroyed lessened the tower's hold on her, but ripping out the weaving hurt so much, and she just wanted to sleep. She wanted her fingers not to be cold and her stomach not to be empty. Even now she could feel the tower wrapping itself around her, coddling her in soothing waves of numbness.

She would never make fun of Elly for being paralyzed by heights again.

She forced herself to sit up. Every muscle screamed and she ordered them to be quiet. No muscle had ever sprung loose through the simple act of sitting up. Morning light had never struck anyone blind and her lungs could not inhale enough air to explode. The urge to lie back down and sleep was nearly overwhelming.

Stupid. All stupid.

She opened her eyes, all the way this time.

"All right," she said to the gap of clear blue sky in front of her. "Here we go." And she slipped into the Work and began ripping.

★ ★ ★

Nate heard Gavin and Elly arguing in the parlor from the end of the corridor. From the pitch and color of their voices, they'd been at it a while. It didn't matter.

"—no good to her dead," Eleanor was saying. "And dead is exactly what you'll be if you try to—"

Gavin cut her off, growling and angry. "I've been training for combat since I was ten years old. You think I can't climb stairs?"

"I think you can't climb those stairs. Not in the shape you're in. Five minutes ago you were unconscious, Gavin! If that happens on that staircase—"

They were standing toe-to-toe. The top of Eleanor's head barely reached Gavin's chin. His fists were clenched tight at his sides; hers were pressed into her hips. Both of their pale Highfall faces were red and angry.

"And why do you think I'm having those pains? She needs me," Gavin said through gritted teeth.

"Yes, but—" Then Elly noticed Nate, watching from the doorway. Her back stiffened and her mouth snapped shut. He knew it was nothing to do with him, personally; it was the argument she didn't want him to see. But the unfriendly look Gavin gave Nate was entirely personal. Even though Nate knew that Elban's last living son could not sense the vial of his dead brother's blood in the satchel, he found his hand wanting to go to it anyway.

Although—all those years linked to Judah. Who knew what the stupid ox of a boy could sense?

"What do you want?" Gavin's tone, belligerent and nasty, reminded Nate of every farm boy who'd ever come after him because Nate lived in a wagon instead of a hut.

Nate ignored that. He ignored Elly, too, focusing all of his attention on Elban's son. "You need to come with me to the tower. The stairs will hold. I can show you where to step. But we have to go now."

Elly, who didn't like being ignored, stepped in between them. "What do you mean?"

"Don't bother," Gavin said. "He'll only lie to you."

She glared at him. "What?"

"He hasn't given Judah any of your notes. That's why she hasn't written back."

Elly's anger became hurt and betrayal. The part of Nate that no longer fully existed made note of how quickly all the food he'd brought her ceased to matter; how quickly she'd turned on him, with nothing more than a word from Elban's son. "Is that true?" she said to Nate.

"You wouldn't understand." Nate turned back to Gavin. "We don't have time to discuss this. The Seneschal wants both of you because of the bond. When he gets here, he'll torture you until she comes down." He let himself hesitate. "Which I'm not sure she can do alone. But if you come with me, we can get her down together."

"What about Theron and Elly?" Gavin said.

"The Seneschal doesn't care about them."

The ruined girl stepped back—unconsciously, Nate suspected—so that she was between Gavin and the door. Her eyes were on Nate. "Can you really get him up the stairs?"

"Yes."

"Then go," she said to Gavin. "Theron and I will stall the Seneschal."

"How?"

"I'll figure out a way." Nate could feel her fierceness even from the doorway. "You said she needs help. Go help her."

One of Gavin's hands went to her arm. Slowly, as if he wasn't sure it belonged there. "Elly—if the Seneschal finds you and not me, he'll hurt you. I might not be able to feel it, but I'll be able to…hear—"

"You'll be able to hear me screaming." The girl was disturbingly calm. "Yes. But the Seneschal might be underestimating what it takes to make me scream."

Gavin shook his head grimly. "If he hurts you enough, you'll scream." Then, like the Lord of Highfall he would never be, "No. If I can't get up those stairs without help, the Seneschal and his guards can't, either."

"They'll bring boards and rope," Elly said. "Go. I'll stall him."

"Listen to her," Nate said.

"How will you stall him?" Gavin said, paying no attention to Nate. "By yelling at him? His guards will move you aside like a doll, Elly."

Elly's smile was cold. "You underestimate me, too."

Gavin turned his head. Although Nate didn't think he knew it, he was facing the tower.

"You know you want to go," Elly said softly. "So go."

He turned back to her. Nate, impatient, didn't know what he was thinking and didn't care. All that mattered was that Gavin did what Nate needed him to do, and in the end, he did. With a curt nod to Elly, he pushed past Nate and out of the parlor.

Nate followed him. Elban's heir would make it up the stairs. The tower would make sure of it.

Every ripped stitch hurt more. Was it the anticipation of how bad it would be that made it worse, or was the tower holding on more tightly to what remained? She could feel the stifling weight of it around her, could feel it reaching into her, trying to pull her back down into torpor. She had managed to drag herself to standing when the door opened; the sight of the magus filled her with hatred and pity as she stood swaying.

But then he stepped through the door and behind him, she saw Gavin. Somehow, impossibly; too thin, but so essentially himself that she felt him like a heat source. He pushed the magus aside, came straight to her, and threw his arms around her. She met them gladly.

"I'm here," he said. "I came for you."

Behind him, she could see the magus kneeling on the floor, rummaging through his satchel. He didn't seem to be paying them any attention, but Judah knew better. She felt the hot prickle of tears in her eyes. "It's not that simple."

"No," the magus said, standing up. "It's not." He'd rolled up his sleeves. On one of his arms, he wore the tooled leather cuff Judah had seen in Caterina's memory, a bloody blade protruding from it; on the other, he'd opened a long gash. In the hand of the bleeding arm he held a small bottle, just like the one Theron's antidote had come in. As Judah watched, he switched it to the knife hand, and poured whatever was inside over his wound. The new liquid was blood-colored, too, but it was darker and seemed to flow unevenly. With a practiced flick of his wrist, the bloody knife blade disappeared back into the cuff. He tossed the vial aside.

Then he began to draw on his own arm. This was wrong. The surface needed to shine, he'd told her. It was all a crutch, an empty ritual, but he believed in the rules.

Gavin made a small strangling sound and fell to his knees next to her. His eyes were wide and panicked, his lips parted. She could see the tip of his tongue poised to speak. No part of him moved. He didn't even blink.

"There," the magus said, sounding tired but satisfied. He dropped down onto the small sofa, as if his legs wouldn't hold him.

Judah looked back and forth between his limp, exhausted form and Gavin's unmoving one. "What did you do?"

"He's fine. He just can't move," the magus said. "I've been practicing. But I'm not strong enough to hold him for very long. We have to hurry."

How will you stall him, Elly?

It was a valid question. Eleanor stood in the parlor and considered it.

She didn't know exactly what was happening, why the Seneschal was coming for Judah or how the magus planned to stop him after he and Gavin retrieved Judah. And why hadn't he passed along her notes? And why had Gavin been awake all night in agony, and where was Theron? She hated not knowing. She was used to feeling like a pawn, and that was bad enough, but now she no longer felt like she understood the game, and that infuriated her.

But she wanted all of them together, where they belonged. Gavin and Judah were together; Eleanor wanted Theron. Gavin and Judah could put up a fight, and they had the magus. Theron had nobody. Theron was a lost kitten. Theron may or may not even notice that another person was in the room. She was not going to leave him at the mercy of the Seneschal's guards, and maybe he could help stall the Seneschal, and how *was* she going to stall the Seneschal, anyway?

As her eyes scanned the room—for Theron, for an idea, for a stray army that had somehow escaped her notice—one of her fingers went to her mouth, the hardened cuticle between her teeth. Her gaze fell on the old stack of books she'd brought from the Lady's Library: herbals, cookery books. One of them had a recipe for a salve to put on sore cuticles. Another to keep children from biting their nails. None contained an army. Although—

Eleanor had spent so many hours reading the diaries of long-dead ladies that they had started to seem alive to her, with all the quirks and faults of living people. Silly Lady Berla filled the pages of her diaries with descriptions of her wardrobe, Lady Agatha with equally exacting descriptions of her physical ailments. Bound by tradition to keep a journal but clearly uninterested, Gavin's mother had—disappointingly—kept only the most perfunctory of notes about her day. (One page, fixed in Eleanor's memory, read simply, *Lost baby. Seneschal kept E away.*)

Her favorite, though, was Lady Margarethe, whose husband had suffered a secret apoplexy, and whose sons, upon learning of their father's infirmity, had laid siege to the House, and their mother in it. After weeks of fighting, the Lady's surviving second son had yielded to her rule, and the Lady herself had written what Eleanor felt was one of the least known and most important historical documents in Highfall history: *Mark well, you defenseless wives, who are allowed no arms at hand; do as I suggest, and keep this in silence as you do so much else, and you will have the knowledge to make a weapon of a single candle.*

It was Lady Margarethe who had first ordered the Passage lined with oiled rushes: not because they were waterproof, but because they would burn. Even the most craven Ladies had soon realized the powerlessness of their position, and Eleanor had never read a single diary that did not contain the same suggestion. *Look back to Lady Margarethe, daughters in Ladyship. She ruled well.*

She'd also been murdered by her second son less than a year after his surrender. But all of those who came after her—including Elly—pretended a horror of damp passages and a deep respect for tradition, and made sure the rushes were well-oiled.

A weapon of a single candle. Eleanor didn't have a candle; what she had was a single remaining match. Tomorrow she would have no matches. Today the Seneschal wanted Gavin and Judah; tomorrow he would still want them.

Wake up each day and figure out how to survive it, she told herself.

She wished she had a whole box of matches. She wished she had Theron. She wished she had an army.

She grabbed her small, lonely match, and ran out of the parlor.

"Working in the physical world takes so much blood," the magus said, wrapping his bleeding arm.

"Gavin." Judah could hear the high note of panic in her voice. "Get up."

He didn't move. He didn't even blink. The magus glanced at Gavin as if he was of very little consequence and said, "I told you, he can't get up. I needed him quiet. He doesn't say anything worth hearing, anyway." Then the magus's eyes, which had been strangely empty, landed on Judah and softened. "Oh, Judah. What have you done to yourself?"

She knew he was talking about the stitches. "I saw you," she said. "I saw you doing this to me."

"I had to." Was that guilt in his voice?

"To make sure I was bound to the tower more than to Gavin?"

He nodded eagerly, relieved that she understood. "Yes. So that you can draw on its power, and so it can draw on him." He nodded his head at Gavin, and a note of complaint crept into his voice. "I didn't have time. There was never enough time."

Judah felt her head lower like an angry bull's, her fists clench. "Why?"

"I told you. Mad Martin bound all the power in the world, and he bound it here. Right under our feet." He practically glowed with purpose. "I never thought it would be so easy to find, but the power drew you here. It wants so badly to be free." He stood and moved closer. Judah saw that he had a knife in his hand: not the strange one from his cuff, but the silver one he'd always used on her for Work. "We have all worked so hard to get you here. In this place. With him." His eyes twitched to Gavin, still motionless, and his mouth curled faintly with disgust. "He was never worthy."

The magus aimed a nasty kick at Gavin's thigh. It landed with a meaty thud. Judah felt the big muscle seize painfully. Gavin didn't move.

Theron wasn't in the solarium, the chapel or the kitchen; when Elly called his name down the catacomb stairs in the pantry, there was no response. Finally, much as she hated it, she gave up. She had to get to the courtyard before the Seneschal came through the Passage. Panting, she made it there just in time to hear the guards approaching, their broad Highfall accents echoing through the winding passage.

She gripped the match in her fingers and waited.

Then the door opened and they were there, with the Seneschal on point, holding a lantern. She couldn't see how many guards were behind him. He saw her, but didn't slow or stop. Eleanor knew this trick; her brothers had pulled it on her often enough. She was supposed to quail and shrink back out of the way. Instead, she squared her shoulders, and didn't move. If he wanted her out of his way, he could do what Gavin had said: pick her up and move her like a doll.

He didn't. She wasn't surprised. With all of his men watching, he would want to move her with the sheer force of his will. To resort to physical force with a mere woman would be beneath him. "Well, Eleanor," he said.

"Seneschal."

"Have you seen the magus?" he said conversationally.

"Up in the tower." They might have been in the rose garden, discussing the previous night's dinner.

"And Gavin?"

"With him, I assume."

"Excellent." He paused. "We have business inside, Eleanor. Kindly step aside."

"What business is that, Seneschal?"

"Judah needs to come down from the tower. I've been very patient."

The guards behind him were carrying some sort of bundles. Boards and rope, she suspected. "Patient?" she said. "Stuck in the tower or stuck in the parlor, she's still behind the Wall. I don't see how it matters."

"It matters," he said, "because I can't get to her in the tower."

Eleanor laughed. "You can't get to her anyway, Seneschal. Your guards can't make her marry you."

Contempt filled his face. "I don't care if she marries me," he said, and remembering how she'd told Judah to do exactly that, Elly felt faintly sick. "It would have made things easier, but it doesn't—to use your word—matter. You're all leaving here today, anyway."

"No," Eleanor said.

He blinked. "Excuse me?"

"No. This is our House. We're not leaving. I haven't done the rushes in months, but the oil still smells rather strongly, don't you think?" she said, and held up the match.

"Like magnets," the magus said. "One side pulls, the other pushes. One side takes, the other gives. His side takes. His entire *line* takes. They have taken and taken and taken for generations. They took the world. They took the life out of it, the power." He pointed at himself, then at her. Whenever his eyes fell on Gavin, they burned with derision, but on her, they just burned. "We're the givers, the ones who would give everything back. Your line. Your family. And mine. His ancestors left us nothing but the thinnest trickles of power, faint shreds of what used to be—but we've learned to use them. Like starving peasants who've learned to eat grass and bark and dirt because people like him take everything else. We used them to create you, Judah. To bring you here, to put you here with him, now. You can open the world. You can fix it. You can make it live again. Only you." Something anguished came into his voice. "We worked so long to make you. So long."

"To make me," Judah said.

He nodded wearily. "You're the end product of five generations of the most powerful Workers we could find. Their lines end in you just as Elban's ends in him." He stood up. Still holding the knife, he used it to point at Gavin. "Like a crystal, focusing the light. And you're bound to him." He flipped the knife over and extended it toward her, hilt out. "Take it," he said when she did nothing. "Derie and Caterina are helping me but I can't hold him much longer."

She stared at the blade. "What do you expect me to do with that?" Her voice was high and nervous.

"Let his blood," Nate said. "You'll need all of it."

Judah took a stumbling step back. She put her hands behind her, as if they might take the knife of their own volition. "You're mad."

He considered. "Maybe. Probably, between you and Derie. It doesn't matter. I'm nothing. You, Judah. You're everything."

She felt as frozen as Gavin.

The magus swallowed hard. She could see him gathering something—strength, his thoughts—and the effort showed. "His blood. And your blood. Let them spill together, then go into the Work and use what you know to break what his ancestors did. You'll have to open and open and open. I'll give you the sigils. You can undo it. All that pent-up power will go back where it belongs."

"That doesn't even make sense."

"You've never seen the world the way it was meant to be, Judah, and neither have I. But you've seen how powerful Work can be." He held up his hand and Judah saw a row of sigils drawn on his skin. "Caterina is here, and Derie. We'll help you. Go into the Work. Break the binding. The tower will take his energy through yours."

"How are you holding him? How can you do anything to him without his blood?" Judah was stalling. She knew the blood was useless, but he didn't.

The magus shrugged. "I used Theron's. But it's hard. Come on, Judah. Cut his throat. End this. We're all suffocating. Most of us don't even know it. Cut him and the binding will break and we can breathe again. Everyone can breathe again."

At some point, he had begun to weep, silently. She didn't think he knew he was doing it. "If he dies, I die," she said. "That's—"

But the magus was shaking his head. "No. The tower will save you. I'll save you. That's what the weaving was for."

Meanwhile, she moved away from him, closer to Gavin. Slowly, so the magus wouldn't notice: thinking that if she could touch Gavin, if she could slip into the Work, she could free him. The two of them could get the knife away from the magus and then—she didn't know what then, but they could figure it out. Even with the knife the magus was no match for both of them. She laid a hand on Gavin's cheek.

And was immediately overwhelmed by a familiar, sinking despair. It was the same despair that had filled him since the coup, anger rotted into hopelessness. The magus's mind was as compartmentalized as the House itself, every memory shut away behind its own door. Gavin, who'd never needed to pretend to be anything other than what he was, still had a mind like a book, one page leading into the next. She had felt it when she'd dug for the truth of the lie about Darid. Now she was more skilled, she could turn the pages of him without leaving too much chaos in her wake, and what she read was that most of Gavin didn't want to live. The world was new and alien and his place in it wasn't what he'd always assumed. He was scared of dying, but he was terrified of being ordinary. He hated his father but his father had been powerful. In Gavin's mind, she read what Gavin himself had read in his father's diaries about the bare stone cell off Elban's parlor, and the people who had been taken there to suffer for Elban's amusement. Men and women, staff and courtier. It couldn't have been a secret: someone cleaned the blood, someone took the bodies to the midden yard. Judah herself had watched the Seneschal move among the crowd at state dinners and balls, seeking out a particular body to be brought to the dais. Judah couldn't remember faces but Elban had written about them and now the words burned in her brain as they did Gavin's. He'd been drawn to people who laughed. Strong or delicate, servile or arrogant, it didn't matter. They all stopped laughing in the end.

Gavin hated his father. He was worried he'd become him. He was ashamed of what Elban had done, but envied him the power to do it, and he was ashamed of that, too.

Judah saw it written, as clear as ink on paper: *If he can save you, do it. Let it end.*

"What are you going to do, Eleanor?" the Seneschal said. "Stand against all my guards, all by yourself?"

Eleanor felt ludicrous, her one tiny body blocking the door and all the giant men crowded into the passageway beyond. But she said, "Four hundred years ago, Lady Margarethe held off both of her sons and an army at this door."

"With her guard, who had swords. You have a single match and some greasy floor mats." The Seneschal shook his head with exasperated pity. "Step aside. None of this concerns you."

She held steady. "If it concerns Gavin and Judah, it concerns me."

Behind the Seneschal, one of the guards muttered something Eleanor couldn't hear. "I think I can talk sense into one girl," the Seneschal said over his shoulder. Then, to Eleanor, he said, "What's stopping you from going back to Tiernan? Is it your brothers? I can arrange to have them killed, if you like. You have good reason to want them dead."

Something lurched in her stomach. The Seneschal smiled. "Yes, I know about your brothers. Your mother actually prostrated herself before me, begging me to take you away. Her one lovely little daughter, among all those brutish stupid sons and her brutish stupid father. We had other candidates for Gavin, you know. Prettier ones from better families. But I took pity on you. I wanted to help you. And now I want to help you again. Go back to Tiernan. When your brothers are dead, it'll be entirely yours, even if you are a woman. I won't interfere at all."

"I don't want Tiernan," she said.

"You can't have Highfall," he said.

She was glad to see the match didn't quiver. "I don't want that, either. I just want to be left in peace. I want all of us left in peace."

His jaw hardened. Quickly, she struck the match on the rough stone wall. It flared to life with a sound like ripping paper. She could feel the heat of it on her fingers.

"That," the Seneschal said, "you can't have." Then he leaned forward and blew out the match.

The magus had begun to shake. The hilt of the knife oscillated wildly in the air and he was nearly sobbing. He seemed about to collapse. Judah was still half in Gavin's mind, but she discovered she could be both places, in the Work and the tower. "We tricked them," the magus said. "We tricked them, to keep

you safe. You don't love him. You only think you love him because you feel what he feels. It's not the same thing. He thinks
he loves you and that's not real, either. He can't love. It's been
bred out of him just as your power has been bred into you."
He laughed through his tears. "Do you know how many people the men of his line have killed? Do you know how many
more have died from cold, or starvation, or a simple lack of
the will to live? I've seen it happen. It's hard to live with no
hope, Judah." He tossed his head, tore at the hair that fell loose
from its queue. "Judah, Judah! That horrible name. When this
is over I'll give you a new one. You'll be free. We both will."

"Gavin won't," she said.

"His death will save thousands," the magus said. "And he's
a monster. If there's a shred of human feeling in him he stole
it from you."

That's probably true, Gavin said in her head.

Shut up. She was replaying everything the magus had said.
There must be a way out of this. There must be a way to free
Gavin, and—

Suddenly she felt as if she were covered in biting insects.
Fighting nausea, she stared at the magus. "Theron's blood?"
she said. "Is that what you said?"

Time shrank into the wisp of smoke rising from the extinguished match. The Seneschal smiled slowly behind it, waiting to see what she would do. "Should we move her, sir?" the
impatient guard behind him said, and the Seneschal answered,
"Give her one more minute to move herself."

The smoke swirled. Dwindled. Died.

"Elly."

She hazarded a glance to the side. Theron stood next to the
open door, against the Wall and out of the Seneschal's line of
sight. His expression was more animated than it had been in

months, almost like his old self. He smiled and lifted something in his hand to show her.

It was the device he'd been working on in the workshop, the device Judah and Gavin had brought down to entice him after his illness. All the bits of spring and wheel that had spent the last few months spread out on the table in Gavin's bedroom, gathering dust: she recognized the pointed key, the green gems. Nested in the middle of the clockwork was a familiar white vial: her last, hoarded vial of gas for the Wilmerian quickstove. She couldn't think when Theron had found time to assemble the thing; she couldn't think why he had chosen now to show it to her.

He wound the key, quickly. It made a comfortable clicking noise. Then he pressed one of the gems, and the big wheel on top began to spin, and the device sparked; caught and burned with a steady purple flame that rose from a tiny post at the top. It was beautiful.

The Seneschal, increasingly amused, waited in the door. He couldn't see Theron, or the clockwork device. Eleanor held out her hand. Theron placed the thing in her palm. It was heavy, but not too heavy; it ticked, but not loudly. It was still burning. She held it at arm's length, where the Seneschal couldn't see it.

"Come on, now, Eleanor," the Seneschal said. "Step aside."

"I told you," she said, "this is our House," and threw the device down onto the oil-soaked mats. The flames leapt up like a crowd to its feet. The Seneschal's eyes went wide with alarm and one of his guards cried out.

Theron slammed the door shut with surprising strength. With glittering merriment in his eyes, he grinned. "Run."

Inside, the men were screaming. Elly laughed, high and horrified, and ran. Theron laughed behind her. She didn't look back.

★ ★ ★

"Elban's heir had to be the last of his line," the magus said. "I'm sorry. We've all done things we're sorry for. When this is over, we'll grieve his brother together."

But grief already boiled inside Gavin, thick and sludgy and hot. Judah couldn't move any more than he could. She felt sick and sad and all the worse for the knowledge that it would have hurt more to lose Theron when he was himself. "Were you the one who poisoned him?" she said.

The magus shook his head emphatically. "No. No. That was Arkady and the Seneschal." He tapped his chest. Behind his spectacles his eyes were wide and luminous. "I was the one who saved him. I gave you the antidote."

Judah felt like a clenched fist. "Why, if you were only going to kill him?"

"For you," the magus said. "I saved him for you."

When she spoke, she could barely hear herself. "To make me trust you."

"Take the knife." The magus moaned. "Can't you hear them? All the voices of all the people who've poured their power into you?"

The horror was that she could. She could feel them in her mind, whispering soft words. Beckoning her. Holding invisible arms out to her, like the tower had: *come, lost one. Come, lonely. Come, you are ours.* She hated how strong it was, the urge to slip into those arms, back into the slow sleepy dullness of all those weeks in the tower. Theron had talked about the voices, about feeling tangled. Was this what it had been like for him all those months? Poor Theron. He hadn't wanted to die. He had never wanted to die. "Get out of me," she said. "Get them out of me."

"Put the knife in his throat and they'll go." Eagerness in the magus's voice.

"Get them out of me!" she screamed.

"Kill him!"

Kill me, Gavin suddenly said. *My brother is dead and my kingdom is gone. Kill me and we can both be free.*

The black desire inside him was so strong. Judah's eyes went to the knife. The magus raised it hopefully toward her. "If you both come down out of this tower alive," he said, "the Seneschal will use you. The bond. He wants to do it to other people. Children. A whole guild of them. The Communicators."

She wanted to tear herself out of her own skin.

"Your life," the magus said, "lived over and over. All the pain of it."

No. No, Gavin said, instantly. *Kill me. Kill me now. The Seneschal won't care about you if I'm dead.*

Judah knew Gavin's face as well as she knew her own. In her head he didn't have this deathly pallor, this faint sheen of sweat darkening the hair at his forehead. In her head his eyes weren't red-rimmed, filled with tears. One spilled over, ran over his fine cheekbone to cling helplessly to the ridge of his jaw. She wiped it away. It felt cold and clean. "Then he'll have no reason to keep me alive," she said to him.

But the magus was shaking his head. "The tower won't let you die."

She took her hand from Gavin, and looked at the magus. "Because the tower needs me?"

He nodded. Again, the eagerness.

"Like the Seneschal needs me."

The magus blinked, confused. "No."

"Yes." All at once the skin-tearing feeling was gone. In its place was something as cold and clean as the tear she'd wiped from Gavin's skin. Her body still hurt. The fingers still grabbed. Theron was still dead. To Gavin, she said, "What about Elly?"

She no longer needed to touch him to hear his response. *Seneschal will send her back to Tiernan. Nothing to gain by killing her.*

"Take the knife." The magus sounded oddly kind. "It's your path. You were made for this."

The voices in her head screamed, grabbed. She leaned down and kissed Gavin's unmoving lips. *I'm sorry*, she told him. *Tell Elly I love her.* Then she stood up.

"I'll pass," she said, and took a step backward, toward the gap in the tower.

Gavin made a strangled noise. The magus stared at him for an uncomprehending moment and then went pale. "No," he said. "Judah. No."

"You can't stop me," she said.

She felt his control over Gavin snap, like the air breaking in half, and suddenly Gavin was on his feet hurtling toward her. The magus was, too. Both of them. Reaching to grab her, just like the voices inside her head grabbed her. To restrain her, just like she had always been restrained. She took a giant step back, a mighty leap. And for a moment she felt held in kind hands, suspended in the air like she belonged there. The empty sky stretching wide and open above her, around her, inside her. The Wall a toy, to be stepped over and left behind. Cold. Terror. Exhilaration. All things: possible.

Then she fell.

CHAPTER TWENTY-ONE

Nathaniel Clare woke into a world that smelled of leather and smoke. His face hurt, as did his chest and gut and legs, in a dozen different places. His eyes were difficult to open and when he licked his lips with a dry tongue he found them crusted with blood. These sensations were all so familiar as to be almost comforting and his first conscious thought was that Derie had beaten him.

His second conscious thought was that Derie was dead. When Judah jumped, he'd felt his old teacher ripped away from life like a climbing vine from a tree, and though there were torn, painful places in him where her tendrils had worked their way in, it was a clean pain, a relief-pain; both a *she-will-never-beat-me-again* pain and a loss pain, because he'd loved Derie, in his way. He'd had no choice but to love her, since so much of his life hinged on her approval. The contradiction didn't trouble him. Humans were complicated and pain was complicated and love was the most complicated thing of all, and also any rawness left in him by Derie's abrupt removal paled in comparison to the searing horror of losing Caterina.

He had felt her go, too. Not a vine on a tree, but a piece of whole cloth, brutally sundered; not raw places left by invading tendrils but great swaths of what Nate thought of as himself. An agonizing emptiness. His mother was gone. His mother was no more. There was no place where his mother was. He was Caterina-less, void of Caterina. The fabric of his world was a pile of tatters on a dirty floor and it was unbearable, he could not live inside himself. He forced his eyes open.

That hurt, too. He found himself in front of a fire: not a roaring fire, just an ordinary flickering fire in a fireplace. A figure sat on a chair across from him. As the world around him came into focus he came to the dull realization that the figure in the chair was the Seneschal, holding a glass of wine.

Judah had jumped. The boy had lived. Nate had failed. Derie was supposed to kill him now, but Derie herself was dead.

But the Seneschal said, "Hello, Nathaniel Clare," and Nate had spent too long at the beck and call of Derie's cruelty not to hear the threat in his voice. Like a dog called by its master, he came the rest of the way awake. Painfully, he pushed himself up to sitting.

"You're in Elban's study," the Seneschal said. "They had you in Eleanor's room. I was always told never to move an unconscious man, but I took the risk of having you brought here, anyway. I think Gavin was determined to beat you to death, a little at a time."

Yes. He remembered that: sudden bursts of pain in the dark, exploding like skyrockets before fading into nothing. He wished the boy had succeeded.

Something white hung off the side of the Seneschal's neck:

a bandage, soft and clumsy. The Seneschal traced his gaze, and touched it. "The Tiernan set fire to the passage. Three of my men died. I didn't. Old Cavellus in Archertown patched me up. He's not half the healer you are."

Apparently Nate was supposed to say something, but his mind was blank. He had failed. He had offered her the knife. She had refused to take it.

"The fire melted the locks and hinges on the inner door," the Seneschal said. "Took us a few days to get back through. I'm sorry about that. You'd be in better shape if we'd been able to get in sooner. Cavellus gave you a tonic to wake you up. He's outside, if you'd like to see him." The gray man held out a glass of wine. "Here. Drink this. You'll feel better."

The musty smell of the wine nauseated him.

"Magus," the Seneschal said, and there was no softening the command in his voice now, "what happened in that tower?"

He'd failed. Judah had refused the knife. His mother had died. Derie had died. They had been with him, in the Work, and Judah had jumped and the tower had burned them like candles to save her. His fault. He was nothing. Why hadn't he died, too?

The Seneschal continued. "Gavin says Judah jumped, but if she were dead he wouldn't be alive to tell me about it, and there's no body in the light well. She's hiding somewhere and we can't find her. We can't find Theron, either. The Tiernan's playing dumb. You're all I have." He sat forward, his eyes intense. "What happened in the tower?"

Nate made his tongue move inside his dry mouth. Ran it over his blood-crusted lips. "My mother," he said. The consonants sounded blunted.

The Seneschal frowned. "Your mother?"

"Dead," Nate said.

The Seneschal glanced toward the massive desk that had

once been Elban's, considering. Then he drew his hand back and hit Nate, open-handed. The force of the blow knocked Nate off the sofa and he landed facedown on a thick rug printed with scarlet flowers. Fresh blood filled his mouth and a drop of brighter scarlet appeared on one of the flowers, then another. They were absorbed instantly.

The Seneschal's strong hand gripped his collar, pulled him up, and dropped him back onto the sofa. Nate felt like a broken doll tossed around a room.

"I'm sorry about that," the Seneschal said. "But I need you thinking clearly. I have men literally tearing apart walls looking for that stupid girl. If you're sad about your mother, I'll buy you a whore and you can tell her all about it, but right now, I need to know where Judah is." The big man pulled at the sleeves of his coat to straighten them. "I need you with me, Nathaniel Magus. Are you with me?"

Nate was not Nathaniel Magus. Nate was nothing. Feeling blood run down his chin, he said, "She's gone."

"Who is? Judah, or your mother?"

"Judah."

"Where?"

Where? He couldn't feel her. But the Judah-places in his head were not torn, did not hurt. So she was still alive. "Somewhere," he said, and then, "Nowhere."

"You need to start being forthcoming with me, magus." The Seneschal's voice was dangerous. "I like you, but I can't afford to be sentimental. Where is she?"

"Somewhere. Nowhere."

This time the hand on his collar lifted him up entirely. A different hand hit him again. It didn't seem like either hand could have anything to do with the Seneschal, whose voice spoke so calmly. "Where is she?"

There was only one answer, only one truth. "Somewhere. Nowhere."

The collar-hand dropped him to his knees. Pain exploded in his side as a boot kicked him. "Magus, please," the Seneschal said, sounding sorry. As if causing pain hurt him, too. "Where's Judah?"

"Somewhere. Nowhere." He'd been beaten before. He was used to being beaten. Being beaten was, in some ways, his natural state. There were no choices to be made during a beating. There was nothing to do at all.

The boot fell again. Something gave in his chest and when he tried to speak again his voice came out in gasps, it was hard to catch his breath. Still: "Somewhere. Nowhere," the nothing-that-was-Nate heard himself say as the boot continued to come, over and over. "Somewhere. Nowhere." As he receded into darkness:

Somewhere. Nowhere.

When the Seneschal returned to the parlor, the knuckles of his right hand were split and bleeding. "I see why the magus looks the way he does," he said to Gavin, who sat on the sofa, his own knuckles neatly bandaged. "He really can be an infuriating little man."

Eleanor sat next to Gavin without touching him. Before the Seneschal's men had taken him, the magus had lain unconscious in her bed for days. During all that time, she hadn't heard him say a word, infuriating or otherwise. "What did he say?" she said now.

"Nothing worth hearing," the Seneschal said, as pleasant as always. "Nonsense, mostly. Eleanor, will you be so good as to fetch some water and clean up this mess he made of my hand?" He lifted the hand as if he had no idea how it had become so battered. As if all of this were merely a chain of unconnected events, out of all control and most certainly not in his.

"No," Eleanor said. "I don't believe I will."

Gavin's mouth twitched at that, which was the closest he'd come to a smile in days. The Seneschal, though, merely blinked at her with faint surprise, said, "Very well," and sat down.

In Judah's chair. Eleanor felt a shivering wave of resentment crawl over her to see him sitting where he did not belong. Thinking of Judah brought her the same agonizing stab of disbelief as always, pain as blinding as the sun. If she went anywhere near that pain, she would not be able to keep herself from screaming, so she pushed it down and away. She was very good at pushing things down and away. She was also very tired of it.

"I've had him taken to Highfall Prison," the Seneschal said. "I think perhaps it will clarify his memory of what happened in the tower. Perhaps it would jog yours, as well, Gavin." Merely a suggestion, the Seneschal's tone said; just trying to be helpful. Eleanor bit hard on the inside of her cheek.

Next to her, she heard Gavin take a long, steady breath. Then he said, "While having the deposed heir imprisoned would be a comforting nod to tradition, there's nothing to jog. I remember everything. We were in the tower. Judah jumped."

"If that were true, you'd be dead."

With the same cool, blank face he'd worn for days, Gavin lifted one shoulder slightly, then let it drop. "Ask the infuriating little man. Before you cut his tongue out, ideally. He's not what he claimed to be." Gavin paused. Then, "He killed my brother." For the first time, his voice was strained and tight.

The Seneschal's watery gray eyes shifted to Elly. Who wanted to scream again, but who contented herself with the smallest shake of her head. She had seen Theron after the magus was in the tower. She had spoken with him. She didn't know where Theron was, but he was somewhere in the House, and she didn't know why Gavin believed the man who'd lied to them for so long in so many ways, instead of her.

With no emotion, the Seneschal said, "If I begin cutting parts of you off, do you think Judah will emerge from wherever she's hidden herself?"

If he'd been hoping for a reaction, he didn't get it. "I doubt it," Gavin said. His bandaged hands slightly clumsy, he pushed up his sleeves. Eleanor gasped: his forearms were covered, front and back, with the same scratched symbol, over and over. Some of the scratches were bloody, some only pink. She didn't know what the mark meant, but she could guess.

Where. Where. Where.

"So she's ignoring you," the Seneschal said.

"No," Gavin said, steady as a clock. "She's not here. She's not dead, but she's not here. I know it doesn't make sense, but it's true."

It didn't make sense. The world was desolate and lonely and Eleanor didn't understand what was happening, but she would not let herself collapse in a heap the way she wanted. With great effort, she kept her attention on the Seneschal. Whatever simmered behind that impassive face, she could feel the heat of it.

"You understand," he finally said, "that I'll tear this House down to the ground to find her, if I have to."

"If you think that'll work, go ahead. Give me a pickaxe. I'll help," Gavin said.

The Seneschal sat back. His expression was patient, even tolerant. "Do you realize the favor I've done you? You would have been a terrible ruler. Not just because you're vain and selfish; because you're weak. Power would have made you stupid. Some pretty little schemer would have led you into a vial and you never would have found your way out." His eyes flicked toward Eleanor. "Honestly, you both would have been miserable, and I would have ended up in charge, anyway."

She felt her cheeks burn with anger, but she said nothing.

"Now," the Seneschal went on, "I'm guessing that the infuriating little man told you about my plan for the guild, and I'm further guessing that Judah didn't like it. She's hidden herself away to keep it from happening. And unlike you, she has the strength to stay hidden no matter what. As long as she's getting your little messages—" he nodded at Gavin's arms "—she'll know you're alive, and that'll be enough." He stood up. "So you're not going to send any more messages. You're not going to be in pain; you're not going to be hungry; you're not going to be cold. No matter where she looks, she won't find you. I think that will drive her mad, don't you?"

Gavin said nothing. The Seneschal called out and the magus he'd brought in from the city entered, accompanied by a guard. Eleanor couldn't remember the magus's name; he was thick around the middle, with thinning hair. He cowered, embarrassed, before the Seneschal. "Bind his hands," the Seneschal said to him. "I want them utterly useless."

The magus did as he was asked, wrapping each of Gavin's fingers individually and then tying them against his palms in loose fists, until each hand was nothing but a useless stump at the end of his arms. Gavin closed his eyes briefly but otherwise didn't react, and Eleanor—watching—told herself that it could be worse; that in fact, it might be, still.

When the magus stepped back, the Seneschal surveyed his work and nodded. "It'll do for now. We'll figure out a more elegant solution at the guildhall."

"What guildhall?" Elly said sharply.

"The guildhall for which you'll be departing at sundown," the Seneschal said. "Secretly, of course. The managers want the House, and I want Judah. As long as she thinks you're here, she won't go far. You may bring what you can carry—within reason, of course. I don't recommend unwrapping his hands, Eleanor. You'll find consequences of that extremely unpleasant." His face was steady. At the last state dinner, when the Wilmerians were there, he had taken Eleanor's arm to help her onto the dais, and told her she looked lovely. It was hard to believe there had ever been kindness in him.

Then he left. Gavin's bound hands lay limp in his lap. Reaching out, Elly took one of them in her own. She intended only to make sure the bandages weren't too tight, but Gavin said, "Don't. He meant what he said. He'll cut your fingers off or something." So she let the clumsy thing drop.

"We have to find Theron," she said.

"Theron is dead," he said.

A shudder went through her. She remembered Theron's thin arm around her, helping her climb the tower stairs; his voice, bright and coaxing and full of life, saying, *Come on, El. A few more steps. I'll keep you safe. I won't let you fall.* But in the tower itself, Gavin believed he'd heard that betraying turn-coat of a magus say he'd killed Theron. Gavin believed he'd been paralyzed, bound by some force he couldn't see. Gavin believed Judah was alive.

She took Gavin's face in her hands—his worn, somber face, the two desolate pits of his eyes like chips of coal. "Tell me again," she said.

"Judah's not dead. She jumped. I saw her jump. But she's not dead." He hesitated. "I can't see my fingers. Can't move them, can't touch anything with them. But I know they're there. I know Judah's somewhere, Elly. I don't know...where—"

The last was barely a whisper. Elly felt her eyes fill with tears, but she pushed them away with the heel of her hand.

"You don't believe Judah's dead," she said. "I don't believe

Theron's dead. Until we learn otherwise, one way or another, we believe each other. All right?"

His eyes still held that odd mix of stubbornness and pity that was becoming so familiar to her, but he said, "All right."

"Good," she said. "In the meantime, we're together. And we'll stay that way as long as we can."

Suddenly, unexpectedly, he dropped his head to her shoulder. His arms, with their bandaged hands, slid around her waist; gripped her tightly, as if to prove she was real. She put her own arms around his shoulders even though she didn't know if she was real, she didn't know if anything was real anymore. She didn't have to know, she told herself. A few more steps; a few more after that. Wake up each day and figure out how to survive it.

She would keep them safe; all of them. She would not let them fall.

SOMEWHERE AND

NOWHERE

There was light—or was it merely the absence of darkness, or was it the absence of anything at all? She saw nothing. Her eyes found nothing to see. She was not sure if she saw light or dark or simply void, absence. Was what she felt truly cool or was it simply the absence of warmth? She was lying down— or was she standing? There was no surface. She simply *was*.

Who was she?

She didn't know. She didn't know how long she had been— here—wherever she was. She was not sure if time passed in the light or the absence or whatever it was, but it seemed to. One idea flowed to the next, at least. They were all shape- less, vague. *This? Not this? Something else?* Eventually she was able to think words like *where?* and *when?* and *who?* If there were names for those things, surely there were names for other things. Surely there were—other things.

Things. Yes. There was a thing called pain; she knew the bite of it. She knew *hurt*, and then *bite*, and then *teeth*, and then suddenly she knew her own teeth, there in her mouth. She had a mouth. She had a head. She had—a body—

She more than was; she had a self. And she realized: this self was not new. There had been a before. This, now, was not an absence but a continuation. Of this one thing, of this first thing, she was certain: she had *been*. She would *be*. She *was*.

I'll stand up.

She was standing up. A gentle ecstasy filled her and with it came words. She thought *feet* and they were there, below her, ten naked toes in the nothing. She thought *dress* and found herself in a gown the color of new grass at dusk, a fine silver vine winding up from its hem. She felt the weight of hair down her back, blinked lidded eyes; thought *air* and discovered breath slipped in and out of her body.

The nothing around her reminded her of fog—*fog!*—and fog reminded her of the orchard—*orchard!*—and somehow she was not surprised when slim trees coalesced out of the absence. Damp ground pressed the soles of her feet. Slowly—as slowly as it had in the beginning of everything—the world formed around her, and there was breeze and there were smells and instead of void her ears filled with the subtle susurration of life itself; and, somewhere above the fog, she knew there was a sun.

She took a step, and then another. The world was beautiful and after the endless time in the void everything she saw dazzled her with its very *there*-ness, and she was walking through it. Toward what, she didn't know. There was something she needed. She would walk until she found it.

★ ★ ★ ★ ★

ACKNOWLEDGMENTS

This is a very long book, so my acknowledgments will be short. Many thanks to Kathy Sagan for taking a chance on this one, as well as Justine Sha, Randy Chan, Ashley MacDonald and everyone else at Mira for shepherding it out into the world; to Gigi Lau, Micaela Alcaino and the rest of the Harlequin Art Department for the gorgeous cover, and for turning my weird lopsided squiggles into lovely non-lopsided maps. Huge thanks, as well, to Elena Stokes and Brianna Robinson, who helped *The Unwilling* find its feet in the big scary world. The McTiernan family loaned me their name for Elly's home province (although they may since have forgotten), so thanks to Linda, Jack and Ewan. Endless gratitude—and that's not hyperbole, my gratitude will seriously never end—to Erin Morgenstern, Kelly Link and Ellen Datlow for wrangling unwieldy early copies, and to Tabitha and Naomi for wrangling even earlier, even more unwieldy versions. Children and books: it really does take a village.

The biggest of hugs and fanciest of candles to my dear friend and agent, Julie Barer, who said, "Maybe you should write the fantasy novel you've been talking about for twenty years," and then went all in on it when I did. I might have written it eventually anyway, but without Julie's support and enthusiasm it might have taken another two decades. She is quite possibly the hardest-working woman in the book business and I am incredibly fortunate to be able to work with her. Thanks also to her assistant, Nicole Cunningham, whose patience is nigh on superheroic.

My mom, Theresa Braffet, is a huge fantasy fan, and it was truly satisfying to write something I knew she would love—so thanks, Mom, for being such an enthusiastic reader, even when I write things that don't have magic in them.

Finally, as always, I am deeply grateful for my family: the small human, who puts up with me spending too much time writing things she's not allowed to read yet, and my partner in all things, Owen King. He read this beast of a novel several million times at last count, and he's the kindest, smartest, most honest and most supportive reader, husband, general human being that I have ever known. With every year that passes I become more and more grateful for him. I can't believe I got so lucky.